BRAM STOKER'S DRACULA OMNIBUS

BRAM STOKER'S DRACULA OMNIBUS

Dracula

◆

The Lair of the White Worm

◆

Dracula's Guest

Introduction by Fay Weldon

ORION

Introduction copyright © Fay Weldon 1992
All rights reserved
The right of Fay Weldon to be identified as the author of the
Introduction to *Bram Stoker's Dracula Omnibus* has been asserted by her
in accordance with the Copyright, Designs and Patents Act 1988.

Dracula first published in Great Britain in 1897.
The Lair of the White Worm first published in Great Britain in 1911.
Dracula's Guest first published in Great Britain in 1914.

The arrangement of this compilation copyright
© Orion Books Ltd 1992

This compilation first published in Great Britain in 1992 by Orion
An imprint of Orion Books Ltd
Orion House, 5 Upper St Martin's Lane, London WC2H 9EA

A CIP catalogue record for this book is available
from the British Library

ISBN 1 85797 040 3 (hardcover)
1 85797 041 1 (trade paperback)

Typeset by Deltatype Ltd, Ellesmere Port
Printed in England by Clays, Ltd, St. Ives plc

Contents

BRAM STOKER

Hello, thank you and goodbye

Some things – not many – you can be sure of.

From the internal evidence of his writing, and from what we know of his life, we can be sure that Abraham (Bram) Stoker, Sagittarian, (November 8th, 1847), red-headed Dubliner, athlete, graduate of Trinity College, manager and companion to the flamboyant actor Henry Irving, married to the beautiful but chilly actress Florence Balcombe, was a man of great energy and fearful, even perverse, imagination.

From what we know of the general enthusiastic response to his books, in particular *Dracula* – here in this volume together with *The Lair of the White Worm* and *Dracula's Guest* (a collection of blood-dripping stories) – we can be sure that this perverse imagination, as the genteel and fastidious chose to see it, finds a general echo in mankind as a whole. And I mean mankind, and young mankind at that; it is young men who line up for the horror movie, for decapitation, flesh slicing, spurting blood and oozing gore, and the girls who, giggling and squealing, accompany the lads and if they'd really prefer a soppy romance and some hand holding, stay quiet about it. And a good time is apparently had by all – some sub-erotic taste satisfied, some cathartic impulse gratified.

And no doubt the impulse was better gratified in the writing of *Dracula* than in its reading. For what a wonderful novel *Dracula* turns out to be: as by sheer accident (I would argue) Bram Stoker hit upon his archetype, and the force and energy of its emergence carried him along, and the reader with him. *Dracula* is so much more satisfying and convincing a read than *The Lair of the White Worm* – or the sub-Poe stories of the *Dracula's Guest* collection – that you can be sure something extraordinary went on in its creation. You may take issue with me over this: *The Lair of the White Worm* has many fervent admirers; Ken Russell, the film-maker, amongst them. Some of the stories are very hard to forget. I wish I could: but then I am the cowardly and coy kind of person who prefers to shut their eyes, not press the VCR pause button, when a head leaves its shoulders in HIGHLANDER II.

Should I explain 'archetype' to the non-Jungians amongst you, and the pre-

Freudians, should there be any innocents left? By archetype I mean one of those submerged, repetitive figures who allegedly inhabit our group unconscious – the heroes, tyrants, priests, queens, scapegoats, charlatans, peasants, seductressess, who live a common life in our joint imagination. They can be identified by our cultural myths – Samson, Catharine the Great, Mata Hari – and are brought to the surface by the art and fiction of our society, be they in the form of Oedipus Rex, Mona Lisa's smile, or Terminator II. When and as they emerge, great, lasting and powerful is the popular response!

Consider, perhaps, as a parallel to Stoker's *Dracula*, how the novelist Jean Rhys quite fortuitously produced an archetype in *Wide Sargasso Sea* – a novel written in her later life, after a long silence, and in a style quite out of keeping with the nervous, albeit exquisite, novels she wrote when young; works which had already lapsed into obscurity. So powerful a novel was *Wide Sargasso Sea* – the life story of Mrs Rochester, the mad wife who creeps from the attic at night to destroy and burn and be revenged – now there's an archetype! as was in the first place Jane Eyre's Mr Rochester, all black moods and burning desire – that its energy reflected back upon Rhys's earlier works and brought them into deserved literary prominence once again.

Dracula moves easily out of Stoker's novel to appear in film, play, cartoon, and comic. The image of the immaculately dressed, courteous gentleman from abroad, who does dreadful things to women behind your back, especially when they're asleep, hovering or bending to strike, with his pointed Mr Spock ears, red eyes, sharp nose and horrid fangs, is familiar to all of us, and strikes us as perfectly believable. Shut the window when the moon is full! Hear the werewolves howling, with their nuzzling noses, and rapacious jaws? Thank you, Bram Stoker, for your warning, or not, as the case may be . . . move over, darling.

The novel is presented with compelling narrative skill, through diaries, letters and news items: Stoker himself stays right out of the book. The incredible, thus subjectively presented, becomes credible: the preposterous possible. No one objective and sensible says 'but these things can't be so'; so no one stands derided. The reader pieces together his own tale from the accounts of others, and is convinced. If young Jonathan Harker, having journeyed to Transylvania to visit Count Dracula on 'legal business', finds his door locked at night and his host creeping about the outside of the castle walls like a lizard, it is almost no more than we expect. 'My very feelings changed to repulsion and terror when I saw the whole man slowly emerge from the window and begin to crawl down the castle wall over that dreadful abyss, *face down* with his cloak spreading out around him like great wings . . . I thought it was some trick of the moonlight, some weird effect of shadows; but I kept looking, and it could be no delusion.' And indeed it could not be. Dracula is out and about on his dreadful business, and what is worse, is determined to travel to that pleasant watering hole, Whitby, Yorkshire, England. Ladies beware! Wash and iron your pretty white summer-muslin dresses as you may, Dracula is on his way . . .

Jonathan is lucky to escape Transylvania with his life and half his wits: Harker's fianceé, Mimi Murray, takes up the story in England, as do later Mimi's friend Lucy and her admirer Dr Arthur Holmwood, and Van Helsing, an expert in vampirism. Van Helsing is too late to save Lucy from Dracula's attention: she becomes in her turn a vampire, one of the un-dead. Only a stake through the heart can bring her peace. A man of science, poor Dr Seward, who has always nourished a hopeless, unreciprocated passion for Lucy, is the one who has to drive the stake. Lucy lies like a nightmare of herself in her coffin, that is to say with bloodstained, voluptuous mouth: she has a carnal and unspiritual appearance, which seems like a devilish mockery of Lucy's own sweet purity. She is simply not herself. Arthur's face is set, and high duty seems to shine through it: he does not falter. The phallic stake is driven, the quivering and writhing of the body becomes less, the teeth seem to champ, the face to quiver, and finally 'it' lies still. The terrible task is over.

Poor Mrs Bram Stoker, elegantly 'frigid'; poor Florence Balcombe, that is to say, actress, much admired by Oscar Wilde. Florence bore Bram a son, and wrote in her introduction to the stories in *Dracula's Guest* (a posthumous collection), albeit affectionately enough, of her husband's 'early strenuous life' – perhaps she was 'frigid' because sex with Bram wasn't much fun? A man must marry and father a child to cover his tracks.

Few 'came out' in those days. Perhaps thankfully, fewer still were aware of how writing could betray the sexual orientation of the writer: who'd ever heard of a sub-text then? If there is no love lost in Bram Stoker's work for female sexuality, he doesn't mind who knows it. Primness and purity is all.

In *The Lair of the White Worm*, Lady Arabella sucks Oolanga –a black man who has dared proposition her elegant, sinuous self – down into her hole. The smell! All the noxious smelling experiences our young hero Adam has ever had – the drainage of war hospitals, of slaughterhouses, the refuse of dissecting rooms, the poisonous effluvium of the bilge of a water-logged ship – worse, still worse. The sight! The fathomless charnel pit, its entrance marked with spots of fresh blood, which seems to go down into the very bowels of the earth, conveying from far down the sighs and sounds of the nethermost hell. Oolanga, the rampant African, is drawn down by Lady Arabella into the gaping aperture, deeper and deeper into the primeval ooze. His shrieks chill our hero Adam's blood – Adam escapes, albeit slipping on the steps in some sticky, acrid mass that felt and smelt like blood.

As I say, poor Florence. If Bram preferred the company of Henry Irving, she may have been glad of it. But people make their own arrangements in these matters, and what should it concern readers what writers do to whom, and how, and of whichever gender? Whatever gets you through the night and the bills paid and the children happy – even if it's their fate, in their turn, to line up outside the horror movies and marvel at the nature of corrupt and corrupting flesh.

Just as the witch has been the focus point of fear and loathing in the West – if God is good, someone must be to blame, and it is our rather remarkable common human determination that God *should* be good and the universe essentially benign – so as you go further East, and into the Slavic world, the vampire becomes more and more the object of fear. In eighteenth century Hungary the uproar against vampires equalled that of the witch hunts of colonial New England. In the West they blamed and burned the witches, women contaminated by the Devil: further East they blamed the un-dead: the living corpse or soulless body who would emerge to drink the blood of the living so that they too grew pale and died – one wonders if TB was perhaps endemic at the time, pallor preceding death? – and became vampires in their turn. The vampire can't rest in his grave; he or she must spend the night searching for a victim. Lights, bells, garlic – these are moderately effective at keeping them out. Certainly worth trying. Like their cousin the werewolf, vampires are at their most dangerous when the moon is full. Would news of them have travelled to Dublin in the 1850s, I wonder, to reach Mrs Stoker, mother of seven? Little Bram was a sickly child, but his mother's favourite, he tells us, and she regaled him as he lay in bed with stories of demons, banshees, ghouls and real life cholera epidemics. Thank you, mother!

A 'strong' woman for her times, nevertheless. Nothing like the Mimis and Lucys who move through the pages of *Dracula*, dainty and thin-blooded, albeit brave and true. Mrs Stoker was a writer, a social worker, a feminist, a friend of Oscar Wilde's mother: she is quoted as saying she didn't care tuppence about her daughters: she much preferred her sons. Was she, do you think, like one of the three women, 'ladies by their dress and manners', who come visiting Jonathan Harker by moonlight? 'They threw no shadow on the floor. All three had brilliant white teeth that shone like pearls against the ruby of their voluptuous lips. There was something about them that made me uneasy, some longing and at the same time some deadly fear. I felt in my heart a wicked, burning desire that they would kiss me with those red lips . . .' As the girl goes on her knees and bends over him, smugly gloating, Jonathan feels the movement of her breath upon him, 'sweet it was in one sense, honey-sweet, and sent the same tingling through the nerves as her voice, but with a bitter underlying of the sweet, a bitter offensiveness, as one smells in blood.'

Mother, mother, beautiful mother, is it your time of the month? How horrid! Strong women both, shall we blame you and Lady Wilde for what your sons became – if blame there be? Did you pay your sons too much loving care and attention? Mother can never get things right; Lady Wilde, by the way, was the author of *Ancient Legends, Mystic Charms and Superstitions of Ireland* (1887). So she was at it too.

Is it more personal still than this? Groddeck – the famous philosopher-doctor who in the 1930s so lamentably treated Katharine Mansfield for the TB which killed her, rather sooner than it would have done without his attentions, and whose famous question was, to a patient in agony, 'but *why* did you break your leg?', suggests that the subliminal smelling of the mother's blood serves as an uncomfortable monthly reminder of the traumas that occurred at birth. Can it then be maternal blood which taints and blights a childhood? What *are* we to do in our search for the perfect upbringing? The very human condition militates against us.

Oh, Dracula, Prince of Darkness, lord of the lands of the unspeakable, scuttling and hovering, glimmering on the edges of all our unconscious. To see him clear you must travel far, leave civilisation behind you, brave the far off lands, journey to Transylvania; only there when the moon is full, in the dark clefts and crevices between the snowy peaks when the black forests toss and turn and the werewolves howl, will you see him for what he is. Sniff him out, as the werewolves do, snuffling and nuzzling – Dracula! Hovering outside the maiden's window (albeit disguised as Bela Lugosi, bobbing up and down on piano wires, but no less terrifying for that) planning to pounce, not a doubt of it, scuttling up the wall and into her room while she sleeps, digging his crescent teeth into her smooth white skin. In the morning just a drop of red blood, escaped blood, to betray his presence . . . the girl becomes a woman, the maiden learns desire, Eve eats the apple, the tender wife becomes a whore and is insatiable for ever after, true love turns elemental, the flesh triumphs over the spirit, and how is any man ever to service all this?

Every four weeks, please notice. And that atmosphere! You can feel it, cut it with a knife just before Dracula arrives: 'There were dark rolling clouds overhead, and in the air the heavy, oppressive sense of thunder.' Oh yes! The cracking and crackling of the femal psyche, in pre-menstrual mode. PMT. They let women off murder charges on account of it, though that's not much comfort to the family. And what woman, these days, ever denied it? PMT has become her license to scowl, to snarl, to kill. When a man turns into a killer werewolf, once a month when the moon is full, he turns *female*: that's the werewolf's secret.

Even the most caring man must be anxious. No wonder your daughter looks so pale today, your wife seems languid, your sister swoons –Dracula's been sucking their blood again. What's to be done about it? Are they going to be *all right*? Supposing it goes on and on and they bleed to death? What then? Why do they put up with it, invite him in? Why do they leave the window open in the first place? What's going on here?

Count Dracula! A *man*? What *is* going on here? If my theory is to hold water, shouldn't Dracula be female? But Countess Dracula would strike us as very odd. No, a man he has to be: and we can argue our way out of even this one. For even menstruation must be controlled by men, it seems. Consider the forceps-bearing obstetrician, the hormone-wielding gynaecologist, the shifter of genes in the fertility lab – men, all men, and determined to take over, such is their envy of the female capacity to create. 'Men have art, women have babies.' I heard it often when I was a child; the crumb of comfort thrown by the rich to the poor; but even that crumb grudged in the heart. Forget penis envy, it's womb envy we're talking about here.

We may have quite a problem, too, with the fact that in Stoker's *Dracula* men as well as women get bitten by vampires. What are we to make of this? Easy! If a man's bitten by Dracula he turns into a raving lunatic: worse even than fading anaemically away. It happened to the unfortunate Penfield, Dr Seward's patient. 'His redeeming quality,' writes Dr Seward, 'is a love of animals though indeed he has such curious turns in it that I sometimes imagine that he is only abnormally cruel. . . .' Penfield's birds, kept as pets in his padded cell, vanish. 'There were a few feathers about the room and on his pillow a drop of blood.' Proximity to a woman at her time of the month can send a man mad, turn him into a devourer of feathered creatures.

Or perhaps Bram Stoker's trouble is that he once had oral sex with a girlfriend and found it was her time of the month and was revolted and the rest of us have been suffering from it ever since? Shutting the window if the moon shines in, in case Dracula's out there? Perhaps it *was* this very trauma which gave Stoker access to his unconscious so that when next he took up his pen out leapt the archetype – a kind of Damaged or Perverse archetype, mind you, for surely in this enlightened age the monthly bleeding of women, the cycle of pain and recovery, should be seen more as the benign evidence of ebb and flow of the life force in women (*pace* Penelope Shuttle and Peter Redgrove in their seminal book, *The Wise Wound*) than something horrid and alarming? And that we readers and viewers have trotted along behind, pursuing a false, misleading and even dangerous archetype? The fear, loathing and wonder of the Great Red Mouth! An image lurking there distorted in the group unconscious: what our parents or teachers told us, in their attempts to be informative about the quite ridiculous, bizarre and wholly unbelievable facts of life, all mixed up with the playground gossip of our own generation. He puts that there; she does this there: I saw them, I heard them; they were actually doing it, but not the way the Biology teacher told us, not one bit. Do they actually *enjoy* it? It's disgusting. Do women get pregnant through their mouths, then? And drops of blood upon the sheets. Fearful, revolting, unnatural!

Mrs Stoker, feminist mother of Bram, and Mr Stoker, civil servant (that is to say, colonial stooge, should you pause to consider or think important the hungry, distressed and angry state of Ireland at the time), what did *you* do? What did little Bram see or hear? What kind of primal scene did he endure?

Has it occurred to you, as it has occurred to me, that while writers such as Jane Austen will be taken to task for ignoring the social condition of the England of her times, writers such as Bram Stoker will be excused the requirement? Can it be that it's because she is female and he is male, and females are expected to look after everything, restore, make just, be 'balanced' in their praise and condemnation? And that male writers are allowed, indeed encouraged, to charge through their own unconsciouses, pulling up the gunge from the bottom, like mud from the depths of a well, and then splash it about without restraint or conscience? You don't get many women horror writers, though Mary Higgins Clark at least had a go. But not a patch on the great bestseller and mind-flayer writers Stephen King, James Herbert, Carpenter and Weaver – aren't these very names in some way archetypal? – ah, the screams of tortured women in the night with which you assail us! Come back, Bram Stoker, all is forgiven!

Has it occurred to you that I have said the most dreadful things about the unfortunate Bram Stoker, and on the flimsiest of evidence? I have accused our writer, if accused is the right word, of homosexuality, bisexuality, not appreciating his wife, being rendered gay by his mother (though it is common wisdom nowadays that homo-eroticism is a matter of nature, not nurture), oral sex (resulting in trauma), womb envy and woman-hatred in general. None of these things need be in the least true, let alone the only truth. I never met the man: I have only what other writers say, combined with the internal evidence of *Dracula, The Lair of the White Worm* and the collected stories of *Dracula's Guest.* but it is the fashion of the times for biographers and critics to be lavish in their suggestion of sexual deviance and scandalous habits and why should I strain against the current?

(My very use of the last phrase might be a sign of some anal fixation or another, of which I may be the last person to be aware. Who is to know about the living, let alone the dead?)

If in Shuttle's and Redgrove's excellent and convincing *The Wise Wound*, it is alleged that Florence Balcombe, Stoker's wife, 'frigid as a statue', is likely to have had an unsatisfactory sex life and so to have had very bad menstrual disturbances, which is why Stoker came up with Dracula, why should I refrain from my own speculations? Why blame the wife when you can blame the mother?

In 1908, three years after Irving's death, four years before his own, Stoker wrote a couple of articles in the monthly review *The 19th Century and After*, in which he took a point of view incompatible with the liberal feeling of his time, and for which he is still taken to task. To argue as he did in 'The Question of a National Theatre' against the founding of such an institution made him unpopular at the time, but his belief that the existence of a National Theatre would detract from the welfare of the theatre as a whole, would take up too high a proportion of available funding money, and that when it comes to theatre small is beautiful and large is inappropriate, seems perfectly acceptable to me. Time, indeed, seems to have made Stoker's point. To suggest, as Stoker does in 'The Censorship of Fiction' – that 'reticence' is an important aspect of art, that if ethical law is not observed, then criminal law must come into operation, and that any attempt to censor must take into account two factors, the weakness of the audience who crave base delights, and the baseness of those who weakly provide them, is not so dreadful. (It may be hypocritical of him, considering the erotic implications of his own writing, but let us suppose Stoker to have written in perfect innocence of his own subtext. A blood-specked pit beside the river's brim, a simple blood speck was to him!) Stoker advocates self-censorship: which is certainly with us. (I could have written in far gorier and more menstrual detail but did not wish to upset your sensibilities.) The individual artist, Stoker suggests, may have to feel, but he need not of necessity speak or write. This is today's view. (I shudder, but keep my shuddering to myself.) Stoker claims that the only emotions which harm are the sex impulses. And this is certainly the view of today's film censors, who will cut sexually explicit scenes, while leaving intact scenes of violence. As much flesh slicing as you like, but never, never, an erect male penis, though female orgasm is grudgingly allowed. Stoker, in his demand for censorship, was no more inconsistent in his day than we are in ours; very little different, though coming to it a different way, from today's film directors, with their scenes of violence, rape and dismemberment, who demand 'no censorship', and simultaneously express anxiety for the welfare of policemen.

'It may be feared,' writes Stoker, 'that writers who deal with lewd subjects generally use the word "problem" either as a shelter for themselves or as a blind for some intentions more base than mere honest investigation. The problem they have in reality set themselves, is to find an easy and prosperous way to their desires without suffering from public ignominy, police interference or the reproaches of conscience.' In other words, the more blood and sex the better something sells: but how do I still go on getting asked out to dinner? 'As it is,' writes Stoker, 'those who prostitute their talents – and amongst them the fairest, imagination – must expect the treatment accorded to the class which they have deliberately joined. The rewards of such – personal luxury and perhaps a measure of wealth – may be theirs, but they must not expect the pleasures or profits of the just – love and honour, troops of friends, and the esteem of good men.' So whatever changed! And with what elegance and persuasiveness Stoker can mount an argument.

Similarly, *Dracula* remains wonderfully readable. Forget, as you turn the pages, Stoker's particular sexuality, about which it is possible endlessly to speculate, though to no particular benefit to the reading experience of the public. Though it is true that to solve the puzzle of his particular and/or peculiar sexual preoccupations may feed through and solve that other puzzle: why it is that young men so enjoy a horror movie: like to press the pause button the better to relish the moment when the knife parts the flesh in the neck: yet seem in no other way unhinged, deranged or perverted. Stoker carries the weight of the charge – of weakly if unknowingly providing base delights – but then that's the fate of the writer. To carry the can.

Dracula, as a piece of writing, is to my mind more effective than *The Lair of the White Worm* or the short stories – all of which you will find in this volume. I would suggest that this is because, by using diaries, letters and press reports to drive his narrative, Stoker is able to hide behind the fear, follies and illusions of his characters. When Stoker appears in his text as all-wise, all-knowing author he is simply not wise enough or knowing enough to transport the reader effectively from the real world to the fantasy world. Doubt sets in. We are left not so much frightened by the unreal as disgusted by the real; generally restless and determined to ask awkward questions. In *The Lair of the White Worm*, why, if Lady Arabella has these agitated, tapering fingers and a reputation as a murderess, do people keep asking her to dinner: why do the police never turn up to move her on? Why, in everyday Dorset, is Mr Caswell *allowed* to fly his kite night and day? It's in the shape of a bird of prey – a hawk – and creates in its monstrous shadow 'a soundless gloom, more dreadful, more disheartening, more soul-killing than any concourse of sounds, no matter how full of fear and dread. Pious individuals put up constant prayers for relief from the intolerable solitude. After a little there were signs of universal depression: that giant spot in high air was a plague of evil influence.' But the hovering man-made hawk, with its power to depress and silence, is nevertheless a wonderful, imaginative, off-key image, and it is worth putting up with poor Oolanga's sucking-down into the fleshy red-mouthed pit to come across it. And if you wonder, if you doubt the mechanics, of exactly how the cat which wishes to kill the crude Texan millionaire manages to slam the door of the Iron Maiden upon him so he dies an excruciating death by spikes, in the story 'The Squaw,' perhaps it doesn't matter. If you relish death by spike, that is. Nasty deaths are the preoccupation of nine-year-olds. Was Stoker a child who never grew up? And off we go again into speculation. Enough.

In spite of a century's drive towards simplicity of expression, the filleting out of adjective and surplus word, a frowning upon repetition, *Dracula*, which commits all possible literary sins, carries the reader along with its wild energy, just as those Transylvanian springs dashed headlong down the mountainsides where the werewolves lurk. You *have* to know what happens next. How well Stoker sets his scene.

Consider now the heroes' return to Transylvania, poor Lucy dead of the vampire's bite, Mimi in a perpetual hypnotic trance (though sleeping within a Holy Circle, and so safe), their horses almost dead from fear – their quest to drive stakes through the hearts of the three voluptuous, insatiable maidens: 'The snow came in flying seeps and with a chill mist. Even in the dark there was a light of some kind, as there ever is over snow: and it seemed though the snow flurries and the wreaths of mist took shape as a woman with trailing garments. All was in dead, grim silence; only the horses whinnied and cowered, as if in terror of the worst. I began to fear, horrible fears . . . The Castle of Dracula now stood out against the red sky, and every stone of its broken battlements was articulated against the light of the setting sun. Oh, my friend John, but it was butcher work! Had I not been nerved by thoughts of others dead, I could not have gone on . . . I could not have endured the horrid screeching as the stake drove home, the plunging of writhing form, and lips of bloody foam.'
Screech and writhe, ladies, as you will, the phallic stake will silence you at last, and all good men, and women too, sleep undisturbed through the rest of the night. Thank you, Mr Stoker, my congratulations, and goodbye.

Fay Weldon
London, June 1992

Dracula

To my dear friend
HOMMY BEG

JONATHAN HARKER'S JOURNAL

(Kept in shorthand)

3 May. Bistritz. – Left Munich at 8.35 p.m. on 1st May, arriving at Vienna early next morning; should have arrived at 6.46, but train was an hour late. Buda-Pesth seems a wonderful place, from the glimpse which I got of it from the train and the little I could walk through the streets. I feared to go very far from the station, as we had arrived late and would start as near the correct time as possible. The impression I had was that we were leaving the West and entering the East; the most Western of splendid bridges over the Danube, which is here of noble width and depth, took us among the traditions of Turkish rule.

We left in pretty good time, and came after nightfall to Klausenburgh. Here I stopped for the night at the Hôtel Royale. I had for dinner, or rather supper, a chicken done up some way with red pepper, which was very good but thirsty. (*Mem.*, get recipe for Mina.) I asked the waiter, and he said it was called 'paprika hendl', and that, as it was a national dish, I should be able to get it anywhere along the Carpathians. I found my smattering of German very useful here; indeed, I don't know how I should be able to get on without it.

Having some time at my disposal when in London, I had visited the British Museum, and made search among the books and maps of the library regarding Transylvania; it had struck me that some foreknowledge of the country could hardly fail to have some importance in dealing with a noble of that country. I find that the district he named is in the extreme east of the country, just on the borders of three states, Transylvania, Moldavia, and Bukovina, in the midst of the Carpathian mountains; one of the wildest and least known portions of Europe. I was not able to light on any map or work giving the exact locality of the Castle Dracula, as there are no maps of this country as yet to compare with our own Ordnance Survey maps; but I found that Bistritz, the post town named by Count Dracula, is a fairly well-known place. I shall enter here some of my notes, as they may refresh my memory when I talk over my travels with Mina.

In the population of Transylvania there are four distinct nationalities: Saxons in the south, and mixed with them the Wallachs, who are the descendants of the Dacians; Magyars in the west; and Szekelys in the east and north. I am going among the latter, who claim to be descended from Attila and the Huns. This may be so, for when the Magyars conquered the country in the eleventh century they found the Huns settled in it. I read that every known superstition in the world is gathered into the horseshoe of the Carpathians, as if it were the centre of some sort of imaginative whirlpool; if so my stay may be very interesting. (*Mem.*, I must ask the Count all about them.)

I did not sleep well, though my bed was comfortable enough, for I had all sorts of queer dreams. There was a dog howling all night long under my window, which may have had something to do with it; or it may have been the paprika, for I had to drink up all the water in my carafe, and was still thirsty. Towards morning I slept and was wakened by the continuous knocking at my door, so I guess I must have been sleeping soundly then. I had for breakfast more paprika, and a sort of porridge of maize flour which they said was 'mamaliga,' and egg-plant stuffed with forcemeat, a very excellent dish, which they call 'impletata.' (*Mem.*, get recipe for this also.) I had to hurry breakfast, for the train started a little before eight, or rather it ought to have done so, for after rushing to the station at 7.30 I had to sit in the carriage for more than an hour before we began to move. It seems to me that the further East you go the more unpunctual are the trains. What ought they to be in China?

All day long we seemed to dawdle through a country which was full of beauty of every kind. Sometimes we saw little towns or castles on the top of steep hills such as we see in old missals; sometimes we ran by rivers and streams which seemed from the wide stony margin on each side of them to be subject to great floods. It takes a lot of water, and running strong, to sweep the outside edge of a river clear. At every station there were groups of people, sometimes crowds, and in all sorts of attire. Some of them were just like peasants at home or those I saw coming through France and Germany, with short jackets and round hats and home-made trousers; but others were very picturesque. The women looked pretty, except when you got near them, but they were all very clumsy about the waist. They had all full white sleeves of some kind or other, and most of them had big belts with a lot of strips of something fluttering from them like the dresses in a ballet, but of course petticoats under them. The strangest figures we saw were the Slovaks, who are more barbarian than the rest, with their big cowboy hats, great baggy dirty-white trousers, white linen shirts, and enormous heavy leather belts, nearly a foot wide, all studded over with brass nails. They wore high boots, with their trousers tucked into them, and had long black hair and heavy black moustaches. They are very picturesque, but do not look prepossessing. On the stage they would be set down at once as some old Oriental band of brigands. They are, however, I am told, very harmless and rather wanting in natural self- assertion.

It was on the dark side of twilight when we got to Bistritz, which is a very interesting old place. Being practically on the frontier – for the Borgo Pass leads from it into Bukovina – it has had a very stormy existence, and it certainly shows marks of it. Fifty years ago a series of great fires took place, which made terrible havoc on five separate occasions. At the very beginning of the seventeenth century it underwent a siege of three weeks and lost 13,000 people, the casualties of war proper being assisted by famine and disease.

Count Dracula had directed me to go to the Golden Krone Hotel, which I found, to my delight, to be thoroughly old-fashioned, for of course I wanted to see all I could of the ways of the country. I was evidently expected, for when I got near the door I faced a cheery-looking elderly woman in the usual peasant dress – white undergarment with long double apron, front and back, of coloured stuff fitting almost too tight for modesty. When I came close she bowed, and said: 'The Herr English-man?' 'Yes,' I said, 'Jonathan Harker.' She smiled, and gave some message to an elderly man in white shirt-sleeves, who had followed her to the door. He went, but immediately returned with a letter:–

'My Friend, – Welcome to the Carpathians. I am anxiously expecting you. Sleep well to-night. At three to-morrow the diligence will start for Bukovina; a place on it is kept for you. At the Borgo Pass my carriage will await you and will bring you to me. I trust that your journey from London has been a happy one, and that you will enjoy your stay in my beautiful land. – Your friend,

'Dracula.'

4 May. – I found that my landlord had got a letter from the Count, directing him to secure the best place on the coach for me; but on making inquiries as to details he seemed somewhat reticent, and pretended that he could not understand my German. This could not be true, because up to then he had understood it perfectly; at least, he answered my questions exactly as if he did. He and his wife, the old lady who had received me, looked at each other in a frightened sort of way. He mumbled out that the money had been sent in a letter, and that was all he knew. When I asked him if he knew Count Dracula, and could tell me anything of his castle, both he and his wife crossed themselves, and, saying that they knew nothing at all, simply refused to speak further. It was so near the time of starting that I had no time to ask anyone else, for it was all very mysterious and not by any means comforting.

Just before I was leaving, the old lady came up to my room and said in a very hysterical way:

'Must you go? Oh! young Herr, must you go?' She was in such an excited state that she seemed to have lost her grip of what German she knew, and mixed it all up with some other language which I did not know at all. I was just able to follow her by asking many questions. When I told her that I must go at once, and that I was engaged on important business, she asked again:

'Do you know what day it is?' I answered that it was the fourth of May. She shook her head as she said again:—

'Oh, yes! I know that, I know that! but do you know what day it is?' On my saying that I did not understand, she went on:

'It is the eve of St George's Day. Do you not know that to-night, when the clock strikes midnight, all the evil things in the world will have full sway? Do you know where you are going, and what you are going to?' She was in such evident distress that I tried to comfort her, but without effect. Finally she went down on her knees and implored me not to go; at least to wait a day or two before starting. It was all very ridiculous, but I did not feel comfortable. However, there was business to be done, and I could allow nothing to interfere with it. I therefore tried to raise her up, and said, as gravely as I could, that I thanked her, but my duty was imperative, and that I must go. She then rose and dried her eyes, and taking a crucifix from her neck offered it to me. I did not know what to do, for, as an English Churchman, I have been taught to regard such things as in some measure idolatrous, and yet it seemed so ungracious to refuse an old lady meaning so well and in such a state of mind. She saw, I suppose, the doubt in my face, for she put the rosary round my neck, and said, 'For your mother's sake,' and went out of the room. I am writing up this part of the diary whilst I am waiting for the coach, which is, of course, late; and the crucifix is still round my neck. Whether it is the old lady's fear, I do not know, but I am not feeling nearly as easy in my mind as usual. If this book should ever reach Mina before I do, let it bring my goodbye. Here comes the coach!

5 May. – *The Castle.* – The grey of the morning has passed, and the sun is high over the distant horizon, which seems jagged, whether with trees or hills I know not, for it is so far off that big things and little are mixed. I am not sleepy, and, as I am not to be called till I awake, naturally I write till sleep comes. There are many odd things to put down, and, lest who reads them may fancy that I dined too well before I left Bistritz, let me put down my dinner exactly. I dined on what they call 'robber steak' – bits of

bacon, onion, and beef, seasoned with red pepper, and strung on sticks and roasted over the fire, in the simple style of the London cat's-meat! The wine was Golden Mediasch, which produces a queer sting on the tongue, which is, however, not disagreeable. I had only a couple of glasses of this, and nothing else.

When I got on the coach the driver had not taken his seat, and I saw him talking with the landlady. They were evidently talking of me, for every now and then they looked at me, and some of the people who were sitting on the bench outside the door – which they call by a name meaning 'word-bearer' – came and listened, and then they looked at me, most of them pityingly. I could hear a lot of words often repeated, queer words, for there were many nationalities in the crowd; so I quietly got my polyglot dictionary from my bag and looked them out. I must say they were not cheering to me, for amongst them were 'Ordog' – Satan, 'pokol' – hell, 'stregoica' – witch, 'vrolok' and 'vlkoslak' – both of which mean the same thing, one being Slovak and the other Servian for something that is either were-wolf or vampire. (*Mem.*, I must ask the Count about these superstitions.)

When we started, the crowd round the inn door, which had by this time swelled to a considerable size, all made the sign of the cross and pointed two fingers towards me. With some difficulty I got a fellow-passenger to tell me what they meant; he would not answer at first, but on learning that I was English, he explained that it was a charm or guard against the evil eye. This was not very pleasant for me, just starting for an unknown place to meet an unknown man; but everyone seemed so kind-hearted, and so sorrowful, and so sympathetic that I could not but be touched. I shall never forget the last glimpse which I had of the inn-yard and its crowd of picturesque figures, all crossing themselves, as they stood round the wide archway, with its background of rich foliage of oleander and orange trees in green tubs clustered in the centre of the yard. Then our driver, whose wide linen drawers covered the whole front of the box-seat – 'gotza' they call them – cracked his big whip over his four small horses, which ran abreast, and we set off on our journey.

I soon lost sight and recollection of ghostly fears in the beauty of the scene as we drove along, although had I known the language, or rather languages, which my fellow-passengers were speaking, I might not have been able to throw them off so easily. Before us lay a green sloping land full of forests and woods, with here and there steep hills, crowned with clumps of trees or with farmhouses, the blank gable end to the road. There was everywhere a bewildering mass of fruit blossom – apple, plum, pear, cherry; and as we drove by I could see the green grass under the trees spangled with the fallen petals. In and out amongst these green hills of what they call here the 'Mittel Land' ran the road, losing itself as it swept round the grassy curve, or was shut out by the straggling ends of pine woods, which here and there ran down the hillsides like tongues of flame. The road was rugged, but still we seemed to fly over it with a feverish haste. I could not understand then what the haste meant, but the driver was evidently bent on losing no time in reaching Borgo Prund. I was told that this road is in summer-time excellent, but that it had not yet been put in order after the winter snows. In this respect it is different from the general run of roads in the Carpathians, for it is an old tradition that they are not to be kept in too good order. Of old the Hospadars would not repair them, lest the Turk should think that they were preparing to bring in foreign troops, and so hasten the war which was always really at loading point.

Beyond the green swelling hills of the Mittel Land rose mighty slopes of forest up to the lofty steeps of the Carpathians themselves. Right and left of us they towered, with the afternoon sun falling upon them and bringing out all the glorious colours of this beautiful range, deep blue and purple in the shadows of the peaks, green and brown where grass and rock mingled, and an endless perspective of jagged rock and pointed crags, till these were themselves lost in the distance, where the snowy peaks rose grandly. Here and there seemed mighty rifts in the mountains, through which, as the sun began to sink, we saw now and again the white gleam of falling water. One of my companions touched my arm as we swept round the base of a hill and opened up the lofty, snow-covered peak of a mountain, which seemed, as we wound on our serpentine way, to be right before us:

'Look! Isten szek!' – 'God's seat!' and he crossed himself reverently. As we wound on our endless way, and the sun sank lower and lower behind us, the shadows of the evening began to creep round us. This was emphasized by the fact that the snowy mountain-top still held the sunset, and seemed to glow out with a delicate cool pink. Here and there we passed Cszeks and Slovaks, all in picturesque attire, but I noticed that goitre was painfully prevalent. By the roadside were many crosses, and as we swept by, my companions all crossed themselves. Here and there was a peasant man or woman kneeling before a shrine, who did not even turn round as we approached, but seemed in the self-surrender of devotion to have neither eyes nor ears for the outer world. There were many things new to me: for instance, hay-ricks in the trees and here and there very beautiful masses of weeping birch, their white stems shining like silver through the delicate green of the leaves. Now and again we passed a leiterwaggon – the ordinary peasant's cart, with its long, snake-like vertebra, calculated to suit the inequalities of the road. On this were sure to be seated quite a group of home-coming peasants, the Cszeks with their white, and the Slovaks with their coloured, sheepskins, the latter carrying lance-fashion their long staves, with axe at end. As the evening fell it began to get very cold, and the growing twilight seemed to merge into one dark mistiness the gloom of the trees, oak, beech, and pine, though in the valleys which ran deep between the spurs of the hills, as we ascended through the Pass, the dark firs stood out here and there against the background of late-lying snow. Sometimes, as the road was cut through the pine woods that seemed in the darkness to be closing down upon us, great masses of greyness, which here and there bestrewed the trees, produced a peculiarly weird and solemn effect, which carried on the thoughts and grim fancies engendered earlier in the evening, when the falling sunset threw into strange relief the ghost-like clouds which amongst the Carpathians seem to wind ceaselessly through the valleys. Sometimes the hills were so steep that, despite our driver's haste, the horses could only go slowly. I wished to get down and walk up them, as we do at home, but the driver would not hear of it. 'No, no,' he said; 'you must not walk here; the dogs are too fierce,' and then he added, with what he evidently meant for grim pleasantry – for he looked round to catch the approving smile of the rest – 'and you may have enough of such matters before you go to sleep.' The only stop he would make was a moment's pause to light his lamps.

When it grew dark there seemed to be some excitement amongst the passengers, and they kept speaking to him, one after the other, as though urging him to further speed. He lashed the horses unmercifully with his long whip, and with wild cries of encouragement urged them on to further exertions. Then through the darkness I could see a sort of patch of grey light ahead of us, as though there were a cleft in the hills. The excitement of the passengers grew greater; the crazy coach rocked on its great leather springs, and swayed like a boat tossed on a stormy sea. I had to hold on. The road grew more level, and we appeared to fly along. Then the mountains seemed to come nearer to us on each side and to frown down upon us; we were entering the Borgo Pass. One by one several of the passengers offered me gifts, which they passed upon me with earnestness which would take no denial; these were certainly of an odd and varied kind, but each was given in simple good faith, with a kindly word, and a blessing, and that strange mixture of fear-meaning movements which I had seen outside the hotel at Bistritz – the sign of the cross and the guard against the evil eye. Then, as we flew along, the driver leaned forward, and on each side the passengers, craning over the edge of the coach, peered eagerly into the darkness. It was evident that something very exciting was either happening or expected, but though I asked each passenger, no one would give me the slightest explanation. This state of excitement kept on for some little time; and at last we saw before us the Pass opening out on the eastern side. There were dark, rolling clouds overhead, and in the air the heavy, oppressive sense of thunder. It seemed as though the mountain range had separated two atmospheres, and that now we had got into the thunderous one. I was now myself looking out for the conveyance which was to take me to the Count. Each moment I expected to see the glare of lamps through the blackness; but all was dark. The only light was the flickering rays of our own lamps, in which steam from our hard-driven horses rose in a white cloud. We could now see the sandy road lying white before us, but there was on it no sign of a vehicle. The passengers drew back with a sigh of gladness, which seemed to mock my own disappointment. I was already thinking what I had best do, when the driver, looking at his watch, said to the others something which I could hardly hear, it was spoken so quietly and in so low a tone; I thought it was, 'An hour less than the time.' Then, turning to me, he said in German worse than my own:

'There is no carriage here. The Herr is not expected, after all. He will now come on to Bukovina, and return to-morrow or the next day; better the next day.' Whilst he was speaking the horses began to neigh and snort and plunge wildly, so that the driver had to hold them up. Then, amongst a chorus of screams from the peasants and a universal crossing of themselves, a calèche, with four horses, drove up behind us, overtook us, and drew up beside the coach. I could see from the flash of our lamps, as the rays fell on them, that the horses were coal-black and splendid animals. They were driven by a tall man, with a long brown beard and a great black hat, which seemed to hide his face from us. I could only see the gleam of a pair of very bright eyes, which seemed red in the lamplight, as he turned to us. He said to the driver:—

'You are early to-night, my friend.' The man stammered in reply:—

'The English Herr was in a hurry,' to which the stranger replied:—

'That is why, I suppose, you wished him to go on to Bukovina. You cannot deceive me, my friend; I know too much, and my horses are swift.' As he spoke he smiled, the lamplight fell on a hard-looking mouth, with very red lips and sharp-looking teeth, as white as ivory. One of my companions whispered to another the line from Burger's 'Lenore':

'Denn die Todten reiten schnell.'—
('For the dead travel fast.')

The strange driver evidently heard the words, for he looked up with a gleaming smile. The passenger turned his face away, at the same time putting out his two fingers and crossing himself. 'Give me the Herr's luggage,' said the driver; and with exceeding alacrity my bags were handed out and put in the calèche. Then I descended from the side of the coach, as the calèche was close alongside, the driver helping me with a hand which caught my arm in a grip of steel; his strength must have been prodigious. Without a word he shook his reins, the horses turned, and we swept into the darkness of the Pass. As I looked back I saw the steam from the horses of the coach by the light of the lamps, and projected against it the figures of my late companions crossing themselves. Then the driver cracked his whip and called to his horses, and off they swept on their way to Bukovina.

As they sank into the darkness I felt a strange chill, and a lonely feeling came over me; but a cloak was thrown over my shoulders, and a rug across my knees, and the driver said in excellent German:

'The night is chill, mein Herr, and my master the Count bade me take all care of you. There is a flask of slivovitz [the plum brandy of the country] underneath the seat, if you should require it.' I did not take any, but it was a comfort to know it was there, all the same. I felt a little strange, and not a little frightened. I think had there been any alternative I should have taken it, instead of prosecuting that unknown night journey. The carriage went at a hard pace straight along, then we made a complete turn and went along another straight road. It seemed to me that we were simply going over and over the same ground again; and so I took note of some salient point, and found that this was so. I would have liked to have asked the driver what this all meant, but I really feared to do so, for I thought that, placed as I was, any protest would have had no effect in case there had been an intention to delay. By and by, however, as I was curious to know how time was passing, I struck a match, and by its flame looked at my watch; it was within a few minutes of midnight. This gave me a sort of shock, for I suppose the general superstition about midnight was increased by my recent experiences. I waited with a sick feeling of suspense.

Then a dog began to howl somewhere in a farmhouse far down the road – a long, agonized wailing, as if from fear. The sound was taken up by another dog, and then another and another, till, borne on the wind which now sighed softly through the Pass, a wild howling began, which seemed to come from all over the country, as far as the imagination could grasp it through the gloom of the night. At the first howl the horses began to strain and rear, but the driver spoke to them soothingly, and they quieted down, but shivered and sweated as though after a runaway from sudden fright. Then, far off in the distance, from the mountains on each side of us began a louder and sharper howling – that of wolves – which affected both the horses and myself in the same way – for I was minded to

9

jump from the calèche and run, whilst they reared again and plunged madly, so that the driver had to use all his great strength to keep them from bolting. In a few minutes, however, my own ears got accustomed to the sound, and the horses so far became quiet that the driver was able to descend and to stand before them. He petted and soothed them, and whispered something in their ears, as I have heard of horse-tamers doing, and with extraordinary effect, for under his caresses they became quite manageable again, though they still trembled. The driver again took his seat, and shaking his reins, started off at a great pace. This time, after going to the far side of the Pass, he suddenly turned down a narrow roadway which ran sharply to the right.

Soon we were hemmed in with trees, which in places arched right over the roadway till we passed as through a tunnel; and again great frowning rocks guarded us boldly on either side. Though we were in shelter, we could hear the rising wind, for it moaned and whistled through the rocks, and the branches of the trees crashed together as we swept along. It grew colder and colder still, and fine powdery snow began to fall, so that soon we and all around us were covered with a white blanket. The keen wind still carried the howling of the dogs, though this grew fainter as we went on our way. The baying of the wolves sounded nearer and nearer, as though they were closing round on us from every side. I grew dreadfully afraid, and the horses shared my fear; but the driver was not in the least disturbed. He kept turning his head to left and right, but I could not see anything through the darkness.

Suddenly, away on our left, I saw a faint flickering blue flame. The driver saw it at the same moment; he at once checked the horses and, jumping to the ground, disappeared into the darkness. I did not know what to do, the less as the howling of the wolves grew closer; but while I wondered the driver suddenly appeared again, and without a word took his seat, and we resumed our journey. I think I must have fallen asleep and kept dreaming of the incident, for it seemed to be repeated endlessly, and now, looking back, it is like a sort of awful nightmare. Once the flame appeared so near the road that even in the darkness around us I could watch the driver's motions. He went rapidly to where the blue flame rose – it must have been very faint, for it did not seem to illuminate the place around it at all – and gathering a few stones, formed them into some device. Once there appeared a strange optical effect: when he stood between me and the flame he did not obstruct it, for I could see its ghostly flicker all the same. This startled me, but as the effect was only momentary, I took it that my eyes deceived me straining through the darkness. Then for a time there were no blue flames, and we sped onwards through the gloom, with the howling of the wolves around us, as though they were following in a moving circle.

At last there came a time when the driver went further afield than he had yet done, and during his absence the horses began to tremble worse than ever and to snort and scream with fright. I could not see any cause for it, for the howling of the wolves had ceased altogether; but just then the moon, sailing through the black clouds, appeared behind the jagged crest of a beetling, pineclad rock, and by its light I saw around us a ring of wolves, with white teeth and lolling red tongues, with long, sinewy limbs and shaggy hair. They were a hundred times more terrible in the grim silence which held them than even when they howled. For myself, I felt a sort of paralysis of fear. It is only when a man feels himself face to face with such horrors that he can understand their true import.

All at once the wolves began to howl as though the moonlight had had some peculiar effect on them. The horses jumped about and reared, and looked helplessly round with eyes that rolled in a way painful to see; but the living ring of terror encompassed them on every side, and they had perforce to remain within it. I called to the coachman to come, for it seemed to me that our only chance was to try to break out through the ring and to aid his approach. I shouted and beat the side of the calèche, hoping by the noise to scare the wolves from that side, so as to give him a chance of reaching the trap. How he came there, I know not, but I heard his voice raised in a tone of imperious command, and looking towards the sound, saw him stand in the roadway. As he swept his long arms, as though brushing aside some impalpable obstacle, the wolves fell back and back further still. Just then a heavy cloud passed across the face of the moon, so that we were again in darkness.

When I could see again the driver was climbing into the calèche, and the wolves had disappeared. This was all so strange and uncanny that a dreadful fear came upon me, and I was afraid to speak or move. The time seemed interminable as we swept on our way, now in almost complete darkness, for the rolling clouds obscured the moon. We kept on ascending, with occasional periods of quick descent, but in the main always ascending. Suddenly I became conscious of the fact that the driver was in the act of pulling up the horses in the courtyard of a vast castle, from whose tall black windows came no ray of light, and whose broken battlements showed a jagged line against the moonlit sky.

2

JONATHAN HARKER'S JOURNAL

(continued)

5 May.– I must have been asleep, for certainly if I had been fully awake I must have noticed the approach to such a remarkable place. In the gloom the courtyard looked of considerable size, and as several dark ways led from it under great round arches it perhaps seemed bigger than it really is. I have not yet been able to see it by daylight.

When the calèche stopped the driver jumped down, and held out his hand to assist me to alight. Again I could not but notice his prodigious strength. His hand actually seemed like a steel vice that could have crushed mine if he had chosen. Then he took out my traps, and placed them on the ground beside me as I stood close to a great door, old and studded with large iron nails, and set in a projecting doorway of massive stone. I could see even in the dim light that the stone was massively carved, but that the carving had been much worn by time and weather. As I stood, the driver jumped again into his seat and shook the reins; the horses started forward, and trap and all disappeared down one of the dark openings.

I stood in silence where I was, for I did not know what to do. Of bell or knocker there was no sign; through these frowning walls and dark window openings it was not likely that my voice could penetrate. The time I waited seemed endless, and I felt doubts and fears crowding upon me. What sort of place had I come to, and among what kind of people? What sort of grim adventure was it on which I had embarked? Was this a customary incident in the life of a solicitor's clerk sent out to explain the purchase of a London estate to a foreigner? Solicitor's clerk! Mina would not like that. Solicitor – for just before leaving London I got word that my examination was successful; and I am now a full-blown solicitor! I began to rub my eyes and pinch myself to see if I were awake. It all seemed like a horrible nightmare to me, and I expected that I should suddenly awake, and find myself at home, with the dawn struggling in through the windows, as I had now and again felt in the morning after a day of overwork. But my flesh answered the pinching test, and my eyes were not to be deceived. I was indeed awake and among the Carpathians. All I could do now was to be patient, and to wait the coming of the morning.

Just as I had come to this conclusion I heard a heavy step approaching behind the great door, and saw through the chinks the gleam of a coming light. Then there was the sound of rattling chains and the clanking of massive bolts drawn back. A key was turned with the loud grating noise of long disuse, and the great door swung back.

Within, stood a tall old man, clean-shaven save for a long white moustache, and clad in black from head to foot, without a single speck of colour about him anywhere. He held in his hand an antique silver lamp, in which the flame burned without chimney or globe of any kind, throwing long, quivering shadows as it flickered in the draught of the open door. The old man motioned me in with his right hand with a courtly gesture, saying in excellent English, but with a strange intonation:

'Welcome to my house! Enter freely and of your own will!' He made no motion of stepping to meet me, but stood like a statue, as though his gesture of welcome had fixed him into stone. The instant, however, that I had stepped over the threshold, he moved impulsively forward, and holding out his hand grasped mine with a strength which made me wince, an effect which was not lessened by the fact that it seemed as cold as ice – more like the hand of a dead than a living man. Again he said:

'Welcome to my house. Come freely. Go safely. And leave something of the happiness you bring!' The strength of the handshake was so much akin to that which I had noticed in the driver, whose face I had not seen, that for a moment I doubted if it were not the same person to whom I was speaking; so, to make sure, I said interrogatively:

'Count Dracula?' He bowed in a courtly way as he replied:–

'I am Dracula. And I bid you welcome, Mr Harker, to my house. Come in; the night air is chill, and you must need to eat and rest.' As he was speaking he put the lamp on a bracket on the wall, and stepping out, took my luggage; he had carried it in before I could forestall him. I protested, but he insisted:

'Nay, sir, you are my guest. It is late, and my people are not available. Let me see to your comfort myself.' He insisted on carrying my traps along the passage, and then up a great winding stair, and along another great passage, on whose stone floor our steps rang heavily. At the end of this he threw open a heavy door, and I rejoiced to see within a well-lit room in which a table was spread for supper, and on whose mighty hearth a great fire of logs flamed and flared.

The Count halted, putting down my bags, closed the door, and crossing the room, opened another door, which led into a small octagonal room lit by a single lamp, and seemingly without a window of any sort. Passing through this, he opened another door, and motioned me to enter. It was a welcome sight; for here was a great bedroom well lighted and warmed with another log fire, which sent a hollow roar up the wide chimney. The Count himself left my luggage inside and withdrew, saying, before he closed the door:

'You will need, after your journey, to refresh yourself by making your toilet. I trust you will find all you wish. When you are ready come into the other room, where you will find your supper prepared.'

The light and warmth and the Count's courteous welcome seemed to have dissipated all my doubts and fears. Having then reached my normal state, I discovered that I was half-famished with hunger; so making a hasty toilet, I went into the other room.

I found supper already laid out. My host, who stood on one side of the great fireplace, leaning against the stone-work, made a graceful wave of his hand to the table, and said:

'I pray you, be seated and sup how you please. You will, I trust, excuse me that I do not join you; but I have dined already, and I do not sup.'

I handed to him the sealed letter which Mr Hawkins had entrusted to me. He opened it and read it gravely; then, with a charming smile, he handed it to me to read. One passage of it, at least, gave me a thrill of pleasure:

'I much regret that an attack of gout, from which malady I am a constant sufferer, forbids absolutely any travelling on my part for some time to come; but I am happy to say I can send a sufficient substitute, one in whom I have every possible confidence. He is a young man, full of energy and talent in his own way, and of a very faithful disposition. He is discreet and silent, and has grown into manhood in my service. He shall be ready to attend on you when you will during his stay, and shall take your instructions in all matters.'

The Count himself came forward and took off the cover of a dish, and I fell to at once on an excellent roast chicken. This, with some cheese and a salad and a bottle of old Tokay, of which I had two glasses, was my supper. During the time I was eating it the Count asked me many questions as to my journey, and I told him by degrees all I had experienced.

By this time I had finished my supper, and by my host's desire had drawn up a chair by the fire and begun to smoke a cigar which he offered me, at the same time excusing himself that he did not smoke. I had now an opportunity of observing him, and found him of a very marked physiognomy.

His face was a strong – a very strong – aquiline, with high bridge of the thin nose and peculiarly arched nostrils; with lofty domed forehead, and hair growing scantily round the temples, but profusely elsewhere. His eyebrows were very massive, almost meeting over the nose, and with bushy hair that seemed to curl in its own profusion. The mouth, so far as I could see it under the heavy moustache, was fixed and rather cruel-looking, with peculiarly sharp white teeth; these protruded over the lips, whose remarkable ruddiness showed astonishing vitality in a man of his years. For the rest, his ears were pale and at the tops extremely pointed; the chin was broad and strong, and the cheeks firm though thin. The general effect was one of extraordinary pallor.

Hitherto I had noticed the backs of his hands as they lay on his knees in the firelight, and they had seemed rather white and fine; but seeing them now close to me, I could not but notice that they were rather coarse – broad, with squat fingers. Strange to say, there were hairs in the centre of the palm. The nails were long and fine, and cut to a sharp point. As the Count leaned over me and his hands touched me, I could not repress a shudder. It may have been that his breath was rank, but a horrible feeling of nausea came over me, which, do what I would, I could not conceal. The Count, evidently noticing it, drew back; and with a grim sort of smile, which showed more than he had yet done his protuberant teeth, sat himself down again on his own side of the fireplace. We were both silent for a while; and as I looked towards the window I saw the first dim streak of the coming dawn. There seemed a strange stillness over everything; but as I listened I heard, as if from down below in the valley, the howling of many wolves. The Count's eyes gleamed, and he said:

'Listen to them – the children of the night. What music they make!' Seeing, I suppose, some expression in my face strange to him, he added:–

'Ah, sir, you dwellers in the city cannot enter into the feelings of the hunter.' Then he rose and said:

'But you must be tired. Your bedroom is all ready, and to-morrow you shall sleep as late as you will. I have to be away till the afternoon; so sleep well and dream well!' and, with a courteous bow, he opened for me himself the door to the octagonal room, and I entered my bedroom. . . .

I am all in a sea of wonders. I doubt; I fear; I think strange things which I dare not confess to my own soul. God keep me, if only for the sake of those dear to me!

7 May. – It is again early morning, but I have rested and enjoyed the last twenty-four hours. I slept till late in the day, and awoke of my own accord. When I had dressed myself I went into the room where we had supped, and found a cold breakfast laid, out with coffee kept hot by the pot being placed on the hearth. There was a card on the table, on which was written:

'I have to be absent for a while. Do not wait for me. D.' So I set to and enjoyed a hearty meal. When I had done, I looked for a bell, so that I might let the servants know I had finished; but I could not find one. There are certainly odd deficiencies in the house, considering the extraordinary evidences of wealth which are round me. The table service is of gold, and so beautifully wrought that it must be of immense value. The curtains and upholstery of the chairs and sofas and the hangings of my bed are of the costliest and most beautiful fabrics, and must have been of fabulous value when they were made, for they are centuries old, though in excellent order. I saw something like them in Hampton Court, but there they were worn and frayed and moth-eaten. But still in none of the rooms is there a mirror. There is not even a toilet glass on my table, and I had to get the little shaving-glass from my bag before I could either shave or brush my hair. I have not yet seen a servant anywhere, or heard a sound near the castle except for the howling of wolves. When I had finished my meal – I do not know whether to call it breakfast or dinner, for it was between five and six o'clock when I had it – I looked about for something to read, for I did not like to go about the castle until I had asked the Count's permission. There was absolutely nothing in the room, book, newspaper, or even writing materials; so I opened another door in the room and found a sort of library. The door opposite mine I tried, but found it locked.

In the library I found, to my great delight, a vast number of English books, whole shelves full of them, and bound volumes of magazines and newspapers. A table in the centre was littered with English magazines and newspapers, though none of them were of very recent date. The books were of the most varied kind – history, geography, politics, political economy, botany, geology, law – all relating to England and English life and customs and manners. There were even such books of reference as the London Directory, the 'Red' and 'Blue' books, Whitaker's Almanack, the Army and Navy Lists, and – it somehow gladdened my heart to see it – the Law List.

Whilst I was looking at the books, the door opened, and the Count entered. He saluted me in a hearty way, and hoped that I had had a good night's rest. Then he went on:

'I am glad you found your way in here, for I am sure there is much that will interest you. These friends' – and he laid his hand on some of the books – 'have been good friends to me, and for some years past, ever since I had the idea of going to London, have given me many, many hours of pleasure. Through them I have come to know your great England; and to know her is to love her. I long to go through the crowded streets of your mighty London, to be in the midst of the whirl and rush of humanity, to share its life, its change, its death, and all that makes it what it is. But alas! as yet I only know your tongue through books. To you, my friend, I look that I know it to speak.'

'But, Count,' I said, 'you know and speak English thoroughly!' He bowed gravely.

'I thank you, my friend, for your all too flattering estimate, but yet I fear that I am but a little way on the road I would travel. True, I know the grammar and the words, but yet I know not how to speak them.'

'Indeed,' I said, 'you speak excellently.'

'Not so,' he answered. 'Well I know that, did I move and speak in your London, none there are who would not know me for a stranger. That is not enough for me. Here I am noble; I am *boyar*; the common people know me, and I am master. But a stranger in a strange land, he is no one; men know him not – and to know not is to care not for. I am content if I am like the rest, so that no man stops if he sees me, or pause in his speaking if he hear my words, to say, "Ha, ha! a stranger!" I have been so long master that I would be master still – or at least that none other should be master of me. You come to me not alone as agent of my friend Peter Hawkins, of Exeter, to tell me all about my new estate in London. You shall, I trust, rest here with me a while, so that by our talking I may learn the English intonation; and I would that you tell me when I make error, even of the smallest, in my speaking. I am sorry that I had to be away so long to-day; but you will, I know, forgive one who has so many important affairs in hand.'

Of course I said all I could about being willing, and asked if I might come into that room when I chose. He answered, 'Yes, certainly,' and added:

'You may go anywhere you wish in the castle, except where the doors are locked, where of course you will not wish to go. There is reason that all things are as they are, and did you see with my eyes and know with my knowledge, you would perhaps better understand.' I said I was sure of this, and then he went on: ·

'We are in Transylvania; and Transylvania is not England. Our ways are not your ways, and there shall be to you many strange things. Nay, from what you have told me of your experiences already, you know something of what strange things here may be.'

This led to much conversation. And as it was evident that he wanted to talk, if only for talking's sake, I asked him many questions regarding things that had already happened to me or come within my notice. Sometimes he sheered off the subject, or turned the conversation by pretending not to understand; but generally he answered all I asked most frankly. Then as time went on, and I had got somewhat bolder, I asked him of some of the strange things of the preceding night, as, for instance, why the coachman went to the places where we had seen the blue flames. Was it indeed true that they showed where gold was hidden? He then explained to me that it was commonly believed that on a certain night of the year – last night, in fact, when all evil spirits are supposed to have unchecked sway – a blue flame is seen over any place where treasure has

17

been concealed. 'That treasure has been hidden,' he went on, 'in the region through which you came last night, there can be but little doubt; for it was the ground fought over for centuries by the Wallachian, the Saxon, and the Turk, Why, there is hardly a foot of soil in all this region that has not been enriched by the blood of men, patriots or invaders. In old days there were stirring times, when the Austrian and the Hungarian came up in hordes, and the patriots went out to meet them – men and women, the aged and the children too – and waited their coming on the rocks above the passes, that they might sweep destruction on them with their artificial avalanches. When the invader was triumphant he found but little, for whatever there was had been sheltered in the friendly soil.'

'But how,' said I, 'can it have remained so long undiscovered, when there is a sure index to it if men will but take the trouble to look?' The Count smiled, and as his lips ran back over his gums, the long, sharp, canine teeth showed out strangely; he answered:

'Because your peasant is at heart a coward and a fool! Those flames only appear on one night. And on that night no man of this land will, if he can help it, stir without his doors. And, dear sir, even if he did he would not know what to do. Why, even the peasant that you tell me of who marked the place of the flame would not know where to look in daylight even for his own work. You would not, I dare be sworn, be able to find these places again?'

'There you are right,' I said. 'I know no more than the dead where even to look for them.' Then we drifted into other matters.

'Come,' he said at last, 'tell me of London and of the house which you have procured for me.' With an apology for my remissness, I went into my own room to get the papers from my bag. Whilst I was placing them in order I heard a rattling of china and silver in the next room, and as I passed through, noticed that the table had been cleared and the lamp lit, for it was by this time deep into the dark. The lamps were also lit in the study or library, and I found the Count lying on the sofa, reading, of all things in the world, an English Bradshaw's Guide. When I came in he cleared the books and papers from the table; and with him I went into plans and deeds and figures of all sorts. He was interested in everything, and asked me a myriad questions about the place and its surroundings. He clearly had studied beforehand all he could get on the subject of the neighbourhood, for he evidently at the end knew very much more than I did. When I remarked this, he answered:

'Well, but, my friend, is it not needful that I should? When I go there I shall be all alone, and my friend Harker Jonathan – nay, pardon me, I fall into my country's habit of putting your patronymic first – my friend Jonathan Harker will not be by my side to correct and aid me. He will be in Exeter, miles away, probably working at papers of the law with my other friend, Peter Hawkins. So!'

We went thoroughly into the business of the purchase of the estate at Purfleet. When I had told him the facts and got his signature to the necessary papers, and had written a letter with them ready to post to Mr Hawkins, he began to ask me how I had come across so suitable a place. I read to him the notes which I had made at the time, and which I inscribe here:

'At Purfleet, on a by-road I came across just such a place as seemed to be required, and where was displayed a dilapidated notice that the place was for sale. It is surrounded by a high wall, of ancient structure, built of heavy stones, and has not been repaired for a large number of years. The closed gates were of heavy old oak and iron, all eaten with rust.

'The estate is called Carfax, no doubt a corruption of the old *Quatre Face*, as the house is four-sided, agreeing with the cardinal points of the compass. It contains in all some twenty acres, quite surrounded by the solid stone wall above mentioned. There are many trees on it, which make it in places gloomy, and there is a deep, dark-looking pond or small lake, evidently fed by some springs, as the water is clear and flows away in a fair-sized stream. The house is very large and of all periods back, I should say, to mediæval times, for one part is of stone immensely thick, with only a few windows high up and heavily barred with iron. It looks like part of a keep, and is close to an old chapel or church. I could not enter it, as I had not the key of the door leading to it from the house, but I have taken with my Kodak views of it from various points. The house has been added to, but in a very straggling way, and I can only guess at the amount of ground it covers, which must be very great. There are but few houses close at hand, one being a very large house only recently added to and formed into a private lunatic asylum. It is not, however, visible from the grounds.'

When I had finished, he said:

'I am glad that it is old and big. I myself am of an old family, and to live in a new house would kill me. A house cannot be made habitable in a day; and, after all, how few days go to make up a century. I rejoice that there is a chapel of old times. We Transylvanian nobles love not to think that our bones may be amongst the common dead. I seek not gaiety nor mirth, not the bright voluptuousness of much sunshine and sparkling waters which please the young and gay. I am no longer young. And my heart, through weary years of mourning over the dead, is not attuned to mirth. Moreover, the walls of my castle are broken; the shadows are many, and the wind breathes cold through the broken battlements and casements. I love the shade and the shadow, and would be alone with my thoughts when I may.'

Somehow his words and his looks did not seem to accord, or else it was that his cast of face made his smile look malignant and saturnine.

Presently, with an excuse, he left me, asking me to put all my papers together. He was some little time away, and I began to look at some of the books around me. One was an atlas, which I found opened naturally at England, as if that map had been much used. On looking at it I found in certain places little rings marked, and on examining these I noticed that one was near London on the east side, manifestly where his new estate was situated; the other two were Exeter, and Whitby on the Yorkshire coast.

It was the better part of an hour when the Count returned. 'Aha!' he said, 'still at your books? Good! But you must not work always. Come; I am informed that your supper is ready.' He took my arm, and we went into the next room, where I found an excellent supper ready on the table. The Count again excused himself, as he had dined out on his being away from home. But he sat as on the previous night, and chatted whilst I ate. After supper I smoked, as on the last evening, and the Count stayed with me, chatting and asking questions on every conceivable subject, hour after hour. I felt that it was getting very late indeed, but I did not say anything, for I felt under obligation to meet my host's wishes in every way. I was not sleepy, as the long sleep yesterday had fortified me; but I could not help experiencing that chill which comes over one at the coming of dawn, which is like, in its way, the turn of the tide. They say people who are near death die generally at the change to the dawn or at the turn of the tide; anyone who has, when tired, and tied as it were to his post, experienced this change in the atmosphere can well believe it. All at once we heard the crow of a cock coming up with preternatural shrillness through the clear morning air; Count Dracula, jumping to his feet, said:

'Why, there is the morning again! How remiss I am to let you stay up so long! You must make your conversation regarding my dear new country of England less interesting, so that I may not forget how time flies by us,' and, with a courtly bow, he left me.

I went into my own room and drew the curtains, but there was little to notice; my window opened into the courtyard; all I could see was the warm grey quickening sky. So I pulled the curtains again, and have written of this day.

8 May. – I began to fear as I wrote in this book that I was getting too diffuse; but now I am glad that I went into detail from the first, for there is something so strange about this place and all in it that I cannot but feel uneasy. I wish I were safe out of it, or that I had never come. It may be that this strange night-existence is telling on me; but would that that were all! If there were anyone to talk to I could bear it, but there is no one. I have only the Count to speak with, and he! – I fear I am myself the only living soul within the place. Let me be prosaic so far as facts can be; it will help me to bear up, and imagination must not run riot with me. If it does I am lost. Let me say at once how I stand – or seem to.

I only slept a few hours when I went to bed, and feeling that I could not sleep any more, got up. I had hung my shaving-glass by the window, and was just beginning to shave. Suddenly I felt a hand on my shoulder, and heard the Count's voice saying to me, 'Good morning.' I started, for it amazed me that I had not seen him, since the reflection of the glass covered the whole room behind me. In starting I had cut myself slightly, but did not notice it at the moment. Having answered the Count's salutation, I turned to the glass again to see how I had been mistaken. This time there could be no error, for the man was close to me, and I could see him over my shoulder. But there was no reflection of him in the mirror! The whole room behind me was displayed; but there was no sign of a man in it, except myself. This was startling, and, coming on the top of so many strange things, was beginning to increase that vague feeling of uneasiness which I always have when the Count is near; but at that instant I saw that the cut had bled a little, and the blood was trickling over my chin. I laid down the razor, turning as I did so half-round to look for some sticking-plaster. When the Count saw my face, his eyes blazed with a sort of demoniac fury, and he suddenly made a grab at my throat. I drew away, and his hand touched the string of beads which held the crucifix. It made an instant change in him, for the fury passed so quickly that I could hardly believe that it was ever there.

'Take care,' he said, 'take care how you cut yourself. It is more dangerous than you think in this country.' Then seizing the shaving-glass, he went on: 'And this is the wretched thing that has done the mischief. It is a foul bauble of man's vanity. Away with it!' and opening the heavy window with one wrench of his terrible hand, he flung out the glass, which was shattered into a thousand pieces on the stones of the courtyard far below. Then he withdrew without a word. It is very annoying, for I do not see how I am to shave, unless in my watch-case or the bottom of the shaving-pot, which is fortunately, of metal.

When I went into the dining-room, breakfast was prepared; but I could not find the Count anywhere. So I breakfasted alone. It is strange that as yet I have not seen the Count eat or drink. He must be a very peculiar man! After breakfast I did a little exploring in the castle. I went out on the stairs and found a room looking towards the south. The view was magnificent, and from where I stood there was every opportunity of seeing it. The castle is on the very edge of a terrible precipice. A stone falling from the window would fall a thousand feet without touching anything! As far as the eye can reach is a sea of green tree-tops, with occasionally a deep rift where there is a chasm. Here and there are silver threads where the rivers wind in deep gorges through the forests.

But I am not in heart to describe beauty, for when I had seen the view I explored further; doors, doors, doors everywhere, and all locked and bolted. In no place save from the windows in the castle walls is there an available exit.

The castle is a veritable prison, and I am a prisoner!

3

JONATHAN HARKER'S JOURNAL

(continued)

When I found that I was a prisoner a sort of wild feeling came over me. I rushed up and down the stairs, trying every door and peering out of every window I could find; but after a little the conviction of my helplessness overpowered all other things. When I look back after a few hours I think I must have been mad for the time, for I behaved much as a rat does in a trap. When, however, the conviction had come to me that I was helpless I sat down quietly – as quietly as I have ever done anything in my life – and began to think over what was best to be done. I am thinking still, and as yet have come to no definite conclusion. Of one thing only am I certain: that it is no use making my ideas known to the Count. He knows well that I am imprisoned; and as he has done it himself, and has doubtless his own motives for it, he would only deceive me if I trusted him fully with the facts. So far as I can see, my only plan will be to keep my knowledge and my fears to myself, and my eyes open. I am, I know, either being deceived, like a baby, by my own fears, or else I am in desperate straits; and if the latter be so, I need, and shall need, all my brains to get through. I had hardly come to this conclusion when I heard the great door below shut, and knew that the Count had returned. He did not come at once into the library, so I went cautiously to my own room and found him making the bed. This was odd, but only confirmed what I had all along thought – that there were no servants in the house. When later I saw him through the chink of the hinges of the door laying the table in the dining-room, I was assured of it; for if he does himself all these menial offices, surely it is proof that there is no one else to do them. This gave me a fright, for if there is no one else in the castle, it must have been the Count himself who was the driver of the coach that brought me here. This is a terrible thought; for if so, what does it mean that he could control the wolves, as he did, by only holding up his hand in silence? How was it that all the people at Bistritz and on the coach had some terrible fear for me? What meant the giving of the crucifix, of the garlic, of the wild rose, of the mountain ash? Bless that good, good woman who hung the crucifix round my neck! for it is a comfort and a strength to me whenever I touch it. It is odd that a thing which I have been taught to regard with disfavour and as idolatrous should in a time of loneliness and trouble be of help. Is it that there is something in the essence of the thing itself, or that it is a medium, a tangible help, in conveying memories of sympathy and comfort? Some time, if it may be, I must examine this matter and try to make up my mind about it. In the meantime I must find out all I can about Count Dracula, as it may help me to understand. To-night he may talk of himself, if I turn the conversation that way. I must be very careful, however, not to awake his suspicion.

Midnight. – I have had a long talk with the Count. I asked him a few questions on Transylvanian history, and he warmed up to the subject wonderfully. In his speaking of things and people, and especially of battles, he spoke as if he had been present at them all. This he afterwards explained by saying that to a *boyar* the pride of his house and name is his own pride, that their glory is his glory, that their fate is his fate. Whenever he spoke of his house he always said 'we', and spoke almost in the plural, like a king speaking. I wish I could put down all he said exactly as he said it, for to me it was most fascinating. It seemed to have in it a whole history of the country. He grew excited as he spoke, and walked about the room pulling his great white moustache and grasping anything on which he laid his hands as though he would crush it by main strength. One thing he said which I shall put down as nearly as I can; for it tells in its way the story of his race:

'We Szekelys have a right to be proud, for in our veins flows the blood of many brave races who fought as the lion fights, for lordship. Here, in the whirlpool of European races, the Ugric tribe bore down from Iceland the fighting spirit which Thor and Wodin gave them, which their Berserkers displayed to such fell intent on the seaboards of Europe, aye, and of Asia and Africa, too, till the peoples thought that the were-wolves themselves had come. Here, too, when they came, they found the Huns, whose warlike fury had swept the earth like a living flame, till the dying peoples held that in their veins ran the blood of those old witches, who, expelled from Scythia, had mated with the devils in the desert. Fools, fools! What devil or what witch was ever so great as Attila, whose blood is in these veins?' He held up his arms. 'Is it a wonder that we were a conquering race; that we were proud; that when the Magyar, the

Lombard, the Avar, the Bulgar, or the Turk poured his thousands on our frontiers, we drove them back? Is it strange that when Arpad and his legions swept through the Hungarian fatherland he found us here when he reached the frontier; that the Honfoglalas was completed there? And when the Hungarian flood swept eastward, the Szekelys were claimed as kindred by the victorious Magyars, and to us for centuries was trusted the guarding of the frontier of Turkeyland; aye, and more than that, endless duty of the frontier guard, for, as the Turks say, "water sleeps, and enemy is sleepless". Who more gladly than we throughout the Four Nations received the "bloody sword", or at its warlike call flocked quicker to the standard of the King? When was redeemed that great shame of my nation, the shame of Cassova, when the flags of the Wallach and the Magyar went down beneath the Crescent; who was it but one of my own race who as Voivode crossed the Danube and beat the Turk on his own ground! This was a Dracula indeed. Who was it that his own unworthy brother, when he had fallen, sold his people to the Turk and brought the shame of slavery on them! Was it not this Dracula, indeed, who inspired that other of his race who in a later age again and again brought his forces over the great river into Turkeyland; who, when he was beaten back, came again, and again, and again, though he had to come alone from the bloody field where his troops were being slaughtered, since he knew that he alone could ultimately triumph? They said that he thought only of himself. Bah! what good are peasants without a leader? Where ends the war without a brain and heart to conduct it? Again, when, after the battle of Mohacs, we threw off the Hungarian yoke, we of the Dracula blood were amongst their leaders, for our spirit would not brook that we were not free. Ah, young sir, the Szekelys – and the Dracula as their heart's blood, their brains, and their swords – can boast a record that mushroom growths like the Hapsburgs and the Romanoffs can never reach. The warlike days are over. Blood is too precious a thing in these days of dishonourable peace; and the glories of the great races are as a tale that is told.'

It was by this time close on morning, and we went to bed. (*Mem.*, this diary seems horribly like the beginning of the 'Arabian Nights', for everything has to break off at cockcrow – or like the ghost of Hamlet's father.)

12 May. – Let me begin with facts – bare, meagre facts, verified by books and figures, and of which there can be no doubt. I must not confuse them with experiences which will have to rest on my own observation or my memory of them. Last evening when the Count came from his room he began by asking me questions on legal matters and on the doing of certain kinds of business. I had spent the day wearily over books, and, simply to keep my mind occupied, went over some of the matters I had been examined in at Lincoln's Inn. There was a certain method in the Count's inquiries, so I shall try to put them down in sequence; the knowledge may somehow or some time be useful to me.

First, he asked if a man in England might have two solicitors, or more. I told him him he might have a dozen if he wished, but that it would not be wise to have more than one solicitor engaged in one transaction, as only one could act at a time, and that to change would be certain to militate against his interest. He seemed thoroughly to understand, and went on to ask if there would be any practical difficulty in having one man to attend, say, to banking, and another to look after shipping, in case local help were needed in a place far from the home of the banking solicitor. I asked him to explain more fully, so that I might not by any chance mislead him, so he said:

'I shall illustrate. Your friend and mine, Mr Peter Hawkins, from under the shadow of your beautiful cathedral at Exeter, which is far from London, buys for me through your good self my place at London. Good! Now here let me say frankly, lest you should think it strange that I have sought the services of one so far off from London instead of someone resident there, that my motive was that no local interest might be served save my wish only; and as one of London resident might, perhaps, have some purpose of himself or friend to serve I went thus afield to seek my agent, whose labours should be only to my interest. Now, suppose I, who have much of affairs, wish to ship goods, say, to Newcastle, or Durham, or Harwich, or Dover, might it not be that it could with more ease be done by consigning to one in those ports?' I answered that certainly it would be most easy, but that we solicitors had a system of agency one for the other, so that local work could be done locally on instruction from any solicitor, so that the client, simply placing himself in the hands of one man, could have his wishes carried out by him without further trouble.

'But,' said he, 'I could be at liberty to direct myself. Is it not so?'

'Of course,' I replied; 'and such is often done by men of business, who do not like the whole of their affairs to be known by any one person.'

'Good!' he said, and then went on to ask about the means of making consignments and the forms to be gone through, and of all sorts of difficulties which might arise, but by forethought could be guarded against. I explained all these things to him to the best of my ability, and he certainly left me under the impression that he would have made a wonderful solicitor, for there was nothing that he did not think of or foresee. For a man who was never in the country, and who did not evidently do much in the way of business, his knowledge and acumen were wonderful. When he had satisfied himself on these points of which he had spoken, and I had verified all as well as I could by the books available, he suddenly stood up and said:

'Have you written since your first letter to our friend Mr Peter Hawkins, or to any other?' It was with some bitterness in my heart that I answered that I had not, that as yet I had not seen any opportunity of sending letters to anybody.

'Then write now, my young friend,' he said, laying a heavy hand on my shoulder; 'write to our friend and to any other; and say, if it will please you, that you shall stay with me until a month from now.'

'Do you wish me to stay so long?' I asked, for my heart grew cold at the thought.

'I desire it much; nay, I will take no refusal. When your master, employer, what you will, engaged that someone should come on his behalf, it was understood that my needs only were to be consulted. I have not stinted. Is it not so?'

What could I do but bow acceptance? It was Mr Hawkins's interest, not mine, and I had to think of him, not myself; and besides, while Count Dracula was speaking, there was that in his eyes and in his bearing which made me remember that I was a prisoner, and that if I wished it I could have no choice. The Count saw his victory in my bow, and his mastery in the trouble of my face, for he began at once to use them, but in his own smooth, resistless way:

'I pray you, my good young friend, that you will not discourse of things other than business in your letters. It will doubtless please your friends to know that you are well, and that you look forward to getting home to them. It is not so?' As he spoke he handed me three sheets of notepaper and three envelopes. They were all of the thinnest foreign post, and looking at them, then at him, and noticing his quiet smile, with the sharp, canine teeth lying over the red under-lip, I understood as well as if he had spoken that I should be careful what I wrote, for he would be able to read it. So I determined to write only formal notes now, but to write fully to Mr Hawkins in secret, and also to Mina, for to her I could write in shorthand, which would puzzle the Count, if he did see it. When I had written my two letters I sat quiet, reading a book whilst the Count wrote several notes, referring as he wrote them to some books on his table. Then he took up my two and placed them with his own, and put by his writing materials, after which, the instant the door had closed behind him, I leaned over and looked at the letters, which were face down on the table. I felt no compunction in doing so, for under the circumstances I felt that I should protect myself in every way I could.

One of the letters was directed to Samuel F. Billington, No. 7, The Crescent, Whitby; another to Herr Leutner, Varna; the third was to

Coutts & Co., London, and the fourth to Herren Klopstock & Billreuth, Buda-Pesth. The second and fourth were unsealed. I was just about to look at them when I saw the door-handle move. I sank back in my seat, having just had time to replace the letters as they had been and to resume my book before the Count, holding still another letter in his hand, entered the room. He took up the letters on the table and stamped them carefully, and then, turning to me, said:

'I trust you will forgive me, but I have much work to do in private this evening. You will, I hope, find all things as you wish.' At the door he turned, and after a moment's pause said:

'Let me advise you, my dear young friend — nay, let me warn you with all seriousness, that should you leave these rooms you will not by any chance go to sleep in any other part of the castle. It is old, and has many memories, and there are bad dreams for those who sleep unwisely. Be warned! Should sleep now or ever overcome you, or be like to do, then haste to your own chamber or to these rooms, for your rest will then be safe. But if you be not careful in this respect, then — ' He finished his speech in a gruesome way, for he motioned with his hands as if he were washing them. I quite understand; my only doubt was as to whether any dream could be more terrible than the unnatural, horrible net of gloom and mystery which seemed closing round me.

Later. — I endorse the last words written, but this time there is no doubt in question. I shall not fear to sleep in any place where he is not. I have placed the crucifix over the head of my bed — I imagine that my rest is thus freer from dreams; and there it shall remain.

When he left me I went to my room. After a little while, not hearing any sound, I came out and went up the stone stair to where I could look out towards the south. There was some sense of freedom in the vast expanse, inaccessible though it was to me, as compared with the narrow darkness of the courtyard. Looking out on this, I felt that I was indeed in prison, and I seemed to want a breath of fresh air, though it were of the night. I am beginning to feel this nocturnal existence tell on me. It is destroying my nerve. I start at my own shadow, and am full of all sorts of horrible imaginings. God knows that there is ground for any terrible fear in this accursed place! I looked out over the beautiful expanse, bathed in soft yellow moonlight till it was almost as light as day. In the soft light the distant hills became melted, and the shadows in the valleys and gorges of velvety blackness. The mere beauty seemed to cheer me; there was peace and comfort in every breath I drew. As I leaned from the window my eye was caught by something moving a story below me, and somewhat to my left, where I imagined, from the lie of the rooms, that the windows of the Count's own room would look out. The window at which I stood was tall and deep, stone-mullioned, and though weather-worn, was still complete; but it was evidently many a day since the case had been there. I drew back behind the stonework, and looked carefully out.

What I saw was the Count's head coming out from the window. I did not see the face, but I knew the man by the neck and the movement of his back and arms. In any case, I could not mistake the hands which I had had so many opportunities of studying. I was at first interested and somewhat amused, for it is wonderful how small a matter will interest and amuse a man when he is a prisoner. But my very feelings changed to repulsion and terror when I saw the whole man slowly emerge from the window and begin to crawl down the castle wall over that dreadful abyss, *face down*, with his cloak spreading out around him like great wings. At first I could not believe my eyes. I thought it was some trick of the moonlight, some weird effect of shadow; but I kept looking, and it could be no delusion. I saw the fingers and toes grasp the corners of the stones, worn clear of the mortar by the stress of years, and by thus using every projection and inequality move downwards with considerable speed, just as a lizard moves along a wall.

What manner of man is this, or what manner of creature is it in the semblance of man? I feel the dread of this horrible place overpowering me; I am in fear – in awful fear – and there is no escape for me; I am encompassed about with terrors that I dare not think of. . . .

15 May. – Once more have I seen the Count go out in his lizard fashion. He moved downwards in a sidelong way, some hundred feet down, and a good deal to the left. He vanished into some hole or window. When his head had disappeared I leaned out to try and see more, but without avail – the distance was too great to allow a proper angle of sight. I knew he had left the castle now, and thought to use the opportunity to explore more than I had dared to do as yet. I went back to the room, and taking a lamp, tried all the doors. They were all locked as I had expected, and the locks were comparatively new; but I went down the stone stairs to the hall where I had entered originally. I found I could pull back the bolts easily enough and unhook the great chains; but the door was locked, and the key was gone! That key must be in the Count's room; I must watch should his door be unlocked, so that I may get it and escape. I went on to make a thorough examination of the various stairs and passages, and to try the doors that opened from them. One or two small rooms near the hall were open, but there was nothing to see in them except old furniture, dusty with age and moth-eaten. At last, however, I found one door at the top of a stairway which, though it seemed to be locked, gave a little under pressure. I tried it harder, and found it was not really locked, but that the resistance came from the fact that the hinges had fallen somewhat, and the heavy door rested on the floor. Here was an opportunity which I might not have again, so I exerted myself, and with many efforts forced it back so that I could enter. I was now in a wing of the castle further to the right than the rooms I knew and a story lower down. From the windows I could see that the suite of rooms lay along to the south of the castle, the windows of the end room looking out both west and south. On the latter side as well as to the former, there was a great precipice. The castle was built on the corner of a great rock, so that on three sides it was quite impregnable, and great windows were placed here where sling, or bow, or culverin could not reach, and consequently light and comfort, impossible to a position which had to be guarded, were secured. To the west was a great valley, and then, rising far away, great jagged mountain fastnesses, rising peak on peak, the sheer rock studded with mountain ash and thorn, whose roots clung in cracks and crevices and crannies of the stone. This was evidently the portion of the castle occupied in bygone days, for the furniture had more air of comfort than any I had seen. The windows were curtainless, and the yellow moonlight, flooding in through the diamond panes, enabled one to see even colours, whilst it softened the wealth of dust which lay over all and disguised in some measure the ravages of time and the moth. My lamp seemed to be of little effect in the brilliant moonlight, but I was glad to have it with me, for there was a dread loneliness in the place which chilled my heart and made my nerves tremble. Still, it was better than living alone in the rooms which I had come to hate from the presence of the Count, and after trying a little to school my nerves, I found a soft quietude come over me. Here I am, sitting at a little oak table where in old times possibly some fair lady sat to pen, with much thought and many blushes, her ill-spelt love-letter, and writing in my diary in shorthand all that has happened since I closed it last. It is nineteenth century up-to-date with a vengeance. And yet, unless my senses deceive me, the old centuries had, and have powers of their own which mere 'modernity' cannot kill.

Later: the Morning of 16 May. – God preserve my sanity, for to this I am reduced. Safety and the assurance of safety are things of the past. Whilst I live on here there is but one thing to hope for: that I may not go mad, if, indeed, I be not mad already. If I be sane, then surely it is maddening to think that of all the foul things that lurk in this hateful place the Count is the least dreadful to me; that to him alone I can look for safety, even though this be only whilst I can serve his purpose. Great God! merciful God! Let me be calm, for out of that way lies madness indeed. I begin to get new lights on certain things which have puzzled me. Up to now I never quite knew what Shakespeare meant when he made Hamlet say:

'My tablets! quick, my tablets!
'Tis meet that I put it down,' etc.,

for now, feeling as though my own brain was unhinged or as if the shock
had come which must end in its undoing, I turn to my diary for repose.
The habit of entering accurately must help to soothe me.

The Count's mysterious warning frightened me at the time; it frightens
me more now when I think of it, for in future he has a fearful hold upon
me. I shall fear to doubt what he may say!

When I had written in my diary and had fortunately replaced the book
and pen in my pocket, I felt sleepy. The Count's warning came into my
mind, but I took a pleasure in disobeying it. The sense of sleep was upon
me, and with it the obstinacy which sleep brings as outrider. The soft
moonlight soothed, and the wide expanse without gave a sense of
freedom which refreshed me. I determined not to return to-night to the
gloom-haunted rooms, but to sleep here, where of old ladies had sat and
sung and lived sweet lives whilst their gentle breasts were sad for their
menfolk away in the midst of remorseless wars. I drew a great couch out
of its place near the corner, so that, as I lay, I could look at the lovely view
to east and south, and unthinking of and uncaring for the dust, composed
myself for sleep.

I suppose I must have fallen asleep; I hope so, but I fear, for all that
followed was startlingly real – so real that now, sitting here in the broad,
full sunlight of the morning, I cannot in the least believe that it was all
sleep.

I was not alone. The room was the same, unchanged in any way since I
came into it; I could see along the floor, in the brilliant moonlight, my
own footsteps marked where I had disturbed the long accumulation of
dust. In the moonlight opposite me were three young women, ladies by
their dress and manner. I thought at the time that I must be dreaming
when I saw them, for, though the moonlight was behind them, they threw
no shadow on the floor. They came close to me and looked at me for some
time and then whispered together. Two were dark, and had high aquiline
noses, like the Count's, and great dark, piercing eyes, that seemed to be
almost red when contrasted with the pale yellow moon. The other was
fair, as fair as can be, with great, wavy masses of golden hair and eyes like
pale sapphires. I seemed somehow to know her face, and to know it in
connection with some dreamy fear, but I could not recollect at the
moment how or where. All three had brilliant white teeth, that shone like
pearls against the ruby of their voluptuous lips. There was something
about them that made me uneasy, some longing and at the same time
some deadly fear. I felt in my heart a wicked, burning desire that they

would kiss me with those red lips. It is not good to note this down, lest some day it should meet Mina's eyes and cause her pain; but it is the truth. They whispered together, and then they all three laughed – such a silvery, musical laugh, but as hard as though the sound never could have come through the softness of human lips. It was like the intolerable, tingling sweetness of water-glasses when played on by a cunning hand. The fair girl shook her head coquettishly, and the other two urged her on. One said:

'Go on! You are first, and we shall follow; yours is the right to begin.' The other added:

'He is young and strong; there are kisses for us all.' I lay quiet, looking out under my eyelashes in an agony of delightful anticipation. The fair girl advanced and bent over me till I could feel the movement of her breath upon me. Sweet it was in one sense, honey-sweet, and sent the same tingling through the nerves as her voice, but with a bitter underlying the sweet, a bitter offensiveness, as one smells in blood.

I was afraid to raise my eyelids, but looked out and saw perfectly under the lashes. The fair girl went on her knees and bent over me, fairly gloating. There was a deliberate voluptuousness which was both thrilling and repulsive, and as she arched her neck she actually licked her lips like an animal, till I could see in the moonlight the moisture shining on the scarlet lips and on the red tongue as it lapped the white sharp teeth. Lower and lower went her head as the lips went below the range of my mouth and chin and seemed about to fasten on my throat. Then she paused, and I could hear the churning sound of her tongue as it licked her teeth and lips, and could feel the hot breath on my neck. Then the skin of my throat began to tingle as one's flesh does when the hand that is to tickle it approaches nearer – nearer. I could feel the soft, shivering touch of the lips on the supersensitive skin of my throat, and the hard dents of two sharp teeth, just touching and pausing there. I closed my eyes in a languorous ecstasy and waited – waited with beating heart.

But at that instant another sensation swept through me as quick as lightning. I was conscious of the presence of the Count, and of his being as if lapped in a storm of fury. As my eyes opened involuntarily I saw his strong hand grasp the slender neck of the fair woman and with giant's power draw it back, the blue eyes transformed with fury, the white teeth champing with rage, and the fair cheeks blazing red with passion. But the Count! Never did I imagine such wrath and fury, even in the demons of the pit. His eyes were positively blazing. The red light in them was lurid, as if the flames of hell-fire blazed behind them. His face was deathly pale, and the lines of it were hard like drawn wires; the thick eyebrows that met over the nose now seemed like a heaving bar of white-hot metal. With a fierce sweep of his arm, he hurled the woman from him, and then motioned to the others, as though he were beating them back; it was the same imperious gesture that I had seen used to the wolves. In a voice which, though low and almost a whisper, seemed to cut through the air and then ring round the room, he exclaimed:

'How dare you touch him, any of you? How dare you cast eyes on him when I had forbidden it? Back, I tell you all! This man belongs to me! Beware how you meddle with him, or you'll have to deal with me.' The fair girl, with laugh of ribald coquetry, turned to answer him:—

'You yourself never loved; you never love!' On this the other women joined, and such a mirthless, hard, soulless laughter rang through the room that it almost made me faint to hear; it seemed like the pleasure of fiends. Then the Count turned, after looking at my face attentively, and said in a soft whisper:

'Yes, I too can love; you yourselves can tell it from the past. Is it not so? Well, now I promise you that when I am done with him, you shall kiss him at your will. Now go! go! I must awaken him, for there is work to be done.'

'Are we to have nothing to-night?' said one of them, with a low laugh, as she pointed to the bag which he had thrown upon the floor, and which moved as though there were some living thing within it. For answer he nodded his head. One of the women jumped forward and opened it. If my ears did not deceive me there was a gasp and a low wail, as of a half-smothered child. The women closed round, whilst I was aghast with horror; but as I looked they disappeared, and with them the dreadful bag. There was no door near them, and they could not have passed me without my noticing. They simply seemed to fade into the rays of the moonlight and pass out through the window, for I could see outside the dim, shadowy forms for a moment before they entirely faded away.

Then the horror overcame me, and I sank down unconscious.

4

JONATHAN HARKER'S JOURNAL

(continued)

I awoke in my own bed. If it be that I had not dreamt, the Count must have carried me here. I tried to satisfy myself on the subject, but could not arrive at any unquestionable result. To be sure, there were certain small evidences, such as that my clothes were folded and laid by in a manner which is not my habit. My watch was still unwound, and I am rigorously accustomed to wind it the last thing before going to bed, and many such details. But these things are no proof, for they may have been evidences that my mind was not as usual, and, from some cause or another, I had certainly been much upset. I must watch for proof. Of one thing I am glad: if it was the Count that carried me here and undressed me, he must have been hurried in his task, for my pockets are intact. I am sure this diary would have been a mystery to him which he would not have brooked. He would have taken or destroyed it. As I look round this room, although it has been to me so full of fear, it is now a sort of sanctuary, for nothing can be more dreadful than those awful women, who were, – who *are* – waiting to suck my blood.

18 May. – I have been down to look at that room again in daylight, for I *must* know the truth. When I got to the doorway at the top of the stairs, I found it closed. It had been so forcibly driven against the jamb that part of the woodwork was splintered. I could see that the bolt of the lock had not been shot, but the door is fastened from the inside. I fear it was no dream, and must act on this surmise.

19 May. – I am surely in the toils. Last night the Count asked me in the suavest tones to write three letters, one saying that my work here was nearly done and that I should start for home within a few days, another that I was starting on the next morning from the time of the letter, and the third that I had left the castle and arrived at Bistritz. I would fain have rebelled, but felt that in the present state of things it would be madness to quarrel openly with the Count whilst I am so absolutely in his power; and to refuse would be to excite his suspicion and to arouse his anger. He knows that I know too much, and that I must not live, lest I be dangerous to him; my only chance is to prolong my opportunities. Something may occur which will give me a chance to escape. I saw in his eyes something of that gathering wrath which was manifest when he hurled that fair woman from him. He explained to me that posts were few and uncertain, and that my writing now would ensure ease of mind to my friends; and he assured me with so much impressiveness that he would countermand the later letters, which would be held over at Bistritz until due time in case chance would admit of my prolonging my stay, that to oppose him would have been to create new suspicion. I therefore pretended to fall in with his views, and asked him what dates I should put on the letters. He calculated a minute, and then said:–

'The first should be June 12, the second June 19, and the third June 29.'

I know now the span of my life. God help me!

28 May. – There is a chance of escape, or at any rate of being able to send word home. A band of Szgany have come to the castle, and are encamped in the courtyard. These Szgany are gipsies; I have notes of them in my book. They are peculiar to this part of the world, though allied to the ordinary gipsies all the world over. There are thousands of them in Hungary and Transylvania who are almost outside all law. They attach themselves as a rule to some great noble or *boyar*, and call themselves by his name. They are fearless and without religion, save superstition, and they talk only their own varieties of the Romany tongue.

I shall write some letters home, and shall try to get them to have them posted. I have already spoken to them through my window to begin an acquaintanceship. They took their hats off and made obeisance and many signs, which, however, I could not understand any more than I could their spoken language. . . .

I have written the letters. Mina's is in shorthand, and I simply ask Mr Hawkins to communicate with her. To her I have explained my situation, but without the horrors which I may only surmise. It would shock and frighten her to death were I to expose my heart to her. Should the letters not carry, then the Count shall not yet know my secret or the extent of my knowledge. . . .

I have given the letters; I threw them through the bars of my window with a gold piece, and made what signs I could to have them posted. The man who took them pressed them to his heart and bowed, and then put them in his cap. I could do no more. I stole back to the study and began to read. As the Count did not come in, I have written here. . . .

The Count has come. He sat down beside me, and said in his smoothest voice as he opened two letters:

'The Szgany has given me these, of which, though I know not whence they come, I shall, of course, take care. See!' – he must have looked at it – 'one is from you, and to my friend Peter Hawkins; the other' – here he caught sight of the strange symbols as he opened the envelope, and the dark look came into his face, and his eyes blazed wickedly – 'the other is a vile thing, an outrage upon friendship and hospitality! It is not signed. Well! so it cannot matter to us.' And he calmly held letter and envelope in the flame of the lamp till they were consumed. Then he went on:

'The letter to Hawkins – that I shall, of course, send on, since it is yours. Your letters are sacred to me. Your pardon, my friend, that unknowingly I did break the seal. Will you not cover it again?' He held out the letter to me, and with a courteous bow handed me a clean envelope. I could only redirect it and hand it to him in silence. When he went out of the room I could hear the key turn softly. A minute later I went over and tried it, and the door was locked.

When, an hour or two after, the Count came quietly into the room, his coming wakened me, for I had gone to sleep on the sofa. He was very courteous and very cheery in his manner, and seeing that I had been sleeping, he said:

'So, my friend, you are tired? Get to bed. There is the surest rest. I may not have the pleasure to talk-to-night, since there are many labours to me; but you will sleep, I pray.' I passed to my room and went to bed, and, strange to say, slept without dreaming. Despair has its own calms.

31 May. – This morning when I woke I thought I would provide myself with some paper and envelopes from my bag and keep them in my pocket, so that I might write in case I should get an opportunity; but again a surprise, again a shock!

Every scrap of paper was gone, and with it all my notes, my memoranda relating to railways and travel, my letter of credit, in fact, all that might be useful to me were I once outside the castle. I sat and pondered a while, and then some thought occurred to me, and I made search of my portmanteau and in the wardrobe where I had placed my clothes.

The suit in which I had travelled was gone, and also my overcoat and rug; I could find no trace of them anywhere. This looked like some new scheme of villainy. . . .

17 June. – This morning, as I was sitting on the edge of my bed cudgelling my brains, I heard without a cracking of whips and pounding and scraping of horses' feet up the rocky path beyond the courtyard. With joy I hurried to the window, and saw drive into the yard two great leiter-waggons, each drawn by eight sturdy horses, and at the head of each pair a Slovak, with his wide hat, great, nail-studded belt, dirty sheepskin, and high boots. They had also their long staves in hand. I ran to the door, intending to descend and try and join them through the main hall, as I thought that way might be opened for them. Again a shock: my door was fastened on the outside.

Then I ran to the window and cried to them. They looked up at me stupidly and pointed, but just then the 'hetman' of the Szgany came out, and seeing them pointing to my window, said something, at which they laughed. Henceforth, no effort of mine, no piteous cry or agonized entreaty, would make them even look at me. They resolutely turned away. The leiter-waggons contained great, square boxes, with handles of thick rope; these were evidently empty by the ease with which the Slovaks handled them, and by their resonance as they were roughly moved. When they were all unloaded and backed in a great heap in one corner of the yard, the Slovaks were given some money by the Szgany, and spitting on it for luck, lazily went each to his horse's head. Shortly afterwards I heard the cracking of their whips die away in the distance.

24 June, before morning. – Last night the Count left me early, and locked himself into his own room. As soon as I dared, I ran up the winding stair, and looked out of the window which opened south. I thought I would watch for the Count, for there is something going on. The Szgany are quartered somewhere in the castle, and are doing work of some kind. I know it, for now and then I hear a far-away, muffled sound as of mattock and spade, and, whatever it is, it must be to the end of some ruthless villainy.

I had been at the window somewhat less than half an hour, when I saw something coming out of the Count's window. I drew back and watched carefully, and saw the whole man emerge. It was a new shock to me to find that he had on the suit of clothes which I had worn whilst travelling here, and slung over his shoulder the terrible bag which I had seen the women take away. There could be no doubt as to this quest, and in my garb, too! This, then, is his new scheme of evil: that he will allow others to see me, as they think, so that he may both leave evidence that I have been seen in the towns or villages posting my own letters, and that any wickedness which he may do shall by the local people be attributed to me.

It makes me rage to think that this can go on, and whilst I am shut up here, a veritable prisoner, but without that protection of the law which is even a criminal's right and consolation.

I thought I would watch for the Count's return, and for a long time sat doggedly at the window. Then I began to notice that there were some quaint little specks floating in the rays of the moonlight. They were like the tiniest grains of dust, and they whirled round and gathered in clusters in a nebulous sort of way. I watched them with a sense of soothing, and a sort of calm stole over me. I leaned back in the embrasure in a more comfortable position, so that I could enjoy more fully the aerial gambolling.

Something made me start up, a low, piteous howling of dogs somewhere far below in the valley, which was hidden from my sight. Louder it seemed to ring in my ears, and the floating motes of dust to take new shapes to the sound as they danced in the moonlight. I felt myself struggling to awake to some call of my instincts; nay, my very soul was struggling, and my half-remembered sensibilities were striving to answer the call. I was becoming hypnotized! Quicker and quicker danced the dust, and the moonbeams seemed to quiver as they went by me into the mass of gloom beyond. More and more they gathered till they seemed to take dim phantom shapes. And then I started, broad awake and in full possession of my senses, and ran screaming from the place. The phantom shapes, which were becoming gradually materialized from the moonbeams, were those of the three ghostly women to whom I was doomed. I fled, and felt somewhat safer in my own room, where there was no moonlight and where the lamp was burning brightly.

When a couple of hours had passed I heard something stirring in the Count's room, something like a sharp wail quickly suppressed; and then there was silence, deep, awful silence, which chilled me. With a beating heart, I tried the door; but I was locked in my prison, and could do nothing. I sat down and simply cried.

As I sat I heard a sound in the courtyard without – the agonized cry of a woman. I rushed to the window, and throwing it up, peered out between the bars. There, indeed, was a woman with dishevelled hair, holding her hands over her heart as one distressed with running. She was leaning against a corner of the gateway. When she saw my face at the window she threw herself forward, and shouted in a voice laden with menace:

'Monster, give me my child!'

She threw herself on her knees, and raising up her hands, cried the same words in tones which wrung my heart. Then she tore her hair and beat her breast, and abandoned herself to all the violences of extravagant emotion. Finally, she threw herself forward, and, though I could not see her, I could hear the beating of her naked hands against the door.

Somewhere high overhead, probably on the tower, I heard the voice of the Count calling in his harsh, metallic whisper. His call seemed to be answered from far and wide by the howling of wolves. Before many minutes had passed a pack of them poured, like a pent-up dam when liberated, through the wide entrance into the courtyard.

There was no cry from the woman, and the howling of the wolves was but short. Before long they streamed away singly, licking their lips.

I could not pity her, for I knew now what had become of her child, and she was better dead.

What shall I do? What can I do? How can I escape from this dreadful thrall of night and gloom and fear?

25 June, morning. – No man knows till he has suffered from the night how sweet and how dear to his heart and eye the morning can be. When the sun grew so high this morning that it struck the top of the great gateway opposite my window, the high spot which it touched seemed to me as if the dove from the ark had lighted there. My fear fell from me as if it had been a vaporous garment which dissolved in the warmth. I must take action of some sort while the courage of the day is upon me. Last night one of my post-dated letters went to post, the first of that fatal series which is to blot out the very traces of my existence from the earth.

Let me not think of it. Action!

It has always been at night-time that I have been molested or threatened, or in some way in danger or in fear. I have not yet seen the

Count in the daylight. Can it be that he sleeps when others wake, that he may be awake whilst they sleep! If I could only get into his room! But there is no possible way. The door is always locked, no way for me.

Yes, there is a way, if one dares to take it. Where his body has gone why may not another body go? I have seen him myself crawl from his window; why should not I imitate him, and go in by his window? The chances are desperate, but my need is more desperate still. I shall risk it. At the worst it can only be death. And a man's death is not a calf's, and the dread Hereafter may still be open to me. God help me in my task! Good-bye, Mina, if I fail: good-bye, my faithful friend and second father; good-bye, all, and last of all Mina!

Same day, later. – I have made the effort, and, God helping me, have come safely back to this room. I must put down every detail in order. I went whilst my courage was fresh straight to the window on the south side, and at once got outside on the narrow ledge of stone which runs round the building on this side. The stones were big and roughly cut, and the mortar had by process of time been washed away between them. I took off my boots, and ventured out on the desperate way. I looked down once, so as to make sure that sudden glimpse of the awful depth would not overcome me, but after that kept my eyes away from it. I knew pretty well the direction and distance of the Count's window, and made for it as well as I could, having regard to the opportunities available. I did not feel dizzy – I suppose I was too excited – and the time seemed ridiculously short till I found myself standing on the window-sill and trying to raise up the sash. I was filled with agitation, however, when I bent down and slid feet foremost in through the window. Then I looked round for the Count, but, with surprise and gladness, made a discovery. The room was empty! It was barely furnished with odd things, which seemed to have never been used; the furniture was something the same style as that in the south rooms, and was covered with dust. I looked for the key, but it was not in the lock, and I could not find it anywhere. The only thing I found was a great heap of gold in one corner – gold of all kinds, Roman, and British, and Austrian, and Hungarian, and Greek and Turkish money, covered with a film of dust, as though it had lain long in the ground. None of it that I noticed was less than three hundred years old. There were also chains and ornaments, some jewelled, but all of them old and stained.

At one corner of the room was a heavy door. I tried it, for, since I could not find the key of the room or the key of the outer door, which was the main object of my search, I must make further examination, or all my efforts would be in vain. It was open, and led through a stone passage to a circular stairway, which went steeply down. I descended, minding carefully where I went, for the stairs were dark, being only lit by loopholes in the heavy masonry. At the bottom there was a dark, tunnel-like passage, through which came a deathly, sickly odour, the odour of old earth newly turned. As I went through the passage the smell grew closer and heavier. At last I pulled open a heavy door which stood ajar, and found myself in an old, ruined chapel, which had evidently been used as a graveyard. The roof was broken, and in two places were steps leading to vaults, but the ground had recently been dug over, and the earth placed in great wooden boxes, manifestly those which had been brought by the Slovaks. There was nobody about, and I made search for any further outlet, but there was none. Then I went over every inch of the ground, so as not to lose a chance. I went down even into the vaults, where the dim light struggled, although to do so was dread to my very soul. Into two of these I went, but saw nothing except fragments of old coffins and piles of dust; in the third, however, I made a discovery.

There, in one of the great boxes, of which there were fifty in all, on a pile of newly dug earth, lay the Count! He was either dead or asleep, I could not say which – for the eyes were open and stony, but without the glassiness of death – and the cheeks had the warmth of life through all their pallor, and the lips were as red as ever. But there was no sign of movement, no pulse, no breath, no beating of the heart. I bent over him, and tried to find any sign of life, but in vain. He could not have lain there long, for the earthy smell would have passed away in a few hours. By the side of the box was its cover, pierced with holes here and there. I thought he might have the keys on him, but when I went to search I saw the dead eyes, and in them, dead though they were, such a look of hate, though unconscious of me or my presence, that I fled from the place, and leaving the Count's room by the window, crawled again up the castle wall. Regaining my own chamber, I threw myself panting upon the bed and tried to think. . . .

29 June. – To-day is the date of my last letter, and the Count has taken steps to prove that it was genuine, for again I saw him leave the castle by the same window, and in my clothes. As he went down the wall, lizard fashion, I wished I had a gun or some lethal weapon, that I might destroy him; but I fear that no weapon wrought alone by man's hand would have any effect on him. I dared not wait to see him return, for I feared to see those weird sisters. I came back to the library, and read there till I fell asleep.

I was awakened by the Count, who looked at me as grimly as a man can look as he said:

'To-morrow, my friend, we must part. You return to your beautiful England, I to some work which may have such an end that we may never meet. Your letter home has been despatched; to-morrow I shall not be here, but all shall be ready for your journey. In the morning come the Szgany, who have some labours of their own here, and also come some Slovaks. When they have gone, my carriage shall come for you, and shall bear you to the Borgo Pass to meet the diligence from Bukovina to Bistritz. But I am in hopes that I shall see more of you at Castle Dracula.' I suspected him, and determined to test his sincerity. Sincerity! It seems like a profanation of the word to write it in connection with such a monster, so I asked him point-blank:—

'Why may I not go to-night?'

'Because, dear sir, my coachman and horses are away on a mission.'

'But I would walk with pleasure. I want to get away at once.' He smiled, such a soft, smooth, diabolical smile that I knew there was some trick behind his smoothness. He said:—

'And your baggage?'

'I do not care about it. I can send for it some other time.'

The Count stood up, and said, with a sweet courtesy which made me rub my eyes, it seemed so real:—

'You English have a saying which is close to my heart, for its spirit is that which rules our *boyars*: "Welcome the coming, speed the parting guest." Come with me, my dear young friend. Not an hour shall you wait in my house against your will, though sad am I at your going, and that you so suddenly desire it. Come!' With a stately gravity, he, with the lamp, preceded me down the stairs and along the hall. Suddenly he stopped.

'Hark!'

Close at hand came the howling of many wolves. It was almost as if the sound sprang up at the raising of his hand, just as the music of a great orchestra seems to leap under the baton of the conductor. After a pause of a moment, he proceeded in his stately way, to the door, drew back the ponderous bolts, unhooked the heavy chains, and began to draw it open.

To my intense astonishment I saw that it was unlocked. Suspiciously I looked all round, but could see no key of any kind.

As the door began to open, the howling of the wolves without grew louder and angrier; their red jaws, with champing teeth, and their blunt-clawed feet as they leaped, came in through the opening door. I knew that to struggle at the moment against the Count was useless. With such allies as these at his command, I could do nothing. But still the door continued slowly to open, and only the Count's body stood in the gap. Suddenly it struck me that this might be the moment and the means of my doom; I was to be given to the wolves, and at my own instigation. There was a diabolical wickedness in the idea great enough for the Count, and as a last chance I cried out:—

'Shut the door; I shall wait till morning!' and covered my face with my hands to hide my tears of bitter disappointment. With one sweep of his powerful arm, the Count threw the door shut, and the great bolts clanged and echoed through the hall as they shot back into their places.

In silence we returned to the library, and after a minute or two I went to my own room. The last I saw of Count Dracula was his kissing his hand to me, with a red light of triumph in his eyes, and with a smile that Judas in hell might be proud of.

When I was in my room and about to lie down, I thought I heard a whispering at my door. I went to it softly and listened. Unless my ears deceived me, I heard the voice of the Count:—

'Back, back, to your own place! Your time is not yet come. Wait. Have patience. To-morrow night, to-morrow night, is yours!' There was a low, sweet ripple of laughter, and in a rage I threw open the door, and saw without the three terrible women licking their lips. As I appeared they all joined in a horrible laugh, and ran away.

I came back to my room and threw myself on my knees. Is it then so near the end? To-morrow! to-morrow! Lord, help me, and those to whom I am dear!

30 June, morning. – These may be the last words I ever write in this diary. I slept till just before the dawn, and when I woke threw myself on my knees, for I determined that if Death came he should find me ready.

At last I felt that subtle change in the air and knew that the morning had come. Then came the welcome cock-crow, and I felt that I was safe. With a glad heart, I opened my door and ran down the hall. I had seen that the door was unlocked and now escape was before me. With hands that trembled with eagerness, I unhooked the chains and drew back the massive bolts.

But the door would not move. Despair seized me. I pulled and pulled at the door, and shook it till, massive as it was, it rattled in its casement. I could see the bolt shot. It had been locked after I left the Count.

Then a wild desire took me to obtain that key at any risk, and I determined then and there to scale the wall again and gain the Count's room. He might kill me, but death now seemed the happier choice of evils. Without a pause I rushed up to the east window and scrambled down the wall, as before, into the Count's room. It was empty, but that was as I expected. I could not see a key anywhere, but the heap of gold remained. I went through the door in the corner and down the winding stair and along the dark passage to the old chapel. I knew now well enough where to find the monster I sought.

The great box was in the same place, close against the wall, but the lid was laid on it, not fastened down, but with the nails ready in their places to be hammered home. I knew I must search the body for the key, so I

41

raised the lid and laid it back against the wall; and then I saw something which filled my very soul with horror. There lay the Count, but looking as if his youth had been half-renewed, for the white hair and moustache were changed to dark iron-grey; the cheeks were fuller, and the white skin seemed ruby-red underneath; the mouth was redder than ever, for on the lips were gouts of fresh blood, which trickled from the corners of the mouth and ran over the chin and neck. Even the deep, burning eyes seemed set amongst swollen flesh, for the lids and pouches underneath were bloated. It seemed as if the whole awful creature were simply gorged with blood; he lay like a filthy leech, exhausted with his repletion. I shuddered as I bent over to touch him, and every sense in me revolted at the contact; but I had to search, or I was lost. The coming night might see my own body a banquet in a similar way to those horrid three. I felt all over the body, but no sign could I find of the key. Then I stopped and looked at the Count. There was a mocking smile on the bloated face which seemed to drive me mad. This was the being I was helping to transfer to London, where, perhaps for centuries to come, he might, amongst its teeming millions, satiate his lust for blood, and create a new and ever widening circle of semi-demons to batten on the helpless. The very thought drove me mad. A terrible desire came upon me to rid the world of such a monster. There was no lethal weapon at hand, but I seized a shovel which the workmen had been using to fill the cases, and lifting it high, struck, with the edge downward, at the hateful face. But as I did so the head turned, and the eyes fell upon me, with all their blaze of basilisk horror. The sight seemed to paralyse me, and the shovel turned in my hand and glanced from the face, merely making a deep gash above the forehead. The shovel fell from my hand across the box, and as I pulled it away the flange of the blade caught the edge of the lid, which fell over again, and hid the horrid thing from my sight. The last glimpse I had was of the bloated face, bloodstained and fixed with a grin of malice which would have held its own in the nethermost hell.

I thought and thought what should be my next move, but my brain seemed on fire, and I waited with a despairing feeling growing over me. As I waited I heard in the distance a gipsy song sung by merry voices coming closer, and through their song the rolling of heavy wheels and the cracking of whips; the Szgany and the Slovaks of whom the Count had spoken were coming. With a last look round and at the box which contained the vile body, I ran from the place and gained the Count's room, determined to rush out at the moment the door should be opened. With strained ears I listened, and heard downstairs the grinding of the key in the great lock and the falling back of the heavy door. There must have been some other means of entry, or someone had a key for one of the

42

locked doors. Then there came the sound of many feet tramping and dying away in some passage which sent up a clanging echo. I turned to run down again towards the vault, where I might find the new entrance; but at that moment there seemed to come a violent puff of wind, and the door to the winding stair blew to with a shock that set the dust from the lintels flying. When I ran to push it open, I found that it was hopelessly fast. I was again a prisoner, and the net of doom was closing round me more closely.

As I write there is in the passage below a sound of many tramping feet and the crash of weights being set down heavily, doubtless the boxes, with their freight of earth. There is a sound of hammering; it is the box being nailed down. Now I can hear the heavy feet tramping again along the hall, with many other idle feet coming behind them.

The door is shut, and the chains rattle; there is a grinding of the key in the lock; I can hear the key withdrawn; then another door opens and shuts; I hear the creaking of lock and bolt.

Hark! in the courtyard and down the rocky way the roll of heavy wheels, the crack of whips, and the chorus of the Szgany as they pass into the distance.

I am alone in the castle with those awful women. Faugh! Mina is a woman, and there is naught in common. They are devils of the Pit!

I shall not remain alone with them; I shall try to scale the castle wall farther than I have yet attempted. I shall take some of the gold with me, lest I want it later. I may find a way from this dreadful place.

And then away for home! away to the quickest and nearest train! away from this cursed spot, from this cursed land, where the devil and his children still walk with earthly feet!

At least God's mercy is better than that of these monsters, and the precipice is steep and high. At its foot man may sleep – as a man. Good-bye, all! Mina!

5

Letter from Miss Mina Murray to Miss Lucy Westenra

'9 May.

'My dearest Lucy, –

'Forgive my long delay in writing, but I have been simply overwhelmed with work. The life of an assistant schoolmistress is sometimes trying. I am longing to be with you, and by the sea, where we can walk together freely and build our castles in the air. I have been working very hard lately, because I want to keep up with Jonathan's studies, and I have been practising shorthand very assiduously. When we are married I shall be able to be useful to Jonathan, and if I can stenograph well enough I can take down what he wants to say in this way and write it out for him on the typewriter, at which I am also practising very hard. He and I sometimes write letters in shorthand, and he is keeping a stenographic journal of his travels abroad. When I am with you I shall keep a diary in the same way. I don't mean one of those two-pages-to-the-week-with-Sunday-squeezed-in-a-corner diaries, but a sort of journal which I can write in whenever I feel inclined. I do not suppose there will be much of interest to other people; but it is not intended for them. I may show it to Jonathan some day if there is in it anything worth sharing, but it is really an exercise-book. I shall try to do what I see lady journalists do: interviewing and writing descriptions and trying to remember conversations. I am told that, with a little practice, one can remember all that goes on or that one hears said during a day. However, we shall see. I shall tell you all my little plans when we meet. I have just had a few hurried lines from Jonathan from Transylvania. He is well, and will be returning in about a week. I am longing to hear all his news. It must be so nice to see strange countries, I wonder if we – I mean Jonathan and I – shall ever see them together. There is the ten o'clock bell ringing. Good-bye.

'Your loving
'MINA.

'Tell me all the news when you write. You have not told me anything for a long time. I hear rumours, and especially of a tall, handsome, curly-haired man? ? ?'

Letter, Lucy Westenra to Mina Murray

'17 Chatham Street,
'Wednesday.

'My dearest Mina, –

'I must say you tax me *very* unfairly with being a bad correspondent. I wrote to you *twice* since we parted, and your last letter was only your *second*. Besides, I have nothing to tell you. There is really nothing to interest you. Town is very pleasant just now, and we go a good deal to picture-galleries and for walks and rides in the park. As to the tall, curly-haired man, I suppose it was the one who was with me at the last Pop. Someone has evidently been telling tales. That was Mr Holmwood. He often comes to see us, and he and mamma get on very well together; they have so many things to talk about in common. We met some time ago a man that would just *do for you*, if you were not already engaged to Jonathan. He is an excellent *parti*, being handsome, well off, and of good birth. He is a doctor and really clever. Just fancy! He is only nine-and-twenty, and he has an immense lunatic asylum all under his own care. Mr Holmwood introduced him to me, and he called here to see us, and often comes now. I think he is one of the most resolute men I ever saw, and yet the most calm. He seems absolutely imperturbable. I can fancy what a wonderful power he must have over his patients. He has a curious habit of looking one straight in the face, as if trying to read one's thoughts. He tries this on very much with me, but I flatter myself he has got a tough nut to crack. I know that from my glass. Do you ever try to read your own face? *I do*, and I can tell you it is not a bad study, and gives you more trouble than you can well fancy if you have never tried it. He says that I afford him a curious psychological study, and I humbly think I do. I do not, as you know, take sufficient interest in dress to be able to describe the new fashions. Dress is a bore. That is slang again, but never mind; Arthur says that every day. There, it is all out. Mina, we have told all our secrets to each other since we were *children*; we have slept together and eaten together, and laughed and cried together; and now, though I have spoken, I would like to speak more. Oh, Mina, couldn't you guess? I love him. I am blushing as I write, for although I *think* he loves me, he has not told me so in words. But, oh, Mina, I love him; I love him; I love him! There, that does me good. I wish I were with you, dear, sitting by the fire undressing, as we used to sit; and I would try to tell you what I feel. I do not know how I am writing this even to you. I am afraid to stop, or I should tear up the letter, and I don't want to stop, for I *do so* want to tell you all. Let me hear from you *at once*, and tell me all that you think about it. Mina, I must stop. Good-night. Bless me in your prayers; and, Mina, pray for my happiness.

'Lucy.

'P.S. – I need not tell you this is a secret. Good-night again.

'L.'

Letter, Lucy Westenra to Mina Murray

'24 May.

'My dearest Mina, –

'Thanks, and thanks, and thanks again for your sweet letter! It was so nice to be able to tell you and to have your sympathy.

'My dear, it never rains but it pours. How true the old proverbs are. Here am I, who will be twenty in September, and yet I never had a proposal till to-day, not a real proposal, and to-day I have had three. Just fancy! THREE proposals in one day! Isn't it awful! I feel sorry, really and truly sorry, for two of the poor fellows. Oh, Mina, I am so happy that I don't know what to do with myself. And three proposals! But, for goodness' sake, don't tell any of the girls, or they would be getting all sorts of extravagant ideas and imagining themselves injured and slighted if in their very first day at home they did not get six at least. Some girls are so vain. You and I, Mina dear, who are engaged and are going to settle down soon soberly into old married women, can despise vanity. Well, I must tell you about the three, but you must keep it a secret, dear, from *everyone*, except, of course, Jonathan. You will tell him, because I would, if I were in your place, certainly tell Arthur. A woman ought to tell her husband everything – don't you think so, dear? – and I must be fair. Men like women, certainly their wives, to be quite as fair as they are; and women, I am afraid, are not always quite as fair as they are; and women, I am afraid, are not always quite as fair as they should be. Well, my dear, number one came just before lunch. I told you of him, Dr John Seward, the lunatic-asylum man, with the strong jaw and the good forehead. He was very cool outwardly, but was nervous all the same. He had evidently been schooling himself as to all sorts of little things, and remembered them; but he almost managed to sit down on his silk hat, which men don't generally do when they are cool, and then when he wanted to appear at ease he kept playing with a lancet in a way that made me nearly scream. He spoke to me, Mina, very straightforwardly. He told me how dear I was to him, though he had known me so little, and what his life would be with me to help and cheer him. He was going to tell me how unhappy he would be if I did not care for him, but when he saw me cry he said that he was a brute and would not add to my present trouble. Then be broke off and asked if I could love him in time; and when I shook my head his hands trembled, and then with some hesitation he asked me if I cared already for anyone else. He put it very nicely, saying that he did not want to wring my confidence from me, but only to know, because if a woman's heart was free a man might have hope. And then, Mina, I felt it a sort of duty to tell him that there was someone. I only told him that much, and then he stood up, and he looked very strong and very grave as he took both my hands in his and said he hoped I would be happy, and that if I ever wanted a friend I must count him one of my best. Oh, Mina dear, I can't help crying; and you must excuse this letter being all blotted. Being proposed to is all very nice and all that sort of thing, but it isn't at all a happy thing when you have to see a poor fellow, whom you know loves you honestly, going away and looking all broken-hearted, and to know that, no matter what he may say at the moment, you are passing quite out of his life. My dear, I must stop here at present, I feel so miserable, though I am so happy.

'Arthur has just gone, and I feel in better spirits than when I left off, so I can go on telling you about the day. Well, my dear, number two came after lunch. He is such a nice fellow, an American from Texas, and he looks so young and so fresh that it seems almost impossible that he has been to so many places and has had such adventures. I sympathize with poor Desdemona when she had such a dangerous stream poured in her ear, even by a black man. I suppose that we women are such cowards that we think a man will save us from fears, and we marry him. I know now what I would do if I were a man and wanted to make a girl love me. No, I don't, for there was Mr Morris telling us his stories, and Arthur never told any, and yet – My dear, I am somewhat previous. Mr Quincey P. Morris found me alone. It seems that a man always does find a girl alone. No, he doesn't, for Arthur tried twice to *make* a chance, and I helping him all I could; I am not ashamed to say it now. I must tell you beforehand that Mr Morris doesn't always speak slang – that is to say, he never does so to strangers or before them, for he is really well educated and has exquisite manners – but he found out that it amused me to hear him talk American slang, and whenever I was present, and there was no one to be shocked, he said such funny things. I am afraid, my dear, he has to invent it all, for it fits exactly into whatever else he has to say. But this is a way slang has. I do not know myself if I shall ever speak slang: I do not know if Arthur likes it, as I have never heard him use any as yet. Well, Mr Morris sat down beside me and looked as happy and jolly as he could, but I could see all the same that he was very nervous. He took my hand in his, and said ever so sweetly:–

' "Miss Lucy, I know I ain't good enough to regulate the fixin's of your little shoes, but I guess if you wait till you find a man that is you will go join them seven young women with the lamps when you quit. Won't you just hitch up alongside of me and let us go down the long road together driving in double harness?"

'Well, he did look so good-humoured and so jolly that it didn't seem half so hard to refuse him as it did poor Dr Seward, so I said, as lightly as I could, that I did not know anything of hitching, and that I wasn't broken to harness at all yet. Then he said that he had spoken in a light manner, and he hoped that if he had made a mistake in doing so on so grave, so momentous, an occasion for him, I would forgive him. He really did look serious when he was saying it, and I couldn't help feeling a bit serious, too. I know, Mina, you will think me a horrid flirt – though I couldn't help feeling a sort of exultation that he was number two in one day. And then, my dear, before I could say a word he began pouring out a perfect torrent of love-making, laying his very heart and soul at my feet. He looked so earnest over it that I shall never again think that a man must be playful always, and never earnest, because he is merry at times. I suppose he saw something in my face which checked him, for he suddenly stopped, and said with a sort of manly fervour that I could have loved him for if I had been free:—

' "Lucy, you are an honest-hearted girl, I know. I should not be here speaking to you as I am now if I did not believe you clean grit, right through to the very depths of your soul. Tell me, like one good fellow to another, is there anyone else that you care for? And if there is, I'll never trouble you a hair's breadth again, but will be, if you will let me, a very faithful friend."

'My dear Mina, why are men so noble when we women are so little worthy of them? Here was I almost making fun of this great-hearted, true gentleman. I burst into tears—I am afraid, my dear, you will think this is a very sloppy letter in more ways than one — and I really felt very badly. Why can't they let a girl marry three men, or as many as want her, and save all this trouble? But this is heresy, and I must not say it. I am glad to say that, though I was crying, I was able to look into Mr Morris's brave eyes, and I told him out straight:—

' "Yes, there is someone I love, though he has not told me yet that he even loves me." I was right to speak to him so frankly, for quite a light came into his face, and he put out both his hands and took mine — I think I put them into his — and said in a hearty way:—

' "That's my brave girl. It's better worth being late for a chance of winning you than being in time for any other girl in the world. Don't cry, my dear. If it's for me, I'm a hard nut to crack; and I take it standing up. If that other fellow doesn't know his happiness, well, he'd better look for it soon, or he'll have to deal with me. Little girl, your honesty and pluck have made me a friend, and that's rarer than a lover; it's more unselfish anyhow. My dear, I'm going to have a pretty lonely walk between this and Kingdom Come. Won't you give me one kiss? It'll be something to keep off the darkness now and then. You can, you know, if you like, for that other good fellow — he must be a good fellow, my dear, and a fine fellow, or you could not love him—hasn't spoken yet." That quite won me, Mina, for it *was* brave and sweet of him, and noble, too, to a rival — wasn't it? — and he so sad; so I leant over and kissed him. He stood up with my two hands in his, and as he looked down into my face — I am afraid I was blushing very much — he said:—

' "Little girl, I hold your hand, and you've kissed me, and if these things don't make us friends nothing ever will. Thank you for your sweet honesty to me, and good-bye." He wrung my hand, and taking up his hat, went straight out of the room without looking back, without a tear or a quiver or a pause; and I am crying like a baby. Oh, why must a man like that be made unhappy when there are lots of girls about who would worship the very ground he trod on? I know I would if I were free – only I don't want to be free. My dear, this quite upset me, and I feel I cannot write of happiness just at once, after telling you of it; and I don't wish to tell of the number three till it can all be happy. – Ever your loving.

'Lucy.

'P.S. – Oh, about number three – I needn't tell you of number three, need I? Besides, it was all so confused; it seemed only a moment from his coming into the room till both his arms were round me, and he was kissing me. I am very, very happy, and I don't know what I have done to deserve it. I must only try in the future to show that I am not ungrateful for all His goodness to me in sending to me such a lover, such a husband, and such a friend.

'Good-bye.'

DR SEWARD'S DIARY

(Kept in phonograph)

25 April. – Ebb tide in appetite to-day. Cannot eat, cannot rest, so diary instead. Since my rebuff of yesterday I have a sort of empty feeling; nothing in the world seems of sufficient importance to be worth the doing. . . . As I knew that the only cure for this sort of thing was work, I went down amongst the patients. I picked out one who has afforded me a study of much interest. He is so quaint in his ideas, and so unlike the normal lunatic, that I have determined to understand him as well as I can. To-day I seemed to get nearer than ever before to the heart of his mystery.

I questioned him more fully than I had ever done, with a view to making myself master of the facts of his hallucination. In my manner of doing it there was, I now see, something of cruelty. I seemed to wish to keep him to the point of his madness – a thing which I avoid with the patients as I would the mouth of hell. (*Mem.*, under what circumstances would I *not* avoid the pit of hell?) *Omnia Romae vernalia sunt.* Hell has its price! *verb. sap.* If there be anything behind this instinct it will be valuable to trace it afterwards *accurately*, so I had better commence to do so, therefore –

R. M. Renfield, aetat. 59 – Sanguine temperament; great physical strength; morbidly excitable; periods of gloom ending in some fixed idea which I cannot make out. I presume that the sanguine temperament itself and the disturbing influence end in a mentally-accomplished finish; a possibly dangerous man, probably dangerous if unselfish. In selfish men caution is as secure an armour for their foes as for themselves. What I think of on this point is, when self is the fixed point the centripetal force is balanced with the centrifugal: when duty, a cause, etc., is the fixed point, the latter force is paramount, and only accident or a series of accidents can balance it.

Letter, Quincey P. Morris to Hon. Arthur Holmwood

'25 *May.*

'My dear Art, –

'We've told yarns by the the camp-fire in the prairies; and dressed one another's wounds after trying a landing at the Marquesas; and drunk healths on the shore of Titicaca. There are more yarns to be told, and other wounds to be healed, and another health to be drunk. Won't you let this be at my camp-fire to-morrow night? I have no hesitation in asking you, as I know a certain lady is engaged to a certain dinner-party, and that you are free. There will only be one other, our old pal at the Korea, Jack Seward. He's coming, too, and we both want to mingle our weeps over the wine-cup, and to drink a health with all our hearts to the happiest man in all the wide world, who has won the noblest heart that God has made and the best worth winning. We promise you a hearty welcome, and a loving greeting, and a health as true as your own right hand. We shall both swear to leave you at home if you drink too deep to a certain pair of eyes. Come!

'Yours, as ever and always,
'QUINCEY P. MORRIS

Telegram from Arthur Holmwood to Quincey P. Morris

'26 *May.*

'Count me in every time. I bear messages which will make both your ears tingle.

ART.'

6

MINA MURRAY'S JOURNAL

24 July. Whitby. – Lucy met me at the station, looking sweeter and lovelier than ever, and we drove up to the house at the Crescent, in which they have rooms. This is a lovely place. The little river, the Esk, runs through a deep valley, which broadens out as it comes near the harbour. A great viaduct runs across, with high piers, through which the view seems, somehow, farther away than it really is. The valley is beautifully green, and it is so steep that when you are on the high land on either side you look right across it, unless you are near enough to see down. The houses of the old town – the side away from us – are all red-roofed, and seem piled up one over the other anyhow, like the pictures we see of Nuremberg. Right over the town is the ruin of Whitby Abbey, which was sacked by the Danes, and which is the scene of part of 'Marmion', where the girl was built up in the wall. It is a most noble ruin, of immense size, and full of beautiful and romantic bits; there is a legend that a white lady is seen in one of the windows. Between it and the town there is another church, the parish one, round which is a big graveyard, all full of tombstones. This is, to my mind, the nicest spot in Whitby, for it lies right over the town, and has a full view of the harbour and all up the bay to where the headland called Kettleness stretches out into the sea. It descends so steeply over the harbour that part of the bank has fallen away, and some of the graves have been destroyed. In one place part of the stonework of the graves stretches out over the sandy pathway far below. There are walks, with seats beside them, through the churchyard; and people go and sit there all day looking at the beautiful view and enjoying the breeze. I shall come and sit here very often myself and work. Indeed, I am writing now, with my book on my knee, and listening to the talk of three old men who are sitting beside me. They seem to do nothing all day but sit up here and talk.

The harbour lies below me, with, on the far side, one long granite wall stretching out into the sea, with a curve outwards at the end of it, in the middle of which is a lighthouse. A heavy sea-wall runs along outside of it. On the near side, the sea-wall makes an elbow crooked inversely, and its end too has a lighthouse. Between the two piers there is a narrow opening into the harbour, which then suddenly widens.

It is nice at high tide; but when the tide is out it shoals away to nothing, and there is merely the stream of the Esk, running between banks of sand, with rocks here and there. Outside the harbour on this side there rises for about half a mile a great reef, the sharp edge of which runs straight out from behind the south lighthouse. At the end of it is a buoy with a bell, which swings in bad weather, and sends in a mournful sound on the wind. They have a legend here that when a ship is lost bells are heard out at sea. I must ask the old man about this; he is coming this way. . . .

He is a funny old man. He must be awfully old, for his face is all gnarled and twisted like the bark of a tree. He tells me that he is nearly a hundred, and that he was a sailor in the Greenland fishing fleet when Waterloo was fought. He is, I am afraid, a very sceptical person, for when I asked him about the bells at sea and the White Lady at the Abbey he said very brusquely:

'I wouldn't fash masel' about them, miss. Them things be all wore out. Mind, I don't say they never was, but I do say that they wasn't in my time. They be all very well for comers and trippers an' the like, but not for a nice young lady like you. Them feet-folks from York and Leeds that be always eatin' cured herrin's an' drinkin' tea an' lookin' out to buy cheap jet would creed aught. I wonder masel' who'd be bothered tellin' lies to them – even the newspapers, which is full of fool-talk.' I thought he would be a good person to learn interesting things from, so I asked him if he would mind telling me something about whale-fishing in the old days. He was just settling himself to begin when the clock struck six, whereupon he laboured to get up, and said:

'I must gang ageeanwards home now, miss. My granddaughter doesn't like to be kept waitin' when the tea is ready, for it takes me time to crammle aboon the grees, for there be a many of 'em; an', miss, I lack belly-timber sairly by the clock.'

He hobbled away, and I could see him hurrying, as well as he could, down the steps. The steps are a great feature of the place. They lead from the town up to the church; there are hundreds of them – I do not know how many – and they wind up in a delicate curve; the slope is so gentle that a horse could easily walk up and down them. I think they must originally have had something to do with the Abbey. I shall go home too. Lucy went out visiting with her mother, and as they were only duty calls, I did not go. They will be home by this.

1 August. – I came up here an hour ago with Lucy, and we had a most interesting talk with my old friend and the two others who always come and join him. He is evidently the Sir Oracle of them, and I should think must have been in his time a most dictatorial person. He will not admit anything, and downfaces everybody. If he can't out-argue them he bullies them, and then takes their silence for agreement with his views. Lucy was looking sweetly pretty in her white lawn frock; she has got a beautiful colour since she has been here. I noticed that the old men did not lose any time in coming up and sitting near her when we sat down. She is so sweet with old people; I think they all fell in love with her on the spot. Even my old man succumbed and did not contradict her, but gave me double share instead. I got him on the subject of the legends, and he went off at once into a sort of sermon. I must try to remember it and put it down:

'It be all fool-talk, lock, stock, and barrel; that's what it be, an' nowt else. These bans an' wafts an' boh-ghosts an' barguests and bogles an' all anent them is only fit to set bairns an' dizzy women a-belderin'. They be nowt but air-blebs! They, an' all grims an' signs an' warnin's, be all invented by parsons an' illsome beuk-bodies an' railway touters to skeer an' scunner hafflin's, an' to get folks to do somethin' that they don't other incline to. It makes me ireful to think o' them. Why, it's them that, not content with printin' lies on paper an' preachin' them out of pulpits, does want to be cuttin' them on the tombstones. Look here all round you in what airt ye will; all them steans, holdin' up their heads as well as they can out of their pride, is acant – simply tumblin' down with the weight o' the lies wrote on them, "Here lies the body" or "Sacred to the memory" wrote on all of them, an' yet in nigh half of them there bean't no bodies at all; an' the memories of them bean't cared a pinch of snuff about, much less sacred. Lies all of them, nothin' but lies of one kind or another! My gog, but it'll be a quare scowderment at the Day of Judgment, when they come tumblin' up here in their death-sarks, all jouped together an' tryin' to drag their tombsteans with them to prove how good they was; some of them trimmlin' and ditherin', with their hands that dozzened an' slippery from lyin' in the sea that they can't even keep ther grup o' them.'

I could see from the old fellow's self-satisfied air and the way in which he looked round for the approval of his cronies that he was 'showing off', so I put in a word to keep him going:

'Oh, Mr Swales, you can't be serious. Surely these tombstones are not all wrong?'

'Yabblins! There may be a poorish few not wrong, savin' where they make out the people too good; for there be folk that do think a balm-bowl be like the sea, if only it be their own. The whole thing be only lies. Now look you here; you come here a stranger, an' you see this kirk-garth.' I nodded, for I thought it better to assent, though I did not quite understand his dialect. I knew it had something to do with the church. He went on: 'And you consate that all these steans be aboon folk that be happed here, snod an' snog?' I assented again. 'Then that be just where the lie comes in. Why, there be scores of these lay-beds that be toom as old Dun's bacca-box on Friday night.' He nudged one of his companions, and they all laughed. 'And my gog! how could they be otherwise? Look at that one, the aftest abaft the bier-bank; read it!' I went over and read:

'Edward Spencelagh, master mariner, murdered by pirates off the coast of Andres, April, 1854, aet. 30.' When I came back Mr Swales went on:

'Who brought him home, I wonder, to hap him here? Murdered off the coast of Andres! an' you consated his body lay under! Why, I could name ye a dozen whose bones lie in the Greenland seas above' – he pointed northwards – 'or where the currents may have drifted them. There be the steans around ye. Ye can, with your young eyes, read the small print of the lies from here. This Braithwaite Lowrey – I knew his father, lost in the *Lively* off Greenland in '20; or Andrew Woodhouse, drowned in the same seas in 1777; or John Paxton, drowned off Cape Farewell a year later; or old John Rawlings, whose grandfather sailed with me, drowned in the Gulf of Finland in '50. Do ye think that all these men will have to make a rush to Whitby when the trumpet sounds? I have me antherums aboot it! I tell ye that when they got here they'd be jommlin' an' jostlin' one another that way that it 'ud be like a fight up on the ice in the old days, when we'd be at one another from daylight to dark, an' tryin' to tie up our cuts by the light of the aurora borealis.' This was evidently local pleasantry, for the old man cackled over it, and his cronies joined in with gusto.

'But,' I said, 'surely you are not quite correct, for you start on the assumption that all the poor people, or their spirits, will have to take their tombstones with them on the Day of Judgment. Do you think that will be really necessary?'

'Well, what else be they tombsteans for? Answer me that, miss!'

'To please their relatives, I suppose.'

'To please their relatives, you suppose!' This he said with intense scorn. 'How will it pleasure their relatives to know that lies is wrote over them, and that everybody in the place knows that they be lies?' He pointed to a stone at our feet which had been laid down as a slab, on which the seat was rested, close to the edge of the cliff. 'Read the lines on that thruffstean,' he said. The letters were upside down to me from where I sat, but Lucy was more opposite to them, so she leant over and read:

' "Sacred to the memory of George Canon, who died, in the hope of a glorious resurrection, on July 29, 1873, falling from the rocks at Kettleness. This tomb is erected by his sorrowing mother to her dearly beloved son. He was the only son of his mother, and she was a widow." Really, Mr Swales, I don't see anything very funny in that!' She spoke her comment very gravely and somewhat severely.

'Ye don't see aught funny! Ha! ha! But that's because ye don't gawm the sorrowin' mother was a hell-cat that hated him because he was acrewk'd – a regular lamiter he was – an' he hated her so that he

54

committed suicide in order that she mightn't get an insurance she put on his life. He blew nigh the top of his head off with an old musket that they had for scarin' the crows with. 'Twarn't for crows then, for it brought the clegs and the dowps to him. That's the way he fell off the rocks. And, as to hopes of a glorious resurrection, I've often heard him say masel' that he hoped he'd go to hell, for his mother was so pious that she'd be sure to go to heaven, an' he didn't want to addle where she was. Now isn't that stean at any rate' – he hammered it with his stick as he spoke – 'a pack of lies? and won't it make Gabriel keckle when Geordie comes pantin' up the grees with the tombstean balanced on his hump, and asks it to be took as evidence!'

I did not know what to say, but Lucy turned the conversation as she said, rising up:

'Oh, why did you tell us of this? It is my favourite seat, and I cannot leave it; and now I find I must go on sitting over the grave of a suicide.'

'That won't harm ye, my pretty; an' it may make poor Geordie gladsome to have so trim a lass sittin' on his lap. That won't hurt ye. Why, I've sat here off an' on for nigh twenty years past, an' it hasn't done me no harm. Don't ye fash about them as lies under ye, or that doesn't lie there either! It'll be time for ye to be getting scart when ye see the tombsteans all run away with, and the place as bare as a stubble-field. There's the clock, an' I must gang. My service to ye, ladies!' And off he hobbled.

Lucy and I sat awhile, and it was all so beautiful before us that we took hands as we sat; and she told me all over again about Arthur and their coming marriage. That made me just a little heart-sick, for I haven't heard from Jonathan for a whole month.

The same day. – I came up here alone, for I am very sad. There was no letter for me. I hope there cannot be anything the matter with Jonathan. The clock has just struck nine. I see the lights scattered all over the town, sometimes in rows where the streets are, and sometimes singly; they run right up the Esk and die away in the curve of the valley. To my left the view is cut off by a black line of roof of the old house next the Abbey. The sheep and lambs are bleating in the fields away behind me, and there is a clatter of a donkey's hoofs up the paved road below. The band on the pier is playing a harsh waltz in good time, and farther along the quay there is a Salvation Army meeting in a back street. Neither of the bands hears the other, but up here I hear and see them both. I wonder where Jonathan is and if he is thinking of me! I wish he were here.

5 June. – The case of Renfield grows more interesting the more I get to understand the man. He has certain qualities very largely developed: selfishness, secrecy, and purpose. I wish I could get at what is the object of the latter. He seems to have some settled scheme of his own, but what it is I do not yet know. His redeeming quality is a love of animals, though, indeed, he has such curious turns in it that I sometimes imagine he is only abnormally cruel. His pets are of odd sorts. Just now his hobby is catching flies. He has at present such a quantity that I have had myself to expostulate. To my astonishment, he did not break out into a fury, as I expected, but took the matter in simple seriousness. He thought for a moment, and then said: 'May I have three days? I shall clear them away.' Of course, I said that would do. I must watch him.

18 June. – He has turned his mind now to spiders, and has got several very big fellows in a box. He keeps feeding them with his flies, and the number of the latter is becoming sensibly diminished, although he has used half his food in attracting more flies from outside to his room.

1 July. – His spiders are now becoming as great a nuisance as his flies, and to-day I told him that he must get rid of them. He looked very sad at this, so I said that he must clear out some of them, at all events. He cheerfully acquiesced in this, and I gave him the same time as before for reduction. He disgusted me much while with him, for when a horrid blow-fly, bloated with some carrion food, buzzed into the room, he caught it, held it exultingly for a few moments between his finger and thumb, and, before I knew what he was going to do, put it into his mouth and ate it. I scolded him for it, but he argued quietly that it was very good and very wholesome; that it was life, strong life, and gave life to him. This gave me an idea, or the rudiment of one. I must watch how he gets rid of his spiders. He has evidently some deep problem in his mind, for he keeps a little note-book in which he is always jotting down something. Whole pages of it are filled with masses of figures, generally single numbers added up in batches, and then the totals added in batches again, as though he was 'focusing' some account, as the auditors put it.

8 July. – There is a method in his madness, and the rudimentary idea in my mind is growing. It will be a whole idea soon, and then, oh, unconscious cerebration! you will have to give the wall to your conscious brother. I kept away from my friend for a few days, so that I might notice if there were any change. Things remained as they were except that he has parted with some of his pets and got a new one. He has managed to get a sparrow, for already the spiders have diminished. Those that do remain, however, are well fed, for he still brings in the flies by tempting them with food.

19 July. – We are progressing. My friend has now a whole colony of sparrows, and his flies and spiders are almost obliterated. When I came in he ran to me and said he wanted to ask me a great favour – a very, very great favour; and as he spoke he fawned on me like a dog. I asked him what it was, and he said, with a sort of rapture in his voice and bearing: 'A kitten, a nice little, sleek, playful kitten, that I can play with, and teach, and feed – and feed – and feed!' I was not unprepared for this request, for I had noticed how his pets went on increasing in size and vivacity, but I did not care that his pretty family of tame sparrows should be wiped out in the same manner as the flies and the spiders; so I said I would see about it, and asked him if he would not rather have a cat than a kitten. His eagerness betrayed him as he answered:

'Oh, yes I would like a cat! I only asked for a kitten lest you should refuse me a cat. No one would refuse me a kitten, would they?' I shook my head, and said that at present I feared it would not be possible, but that I would see about it. His face fell, and I could see a warning of danger in it, for there was a sudden fierce, sidelong look which meant killing. The man is an undeveloped homicidal maniac. I shall test him with his present craving and see how it will work out; then I shall know more.

10 p.m. – I have visited him again and found him sitting in a corner brooding. When I came in he threw himself on his knees before me and implored me to let him have a cat; that his salvation depended upon it. I was firm, however, and told him that he could not have it, whereupon he went without a word, and sat down, gnawing his fingers, in the corner where I had found him. I shall see him in the morning early.

20 July. – Visited Renfield very early, before the attendant went his rounds. Found him up and humming a tune. He was spreading out his sugar, which he had saved, in the window, and was manifestly beginning his fly-catching again; and beginning cheerfully and with a good grace. I looked around for his birds, and not seeing them, asked him where they were. He replied, without turning round, that they had all flown away. There were a few feathers about the room and on his pillow a drop of blood. I said nothing, but went and told the keeper to report to me if there were anything odd about him during the day.

11 a.m. – The attendant has just been to me to say that Renfield has been very sick and has disgorged a whole lot of feathers. 'My belief is, doctor,' he said, 'that he has eaten his birds, and that he just took and ate them raw!'

11 p.m. – I gave Renfield a strong opiate to-night, enough to make even him sleep, and took away his pocket-book to look at it. The thought that has been buzzing about my brain lately is complete, and the theory proved. My homicidal maniac is of a peculiar kind. I shall have to invent a new classification for him, and call him a zoophagous (life-eating) maniac; what he desires is to absorb as many lives as he can, and he has laid himself out to achieve it in a cumulative way. He gave many flies to one spider and many spiders to one bird, and then wanted a cat to eat the many birds. What would have been his later steps? It would almost be worth while to complete the experiment. It might be done if there were only a sufficient cause. Men sneered at vivisection, and yet look at its results to-day! Why not advance science in its most difficult and vital aspect – the knowledge of the brain? Had I even the secret of one such mind – did I hold the key to the fancy of even one lunatic – I might advance my own branch of science to a pitch compared with which Burdon-Sanderson's physiology or Ferrier's brain knowledge would be as nothing. If only there were a sufficient cause! I must not think too much of this, or I may be tempted; a good cause might turn the scale with me, for may not I too be of an exceptional brain, congenitally?

How well the man reasoned; lunatics always do within their own scope. I wonder at how many lives he values a man, or if at only one. He has closed the account most accurately, and to-day begun a new record. How many of us begin a new record with each day of our lives?

To me it seems only yesterday that my whole life ended with my new hope, and that truly I began a new record. So it will be until the Great Recorder sums me up and closes my ledger account with a balance to profit or loss. Oh, Lucy, Lucy, I cannot be angry with you, nor can I be angry with my friend whose happiness is yours; but I must only wait on hopeless and work. Work! work!

If I only could have as strong a cause as my poor mad friend there, a good, unselfish cause to make me work, that would be indeed happiness.

MINA MURRAY'S JOURNAL

26 July. – I am anxious, and it soothes me to express myself here; it is like a whispering to one's self and listening at the same time. And there is also something about the shorthand symbols that makes it different from writing. I am unhappy about Lucy and about Jonathan. I had not heard from Jonathan for some time, and was very concerned; but yesterday dear Mr Hawkins, who is always so kind, sent me a letter from him. I had written asking him if he had heard, and he said the enclosed had just been received. It is only a line dated from Castle Dracula, and says that he is just starting for home. That is not like Jonathan; I do not understand it, and it makes me uneasy. Then, too, Lucy, although she is so well, has lately taken to her old habit of walking in her sleep. Her mother has spoken to me about it, and we have decided that I am to lock the door of our room every night. Mrs Westenra has got an idea that sleep-walkers always go out on roofs of houses and along the edges of cliffs, and then get suddenly awakened and fall over with a despairing cry that echoes all over the place. Poor dear, she is naturally anxious about Lucy, and she tells me that her husband, Lucy's father, had the same habit; that he would get up in the night and dress himself and go out, if he were not stopped. Lucy is to be married in the autumn, and she is already planning out her dresses and how her house is to be arranged. I sympathize with her, for I do the same, only Jonathan and I will start in life in a very simple way, and shall have to try to make both ends meet. Mr Holmwood – he is the Hon. Arthur Holmwood, only son of Lord Godalming – is coming up here very shortly – as soon as he can leave town, for his father is not very well, and I think dear Lucy is counting the moments till he comes. She wants to take him up to the seat on the churchyard cliff and show him the beauty of Whitby. I daresay it is the waiting which disturbs her; she will be all right when he arrives.

27 July. – No news from Jonathan. I am getting quite uneasy about him, though why I should I do not know; but I *do* wish that he would write, if it were only a single line. Lucy walks more than ever, and each night I am awakened by her moving about the room. Fortunately, the weather is so hot that she cannot get cold; but still the anxiety and the perpetually being awakened is beginning to tell on me, and I am getting nervous and wakeful myself. Thank God, Lucy's health keeps up. Mr Holmwood has been suddenly called to Ring to see his father, who has been taken seriously ill. Lucy frets at the postponement of seeing him, but it does not touch her looks; she is a trifle stouter, and her cheeks are a lovely rose pink. She has lost that anaemic look which she had. I pray it will all last.

3 August. – Another week gone, and no news from Jonathan, not even to Mr Hawkins, from whom I have heard. Oh, I do hope he is not ill. He surely would have written. I look at that last letter of his, but somehow it does not satisfy me. It does not read like him, and yet it is his writing. There is no mistake of that. Lucy has not walked much in her sleep the last week, but there is an odd concentration about her which I do not understand; even in her sleep she seems to be watching me. She tries the door, and finding it locked, goes about the room searching for the key.

6 August. – Another three days, and no news. This suspense is getting dreadful. If I only knew where to write to or where to go to, I should feel easier; but no one has heard a word of Jonathan since that last letter. I must only pray to God for patience. Lucy is more excitable than ever, but is otherwise well. Last night was very threatening, and the fishermen say that we are in for a storm. I must try to watch it and learn the weather signs. To-day is a grey day, and the sun as I write is hidden in thick clouds, high over Kettleness. Everything is grey – except the green grass, which seems like emerald amongst it; grey earthy rock; grey clouds, tinged with the sunburst at the far edge, hang over the grey sea, into which the sand-points stretch like grey fingers. The sea is tumbling in over the shallows and the sandy flats with a roar, muffled in the sea-mists drifting inland. The horizon is lost in a grey mist. All is vastness; the clouds are piled up like giant rocks, and there is a 'brool' over the sea that sounds like some presage of doom. Dark figures are on the beach here and there, sometimes half shrouded in the mist, and seem 'men like trees walking'. The fishing-boats are racing for home, and rise and dip in the ground swell as they sweep into the harbour, bending to the scuppers. Here comes old Mr Swales. He is making straight for me, and I can see, by the way he lifts his hat, that he wants to talk. . . .

I have been quite touched by the change in the poor old man. When he sat down beside me, he said in a very gentle way:

'I want to say something to you, miss.' I could see he was not at ease, so I took his poor old wrinkled hand in mine and asked him to speak fully; so he said, leaving his hand in mine:

'I'm afraid, my deary, that I must have shocked you by all the wicked things I've been sayin' about the dead, and suchlike, for weeks past; but I didn't mean them, and I want ye to remember that when I've gone. We aud folks that be daffled, and with one foot abaft the krok-hooal, don't altogether like to think of it, and we don't want to feel scart of it; an' that's why I've took to makin' light of it, so that I'd cheer up my own heart a bit. But, Lord love ye, miss, I ain't afraid of dyin' not a bit; only I don't want to die if I can help it. My time must be nigh at hand now, for I be aud, and a hundred years is too much for any man to expect; and I'm so nigh it that the Aud Man is already whettin' his scythe. Ye see, I can't get out o' the habit of caffin' about it all at once; the chafts will wag as they used to. Some day soon the Angel of Death will sound his trumpet for me. But don't ye dooal an' greet, my deary!' – for he saw that I was crying – 'if he should come this very night I'd not refuse to answer his call. For life be, after all, only a waitin' for somethin' else than what we're doin'; and death be all that we can rightly depend on. But I'm content, for it's comin' to me, my deary, and comin' quick. It may be comin' while we be lookin' and wonderin'. Maybe it's in that wind out over the sea that's bringin' with it loss and wreck, and sore distress, and sad hearts. Look! look!' he cried suddenly. 'There's something in that wind and in the hoast beyont that sounds, and looks, and tastes, and smells like death. It's in the air; I feel it comin'. Lord, make me answer cheerful when my call comes!' He held up his arms devoutly, and raised his hat. His mouth moved as though he were praying. After a few minutes' silence, he got up, shook hands with me, and blessed me, and said good-bye, and hobbled off. It all touched me, and upset me very much. I was glad when the coastguard came along, with his spy-glass under his arm. He stopped to talk with me, as he always does, but all the time looking at a strange ship.

'I can't make her out,' he said; 'she's a Russian, by the look of her, but she's knocking about in the queerest way. She doesn't know her mind a bit; she seems to see the storm coming, but can't decide whether to run up north in the open, or to put in here. Look there again! She is steered mighty strangely, for she doesn't mind the hand on the wheel; changes about with every puff of wind. We'll hear more of her before this time to-morrow.'

7

CUTTING FROM 'The Dailygraph', 8 AUGUST

(Pasted in Mina Murray's Journal)

From a Correspondent

Whitby.

One of the greatest and suddenest storms on record has just been experienced here, with results both strange and unique. The weather had been somewhat sultry, but not to any degree uncommon in the month of August. Saturday evening was as fine as ever was known, and the great body of holiday-makers set out yesterday for visits to Mulgrave Woods, Robin Hood's Bay, Rig Mill, Runswick, Staithes, and the various trips in the neighbourhood of Whitby. The steamers *Emma* and *Scarborough* made excursions along the coast, and there was an unusual amount of 'tripping' both to and from Whitby. The day was unusually fine till the afternoon, when some of the gossips who frequent the East Cliff churchyard, and from that commanding eminence watch the wide sweep of sea visible to the north and east, called attention to a sudden show of 'mares'-tails' high in the sky to the north-west. The wind was then blowing from the south-west in the mild degree which in barometrical language is ranked 'No. 2: light breeze'. The coastguard on duty at once made report, and one old fisherman, who for more than half a century has kept watch on weather signs from the East Cliff, foretold in an emphatic manner the coming of a sudden storm. The approach of sunset was so very beautiful, so grand in its masses of splendidly-coloured clouds, that there was quite an assemblage on the walk along the cliff in the old churchyard to enjoy the beauty. Before the sun dipped below the black mass of Kettleness, standing boldly athwart the western sky, its downward way was marked by myriad clouds of every sunset-colour – flame, purple, pink, green, violet, and all the tints of gold; with here and there masses not large, but seemingly of absolute blackness, in all sorts of shapes, as well outlined as colossal silhouettes. The experience was not lost on the painters, and doubtless some of the sketches of the 'Prelude to the Great Storm' will grace the R.A. and R.I. walls in May next. More than one captain made up his mind then and there that his 'cobble' or his 'mule', as they term the different classes of boats, would remain in the harbour till the storm had passed. The wind fell away entirely during the evening, and at midnight there was a dead calm, a sultry heat, and that prevailing intensity which, on the approach of thunder, affects persons of a sensitive nature. There were but few lights in sight at sea, for even the coasting steamers, which usually 'hug' the shore so closely, kept well to seaward, and but few fishing-boats were in sight. The only sail noticeable was a foreign schooner with all sails set, which was seemingly going westwards. The foolhardiness or ignorance of her officers was a prolific theme for comment whilst she remained in sight, and efforts were made to signal her to reduce sail in face of her danger. Before the night shut down she was seen with sails idly flapping as she gently rolled on the undulating swell of the sea.

'As idle as a painted ship upon a painted ocean.'

Shortly before ten o'clock the stillness of the air grew quite oppressive, and the silence was so marked that the bleating of a sheep inland or the barking of a dog in the town was distinctly heard, and the band on the pier, with its lively French air, was like a discord in the great harmony of nature's silence. A little after midnight came a strange sound from over the sea, and high overhead the air began to carry a strange, faint hollow booming.

Then without warning the tempest broke. With a rapidity which, at the time, seemed incredible, and even afterwards is impossible to realize, the whole aspect of nature at once became convulsed. The waves rose in growing fury, each over-topping its fellow, till in a very few minutes the lately glassy sea was like a roaring and devouring monster. White-crested waves beat madly on the level sands and rushed up the shelving cliffs; others broke over the piers, and with their spume swept the lanthorns of the lighthouses which rise from the end of either pier of Whitby Harbour.

The wind roared like thunder, and blew with such force that it was with difficulty that even strong men kept their feet, or clung with grim clasp to the iron stanchions. It was found necessary to clear the entire piers from the mass of onlookers, or else the fatalities of the night would have been increased manyfold. To add to the difficulties and dangers of the time, masses of sea-fog came drifting inland – white, wet clouds, which swept by in ghostly fashion, so dank and damp and cold that it needed but little effort of imagination to think that the spirits of those lost at sea were touching their living brethren with the clammy hands of death, and many a one shuddered as the wreaths of sea-mist swept by. At times the mist cleared, and the sea for some distance could be seen in the glare of the lightning, which now came thick and fast, followed by such sudden peals of thunder that the whole sky overhead seemed trembling under the shock of the footsteps of the storm. Some of the scenes thus revealed were of immeasurable grandeur and of absorbing interest – the sea, running mountains high, threw skywards with each wave mighty masses of white foam, which the tempest seemed to snatch at and whirl away into space; here and there a fishing-boat, with a rag of sail, running madly for shelter before the blast; now and again the white wings of a storm-tossed sea-bird. On the summit of the East Cliff the new searchlight was ready for experiment, but had not yet been tried. The officers in charge of it got it into working order, and in the pauses of the inrushing mist swept with it the surface of the sea. Once or twice its service was most effective, as when a fishing-boat, with gunwale under water, rushed into the harbour, able, by the guidance of the sheltering light, to avoid the danger of dashing against the piers. As each boat achieved the safety of the port there was a shout of joy from the mass of people on shore, a shout which for a moment seemed to cleave the gale and was then swept away in its rush. Before long the searchlight discovered some distance away a schooner with all sails set, apparently the same vessel which had been noticed earlier in the evening. The wind had by this time backed to the east, and there was a shudder amongst the watchers on the cliff as they realized the terrible danger in which she now was. Between her and the port lay the great flat reef on which so many good ships have from time to time suffered, and, with the wind blowing from its present quarter, it would be quite impossible that she should fetch the entrance of the harbour. It was now nearly the hour of high tide, but the waves were so great that in their troughs the shallows of the shore were almost visible, and the schooner, with all sails set, was rushing with such speed that, in the words of one old salt, 'she must fetch up somewhere, if it was only in hell.' Then came another rush of sea-fog, greater than any hitherto – a mass of dank mist, which seemed to close on all things like a grey pall, and left available to men only the organ of hearing, for the roar of the tempest, and the crash of the thunder, and the booming of the mighty bellows came through the damp oblivion even louder than before. The rays of the searchlight were kept fixed on the harbour mouth across the East Pier, where the shock was expected, and men waited breathless. The wind suddenly shifted to the north-east, and the remnant of the sea-fog melted in the blast; and then, *mirabile dictu*, between the piers, leaping from wave to wave as it rushed at headlong speed, swept the strange schooner before the blast, with all sail set, and gained the safety of the harbour. The searchlight followed her, and a shudder ran through all who saw her, for lashed to the helm was a corpse, with drooping head, which swung horribly to and fro at each motion of the ship. No other form could be seen on deck at all. A great awe came on all as they realized that the ship, as if by a miracle, had found the harbour, unsteered save by the hand of a dead man! However, all took place more quickly than it takes to write these words. The schooner paused not, but rushing across the harbour, pitched herself on that accumulation of sand and gravel washed by many tides and many storms into the south-east corner of the pier jutting under the East Cliff, known locally as Tate Hill Pier.

There was of course a considerable concussion as the vessel drove up on the sand-heap. Every spar, rope, and stay was strained, and some of the 'top-hamper' came crashing down. But, strangest of all, the very instant the shore was touched, an immense dog sprang up on deck from below, as if shot up by the concussion, and running forward, jumped from the bow on to the sand. Making straight for the steep cliff, where the churchyard hangs over the laneway to the East Pier so steeply that some of the flat tombstones – 'thruff-steans' or 'through-stones', as they call them in the Whitby vernacular – actually project over where the sustaining cliff has fallen away, it disappeared in the darkness, which seemed intensified just beyond the focus of the searchlight.

It so happened that there was no one at the moment on Tate Hill Pier, as all those whose houses are in close proximity were either in bed or were out on the heights above. Thus the coastguard on duty on the eastern side of the harbour, who at once ran down to the little pier, was the first to climb on board. The men working the searchlight, after scouring the entrance of the harbour without seeing anything, then turned the light on the derelict and kept it there. The coastguard ran aft, and when he came beside the wheel, bent over to examine it and recoiled at once as though under some sudden emotion. This seemed to pique the general curiosity, and quite a number of people began to run. It is a good way round from the West Cliff by the Drawbridge to Tate Hill Pier, but your correspondent is a fairly good runner, and came well ahead of the crowd. When I arrived, however, I found already assembled on the pier a crowd, whom the coastguard and police refused to allow to come on board. By the courtesy of the chief boatman, I was, as your correspondent, permitted to climb on deck, and was one of a small group who saw that dead seaman whilst actually lashed to the wheel.

It was no wonder that the coastguard was surprised, or even awed, for not often can such a sight have been seen. The man was simply fastened by his hands, tied one over the other, to a spoke of the wheel. Between the inner hand and the wood was a crucifix, the set of beads on which it was fastened being around both wrists and wheel, and all kept fast by the binding cords. The poor fellow may have been seated at one time, but the flapping and buffeting of the sails had worked through the rudder of the wheel and dragged him to and fro, so that the cords with which he was tied had cut the flesh to the bone. Accurate note was made of the state of things, and a doctor – Surgeon J. M. Caffyn, of 33, East Elliot Place – who came immediately after me, declared, after making examination, that the man must have been dead for quite two days. In his pocket was a bottle, carefully corked, empty save for a little roll of paper, which proved to be the addendum to the log. The coastguard said the man must have tied up his own hands, fastening the knots with his teeth. The fact that a coastguard was the first on board may save some complications, later on, in the Admiralty Court; for the coastguards cannot claim the salvage which is the right of the first civilian entering on a derelict. Already, however, the legal tongues are wagging, and one young law student is loudly asserting that the rights of the owner are already completely sacrificed, his property being held in contravention of the statutes of mortmain, since the tiller, as emblemship, if not proof, of delegated possession, is held in a *dead hand*. It is needless to say that the dead steersman has been reverently removed from the place where he held his honourable watch and ward till death – a steadfastness as noble as that of the young Casabianca – and placed in the mortuary to await inquest.

Already the sudden storm is passing, and its fierceness is abating; the crowds are scattering homewards, and the sky is beginning to redden over the Yorkshire wolds. I shall send, in time for your next issue, further details of the derelict ship which found her way so miraculously into harbour in the storm.

Whitby.

9 *August.* – The sequel to the strange arrival of the derelict in the storm last night is almost more startling than the thing itself. It turns out that the schooner is a Russian from Varna, and is called the *Demeter*. She is

almost entirely in ballast of silver sand, with only a small amount of cargo – a number of great wooden boxes filled with mould. This cargo was consigned to a Whitby solicitor, Mr S. F. Billington, of 7, The Crescent, who this morning went aboard and formally took possession of the goods consigned to him. The Russian consul, too, acting for the charter-party, took formal possession of the ship, and paid all harbour dues, etc. Nothing is talked about here to-day except the strange coincidence; the officials of the Board of Trade have been most exacting in seeing that every compliance has been made with existing regulations. As the matter is to be a 'nine days' wonder', they are evidently determined that there shall be no cause of after complaint. A good deal of interest was abroad concerning the dog which landed when the ship struck, and more than a few of the members of the S.P.C.A., which is very strong in Whitby, have tried to befriend the animal. To the general disappointment, however, it was not to be found; it seems to have disappeared entirely from the town. It may be that it was frightened and made its way on to the moors, where it is still hiding in terror. There are some who look with dread on such a possibility, lest later on it should in itself become a danger, for it is evidently a fierce brute. Early this morning a large dog, a half-bred mastiff, belonging to a coal merchant close to Tate Hill Pier, was found dead in the roadway opposite its master's yard. It had been fighting, and manifestly had had a savage opponent, for its throat was torn away, and its belly slit open as if with a savage claw.

Later. – By the kindness of the Board of Trade inspector, I have been permitted to look over the log-book of the *Demeter*, which was in order up to within three days, but contained nothing of special interest except as to facts of missing men. Th greater interest, however, is with regard to the paper found in the bottle, which was to-day produced at the inquest; and a more strange narrative than the two between them unfold it has not been my lot to come across. As there is no motive for concealment, I am permitted to use them, and accordingly send you a rescript, simply omitting technical details of seamanship and supercargo. It almost seems as though the captain had been seized with some kind of mania before he had got well into blue water, and that this had developed persistently throughout the voyage. Of course my statement must be taken *cum grano*, since I am writing from the dictation of a clerk of the Russian consul, who kindly translated for me, time being short.

LOG OF THE 'DEMETER'

Varna to Whitby

Written 18 July, things so strange happening, that I shall keep accurate note henceforth till we land.

On 6 July we finished taking in cargo, silver sand and boxes of earth. At noon set sail. East wind, fresh, Crew, five hands . . . two mates, cook, and myself (captain).

On 11 July at dawn entered Bosphorus. Boarded by Turkish Customs officers. Backsheesh. All correct. Under way at 4 p.m.

On 12 July through Dardanelles. More Customs officers and flagboat of guarding squadron. Backsheesh again. Work of officers thorough, but quick. Want us off soon. At dark passed into Archipelago.

On 13 July passed Cape Matapan. Crew dissatisfied about something. Seemed scared, but would not speak out.

On 14 July was somewhat anxious about crew. Men all steady fellows, who sailed with me before. Mate could not make out what was wrong; they only told him there was *something*, and crossed themselves. Mate lost temper with one of them that day and struck him. Expected fierce quarrel, but all was quiet.

On 16 July mate reported in the morning that one of crew, Petrofsky, was missing. Could not account for it. Took larboard watch eight bells last night; was relieved by Abramoff, but did not go to bunk. Men more downcast than ever. All said they expected something of the kind, but would not say more than that there was *something* aboard. Mate getting very impatient with them; feared some trouble ahead.

On 17 July, yesterday, one of the men, Olgaren, came to my cabin, and in an awestruck way confided to me that he thought there was a strange man aboard the ship. He said that in his watch he had been sheltering behind the deckhouse, as there was a rain-storm, when he saw a tall, thin man, who was not like any of the crew, come up the companion way, and go along the deck forward, and disappear. He followed cautiously, but when he got to bows found no one, and the hatchways were all closed. He was in a panic of superstitious fear, and I am afraid the panic may spread. To allay it, I shall to-day search entire ship carefully from stem to stern.

Later in the day I got together the whole crew, and told them, as they evidently thought there was someone in the ship, we should search from stem to stern. First mate angry; said it was folly, and to yield to such foolish ideas would demoralize the men; said he would engage to keep them out of trouble with a handspike. I let him take the helm, while the rest began thorough search, all keeping abreast, with lanterns; we left no corner unsearched. As there were only the big wooden boxes, there were no odd corners where a man could hide. Men much relieved when search over, and went back to work cheerfully. First mate scowled, but said nothing.

22 July. – Rough weather last three days, and all hands busy with sails – no time to be frightened. Men seem to have forgotten their dread. Mate cheerful again, and all on good terms. Praised men for work in bad weather. Passed Gibraltar and out through Straits. All well.

24 July. – There seems some doom over this ship. Already a hand short, and entering on the Bay of Biscay with wild weather ahead, and yet last night another man lost – disappeared. Like the first, he came off his watch and was not seen again. Men all in a panic of fear; sent a round robin, asking to have double watch, as they fear to be alone. Mate violent. Fear there will be some trouble, as either he or the men will do some violence.

28 July. – Four days in hell, knocking about in a sort of maelstrom, and the wind a tempest. No sleep for any one. Men all worn out. Hardly know how to set a watch since no one fit to go on. Second mate volunteered to steer and watch, and let men snatch a few hours' sleep. Wind abating; seas still terrific, but feel them less, as ship is steadier.

29 July. – Another tragedy. Had single watch to-night, as crew too tired to double. When morning watch came on deck could find no one except steersman. Raised outcry, and all came on deck. Thorough search, but no one found. Are now without second mate, and crew in a panic. Mate and I agreed to go armed henceforth and wait for any sign of cause.

30 July. – Last night. Rejoined we are nearing England. Weather fine, all sails set. Retired worn out; slept soundly; awaked by mate telling me that both men on watch and steersman missing. Only self and mate and two hands left to work ship.

1 August. – Two days of fog, and not a sail sighted. Had hoped when in the English Channel to be able to signal for help or get in somewhere. Not having power to work sails, have to run before wind. Dare not lower, as could not raise them again. We seem to be drifting to some terrible doom. Mate now more demoralized than either of them. His stronger nature seems to have worked inwardly against him. Men are beyond fear, working stolidly and patiently, with minds made up to worst. They are Russian, he Roumanian.

2 August, midnight. – Woke up from few minutes' sleep by hearing a cry, seemingly outside my port. Could see nothing in fog. Rushed on deck, and ran against mate. Tells me heard cry and ran, but no sign of man on watch. One more gone. Lord, help us! Mate says we must be past Straits of Dover, as in a moment of fog lifting he saw North Foreland just as he heard the man cry out. If so we are now off in the North Sea, and only God can guide us in the fog, which seems to move with us; and God seems to have deserted us.

3 August. – At midnight I went to relieve the man at the wheel, but when I got to it found no one there. The wind was steady, and as we ran before it there was no yawing. I dared not leave it, so shouted for the mate. After a few seconds he rushed up on deck in his flannels. He looked wild-eyed and haggard, and I greatly fear his reason has given way. He came close to me and whispered hoarsely, with his mouth to my ear, as though fearing the very air might hear: 'It is here; I know it, now. On the watch last night I saw It, like a man, tall and thin, and ghastly pale. It was in the bows, and looking out. I crept behind It, and gave It my knife; but the knife went through It, empty as the air.' And as he spoke he took his knife and drove it savagely into space. Then he went on: 'But It is here, and I'll find it. It is in the hold, perhaps, in one of those boxes. I'll unscrew them one by one and see. You work the helm.' And, with a warning look and his finger on his lip, he went below. There was springing up a choppy wind, and I could not leave the helm. I saw him come out on deck again with a tool-chest and a lantern, and go down the forward hatchway. He is mad, stark, raving mad, and it's no use my trying to stop him. He can't hurt those big boxes; they are invoiced as 'clay', and to pull them about is as harmless a thing as he can do. So here I stay, and mind the helm, and write these notes. I can only trust in God and wait till the fog clears. Then, if I can't steer to any harbour with the wind that is, I shall cut down sails and lie by, and signal for help. . . .

It is nearly all over now. Just as I was beginning to hope that the mate would come out calmer – for I heard him knocking away at something in the hold, and work is good for him – there came up the hatchway a sudden, startled scream, which made my blood run cold, and up on the deck he came as if shot from a gun – a raging madman, with his eyes rolling and his face convulsed with fear. 'Save me! save me!' he cried, and then looked round on the blanket of fog. His horror turned to despair, and in a steady voice he said: 'You had better come too, captain, before it is too late. *He* is there. I know the secret now. The sea will save me from Him, and it is all that is left!' Before I could say a word, or move forward to seize him, he sprang on the bulwark and deliberately threw himself into the sea. I suppose I know the secret too, now. It was this madman who had got rid of the men one by one, and now he has followed them himself. God help me! How am I to account for all these horrors when I get to port? *When* I get to port! Will that ever be?

4 August. – Still fog, which the sunrise cannot pierce. I know there is sunrise because I am a sailor, why else I know not. I dared not go below, I dared not leave the helm so here all night I stayed, and in the dimness of the night I saw It – Him! God forgive me, but the mate was right to jump overboard. It is better to die like a man; to die like a sailor in blue water no man can object. But I am captain, and I must not leave my ship. But I shall baffle this fiend or monster, for I shall tie my hands to the wheel when my strength begins to fail, and along with them I shall tie that which He – It! – dare not touch; and then, come good wind or foul, I shall save my soul, and my honour as a captain. I am growing weaker, and the night is coming on. If He can look me in the face again, I may not have time to act. . . . If we are wrecked, mayhap this bottle may be found, and those who find it may understand; if not, . . . well, then all men shall know that I have been true to my trust. God and the Blessed Virgin and the saints help a poor ignorant soul trying to do his duty. . . .

Of course the verdict was an open one. There is no evidence to adduce; and whether or not the man himself committed the murders there is now none to say. The folk hold almost universally here that the captain is simply a hero, and he is to be given a public funeral. Already it is arranged that his body is to be taken with a train of boats up the Esk for a piece and then brought back to Tate Hill Pier and up the Abbey steps; for he is to be buried in the churchyard on the cliff. The owners of more than a hundred boats have already given in their names as wishing to follow him to the grave.

No trace has ever been found of the great dog; at which there is much mourning, for, with public opinion in its present state, he would, I believe, be adopted by the town. To-morrow will see the funeral; and so will end this one more 'mystery of the sea'.

MINA MURRAY'S JOURNAL

8 August. – Lucy was very restless all night, and I, too, could not sleep. The storm was fearful, and as it boomed loudly among the chimney-pots, it made me shudder. When a sharp puff came it seemed to be like a distant gun. Strangely enough, Lucy did not wake; but she got up twice and dressed herself. Fortunately, each time I awoke in time, and managed to undress her without waking her, and got her back to bed. It is a very strange thing, this sleep-walking, for as soon as her will is thwarted in any physical way, her intention, if there be any, disappears, and she yields herself almost exactly to the routine of her life.

Early in the morning we both got up and went down to the harbour to see if anything had happened in the night. There were very few people about, and though the sun was bright, and the air clear and fresh, the big, grim-looking waves, that seemed dark themselves because the foam that topped them was like snow, forced themselves in through the narrow mouth of the harbour – like a bullying man going through a crowd.

Somehow I felt glad that Jonathan was not on the sea last night, but on land. But, oh, is he on land or sea? Where is he, and how? I am getting fearfully anxious about him. If I only knew what to do, and could do anything?

10 August. – The funeral of the poor sea-captain to-day was most touching. Every boat in the harbour seemed to be there, and the coffin was carried by captains all the way from Tate Hill Pier up to the churchyard. Lucy came with me, and we went early to our old seat, whilst the cortège of boats went up the river to the Viaduct and came down again. We had a lovely view, and saw the procession nearly all the way. The poor fellow was laid to rest quite near our seat, so that we stood on it when the time came and saw everything. Poor Lucy seemed much upset. She was restless and uneasy all the time, and I cannot but think that her dreaming at night is telling on her. She is quite odd in one thing: she will not admit to me that there is any cause for restlessness; or if there be, she does not understand it herself. There is an additional cause in that poor old Mr Swales was found dead this morning on our seat, his neck being broken. He had evidently, as the doctor said, fallen back in the seat in some sort of fright, for there was a look of fear and horror on his face that the men said made them shudder. Poor dear old man! Perhaps he had seen Death with his dying eyes! Lucy is so sweet and sensitive that she feels influences more acutely than other people do. Just now she was quite upset by a little thing which I did not much heed, though I am myself very fond of animals. One of the men who come up here often to look for the boats was followed by his dog. The dog is always with him. They are both quiet persons, and I never saw the man angry, nor heard the dog bark. During the service the dog would not come to its master, who was on the seat with us, but kept a few yards off, barking and howling. Its master spoke to it gently, and then harshly, and then angrily; but it would neither come nor cease to make a noise. It was in a sort of fury, with its eyes savage, and all its hairs bristling out like a cat's tail when puss is on the war-path. Finally the man, too, got angry, and jumped down and kicked the dog, and then took it by the scruff of the neck and half dragged and half threw it on the tombstone on which the seat is fixed. The moment it touched the stone the poor thing became quiet and fell all into a tremble. It did not try to get away, but crouched down, quivering and cowering, and was in such a pitiable state of terror that I tried, though without effect, to comfort it. Lucy was full of pity, too, but she did not attempt to touch the dog, but looked at in an agonized sort of way. I greatly fear that she is of too super-sensitive a nature to go through the world without trouble. She will be dreaming of this to-night, I am sure. The whole agglomeration of things – the ship steered into port by a dead man; his attitude, tied to the wheel with a crucifix and beads; the touching funeral; the dog, now furious and now in terror – will all afford material for her dreams.

I think it will be best for her to go to bed tired out physically, so I shall take her for a long walk by the cliffs to Robin Hood's Bay and back. She ought not to have much inclination for sleep-walking then.

8

MINA MURRAY'S JOURNAL

Same day, 11 o'clock p.m. – Oh, but I am tired! If it were not that I have made my diary a duty I should not open it to-night. We had a lovely walk. Lucy, after a while, was in gay spirits, owing, I think, to some dear cows who came nosing towards us in a field close to the lighthouse, and frightened the wits out of us. I believe we forgot everything, except, of course, personal fear, and it seemed to wipe the slate clean and give us a fresh start. We had a capital 'severe tea' at Robin Hood's Bay in a sweet little old-fashioned inn, with a bow-window right over the seaweed-covered rocks of the strand. I believe we should have shocked the 'New Woman' with our appetites. Men are more tolerant, bless them! Then we walked home with some, or rather many, stoppages to rest, and with our hearts full of a constant dread of wild bulls. Lucy was really tired, and we intended to creep off to bed as soon as we could. The young curate came in, however, and Mrs Westenra asked him to stay for supper. Lucy and I had both a fight for it with the dusty miller; I know it was a hard fight on my part, and I am quite heroic. I think that some day the bishops must get together and see about breeding up a new class of curates, who don't take supper, no matter how they may be pressed to, and who will know when girls are tired. Lucy is asleep and breathing softly. She has more colour in her cheeks than usual, and looks, oh, so sweet. If Mr Holmwood fell in love with her seeing her only in the drawing-room, I wonder what he would say if he saw her now. Some of the 'New Woman' writers will some day start an idea that men and women should be allowed to see each other asleep before proposing or accepting. But I suppose the New Woman won't condescend in future to accept; she will do the proposing herself. And a nice job she will make of it, too! There's some consolation in that. I am so happy to-night, because dear Lucy seems better. I really believe she has turned the corner, and that we are over her troubles with dreaming. I should be quite happy if I only knew if Jonathan . . . God bless and keep him.

11 August, 3 a.m. – Diary again. No sleep now, so I may as well write. I am too agitated to sleep. We have had such an adventure, such an agonizing experience. I fell asleep as soon as I had closed my diary. . . . Suddenly I became broad awake, and sat up, with a horrible sense of fear upon me, and of some feeling of emptiness around me. The room was dark, so I could not see Lucy's bed; I stole across and felt for her. The bed was empty. I lit a match, and found that she was not in the room. The door was shut, but not locked, as I had left it. I feared to wake her mother, who has been more than usually ill lately, so threw on some clothes and got ready to look for her. As I was leaving the room it struck me that the clothes she wore might give me some clue to her dreaming intention. Dressing-gown would mean house; dress, outside. Dressing-gown and dress were both in their places. 'Thank God,' I said to myself, 'she cannot be far, as she is only in her nightdress.' I ran downstairs and looked in the sitting-room. Not there! Then I looked in all the other open rooms of the house, with an ever-growing fear chilling my heart. Finally I came to the hall-door and found it open. It was not wide open, but the catch of the lock had not caught. The people of the house are careful to lock the door every night, so I feared that Lucy must have gone out as she was. There was no time to think of what might happen; a vague, overmastering fear obscured all details. I took a big, heavy shawl and ran out. The clock was striking one as I was in the Crescent, and there was not a soul in sight. I ran along the North Terrace, but could see no sign of the white figure which I expected. At the edge of the West Cliff above the pier I looked across the harbour to the East Cliff, in the hope or fear – I don't know which – of seeing Lucy in our favourite seat. There was a bright full moon, with heavy black, driving clouds, which threw the whole scene into a fleeting diorama of light and shade as they sailed across. For a moment or two I could see nothing, as the shadow of a cloud obscured St Mary's Church and all around it. Then as the cloud passed I could see the ruins of the Abbey coming into view; and as the edge of a narrow band of light as sharp as a sword-cut moved along, the church and the churchyard became gradually visible. Whatever my expectation was, it was not disappointed, for there, on our favourite seat, the silver light of the moon struck a half-reclining figure, snowy white. The coming of the cloud was too quick for me to see much, for shadow shut down on light almost immediately; but it seemed to me as though something dark stood behind the seat where the white figure shone, and bent over it. What it was, whether man or beast, I could not tell; I did not wait to catch another glance, but flew down the steep steps to the pier and along by the fish-market to the bridge, which was the only way to reach the East Cliff. The town seemed as dead, for not a soul did I see; I rejoiced that it was so, for I wanted no witness of poor Lucy's condition. The time and distance seemed endless, and my knees trembled and my breath came laboured as I toiled up the endless steps to the Abbey. I must have gone fast, and yet it seemed to me as if my feet were weighted with lead, and as though every joint in my body were rusty. When I got almost to the top I could see the seat and the white figure, for I was now close enough to distinguish it even through the spells of shadow. There was undoubtedly something, long and black, bending over the half-reclining white figure. I called in fright, 'Lucy! Lucy!' and something raised a head, and from where I was I could see a white face and red, gleaming eyes. Lucy did not answer, and I ran on to the entrance of the churchyard. As I entered, the church was between me and the seat, and for a minute or so I lost sight of her. When I came in view again the cloud had passed, and the moonlight struck so brilliantly that I could see Lucy half-reclining with her head lying over the back of the seat. She was quite alone, and there was not a sign of any living thing about.

When I bent over her I could see that she was still asleep. Her lips were parted, and she was breathing – not softly, as usual with her, but in long, heavy gasps, as though striving to get her lungs full at every breath. As I came close, she put up her hand in her sleep and pulled the collar of her nightdress close round her throat. Whilst she did so there came a little shudder through her, as though she felt the cold. I flung the warm shawl over her, and drew the edges tight round her neck, for I dreaded lest she should get some deadly chill from the night air, unclad as she was. I feared to wake her all at once, so, in order to have my hands free that I might help her, I fastened the shawl at her throat with a big safety-pin; but I must have been clumsy in my anxiety and pinched or pricked her with it, for by-and-by, when her breathing became quieter, she put her hand to her throat again and moaned. When I had her carefully wrapped up I put my shoes on her feet, and then began very gently to wake her. At first she did not respond; but gradually she became more and more uneasy in her sleep, moaning and sighing occasionally. At last, as time was passing fast, and for many other reasons, I wished to get her home at once, I shook her more forcibly, till finally she opened her eyes and awoke. She did not seem surprised to see me, as, of course, she did not realize all at once where she was. Lucy always wakes prettily, and even at such a time, when her body must have been chilled with cold, and her mind somewhat appalled at waking unclad in a churchyard at night, she did not lose her grace. She trembled a little, and clung to me; when I told her to come at once with me home she rose without a word, with the obedience of a child. As we passed along, the gravel hurt my feet, and Lucy noticed me wince. She stopped and wanted to insist upon my taking my shoes; but I would not. However, when we got to the pathway outside the churchyard, where there was a puddle of water remaining from the storm, I daubed my feet with mud, using each foot in turn on the other, so that as we went home no one, in case we should meet anyone, should notice my bare feet.

Fortune favoured us, and we got home without meeting a soul. Once we saw a man, who seemed not quite sober, passing along a street in front of us; but we hid in a door till he had disappeared up an opening such as there are here, steep little closes, or 'wynds', as they call them in Scotland. My heart beat so loud all the time that sometimes I thought I should faint. I was filled with anxiety about Lucy, not only for her health, lest she should suffer from the exposure, but for her reputation in case the story should get wind. When we got in, and had washed our feet, and had said a prayer of thankfulness together, I tucked her into bed. Before falling asleep she asked – even implored – me not to say a word to any one, even her mother, about her sleep-walking adventure. I hesitated at first to promise; but on thinking of the state of her mother's health, and how the knowledge of such a thing would fret her, and thinking, too, of how such a story might become distorted – nay, infallibly would – in case it should leak out I thought it wiser to do so. I hope I did right. I have locked the door, and the key is tied to my wrist, so perhaps I shall not be again disturbed. Lucy is sleeping soundly; the reflex of the dawn is high and far over the sea. . . .

Same day, noon. – All goes well. Lucy slept till I woke her, and seemed not to have even changed her side. The adventure of the night does not seem to have harmed her; on the contrary, it has benefited her, for she looks better this morning than she has done for weeks. I was sorry to notice that my clumsiness with the safety-pin hurt her. Indeed, it might have been serious, for the skin of her throat was pierced. I must have pinched up a piece of loose skin and have transfixed it, for there are two little red points like pin-pricks, and on the band of her nightdress was a drop of blood. When I apologized and was concerned about it, she laughed and petted me, and said she did not even feel it. Fortunately it cannot leave a scar, as it is so tiny.

Same day, night. – We passed a happy day. The air was clear, and the sun bright and there was a cool breeze. We took our lunch to Mulgrave Woods, Mrs Westenra driving by the road and Lucy and I walking by the cliff path and joining her at the gate. I felt a little sad myself, for I could not but feel how *absolutely* happy it would have been had Jonathan been with me. But there! I must only be patient. In the evening we strolled in the Casino Terrace, and heard some good music by Spohr and Mackenzie, and went to bed early. Lucy seems more restful than she has been for some time, and fell asleep at once. I shall lock the door and secure the key the same as before, though I do not expect any trouble to-night.

12 August. – My expectations were wrong, for twice during the night I was awakened by Lucy trying to get out. She seemed, even in her sleep, to be a little impatient at finding the door shut, and went back to bed under a sort of protest. I woke with the dawn, and heard the birds chirping outside of the window. Lucy woke, too, and, I was glad to see, was even better than on the previous morning. All her old gaiety of manner seemed to have come back, and she came and snuggled in beside me, and told me all about Arthur; I told her how anxious I was about Jonathan, and then she tried to comfort me. Well, she succeeded somewhat, for, though sympathy can't alter facts, it can help to make them more bearable.

13 August. – Another quiet day, and to bed with the key on my wrist as before. Again I woke in the night, and found Lucy sitting up in bed, still asleep, pointing to the window. I got up quietly, and pulling aside the blind, looked out. It was brilliant moonlight, and the soft effect of the light over the sea and sky – merged together in one great, silent mystery – was beautiful beyond words. Between me and the moonlight flitted a great bat, coming and going in great, whirling circles. Once or twice it came quite close, but was, I suppose, frightened at seeing me, and flitted away across the harbour towards the Abbey. When I came back from the window Lucy had lain down again, and was sleeping peacefully. She did not stir again all night.

14 August. – On the East Cliff, reading and writing all day. Lucy seems to have become as much in love with the spot as I am, and it is hard to get her away from it when it is time to come home for lunch or tea or dinner. This afternoon she made a funny remark. We were coming home for dinner, and had come to the top of the steps up from the West Pier and stopped to look at the view, as we generally do. The setting sun, low down in the sky, was just dropping behind Kettleness; the red light was thrown over on the East Cliff and the old Abbey, and seemed to bathe everything in a beautiful rosy glow. We were silent for a while, and suddenly Lucy murmured as if to herself:–

'His red eyes again! They are just the same.' It was such an odd expression, coming *apropos* of nothing, that it quite startled me. I slewed round a little, so as to see Lucy well without seeming to stare at her, and saw that she was in a half-dreamy state, with an odd look on her face that I could not quite make out; so I said nothing, but followed her eyes. She appeared to be looking over at our seat, whereon was a dark figure seated alone. I was a little startled myself, for it seemed for an instant as if the stranger had great eyes like burning flames; but a second look dispelled the illusion. The red sunlight was shining on the windows of St Mary's Church behind our seat, and as the sun dipped there was just sufficient change in the refraction and reflection to make it appear as if the light moved. I called Lucy's attention to the peculiar effect, and she became herself with a start, but she looked sad all the same; it may have been that she was thinking of that terrible night up there. We never refer to it; so I said nothing, and we went home to dinner. Lucy had a headache and went early to bed. I saw her asleep, and went out for a little stroll myself; I walked along the cliffs to the westward, and was full of sweet sadness, for I was thinking of Jonathan. When coming home – it was then bright moonlight, so bright that, though the front of our part of the Crescent was in shadow, everything could be well seen – I threw a glance up at our window, and saw Lucy's head leaning out. I thought that perhaps she was looking out for me, so I opened my handkerchief and waved it. She did not notice or make any movement whatever. Just then, the moonlight crept round an angle of the building, and the light fell on the window. There distinctly was Lucy with her head lying up against the side of the window-sill and her eyes shut. She was fast asleep, and by her, seated on the window-sill, was something that looked like a good-sized bird. I was afraid she might get a chill, so I ran upstairs, but as I came into the room she was moving back to her bed, fast asleep, and breathing heavily; she was holding her hand to her throat, as though to protect it from cold. I did not wake her, but tucked her up warmly. I have taken care that the door is locked and the window securely fastened.

She looks so sweet as she sleeps; but she is paler than is her wont, and there is a drawn, haggard look under her eyes which I do not like. I fear she is fretting about something. I wish I could find out what it is.

15 August. – Rose later than usual. Lucy was languid and tired, and slept on after we had been called. We had a happy surprise at breakfast. Arthur's father is better, and wants the marriage to come off soon. Lucy is full of quiet joy, and her mother is glad and sorry at once. Later on in the day she told me the cause. She is grieved to lose Lucy as her very own, but she is rejoiced that she is soon to have someone to protect her. Poor dear, sweet lady! She confided to me that she has got her death-warrant. She has not told Lucy, and made me promise secrecy; her doctor told her that within a few months, at most, she must die, for her heart is weakening. At any time, even now, a sudden shock would be almost sure to kill her. Ah, we were wise to keep from her the affair of the dreadful night of Lucy's sleep-walking.

17 August. – No diary for two whole days. I have not had the heart to write. Some sort of shadowy pall seems to be coming over our happiness. No news from Jonathan, and Lucy seems to be growing weaker, whilst her mother's hours are numbering to a close. I do not understand Lucy's fading away as she is doing. She eats well and sleeps well, and enjoys the fresh air; but all the time the roses in her cheeks are fading, and she gets weaker and more languid day by day; at night I hear her gasping as if for air. I keep the key of our door always fastened to my wrist at night, but she gets up and walks about the room, and sits at the open window. Last night I found her leaning out when I woke up, and when I tried to wake her I could not; she was in a faint. When I managed to restore her she was as weak as water, and cried silently between long, painful struggles for breath. When I asked her how she came to be at the window she shook her head and turned away. I trust her feeling ill may not be from that unlucky prick of the safety-pin. I looked at her throat just now as she lay asleep, and the tiny wounds seem not to have healed. They are still open, and, if anything, larger, than before, and the edges of them are faintly white. They are like little white dots with red centres. Unless they heal within a day or two, I shall insist on the doctor seeing about them.

Letter, Samuel F. Billington & Son, Solicitors, Whitby, to Messrs. Carter, Paterson & Co., London

'17 *August*.

'Dear Sirs, –

'Herewith please receive invoice of goods sent by Great Northern Railway. Same are to be delivered to Carfax, near Purfleet, immediately on receipt at goods station King's Cross. The house is at present empty, but enclosed please find keys, all of which are labelled.

'You will please deposit the boxes, fifty in number, which form the consignment, in the partially ruined building forming part of the house and marked "A" on rough diagram enclosed. Your agent will easily recognize the locality, as it is the ancient chapel of the mansion. The goods leave by the train at 9.30 to-night, and will be due at King's Cross at 4.30 to-morrow afternoon. As our client wishes the delivery made as soon as possible, we shall be obliged by your having teams ready at King's Cross at the time named and forthwith conveying the goods to destination. In order to obviate any delays possible through any routine requirements as to payment in your departments, we enclose cheque herewith for ten pounds (£10), receipt of which please acknowledge. Should the charge be less than this amount, you can return balance; if greater, we shall at once send cheque for difference on hearing from you. You are to leave the keys on coming away in the main hall of the house, where the proprietor may get them on his entering the house by means of his duplicate key.

'Pray do not take us as exceeding the bounds of business courtesy in pressing you in all ways to use the utmost expedition.

'We are, dear Sirs,
'Faithfully yours,
'SAMUEL F. BILLINGTON & SON.'

*Letter, Messrs. Carter, Paterson & Co, London to Messrs.
Billington & Son, Whitby*

'*21 August.*

'Dear Sirs, –
   'We beg to acknowledge £10 received and to return cheque £1 17s.9d.,
amount of overplus, as shown in receipted account herewith. Goods are
delivered in exact accordance with instructions, and keys left in parcel in
main hall, as directed.
'We are, dear Sirs,
'Yours respectfully,
'*Pro* CARTER, PATERSON & CO.'

MINA MURRAY'S JOURNAL

18 August. – I am happy to-day, and write sitting on the seat in the
churchyard. Lucy is ever so much better. Last night she slept well all night,
and did not disturb me once. The roses seem coming back already to her
cheeks, though she is still sadly pale and wan-looking. If she were in any
way anaemic I could understand it, but she is not. She is in gay spirits and
full of life and cheerfulness. All the morbid reticence seems to have passed
from her, and she has just reminded me, as if I needed any reminding, of
that night, and that it was here, on this very seat, I found her asleep. As she
told me she tapped playfully with the heel of her boot on the stone slab
and said:–
   'My poor little feet didn't make much noise then! I daresay poor old Mr
Swales would have told me that it was because I didn't want to wake up
Geordie.' As she was in such a communicative humour, I asked her if she
had dreamed at all that night. Before she answered, that sweet, puckered
look came into her forehead, which Arthur – I call him Arthur from her
habit – says he loves; and, indeed, I don't wonder that he does. Then she
went on in a half-dreaming kind of way, as if trying to recall it to herself:–
   'I didn't quite dream; but it all seemed to be real. I only wanted to be
here in this spot – I don't know why, for I was afraid of something – I
don't know what. I remember, though I suppose I was asleep, passing
through the streets and over the bridge. A fish leaped as I went by, and I

79

leaned over to look at it, and I heard a lot of dogs howling – the whole town seemed as if it must be full of dogs all howling at once – as I went up the steps. Then I have a vague memory of something long and dark with red eyes, just as we saw in the sunset, and something very sweet and very bitter all around me at once; and then I seemed sinking into deep green water, and there was a singing in my ears, as I have heard there is to drowning men; and then everything seemed passing away from me; my soul seemed to go out from my body and float about the air. I seemed to remember that once the West Lighthouse was right under me, and then there was a sort of agonizing feeling, as if I were in an earthquake, and I came back and found you shaking my body. I saw you do it before I felt you.'

Then she began to laugh. It seemed a little uncanny to me, and I listened to her breathlessly. I did not quite like it, and thought it better not to keep her mind on the subject, so we drifted on to other subjects, and Lucy was like her old self again. When we got home the fresh breeze had braced her up, and her pale cheeks were really more rosy. Her mother rejoiced when she saw her, and we all spent a very happy evening together.

19 August. – Joy, joy, joy! although not all joy. At last, news of Jonathan. The dear fellow has been ill, that is why he did not write. I am not afraid to think it or to say it, now that I know. Mr Hawkins sent me on the letter, and wrote himself oh, so kindly. I am to leave in the morning and to go over to Jonathan, and to help nurse him if necessary, and to bring him home. Mr Hawkins says it would not be a bad thing if we were to be married out there. I have cried over the good Sister's letter till I can feel it wet against my bosom, where it lies. It is of Jonathan, and must be next my heart, for he is *in* my heart. My journey is all mapped out, and my luggage ready. I am only taking one change of dress; Lucy will bring my trunk to London and keep it till I send for it, for it may be that . . . I must write no more; I must keep it to say to Jonathan, my husband. The letter that he has seen and touched must comfort me till we meet.

Letter, Sister Agatha, Hospital of St Joseph and Ste Mary, Buda-Pesth, to Miss Wilhelmina Murray

'*12 August.*

'Dear Madam, –
'I write by desire of Mr Jonathan Harker, who is himself not strong enough to write, though progressing well, thanks to God and St Joseph and Ste Mary. He has been under our care for nearly six weeks, suffering from a violent brain fever. He wishes me to convey his love, and to say that by this post I write for him to Mr Peter Hawkins, Exeter, to say, with

his dutiful respects, that he is sorry for this delay, and that all his work is completed. He will require some few weeks' rest in our sanatorium in the hills, but will then return. He wishes me to say that he has not sufficient money with him, and that he would like to pay for his staying here, so that others who need shall not be wanting for help.

'Believe me,
'Yours, with sympathy and all blessings,
SISTER AGATHA.

'P.S. – My patient being asleep, I open this to let you know something more. He has told me all about you, and that you are shortly to be his wife. All blessings to you both! He has had some fearful shock – so says our doctor – and in his delirium his ravings have been dreadful; of wolves and poison and blood; of ghosts and demons; and I fear to say of what. Be careful with him always that there may be nothing to excite him of this kind for a long time to come; the traces of such an illness as his do not lightly die away. We should have written long ago, but we knew nothing of his friends, and there was on him nothing that any one could understand. He came in the train from Klausenburgh, and the guard was told by the station-master there that he rushed into the station shouting for a ticket for home. Seeing from his violent demeanour that he was English, they gave him a ticket for the farthest station on the way thither that the train reached.

'Be assured that he is well cared for. He has won all hearts by his sweetness and gentleness. He is truly getting on well, and I have no doubt will in a few weeks be all himself. But be careful of him for safety's sake. There are, I pray God and St Joseph and Ste Mary, many, many happy years for you both.'

DR SEWARD'S DIARY

19 August. – Strange and sudden change in Renfield last night. About eight o'clock he began to get excited and to sniff about as a dog does when setting. The attendant was struck by his manner, and knowing my interest in him, encouraged him to talk. He is usually respectful to the attendant, and at times servile; but to-night, the man tells me, he was quite haughty. Would not condescend to talk with him at all. All he would say was:–

'I don't want to talk to you; you don't count now; the Master is at hand.'

The attendant thinks it is some sudden form of religious mania which has seized him. If so, we must look out for squalls, for a strong man with

81

homicidal and religious mania at once might be dangerous. The combination is a dreadful one. At nine o'clock I visited him myself. His attitude to me was the same as that to the attendant; in his sublime self-feeling the difference between myself and attendant seemed to him as nothing. It looks like religious mania, and he will soon think that he himself is God. These infinitesimal distinctions between man and man are too paltry for an Omnipotent being. How these madmen give themselves away! The real God taketh heed lest a sparrow fall; but the God created from human vanity sees no difference between an eagle and a sparrow. Oh, if men only knew!

For half an hour or more Renfield kept getting excited in greater and greater degree. I did not pretend to be watching him, but I kept strict observation all the same. All at once that shifty look came into his eyes which we always see when a madman has seized an idea, and with it the shifty movement of the head and back which asylum attendants come to know so well. He became quite quiet, and went and sat on the edge of his bed resignedly, and looked into space with lack-lustre eyes. I thought I would find out if his apathy were real or only assumed, and tried to lead him to talk of his pets, a theme which never failed to excite his attention. At first he made no reply, but at length said testily:—

'Bother them all! I don't care a pin about them.'

'What?' I said. 'You don't mean to tell me that you don't care about spiders?' (Spiders at present are his hobby, and the note-book is filling up with columns of small figures.) To this he answered enigmatically:—

'The bride-maidens rejoice the eyes that wait the coming of the bride; but when the bride draweth nigh, then the maidens shine not to the eyes that are filled.'

He would not explain himself, but remained obstinately seated on his bed all the time I remained with him.

I am weary to-night and low in spirits. I cannot but think of Lucy, and how different things might have been. If I don't sleep at once, chloral, the modern Morpheus — $C_2HCl_3O.H_2O$! I must be careful not to let it grow into a habit. No, I shall take none to-night! I have thought of Lucy, and I shall not dishonour her by mixing the two. If need be, to-night shall be sleepless. . . .

Glad I made the resolution; gladder that I kept to it. I had lain tossing about, and had heard the clock strike only twice, when the night-watchman came to me, sent up from the ward, to say that Renfield had escaped. I threw on my clothes and ran down at once; my patient is too dangerous a person to be roaming about. Those ideas of his might work out dangerously with strangers. The attendant was waiting for me. He said he had seen him not ten minutes before, seemingly asleep in his bed, when he had looked through the observation-trap in the door. His attention was called by the sound of the window being wrenched out. He ran back and saw his feet disappear through the window, and had at once sent up for me. He was only in his night-gear, and cannot be far off. The attendant thought it would be more useful to watch where he should go than to follow him, as he might lose sight of him whilst getting out of the building by the door. He is a bulky man, and couldn't get through the window. I am thin, so, with his aid, I got out, but feet foremost, and, as we were only a few feet above ground, landed unhurt. The attendant told me the patient had gone to the left and had taken a straight line, so I ran as quickly as I could. As I got through the belt of trees I saw a white figure scale the high wall which separates our grounds from those of the deserted house.

I ran back at once, and told the watchman to get three or four men immediately and follow me into the grounds of Carfax, in case our friend might be dangerous. I got a ladder myself, and crossing the wall, dropped down on the other side. I could see Renfield's figure just disappearing behind the angle of the house, so I ran after him. On the far side of the house I found him pressed close against the old iron-bound oak door of the chapel. He was talking, apparently to someone, but I was afraid to go near enough to hear what he was saying, lest I might frighten him, and he should run off. Chasing an errant swarm of bees is nothing to following a naked lunatic when the fit of escaping is upon him! After a few minutes, however, I could see that he did not take note of anything around him, and so ventured to draw nearer to him – the more so as my men had now crossed the wall and were closing him in. I heard him say:–

'I am here to do Your bidding, Master. I am Your slave, and You will reward me, for I shall be faithful. I have worshipped You long and afar off. Now that You are near, I await Your commands, and You will not pass me by, will You, dear Master, in Your distribution of good things?'

He *is* a selfish old beggar anyhow. He thinks of the loaves and fishes even when he believes he is in a Real Presence. His manias make a startling combination. When we closed in on him he fought like a tiger. He is immensely strong, and he was more like a wild beast than a man. I never saw a lunatic in such a paroxysm of rage before; and I hope I shall not again. It is a mercy that we have found out his strength and his danger in good time. With strength and determination like his, he might have done wild work before he was caged. He is safe now at any rate. Jack Sheppard himself couldn't get free from the strait-waistcoat that keeps him restrained, and he's chained to the wall in the padded room. His cries are at times awful, but the silences that follow are more deadly still, for he means murder in every turn and movement.

Just now he spoke coherent words for the first time:—

'I shall be patient, Master. It is coming – coming – coming!'

So I took the hint, and came too. I was too excited to sleep, but this diary has quieted me, and I feel I shall get some sleep to-night.

9

Letter, Mina Harker to Lucy Westenra

'Buda-Pesth, 24 August.

'My dearest Lucy, –

'I know you will be anxious to hear all that has happened since we parted at the railway station at Whitby. Well, my dear, I got to Hull all right, and caught the boat to Hamburg, and then the train on here. I feel I can hardly recall anything of the journey, except that I knew I was coming to Jonathan, and that, as I should have to do some nursing, I had better get all the sleep I could. . . . I found my dear one, oh, so thin and pale and weak-looking. All the resolution has gone out of his dear eyes, and that quiet dignity which I told you was in his face has vanished. He is only a wreck of himself, and he does not remember anything that has happened to him for a long time past. At least, he wants me to believe so, and I shall never ask. He has had some terrible shock, and I fear it might tax his poor brain if he were to try to recall it. Sister Agatha who is a good creature and a born nurse, tells me that he raved of dreadful things whilst he was off his head. I wanted her to tell me what they were; but she would only cross herself, and say she would never tell; that the ravings of the sick were the secrets of God, and that if a nurse through her vocation should hear them, she should respect her trust. She is a sweet, good soul, and the next day, when she saw I was troubled, she opened up the subject again, and after saying that she could never mention what my poor dear raved about, added: "I can tell you this much, my dear: that it was not about anything which he has done wrong himself; and you, as his wife to be, have no cause to be concerned. He has not forgotten you or what he owes to you. His fear was of great and terrible things, which no mortal can treat of." I believe the dear soul thought I might be jealous lest my poor dear should have fallen in love with any other girl. The idea of *my* being jealous about Jonathan! And yet, my dear, let me whisper, I felt a thrill of joy through me when I *knew* that no other woman was a cause of trouble. I am now sitting by his bedside, where I can see his face while he sleeps. He is waking! . . . When he woke he asked me for his coat, as he wanted to get something from the pocket; I asked Sister Agatha, and she brought all his things. I saw that amongst them was his note-book, and was going to ask him to let me look at it – for I knew then that I might find some clue to his trouble – but I suppose he must have seen my wish in my eyes, for he sent me over to the window, saying he wanted to be quite alone for a moment. Then he called me back, and when I came he had his hand over the note-book, and he said to me very solemnly:–

' "Wilhelmina" – I knew then that he was in deadly earnest for he has never called me by that name since he asked me to marry him – "you know, dear, my ideas of the trust between husband and wife: there should be no secret, no concealment. I have had a great shock, and when I try to think of what it is I feel my head spin round, and I do not know if it was all real or the dreaming of a madman. You know I have had brain fever, and that is to be mad. The secret is here, and I do not want to know it. I want to take up my life here, with our marriage." For, my dear, we had decided to be married as soon as the formalities are complete. "Are you willing, Wilhelmina, to share my ignorance? Here is the book. Take it and keep it, read it if you will, but never let me know; unless, indeed, some solemn duty should come upon me to go back to the bitter hours, asleep or awake, sane or mad, recorded here." He fell back, exhausted, and I put the book under his pillow, and kissed him. I have asked Sister Agatha to beg the Superior to let our wedding be this afternoon, and am waiting her reply. . . .

'She has come and told me that the chaplain of the English mission church has been sent for. We are to be married in an hour, or as soon after as Jonathan awakes. . . .

'Lucy, the time has come and gone. I feel very solemn, but very, very happy. Jonathan woke a little after the hour, and all was ready, and he sat up in bed, propped up with pillows. He answered his "I will" firmly and strongly. I could hardly speak; my heart was so full that even these words seemed to choke me. The dear Sisters were so kind. Please God, I shall never, never forget them, nor the grave and sweet responsibilities I have taken upon me. I must tell you of my wedding present. When the chaplain and the Sisters had left me alone with my husband – oh, Lucy, it is the first time I have written the words "my husband" – left me alone with my husband, I took the book from under his pillow, and wrapped it up in white paper, and tied it with a little bit of pale blue ribbon which was wound round my neck, and sealed it over the knot with sealing-wax, and for my seal I used my wedding ring. Then I kissed it and showed it to my husband, and told him that I would keep it so, and then it would be an outward and visible sign for us all our lives that we trusted each other; that I would never open it unless it were for his own dear sake, or for the sake of some stern duty. Then he took my hand in his, and oh, Lucy, it was the first time he took *his wife's* hand, and said that it was the dearest thing in all the wide world, and that he would go through all the past again to win it, if need be. The poor dear meant to have said a part of the past; but he cannot think of time yet, and I shall not wonder if at first he mixes up not only the month, but the year.

'Well, my dear, what could I say? I could only tell him that I was the happiest woman in all the wide world, and that I had nothing to give him except myself, my life, and my trust, and that with these went my love and duty for all the days of my life. And, my dear, when he kissed me, and drew me to him with his poor weak hands, it was like a very solemn pledge between us. . . .

'Lucy dear, do you know why I tell you all this? It is not only because it is all sweet to me, but because you have been, and are, very dear to me. It was my privilege to be your friend and guide when you came from the schoolroom to prepare for the world of life. I want you to see now, and with the eyes of a very happy wife, whither duty has led me; so that in your own married life you too may be all happy as I am. My dear, please Almighty God, your life may be all it promises: a long day of sunshine, with no harsh wind, no forgetting duty, no distrust. I must not wish you no pain, for that can never be; but I do hope you will be *always* as happy as I am *now*. Good-bye, my dear. I shall post this at once, and, perhaps, write you very soon again. I must stop, for Jonathan is waking – I must attend to my husband!

> 'Your ever-loving
> 'MINA HARKER.'

Letter, Lucy Westenra to Mina Harker

> '*Whitby, 30 August.*

'My dearest Mina, –

'Oceans of love and millions of kisses, and may you soon be in your own home with your husband. I wish you could be coming home soon enough to stay with us here. This strong air would soon restore Jonathan; it has quite restored me. I have an appetite like a cormorant, am full of life, and sleep well. You will be glad to know that I have quite given up walking in my sleep. I think I have not stirred out of my bed for a week, that is, when I once got into it at night. Arthur says I am getting fat. By the way, I forgot to tell you that Arthur is here. We have such walks and drives, and rides, and rowing, and tennis, and fishing together; and I love him more than ever. He *tells me* that he loves me more, but I doubt that, for at first he told me that he couldn't love me more than he did then. But this is nonsense. There he is calling to me. So no more just at present from your loving

'LUCY.

'P.S. – Mother sends her love. She seems better, poor dear.
'P.P.S. – We are to be married on 28 September.'

DR SEWARD'S DIARY

20 August. – The case of Renfield grows even more interesting. He has now so far quieted that there are spells of cessation from his passion. For the first week after his attack he was perpetually violent. Then one night, just as the moon rose, he grew quiet, and kept murmuring to himself: 'Now I can wait; now I can wait.' The attendant came to tell me, so I ran down at once to have a look at him. He was still in the strait-waistcoat and in the padded room, but the suffused look had gone from his face, and his eyes had something of their old pleading – I might almost say, 'cringing' – softness. I was satisfied with his present condition, and directed him to be relieved. The attendants hesitated, but finally carried out my wishes without protest. It was a strange thing that the patient had humour enough to see their distrust, for, coming close to me, he said in a whisper, all the while looking furtively at them:–

'They think I could hurt you! Fancy *me* hurting *you*! The fools!'

It was soothing, somehow, to the feelings to find myself dissociated even in the mind of this poor madman from the others; but all the same I do not follow his thought. Am I to take it that I have anything in common with him, so that we are, as it were, to stand together; or has he to gain from me some good so stupendous that my well-being is needful to him? I must find out later on. To-night he will not speak. Even the offer of a kitten or even a full-grown cat will not tempt him. He will only say: 'I don't take any stock in cats. I have more to think of now, and I can wait; I can wait.'

After a while I left him. The attendant tells me that he was quiet until just before dawn, and then he began to get uneasy, and at length violent, until at last he fell into a paroxysm which exhausted him so that he swooned into a sort of coma.

. . . Three nights has the same thing happened – violent all day, then quiet from moonrise to sunrise. I wish I could get some clue to the cause. It would almost seem as if there was some influence which came and went. Happy thought! We shall to-night play sane wits against mad ones. He escaped before without our help; to-night he shall escape with it. We shall give him a chance, and have the men ready to follow in case they are required. . . .

23 August. – 'The unexpected always happens.' How well Disraeli knew life! Our bird when he found the cage open would not fly, so all our subtle arrangements went for naught. At any rate, we have proved one thing: that the spells of quietness last a reasonable time. We shall in future be able to ease his bond for a few hours each day. I have given orders to the night attendant merely to shut him in the padded room, when once he is quiet, until an hour before sunrise. The poor soul's body will enjoy the relief even if his mind cannot appreciate it. Hark! The unexpected again! I am called; the patient has once more escaped.

Later. – Another night adventure. Renfield artfully waited until the attendant was entering the room to inspect. Then he dashed out past him and flew down the passage. I sent word for the attendants to follow. Again we went into the ground of the deserted house, and we found him in the same place, pressed against the old chapel door. When he saw me he became furious, and had not the attendants seized him in time, he would have tried to kill me. As we were holding him a strange thing happened. He suddenly redoubled his efforts, and then he suddenly grew calm. I looked round instinctively, but could see nothing. Then I caught the patient's eye and followed it, but could trace nothing as it looked into the moonlit sky except a big bat, which was flapping its silent and ghostly way to the west. Bats usually wheel and flit about but this one seemed to go straight on, as if it knew where it was bound for or had some intention of its own. The patient grew calmer every instant, and presently said:–

'You needn't tie me; I shall go quietly!' Without trouble we came back to the house. I feel there is something ominous in his calm, and shall not forget this night. . . .

LUCY WESTENRA'S DIARY

Hillingham, 24 August. – I must imitate Mina, and keep writing things down. Then we can have long talks when we do meet. I wonder when it will be. I wish she were with me again, for I feel so unhappy. Last night I seemed to be dreaming again just as I was at Whitby. Perhaps it is the change of air, or getting home again. It is all dark and horrid to me, for I can remember nothing; but I am full of vague fear, and I feel so weak and worn out. When Arthur came to lunch he looked quite grieved when he saw me, and I hadn't the spirit to be cheerful. I wonder if I could sleep in mother's room to-night. I shall make an excuse and try.

25 August. – Another bad night. Mother did not seem to take to my proposal. She seems not too well herself, and doubtless she fears to worry me. I tried to keep awake, and succeeded for a while; but when the clock struck twelve it waked me from a doze, so I must have been falling asleep. There was a sort of scratching or flapping at the window, but I did not mind it, and as I remember no more, I suppose I must then have fallen asleep. More bad dreams. I wish I could remember them. This morning I am horribly weak. My face is ghastly pale, and my throat pains me. It must be something wrong with my lungs, for I don't seem ever to get air enough. I shall try to cheer up when Arthur comes, or else I know he will be miserable to see me so.

Letter, Arthur Holmwood to Dr Seward

'*Albemarle Hotel, 31 August.*

'My dear Jack, –

'I want you to do me a favour. Lucy is ill; that is, she has no special disease, but she looks awful, and is getting worse every day. I have asked her if there is any cause; I do not dare to ask her mother, for to disturb the poor lady's mind about her daughter in her present state of health would be fatal. Mrs Westenra has confided to me that her doom is spoken – disease of the heart – though poor Lucy does not know it yet. I am sure that there is something preying on my dear girl's mind. I am almost distracted when I think of her; to look at her gives me a pang. I told her I should ask you to see her, and though she demurred at first – I know why, old fellow – she finally consented. It will be a painful task for you, I know, old friend, but it is for *her* sake, and I must not hesitate to ask, or you to act. You are to come to lunch at Hillingham to-morrow, two o'clock, so as not to arouse any suspicion in Mrs Westenra, and after lunch Lucy will take an opportunity of being alone with you. I shall come in for tea, and we can go away together. I am filled with anxiety, and want to consult with you alone as soon as I can after you have seen her. Do not fail!

'ARTHUR.'

Telegram, Arthur Holmwood to Seward

'*1 September.*

'Am summoned to see my father, who is worse. Am writing. Write me fully by to-night's post to Ring. Wire me if necessary.'

Letter from Dr Seward to Arthur Holmwood

'2 September.

'My dear old fellow, –

'With regard to Miss Westenra's health, I hasten to let you know at once that in my opinion there is not any functional disturbance or any malady that I know of. At the same time, I am not by any means satisfied with her appearance; she is woefully different from what she was when I saw her last. Of course you must bear in mind that I did not have full opportunity of examination such as I should wish; our very friendship makes a little difficulty which not even medical science or custom can bridge over. I had better tell you exactly what happened, leaving you to draw, in a measure, your own conclusions. I shall then say what I have done and propose doing.

'I found Miss Westenra in seemingly gay spirits. Her mother was present, and in a few seconds I made up my mind that she was trying all she knew to mislead her mother and prevent her from being anxious. I have no doubt she guesses, if she does not know, what need of caution there is. We lunched alone, and as we all exerted ourselves to be cheerful, we got, as some kind of reward for our labours, some real cheerfulness amongst us. Then Mrs Westenra went to lie down, and Lucy was left with me. We went into her boudoir, and till we got there her gaiety remained, for the servants were coming and going. As soon as the door was closed, however, the mask fell from her face, and she sank down into a chair with a great sigh, and hid her eyes with her hand. When I saw that her high spirits had failed, I at once took advantage of her reaction to make a diagnosis. She said to me very sweetly:–

' "I cannot tell you how I loathe talking about myself." I reminded her that a doctor's confidence was sacred, but that you were grievously anxious about her. She caught on to my meaning at once, and settled that matter in a word. "Tell Arthur everything you choose. I do not care for myself, but all for him!" So I am quite free.

'I could easily see that she is somewhat bloodless, but I could not see the usual anaemic signs, and by a chance I was actually able to test the quality of her blood, for in opening a window which was stiff a cord gave way, and she cut her hand slightly with broken glass. It was a slight matter in itself, but it gave me an evident chance, and I secured a few drops of the blood and have analysed them. The qualitative analysis gives a quite

90

normal condition, and shows, I should infer, in itself a vigorous state of health. In other physical matters I was quite satisfied that there is no need for anxiety; but as there must be a cause somewhere, I have come to the conclusion that it must be something mental. She complains of difficulty in breathing satisfactorily at times, and of heavy, lethargic sleep, with dreams that frighten her, but regarding which she can remember nothing. She says that as a child she used to walk in her sleep, and that when in Whitby the habit came back, and that once she walked out in the night and went to the East Cliff, where Miss Murray found her: but she assures me that of late the habit has not returned. I am in doubt, and so have done the best thing I know of: I have written to my old friend and master, Professor Van Helsing, of Amsterdam, who knows as much about obscure diseases as anyone in the world. I have asked him to come over, and as you told me that all things were to be at your charge, I have mentioned to him who you are and your relations to Miss Westenra. This, my dear fellow, is only in obedience to your wishes, for I am only too proud and happy to do anything I can for her. Van Helsing would, I know, do anything for me for a personal reason. So, no matter on what ground he comes, we must accept his wishes. He is a seemingly arbitrary man, but this is because he knows what he is talking about better than anyone else. He is a philosopher and a metaphysician, and one of the most advanced scientists of his day; and he has I believe, an absolutely open mind. This, with an iron nerve, a temper of the ice brook, an indomitable resolution, self-command and toleration exalted from virtues to blessings, and the kindest and truest heart that beats – these form his equipment for the noble work that he is doing for mankind – work both in theory and practice, for his views are as wide as his all-embracing sympathy. I tell you these facts that you may know why I have such confidence in him. I have asked him to come at once. I shall see Miss Westenra to-morrow again. She is to meet me at the Stores, so that I may not alarm her mother by too early a repetition of my call.

'Yours always
'JOHN SEWARD.'

Letter, Abraham Van Helsing, M.D., D.Ph., D.Litt., etc., etc.,
to Dr Seward

'2 September.

'My good Friend, –
'When I have received your letter I am already coming to you. By good fortune I can leave just at once, without wrong to any of those who have

trusted me. Were fortune other, then it were bad for those who have trusted, for I come to my friend when he call me to aid those he holds dear. Tell your friend that when that time you suck from my wound so swiftly the poison of the grangrene from that knife that our other friend, too nervous, let slip, you did more for him when he wants my aids and you call for them than all his great fortune could do. But it is pleasure added to do for him, your friend; it is to you that I come. Have then rooms for me at the Great Eastern Hotel, so that I may be near to hand, and please it so arrange that we may see the young lady not too late on to-morrow, for it is likely that I may have to return here that night. But if need be I shall come again in three days, and stay longer if it must. Till then good-bye, my friend John.

'VAN HELSING.'

Letter, Dr Seward to Hon. Arthur Holmwood

'3 September.

'My dear Art, –

'Van Helsing has come and gone. He came on with me to Hillingham, and found that, by Lucy's discretion, her mother was lunching out, so that we were alone with her. Van Helsing made a very careful examination of the patient. He is to report to me, and I shall advise you, for of course I was not present all the time. He is, I fear, much concerned, but says he must think. When I told him of our friendship and how you trust to me in the matter, he said: "You must tell him all you think. Tell him what I think, if you can guess it, if you will. Nay, I am not jesting. This is no jest, but life and death, perhaps more." I asked what he meant by that, for he was very serious. This was when we had come back to town, and he was having a cup of tea before starting on his return to Amsterdam. He would not give me any further clue. You must not be angry with him, Art, because his very reticence means that all his brains are working for her good. He will speak plainly enough when the time comes, be sure. So I told him I would simply write an account of our visit, just as if I were doing a descriptive special article for *The Daily Telegraph*. He seemed not to notice, but remarked that the smuts in London were not quite so bad as they used to be when he was a student here. I am to get his report to-morrow if he can possibly make it. In any case I am to have a letter.

'Well, as to the visit. Lucy was more cheerful than on the day I first saw her, and certainly looked better. She had lost something of the ghastly look that so upset you, and her breathing was normal. She was very sweet to the Professor (as she always is), and tried to make him feel at ease; though I could see that the poor girl was making a hard struggle for it. I believe Van Helsing saw it, too, for I saw the quick look under his bushy brows that I knew of old. Then he began to chat of all things except ourselves and diseases, and with such an infinite geniality that I could see poor Lucy's pretence of animation merge into reality. Then, without any seeming change, he brought the conversation gently round to his visit, and suavely said:–

' "My dear young miss. I have the so great pleasure because you are much beloved. That is much, my dear, even were there that which I do not see. They told me you were in the spirit, and that you were of a ghastly pale. To them I say: 'Pouf!' " And he snapped his fingers at me and went on: "But you and I shall show them how wrong they are. How can he" – and he pointed at me with the same look and gesture as that with which once he pointed me out to his class, on, or rather after, a particular occasion which he never fails to remind me of – "know anything of a young ladies? He has his madmans to play with, and to bring them back to happiness and to those that love them. It is much to do, and, oh, but there are rewards, in that we can bestow such happiness. But the young ladies! He has no wife nor daughter, and the young do not tell themselves to the young, but to the old, like me, who have known so many sorrows and the causes of them. So, my dear, we will send him away to smoke the cigarette in the garden, whiles you and I have little talk all to ourselves." I took the hint, and strolled about, and presently the Professor came to the window and called me in. He looked grave, but said: "I have made careful examination, but there is no functional cause. With you I agree that there has been much blood lost, it has been, but is not. But the conditions of her are in no way anaemic. I have asked her to send me her maid that I may asked just one or two questions, that so I may not chance to miss nothing. I know well what she will say. And yet there is cause; there is always cause for everything. I must go back home and think. You must send to me the telegram every day; and if there be cause I shall come again. The disease – for not to be all well is a disease – interest me, and the sweet young dear, she interest me too. She charm me, and for her, if not for you or disease, I come."

'As I tell you, he would not say a word more, even when we were alone. And so now, Art, you know all I know. I shall keep stern watch. I trust your poor father is rallying. It must be a terrible thing to you, my dear old fellow, to be placed in such a position between two people who are both so dear to you. I know your idea of duty to your father, and you are right to stick to it; but, if need be, I shall send you word to come at once to Lucy; so do not be over-anxious unless you hear from me.'

4 September. – Zoophagous patient still keeps up our interest in him. He had only one outburst, and that was yesterday at an unusual time. Just before the stroke of noon he began to grow restless. The attendant knew the symptoms, and at once summoned aid. Fortunately the men came at a run, and were just in time, for at the stroke of noon he became so violent that it took all their strength to hold him. In about five minutes, however, he began to get more and more quiet, and finally sank into a sort of melancholy, in which state he has remained up to now. The attendant tells me that his screams whilst in the paroxysm were really appalling; I found my hands full when I got in, attending to some of the other patients who were frightened by him. Indeed, I can quite understand the effect, for the sounds disturbed even me, though I was some distance away. It is now after the dinner-hour of the asylum, and as yet my patient sits in a corner brooding, with a dull, sullen, woebegone look in his face, which seems rather to indicate than to show something directly. I cannot quite understand it.

Later. – Another change in my patient. At five o'clock I looked in on him, and found him seemingly as happy and contented as he used to be. He was catching flies and eating them, and was keeping note of his capture by making nail-marks on the edge of the door between the ridges of padding. When he saw me, he came over and apologized for his bad conduct, and asked me in a very humble, cringing way to be let back to his own room and to have his note-book again. I thought it well to humour him; so he is back in his room, with the window open. He has the sugar of his tea spread out on the windowsill, and is reaping quite a harvest of flies. He is not now eating them, but putting them in a box, as of old, and is already examining the corners of his room to find a spider. I tried to get him to talk about the past few days, for any clue of his thoughts would be of immense help to me; but he would not rise. For a moment or two he looked very sad, and said in a sort of far-away voice, as though saying it rather to himself than to me:–

'All over! all over! He has deserted me. No hope for me now unless I do it for myself!' Then suddenly turning to me in a resolute way, he said: 'Doctor, won't you be very good to me and let me have a little more sugar? I think it would be good for me.'

'And the flies?' I said.

'Yes! The flies like it, too, and I like the flies; therefore I like it.' And there are people who know so little as to think that madmen do not argue. I procured him a double supply, and left him as happy a man as, I suppose, any in the world. I wish I could fathom his mind.

Midnight. – Another change in him. I had been to see Miss Westenra, whom I found much better, and had just returned, and was standing at our own gate looking at the sunset, when once more I heard him yelling. As his room is on this side of the house, I could hear it better than in the morning. It was a shock to me to turn from the wonderful smoky beauty of a sunset over London, with its lurid lights and inky shadows and all the marvellous tints that come on foul clouds even as on foul water, and to realize all the grim sternness of my own cold stone building, with its wealth of breathing misery, and my own desolate heart to endure it all. I reached him just as the sun was going down, and from his window saw the red disc sink. As it sank he became less and less frenzied; and just as it dipped he slid from the hands that held him, an inert mass, on the floor. It is wonderful, however, what intellectual recuperative power lunatics have, for within a few minutes he stood up quite calmly and looked around him. I signalled to the attendants not to hold him, for I was anxious to see what he would do. He went straight over to the window and brushed out the crumbs of sugar; then he took his fly-box and emptied it outside, and threw away the box; then he shut the window, and crossing over, sat down on his bed. All this surprised me, so I asked him: 'Are you not going to keep flies any more?'

'No, said he; 'I am sick of all that rubbish!' He certainly is a wonderfully interesting study. I wish I could get some glimpse of his mind or of the cause of his sudden passion. Stop; there may be a clue after all, if we can find why to-day his paroxysms came on at high noon and at sunset. Can it be that there is a malign influence of the sun at periods which affects certain natures – as at times the moon does others? We shall see.

Telegram, Seward, London, to Van Helsing, Amsterdam

'*4 September.* – Patient still better to-day.'

Telegram, Seward, London, to Van Helsing, Amsterdam

'*5 September.* – Patient greatly improved. Good appetite; sleeps naturally; good spirits, colour coming back.'

'*6 September*. – Terrible change for the worse. Come at once; do not lose an hour. I hold over telegram to Holmwood till have seen you.'

10

Letter, Dr Seward to Hon. Arthur Holmwood

'6 September.

'My dear Art, –

'My news to-day is not so good. Lucy this morning had gone back a bit. There is, however, one good thing which has arisen from it: Mrs Westenra was naturally anxious concerning Lucy, and has consulted me professionally about her. I took advantage of the opportunity, and told her that my old master, Van Helsing, the great specialist, was coming to stay with me, and that I would put her in his charge conjointly with myself; so now we can come and go without alarming her unduly, for a shock to her would mean sudden death, and this, in Lucy's weak condition, might be disastrous to her. We are hedged in with difficulties, all of us, my poor old fellow; but please God, we shall come through them all right. If any need I shall write, so that, if you do not hear from me, take it for granted that I am simply waiting for news. In haste.

'Yours ever,
JOHN SEWARD.'

DR SEWARD'S DIARY

7 September. – The first thing Van Helsing said to me when we met at Liverpool Street was:–

'Have you said anything to our young friend the lover of her?'

'No,' I said. 'I waited till I had seen you, as I said in my telegram. I wrote him a letter simply telling him that you were coming, as Miss Westenra was not so well, and that I should let him know if need be.'

'Right, my friend,' he said, 'quite right! Better he not know as yet; perhaps he shall never know. I pray so; but if it be needed, then he shall know all. And, my good friend John, let me caution you. You deal with the madmen. All men are mad in some way or the other; and inasmuch as you deal discreetly with your madmen, so deal with God's madmen, too – the rest of the world. You tell not your madmen what you do nor why you do it; you tell them not what you think. So you shall keep knowledge in its place, where it may rest – where it may gather its kind around it and breed. You and I shall keep as yet what we know here, and here.' He touched me on the heart and on the forehead, and then touched himself the same way. 'I have for myself thoughts at the present. Later I shall unfold to you.'

'Why not now?' I asked. 'It may do some good; we may arrive at some decision.' He stopped and looked at me, and said:–

'My friend John, when the corn is grown, even before it has ripened – while the milk of its mother-earth is in him, and the sunshine has not yet begun to paint him with his gold, the husbandman he pull the ear and rub him between his rough hands, and blow away the green chaff, and say to you: "Look! he's good corn; he will make good crop when the time comes." ' I did not see the application, and told him so. For reply he reached over and took my ear in his hand and pulled it playfully, as he used long ago to do at lectures, and said: 'The good husbandman tell you so then because he knows, but not till then. But you do not find the good husbandman dig up his planted corn to see if he grow; that is for the children who play at husbandry, and not for those who take it as of the work of their life. See you now, friend John! I have sown my corn, and Nature has her work to do in making it sprout; if he sprout at all, there's some promise; and I wait till the ear begins to swell.' He broke off, for he evidently saw that I understood. Then he went on, and very gravely:–

'You were always a careful student, and your case-book was ever more full than the rest. You were only student then; now you are master, and I trust that good habit have not fail. Remember, my friend, that knowledge is stronger than memory, and we should not trust the weaker. Even if you have not kept the good practice, let me tell you that this case of our dear miss is one that may be – mind, I say *may be* – of such interest to us and others that all the rest may not make him kick the beam, as your peoples say. Take then good note of it. Nothing is too small. I counsel you, put down in record even your doubts and surmises. Hereafter it may be of interest to you to see how true you guess. We learn from failure, not from success!'

When I described Lucy's symptoms – the same as before, but definitely more marked – he looked very grave, but said nothing. He took with him a bag in which were many instruments and drugs, 'the ghastly paraphernalia of our beneficial trade', as he once called, in one of his lectures, the equipment of a professor of the healing craft. When we were shown in, Mrs Westenra met us. She was alarmed, but not nearly so much as I

97

expected to find her. Nature in one of her beneficent moods has ordained that even death has some antidote to its own terrors. Here, in a case where any shock may prove fatal, matters are so ordered that, from some cause or other, the things not personal – even the terrible change in her daughter to whom she is so attached – do not seem to reach her. It is something like the way Dame Nature gathers round a foreign body an envelope of some insensitive tissue which can protect from evil that which it would otherwise harm by contact. If this be an ordered selfishness, then we should pause before we condemn any one of the vice of egoism, for there may be deeper roots for its causes than we have knowledge of.

I used my knowledge of this phase of spiritual pathology, and laid down a rule that she should not be present with Lucy or think of her illness more than was absolutely required. She assented readily, so readily that I saw again the hand of Nature fighting for life. Van Helsing and I were shown up to Lucy's room. If I was shocked when I saw her yesterday, I was horrified when I saw her to-day. She was ghastly, chalkily pale; the red seemed to have gone even from her lips and gums, and the bones of her face stood out prominently; her breathing was painful to see or hear. Van Helsing's face grew set as marble, and his eyebrows converged till they almost touched over his nose. Lucy lay motionless and did not seem to have strength to speak, so for a while we were all silent. Then Van Helsing beckoned to me, and we went gently out of the room. The instant we had closed the door he stepped quickly along the passage to the next door, which was open. Then he pulled me quickly in with him and closed the door.

'My God!' he said: 'this is dreadful. There is no time to be lost. She will die for sheer want of blood to keep the heart's action as it should be. There must be a transfusion of blood at once. Is it you or me?'

'I am younger and stronger, Professor. It must be me.'

'Then get ready at once. I will bring up my bag. I am prepared.'

I went downstairs with him and as we were going there was a knock at the hall-door. When we reached the hall the maid had just opened the door, and Arthur was stepping quickly in. He rushed up to me, saying in an eager whisper:–

'Jack, I was so anxious. I read between the lines of your letter, and have been in an agony. The dad was better, so I ran down here to see for myself. Is not that gentleman Dr Van Helsing? I am so thankful to you, sir, for coming.' When first the Professor's eye had lit upon him he had been angry at any interruption at such a time; but now, as he took in his stalwart proportions and recognized the strong young manhood which seemed to emanate from him, his eyes gleamed. Without a pause he said to him gravely as he held out his hand:–

'Sir, you have come in time. You are the lover of our dear miss. She is bad, very, very bad. Nay, my child, do not go like that.' For he suddenly grew pale and sat down in a chair almost fainting. 'You are to help her. You can do more than any that live, and your courage is your best help.'

'What can I do?' asked Arthur hoarsely. 'Tell me, and I shall do it. My life is hers, and I would give the last drop of blood in my body for her.' The Professor has a strongly humorous side, and I could from old detect a trace of its origin in his answer:—

'My young sir, I do not ask so much as that – not the last!'

'What shall I do?' There was fire in his eyes, and his open nostrils quivered with intent. Van Helsing slapped him on the shoulder. 'Come!' he said. 'You are a man, and it is a man we want. You are better than me, better than my friend John.' Arthur looked bewildered, and the Professor went on by explaining in a kindly way:—

'Young miss is bad, very bad. She wants blood, and blood she must have or die. My friend John and I have consulted; and we are about to perform what we call transfusion of blood – to transfer from full veins of one to the empty veins which pine for him. John was to give his blood, as he is the more young and strong than me' – here Arthur took my hand and wrung it hard in silence – 'but, now you are here, you are more good than us, old or young, who toil much in the world of thought. Our nerves are not so calm and our blood not so bright than yours!' Arthur turned to him and said:—

'If you only knew how gladly I would die for her you would understand – '

He stopped, with a sort of choke in his voice.

'Good boy!' said Van Helsing. 'In the not-so-far-off you will be happy that you have done all for her you love. Come now and be silent. You shall kiss her once before it is done, but then you must go; and you must leave at my sign. Say no word to Madame; you know how it is with her! There must be no shock; any knowledge of this would be one. Come!'

We all went up to Lucy's room. Arthur by direction remained outside. Lucy turned her head and looked at us, but said nothing. She was not asleep, but she was simply too weak to make the effort. Her eyes spoke to us; that was all. Van Helsing took some things from his bag and laid them on a little table out of sight. Then he mixed a narcotic, and coming over to the bed, said cheerily:—

'Now, little miss, here is your medicine. Drink it off, like a good child. See, I lift you so that to swallow is easy. Yes.' She had made the effort with success.

It astonished me how long the drug took to act. This, in fact, marked the extent of her weakness. The time seemed endless until sleep began to flicker in her eyelids. At last, however, the narcotic began to manifest its potency; and she fell into a deep sleep. When the Professor was satisfied he called Arthur into the room, and bade him strip off his coat. Then he added: 'You may take that one little kiss whiles I bring over the table. Friend John, help to me!' So neither of us looked whilst he bent over her.

Van Helsing, turning to me, said:—

'He is so young and strong and of blood so pure that we need not defibrinate it.'

Then with swiftness, but with absolute method, Van Helsing performed the operation. As the transfusion went on something like life seemed to come back to poor Lucy's cheeks, and through Arthur's growing pallor the joy of his face seemed absolutely to shine. After a bit I began to grow anxious, for the loss of blood was telling on Arthur, strong man as he was. It gave me an idea of what a terrible strain Lucy's system must have undergone that what weakened Arthur only partially restored her. But the Professor's face was set, and he stood watch in hand and with his eyes fixed now on the patient and now on Arthur. I could hear my own heart beat. Presently he said in a soft voice: 'Do not stir an instant. It is enough. You attend him; I will look to her.' When all was over I could see how much Arthur was weakened. I dressed the wound and took his arm to bring him away, when Van Helsing spoke without turning round – the man seems to have eyes in the back of his head:—

'The brave lover I think deserve another kiss, which he shall have presently.' And as he had now finished his operation, he adjusted the pillow to the patient's head. As he did so the narrow black velvet band which she seemed always to wear round her throat, buckled with an old diamond buckle which her lover had given her, was dragged a little up, and showed a red mark on her throat. Arthur did not notice it, but I could hear the deep hiss of indrawn breath which is one of Van Helsing's ways of betraying emotion. He said nothing at the moment, but turned to me, saying: 'Now take down our brave young lover, give him of the port wine, and let him lie down a while. He must then go home and rest, sleep much and eat much, that he may be recruited of what he has so given to his love. He must not stay here. Hold! a moment. I may take it, sir, that you are anxious of results. Then bring it with you that in all ways the operation is successful. You have saved her life this time, and you can go home and rest easy in mind that all that can be is. I shall tell her all when she is well; she shall love you none the less for what you have done. Good-bye.'

When Arthur had gone I went back to the room. Lucy was sleeping gently, but her breathing was stronger; I could see the counterpane move as her breast heaved. By the bedside sat Van Helsing, looking at her intently. The velvet band again covered the red mark. I asked the Professor in a whisper:–

'What do you make of that mark on her throat?'

'What do you make of it?'

'I have not seen it yet,' I answered, and then and there proceeded to loose the band. Just over the external jugular vein there were two punctures, not large, but not wholesome-looking. There was no sign of disease, but the edges were white and worn-looking, as if by some trituration. It at once occurred to me that this wound, or whatever it was, might be the means of that manifest loss of blood; but I abandoned the idea as soon as formed, for such a thing could not be. The whole bed would have been drenched to a scarlet with the blood which the girl must have lost to leave such a pallor as she had before the transfusion.

'Well?' said Van Helsing.

'Well,' said I, 'I can make nothing of it.' The Professor stood up. 'I must go back to Amsterdam to-night,' he said. 'There are books and things there which I want. You must remain here all the night, and you must not let your sight pass from her.'

'Shall I have a nurse?' I asked.

'We are the best nurses, you and I. You keep watch all night; see that she is well fed, and that nothing disturbs her. You must not sleep all the night. Later on we can sleep, you and I. I shall be back as soon as possible. And then we may begin.'

'May begin?' I said. 'What on earth do you mean?'

'We shall see!' he answered as he hurried out. He came back a moment later and put his head inside the door, and said, with warning finger held up:–

'Remember, she is your charge. If you leave her, and harm befall, you shall not sleep easy hereafter!'

DR SEWARD'S DIARY (continued)

8 September. – I sat up all night with Lucy. The opiate worked itself off towards dusk, and she waked naturally; she looked a different being from what she had been before the operation. Her spirits even were good, and she was full of a happy vivacity, but I could see evidences of the absolute prostration which she had undergone. When I told Mrs Westenra that Dr Van Helsing had directed that I should sit up with her she almost pooh-poohed the idea, pointing out her daughter's renewed strength and excellent spirits. I was firm, however, and made preparations for my long vigil. When her maid had prepared her for the night I came in, having in the meantime had supper, and took a seat by the bedside. She did not in any way make objection, but looked at me gratefully whenever I caught her eye. After a long spell she seemed sinking off to sleep, but with an effort seemed to pull herself together and shook it off. This was repeated several times, with greater effort and with shorter pauses as the time moved on. It was apparent that she did not want to sleep, so I tackled the subject at once:–

'You do not want to go to sleep?'

'No; I am afraid.'

'Afraid to go to sleep! Why so? It is the boon we all crave for.'

'Ah, not if you were like me – if sleep was to you a presage of horror!'

'A presage of horror! What on earth do you mean?'

'I don't know; oh, I don't know. And that is what is so terrible. All this weakness comes to me in sleep; until I dread the very thought.'

'But my dear girl, you may sleep to-night. I am here watching you, and I can promise that nothing will happen.'

'Ah, I can trust you!' I seized the opportunity, and said: 'I promise you that if I see any evidence of bad dreams I will wake you at once.'

'You will? Oh, will you really? How good you are to me! Then I will sleep!' And almost at the word she gave a deep sigh of relief, and sank back, asleep.

All night long I watched her. She never stirred, but slept on and on in a deep, tranquil, life-giving, health-giving sleep. Her lips were slightly parted, and her breast rose and fell with the regularity of a pendulum. There was a smile on her face, and it was evident that no bad dreams had come to disturb her peace of mind.

In the early morning her maid came, and I left her in her care and took myself back home, for I was anxious about many things. I sent a short wire to Van Helsing and to Arthur, telling them of the excellent result of the operation. My own work, with its manifold arrears, took me all day to clear off; it was dark when I was able to inquire about my zoophagous patient. The report was good: he had been quite quiet for the past day and night. A telegram came from Van Helsing at Amsterdam whilst I was at dinner, suggesting that I should be at Hillingham to-night, as it might be well to be at hand, and stating that he was leaving by the night mail and would join me early in the morning.

9 September. – I was pretty tired and worn-out when I got to Hillingham. For two nights I had hardly had a wink of sleep, and my brain was beginning to feel that numbness which marks cerebral exhaustion. Lucy was up and in cheerful spirits. When she shook hands with me she looked sharply in my face and said:–

'No sitting up to-night for you. You are worn-out. I am quite well again; indeed, I am; and if there is to be any sitting up, it is I who will sit up with you.' I would not argue the point, but went and had my supper. Lucy came with me, and, enlivened by her charming presence, I made an excellent meal, and had a couple of glasses of the more than excellent port. Then Lucy took me upstairs and showed me a room next to her own, where a cosy fire was burning. 'Now,' she said, 'you must stay here. I shall leave this door open and my door too. You can lie on the sofa, for I know that nothing would induce any of you doctors to go to bed whilst there is a patient above the horizon. If I want anything I shall call out, and you can come to me at once.' I could not but acquiesce, for I was 'dog-tired', and could not have sat up had I tried. So, on her renewing her promise to call me if she should want anything, I lay on the sofa, and forgot all about everything.

LUCY WESTENRA'S DIARY

9 September. – I feel so happy to-night. I have been so miserably weak, that to be able to think and move about is like feeling sunshine after a long spell of east wind out of a steel sky. Somehow Arthur feels very, very close to me. I seem to feel his presence warm about me. I suppose it is that sickness and weakness are selfish things and turn our inner eyes and sympathy on ourselves, whilst health and strength give Love rein, and in thought and feeling he can wander where he wills. I know where my thoughts are. If Arthur only knew! My dear, my dear, your ears must tingle as you sleep, as mine do waking. Oh, the blissful rest of last night! How I slept with that dear, good Dr Seward watching me. And to-night I shall not fear to sleep, since he is close at hand and within call. Thank everybody for being so good to me! Thank God! Good-night, Arthur.

DR SEWARD'S DIARY

10 September. – I was conscious of the Professor's hand on my head, and started awake all in a second. That is one of the things that we learn in an asylum, at any rate.
    'And how is our patient?'
    'Well, when I left her, or rather when she left me,' I answered.
    'Come, let us see,' he said. And together we went into the room.
    The blind was down, and I went over to raise it gently, whilst Van Helsing stepped, with his soft, cat-like tread, over to the bed.
    As I raised the blind, and the morning sunlight flooded the room, I heard the Professor's low hiss of inspiration, and knowing its rarity, a

deadly fear shot through my heart. As I passed over he moved back, and his exclamation of horror, 'Gott in Himmel!' needed no enforcement from his agonized face. He raised his hand and pointed to the bed, and his iron face was drawn and ashen white. I felt my knees begin to tremble.

There on the bed, seemingly in a swoon, lay poor Lucy, more horribly white and wan-looking than ever. Even the lips were white, and the gums seemed to have shrunken back from the teeth, as we sometimes see in a corpse after a prolonged illness. Van Helsing raised his foot to stamp in anger, but the instinct of his life and all the long years of habit stood to him, and he put it down again softly. 'Quick!' he said. 'Bring the brandy.' I flew to the dining-room, and returned with the decanter. He wetted the poor white lips with it, and together we rubbed palm and wrist and heart. He felt her heart, and after a few moments of agonizing suspense said:—

'It is not too late. It beats, though but feebly. All our work is undone; we must begin again. There is no young Arthur here now; I have to call on you yourself this time, friend John.' As he spoke, he was dipping into his bag and producing the instruments for transfusion; I had taken off my coat and rolled up my shirt-sleeve. There was no possibility of an opiate just at present, and no need of one; and so, without a moment's delay, we began the operation. After a time — it did not seem a short time either, for the draining away of one's blood, no matter how willingly it be given, is a terrible feeling — Van Helsing held up a warning finger. 'Do not stir,' he said, 'but I fear that with growing strength she may wake; and that would make danger, oh, so much danger. But I shall precaution take. I shall give hypodermic injection of morphia.' He proceeded then, swiftly and deftly, to carry out his intent. The effect on Lucy was not bad, for the faint seemed to merge subtly into the narcotic sleep. It was with a feeling of personal pride that I could see a faint tinge of colour steal back into the pallid cheeks and lips. No man knows till he experiences it, what it is to feel his own life-blood drawn away into the veins of the woman he loves.

The Professor watched me critically. 'That will do,' he said. 'Already?' I remonstrated. 'You took a great deal more from Art.' To which he smiled a sad sort of smile as he replied:—

'He is her lover, her *fiancé*. You have work, much work, to do for her and for others; and the present will suffice.'

When we stopped the operation, he attended to Lucy, whilst I applied digital pressure to my own incision. I lay down, whilst I waited his leisure to attend me, for I felt faint and a little sick. By-and-by he bound up my wound, and sent me downstairs to get a glass of wine for myself. As I was leaving the room, he came after me, and half whispered:—

'Mind, nothing must be said of this. If our young lover should turn up unexpected, as before, no word to him. It would at once frighten him and enjealous him, too. There must be none. So!'

When I came back he looked at me carefully, and then said:—

'You are not much the worse. Go into the room, and lie on your sofa, and rest awhile; then have much breakfast, and come here to me.'

I followed out his orders, for I knew how right and wise they were. I had done my part, and now my next duty was to keep up my strength. I felt very weak, and in the weakness lost something of the amazement at what had occurred. I fell asleep on the sofa, however, wondering over and over again how Lucy had made such a retrograde movement, and how she could have been drained of so much blood with no sign anywhere to show for it. I think I must have continued my wonder in my dreams, for sleeping and waking, my thoughts always came back to the little punctures in her throat and the ragged, exhausted appearance of their edges – tiny though they were.

Lucy slept well into the day; and when she woke she was fairly well and strong, though not nearly so much as the day before. When Van Helsing had seen her, he went out for a walk, leaving me in charge, with strict injunctions that I was not to leave her for a moment. I could hear his voice in the hall, asking the way to the nearest telegraph office.

Lucy chatted with me freely, and seemed quite unconscious that anything had happened. I tried to keep her amused and interested. When her mother came up to see her, she did not seem to notice any change whatever, but said to me gratefully:—

'We owe you so much, Dr Seward, for all you have done, but you really must now take care not to overwork yourself. You are looking pale yourself. You want a wife to nurse and look after you a bit; that you do!' As she spoke Lucy turned crimson, though it was only momentarily, for her poor wasted veins could not stand for long such an unwonted drain to the head. The reaction came in excessive pallor as she turned imploring eyes on me. I smiled and nodded, and laid my finger on my lips; with a sigh, she sank back amid her pillows.

Van Helsing returned in a couple of hours, and presently said to me: 'Now you go home, and eat much and drink enough. Make yourself strong. I stay here to-night, and I shall sit up with little miss myself. You and I must watch the case, and we must have none other to know. I have grave reasons. No, do not ask them; think what you will. Do not fear to think even the most not-probable. Good-night.'

In the hall two of the maids came to me, and asked if they or either of them might not sit up with Miss Lucy. They implored me to let them; and when I said it was Dr Van Helsing's wish that either he or I should sit up, they asked me quite piteously to intercede with the 'foreign gentleman'. I was much touched by their kindness. Perhaps it is because I am weak at present, and perhaps it was on Lucy's account that their devotion was manifested; for over and over again have I seen similar instances of woman's kindness. I got back here in time for a late dinner; went my rounds – all well; and set this down whilst waiting for sleep. It is coming.

11 September. – This afternoon I went over to Hillingham. Found Van Helsing in excellent spirits, and Lucy much better. Shortly after I had arrived, a big parcel from abroad came for the Professor. He opened it with much impressment – assumed, of course – and showed a great bundle of white flowers.

'These are for you, Miss Lucy,' he said.

'For me? Oh, Dr Van Helsing!'

'Yes, my dear, but not for you to play with. These are medicines.' Here Lucy made a wry face. 'Nay, but they are not to take in a decoction or in nauseous form, so you need not snub that so charming nose, or I shall point out to my friend Arthur what woes he may have to endure in seeing so much beauty that he so loves so much distort. Aha, my pretty miss, that bring the so nice nose all straight again. This is medicinal, but you do not know how. I put him in your window, I make pretty wreath, and hang him round your neck, so that you sleep well. Oh yes! they, like the lotus flower, make your trouble forgotten. It smell so like the waters of Lethe, and of that fountain of youth that the Conquistadores sought for in the Floridas, and find him all too late.'

Whilst he was speaking, Lucy had been examining the flowers and smelling them. Now she threw them down, saying, with half-laughter and half-disgust:–

'Oh, Professor, I believe you are only putting up a joke on me. Why, these flowers are only common garlic.'

To my surprise, Van Helsing rose up and said with all his sternness, his iron jaw set and his bushy eyebrows meeting:–

'No trifling with me! I never jest! There is grim purpose in all I do; and I warn you that you do not thwart me. Take care, for the sake of others if not for your own.' Then seeing poor Lucy scared, as she might well be, he went on more gently: 'Oh, little miss, my dear, do not fear me. I only do for your good; but there is much virtue to you in those so common flower. See, I place them myself in your room. I make myself the wreath that you are to wear. But hush! no telling to others that make so inquisitive questions. We must obey, and silence is part of obedience; and obedience is to bring you strong and well into loving arms that wait for you. Now sit still awhile. Come with me, friend John, and you shall help me deck the room with my garlic, which is all the way from Haarlem, where my friend

Vanderpool raise herb in his glasshouses all the year. I had to telegraph yesterday, or they would not have been here.'

We went into the room, taking the flowers with us. The Professor's actions were certainly odd, and not to be found in any pharmacopoeia that I ever heard of. First, he fastened up the windows and latched them securely; next, taking a handful of the flowers, he rubbed them all over the sashes, as though to ensure that every whiff of air that might get in would be laden with the garlic smell. Then with the wisp he rubbed all over the jamb of the door, above, below, and at each side, and round the fireplace in the same way. It all seemed grotesque to me, and presently I said:—

'Well, Professor, I know you always have a reason for what you do, but this certainly puzzles me. It is well we have no sceptic here, or he would say that you were working some spell to keep out an evil spirit.'

'Perhaps I am!' he answered quietly as he began to make the wreath which Lucy was to wear round her neck.

We then waited whilst Lucy made her toilet for the night, and when she was in bed he came and himself fixed the wreath of garlic round her neck. The last words he said to her were:—

'Take care you do not disturb it; and even if the room feel close, do not to-night open the window or the door.'

'I promise,' said Lucy, 'and thank you both a thousand times for all your kindness to me! Oh, what have I done to be blessed with such friends?'

As we left the house in my fly, which was waiting, Van Helsing said:—

'To-night I can sleep in peace, and sleep I want – two nights of travel, much reading in the day between, and much anxiety on the day to follow, and a night to sit up, without to wink. To-morrow in the morning early you call for me, and we come together to see our pretty miss, so much more strong for my "spell" which I have work. Ho! ho!'

He seemed so confident that I, remembering my own confidence two nights before and with the baneful result, felt awe and vague terror. It must have been my weakness that made me hesitate to tell it to my friend, but I felt it all the more, like unshed tears.

11

LUCY WESTENRA'S DIARY

12 September. – How good they all are to me! I quite love that dear Dr Van Helsing. I wonder why he was so anxious about these flowers. He positively frightened me, he was so fierce. And yet he must have been right, for I feel comfort from them already. Somehow, I do not dread being alone to-night, and I can go to sleep without fear. I shall not mind any flapping outside the window. Oh, the terrible struggle that I have had against sleep so often of late; the pain of the sleeplessness, or the pain of the fear of sleep, with such unknown horrors as it has for me! How blessed are some people, whose lives have no fears, no dreads; to whom sleep is a blessing that comes nightly, and brings nothing but sweet dreams. Well, here I am to-night, hoping for sleep, and lying like Ophelia in the play, with 'virgin crants and maiden strewments'. I never liked garlic before, but to-night it is delightful! There is peace in its smell; I feel sleep coming already. Good-night everybody.

DR SEWARD'S DIARY

13 September. – Called at the Berkeley and found Van Helsing, as usual, up to time. The carriage ordered from the hotel was waiting. The Professor took his bag, which he always brings with him now.

Let all be put down exactly. Van Helsing and I arrived at Hillingham at eight o'clock. It was a lovely morning; the bright sunshine and all the fresh feeling of early autumn seemed like the completion of nature's annual work. The leaves were turning to all kinds of beautiful colours, but had not yet begun to drop from the trees. When we entered we met Mrs Westenra coming out of the morning-room. She is always an early riser. She greeted us warmly and said:–

'You will be glad to know that Lucy is better. The dear child is still asleep. I looked into her room and saw her, but did not go in, lest I should disturb her.' The Professor smiled, and looked quite jubilant. He rubbed his hands together, and said:–

'Aha! I thought I had diagnosed the case. My treatment is working,' to which she answered:–

'You must not take all the credit to yourself, doctor. Lucy's state this morning is due in part to me.'

'How do you mean, ma'am?' asked the Professor.

'Well, I was anxious about the dear child in the night, and went into her room. She was sleeping soundly – so soundly that even my coming did not wake her. But the room was awfully stuffy. There were a lot of those horrible strong-smelling flowers about everywhere, and she had actually a bunch of them round her neck. I feared that the heavy odour would be too much for the dear child in her weak state, so I took them all away and opened a bit of the window to let in a little fresh air. You will be pleased with her, I am sure.'

She moved off into her boudoir, where she usually breakfasted early. As she had spoken, I watched the Professor's face, and saw it turn ashen grey. He had been able to retain his self-command whilst the poor lady was present, for he knew her state and how mischievous a shock would be; he actually smiled on her as he held open the door for her to pass into her room. But the instant she had disappeared he pulled me, suddenly and forcibly, into the dining-room and closed the door.

Then, for the first time in my life, I saw Van Helsing break down. He raised his hands over his head in a sort of mute despair, and then beat his palms together in a helpless way; finally he sat down on a chair, and putting his hands before his face, began to sob, with loud, dry sobs that seemed to come from the very racking of his heart. Then he raised his arms again, as though appealing to the whole universe. 'God! God! God!' he said. 'What have we done, what has this poor thing done, that we are so sore beset? Is there fate amongst us still, sent down from the pagan world of old, that such things must be, and in such a way? This poor mother, all unknowing, and all for the best as she think, does such thing as lose her daughter body and soul; and we must not tell her, we must not even warn her, or she die, and then both die. Oh, how we are beset! How are all the powers of the devils against us!' Suddenly he jumped to his feet. 'Come,' he said, 'come, we must see and act. Devils or no devils, or all the devils at once, it matters not; we fight him all the same.' He went to the hall-door for his bag; and together we went up to Lucy's room.

Once again I drew up the blind, whilst Van Helsing went towards the bed. This time he did not start as he looked on the poor face with the same awful, waxen pallor as before. He wore a look of stern sadness and infinite pity.

'As I expected,' he murmured, with that hissing inspiration of his which meant so much. Without a word he went and locked the door, and then began to set out on the little table the instruments for yet another operation of transfusion of blood. I had long ago recognized the necessity, and begun to take off my coat, but he stopped me with a warning hand. 'No!' he said. 'To-day you must operate, I shall provide. You are weakened already.' As he spoke he took off his coat and rolled up his shirt-sleeve.

Again the operation; again the narcotic; again some return of colour to the ashy cheeks, and the regular breathing of healthy sleep. This time I watched whilst Van Helsing recruited himself and rested.

Presently he took an opportunity of telling Mrs Westenra that she must not remove anything from Lucy's room without consulting him; that the flowers were of medicinal value, and that the breathing of their odour was a part of the system of cure. Then he took over the care of the case himself, saying that he would watch this night and the next and would send me word when to come.

After another hour Lucy waked from her sleep, fresh and bright, and seemingly not much the worse from her terrible ordeal.

What does it all mean? I am beginning to wonder if my long habit of life amongst the insane is beginning to tell upon my own brain.

LUCY WESTENRA'S DIARY

17 September. – Four days and nights of peace. I am getting so strong again that I hardly know myself. It is as if I had passed through some long nightmare, and had just awakened to see the beautiful sunshine and feel the fresh air of the morning around me. I have a dim half-remembrance of long, anxious times of waiting and fearing; darkness in which there was not even the pain of hope to make present distress more poignant; and then long spells of oblivion, and the rising back to life as a diver coming up through a great press of water. Since, however, Dr Van Helsing has been with me, all this bad dreaming seems to have passed away; the noises that used to frighten me out of my wits – the flapping against the windows, the distant voices which seemed so close to me, the harsh sounds that came from I know not where and commanded me to do I know not what – have all ceased. I go to bed now without any fear of sleep. I do not even try to keep awake. I have grown quite fond of the garlic, and a boxful arrives for me every day from Haarlem. To-night Dr Van Helsing is going away, as he has to be for a day in Amsterdam. But I need not be watched; I am well enough to be left alone. Thank God for mother's sake, and dear Arthur's, and for all our friends who have been so kind! I shall not even feel the change, for last night Dr Van Helsing slept in his chair a lot of the time. I found him asleep twice when I awoke; but I did not fear to go to sleep again, although the boughs or bats or something flapped almost angrily against the window-panes.

'The Pall Mall Gazette', 18 September

THE ESCAPED WOLF

PERILOUS ADVENTURE OF OUR INTERVIEWER

Interview with the Keeper in the Zoological Gardens

After many inquiries and almost as many refusals, and perpetually using the words *Pall Mall Gazette* as a sort of talisman I managed to find the keeper of the section of the Zoological Gardens in which the wolf department is included. Thomas Bilder lives in one of the cottages in the enclosure behind the elephant-house, and was just sitting down to his tea when I found him. Thomas and his wife are hospitable folk, elderly, and without children, and if the specimen I enjoyed of their hospitality be of the average kind, their lives must be pretty comfortable.

The keeper would not enter on what he called 'business' until the supper was over, and we were all satisfied. Then when the table was cleared, and he had lit his pipe, he said:—

'Now, sir, you can go on and arsk me what you want. You'll excoose me refoosin' to talk of perfeshunal subjects afore meals. I gives the wolves and the jackals and the hyenas in all our section their tea afore I begins to arsk them questions.'

'How do you mean, ask them questions?' I queried, wishing to get him into a talkative murmour.

''Ittin' of them over the 'ead with a pole is one way; scratchin' of their hears is another, when gents as is flush wants a bit of a show-orf to their gals. I don't so much mind the fust – the 'ittin' with a pole afore I chucks in their dinner; but I waits till they've 'ad their sherry and kawfee, so to speak, afore I tries on with the ear-scratchin'. Mind you,' he added philosophically, 'there's a deal of the same nature in us as in them there animiles. Here's you a-comin' and arskin' of me questions about my business, and I that grumpy-like that only for your bloomin' arf-quid I'd 'a' seen you blowed fust 'fore I'd answer. Not even when you arsked me sarcastic-like if I'd like you to arsk the Superintendent if you might arsk me questions. Without offence, did I tell yer to go to 'ell?'

'You did.'

'An' when you said you'd report me for usin' of obscene language, that was 'itten' me over the 'ead; but the 'arf-quid made that all right. I weren't a-goin' to fight, so I waited for the food, and did with my 'owl as the wolves, and lions, and tigers does. But, Lor' love yer 'art, now that the old 'ooman has stuck a chunk of her tea-cake in me, an' rinsed me out with her bloomin' old teapot, and I've lit up, you may scratch my ears for all you're worth, and won't get even a growl out of me. Drive along with your questions. I know what yer a-comin' at, that 'ere escaped wolf.'

'Exactly. I want you to give me your view of it. Just tell me how it happened; and when I know the facts I'll get you to say what you consider was the cause of it, and how you think the whole affair will end.'

'All right, guv'nor. This 'ere is about the 'ole story. That 'ere wolf what we called Bersicker was one of three grey ones that came from Norway to Jamrach's, which we bought off him four year ago. He was a nice well-behaved wolf, that never gave no trouble to talk of. I'm more surprised at

111

'im for wantin' to get out nor any other animile in the place. But, there, you can't trust wolves no more nor women.'

'Don't you mind him, sir!' broke in Mrs Tom, with a cheery laugh. "E's got mindin' the animiles so long that blest if he ain't like a old wolf 'isself! But there ain't no 'arm in 'im.'

'Well, sir, it was about two hours after feedin' yesterday when I first hear any disturbance. I was makin' up a litter in the monkey-house for a young puma which is ill; but when I heard the yelpin' and 'owlin' I kem away straight. There was Bersicker a-tearin' like a mad thing at the bars as if he wanted to get out. There wasn't much people about that day, and close at hand was only one man, a tall, thin chap, with a 'ook nose and a pointed beard, with a few white hairs runnin' through it. He had a 'ard, cold look and red eyes, and I took a sort of mislike to him, for it seemed as if it was 'im as they was hirritated at. He 'ad white kid gloves on 'is 'ands, and he pointed out the animiles to me and says: "Keeper, these wolves seem upset at something."

' "Maybe it's you," says I, for I did not like the airs as he give 'isself. He didn't get angry, as I 'oped he would but he smiled a kind of insolent smile, with a mouth full of white, sharp teeth. "Oh, no, they wouldn't like me," 'e says.

' "Ow yes, they would," says I, a-imitatin' of him. "They always like a bone or two to clean their teeth on about tea-time, which you 'as a bagful."

'Well, it was a odd thing, but when the animiles see us a-talkin' they lay down, and when I went over to Bersicker he let me stroke his ears same as ever. That there man kem over, and blessed but if he didn't put in his hand and stroke the old wolf's ears too!

' "Tyke care," says I. "Bersicker is quick."

' "Never mind," he says. "I'm used to 'em!"

' "Are you in the business yourself?" I says, tyking off my 'at, for a man what trades in wolves, anceterer, is a good friend to keepers.

' "No," says he, "not exactly in the business, but I 'ave made pets of several." And with that he lifts his 'at as perlite as a lord, and walks away. Old Bersicker kep' a-lookin' arter 'im till 'e was out of sight, and then went and lay down in a corner, and wouldn't come hout the 'ole hevening. Well, larst night, so soon as the moon was hup, the wolves here all began a-'owling. There warn't nothing for them to 'owl at. There warn't no one near, except someone that was evidently a-callin' a dog somewheres out back of the gardings in the Park road. Once or twice I went out to see that all was right, and it was, and then the 'owling stopped. Just before twelve o'clock I just took a look round afore turnin' in, an', bust me, but when I kem opposite to old Bersicker's cage I see the rails broken and twisted about and the cage empty. And that's all I know for certing.'

'Did anyone else see anything?'

'One of our gard'ners was a-comin' 'ome about that time from a 'armony, when he sees as big grey dog comin' out through the gardin 'edges. At least, so he says; but I don't give much for it myself, for if he did 'e never said a word about it to his missis when 'e got 'ome, and it was only after the escape of the wolf was made known, and we had been up all night a-huntin' of the Park for Bersicker, that he remembered seein' anything. My own belief was that the 'armony 'ad got into his 'ead.'

'Now, Mr Bilder, can you account in any way for the escape of the wolf?'

'Well, sir,' he said, with a suspicious sort of modesty, 'I think I can; but I don't know as 'ow you'd be satisfied with the theory.'

'Certainly I shall. If a man like you, who knows the animals from experience, can't hazard a good guess at any rate, who is even to try?'

'Well then, sir, I accounts for it this way: it seems to me that 'ere wolf escaped – simply because he wanted to get out.'

From the hearty way that both Thomas and his wife laughed at the joke I could see that it had done service before, and that the whole explanation was simply an elaborate sell. I couldn't cope in badinage with the worthy Thomas, but I thought I knew a surer way to his heart, so I said:–

'Now, Mr Bilder, we'll consider that first half-sovereign worked off, and this brother of his is waiting to be claimed when you've told me what you think will happen.'

'Right y'are, sir,' he said briskly. 'Ye'll excoose me, I know, for a-chaffin' of ye, but the old woman here winked at me, which was as much as telling me to go on.'

'Well, I never!' said the old lady.

'My opinion is this: that 'ere wolf is a-'idin' of, somewheres. The gard'ner wot didn't remember said he was a-gallopin' northward faster than a horse could go; but I don't believe him, for, yer see, wolves don't gallop no more than dogs does, they not bein' built that way. Wolves is fine things in a story-book, and I dessay when they gets in packs and does be chivvin' somethin' that's more afeared than they is they can make a devil of a noise and chop it up, whatever it is. But, Lor' bless you, in real life a wolf is only a low creature, not half so clever as a good dog; and not half a quarter so much fight in 'im. This one ain't been used to fightin' or even to providin' for hisself, and more like he's somewhere round the Park a-'idin' an' a-shiverin' of, and, if he thinks at all, wonderin' where he is to get his breakfast from; or maybe he's got down some area and is in a coal-cellar. My eye, won't some cook get a rum start when she sees his green eyes a-shining at her out of the dark! If he can't get food he's bound to look for it, and mayhap he may chance to light on a butcher's shop in

113

time. If he doesn't, and some nursemaid goes a-walkin' orf with a soldier, leavin' of the hinfant in the perambulator – well then I shouldn't be surprised if the census is one babby the less. That's all.'

I was handing him the half-sovereign, when something came bobbing up against the window, and Mr Bilder's face doubled its natural length with surprise.

'God bless me!' he said. 'If there ain't old Bersicker come back by 'isself!'

He went to the door and opened it; a most unnecessary proceeding it seemed to me. I have always thought that a wild animal never looks so well as when some obstacle of pronounced durability is between us; a personal experience has intensified rather than diminished that idea.

After all, however, there is nothing like custom, for neither Bilder nor his wife thought any more of the wolf than I should of a dog. The animal itself was as peaceful and well-behaved as that father of all picture-wolves, Red Riding Hood's quondam friend, whilst seeking her confidence in masquerade.

The whole scene was an unutterable mixture of comedy and pathos. The wicked wolf that for half a day had paralysed London and set all the children in the town shivering in their shoes, was there in a sort of penitent mood, and was received and petted like a sort of vulpine prodigal son. Old Bilder examined him all over with most tender solicitude, and when he had finished with his penitent said:

'There, I knew the poor old chap would get into some kind of trouble; didn't I say it all along? Here's his head all cut and full of broken glass. 'E's been a-gettin' over some bloomin' wall or other. It's a shyme that people are allowed to top their walls with broken bottles. This 'ere's what comes of it. Come along, Bersicker.'

He took the wolf and locked him up in a cage, with a piece of meat that satisfied, in quantity at any rate, the elementary conditions of the fatted calf, and went off to report.

I came off, too, to report the only exclusive information that is given to-day regarding the strange escapade at the Zoo.

DR SEWARD'S DIARY

17 September. – I was engaged after dinner in my study posting up my books, which, through press of other work and the many visits to Lucy, had fallen sadly into arrear. Suddenly the door was burst open, and in rushed my patient, with his face distorted with passion. I was thunderstruck, for such a thing as a patient getting of his own accord into the

Superintendent's study is almost unknown. Without an instant's pause he made straight at me. He had a dinner-knife in his hand, and, as I saw he was dangerous, I tried to keep the table between us. He was too quick and too strong for me, however; for before I could get my balance he had struck at me and cut my left wrist rather severely. Before he could strike again, however, I got in my right, and he was sprawling on his back on the floor. My wrist bled freely, and quite a little pool trickled on to the carpet. I saw that my friend was not intent on further effort, and occupied myself binding up my wrist, keeping a wary eye on the prostrate figure all the time. When the attendants rushed in, and we turned our attention to him, his employment positively sickened me. He was lying on his belly on the floor licking up, like a dog, the blood which had fallen from my wounded wrist. He was easily secured, and, to my surprise, went with the attendants quite placidly, simply repeating over and over again: 'The blood is the life! the blood is the life!'

I cannot afford to lose blood just at present: I have lost too much of late for my physical good, and the then prolonged strain of Lucy's illness and its horrible phases is telling on me. I am over-excited and weary, and I need rest, rest, rest. Happily Van Helsing has not summoned me, so I need not forgo my sleep; to-night I could not well do without it.

Telegram, Van Helsing, Antwerp, to Seward, Carfax

(Sent to Carfax, Sussex, as no county given; delivered late by twenty-two hours.)

'*17 September*. – Do not fail to be at Hillingham to-night. If not watching all the time, frequently visit to see that flowers are as placed; very important; do not fail. Shall be with you as soon as possible after arrival.'

DR SEWARD'S DIARY

18 September. – Just off for train to London. The arrival of Van Helsing's telegram filled me with dismay. A whole night lost, and I know by bitter experience what may happen in a night. Of course it is possible that all may be well, but what *may* have happened? Surely there is some horrible doom hanging over us that every possible accident should thwart us in all we try to do. I shall take this cylinder with me, and then I can complete my entry on Lucy's phonograph.

MEMORANDUM LEFT BY LUCY WESTENRA

17 September. Night. – I write this and leave it to be seen, so that no one may by chance get into any trouble through me. This is an exact record of what took place to-night. I feel I am dying of weakness, and have barely strength to write, but it must be done if I die in the doing.

I went to bed as usual, taking care that the flowers were placed as Dr Van Helsing directed, and soon fell asleep.

I was waked by the flapping at the window, which had begun after the sleep-walking on the cliff at Whitby when Mina saved me, and which now I know so well. I was not afraid, but I did wish that Dr Seward was in the next room – as Dr Van Helsing said he would be – so that I might have called him. I tried to go to sleep, but could not. Then there came to me the old fear of sleep, and I determined to keep awake. Perversely sleep would try to come when I did not want it, so, as I feared to be alone, I opened my door and called out: 'Is there anybody there?' There was no answer. I was afraid to wake mother, and so closed my door again. Then outside in the shrubbery I heard a sort of howl like a dog's, but more fierce and deeper. I went to the window and looked out, but could see nothing, except a big bat, which had evidently been buffeting its wings against the window. So I went back to bed again, but determined to go to sleep. Presently the door opened, and mother looked in; seeing by my moving that I was not asleep, came in, and sat by me. She said to me even more sweetly and softly than her wont:–

'I was uneasy about you, darling, and came in to see that you were all right.'

I feared she might catch cold sitting there, and asked her to come in and sleep with me, so she came into bed, and lay down beside me; she did not take off her dressing-gown, for she said she would only stay awhile and then go back to her own bed. As she lay there in my arms, and I in hers, the flapping and buffeting came to the window again. She was startled and a little frightened, and cried out: 'What is that?' I tried to pacify her, and at last succeeded, and she lay quiet; but I could hear her poor dear heart still beating terribly. After a while there was the low howl again out in the shrubbery, and shortly after there was a crash at the window, and a lot of broken glass was hurled on the floor. The window blind blew back with the wind that rushed in, and in the aperture of the broken panes there was the head of a great gaunt grey wolf. Mother cried out in a fright, and struggled up into a sitting posture, and clutched wildly at anything that would help her. Amongst other things, she clutched the wreath of flowers that Dr Van Helsing insisted on my wearing round my neck, and tore it away from me. For a second or two she sat up, pointing at the wolf, and there was a strange and horrible gurgling in her throat; then she fell over, as if struck with lightning, and her head hit my forehead and made me dizzy for a moment or two. The room and all round seemed to spin round. I kept my eyes fixed on the window, but the wolf drew his head back, and a whole myriad of little specks seemed to come blowing in through the broken window, and wheeling and circling round like the pillar of dust that travellers describe when there is a simoom in the desert. I tried to stir, but there was some spell upon me, and dear mother's poor body, which seemed to grow cold already – for her dear heart had ceased to beat – weighed me down; and I remembered no more for a while.

The time did not seem long, but very, very awful, till I recovered consciousness again. Somewhere near, a passing bell was tolling; the dogs all round the neighbourhood were howling; and in our shrubbery, seemingly just outside, a nightingale was singing. I was dazed and stupid with pain and terror and weakness, but the sound of the nightingale seemed like the voice of my dead mother come back to comfort me. The sounds seemed to have awakened the maids, too, for I could hear their bare feet pattering outside my door. I called to them, and they came in, and when they saw what had happened, and what it was that lay over me in the bed, they screamed out. The wind rushed in through the broken window, and the door slammed to. They lifted off the body of my dear mother and laid her, covered up with a sheet, on the bed after I had got up. They were all so frightened and nervous that I directed them to go to the dining-room and have each a glass of wine. The door flew open for an instant and closed again. The maids shrieked, and then went in a body to the dining-room; and I laid what flowers I had on my dear mother's breast. When they were there I remembered what Dr Van Helsing had told me, but I didn't like to remove them, and, besides, I would have some of the servants to sit up with me now. I was surprised that the maids did not come back. I called them, but got no answer, so I went to the dining-room to look for them.

My heart sank when I saw what had happened. They all four lay helpless on the floor, breathing heavily. The decanter of sherry was on the table half full, but there was a queer, acrid smell about. I was suspicious, and examined the decanter. It smelt of laudanum, and looking on the sideboard, I found that the bottle which mother's doctor uses for her – oh! did use – was empty. What am I to do? What am I to do? I am back in the room with mother. I cannot leave her, and I am alone, save for the sleeping servants, whom someone has drugged. Alone with the dead! I dare not go out, for I can hear the low howl of the wolf through the broken window.

The air seems full of specks, floating and circling in the draught from the window, and the lights burn blue and dim. What am I to do? God shield me from harm this night! I shall hide this paper in my breast, where they shall find it when they come to lay me out. My dear mother gone! It is time that I go too. Good-bye, dear Arthur, if I should not survive this night. God keep you, dear, and God help me!

12

DR SEWARD'S DIARY

18 September. – I drove at once to Hillingham and arrived early. Keeping my cab at the gate, I went up the avenue alone. I knocked gently and rang as quietly as possible, for I feared to disturb Lucy or her mother, and hoped to bring only a servant to the door. After a while, finding no response, I knocked and rang again; still no answer. I cursed the laziness of the servants that they should lie abed at such an hour – for it was now ten o'clock – and so rang and knocked again, but more impatiently, and still without response. Hitherto I had blamed only the servants, but now a terrible fear began to assail me. Was this desolation but another link in the chain of doom which seemed drawing tight around us? Was it indeed a house of death to which I had come too late? I knew that minutes, even seconds of delay might mean hours of danger to Lucy, if she had had again one of those frightful relapses; and I went round the house to try if I could to find by chance an entry anywhere.

I could find no means of ingress. Every window and door was fastened and locked, and I returned baffled to the porch. As I did so, I heard the rapid pit-pat of a swiftly driven horse's feet. They stopped at the gate, and a few seconds later I met Van Helsing running up the avenue. When he saw me, he gasped out:

'Then it was you, and just arrived. How is she? Are we too late? Did you get my telegram?'

I answered as quickly and coherently as I could that I had only got his telegram early in the morning and had not lost a minute in coming here, and that I could not make anyone in the house hear me. He paused and raised his hat as he said solemnly:

'Then I fear we are too late. God's will be done!' With his usual recuperative energy, he went on: 'Come. If there be no way open to get in, we must make one. Time is all in all to us now.'

We went round to the back of the house, where there was a kitchen window. The Professor took a small surgical saw from his case, and handing it to me, pointed to the iron bars which guarded the window. I attacked them at once and had very soon cut through three of them. Then with a long, thin knife we pushed back the fastening of the sashes and opened the window. I helped the Professor in and followed him. There was no one in the kitchen or in the servants' rooms, which were close at hand. We tried all the rooms as we went along, and in the dining-room, dimly lit by rays of light through the shutters, found four servant-women lying on the floor. There was no need to think them dead, for their stertorous breathing and the acrid smell of laudanum in the room left no doubt as to their condition. Van Helsing and I looked at each other, and as we moved away he said: 'We can attend to them later.' Then we ascended to Lucy's room. For an instant or two we paused at the door to listen, but there was no sound that we could hear. With white faces and trembling hands, we opened the door gently, and entered the room.

How shall I describe what we saw? On the bed lay two women, Lucy and her mother. The latter lay farthest in, and she was covered with a white sheet, the edge of which had been blown back by the draught through the broken window, showing the drawn, white face, with a look of terror fixed upon it. By her side lay Lucy, with face white and still more drawn. The flowers which had been round her neck we found upon her mother's bosom, and her throat was bare, showing the two little wounds which we had noticed before, but looking horribly white and mangled. Without a word the Professor bent over the bed, his head almost touching poor Lucy's breast; then he gave a quick turn of his head, as of one who listens, and leaping to his feet, he cried out to me:

'It is not yet too late! Quick! Quick! Bring the brandy!'

I flew downstairs and returned with it, taking care to smell and taste it, lest it, too, were drugged like the decanter of sherry which I found on the table. The maids were still breathing, but more restlessly, and I fancied that the narcotic was wearing off. I did not stay to make sure, but returned to Van Helsing. He rubbed the brandy, as on another occasion, on her lips and gums and on her wrists and the palms of her hands. He said to me:

'I can do this, all that can be at the present. You go wake those maids. Flick them in the face with a wet towel, and flick them hard. Make them get heat and fire and a warm bath. This poor soul is nearly as cold as that beside her. She will need be heated before we can do anything more.'

I went at once, and found little difficulty in waking three of the women. The fourth was only a young girl, and the drug had evidently affected her more strongly, so I lifted her on the sofa and let her sleep. The others were dazed at first, but as remembrance came back to them they cried and sobbed in a hysterical manner. I was stern with them, however, and would not let them talk. I told them that one life was bad enough to lose, and that if they delayed they would sacrifice Miss Lucy. So, sobbing and crying, they went about their way, half-clad as they were, and prepared fire and water. Fortunately, the kitchen and boiler fires were still alive, and there was no lack of hot water. We got a bath, and carried Lucy out as she was and placed her in it. Whilst we were busy chafing her limbs there was a knock on the hall-door. One of the maids ran off, hurried on some more clothes, and opened it. Then she returned and whispered to us that there was a gentleman who had come with a message from Mr Holmwood. I bade her simply tell him that he must wait, for we could see no one now. She went away with the message, and, engrossed with our work, I clean forgot all about him.

I never saw in all my experience the Professor work in such deadly earnest. I knew – as he knew – that it was a stand-up fight with death, and in a pause told him so. He answered me in a way that I did not understand, but with the sternest look that his face could wear:–

'If that were all, I would stop here where we are now, and let her fade away in peace, for I see no light in life over her horizon.' He went on with his work with, if possible, renewed and more frenzied vigour.

Presently we both began to be conscious that the heat was beginning to be of some effect. Lucy's heart beat a trifle more audibly to the stethoscope, and her lungs had a perceptible movement. Van Helsing's face almost beamed, and as we lifted her from the bath and rolled her in a hot sheet to dry her he said to me:–

'The first gain is ours! Check to the king!'

We took Lucy into another room, which had by now been prepared, and laid her in bed and forced a few drops of brandy down her throat. I noticed that Van Helsing tied a soft silk handkerchief round her throat. She was still unconscious, and was quite as bad as, if not worse than, we had ever seen her.

Van Helsing called in one of the women, and told her to stay with her and not to take her eyes off her till we returned, and then beckoned me out of the room.

'We must consult as to what is to be done,' he said as we descended the stairs. In the hall he opened the dining-room door, and we passed in, he closing the door carefully behind him. The shutters had been opened, but the blinds were already down, with that obedience to the etiquette of death which the British woman of the lower classes always rigidly observes. The room was, therefore, dimly dark. It was, however, light enough for our purposes. Van Helsing's sternness was somewhat relieved by a look of perplexity. He was evidently torturing his mind about something, so I waited for an instant, and he spoke:–

'What are we to do now? Where are we to turn for help? We must have another transfusion of blood, and that soon, or that poor girl's life won't be worth an hour's purchase. You are exhausted already; I am exhausted too. I fear to trust those women, even if they would have courage to submit. What are we to do for someone who will open his veins for her?'

'What's the matter with me, anyhow?'

The voice came from the sofa across the room, and its tones brought relief and joy to my heart, for they were those of Quincey Morris. Van Helsing started angrily at the first sound, but his face softened and a glad look came into his eyes as I cried out: 'Quincey Morris!' and rushed towards him with outstretched hands.

'What brought you here?' I cried as our hands met.

'I guess Art is the cause.'

He handed me a telegram:–

'Have not heard from Seward for three days, and am terribly anxious. Cannot leave. Father still in same condition. Send me word how Lucy is. Do not delay. – HOLMWOOD.'

'I think I came just in the nick of time. You know you have only to tell me what to do.'

Van Helsing strode forward and took his hand, looking him straight in the eyes as he said:–

'A brave man's blood is the best thing on this earth when a woman is in trouble. You're a man, and no mistake. Well, the devil may work against us for all he's worth, but God sends us men when we want them.'

Once again we went through that ghastly operation. I have not the heart to go through with the details. Lucy had got a terrible shock, and it told on her more than before, for though plenty of blood went into her veins, her body did not respond to the treatment as well as on the other occasions. Her struggle back into life was something frightful to see and hear. However, the action of both heart and lungs improved, and Van Helsing made a subcutaneous injection of morphia, as before, and with good effect. Her faint became a profound slumber. The Professor watched whilst I went downstairs with Quincey Morris, and sent one of the maids to pay off one of the cabmen who were waiting. I left Quincey lying down after having a glass of wine, and told the cook to get ready a good breakfast. Then a thought struck me, and I went back to the room where Lucy now was. When I came softly in, I found Van Helsing with a sheet or two of note-paper in his hand. He had evidently read it, and was thinking it over as he sat with his hand to his brow. There was a look of grim satisfaction in his face, as of one who has had a doubt solved. He handed me the paper, saying only: 'It dropped from Lucy's breast when we carried her to the bath.'

121

When I had read it, I stood looking at the Professor, and after a pause asked him: 'In God's name, what does it all mean? Was she, or is she, mad: or what sort of horrible danger is it?' I was so bewildered that I did not know what to say more. Van Helsing put out his hand and took the paper, saying:–

'Do not trouble about it now. Forget it for the present. You shall know and understand it all in good time; but it will be later. And now what is that you came to me to say?' This brought me back to fact, and I was all myself again.

'I came to speak about the certificate of death. If we do not act properly and wisely, there may be an inquest, and that paper would have to be produced. I am in hopes that we need have no inquest, for if we had it would surely kill poor Lucy, if nothing else did. I know, and you know, and the other doctor who attended her knows, that Mrs Westenra had disease of the heart, and we can certify that she died of it. Let us fill up the certificate at once, and I shall take it myself to the registrar and go on to the undertaker.'

'Good, oh my friend John! Well thought of! Truly Miss Lucy, if she be sad in the foes that beset her, is at least happy in the friends that love her. One, two, three, all open their veins for her, besides one old man. Ah yes, I know, friend John; I am not blind! I love you all the more for it! Now go.'

In the hall I met Quincey Morris, with a telegram for Arthur telling him that Mrs Westenra was dead; that Lucy also had been ill, but was now going on better; and that Van Helsing and I were with her. I told him where I was going, and he hurried me out, but as I was going said:–

'When you come back, Jack, may I have two words with you all to ourselves?' I nodded in reply and went out. I found no difficulty about the registration, and arranged with the local undertaker to come up in the evening to measure for the coffin and to make arrangements.

When I got back Quincey was waiting for me. I told him I would see him as soon as I knew about Lucy, and went up to her room. She was still sleeping, and the Professor seemingly had not moved from his seat at her side. From his putting his finger to his lips, I gathered that he expected her to wake before long and was afraid of forestalling nature. So I went down to Quincey and took him into the breakfast-room, where the blinds were not drawn down, and which was a little more cheerful, or rather less cheerless, than the other rooms. When we were alone, he said to me:–

'Jack Seward, I don't want to shove myself in anywhere where I've no right to be; but this is no ordinary case. You know I loved that girl and wanted to marry her; but, although that's all past and gone, I can't help feeling anxious about her all the same. What is it that's wrong with her? The Dutchman – and a fine old fellow he is; I can see that – said, that time you two came into the room, that you must have *another* transfusion of blood, and that both you and he were exhausted. Now I know well that you medical men speak *in camera*, and that a man must not expect to know what they consult about in private. But this is no common matter, and, whatever it is, I have done my part. Is not that so?'

'That's so,' I said, and he went on:–

'I take it that both you and Van Helsing had done already what I did to-day. Is not that so?'

'That's so.'

'And I guess Art was in it too. When I saw him four days ago down at his own place he looked queer. I have not seen anything pulled down so quick since I was on the Pampas and had a mare that I was fond of go to grass all in a night. One of those big bats that they call vampires had got to her in the night, and, what with his gorge and the vein left open, there wasn't enough blood in her to let her stand up, and I had to put a bullet through her as she lay. Jack, if you may tell me without betraying confidence, Arthur was the first; is not that so?' As he spoke the poor follow looked terribly anxious. He was in a torture of suspense regarding the woman he loved, and his utter ignorance of the terrible mystery which seemed to surround her intensified his pain. His very heart was bleeding, and it took all the manhood of him – and there was a royal lot of it, too – to keep him from breaking down. I paused before answering, for I felt that I must not betray anything which the Professor wished kept secret, but already he knew so much, and guessed so much, that there could be no reason for not answering, so I answered in the same phrase: 'That's so.'

'And how long has this been going on?'

'About ten days.'

'Ten days! Then I guess, Jack Seward, that that poor pretty creature that we all love has had put into her veins within that time the blood of four strong men. Man alive, her whole body wouldn't hold it.' Then, coming close to me, he spoke in a fierce half-whisper: 'What took it out?'

I shook my head. 'That,' I said, 'is the crux. Van Helsing is simply frantic about it, and I am at my wits' end. I can't even hazard a guess. There has been a series of little circumstances which have thrown out all our calculations as to Lucy being properly watched. But these shall not occur again. Here we stay until all be well – or ill.' Quincey held out his hand.

'Count me in,' he said. 'You and the Dutchman will tell me what to do, and I'll do it.'

When she woke late in the afternoon, Lucy's first movement was to feel in her breast, and, to my surprise, produced the paper which Van Helsing had given me to read. The careful Professor had replaced it where it had

123

come from, lest on waking she should be alarmed. Her eye then lit on Van Helsing and on me too, and gladdened. Then she looked round the room, and seeing where she was, shuddered; she gave a loud cry, and put her poor thin hands before her pale face. We both understood what that meant – that she had realized to the full her mother's death; so we tried what we could to comfort her. Doubtless sympathy eased her somewhat, but she was very low in thought and spirit, and wept silently and weakly for a long time. We told her that either or both of us would now remain with her all the time, and that seemed to comfort her. Towards dusk she fell into a doze. Here a very odd thing occurred. Whilst still asleep she took the paper from her breast and tore it in two. Van Helsing stepped over and took the pieces from her. All the same, however, she went on with the action of tearing, as though the material were still in her hands; finally she lifted her hands and opened them as though scattering the fragments. Van Helsing seemed surprised, and his brows gathered as if in thought, but he said nothing.

19 September. – All last night she slept fitfully, being always afraid to sleep, and something weaker when she woke from it. The Professor and I took it in turns to watch, and we never left her for a moment unattended. Quincey Morris said nothing about his intention, but I knew that all night long he patrolled round and round the house.

When the day came, its searching light showed the ravages in poor Lucy's strength. She was hardly able to turn her head, and the little nourishment which she could take seemed to do her no good. At times she slept, and both Van Helsing and I noticed the difference in her, between sleeping and waking. Whilst asleep she looked stronger, although more haggard, and her breathing was softer; her open mouth showed the pale gums drawn back from the teeth, which thus looked positively longer and sharper than usual; when she woke the softness of her eyes evidently changed the expression, for she looked her own self, although a dying one. In the afternoon she asked for Arthur, and we telegraphed for him. Quincey went off to meet him at the station.

When he arrived it was nearly six o'clock, and the sun was setting full and warm, and the red light streamed in through the window and gave more colour to the pale cheeks. When he saw her, Arthur was simply choked with emotion, and none of us could speak. In the hours that had passed, the fits of sleep, or the comatose condition that passed for it, had grown more frequent, so that the pauses when conversation was possible were shortened. Arthur's presence, however, seemed to act as a stimulant; she rallied a little, and spoke to him more brightly than she had done since we arrived. He too pulled himself together, and spoke as cheerily as he could, so that the best was made of everything.

It is now nearly one o'clock, and he and Van Helsing are sitting with her. I am to relieve them in a quarter of an hour, and I am entering this on Lucy's phonograph. Until six o'clock they are to try to rest. I fear that to-morrow will end our watching, for the shock has been too great; the poor child cannot rally. God help us all.

Letter, Mina Harker to Lucy Westenra

(Unopened by her)

'17 September.

'My dearest Lucy,–

'It seems *an age* since I heard from you, or indeed since I wrote. You will pardon me, I know, for all my faults when you have read all my budget of news. Well, I got my husband back all right; when we arrived at Exeter there was a carriage waiting for us, and in it, though he had an attack of gout, Mr Hawkins. He took us to his own house, where there were rooms for us all nice and comfortable, and we dined together. After dinner Mr Hawkins said:–

' "My dears, I want to drink your health and prosperity; and may every blessing attend you both. I know you both from children, and have, with love and pride, seen you grow up. Now I want you to make your home here with me. I have left to me neither chick nor child; all are gone, and in my will I have left you everything." I cried, Lucy dear, as Jonathan and the old man clasped hands. Our evening was a very, very happy one.

'So here we are, installed in this beautiful old house, and from both my bedroom and drawing-room I can see the great elms of the cathedral close, with their great black stems standing out against the old yellow stone of the cathedral; and I can hear the rooks overhead cawing and cawing and chattering and gossiping all day, after the manner of rooks – and humans. I am busy, I need not tell you, arranging things and house-keeping. Jonathan and Mr Hawkins are busy all day; for, now that Jonathan is a partner, Mr Hawkins wants to tell him all about the clients.

'How is your dear mother getting on? I wish I could run up to town for a day or two to see you, dear, but I dare not go yet, with so much on my shoulders; and Jonathan wants looking after still. He is beginning to put some flesh on his bones again, but he was terribly weakened by the long illness; even now he sometimes starts out of his sleep in a sudden way and awakes all trembling until I can coax him back to his usual placidity. However, thank God, these occasions grow less frequent as the days go on, and they will in time pass away altogether, I trust. And now I have told you my news, let me ask yours. When are you to be married, and where,

125

and who is to perform the ceremony, and what are you to wear, and is it to be a public or a private wedding? Tell me all about it, dear; tell me all about everything, for there is nothing which interests you which will not be dear to me. Jonathan asks me to send his "respectful duty", but I do not think that is good enough from the junior partner of the important firm of Hawkins and Harker; and so, as you love me, and he loves me, and I love you with all the moods and tenses of the verb, I send you simply his "love" instead. Good-bye, my dearest Lucy, and all blessings on you.

'Yours,
'MINA HARKER.'

Report from Patrick Hennessey, M.D., M.R.C.S, L.K.Q.C.P.I., etc., etc., to John Seward, M.D.

'20 September.

'My dear Sir,–
'In accordance with your wishes, I enclose report of the conditions of everything left in my charge. . . . With regard to patient, Renfield, there is more to say. He has had another outbreak which might have had a dreadful ending, but which, as it fortunately happened, was unattended with any unhappy results. This afternoon a carrier's cart with two men made a call at the empty house whose grounds abut on ours – the house to which, you will remember, the patient twice ran away. The men stopped at our gate to ask the porter their way, as they were strangers. I was myself looking out of the study window, having a smoke after dinner, and saw one of them come up to the house. As he passed the window of Renfield's room, the patient began to rate him from within, and called him all the foul names he could lay his tongue to. The man, who seemed a decent fellow enough, contented himself by telling him to "shut up for a foul-mouthed beggar", whereon our man accused him of robbing him and wanting to murder him and said that he would hinder him if he were to swing for it. I opened the window and signed to the man not to notice, so he contented himself after looking the place over and making up his mind as to what kind of place he had got to by saying: "Lor' bless yer, sir, I wouldn't mind what was said to me in a bloomin' madhouse. I pity ye and the guv'nor for havin' to live in the house with a wild beast like that." Then he asked the way civilly enough, and I told him where the gate of the empty house was; he went away, followed by threats and curses and revilings from our man. I went down to see if I could make out any cause for his anger, since he is usually such a well-behaved man, and except his violent fits nothing of the kind had ever occurred. I found him, to my

astonishment, quite composed and most genial in his manner. I tried to get him to talk of the incident, but he blandly asked me questions as to what I meant, and led me to believe that he was completely oblivious of the affair. It was, I am sorry to say, however, only another instance of his cunning, for within half an hour I heard of him again. This time he had broken out through the window of his room, and was running down the avenue. I called to the attendants to follow me, and ran after him, for I feared he was intent on some mischief. My fear was justified when I saw the same cart which had passed before coming down the road, having on it some great wooden boxes. The men were wiping their foreheads, and were flushed in the face, as if with violent exercise. Before I could get up to him the patient rushed at them, and pulling one of them off the cart, began to knock his head against the ground. If I had not seized him just at the moment I believe he would have killed the man there and then. The other fellow jumped down and struck him over the head with the butt-end of his heavy whip. It was a terrible blow; but he did not seem to mind it, but seized him also, and struggled with the three of us, pulling us to and fro as if we were kittens. You know I am no light weight, and the others were both burly men. At first he was silent in his fighting; but as we began to master him, and the attendants were putting a strait-waistcoat on him, he began to shout: "I'll frustrate them! They shan't rob me! they shan't murder me by inches! I'll fight for my Lord and Master!" and all sorts of similar incoherent ravings. It was with very considerable difficulty that they got him back to the house and put him in the padded room. One of the attendants, had a finger broken. However, I set it all right; and he is going on well.

'The two carriers were at first loud in their threats of actions for damages, and promised to rain all the penalties of the law on us. Their threats were, however, mingled with some sort of indirect apology for the defeat of the two of them by a feeble madman. They said that if it had not been for the way their strength had been spent in carrying and raising the heavy boxes to the cart they would have made short work of him. They gave as another reason for their defeat the extraordinary state of drouth to which they had been reduced by the dusty nature of their occupation and the reprehensible distance from the scene of their labours of any place of public entertainment. I quite understood their drift, and after a stiff glass of grog, or rather more of the same, and with each a sovereign in hand, they made light of the attack, and swore that they would encounter a worse madman any day for the pleasure of meeting so "bloomin' good a bloke" as your correspondent. I took their names and addresses, in case they might be needed. They are as follows:– Jack Smollet, of Dudding's Rents, King George's Road, Great Walworth, and Thomas Snelling, Peter

127

Parley's Row, Guide Court, Bethnal Green. They are both in the employment of Harris & Sons, Moving and Shipment Company, Orange Master's Yard, Soho.

'I shall report to you any matter of interest occurring here, and shall wire you at once if there is anything of importance.

'Believe me, dear Sir,
'Yours faithfully,
'PATRICK HENNESSEY.'

Letter, Mina Harker to Lucy Westenra

(Unopened by her)

'*18 September*.

'My dearest Lucy,–
    'Such a sad blow has befallen us. Mr Hawkins has died very suddenly. Some may not think it so sad for us, but we had both come to so love him that it really seemed as though we had lost a father. I never knew either father or mother, so that the dear old man's death is a real blow to me. Jonathan is greatly distressed. It is not only that he feels sorrow, deep sorrow, for the dear, good man who has befriended him all his life, and now at the end has treated him like his own son and left him a fortune which to people of our modest bringing up is wealth beyond the dream of avarice, but Jonathan feels it on another account. He says the amount of responsibility which it puts upon him makes him nervous. He begins to doubt himself. I try to cheer him up, and *my* belief in *him* helps him to have a belief in himself. But it is here that the grave shock that he experienced tells upon him most. Oh, it is too hard that a sweet, noble, strong nature such as his – a nature which enabled him, by our dear, good friend's aid, to rise from clerk to master in a few years – should be so injured that the very essence of its strength is gone. Forgive me, dear, if I worry you with my troubles in the midst of your own happiness; but, Lucy dear, I must tell someone, for the strain of keeping up a brave and cheerful appearance to Jonathan tries me, and I have no one here that I can confide in. I dread coming up to London, as we must do the day after to-morrow; for poor Mr Hawkins left in his will that he was to be buried in the grave with his father. As there are no relations at all, Jonathan will have to be chief mourner. I shall try to run over to see you, dearest, if only for a few minutes. Forgive me for troubling you. With all blessings,

'Your loving
MINA HARKER.'

128

20 September. – Only resolution and habit can let me make an entry to-night. I am too miserable, too low-spirited, too sick of the world and all in it, including life itself, and I would not care if I heard this moment the flapping of the wings of the angel of death. And he has been flapping those wings to some purpose of late – Lucy's mother and Arthur's father, and now. . . . Let me get on with my work.

I duly relieved Van Helsing in his watch over Lucy. We wanted Arthur to go to rest also, but he refused at first. It was only when I told him that we should want him to help us during the day, and that we must not all break down for want of rest, lest Lucy should suffer, that he agreed to go. Van Helsing was very kind to him. 'Come, my child,' he said; 'come with me. You are sick and weak, and have had much sorrow and much mental pain, as well as that tax on your strength that we know of. You must not be alone; for to be alone is to be full of fears and alarms. Come to the drawing-room, where there is a big fire, and there are two sofas. You shall lie on one, and I on the other, and our sympathy will be comfort for each other, even though we do not speak, and even if we sleep.' Arthur went off with him, casting back a longing look on Lucy's face, which lay on her pillow, almost whiter than the lawn. She lay quite still, and I looked round the room to see that all was as it should be. I could see that the Professor had carried out in this room, as in the other, his purpose of using the garlic; the whole of the window-sashes reeked with it, and round Lucy's neck, over the silk handkerchief which Van Helsing made her keep on, was a rough chaplet of the same odorous flowers. Lucy was breathing somewhat stertorously, and her face was at its worst, for the open mouth showed the pale gums. Her teeth, in the dim, uncertain light, seemed longer and sharper than they had been in the morning. In particular, by some trick of the light, the canine teeth looked longer and sharper than the rest. I sat down by her, and presently she moved uneasily. At the same moment there came a sort of dull flapping or buffeting at the window. I went over to it softly, and peeped out by the corner of the blind. There was a full moonlight, and I could see that the noise was made by a great bat, which wheeled round – doubtless attracted by the light, although so dim – and every now and again struck the window with its wings. When I came back to my seat I found that Lucy had moved slightly, and had torn away the garlic flowers from her throat. I replaced them as well as I could, and sat watching her.

Presently she woke, and I gave her food, as Van Helsing had prescribed. She took but a little, and that languidly. There did not seem to be with her now the unconscious struggle for life and strength that had hitherto so marked her illness. It struck me as curious that the moment she became conscious she pressed the garlic flowers close to her. It was certainly odd that whenever she got into that lethargic state, with the stertorous breathing, she put the flowers from her; but that when she waked she clutched them close. There was no possibility of making any mistake about this, for in the long hours that followed, she had many spells of sleeping and waking, and repeated both actions many times.

At six o'clock Van Helsing came to relieve me. Arthur had then fallen into a doze, and he mercifully let him sleep on. When he saw Lucy's face I could hear the hissing indraw of his breath, and he said to me in a sharp whisper: 'Draw up the blind; I want light!' Then he bent down, and, with his face almost touching Lucy's, examined her carefully. He removed the flowers and lifted the silk handkerchief from her throat. As he did so he started back, and I could hear his ejaculation, 'Mein Gott!' as it was smothered in his throat. I bent over and looked too, and as I noticed some queer chill came over me.

The wounds on the throat had absolutely disappeared.

For fully five minutes Van Helsing stood looking at her, with his face at its sternest. Then he turned to me and said calmly:–

'She is dying. It will not be long now. It will be much difference, mark me, whether she dies conscious or in her sleep. Wake that poor boy, and let him come and see the last; he trusts us, and we have promised him.'

I went to the dining-room and waked him. He was dazed for a moment, but when he saw the sunlight streaming in through the edges of the shutters he thought he was late, and expressed his fear. I assured him that Lucy was still asleep, but told him as gently as I could that both Van Helsing and I feared that the end was near. He covered his face with his hands, and slid down on his knees by the sofa, where he remained, perhaps a minute, with his hands buried, praying, whilst his shoulders shook with grief. I took him by the hand and raised him up. 'Come,' I said, 'my dearest old fellow, summon all your fortitude; it will be best and easiest for *her*.'

When we came into Lucy's room I could see that Van Helsing had, with his usual forethought, been putting matters straight and making everything look as pleasing as possible. He had even brushed Lucy's hair, so that it lay on the pillow in its usual shiny ripples. When we came into the room she opened her eyes, and seeing him, whispered softly:–

'Arthur! Oh, my love, I am glad you have come!' He was stooping to kiss her, when Van Helsing motioned him back. 'No,' he whispered, 'not yet! Hold her hand: it will comfort her more.'

So Arthur took her hand and knelt beside her, and she looked her best, with all the soft lines matching the angelic beauty of her eyes. Then gradually her eyes closed, and she sank to sleep. For a little bit her breast heaved softly, and her breath came and went like a tired child's.

And then insensibly there came the strange change which I had noticed in the night. Her breathing grew stertorous, the mouth opened, and the pale gums, drawn back, made the teeth look longer and sharper than ever. In a sort of sleep-waking, vague, unconscious way she opened her eyes, which were now dull and hard at once, and said in a soft voluptuous voice, such as I had never heard from her lips:—

'Arthur! Oh, my love, I am so glad you have come! Kiss me!' Arthur bent eagerly over to kiss her; but at that instant Van Helsing, who, like me, had been startled by her voice, swooped upon him, and catching him by the neck with both hands, dragged him back with a fury of strength which I never thought he could have possessed, and actually hurled him almost across the room.

'Not for your life!' he said; 'not for your living soul and hers!' And he stood between them like a lion at bay.

Arthur was so taken aback that he did not for a moment know what to do or say; and before any impulse of violence could seize him he realized the place and the occasion, and he stood silent, waiting.

I kept my eyes fixed on Lucy, as did Van Helsing, and we saw a spasm as of rage flit like a shadow over her face; the sharp teeth champed together. Then her eyes closed, and she breathed heavily.

Very shortly after she opened her eyes in all their softness, and putting out her poor pale, thin hand, took Van Helsing's great brown one; drawing it to her, she kissed it. 'My true friend,' she said, in a faint voice, but with untellable pathos, 'my true friend, and his! Oh, guard him, and give him peace!'

'I swear it!' said he solemnly, kneeling beside her and holding up his hand, as one who registers an oath. Then he turned to Arthur, and said to him: 'Come, my child, take her hand in yours, and kiss her on the forehead, and only once.'

Their eyes met instead of their lips; and so they parted.

Lucy's eyes closed; and Van Helsing, who had been watching closely, took Arthur's arm, and drew him away.

And then Lucy's breathing became stertorous again, and all at once it ceased.

'It is all over,' said Van Helsing. 'She is dead!'

I took Arthur by the arm, and led him away to the drawing-room, where he sat down, and covered his face with his hands sobbing in a way that nearly broke me down to see.

I went back to the room, and found Van Helsing looking at poor Lucy, and his face was sterner than ever. Some change had come over her body.

Death had given back part of her beauty, for her brow and cheeks had recovered some of their flowing lines; even the lips had lost their deadly pallor. It was as if the blood, no longer needed for the working of the heart, had gone to make the harshness of death as little rude as might be.

> 'We thought her dying whilst she slept
> And sleeping when she died.'

I stood beside Van Helsing, and said:–
'Ah, well, poor girl, there is peace for her at least. It is the end!'
He turned to me, and said with grave solemnity:–
'Not so! alas! not so. It is only the beginning!'
When I asked him what he meant, he only shook his head and answered:–
'We can do nothing as yet. Wait and see.'

13

DR SEWARD'S DIARY

(continued)

The funeral was arranged for the next succeeding day, so that Lucy and her mother might be buried together. I attended to all the ghastly formalities, and the urbane undertaker proved that his staff were afflicted – or blessed – with something of his own obsequious suavity. Even the woman who performed the last offices for the dead remarked to me, in a confidential, brother-professional way, when she had come out from the death-chamber:–
'She makes a very beautiful corpse, sir. It's quite a privilege to attend on her. It's not too much to say that she will do credit to our establishment!'
I noticed that Van Helsing never kept far away. This was possible from the disordered state of things in the household. There were no relatives at hand; and as Arthur had to be back the next day to attend at his father's funeral, we were unable to notify anyone who should have been bidden. Under the circumstances, Van Helsing and I took it upon ourselves to examine papers, etc. He insisted upon looking over Lucy's papers himself. I asked him why, for I feared that he, being a foreigner, might not be quite aware of English legal requirements, and so might in ignorance make some unnecessary trouble. He anwered me:–
'I know; I know. You forget that I am a lawyer as well as a doctor. But this is not altogether for the law. You knew that, when you avoided the

coroner. I have more than him to avoid. There may be papers – such as this.'

As he spoke he took from his pocket-book the memorandum which had been in Lucy's breast, and which she had torn in her sleep.

'When you find anything of the solicitor who is for the late Mrs Westenra, seal all her papers, and write him to-night. For me, I watch here in the room and in Miss Lucy's old room all night, and I myself search for what may be. It is not well that her very thoughts go into the hands of strangers.'

I went on with my part of the work, and in another half-hour had found the name and address of Mrs Westenra's solicitor and had written to him. All the poor lady's papers were in order; explicit directions regarding the place of burial were given. I had hardly sealed the letter, when, to my surprise, Van Helsing walked into the room saying:–

'Can I help you, friend John? I am free, and if I may, my service is to you.'

'Have you got what you looked for?' I asked, to which he replied:–

'I did not look for any specific thing. I only hoped to find, and find I have, all that there was – only some letters and a few memoranda, and a diary new begun. But I have them here, and we shall for the present say nothing of them. I shall see that poor lad to-morrow evening, and, with his sanction, I shall use some.'

When we had finished the work in hand, he said to me:–

'And now, friend John, I think we may to bed. We want sleep, both you and I, and rest to recuperate. To-morrow we shall have much to do, but for the to-night there is no need of us. Alas!'

Before turning in we went to look at poor Lucy. The undertaker had certainly done his work well, for the room was turned into a small *chapelle ardente*. There was a wilderness of beautiful white flowers, and death was made as little repulsive as might be. The end of the winding-sheet was laid over the face; when the Professor bent over and turned it gently back, we both started at the beauty before us, the tall wax candles showing a sufficient light to note it well. All Lucy's loveliness had come back to her in death, and the hours that had passed, instead of leaving traces of 'decay's effacing fingers', had but restored the beauty of life, till positively I could not believe my eyes that I was looking at a corpse.

The Professor looked sternly grave. He had not loved her as I had, and there was no need for tears in his eyes. He said to me: 'Remain till I return,' and left the room. He came back with a handful of wild garlic from the box waiting in the hall, but which had not been opened, and placed the flowers amongst the others on and around the bed. Then he took from his neck, inside his collar, a little golden crucifix, and placed it over the mouth. He restored the sheet to its place, and we came away.

I was undressing in my own room, when, with a premonitory tap at the door, he entered, and at once began to speak:—

'To-morrow I want you to bring me, before night, a set of post-mortem knives.'

'Must we make an autopsy?' I asked.

'Yes, and no. I want to operate, but not as you think. Let me tell you now, but not a word to another. I want to cut off her head and take out her heart. Ah! you a surgeon, and so shocked! You, whom I have seen with no tremble of hand or heart, do operations of life and death that make the rest shudder. Oh, but I must not forget, my dear friend John, that you loved her; and I have not forgotten it, for it is I that shall operate, and you must only help. I would like to do it to-night, but for Arthur I must not; he will be free after his father's funeral to-morrow, and he will want to see her – to see *it*. Then, when she is coffined ready for the next day, you and I shall come when all sleep. We shall unscrew the coffin-lid, and shall do our operation; and then replace all, so that none know, save we alone.'

'But why do it at all? The girl is dead. Why mutilate her poor body without need? And if there is no necessity for a post-mortem and nothing to gain by it – no good to her, to us, to science, to human knowledge – why do it? Without such it is monstrous.'

For answer he put his hand on my shoulder, and said, with infinite tenderness:—

'Friend John, I pity your poor bleeding heart; and I love you the more because it does so bleed. If I could, I would take on myself the burden that you do bear. But there are things that you know not, but that you shall know, and bless me for knowing, though they are not pleasant things. John, my child, you have been my friend now many years, and yet did you ever know me to do any without good cause? I may err – I am but man; but I believe in all I do. Was it not for these causes that you send for me when the great trouble came? Yes! Were you not amazed, nay horrified, when I would not let Arthur kiss his love – though she was dying – and snatched him away by all my strength? Yes! And yet you saw how she thanked me, with her so beautiful dying eyes, her voice, too, so weak, and she kissed my rough old hand and bless me? Yes! and did you not hear me swear promise to her, that so she closed her eyes grateful? Yes!

'Well, I have good reason now for all I want to do. You have for many years trust me; you have believe me weeks past, when there be things so strange that you might have well doubt. Believe me yet a little, friend John. If you trust me not, then I must tell what I think; and that is not perhaps well. And if I work – as work I shall, no matter trust or no trust – without my friend trust in me, I work with heavy heart, and feel, oh! so lonely when I want all help and courage that may be!' He paused a moment, and went on solemnly: 'Friend John, there are strange and terrible days before us. Let us not be two, but one, that so we work to a good end. Will you not have faith in me?'

I took his hand, and promised him. I held my door open as he went away, and watched him go into his room and close the door. As I stood without moving, I saw one of the maids pass silently along the passage – she had her back towards me, so did not see me – and go into the room where Lucy lay. The sight touched me. Devotion is so rare, and we are so grateful to those who show it unasked to those we love. Here was a poor girl putting aside the terrors which she naturally had of death to go watch alone by the bier of the mistress whom she loved, so that the poor clay might not be lonely till laid to eternal rest. . . .

I must have slept long and soundly, for it was broad daylight when Van Helsing waked me by coming into my room. He came over to my bedside and said:–

'You need not trouble about the knives; we shall not do it.'

'Why not?' I asked. For his solemnity of the night before had greatly impressed me.

'Because,' he said sternly, 'it is too late – or too early. See!' Here he held up the little golden crucifix. 'This was stolen in the night.'

'How stolen,' I asked in wonder, 'since you have it now?'

'Because I get it back from the worthless wretch who stole it, from the woman who robbed the dead and the living. Her punishment will surely come, but not through me; she knew not altogether what she did, and thus unknowing, she only stole. Now we must wait.'

He went away on the word, leaving me with a new mystery to think of, a new puzzle to grapple with.

The forenoon was a dreary time, but at noon the solicitor came: Mr Marquand, of Wholeman, Sons, Marquand and Lidderdale. He was very genial and very appreciative of what we had done, and took off our hands all cares as to details. During lunch he told us that Mrs Westenra had for some time expected sudden death from her heart, and had put her affairs in absolute order; he informed us that, with the exception of a certain entailed property of Lucy's father which now, in default of direct issue, went back to a distant branch of the family, the whole estate, real and personal, was left absolutely to Arthur Holmwood. When he had told us so much he went on:–

'Frankly we did our best to prevent such a testamentary disposition, and pointed out certain contingencies that might leave her daughter either penniless or not so free as she should be to act regarding a matrimonial alliance. Indeed, we pressed the matter so far that we almost came into collision, for she asked us if we were or were not prepared to carry out her wishes. Of course, we had then no alternative but to accept. We were right in principle, and ninety-nine times out of a hundred we should have proved, by the logic of events, the accuracy of our judgment. Frankly, however, I must admit that in this case any other form of disposition would have rendered impossible the carrying out of her wishes. For by her predeceasing her daughter the latter would have come into possession of the property, and, even had she only survived her mother by five minutes, her property would, in case there were no will – and a will was a practical impossibility in such a case – have been treated at her decease as under intestacy. In which case, Lord Godalming, though so dear a friend, would have had no claim in the world; and the inheritors, being remote, would not be likely to abandon their just rights for sentimental reasons regarding an entire stranger. I assure you, my dear sirs, I am rejoiced at the result, perfectly rejoiced.'

He was a good fellow, but his rejoicing at the one little part – in which he was officially interested – of so great a tragedy was an object-lesson in the limitations of sympathetic understanding.

He did not remain long, but said he would look in later in the day and see Lord Godalming. His coming, however, had been a certain comfort to us, since it assured us that we should not have to dread hostile criticism as to any of our acts. Arthur was expected at five o'clock, so a little before that time we visited the death-chamber. It was so in very truth, for now both mother and daughter lay in it. The undertaker, true to his craft, had made the best display he could of his goods, and there was a mortuary air about the place that lowered our spirits at once. Van Helsing ordered the former arrangement to be adhered to, explaining that, as Lord Godalming was coming very soon, it would be less harrowing to his feelings to see all that was left of his *fiancé* quite alone. The undertaker seemed shocked at his own stupidity, and exerted himself to restore things to the condition in which we left them the night before, so that when Arthur came such shocks to his feelings as we could avoid were saved.

Poor fellow! He looked desperately sad and broken; even his stalwart manhood seemed to have shrunk somewhat under the strain of his much-tried emotions. He had, I knew, been very genuinely and devotedly attached to his father; and to lose him, and at such a time, was a bitter blow to him. With me he was warm as ever, and to Van Helsing he was sweetly courteous; but I could not help seeing that there was some constraint with him. The Professor noticed it, too, and motioned me to bring him upstairs. I did so, and left him at the door of the room, as I felt he would like to be quite alone with her; but he took my arm and led me in, saying huskily:–

'You loved her too, old fellow; she told me all about it, and there was no friend had a closer place in her heart than you. I don't know how to thank you for all you have done for her. I can't think yet. . . .'

Here he suddenly broke down, and threw his arms round my shoulders and laid his head on my breast, crying:—

'Oh, Jack, Jack! What shall I do? The whole of life seems gone from me all at once, and there is nothing in the wide world for me to live for.'

I comforted him as well as I could. In such cases men do not need much expression. A grip of the hand, the tightening of an arm over the shoulder, a sob in unison, are expressions of sympathy dear to a man's heart. I stood still and silent till his sobs died away, and then I said softly to him:—

'Come and look at her.'

Together we moved over to the bed, and I lifted the lawn from her face. God! how beautiful she was. Every hour seemed to be enhancing her loveliness. It frightened and amazed me somewhat; and as for Arthur, he fell a-trembling, and finally was shaken with doubt as with an ague. At last, after a long pause, he said to me in a faint whisper:—

'Jack, is she really dead?'

I assured him sadly that it was so, and went on to suggest — for I felt that such a horrible doubt should not have life for a moment longer than I could help — that it often happened that after death faces became softened and even resolved into their youthful beauty; that this was especially so when death had been preceded by any acute or prolonged suffering. It seemed to quite do away with any doubt, and, after kneeling beside the couch for a while and looking at her lovingly and long, he turned aside. I told him that that must be good-bye, as the coffin had to be prepared; so he went back and took her dead hand in his and kissed it, and bent over and kissed her forehead. He came away, fondly looking back over his shoulder at her as he came.

I left him in the drawing-room, and told Van Helsing that he had said good-bye; so the latter went to the kitchen to tell the undertaker's men to proceed with the preparations and to screw up the coffin. When he came out of the room again I told him of Arthur's question, and he replied:—

'I am not surprised. Just now I doubted for a moment myself!'

We all dined together, and I could see that poor Art was trying to make the best of things. Van Helsing had been silent all dinner-time, but when we had lit our cigars he said:—

'Lord —'; but Arthur interrupted him:—

'No, no, not that, for God's sake! not yet at any rate. Forgive me, sir: I did not mean to speak offensively; it is only because my loss is so recent.'

The Professor answered very sweetly:—

'I only used that name because I was in doubt. I must not call you

"Mr", and I have grown to love you – yes, my dear boy, to love you – as Arthur.'

Arthur held out his hand, and took the old man's warmly.

'Call me what you will,' he said. 'I hope I may always have the title of a friend. And let me say that I am at a loss for words to thank you for your goodness to my poor dear.' He paused a moment, and went on: 'I know that she understood your goodness even better than I do; and if I were rude or in any way wanting at that time you acted so – you remember' – the Professor nodded – 'you must forgive me.'

He answered with a grave kindness:–

'I know it was hard for you to quite trust me then, for to trust such violence needs to understand; and I take it that you do not – that you cannot – trust me now, for you do not yet understand. And there may be more times when I shall want you to trust when you cannot – and may not – and must not yet understand. But the time will come when your trust shall be whole and complete in me, and when you shall understand as though the sunlight himself shone through. Then you shall bless me from first to last for your own sake, and for the sake of others, and for her dear sake to whom I swore to protect.'

'And, indeed, indeed, sir,' said Arthur warmly, 'I shall in all ways trust you. I know and believe you have a very noble heart, and you are Jack's friend, and you were hers. You shall do what you like.'

The Professor cleared his throat a couple of times, as though about to speak, and finally said:–

'May I ask you something now?'

'Certainly.'

'You know that Mrs Westenra left you all her property?'

'No, poor dear; I never thought of it.'

'And as it is all yours, you have a right to deal with it as you will. I want you to give me permission to read all Miss Lucy's papers and letters. Believe me, it is no idle curiosity. I have a motive of which, be sure, she would have approved. I have them all here. I took them before we knew that all was yours, so that no strange hand might touch them – no strange eye look through words into her soul. I shall keep them, if I may; even you may not see them yet, but I shall keep them safe. No word shall be lost; and in the good time I shall give them back to you. It's a hard thing I ask, but you will do it, will you not, for Lucy's sake?'

Arthur spoke out heartily, like his old self:–

'Dr Van Helsing, you may do what you will. I feel that in saying this I am doing what my dear one would have approved. I shall not trouble you with questions till the time comes.'

The old Professor stood up as he said solemnly:–

'And you are right. There will be pain for us all; but it will not be all pain, nor will this pain be the last. We and you too – you most of all, my dear boy – will have to pass through the bitter water before we reach the sweet. But we must be brave of heart and unselfish, and do our duty, and all will be well!'

I slept on a sofa in Arthur's room that night. Van Helsing did not go to bed at all. He went to and fro, as if patrolling the house, and was never out of sight of the room where Lucy lay in her coffin, strewn with the wild garlic flowers, which sent, through the odour of lily and rose, a heavy, overpowering smell into the night.

MINA HARKER'S JOURNAL

22 September. – In the train to Exeter. Jonathan sleeping.

It seems only yesterday that the last entry was made, and yet how much beween them, in Whitby and all the world before me, Jonathan away and no news of him; and now, married to Jonathan, Jonathan a solicitor, a partner, rich, master of his business, Mr Hawkins dead and buried, and Jonathan with another attack that may harm him. Some day he may ask me about it. Down it all goes. I am rusty in my shorthand – see what unexpected prosperity does for us – so it may be as well to freshen it up again with an exercise anyhow. . . .

The service was very simple and very solemn. There were only ourselves and the servants there, one or two old friends of his from Exeter, his London agent, and a gentleman representing Sir John Paxton, the President of the Incorporated Law Society. Jonathan and I stood hand in hand, and we felt that our best and dearest friend was gone from us. . . .

We came back to town quietly, taking a 'bus to Hyde Park Corner. Jonathan thought it would interest me to go into the Row for a while, so we sat down; but there were very few people there, and it was sad-looking and desolate to see so many empty chairs. It made us think of the empty chair at home; so we got up and walked down Piccadilly. Jonathan was holding me by the arm, the way he used to in old days before I went to school. I felt it very improper, for you can't go on for some years teaching etiquette and decorum to other girls without the pedantry of it biting into yourself a bit; but it was Jonathan, and he was my husband, and we didn't know anybody who saw us – and we didn't care if they did – so on we walked. I was looking at a very beautiful girl, in a big cart-wheel hat, sitting in a victoria outside Giuliano's when I felt Jonathan clutch my arm so tight that he hurt me, and he said under his breath. 'My God!' I am always anxious about Jonathan, for I fear that some nervous fit may upset him again; so I turned to him quickly, and asked him what it was that disturbed him.

He was very pale, and his eyes seemed bulging out as, half in terror and half in amazement, he gazed at a tall, thin man, with a beaky nose and black moustache and pointed beard, who was also observing the pretty girl. He was looking at her so hard that he did not see either of us, and so I had a good view of him. His face was not a good face; it was hard, and cruel, and sensual, and his big white teeth, that looked all the whiter because his lips were so red, were pointed like an animal's. Jonathan kept staring at him, till I was afraid he would notice. I feared he might take it ill, he looked so fierce and nasty. I asked Jonathan why he was so disturbed, and he answered, evidently thinking that I knew as much about it as he did: 'Do you see who it is?'

'No, dear,' I said; 'I don't know him; who is it?' His answer seemed to shock and thrill me, for it was said as if he did not know that it was to me, Mina, to whom he was speaking:–

'It is the man himself!'

The poor dear was evidently terrified at something – very greatly terrified; I do believe that if he had not had me to lean on and to support him, he would have sunk down. He kept staring; a man came out of the shop with a small parcel, and gave it to the lady, who then drove off. The dark man kept his eyes fixed on her, and when the carriage moved up Piccadilly he followed in the same direction, and hailed a hansom. Jonathan kept looking after him, and said, as if to himself:–

'I believe it is the Count, but he has grown young. My God, if this be so! Oh, my God! my God! If I only knew! if I only knew!' He was distressing himself so much that I feared to keep his mind on the subject by asking him any questions, so I remained silent. I drew him away quietly, and he, holding my arm, came easily. We walked a little further, and then went in and sat for a while in the Green Park. It was a hot day for autumn, and there was a comfortable seat in a shady place. After a few minutes' staring at nothing, Jonathan's eyes closed, and he went quietly into a sleep, with his head on my shoulder. I thought it was the best thing for him, so did not disturb him. In about twenty minutes he woke up, and said to me quite cheerfully:–

'Why, Mina, have I been asleep? Oh, do forgive me for being so rude. Come, and we'll have a cup of tea somewhere.' He had evidently forgotten all about the dark stranger, as in his illness he had forgotten all that this episode had reminded him of. I don't like this lapsing into forgetfulness; it may make or continue some injury to the brain. I must not ask him, for fear I shall do more harm than good; but I must somehow learn the facts of his journey abroad. The time is come, I fear, when I must open that parcel and know what is written. Oh, Jonathan, you will, I know, forgive me if I do wrong but it is for your own dear sake.

Later. – A sad home-coming in every way – the house empty of the dear soul who was so good to us; Jonathan still pale and dizzy under a slight relapse of his malady; and now a telegram from Van Helsing, whoever he may be:–

'You will be grieved to hear that Mrs Westenra died five days ago, and that Lucy died the day before yesterday. They were both buried to-day.'

Oh, what a wealth of sorrow in a few words! Poor Mrs Westenra! poor Lucy! Gone, gone, never to return to us! And poor, poor Arthur, to have lost such sweetness out of his life! God help us all to bear our troubles.

DR SEWARD'S DIARY

22 September. – It is all over. Arthur has gone back to Ring, and has taken Quincey Morris with him. What a fine fellow is Quincey! I believe in my heart of hearts that he suffered as much about Lucy's death as any of us; but he bore himself through it like a moral Viking. If America can go on breeding men like that, she will be a power in the world indeed. Van Helsing is lying down, having a rest preparatory to his journey. He goes over to Amsterdam to-night, but says he returns to-morrow night; that he only wants to make some arrangements which can only be made personally. He is to stop with me then, if he can; he says he has work to do in London which may take him some time. Poor old fellow! I fear that the strain of the past week has broken down even his iron strength. All the time of the burial he was, I could see, putting some terrible restraint on himself. When it was all over, we were standing beside Arthur, who, poor fellow, was speaking of his part in the operation where his blood had been transfused to his Lucy's veins; I could see Van Helsing's face grow white and purple by turns. Arthur was saying that he felt since then as if they two had been really married, and that she was his wife in the sight of God. None of us said a word of the other operations, and none of us ever shall. Arthur and Quincey went away together to the station, and Van Helsing and I came on here. The moment we were alone in the carriage he gave way to a regular fit of hysterics. He has denied to me since that it was hysterics, and insisted that it was only his sense of humour asserting itself under very terrible conditions. He laughed till he cried and I had to draw down the blinds lest anyone should see us and misjudge; and then he cried till he laughed again; and laughed and cried together, just as a woman does. I tried to be stern with him, as one is to a woman under the circumstances; but it had no effect. Men and women are so different in manifestations of nervous strength or weakness! Then when his face grew grave and stern again I asked him why his mirth, and why at such a time. His reply was in a way characteristic of him, for it was logical and forceful and mysterious. He said:

'Ah, you don't comprehend, friend John. Do not think that I am not sad, though I laugh. See, I have cried even when the laugh did choke me. But no more think that I am all sorry when I cry, for the laugh he come just the same. Keep it always with you that laughter who knock at your door and say: "May I come in?" is not the true laughter. No! he is a king, and he come when and how he like. He ask no person; he choose no time of suitability. He say: "I am here." Behold, in example, I grieve my heart out for that so sweet young girl; I give my blood for her, though I am old and worn; I give my time, my skill, my sleep; I let my other sufferers want that she may have all. And yet I can laugh at her very grave – laugh when the clay from the spade of the sexton drop upon her coffin and say: "Thud! thud!" to my heart, till it send back the blood from my cheek. My heart bleed for that poor boy – that dear boy, so of the age of mine own boy had I been so blessed that he live, and with his hair and eyes the same. There, you know now why I love him so. And yet when he say things that touch my husband-heart to the quick, and make my father-heart yearn to him as to no other man – not even to you, friend John, for we are more level in experiences than father and son – yet even at such moment King Laugh he come to me and shout and bellow in my ear: "Here I am! Here I am!" till the blood come dance back and bring some of the sunshine that he carry with him to my cheek. Oh, friend John, it is a strange world, a sad world, a world full of miseries, and woes, and troubles; and yet when King Laugh come he make them all dance to the tune he play. Bleeding hearts, and dry bones of the churchyard, and tears that burn as they fall – all dance together to the music that he make with that smileless mouth of him. And believe me, friend John, that he is good to come, and kind. Ah, we men and women are like ropes drawn tight with strain that pull us different ways. Then tears come; and, like the rain on the ropes, they brace us up, until perhaps the strain become too great, and we break. But King Laugh he come like the sunshine, and he ease off the strain again; and we bear to go on with our labour, what it may be.'

I did not like to wound him by pretending not to see his idea; but, as I did not yet understand the cause of his laughter, I asked him. As he answered me his face grew stern, and he said in quite a different tone:–

'Oh, it was the grim irony of it all – this so lovely lady garlanded with flowers, that looked so fair as life, till one by one we wondered if she were truly dead; she laid in that so fine marble house in that lonely churchyard, where rest so many of her kin, laid there with the mother who loved her, and whom she loved; and that sacred bell going "Toll! toll! toll!" so sad and slow; and those holy men, with the white garments of the angel, pretending to read books, and yet all the time their eyes never on the page; and all us with the bowed head. And all for what? She is dead; so! Is it not?'

'Well, for the life of me, Professor,' I said, 'I can't see anything to laugh at in all that. Why, your explanation makes it a harder puzzle than before. But even if the burial service was comic, what about poor Art and his trouble? Why, his heart was simply breaking.'

'Just so. Said he not that the transfusion of his blood to her veins had made her truly his bride?'

'Yes, and it was a sweet and comforting idea for him.'

'Quite so. But there was a difficulty, friend John. If so that, then what about the others? Ho, ho! Then this so sweet maid is a polyandrist, and me, with my poor wife dead to me, but alive by Church's law, though no wits, all gone – even I, who am faithful husband to this now-no-wife, am bigamist.'

'I don't see where the joke comes in there either!' I said; and I did not feel particularly pleased with him for saying such things. He laid his hand on my arm, and said:–

'Friend John, forgive me if I pain. I showed not my feeling to others when it would wound, but only to you, my old friend, whom I can trust. If you could have looked into my very heart then when I want to laugh; if you could have done so when the laugh arrived; if you could do so now, when King Laugh have pack up his crown and all that is to him – for he go far, far away from me, and for a long, long time – maybe you would perhaps pity me the most of all.'

I was touched by the tenderness of his tone, and asked why.

'Because I know!'

And now we are all scattered; and for many a long day loneliness will sit over our roofs with brooding wings. Lucy lies in the tomb of her kin, a lordly death-house in a lonely churchyard, away from teeming London; where the air is fresh; and the sun rises over Hampstead Hill, and where wild flowers grow of their own accord.

So I can finish this diary; and God only knows if I shall ever begin another. If I do, or if I ever open this again, it will be to deal with different people and different themes; for here at the end, where the romance of my life is told, ere I go back to take up the thread of my life-work, I say sadly and without hope,

'FINIS'

A HAMPSTEAD MYSTERY

The neighbourhood of Hampstead is just at present exercised with a series of events which seem to run on lines parallel to those of what was known to the writers of headlines as 'The Kensington Horror', or 'The Stabbing Woman', or 'The Woman in Black'. During the past two or three days several cases have occurred of young children straying from home or neglecting to return from their playing on the Heath. In all these cases the children were too young to give any properly intelligible account of themselves, but the consensus of their excuses is that they had been with a 'bloofer lady'. It has always been late in the evening when they have been missed, and on two occasions the children have not been found until early in the following morning. It is generally supposed in the neighbourhood that, as the first child missed gave as his reason for being away that a 'bloofer lady' had asked him to come for a walk, the others had picked up the phrase and used it as occasion served. This is the more natural as the favourite game of the little ones at present is luring each other away by wiles. A correspondent writes us that to see some of the tiny tots pretending to be the 'bloofer lady' is supremely funny. Some of our caricaturists might, he says, take a lesson in the irony of grotesque by comparing the reality and the picture. It is only in accordance with general principles of human nature that the 'bloofer lady' should be the popular rôle at these *al Fresco* performances. Our correspondent naïvely says that even Ellen Terry could not be so winningly attractive as some of these grubby-faced little children pretend – and even imagine themselves – to be.

There is, however, possibly a serious side to the question, for some of the children, indeed all who have been missed at night, have been slightly torn or wounded in the throat. The wounds seem such as might be made by a rat or small dog, and although of not much importance individually, would tend to show that whatever animal inflicts them has a system or method of its own. The police of the division have been instructed to keep a sharp lookout for straying children, especially when very young, in and around Hampstead Heath, and for any stray dog which may be about.

The 'Westminster Gazette', 25 September

Extra Special

THE HAMPSTEAD HORROR

ANOTHER CHILD INJURED

The 'Bloofer Lady'

We have just received intelligence that another child, missed last night, was only discovered late in the morning under a furze bush at the Shooter's Hill side of Hampstead Heath, which is, perhaps, less frequented than the other parts. It has the same tiny wound in the throat as has been noticed in other cases. It was terribly weak, and looked quite emaciated. It too, when partially restored, had the common story to tell of being lured away by the 'bloofer lady'.

14

MINA HARKER'S JOURNAL

23 September. – Jonathan is better after a bad night. I am so glad that he has plenty of work to do, for that keeps his mind off the terrible things; and oh, I am rejoiced that he is not now weighed down with the responsibility of his new position. I knew he would be true to himself, and now how proud I am to see my Jonathan rising to the height of his advancement and keeping pace in all ways with the duties that come upon him. He will be away all day till late, for he said he could not lunch at home. My household work is done, so I shall take his foreign journal, and lock myself up in my room and read it. . . .

24 September. – I hadn't the heart to write last night; that terrible record of Jonathan's upset me so. Poor dear! How he must have suffered, whether it be true or only imagination. I wonder if there is any truth in it at all. Did he get his brain fever, and then write all those terrible things; or had he some cause for it all? I suppose I shall never know, for I dare not open the subject to him. . . . And yet that man we saw yesterday! He seemed quite certain of him. . . . Poor fellow! I suppose it was the funeral upset him and sent his mind back on some train of thought. . . . He believes it all himself. I remember how on our wedding-day he said: 'Unless some solemn duty come upon me to go back to the bitter hours, asleep or awake, mad or sane.' There seems to be through it all some thread of continuity. . . . That fearful Count was coming to London, with its teeming millions. . . . There may be a solemn duty; and if it come we must not shrink from it. . . . I shall be prepared. I shall get my typewriter this very hour and begin transcribing. Then we shall be ready for other eyes if required. And if it be wanted, then, perhaps, if I am ready, poor Jonathan may not be upset, for I can speak for him and never let him be troubled or worried with it all. If ever Jonathan quite gets over the nervousness he may want to tell me of it all, and I can ask him questions and find out things, and see how I may comfort him.

Letter, Van Helsing to Mrs Harker

'24 September.
'Dear Madam,   (Confidence).
  'I pray you to pardon my writing, in that I amso far friend as that I send to you sad news of Miss Lucy Westenra's death. By the kindness of Lord Godalming, I am empowered to read her letters and papers, for I am deeply concerned about certain matters vitally important. In them I find some letters from you, which show how great friends you were and how you love her. Oh, Madam Mina, by that love, I implore you, help me. It is for others' good that I ask – to redress great wrong, and to lift much and terrible troubles – that may be more great then you can know. May it be that I see you? You can trust me. I am a friend of Dr John Seward and of Lord Godalming (that was Arthur of Miss Lucy). I must keep it private for the present from all. I should come to Exeter to see you at once if you tell me I am privilege to come, and where and when. I implore your pardon, madam. I have read your letters to poor Lucy, and know how good you are and how your husband suffer; so I pray you, if it may be, enlighten him not, lest it may harm. Again your pardon, and forgive me.

'VAN HELSING.'

'*25 September.* – Come to-day by quarter-past ten train if you can catch it. Can see you any time you call.

WILHELMINA HARKER.'

MINA HARKER'S JOURNAL

25 September. – I cannot help feeling terribly excited as the time draws near for the visit of Dr Van Helsing, for somehow I expect it will throw some light upon Jonathan's sad experience; and as he attended poor dear Lucy in her last illness, he can tell me all about her. That is the reason for his coming; it is concerning Lucy and her sleep-walking, and not about Jonathan. Then I shall never know the real truth now! How silly I am. That awful journal gets hold of my imagination and tinges everything with something of its own colour. Of course it is about Lucy. That habit came back to the poor dear, and that awful night on the cliff must have made her ill. I had almost forgotten in my own affairs how ill she was afterwards. She must have told him of her sleep-walking adventure on the cliff, and that I knew all about it; and now he wants me to tell him about it, so that he may understand. I hope I did right in not saying anything of it to Mrs Westenra; I should never forgive myself if any act of mine, were it even a negative one, brought harm on poor dear Lucy. I hope, too, Dr Van Helsing will not blame me; I have had so much trouble and anxiety of late that I feel I cannot bear more just at present.

I suppose a cry does us all good at times – clears the air as other rain does. Perhaps it was reading the journal yesterday that upset me, and then Jonathan went away this morning to stay away from me a whole day and night, the first time we have been parted since our marriage. I do hope the dear fellow will take care of himself, and that nothing will occur to upset him. It is two o'clock and the doctor will be here soon now. I shall say nothing of Jonathan's journal unless he asks me. I am so glad I have typewritten out my own journal, so that, in case he asks about Lucy, I can hand it to him; it will save much questioning.

Later. – He has come and gone. Oh, what a strange meeting, and how it all makes my head whirl round! I feel like one in a dream. Can it be all possible, or even a part of it? If I had not read Jonathan's journal first, I should never have accepted even a possibility. Poor, poor, dear Jonathan! How he must have suffered. Please the good God all this may not upset him again. I shall try to save him from it; but it may be even a consolation and a help to him – terrible though it be and awful in its consequences – to know for certain that his eyes and ears and brain did not deceive him, and that it is all true. It may be that it is the doubt which haunts him; that when the doubt is removed, no matter which – waking or dreaming – may prove the truth, he will be more satisfied and better able to bear the shock. Dr Van Helsing must be a good man as well as a clever one if he is Arthur's friend and Dr Seward's, and if they brought him all the way from Holland to look after Lucy. I feel from having seen him that he is good and kind and of a noble nature. When he comes to-morrow I shall ask him about Jonathan; and then, please God, all this sorrow and anxiety may lead to a good end. I used to think I would like to practise interviewing; Jonathan's friend on the *Exeter News* told him that memory was everything in such work – that you must be able to put down exactly almost every word spoken, even if you had to refine some of it afterwards. Here was a rare interview; I shall try to record it *verbatim*.

It was half-past two o'clock when the knock came. I took my courage *à deux mains* and waited. In a few minutes Mary opened the door, and announced 'Dr Van Helsing.'

I rose and bowed, and he came towards me; a man of medium height, strongly built, with his shoulders set back over a broad, deep chest and a neck well balanced on the trunk as the head is on the neck. The poise of the head strikes one at once as indicative of thought and power; the head is noble, well-sized, broad, and large behind the ears. The face, clean-shaven, shows a hard, square chin, a large, resolute, mobile mouth, a good-sized nose, rather straight, but with quick, sensitive nostrils, that seem to broaden as the big, bushy eyebrows come down and the mouth tightens. The forehead is broad and fine, rising at first almost straight and then sloping back above two bumps or ridges wide apart; such a forehead that the reddish hair cannot possibly tumble over it, but falls naturally back and to the sides. Big, dark blue eyes are set widely apart, and are quick and tender or stern with the man's moods. He said to me:–

'Mrs Harker, is it not?' I bowed assent.

'That was Miss Mina Murray?' Again I assented.

'It is Mina Murray that I came to see, that was friend of that poor dear child Lucy Westernra. Madam Mina, it is on account of the dead I come.'

'Sir,' I said, 'you could have no better claim on me than that you were a friend and helper of Lucy Westenra.' And I held out my hand. He took it and said tenderly:–

'Oh, Madam Mina, I knew that the friend of that poor lily girl must be good, but I had yet to learn –' He finished his speech with a courtly bow. I asked him what it was that he wanted to see me about, so he at once began:–

'I have read your letters to Miss Lucy. Forgive me, but I had to begin to inquire somewhere, and there was none to ask. I know that you were with her at Whitby. She sometimes kept a diary – you need not look surprised, Madam Mina; it was begun after you left, and was made in imitation of you – and in that diary she traces by inference certain things to a sleep-walking in which she puts down that you saved her. In great perplexity then I come to you, and ask you out of your so much kindness to tell me all of it that you remember.'

'I can tell you, I think, Dr Van Helsing, all about it.'

'Ah, then you have a good memory for facts, for details? It is not always so with young ladies.'

'No, doctor, but I wrote it all down at the time. I can show it to you if you like.'

'Oh, Madam Mina, I will be grateful; you will do me much favour.' I could not resist the temptation of mystifying him a bit – I suppose it is some of the taste of the original apple that remains still in our mouths – so I handed him the shorthand diary. He took it with a greatful bow, and said:–

'May I read it?'

'If you wish,' I answered as demurely as I could. He opened it, and for the instant his face fell. Then he stood up and bowed.

'Oh, you so clever woman!' he said. 'I long knew that Mr Jonathan was a man of much thankfulness; but see, his wife have all the good things. And will you not so much honour me and so help me as to read it for me? Alas! I know not the shorthand.' By this time my little joke was over, and I was almost ashamed; so I took the typewritten copy from my work-basket and handed it to him.

'Forgive me,' I said: 'I could not help it; but I had been thinking that it was of dear Lucy that you wished to ask, and so that you might not have to wait – not on my account, but because I know your time must be precious – I have written it out on the typewriter for you.'

He took it, and his eyes glistened. 'You are so good,' he said. 'And may I read it now? I may want to ask you some things when I have read.'

'By all means,' I said, 'read it over whilst I order lunch; and then you can ask me questions whilst we eat.' He bowed and settled himself in a chair with his back to the light, and became absorbed in the papers, whilst I went to see after lunch, chiefly in order that he might not be disturbed. When I came back I found him walking hurriedly up and down the room, his face all ablaze with excitement. He rushed up to me and took me by both hands.

'Oh, Madam Mina,' he said, 'how can I say what I owe to you? This paper is as sunshine. It opens the gate to me. I am daze, I am dazzle, with so much light; and yet clouds roll in behind the light every time. But that you do not, cannot, comprehend. Oh, but I am grateful to you, you so clever woman. Madam' – he said this very solemnly – 'if ever Abraham Van Helsing can do anything for you or yours, I trust you will let me know. It will be pleasure and delight if I may serve you as a friend; as a friend, but all I have ever learned, all I can ever do, shall be for you and those you love. There are darknesses in life, and there are lights; you are one of the lights. You will have happy life and good life, and your husband will be blessed in you.'

'But, doctor, you praise me too much, and – and you do not know me.'

'Not know you – I, who am old, and who have studied all my life men and women; I, who have made my speciality the brain and all that belongs to him and all that follow from him! And I have read your diary that you have so goodly written for me, and which breathes out truth in every line. I, who have read your so sweet letter to poor Lucy of your marriage and your trust, not know you! Oh, Madam Mina, good women tell all their lives, and by day and by hour and by minute, such things that angels can read; and we men who wish to know have in us something of angel's eyes. Your husband is noble nature, and you are noble too, for you trust, and trust cannot be where there is mean nature. And your husband – tell me of him. Is he quite well? Is all that fever gone, and is he strong and hearty?' I saw here an opening to ask him about Jonathan, so I said:–

'He has almost recovered, but he has been greatly upset by Mr Hawkin's death.' He interrupted:–

'Oh yes, I know, I know. I have read your last two letters.' I went on:–

'I suppose this upset him, for when we were in town on Thursday last he had a sort of shock.'

'A shock, and after brain fever so soon! That was not good. What kind of shock was it?'

'He thought he saw someone who recalled something terrible, something which led to his brain fever.' And here the whole thing seemed to overwhelm me in a rush. The pity for Jonathan, the horror which he experienced, the whole fearful mystery of his diary, and the fear that has been brooding over me ever since, all came in a tumult. I suppose I was hysterical, for I threw myself on my knees and held up my hands to him, and implored him to make my husband well again. He took my hands and raised me up, and made me sit on the sofa, and sat by me; he held my hand in his, and said to me with, oh, such infinite sweetness:–

'My life is a barren and lonely one, and so full of work that I have not had much time for friendships; but since I have been summoned to here by my friend John Seward I have known so many good people and seen such nobility that I feel more than ever – and it has grown with my advancing years – the loneliness of my life. Believe me, then, that I come here full of respect for you, and you have given me hope – hope, not in what I am seeking of, but that there are good women still left to make life happy – good women, whose lives and whose truths may make good lesson for the children that are to be. I am glad, glad, that I may here be of some use to you; for if your husband suffer, he suffer within the range of my study and experience. I promise you that I will gladly do *all* for him that I can – all to make his life strong and manly, and your life a happy one. Now you must eat. You are over-wrought and perhaps over-anxious. Husband Jonathan would not like to see you so pale; and what he like not where he love, is not to his good. Therefore for his sake you must eat and smile. You have told me all about Lucy, and so now we shall not speak of it, lest it distress. I shall stay in Exeter to-night, for I want to think over what you have told me, and when I have thought I will ask you questions, if I may. And then, too, you will tell me of husband Jonathan's trouble so far as you can, but not yet. You must eat now; afterwards you shall tell me all.'

After lunch, when we went back to the drawing-room he said to me:–

'And now tell me all about him.' When it came to speaking to this great, learned man, I began to fear that he would think me a weak fool, and Jonathan a madman – that journal is all so strange – and I hesitated to go on. But he was so sweet and kind, and he had promised to help, and I trusted him, so I said:–

'Dr Van Helsing, what I have to tell you is so queer that you must not laugh at me or at my husband. I have been since yesterday in a sort of fever of doubt; you must be kind to me, and not think me foolish that I have even half believed some very strange things.' He reassured me by his manner as well as his words when he said:–

'Oh, my dear, if you only knew how strange is the matter regarding which I am here, it is you who would laugh. I have learned not to think little of any one's belief, no matter how strange it be. I have tried to keep an open mind; and it is not the ordinary things of life that could close it, but the strange things, the extraordinary things, the things that make one doubt if they be mad or sane.'

'Thank you, thank you, a thousand times! You have taken a weight off my mind. If you will let me, I shall give you a paper to read. It is long, but I have typewritten it out. It will tell you my trouble and Jonathan's. It is the copy of his journal when abroad, and all that happened. I dare not say anything of it; you will read for yourself and judge. And then when I see you, perhaps, you will be very kind and tell me what you think.'

'I promise,' he said as I gave him the papers; 'I shall in the morning, so soon as I can, come to see you and your husband, if I may.'

'Jonathan will be here at half-past eleven, and you must come to lunch with us and see him then; you could catch the quick 3.45 train, which will leave you at Paddington before eight.' He was surprised at my knowledge of the trains off-hand, but he does not know that I have made up all the trains to and from Exeter, so that I may help Jonathan in case he is in a hurry.

So he took the papers with him and went away, and I sit here thinking – thinking I don't know what.

Letter (by hand), Van Helsing to Mrs Harker

'*25 September, 6 o'clock.*

'Dear Madam Mina,

'I have read your husband's so wonderful diary. You may sleep without doubt. Strange and terrible as it is, it is *true*! I will pledge my life on it. It may be worse for others; but for him and you there is no dread. He is a noble fellow; and let me tell you from experience of men, that one who would do as he did in going down that wall and to that room – ay, and going a second time – is not one to be injured in permanence by a shock. His brain and his heart are all right; this I swear, before I have even seen him; so be at rest. I shall have much to ask him of other things. I am blessed that to-day I come to see you, for I have learn all at once so much and again I am dazzle – dazzle more than ever, and I must think.

'Yours the most faithful,
'ABRAHAM VAN HELSING.'

Letter, Mrs Harker to Van Helsing

'*25 September, 6.30 p.m.*

'My dear Dr Van Helsing,

'A thousand thanks for your kind letter, which has taken a great weight off my mind. And yet, if it be true, what terrible things there are in the world, and what an awful thing if that man, that monster, be really in London! I fear to think. I have this moment, whilst writing, had a wire from Jonathan saying that he leaves by the 6.25 to-night from Launceston and will be here at 10.18, so that I shall have no fear to-night. Will you therefore, instead of lunching with us, please come to breakfast, at eight o'clock, if this be not too early for you? You can get away, if you are in a hurry, by the 10.30 train, which will bring you to Paddington by 2.35. Do not answer this, as I shall take it that, if I do not hear, you will come to breakfast.

'Believe me,
'Your faithful and grateful friend,
'MINA HARKER.'

152

26 September. – I thought never to write in this diary again, but the time has come. When I got home last night Mina had supper ready, and when we had supped she told me of Van Helsing's visit, and of her having given him the two diaries copied out, and of how anxious she had been about me. She showed me in the doctor's letter that all I wrote down was true. It seems to have made a new man of me. It was the doubt as to the reality of the whole thing that knocked me over. I felt impotent, and in the dark, and distrustful. But, now that I *know*, I am not afraid, even of the Count. He has succeeded after all, then, in his design in getting to London, and it was he I saw. He has got younger, and how? Van Helsing is the man to unmask him and hunt him out, if he is anything like what Mina says. We sat late, and talked it all over. Mina is dressing, and I shall call at the hotel in a few minutes and bring him over. . . .

He was, I think, surprised to see me. When I came into the room where he was, and introduced myself, he took me by the shoulder and turned my face round to the light, and said, after a sharp scrutiny:–

'But Madam Mina told me you were ill, that you had had a shock.' It was so funny to hear my wife called 'Madam Mina' by this kindly, strong-faced old man. I smiled, and said:–

'I *was* ill, I *have* had a shock: but you have cured me already.'

'And how?'

'By your letter to Mina last night. I was in doubt, and then everything took a hue of unreality, and I did not know what to trust, even the evidence of my own senses. Not knowing what to trust, I did not know what to do; and so had only to keep on working in what had hitherto been the groove of my life. The groove ceased to avail me, and I mistrusted myself. Doctor, you don't know what it is to doubt everything, even yourself. No, you don't; you couldn't with eyebrows like yours.' He seemed pleased, and laughed as he said:–

'So! You are physiognomist. I learn more here with each hour. I am with so much pleasure coming to you to breakfast; and, oh, sir, you will pardon praise from an old man, but you are blessed in your wife.' I would listen to him go on praising Mina for a day, so I simply nodded and stood silent.

'She is one of God's women fashioned by His own hand to show us men and other women that there is a heaven where we can enter, and that its light can be here on earth. So true, so sweet, so noble, so little an egoist – and that, let me tell you, is much in this age, so sceptical and selfish. And you, sir – I have read all the letters to poor Miss Lucy and some of them speak of you, so I know you since some days from the knowing of others;

but I have seen your true self since last night. You will give me your hand, will you not? And let us be friends for all our lives.'

We shook hands, and he was so earnest and so kind that it made me quite choky.

'And now,' he said, 'may I ask you for some more help? I have a great task to do, and at the beginning it is to know. You can help me here. Can you tell me what went before your going to Transylvania? Later on I may ask more help and of a different kind; but at first this will do.'

'Look here, sir,' I said, 'does what you have to do concern the Count?'

'It does,' he said solemnly.

'Then I am with you heart and soul. As you go by the 10.30 train, you will not have time to read them; but I shall get the bundle of papers. You can take them with you and read them on the train.'

After breakfast I saw him to the station. When we were parting he said: 'Perhaps you will come to town if I send to you, and take Madam Mina too.'

'We shall both come when you will,' I said.

I had got him the morning papers and the London papers of the previous night, and while we were talking at the carriage window, waiting for the train to start, he was turning them over. His eye suddenly seemed to catch something in one of them, the *Westminster Gazette* – I knew it by the colour – and he grew quite white. He read something intently, groaning to himself: 'Mein Gott! Mein Gott! So soon! so soon!' I do not think he remembered me at the moment. Just then the whistle blew, and the train moved off. This recalled him to himself, and he leaned out of the window and waved his hand, calling out: 'Love to Madam Mina; I shall write so soon as ever I can.'

DR SEWARD'S DIARY

26 September. – Truly there is no such thing as finality. Not a week since I said 'Finis', and yet here I am starting fresh again, or rather going on with the same record. Until this afternoon I had no cause to think of what is done. Renfield had become, to all intents, as sane as he ever was. He was already well ahead with his fly business; and he had just started in the spider line also; so he had not been any trouble to me. I had a letter from Arthur, written on Sunday, and from it I gather that he is bearing up wonderfully well. Quincey Morris is with him, and that is much of a help, for he himself is a bubbling well of good spirits. Quincey wrote me a line too, and from him I hear that Arthur is beginning to recover something of his old buoyancy; so as to them all my mind is at rest. As for myself, I was settling down to my work with the enthusiasm which I used to have for it, so that I might fairly have said that the wound which poor Lucy left on me was becoming cicatrized. Everything is, however, now reopened; and what is to be the end God only knows. I have an idea that Van Helsing thinks he knows too, but he will only let out enough at a time to whet curiosity. He went to Exeter yesterday, and stayed there all night. To-day he came back, and almost bounded into my room at about half-past five o'clock, and thrust last night's *Westminster Gazette* into my hand.

'What do you think of that?' he asked as he stood back and folded his arms.

I looked over the paper, for I really did not know what he meant; but he took it from me and pointed out a paragraph about children being decoyed away at Hampstead. It did not convey much to me, until I reached a passage where it described small punctured wounds on their throats. An idea struck me, and I looked up. 'Well?' he said.

'It is like poor Lucy's.'

'And what do make of it?'

'Simply that there is some cause in common. Whatever it was that injured her has injured them.' I did not quite understand his answer:–

'That is true indirectly, but not directly.'

'How do you mean, Professor?' I asked. I was a little inclined to take his seriousness lightly – for, after all, four days of rest and freedom from burning, harrowing anxiety does help to restore one's spirits – but when I saw his face it sobered me. Never, even in the midst of our despair about poor Lucy, had he looked more stern.

'Tell me!' I said. 'I can hazard no opinion. I do not know what to think, and I have no data on which to found a conjecture.'

'Do you mean to tell me, friend John, that you have no suspicion as to what poor Lucy died of; not after all the hints given, not only by events, but by me?'

'Of nervous prostration following on great loss or waste of blood.'

'And how the blood lost or waste?' I shook my head. He stepped over and sat down beside me, and went on:–

'You are clever man, friend John; you reason well, and your wit is bold; but you are too prejudiced. You do not let your eyes see nor your ears hear, and that which is outside your daily life is not of account to you. Do you not think that there are things which you cannot understand, and yet which are; that some people see things that others cannot? But there are things old and new which must not be contemplate by men's eyes, because they know – or think they know – some things which other men have told them. Ah, it is the fault of our science that it wants to explain all; and if it explain not, then it says there is nothing to explain. But yet we see around us every day the growth of new beliefs, which think themselves new; and which are yet but the old, which pretend to be young – like the fine ladies at the opera. I suppose now you do not believe in corporeal transference. No? Nor in materialization. No? Nor in astral bodies. No? Nor in the reading of thought. No? Nor in hypnotism –'

'Yes,' I said. 'Charcot has proved that pretty well.' He smiled as he went on: 'Then you are satisfied as to it. Yes? And of course then you understand how it act, and can follow the mind of the great Charcot – alas that he is no more! – into the very soul of the patient that he influence. No? Then, friend John, am I to take it that you simply accept fact, and are satisfied to let from premise to conclusion be a blank? No? Then tell me – for I am student of the brain – how you accept the hypnotism and reject the thought-reading. Let me tell you, my friend, that there are things done to-day in electrical science which would have been deemed unholy by the very men who discovered electricity – who would themselves not so long before have been burned as wizards. There are always mysteries in life. Why was it that Methuselah lived nine hundred years, and "Old Parr" one hundred and sixty-nine, and yet that poor Lucy, with four men's blood in her poor veins, could not live even one day! For, had she lived one more day, we could have save her. Do you know all the mystery of life and death? Do you know the altogether of comparative anatomy, and can say wherefore the qualities of brutes are in some men, and not in others? Can you tell me why, when other spiders die small and soon, that one great spider lived for centuries in the tower of the old Spanish church and grew and grew, till, on descending, he could drink the oil of all the church lamps? Can you tell me why in the Pampas, ay and elsewhere, there are bats that come at night and open the veins of cattle and horses and suck dry their veins; how in some islands of the Western seas there are bats which hang on the trees all day, that those who have seen describe as like giant nuts or pods, and that when the sailors sleep on the deck, because that it is hot, flit down on them, and then – and then in the morning are found dead men, white as even Miss Lucy was?'

'Good God, Professor!' I said, starting up. 'Do you mean to tell me that Lucy was bitten by such a bat; and that such a thing is here in London in the nineteenth century?' He waved his hand for silence, and went on:–

'Can you tell me why the tortoise lives more long than generations of men; why the elephant goes on and on till he have seen dynasties; and why the parrot never die only of bite of cat or dog or other complaint? Can you tell me why men believe in all ages and places that there are some few who live on always if they be permit; that there are men and women who cannot die? We all know – because science has vouched for the fact – that there have been toads shut up in rocks for thousands of years, shut in one so small hole that only hold him since the youth of the world. Can you tell me how the Indian fakir can make himself to die and have been buried, and his grave sealed and corn sowed on it, and the corn reaped and be cut and sown and reaped and cut again, and then men come and take away the unbroken seal, and that there lie the Indian fakir, not dead, but that rise up and walk amongst them as before?' Here I interrupted him. I was getting bewildered; he so crowded on my mind his list of nature's eccentricities and possible impossibilities that my imagination was getting fired. I had a dim idea that he was teaching me some lesson, as long ago he used to do in his study at Amsterdam; but he used then to tell me the thing, so that I could have the object of thought in mind all the time. But now I was without his help, yet I wanted to follow him, so I said:

'Professor, let me be your pet student again. Tell me the thesis, so that I may apply your knowledge as you go on. At present I am going in my mind from point to point as a mad man, and not a sane one, follows an idea. I feel like a novice blundering through a bog in a mist, jumping from one tussock to another in the mere blind effort to move on without knowing where I am going.'

'That is good image,' he said. 'Well, I shall tell you. My thesis is this: I want you to believe.'

'To believe what?'

'To believe in things that you cannot. Let me illustrate. I heard once of an American who so defined faith: "that which enables us to believe things which we know to be untrue". For one, I follow that man. He meant that we shall have an open mind, and not let a little bit of truth check the rush of a big truth, like a small rock does a railway truck. We get the small truth first. Good! We keep him, and we value him; but all the same we must not let him think himself all the truth in the universe.'

'Then you want me not to let some previous conviction injure the receptivity of my mind with regard to some strange matter. Do I read your lesson aright?'

'Ah, you are my favourite pupil still. It is worth to teach you. Now that you are willing to understand, you have taken the first step to understand. You think then that those so small holes in the children's throats were made by the same that made the hole in Miss Lucy?'

'I suppose so.' He stood up and said solemnly:—

'Then you are wrong. Oh, would it were so! but alas! no. It is worse, far, far worse.'

'In God's name, Professor Van Helsing, what do you mean?' I cried.

He threw himself with a despairing gesture into a chair, and placed his elbows on the table, covering his face with his hands as he spoke:— 'They were made by Miss Lucy!'

157

15

DR SEWARD'S DIARY

(continued)

For a while sheer anger mastered me; it was as if he had during her life struck Lucy on the face. I smote the table hard and rose up as I said to him:–

'Dr Van Helsing, are you mad?' He raised his head and looked at me, and somehow the tenderness of his face calmed me at once. 'Would I were!' he said. 'Madness were easy to bear compared with truth like this. Oh, my friend, why, think you, did I go so far round; why take so long to tell you so simple a thing? Was it because I hate you and have hated you all my life? Was it because I wished to give you pain? Was it that I wanted, now so late, revenge for that time when you saved my life, and from a fearful death? Ah no!'

'Forgive me,' said I. He went on:–

'My friend, it was because I wished to be gentle in the breaking to you, for I know that you have loved that so sweet lady. But even yet I do not expect you to believe. It is so hard to accept at once any abstract truth, that we may doubt such to be possible when we have always believed the "no" of it; it is more hard still to accept so sad a concrete truth, and of such a one as Miss Lucy. To-night I go to prove it. Dare you come with me?'

This staggered me. A man does not like to prove such a truth; Byron excepted from the category, jealousy.

'And prove the very truth he most abhorred.'

He saw my hesitation, and spoke:–

'The logic is simple, no madman's logic this time, jumping from tussock to tussock in a misty fog. If it be not true, then proof will be relief; at worst it will not harm. If it be true! Ah, there is the dread; yet very dread should help my cause, for in it is some need of belief. Come, I tell you what I propose: first, that we go off now and see that child in the hospital. Dr Vincent of the North Hospital, where the papers say the child is, is friend of mine, and I think of yours since you were in class at Amsterdam. He will let two scientists see his case, if he will not let two friends. We shall tell him nothing, but only that we wish to learn. And then – '

'And then?' He took a key from his pocket and held it up.

'And then we spend the night, you and I, in the churchyard where Lucy lies. This is the key that lock the tomb. I had it from the coffin-man to give to Arthur.' My heart sank within me, for I felt that there were some fearful ordeal before us. I could do nothing, however, so I plucked up what heart I could and said that we had better hasten, as the afternoon was passing. . . .

We found the child awake. It had had a sleep and taken some food, and altogether was going on well. Dr Vincent took the bandage from its throat, and showed us the punctures. There was no mistaking the similarity to those which had been on Lucy's throat. They were smaller, and the edges looked fresher; that was all. We asked Vincent to what he attributed them, and he replied that it must have been a bite of some animal, perhaps a rat; but, for his own part, he was inclined to think that it was one of the bats which are so numerous on the northern heights of London. 'Out of so many harmless ones,' he said, 'there may be some wild specimen from the South of a more malignant species. Some sailor may have brought one home, and it managed to escape; or even from the Zoological Gardens a young one may have got loose, or one be bred there from a vampire. These things do occur, you know. Only ten days ago a wolf got out, and was, I believe, traced up in this direction. For a week after, the children were playing nothing but Red Riding Hood on the Heath and in every alley in the place until this "bloofer lady" scare came along, since when it has been quite a gala-time with them. Even this poor little mite, when he woke up to-day, asked the nurse if he might go away. When she asked him why he wanted to go, he said wanted to play with the "bloofer lady".'

'I hope,' said Van Helsing, 'that when you are sending the child home you will caution its parents to keep strict watch over it. These fancies to stray are most dangerous; and if the child were to remain out another night, it would probably be fatal. But in any case I suppose you will not let it away for some days?'

'Certainly not, not for a week at least; longer if the wound is not healed.'

Our visit to the hospital took more time than we had reckoned on, and the sun had dipped before we came out. When Van Helsing saw how dark it was, he said:—

'There is no hurry. It is more late than I thought. Come, let us seek somewhere that we may eat, and then we shall go on our way.'

We dined at 'Jack Straw's Castle' along with a little crowd of bicyclists and others who were genially noisy. About ten o'clock we started from the inn. It was then very dark, and the scattered lamps made the darkness greater when we were once outside their individual radius. The Professor had evidently noted the road we were to go, for he went on unhesitatingly; but as for me, I was in quite a mix-up as to locality. As we went further, we met fewer and fewer people, till at last we were somewhat surprised when we met even the patrol of horse police going their usual suburban round. At last we reached the wall of the churchyard, which we climbed over. With some little difficulty – for it was very dark, and the whole place seemed so strange to us – we found the Westenra tomb. The Professor took the key, opened the creaky door, and standing back, politely, but quite unconsciously, motioned me to precede him. There was a delicious irony in the offer, in the courtliness of giving preference on such a ghastly occasion. My companion followed me quickly, and cautiously drew the door to, after carefully ascertaining that the lock was a falling, and not a spring one. In the latter case we should have been in a bad plight. Then he fumbled in his bag, and taking out a match-box and a piece of candle, proceeded to make a light. The tomb in the daytime, and when wreathed with fresh flowers, had looked grim and gruesome enough; but now some days afterwards, when the flowers hung lank and dead, their whites turning to rust and their greens to browns; when the spider and the beetle had resumed their accustomed dominance; when time-discoloured stone, and dust-encrusted mortar, and rusty, dank iron, and tarnished brass and clouded silver-plating gave back the feeble glimmer of a candle, the effect was more miserable and sordid than could have been imagined. It conveyed irresistibly the idea that life – animal life – was not the only thing which could pass away.

Van Helsing went about his work systematically. Holding his candle so that he could read the coffin plates, and so holding it that the sperm dropped in white patches which congealed as they touched the metal, he made assurance of Lucy's coffin. Another search in his bag, and he took out a turnscrew.

'What are you going to do?' I asked.

'To open the coffin. You shall yet be convinced.' Straightway he began taking out the screws, and finally lifted off the lid, showing the casing of lead beneath. The sight was almost too much for me. It seemed to be as much an affront to the dead as it would have been to have stripped off her clothing in her sleep whilst living; I actually took hold of his hand to stop him. He only said: 'You shall see,' and again fumbling in his bag, took out a tiny fret-saw. Striking the turnscrew through the lead with a swift downward stab, which made me wince, he made a small hole, which was, however, big enough to admit the point of the saw. I had expected a rush of gas from the week-old corpse. We doctors, who have had to study our dangers, have to become accustomed to such things, and I drew back towards the door. But the Professor never stopped for a moment; he sawed down a couple of feet along one side of the lead coffin, and then across, and down the other side. Taking the edge of the loose flange, he bent it back towards the foot of the coffin, and holding up the candle into the aperture, motioned to me to look.

I drew near and looked. The coffin was empty.

It was certainly a surprise to me, and gave me a considerable shock, but Van Helsing was unmoved. He was now more sure than ever of his ground, and so emboldened to proceed in his task. 'Are you satisfied now, friend John?' he asked.

I felt all the dogged argumentativeness of my nature awake within me as I answered him:

'I am satisfied that Lucy's body is not in that coffin; but that only proves one thing.'

'And what is that, friend John?'

'That it is not there.'

'That is good logic,' he said, 'so far as it goes. But how do you – how can you – account for it not being there?'

'Perhaps a body-snatcher,' I suggested. 'Some of the undertaker's people may have stolen it.' I felt that I was speaking folly, and yet it was the only real cause which I could suggest. The Professor sighed. 'Ah well!' he said, 'we must have more proof. Come with me.'

He put on the coffin-lid again, gathered up all his things and placed them in the bag, blew out the light, and placed the candle also in the bag. We opened the door, and went out. Behind us he closed the door and locked it. He handed me the key, saying: 'Will you keep it? You had better be assured.' I laughed – it was not a very cheerful laugh, I am bound to say – as I motioned him to keep it. 'A key is nothing,' I said; 'there may be duplicates; and anyhow it is not difficult to pick a lock of that kind.' He said nothing, but put the key in his pocket. Then he told me to watch at one side of the churchyard whilst he could watch at the other. I took up my place behind a yew-tree, and I saw his dark figure move until the intervening headstones and trees hid it from my sight.

It was a lonely vigil. Just after I had taken my place I heard a distant clock strike twelve, and in time came one and two. I was chilled and unnerved, and angry with the Professor for taking me on such an errand and with myself for coming. I was too cold and too sleepy to be keenly observant, and not sleepy enough to betray my trust; so altogether I had a dreary, miserable time.

Suddenly, as I turned round, I thought I saw something like a white streak, moving between two dark yew-trees at the side of the churchyard farthest from the tomb; at the same time a dark mass moved from the Professor's side of the ground, and hurriedly went towards it. Then I too moved; but I had to go round headstones and railed-off tombs, and I stumbled over graves. The sky was overcast, and somewhere far off an early cock crew. A little way off, beyond the line of scattered juniper-trees, which marked the pathway to the church, a white, dim figure flitted in the direction of the tomb. The tomb itself was hidden by trees, and I could not see where the figure disappeared. I heard the rustle of actual movement where I had first seen the white figure, and coming over, found the Professor holding in his arms a tiny child. When he saw me he held it out to me, and said:—

'Are you satisfied now?'

'No,' I said, in a way that I felt was aggressive.

'Do you not see the child?'

'Yes, it is a child, but who brought it here? And is it wounded?' I asked.

'We shall see,' said the Professor, and with one impulse we took our way out of the churchyard, he carrying the sleeping child.

When we had got some little distance away, we went into a clump of trees, and struck a match, and looked at the child's throat. It was without a scratch or scar of any kind.

'Was I right?' I asked triumphantly.

'We were just in time,' said the Professor thankfully.

We had now to decide what we were to do with the child, and so consulted about it. If we were to take it to a police station we should have to give some account of our movements during the night; at least, we should have had to make some statement as to how we had come to find the child. So finally we decided that we would take it to the Heath, and when we heard a policeman coming, would leave it where he could not fail to find it; we would then seek our way home as quickly as we could. All fell out well. At the edge of Hampstead Heath we heard a policeman's heavy tramp, and laying the child on the pathway, we waited and watched until he saw it as he flashed his lantern to and fro. We heard his exclamation of astonishment, and then we went away silently. By good chance we got a cab near the 'Spaniards', and drove to town.

I cannot sleep, so I make this entry. But I must try to get a few hours' sleep, as Van Helsing is to call for me at noon. He insists that I shall go with him on another expedition.

27 September. – It was two o'clock before we found a suitable opportunity for our attempt. The funeral held at noon was all completed, and the last stragglers of the mourners had taken themselves lazily away, when, looking carefully from behind a clump of alder-trees, we saw the sexton lock the gate after him. We knew then that we were safe till morning did we desire it; but the Professor told me that we should not want more than an hour at most. Again I felt that horrid sense of the reality of things, in which any effort of imagination seemed out of place; and I realized distinctly the perils of the law which we were incurring in our unhallowed work. Besides, I felt it was all so useless. Outrageous as it was to open a leaden coffin, to see if a woman dead nearly a week were really dead, it now seemed the height of folly to open the tomb again, when we knew, from the evidence of our own eyesight, that the coffin was empty. I shrugged my shoulders, however, and rested silent, for Van Helsing had a way of going on his own road, no matter who remonstrated. He took the key, opened the vault, and again courteously motioned me to precede. The place was not so gruesome as last night, but oh, how unutterably mean-looking when the sunshine streamed in. Van Helsing walked over to Lucy's coffin, and I followed. He bent over and again forced back the leaden flange; and then a shock of surprise and dismay shot through me.

There lay Lucy, seemingly just as we had seen her the night before her funeral. She was, if possible, more radiantly beautiful than ever; and I could not believe that she was dead. The lips were red, nay redder than before; and on the cheeks was a delicate bloom.

'Is this a juggle?' I said to him.

'Are you convinced now?' said the Professor in response, and as he spoke he put over his hand, and in a way that made me shudder, pulled back the dead lips and showed the white teeth.

'See,' he went on, 'see, they are even sharper than before. With this and this' – and he touched one of the canine teeth and that below it – 'the little children can be bitten. Are you of belief now, friend John?' Once more, argumentative hostility woke within me. I *could* not accept such an overwhelming idea as he suggested; so, with an attempt to argue of which I was even at the moment ashamed, I said:–

'She may have been placed here since last night.'

'Indeed? That is so, and by whom?'

'I do not know. Someone has done it.'

'And yet she has been dead one week. Most peoples in that time would not look so.' I had no answer for this, so was silent. Van Helsing did not seem to notice my silence; at any rate, he showed neither chagrin nor triumph. He was looking intently at the face of the dead woman, raising the eyelids and looking at the eyes, and once more opening the lips and examining the teeth. Then he turned to me and said:–

'Here, there is one thing which is different from all recorded: here is some dual life that is not as the common. She was bitten by the vampire when she was in a trance, sleep-walking – oh, you start, you do not know that, friend John, but you shall know it all later – and in trance could he best come to take more blood. In trance she died, and in trance she is Un-Dead, too. So it is that she differ from all other. Usually when the Un-Dead sleep at home' – as he spoke he made a comprehensive sweep of his arm to designate what to a vampire was 'home' – 'their face show what they are, but this so sweet that-was when she not Un-Dead she go back to the nothings of the common dead. There is no malign there, see, and so it make hard that I must kill her in her sleep.' This turned my blood cold, and it began to dawn upon me that I was accepting Van Helsing's theories; but if she were really dead, what was there of terror in the idea of killing her? He looked up at me, and evidently saw the change in my face, for he said almost joyously:–

'Ah, you believe now?'

I answered: 'Do not press me too hard all at once. I am willing to accept. How will you do this bloody work?'

'I shall cut off her head and fill her mouth with garlic, and I shall drive a stake through her body.' It made me shudder to think of so mutilating the body of the woman whom I had loved. And yet the feeling was not so strong as I had expected. I was, in fact, beginning to shudder at the presence of this being, this Un-Dead, as Van Helsing called it, and to loathe it. Is it possible that love is all subjective, or all objective?

I waited a considerable time for Van Helsing to begin, but he stood as if wrapped in thought. Presently he closed the catch of his bag with a snap, and said:–

'I have been thinking, and have made up my mind as to what is best. If I did simply follow my inclining I would do now, at this moment, what is to be done; but there are other things to follow, and things that are thousand times more difficult in that them we do not know. This is simple. She have yet no life taken, though that is of time; and to act now would be to take danger from her for ever. But then we may have to want Arthur, and how shall we tell him of this? If you, who saw the wounds on Lucy's throat, and saw the wounds so similar on the child's at the hospital; if you, who saw the coffin empty last night and full to-day with a woman who have not change only to be more rose and more beautiful in a whole week after she die – if you know of this and know of the white figure last night that brought the child to the churchyard, and yet of your own senses you did not believe, how, then, can I expect Arthur, who know none of those things, to believe? He doubted me when I took him from her kiss when she was dying. I know he has forgiven me because in some mistaken idea I have done things that prevent him say good-bye as he ought; and he may think that in some more mistaken idea this woman was buried alive; and that in most mistake of all we have killed her. He will then argue back that it is we, mistaken ones, that have killed her by our ideas; and so he will be much unhappy always. Yet he never can be sure; and that is the worst of all. And he will sometimes think that she he loved was buried alive, and that will paint his dreams with horrors of what she must have suffered;

and, again, he will think that we may be right, and that his so beloved was, after all, an Un-Dead. No! I told him once, and since then I learn much. Now, since I know it is all true, a hundred thousand times more do I know that he must pass through the bitter waters to reach the sweet. He, poor fellow, must have one hour that will make the very face of heaven grow black to him; then we can act for good all round and send him peace. My mind is made up. Let us go. You return home for to-night to your asylum, and see that all be well. As for me, I shall spend the night here in this churchyard in my own way. To-morrow night you will come to me to the Berkeley Hotel at ten of the clock. I shall send for Arthur to come too, and also that so fine young man of America that gave his blood. Later we shall all have work to do. I come with you so far as Piccadilly and there dine, for I must be back here before the sun set.'

So we locked the tomb and came away, and got over the wall of the churchyard, which was not much of a task, and drove back to Piccadilly.

Note left by Van Helsing in his portmanteau, Berkeley Hotel, directed to John Seward, M.D.
(Not delivered)

'*27 September.*

'Friend John,–

'I write this in case anything should happen. I go alone to watch in that churchyard. It pleases me that the Un-Dead, Miss Lucy, shall not leave to-night, that so on the morrow night she may be more eager. Therefore I shall fix some things she like not – garlic and a crucifix – and so seal up the door of the tomb. She is young as Un-Dead, and will heed. Moreover, these are only to prevent her coming out; they may not prevail on her wanting to get in; for then the Un-Dead is desperate, and must find the line of least resistance, whatsoever it may be. I shall be at hand all the night from sunset till after the sunrise, and if there be aught that may be learned I shall learn it. For Miss Lucy, or from her, I have no fear: but that other to whom is there that she is Un-Dead, he have now the power to seek her tomb and find shelter. He is cunning, as I know from Mr Jonathan and from the way that all along he have fooled us when he played with us for Miss Lucy's life, and we lost; and in many ways the Un-Dead are strong. He have always the strength in his hand of twenty men; even we four who gave our strength to Miss Lucy it also is all to him. Besides, he can summon his wolf and I know not what. So if it be that he come thither on this night he shall find me; but none other shall – until it be too late. But it may be that he will not attempt the place. There is no reason why he should; his hunting ground is more full of game than the churchyard where the Un-Dead woman sleep, and one old man watch.

'Therefore I write this in case. . . . Take the papers that are with this, the diaries of Harker and the rest, and read them, and then find this great Un-Dead, and cut off his head and burn his heart or drive a stake through it, so that the world may rest from him.

'If it be so, farewell.

'VAN HELSING.'

DR SEWARD'S DIARY

28 September. – It is wonderful what a good night's sleep will do for one. Yesterday I was almost willing to accept Van Helsing's monstrous ideas; but now they seem to start out lurid before me as outrages on common sense. I have no doubt that he believes it all. I wonder if his mind can have become in any way unhinged. Surely there must be *some* rational explanation of all these mysterious things. Is it possible that the Professor can have done it himself? He is so abnormally clever that if he went off his head he would carry out his intent with regard to some fixed idea in a wonderful way. I am loath to think it, and indeed it would be almost as great a marvel as the other to find that Van Helsing was mad; but anyhow I shall watch him carefully. I may get some light on the mystery.

29 September, morning. . . . . Last night, at a little before ten o'clock, Arthur and Quincey came into Van Helsing's room; he told us all what he wanted us to do, but especially addressing himself to Arthur, as if all our wills were centred in his. He began by saying that he hoped we would all come with him too, 'for,' he said, 'there is a grave duty to be done there. You were doubtless surprised at my letter?' This query was directly addressed to Lord Godalming.

'I was. It rather upset me for a bit. There has been so much trouble around my house of late that I could do without any more. I have been curious, too, as to what you mean. Quincey and I talked it over; but the more we talked, the more puzzled we got, till now I can say for myself that I'm about up a tree as to any meaning about anything.'

'Me, too,' said Quincey Morris laconically.

'Oh,' said the Professor, 'then you are nearer the beginning, both of you, than friend John here, who has to go a long way back before he can even get so far as to begin.'

It was evident that he recognized my return to my old doubting frame of mind without my saying a word. Then, turning to the other two, he said with intense gravity:–

'I want your permission to do what I think good this night. It is, I know, much to ask; and when you know what it is I propose to do you will know, and only then, how much. Therefore may I ask that you promise me in the dark, so that afterwards, though you may be angry with me for a time – I must not disguise from myself the possibility that such may be – you shall not blame yourselves for anything.'

'That's frank anyhow,' broke in Quincey. 'I'll answer for the Professor. I don't quite see his drift, but I swear he's honest; and that's good enough for me.'

'I thank you, sir,' said Van Helsing proudly. 'I have done myself the honour of counting you one trusting friend, and such endorsement is dear to me.' He held out a hand, which Quincey took.

Then Arthur spoke out:–

'Dr Van Helsing, I don't quite like to buy a "pig in a poke", as they say in Scotland, and if it be anything in which my honour as a gentleman or my faith as a Christian is concerned, I cannot make such a promise. If you can assure me that what you intend does not violate either of these two, then I give my consent at once; though, for the life of me, I cannot understand what you are driving at.'

'I accept your limitation,' said Van Helsing, 'and all I ask of you is that if you feel it necessary to condemn any act of mine, you will first consider it well and be satisfied that it does not violate your reservations.'

'Agreed!' said Arthur; 'that is only fair. And now that the *pourparlers* are over, may I ask what it is we are to do?'

'I want you to come with me, and to come in secret, to the churchyard at Kingstead.'

Arthur's face fell as he said in an amazed sort of way:–

'Where poor Lucy is buried?' The Professor bowed. Arthur went on: 'And when there?'

'To enter the tomb!' Arthur stood up.

'Professor, are you in earnest; or is it some monstrous joke? Pardon me, I see that you are in earnest.' He sat down again, but I could see that he sat firmly and proudly, as one who is on his dignity. There was silence until he asked again:–

'And when in the tomb?'

'To open the coffin.'

'This is too much!' he said, angrily rising again. 'I am willing to be patient in all things that are reasonable; but in this – this desecration of the grave – of one who – ' He fairly choked with indignation. The Professor looked pityingly at him.

'If I could spare you one pang, my poor friend,' he said, 'God knows I would. But this night our feet must tread in thorny paths; or later, and for ever, the feet you love must walk in paths of flame!'

Arthur looked up with set, white face and said:–

'Take care, sir, take care!'

'Would it not be well to hear what I have to say?' said Van Helsing. 'And then you will at least know the limit of my purpose. Shall I go on?'

'That's fair enough,' broke in Morris.

After a pause Van Helsing went on, evidently with an effort:–

'Miss Lucy is dead; is it not so? Then there can be no wrong to her. But if she be not dead – '

Arthur jumped to his feet.

'Good God!' he cried. 'What do you mean? Has there been any mistake; has she been buried alive?' He groaned in anguish that not even hope could soften.

'I did not say she was alive, my child; I did not think it. I go no further than to say that she might be Un-Dead.'

'Un-Dead! Not alive! What do you mean? Is this all a nightmare, or what is it?'

'There are mysteries which men can only guess at, which age by age they may solve only in part. Believe me, we are now on the verge of one. But I have not done. May I cut off the head of dead Miss Lucy?'

'Heavens and earth, no!' cried Arthur in a storm of passion. 'Not for the wide world will I consent to any mutilation of her dead body. Dr Van Helsing, you try me too far. What have I done to you that you should torture me so? What did that poor, sweet girl do that you should want to cast such dishonour on her grave? Are you mad that speak such things, or am I mad that listen to them? Don't dare to think more of such a desecration; I shall not give my consent to anything you do. I have a duty to do in protecting her grave from outrage; and, by God, I shall do it!'

Van Helsing rose up from where he had all the time been seated, and said, gravely and sternly:–

'My Lord Godalming, I, too, have a duty to do, a duty to others, a duty to you, a duty to the dead; and, by God, I shall do it! All I ask you now is that you come with me, that you look and listen; and if when later I make the same request you do not be more eager for its fulfilment even than I am, then – then I shall do my duty, whatever it may seem to me. And then, to follow of your Lordship's wishes, I shall hold myself at your disposal to render an account to you, when and where you will.' His voice broke a little, and he went on with an accent full of pity:–

'But, I beseech you, do not go forth in anger with me. In a long life of acts which were often not pleasant to do, and which sometimes did wring my heart, I have never had so heavy a task as now. Believe me that if the time comes for you to change your mind towards me, one look from you will wipe away all this so sad hour, for I would do what a man can to save you from sorrow. Just think. For why should I give myself so much of labour and so much of sorrow? I have come here from my own land to do what I can of good; at the first to please my friend John, and then to help a sweet young lady, whom, too, I came to love. For her – I am ashamed to say so much, but I say it in kindness – I gave what you gave: the blood of my veins; I gave it, I, who was not, like you, her lover, but only her physician and her friend. I gave to her my nights and days – before death, after death; and if my death can do her good even now, when she is the dead Un-Dead, she shall have it freely.' He said this with a very grave, sweet pride, and Arthur was much affected by it. He took the old man's hand and said in a broken voice:–

'Oh, it is hard to think of it, and I cannot understand; but at least I will go with you and wait.'

16

DR SEWARD'S DIARY

(continued)

It was just a quarter before twelve o'clock when we got into the churchyard over the low wall. The night was dark, with occasional gleams of moonlight between the rents of the heavy clouds that scudded across the sky. We all kept somehow close together, with Van Helsing slightly in front as he led the way. When we had come close to the tomb I looked well at Arthur, for I feared that the proximity to a place laden with so sorrowful a memory would upset him; but he bore himself well. I took it that the very mystery of the proceeding tended in some way to counteract his grief. The Professor unlocked the door, and seeing a natural hesitation amongst us for various reasons, solved the difficulty by entering first himself. The rest of us followed, and he closed the door. He then lit a dark lantern and pointed to the coffin. Arthur stepped forward hesitatingly; Van Helsing said to me:–

'You were with me here yesterday. Was the body of Miss Lucy in that coffin?'

'It was.' The Professor turned to the rest, saying:–

'You hear; and yet there is one who does not believe with me.' He took his screwdriver and again took off the lid of the coffin. Arthur looked on, very pale but silent; when the lid was removed he stepped forward. He evidently did not know that there was a leaden coffin, or, at any rate, had not thought of it. When he saw the rent in the lead, the blood rushed to his face for an instant, but as quickly fell away again, so that he remained of a ghastly whiteness; he was still silent. Van Helsing forced back the leaden flange, and we all looked in and recoiled.

The coffin was empty!

For several minutes no one spoke a word. The silence was broken by Quincey Morris:—

'Professor, I answered for you. Your word is all I want. I wouldn't ask such a thing ordinarily – I wouldn't so dishonour you as to imply a doubt; but this is a mystery that goes beyond any honour or dishonour. Is this your doing?'

'I swear to you by all that I hold sacred that I have not removed nor touched her. What happened was this: Two nights ago my friend Seward and I came here – with good purpose, believe me. I opened that coffin, which was then sealed up, and we found it, as now, empty. We then waited, and saw something white come through the trees. The next day we came here in daytime, and she lay there. Did she not, friend John?'

'Yes.'

'That night we were just in time. One more so small child was missing, and we find it, thank God, unharmed amongst the graves. Yesterday I came here before sundown, for at sundown the Un-Dead can move. I waited here all the night till the sun rose, but I saw nothing. It was most probable that it was because I had laid over the clamps of those doors garlic, which the Un-Dead cannot bear, and other things which they shun. Last night there was no exodus, so to-night before the sundown I took away my garlic and other things. And so it is we find this coffin empty. But bear with me. So far there is much that is strange. Wait you with me outside, unseen and unheard, and things much stranger are yet to be. So' – here he shut the dark slide of his lantern – 'now to the outside.' He opened the door, and we filed out, he coming last and locking the door behind him.

Oh! but it seemed fresh and pure in the night air after the terror of that vault. How sweet it was to see the clouds race by, and the brief gleams of the moonlight between the scudding clouds crossing and passing – like the gladness and sorrow of a man's life; how sweet it was to breathe the fresh air, that had no taint of death and decay; how humanizing to see the red lighting of the sky beyond the hill, and to hear far away the muffled roar that marks the life of a great city. Each in his own way was solemn and overcome. Arthur was silent, and was, I could see, striving to grasp the purpose and the inner meaning of the mystery. I was myself tolerably patient, and half inclined again to throw aside doubt and to accept Van Helsing's conclusions. Quincey Morris was phlegmatic in the way of a man who accepts all things, and accepts them in the spirit of cool bravery, with hazard of all he has to stake. Not being able to smoke, he cut himself a good-sized plug of tobacco and began to chew. As to Van Helsing, he was employed in a definite way. First he took from his bag a mass of what looked like thin, wafer-like biscuit, which was carefully rolled up in a white napkin; next he took out a double-handful of some whitish stuff, like dough or putty. He crumbled the wafer up fine and worked it into the mass between his hands. This he then took, and rolling it into thin strips, began to lay them into the crevices between the door and its setting in the tomb. I was somewhat puzzled at this, and being close, asked him what it was that he was doing. Arthur and Quincey drew near also, as they too were curious. He answered:–

'I am closing the tomb, so that the Un-Dead may not enter.'

'And is that stuff you have put there going to do it?' asked Quincey. 'Great Scott! Is this a game?'

'It is.'

'What is that which you are using?' This time the question was by Arthur. Van Helsing reverently lifted his hat as he answered:–

'The Host. I brought it from Amsterdam. I have an Indulgence.' It was an answer that appalled the most sceptical of us, and we felt individually that in the presence of such earnest purpose as the Professor's, a purpose which could thus use the to him most sacred of things, it was impossible to distrust. In respectful silence we took the places assigned to us close round the tomb, but hidden from the sight of anyone approaching. I pitied the others, especially Arthur. I had myself been apprenticed by my former visits to this watching horror; and yet I, who had up to an hour ago repudiated the proofs, felt my heart sink within me. Never did tombs look so ghastly white; never did cypress, or yew, or juniper so seem the embodiment of funeral gloom; never did tree or grass wave or rustle so ominously; never did bough creak so mysteriously; and never did the far-away howling of dogs send such a woeful presage through the night.

There was a long spell of silence, a big, aching void, and then from the Professor a keen 'S-s-s-s!' He pointed; and far down the avenue of yews we saw a white figure advance – a dim white figure, which held something dark at its breast. The figure stopped, and at the moment a ray of moonlight fell between the masses of driving clouds and showed in startling prominence a dark-haired woman, dressed in the cerements of the grave. We could not see the face, for it was bent down over what we saw to be a fair-haired child. There was a pause and a sharp little cry, such as a child gives in sleep, or a dog as it lies before the fire and dreams. We were starting forward, but the Professor's warning hand, seen by us as he stood behind a yew-tree, kept us back; and then as we looked the white figure moved forward again. It was now near enough for us to see clearly, and the moonlight still held. My own heart grew cold as ice, and I could hear the gasp of Arthur as we recognized the features of Lucy Westenra. Lucy Westenra, but yet how changed. The sweetness was turned to adamantine, heartless cruelty, and the purity to voluptuous wantonness. Van Helsing stepped out, and, obedient to his gesture, we all advanced too; the four of us ranged in a line before the door of the tomb. Van Helsing raised his lantern and drew the slide; by the concentrated light that fell on Lucy's face we could see that the lips were crimson with fresh blood, and that the stream had trickled over her chin and stained the purity of her lawn death-robe.

We shuddered with horror. I could see by the tremulous light that even Van Helsing's iron nerve had failed. Arthur was next to me, and if I had not seized his arm and held him up, he would have fallen.

When Lucy – I call the thing that was before us Lucy because it bore her shape – saw us she drew back with an angry snarl, such as a cat gives when taken unawares; then her eyes ranged over us. Lucy's eyes in form and colour; but Lucy's eyes unclean and full of hell-fire, instead of the pure, gentle orbs we knew. At that moment the remnant of my love passed into hate and loathing; had she then to be killed, I could have done it with savage delight. As she looked, her eyes blazed with unholy light, and the face became wreathed with a voluptuous smile. Oh, God, how it made me shudder to see it! With a careless motion, she flung to the ground, callous as a devil, the child that up to now she had clutched strenuously to her breast, growling over it as a dog growls over a bone. The child gave a sharp cry, and lay there moaning. There was a cold-bloodedness in the act which wrung a groan from Arthur; when she advanced to him with outstretched arms and a wanton smile, he fell back and hid his face in his hands.

She still advanced, however, and with languorous, voluptuous grace, said:–

'Come to me, Arthur. Leave these others and come to me. My arms are hungry for you. Come, and we can rest together. Come, my husband, come!'

There was something diabolically sweet in her tones – something of the tingling of glass when struck – which rang through the brains even of us who heard the words addressed to another. As for Arthur, he seemed under a spell; moving his hands from his face, he opened wide his arms. She was leaping for them, when Van Helsing sprang forward and held between them his little golden crucifix. She recoiled from it, and, with a suddenly distorted face, full of rage, dashed past him as if to enter the tomb.

When within a foot or two of the door, however, she stopped as if arrested by some irresistible force. Then she turned, and her face was shown in the clear burst of moonlight and by the lamp, which had now no quiver from Van Helsing's iron nerves. Never did I see such baffled malice on a face; and never, I trust, shall such ever be seen again by mortal eyes. The beautiful colour became livid, the eyes seemed to throw out sparks of hell-fire, the brows were wrinkled as though the folds of the flesh were the coils of Medusa's snakes, and the lovely, blood-stained mouth grew to an open square, as in the passion masks of the Greeks and Japanese. If ever a face meant death – if looks could kill – we saw it at that moment.

And so for a full half minute, which seemed an eternity, she remained between the lifted crucifix and the sacred closing of her means of entry. Van Helsing broke the silence by asking Arthur:–

'Answer me, oh my friend! Am I to proceed in my work?'

Arthur threw himself on his knees, and hid his face in his hands, as he answered:–

'Do as you will, friend; do as you will. There can be no horror like this ever any more!' and he groaned in spirit. Quincey and I simultaneously moved towards him, and took his arms. We could hear the click of the closing lantern as Van Helsing held it down; coming close to the tomb, he began to remove from the chinks some of the sacred emblem which he had placed there. We all looked on in horrified amazement as we saw, when he stood back, the woman, with a corporeal body as real at the moment as our own, pass in through the interstice where scarce a knife-blade could have gone. We all felt a glad sense of relief when we saw the Professor calmly restoring the strings of putty to the edges of the door.

When this was done, he lifted the child and said:–

'Come now, my friends; we can do no more till to-morrow. There is a funeral at noon, so here we shall all come before long after that. The friends of the dead will all be gone by two, and when the sexton locks the gate we shall remain. Then there is more to do; but not liks this of to-night. As for this little one, he is not much harm, and by to-morrow night he shall be well. We shall leave him where the police will find him, as on the other night; and then to home.' Coming close to Arthur, he said:–

'My friend Arthur, you have had sore trial; but after, when you will look back, you will see how it was necessary. You are now in the bitter waters, my child. By this time to-morrow, you will, please God, have passed them, and have drunk of the sweet waters; so do not mourn overmuch. Till then I shall not ask you to forgive me.'

Arthur and Quincey came home with me, and we tried to cheer each other on the way. We had left the child in safety, and were tired; so we all slept with more or less reality of sleep.

29 September, night. – A little before twelve o'clock we three – Arthur, Quincey Morris, and myself – called for the Professor. It was odd to notice that by common consent we had all put on black clothes. Of course, Arthur wore black, for he was in deep mourning, but the rest of us wore it by instinct. We got to the churchyard by half-past one, and strolled about, keeping out of official observation, so that when the gravediggers had completed their task, and the sexton, under the belief that everyone had gone, had locked the gate, we had the place all to ourselves. Van Helsing, instead of his little black bag, had with him a long leather one, something like a cricketing bag; if was manifestly of fair weight.

When we were alone and had heard the last of the footsteps die out up the road, we silently, and as if by ordered intention, followed the Professor to the tomb. He unlocked the door, and we entered, closing it behind us. Then he took from his bag the lantern, which he lit, and also two wax candles, which, when lighted, he stuck, by melting their own ends, on other coffins, so that they might give light sufficient to work by. When he again lifted the lid off Lucy's coffin we all looked – Arthur trembling like an aspen – and saw that the body lay there in all its death-beauty. But there was no love in my own heart, nothing but loathing for the foul Thing which had taken Lucy's shape without her soul. I could see even Arthur's face grow hard as he looked. Presently he said to Van Helsing:–

'Is this really Lucy's body, or only a demon in her shape?'

'It is her body, and yet not it. But wait a while, and you shall see her as she was, and is.'

She seemed like a nightmare of Lucy as she lay there; the pointed teeth, the bloodstained, voluptuous mouth – which it made one shudder to see – the whole carnal and unspiritual appearance, seeming like a devilish mockery of Lucy's sweet purity. Van Helsing, in his methodical manner, began taking the various contents from his bag and placing them ready for use. First he took out a soldering iron and some plumbing solder, and then a small oil-lamp, which gave out, when lit in a corner of the tomb, gas which burned at fierce heat with a blue flame; then his operating knives, which he placed to hand; and last a round wooden stake, some two and half or three inches thick and about three feet long. One end of it was hardened by charring in the fire, and was sharpened to a fine point. With this stake came a heavy hammer, such as in households is used in the coal-cellar for breaking the lumps. To me, a doctor's preparations of any kind are stimulating and bracing, but the effect of these things on both Arthur and Quincey was to cause them a sort of consternation. They both, however, kept their courage, and remained silent and quiet.

When all was ready, Van Helsing said:–

'Before we do anything, let me tell you this; it is out of the lore and experience of the ancients and of all those who have studied the powers of the Un-Dead. When they become such, there comes with the change the curse of immortality; they cannot die, but must go on age after age adding new victims and multiplying the evils of the world; for all that die from the preying of the Un-Dead become themselves Un-Dead, and prey on their kind. And so the circle goes on ever widening, like as the ripples from a stone thrown in the water. Friend Arthur, if you had met that kiss which you know of before poor Lucy die; or again, last night when you open your arms to her, you would in time, when you had died, have become *nosferatu*, as they call it in Eastern Europe, and would all time make more of those Un-Deads that so have filled us with horror. The career of this so unhappy dear lady is but just begun. Those children whose blood she suck are not as yet so much the worse; but if she live on, Un-Dead, more and more they lose their blood, and by her power over them they come to her; and so she draw their blood with that so wicked mouth. But if she die in truth, then all cease; the tiny wounds of the throat disappear, and they go back to their plays unknowing ever of what has been. But of the most blessed of all, when this now Un-Dead be made to rest as true dead, then the soul of the poor lady whom we love shall again be free. Instead of working wickedness by night and growing more debased in the assimilation of it by day, she shall take her place with the other Angels. So that, my friend, it will be a blessed hand for her that shall strike the blow that sets her free. To this I am willing; but is there none amongst us who has a better right? Will it be no joy to think hereafter in the silence of the night when sleep is not: "It was my hand that sent her to the stars; it was the hand of him that loved her best; the hand of all she would herself have chosen, had it been to her to choose"? Tell me if there be such a one amongst us.'

We all looked at Arthur. He saw, too, what we all did, the infinite kindness which suggested that his should be the hand which would restore Lucy to us as a holy, and not an unholy, memory; he stepped forward and said bravely, though his hand trembled, and his face was as pale as snow:–

'My true friend, from the bottom of my broken heart I thank you. Tell me what I am to do, and I shall not falter!' Van Helsing laid a hand on his shoulder, and said:–

'Brave lad! A moment's courage, and it is done. This stake must be driven through her. It will be a fearful ordeal – be not deceived in that – but it will be only a short time, and you will then rejoice more than your pain was great; from this grim tomb you will emerge as though you tread on air. But you must not falter once you have begun. Only think that we, your true friends, are round you, and that we pray for you all the time.'

'Go on,' said Arthur hoarsely. 'Tell me what I am to do.'

'Take this stake in your left hand, ready to place the point over the heart, and the hammer in your right. Then when we begin our prayer for the dead – I shall read him; I have here the book, and the others shall follow – strike in God's name, that so all may be well with the dead that we love, and that the Un-Dead pass away.'

Arthur took the stake and the hammer, and when once his mind was set on action his hands never trembled nor even quivered. Van Helsing opened his missal and began to read, and Quincey and I followed as well as we could. Arthur placed the point over the heart, and as I looked I could see its dint in the white flesh. Then he struck with all his might.

The Thing in the coffin writhed; and a hideous, blood-curdling screech came from the opened red lips. The body shook and quivered and twisted in wild contortions; the sharp white teeth clamped together till the lips were cut and the mouth was smeared with crimson foam. But Arthur never faltered. He looked like a figure of Thor as his untrembling arm rose and fell, driving deeper and deeper the mercy-bearing stake, whilst the blood from the pierced heart welled and spurted up around it. His face was set, and high duty seemed to shine through it; the sight of it gave us courage, so that our voices seemed to ring through the little vault.

And then the writhing and quivering of the body became less, and the teeth ceased to champ, and the face to quiver. Finally it lay still. The terrible task was over.

The hammer fell from Arthur's hand. He reeled and would have fallen had we not caught him. Great drops of sweat sprang out on his forehead, and his breath came in broken gasps. It had indeed been an awful strain on him; and had he not been forced to his task by more than human considerations he could never have gone through with it. For a few minutes we were so taken up with him that we did not look towards the coffin. When we did, however, a murmur of startled surprise ran from one to the other of us. We gazed so eagerly that Arthur rose, for he had been seated on the ground, and came and looked too; and then a glad, strange light broke over his face and dispelled altogether the gloom and the horror that lay upon it.

There in the coffin lay no longer the foul Thing that we had so dreaded and grown to hate that the work of her destruction was yielded as a privilege to the one best entitled to it, but Lucy as we had seen her in her life, with her face of unequalled sweetness and purity. True that there was there, as we had seen them in life, the traces of care and pain and waste; but these were all dear to us, for they marked her truth to what we knew. One and all we felt that the holy calm that lay like sunshine over the wasted face and form was only an earthly token and symbol of the calm that was to reign for ever.

Van Helsing came and laid his hand on Arthur's shoulder, and said to him:–

'And now, Arthur, my friend, dear lad, am I not forgiven?'

The reaction of the terrible strain came as he took the old man's hand in his, and raising it to his lips, pressed it, saying:–

'Forgiven! God bless you that you have given my dear one her soul again, and me peace.' He put his hands on the Professor's shoulder, and laying his head on his breast, cried for a while silently, whilst we stood unmoving. When he raised his head Van Helsing said to him:–

'And now, my child, you may kiss her. Kiss her dead lips if you will, as she would have you to, if for her to choose. For she is not a grinning devil now – not any more a foul Thing for all eternity. No longer she is the devil's Un-Dead. She is God's true dead, whose soul is with Him!'

Arthur bent and kissed her, and then we sent him and Quincey out of the tomb; the Professor and I sawed the top off the stake, leaving the point of it in the body. Then we cut off the head and filled the mouth with garlic. We soldered up the leaden coffin, screwed on the coffin-lid, and gathering up our belongings, came away. When the Professor locked the door he gave the key to Arthur.

Outside the air was sweet, and the sun shone, and the birds sang, and it seemed as if all nature were tuned to a different pitch. There was gladness and mirth and peace everywhere, for we were at rest ourselves on one account, and we were glad, though it was with a tempered joy.

Before we moved away Van Helsing said:–

'Now, my friends, one step of our work is done, one the most harrowing to ourselves. But there remains a greater task: to find out the author of this our sorrow and to stamp him out. I have clues which we can follow; but it is a long task, and a difficult, and there is danger in it, and pain. Shall you not all help me? We have learned to believe, all of us – is it not so? And since so, do we not see our duty? Yes! And do we not promise to go on to the bitter end?'

Each in turn, we took his hand, and the promise was made. Then said the Professor as we moved off:–

'Two nights hence you shall meet with me and dine together at seven of the clock with friend John. I shall entreat two others, two that you know not as yet; and I shall be ready to all our work show and our plans unfold. Friend John, you come with me home, for I have much to consult about, and you can help me. To-night I leave for Amsterdam, but shall return to-morrow night. And then begins our great quest. But first I shall have much to say, so that you may know what is to do and to dread. Then our promise shall be made to each other anew; for there is a terrible task before us, and once our feet are on the ploughshare, we must not draw back.'

17

DOCTOR SEWARD'S DIARY

(continued)

When we arrived at the Berkeley Hotel, Van Helsing found a telegram waiting for him:–

'Am coming up by train. Jonathan at Whitby. Important news. – MINA HARKER.'

The Professor was delighted. 'Ah, that wonderful Madam Mina,' he said, 'pearl among women! She arrive, but I cannot stay. She must go to your house, friend John. You must meet her at the station. Telegraph her *en route*, so that she may be prepared.'

When the wire was despatched he had a cup of tea; over it he told me of a diary kept by Jonathan Harker when abroad, and gave me a typewritten copy of it, as also of Mrs Harker's diary at Whitby. 'Take these,' he said, 'and study them well. When I have returned you will be master of all the facts, and we can then better enter on our inquisition. Keep them safe, for there is in them much of treasure. You will need all your faith, even you who have had such an experience as that of to-day. What is here told,' he laid his hand heavily and gravely on the packet of papers as he spoke, 'may be the beginning of the end to you and me and many another; or it may sound the knell of the Un-Dead who walk the earth. Read all, I pray you, with the open mind; and if you can add in any way to the story here told do so, for it is all-important. You have kept diary of all these so strange things; is it not so? Yes! Then we shall go through all these together when that we meet.' He then made ready for his departure, and shortly after drove off to Liverpool Street. I took my way to Paddington, where I arrived about fifteen minutes before the train came in.

The crowd melted away after the bustling fashion common to arrival platforms; and I was beginning to feel uneasy, lest I might miss my guest, when a sweet-faced, dainty-looking girl stepped up to me, and, after a quick glance, said: 'Dr Seward, is it not?'

'And you are Mrs Harker!' I answered at once; whereupon she held out her hand.

'I knew you from the description of poor dear Lucy; but – ' She stopped suddenly, and a quick blush overspread her face.

The blush that rose to my own cheeks somehow set us both at ease, for it was a tacit answer to her own. I got her luggage, which included a typewriter, and we took the Underground to Fenchurch Street, after I had sent a wire to my housekeeper to have a sitting-room and bedroom prepared at once for Mrs Harker.

In due time we arrived. She knew, of course, that the place was a lunatic asylum, but I could see that she was unable to repress a slight shudder when we entered.

She told me that, if she might, she would come presently to my study, as she had much to say. So here I am finishing my entry on my phonograph diary whilst I await her. As yet I have not had the chance of looking at the papers which Van Helsing left with me, though they lie open before me. I must get her interested in something, so that I may have an opportunity of reading them. She does not know how precious time is, or what a task we have in hand. I must be careful not to frighten her. Here she is!

MINA HARKER'S JOURNAL

29 September. – After I had tidied myself, I went down to Dr Seward's study. At the door I paused a moment, for I thought I heard him talking with someone. As, however, he had pressed me to be quick, I knocked at the door, and on his calling out, 'Come in,' I entered.

To my intense surprise, there was no one with him. He was quite alone, and on the table opposite him was what I knew at once from the description to be a phonograph. I had never seen one, and was much interested.

'I hope I did not keep you waiting,' I said; 'but I stayed at the door as I heard you talking, and thought there was someone with you.'

'Oh,' he replied, with a smile, 'I was only entering my diary.'

'Your diary?' I asked him in surprise.

'Yes,' he answered. 'I keep it in this.' As he spoke he laid his hand on the phonograph. I felt quite excited over it, and blurted out:–

'Why, this beats even shorthand! May I hear it say something?'

'Certainly,' he replied with alacrity, and stood up to put it in train for speaking. Then he paused, and a troubled look overspread his face.

'The fact is,' he began awkwardly, 'I only keep my diary in it; and as it is entirely – almost entirely – about my cases, it may be awkward – that is, I mean – ' He stopped, and I tried to help him out of his embarrassment:

'You helped to attend dear Lucy at the end. Let me hear how she died; for all that I can know of her, I shall be very grateful. She was very, very dear to me.'

To my surprise, he answered, with a horrorstruck look in his face:–

'Tell you of her death? Not for the wide world!'

'Why not?' I asked, for some grave, terrible feeling was coming over me. Again he paused, and I could see that he was trying to invent an excuse. At length he stammered out:–

'You see, I do not know how to pick out any particular part of the diary.' Even while he was speaking an idea had dawned upon him, and he said with unconscious simplicity, in a different voice, and with the naïveté of a child: 'That's quite true, upon my honour. Honest Indian!' I could not but smile, at which he grimaced. 'I gave myself away that time!' he said. 'But do you know that, although I have kept the diary for months past, it never once struck me how I was going to find any particular part of it in case I wanted to look it up?' By this time my mind was made up that the diary of a doctor who attended Lucy might have something to add to the sum of our knowledge of that terrible Being, and I said boldly:–

'Then, Dr Seward, you had better let me copy it out for you on my typewriter.' He grew to a positively deathly pallor as he said:–

'No! no! no! For all the world, I wouldn't let you know that terrible story!'

Then it was terrible; my intuition was right! For a moment I thought, and as my eyes ranged the room, unconsciously looking for something or some opportunity to aid me, they lit on the great batch of typewriting on the table. His eyes caught the look in mine, and, without thinking, followed their direction. As they saw the parcel he realized my meaning.

'You do not know me,' I said. 'When you have read those papers – my own diary and my husband's also, which I have typed – you will know me better. I have not faltered in giving every thought of my own heart in this cause; but, of course, you do not know me – yet; and I must not expect you to trust me so far.'

He is certainly a man of noble nature; poor dear Lucy was right about him. He stood up and opened a large drawer, in which were arranged in order a number of hollow cylinders of metal covered with dark wax, and said:–

'You are quite right. I did not trust you because I did not know you. But I know you now; and let me say that I should have known you long ago. I know that Lucy told you of me; she told me of you too. May I make the only atonement in my power? Take the cylinders and hear them – the first half-dozen of them are personal to me, and they will not horrify you; then you will know me better. Dinner will by then be ready. In the meantime I shall read over some of these documents, and shall be better able to understand certain things.' He carried the phonograph himself up to my sitting-room and adjusted it for me. Now I shall learn something pleasant, I am sure; for it will tell me the other side of a true love episode of which I know one side already. . . .

DR SEWARD'S DIARY

29 September. – I was so absorbed in that wonderful diary of Jonathan Harker and that other of his wife that I let the time run on without thinking. Mrs Harker was not down when the maid came to announce dinner, so I said: 'She is possibly tired; let dinner wait an hour'; and I went on with my work. I had just finished Mrs Harker's diary, when she came in. She looked sweetly pretty, but very sad, and her eyes were flushed with crying. This somehow moved me much. Of late I have had cause for tears, God knows! but the relief of them was denied me; and now the sight of those sweet eyes, brightened with recent tears, went straight to my heart. So I said as gently as I could:–

'I greatly fear I have distressed you.'

'Oh no, not distressed me,' she replied, 'but I have been more touched than I can say by your grief. That is a wonderful machine, but it is cruelly true. It told me, in its very tones, the anguish of your heart. It was like a soul crying out to almighty God. No one must hear them spoken ever again! See, I have tried to be useful. I have copied out the words on my typewriter, and none other need now hear your heart beat, as I did.'

'No one need ever know, shall ever know,' I said in a low voice. She laid her hand on mine and said gravely:–

'Ah, but they must!'

'Must! But why?' I asked.

'Because it is a part of the terrible story, a part of poor dear Lucy's death and all that led to it; because in the struggle which we have before us to rid the earth of this terrible monster we must have all the knowledge and all the help which we can get. I think that the cylinders which you gave me contained more than you intended me to know; but I can see that there are in your record many lights to this dark mystery. You will let me help, will you not? I know all up to a certain point, and I see already, though your diary only took me to 7 September, how poor Lucy was beset, and how her terrible doom was being wrought out. Jonathan and I have been working day and night since Professor Van Helsing saw us. He is gone to Whitby to get more information, and he will be here to-morrow to help us. We need have no secrets amongst us; working together and with absolute trust, we can surely be stronger than if some of us were in the dark.' She looked at me so appealingly, and at the same time manifested such courage and resolution in her bearing, that I gave in at once to her wishes. 'You shall,' I said, 'do as you like in the matter. God forgive me if I do wrong! There are terrible things yet to learn of; but if you have so far travelled on the road to poor Lucy's death, you will not be content, I know, to remain in the dark. Nay, the end – the very end – may give you a gleam of peace. Come, there is dinner. We must keep one another strong for what is before us; we have a cruel and dreadful task. When you have eaten you shall learn the rest, and I will answer any questions you ask – if there be anything which you do not understand, though it was apparent to us who were present.'

MINA HARKER'S JOURNAL

29 September. – After dinner I came with Dr Seward to his study. He brought back the phonograph from my room, and I took my typewriter. He placed me in a comfortable chair, and arranged the phonograph so that I could touch it without getting up, and showed me how to stop it in case I should want to pause. Then he very thoughtfully took a chair, with his back to me, so that I might be as free as possible, and began to read. I put the forked metal to my ears and listened.

When the terrible story of Lucy's death, and – and all that followed, was done, I lay back in my chair powerless. Fortunately I am not of a fainting disposition. When Dr Seward saw me he jumped up with a horrified exclamation, and hurriedly taking a case-bottle from a cupboard, gave me some brandy, which in a few minutes somewhat restored me. My brain was all in a whirl, and only that there came through all the multitude of horrors the holy ray of light that my dear, dear Lucy was at last at peace, I do not think I could have borne it without making a scene. It is all so wild, and mysterious, and strange, that if I had not known Jonathan's experience in Transylvania I could not have believed. As it was, I didn't know what to believe, and so got out of my difficulty by attending to something else. I took the cover off my typewriter, and said to Dr Seward:–

'Let me write this all out now. We must be ready for Dr Van Helsing when he comes. I have sent a telegram to Jonathan to come on here when he arrives in London from Whitby. In this matter dates are everything, and I think if we get all our material ready, and have every item put in chronological order, we shall have done much. You tell me that Lord Godalming and Mr Morris are coming too. Let us be able to tell them when they come.' He accordingly set the phonograph at a slow pace, and I began to typewrite from the beginning of the seventh cylinder. I used manifold, and so took three copies of the diary, just as I had done with all the rest. It was late when I got through, but Dr Seward went about his work of going his round of the patients; when he had finished he came back and sat near me, reading, so that I did not feel too lonely whilst I worked. How good and thoughtful he is; the world seems full of good men – even if there *are* monsters in it. Before I left him I remembered what

Jonathan put in his diary of the Professor's perturbation at reading something in an evening paper at the station at Exeter; so, seeing that Dr Seward keeps his newspapers, I borrowed the files of the *Westminster Gazette* and the *Pall Mall Gazette*, and took them to my room. I remember how much the *Dailygraph* and the *Whitby Gazette*, of which I had made cuttings, helped us to understand the terrible events at Whitby when Count Dracula landed, so I shall look through the evening papers since then, and perhaps I shall get some new light. I am not sleepy, and the work will help to keep me quiet.

DR SEWARD'S DIARY

30 September. – Mr Harker arrived at nine o'clock. He had got his wife's wire just before starting. He is uncommonly clever, if one can judge from his face, and full of energy. If his journal be true – and judging by one's own wonderful experiences it must be – he is also a man of great nerve. That going down to the vault a second time was a remarkable piece of daring. After reading his account of it I was prepared to meet a good specimen of manhood, but hardly the quiet, business-like gentleman who came here to-day.

Later. – After lunch Harker and his wife went back to their own room, and as I passed a while ago I heard the click of the typewriter. They are hard at it. Mrs Harker says that they are knitting together in chronological order every scrap of evidence they have. Harker has got the letters between the consignee of the boxes at Whitby and the carriers in London who took charge of them. He is now reading his wife's typescript of my diary. I wonder what they make out of it. Here it is. . . .

Strange that it never struck me that the very next house might be the Count's hiding-place! Goodness knows that we had enough clues from the conduct of the patient Renfield! The bundle of letters relating to the purchase of the house were with the typescript. Oh, if we had only had them earlier we might have saved poor Lucy! Stop; that way madness lies! Harker has gone back, and is again collating his material. He says that by dinner-time they will be able to show a whole connected narrative. He thinks that in the meantime I should see Renfield, as hitherto he had been a sort of index to the coming and going of the Count. I hardly see this yet, but when I get at the dates I suppose I shall. What a good thing that Mrs Harker put my cylinders into type! We never could have found the dates otherwise. . . .

I found Renfield sitting placidly in his room with his hands folded, smiling benignly. At the moment he seemed as sane as anyone I ever saw. I sat down and talked with him on a lot of subjects, all of which he treated naturally. He then, of his own accord, spoke of going home, a subject he has never mentioned to my knowledge during his sojourn here. In fact, he spoke quite confidently of getting his discharge at once. I believe that, had I not had the chat with Harker and read the letters and the dates of his outbursts, I should have been prepared to sign for him after a brief time of observation. As it is, I am darkly suspicious. All those outbreaks were in some way linked with the proximity of the Count. What then does this absolute content mean? Can it be that his instinct is satisfied as to the vampire's ultimate triumph? Stay; he is himself zoophagous, and in his wild ravings outside the chapel door of the deserted house he always spoke of 'master'. This all seems confirmation of our idea. However, after a while I came away; my friend is just a little too sane at present to make it safe to probe him too deep with questions. He might begin to think, and then – ! So I came away. I mistrust these quiet moods of his; so I have given the attendant a hint to look closely after him, and to have a strait-waistcoat ready in case of need.

JONATHAN HARKER'S JOURNAL

29 September, in train to London. – When I received Mr Billington's courteous message that he would give me any information in his power, I thought it best to go down to Whitby and make, on the spot, such inquiries as I wanted. It was now my object to trace that horrid cargo of the Count's to its place in London. Later, we may be able to deal with it. Billington junior, a nice lad, met me at the station, and brought me to his father's house, where they had decided that I must stay the night. They are hospitable, with true Yorkshire hospitality: give a guest everything, and leave him free to do as he likes. They all knew that I was busy, and that my stay was short, and Mr Billington had ready in his office all the papers concerning the consignment of boxes. It gave me almost a turn to see again one of the letters which I had seen on the Count's table before I knew of his diabolical plans. Everything had been carefully thought out, and done systematically and with precision. He seemed to have been prepared for every obstacle which might be placed by accident in the way of his intentions being carried out. To use an Americanism, he had 'taken no chances', and the absolute accuracy with which his instructions were fulfilled was simply the logical result of his care. I saw the invoice, and took note of it: 'Fifty cases of common earth, to be used for experimental purposes.' Also the copy of letter to Carter Paterson, and their reply; of both of these I got copies. This was all the information Mr Billington could give me, so I went down to the port and saw the coastguards, the Customs officers, and the harbour-master. They had all something to say of the strange entry of the ship, which is already taking its place in local tradition; but no one could add to the simple description: 'Fifty cases of common earth.' I then saw the station-master, who kindly put me in communication with the men who had actually received the boxes. Their tally was exact with the list, and they had nothing to add except that the boxes were 'main and mortal heavy', and that shifting them was dry work. One of them added that it was hard lines that there wasn't any gentlemen 'such-like as yourself, squire', to show some sort of appreciation of their efforts in a liquid form; another put in a rider that the thirst then generated was such that even the time which had elapsed had not completely allayed it. Needless to add, I took care before leaving to lift, for ever and adequately, this source of reproach.

30 September. – The station-master was good enough to give me a line to his old companion the station-master at King's Cross, so that when I arrived there in the morning I was able to ask him about the arrival of the boxes. He, too, put me at once in communication with the proper officials, and I saw that their tally was correct with the original invoice. The opportunities of acquiring an abnormal thirst had been here limited; a noble use of them had, however, been made, and again I was compelled to deal with the result in an *ex post facto* manner.

From thence I went on to Carter Paterson's central office, where I met with the utmost courtesy. They looked up the transaction in their day-book and letter-book, and at once telephoned to their King's Cross office for more details. By good fortune, the men who did the teaming were waiting for work, and the official at once sent them over, sending also by one of them the way-bill and all the papers connected with the delivery of the boxes at Carfax. Here again I found the tally agreeing exactly; the carriers' men were able to supplement the paucity of the written words with a few details. These were, I shortly found, connected almost solely with the dusty nature of the job, and of the consequent thirst engendered in the operators. On my affording opportunity, through the medium of the currency of the realm, of the allaying at a later period this beneficent evil, one of the men remarked:–

'That 'ere 'ouse, guv'nor, is the rummiest I ever was in. Blyme! but it ain't been touched sence a hundred years. There was dust that thick in the place that you might have slep' on it without 'urtin' of yer bones; an' the place was that neglected that yer might 'ave smelled ole Jerusalem in it. But the ole chapel – that took the cike, that did! Me and my mate, we thort we wouldn't never git out quick enough. Lor', I wouldn't take less nor a quid a moment to stay there arter dark.' Having been in the house, I could well believe him; but if he knew what I know, he would, I think, have raised his terms.

Of one thing I am now satisfied: that *all* the boxes which arrived at Whitby from Varna in the *Demeter* were safely deposited in the old chapel of Carfax. There should be fifty of them there, unless any have since been removed – as from Dr Seward's diary I fear.

I shall try to see the carter who took away the boxes from Carfax when Renfield attacked them. By following up this clue we may learn a good deal.

Later. – Mina and I have worked all day, and we have put all the papers into order.

MINA HARKER'S JOURNAL

30 September. – I am so glad that I hardly know how to contain myself. It is, I suppose, the reaction from the haunting fear which I have had: that this terrible affair and the reopening of his old wound might act detrimentally on Jonathan. I saw him leave for Whitby with as brave a face as I could, but I was sick with apprehension. The effort has, however, done him good. He was never so resolute, never so strong, never so full of volcanic energy, as at present. It is just as that dear, good Professor Van Helsing said: he is true grit, and he improves under strain that would kill a weaker nature. He came back full of life and hope and determination; we have got everything in order for to-night. I feel myself quite wild with excitement. I suppose one ought to pity anything so hunted as is the Count. That is just it: this Thing is not human – not even beast. To read Dr Seward's account of poor Lucy's death, and what followed, is enough to dry up the springs of pity in one's heart.

Later. – Lord Godalming and Mr Morris arrived earlier than we expected. Dr Seward was out on business and had taken Jonathan with him, so I had to see them. It was to me a painful meeting, for it brought back all poor dear Lucy's hopes of only a few months ago. Of course they had heard Lucy speak of me, and it seemed that Dr Van Helsing, too, had been quite 'blowing my trumpet', as Mr Morris expressed it. Poor fellows, neither of them is aware that I know all about the proposals they made to Lucy. They did not quite know what to say or do, as they were ignorant of the amount of my knowledge; so they had to keep on neutral subjects. However, I thought the matter over, and came to the conclusion that the best thing I could do would be to post them in affairs right up to date. I knew from Dr Seward's diary that they had been at Lucy's death – her real death – and that I need not fear to betray any secret before the time. So I told them, as well as I could, that I had read all the papers and diaries, and that my husband and I, having type-written them, had finished putting them in order. I gave them each a copy to read in the library. When Lord Godalming got his and turned it over – it does make a pretty good pile – he said:–

'Did you write all this, Mrs Harker?'

I nodded, and he went on:–

'I don't quite see the drift of it; but you people are all so good and kind, and have been working so earnestly and so energetically, that all I can do is to accept your ideas blindfold and try to help you. I have had one lesson already in accepting facts that should make a man humble to the last hour of his life. Besides, I know you loved my poor Lucy – ' Here he turned away and covered his face with his hands. I could hear the tears in his voice. Mr Morris, with instinctive delicacy, just laid a hand for a moment on his shoulder, and then walked quietly out of the room. I suppose there is something in woman's nature that makes a man free to break down before her and express his feelings on the tender or emotional side without feeling it derogatory to his manhood; for when Lord Godalming found himself alone with me he sat down on the sofa and gave way utterly and openly. I sat down beside him and took his hand. I hope he didn't think it forward of me, and that if he ever thinks of it afterwards he never will have such a thought. There I wrong him; I *know* he never will – he is too true a gentleman. I said to him, for I could see that his heart was breaking:–

'I loved dear Lucy, and I know what she was to you, and what you were to her. She and I were like sisters; and now she is gone, will you not let me be like a sister to you in your trouble? I know what sorrows you have had, though I cannot measure the depth of them. If sympathy and pity can help in your affliction, won't you let me be of some little service – for Lucy's sake?'

In an instant the poor dear fellow was overwhelmed with grief. It seemed to me that all that he had of late been suffering in silence found a vent at once. He grew quite hysterical, and raising his open hands, beat his palms together in a perfect agony of grief. He stood up and then sat down again, and the tears rained down his cheeks. I felt an infinite pity for him, and opened my arms unthinkingly. With a sob he laid his head on my shoulder, and cried like a wearied child, whilst he shook with emotion.

We women have something of the mother in us that makes us rise above smaller matters when the mother-spirit is invoked; I felt this big, sorrowing man's head resting on me, as though it were that of the baby that some day may lie on my bosom, and I stroked his hair as though he were my own child. I never thought at the time how strange it all was.

After a little bit his sobs ceased, and he raised himself with an apology, though he made no disguise of his emotion. He told me that for days and nights past – weary days and sleepless nights – he had been unable to speak with anyone, as a man must speak in his time of sorrow. There was no woman whose sympathy could be given to him, or with whom, owing to the terrible circumstances with which his sorrow was surrounded, he could speak freely. 'I know now how I suffered,' he said, as he dried his eyes, 'but I do not know even yet – and none other can ever know – how much your sweet sympathy has been to me to-day. I shall know better in time; and believe me that, though I am not ungrateful now, my gratitude will grow with my understanding. You will let me be like a brother, will you now, for all our lives – for dear Lucy's sake?'

'For dear Lucy's sake,' I said as we clasped hands. 'Ay, and for your own sake,' he added, 'for if a man's esteem and gratitude are ever worth the winning, you have won mine to-day. If ever the future should bring to you a time when you need a man's help, believe me, you will not call in vain. God grant that no such time may ever come to you to break the sunshine of your life; but if it should ever come, promise me that you will let me know.' He was so earnest, and his sorrow was so fresh, that I felt it would comfort him, so I said:–

'I promise.'

As I came along the corridor I saw Mr Morris looking out of a window. He turned as he heard my footsteps. 'How is Art?' he said. Then noticing my red eyes, he went on: 'Ah, I see you have been comforting him. Poor old fellow! he needs it. No one but a woman can help a man when he is in trouble of the heart; and he had no one to comfort him.'

He bore his own trouble so bravely that my heart bled for him. I saw the manuscript in his hand, and I knew that when he read it he would realize how much I knew; so I said to him:–

'I wish I could comfort all who suffer from the heart. Will you let me be your friend, and will you come to me for comfort if you need it? You will know, later on, why I speak.' He saw that I was in earnest, and stooping, took my hand, and raising it to his lips, kissed it. It seemed but poor comfort to so brave and unselfish a soul, and impulsively I bent over and kissed him. The tears rose in his eyes, and there was a momentary choking in his throat; he said quite calmly:–

'Little girl, you will never regret that true-hearted kindness, so long as ever you live!' Then he went into the study to his friend.

'Little girl!' – the very words he had used to Lucy, and oh, but he proved himself a friend!

18

DR SEWARD'S DIARY

30 September. – I got home at five o'clock, and found that Godalming and Morris had not only arrived, but had already studied the transcript of the various diaries and letters which Harker and his wonderful wife had made and arranged. Harker had not yet returned from his visit to the carriers' men, of whom Dr Hennessey had written to me. Mrs Harker gave us a cup of tea, and I can honestly say that, for the first time since I have lived in it, this old house seemed like *home.* When we had finished, Mrs Harker said:–

'Dr Seward, may I ask a favour? I want to see your patient, Mr Renfield. Do let me see him. What you have said of him in your diary interests me so much!' She looked so appealing and so pretty that I could not refuse her, and there was no possible reason why I should; so I took her with me. When I went into the room, I told the man that a lady would like to see him; to which he simply answered: 'Why?'

'She is going through the house, and wants to see every one in it,' I answered. 'Oh, very well,' he said: 'let her come in, by all means; but just wait a minute till I tidy up the place.' His method of tidying was peculiar: he simply swallowed all the flies and spiders in the boxes before I could stop him. It was quite evident that he feared, or was jealous of, some interference. When he had got through his disgusting task, he said cheerfully: 'Let the lady come in,' and sat down on the edge of his bed with his head down, but with his eyelids raised so that he could see her as she entered. For a moment I thought that he might have some homicidal intent; I remembered how quiet he had been just before he attacked me in my own study, and I took care to stand where I could seize him at once if he attempted to make a spring at her. She came into the room with an easy gracefulness which would at once command the respect of any lunatic – for easiness is one of the qualities mad people most respect. She walked over to him, smiling pleasantly, and held out her hand.

'Good evening, Mr Renfield,' said she. 'You see, I know you, for Dr Seward has told me of you.' He made no immediate reply, but eyed her all over intently with a set frown on his face. This look gave way to one of wonder, which merged in doubt; then, to my intense astonishment, he said:–

'You're not the girl the doctor wanted to marry, are you? You can't be, you know, for she's dead.' Mrs Harker smiled sweetly as she replied:–

'Oh no! I have a husband of my own, to whom I was married before I ever saw Dr Seward, or he me. I am Mrs Harker.'

'Then what are you doing here?'

'My husband and I are staying on a visit with Dr Seward.'

'Then don't stay.'

'But why not?' I thought that this style of conversation might not be pleasant to Mrs Harker, any more than it was to me, so I joined in:—

'How did you know I wanted to marry anyone?' His reply was simply contemptuous, given in a pause in which he turned his eyes from Mrs Harker to me, instantly turning them back again:—

'What an asinine question!'

'I don't see that at all, Mr Renfield,' said Mrs Harker, at once championing me. He replied to her with as much courtesy and respect as he had shown contempt to me:—

'You will, of course, understand, Mrs Harker, that when a man is loved and honoured as our host is, everything regarding him is of interest in our little community. Dr Seward is loved not only by his household and his friends, but even by his patients, who, being some of them hardly in mental equilibrium, are apt to distort causes and effects. Since I myself have been an inmate of a lunatic asylum, I cannot but notice that the sophistic tendancies of some of its inmates lean towards the errors of *non causae* and *ignoratio elenchi*.' I positively opened my eyes at this new development. Here was my own pet lunatic – the most pronounced of his type that I had ever met with – talking elemental philosophy, and with the manner of a polished gentleman. I wonder if it was Mrs Harker's presence which had touched some chord in his memory. If this new phase was spontaneous, or in any way due to her unconscious influence, she must have some rare gift or power.

We continued to talk for some time; and, seeing that he was seemingly quite reasonable, she ventured, looking at me questioningly as she began, to lead him to his favourite topic. I was again astonished, for he addressed himself to the question with the impartiality of the completest sanity; he even took himself as an example when he mentioned certain things.

'Why, I myself am an instance of a man who had a strange belief. Indeed, it was no wonder that my friends were alarmed, and insisted on my being put under control. I used to fancy that life was a positive and perpetual entity, and that by consuming a multitude of live things, no matter how low in the scale of creation, one might indefinitely prolong life. At times I held the belief so strongly that I actually tried to take human life. The doctor here will bear me out that on one occasion I tried to kill him for the purpose of strengthening my vital powers by the assimilation with my own body of his life through the medium of his blood – relying, of course, upon the Scriptural phrase, "For the blood is the life." Though, indeed, the vendor of a certain nostrum has vulgarized the truism to the very point of contempt. Isn't that true, doctor?' I nodded assent, for I was so amazed that I hardly knew what I ought to think or say; it was hard to imagine that I had seen him eat up his spiders and flies not five minutes before. Looking at my watch, I saw that I should go to the station to meet Van Helsing, so I told Mrs Harker that it was time to leave. She came at once, after saying pleasantly to Mr Renfield:'Good-bye, and I hope I may see you often, under auspices pleasanter to yourself,' to which, to my astonishment, he replied:–

'Good-bye, my dear. I pray God I may never see your sweet face again. May He bless and keep you!'

When I went to the station to meet Van Helsing I left the boys behind me. Poor Art seemed more cheerful than he has been since Lucy first took ill, and Quincey is more like his own bright self than he has been for many a long day.

Van Helsing stepped from the carriage with the eager nimbleness of a boy. He saw me at once, and rushed up to me, saying:–

'Ah, friend John, how goes all? Well? So! I have been busy, for I come here to stay if need be. All affairs are settled with me, and I have so much to tell. Madam Mina is with you? Yes. And her so fine husband? And Arthur and my friend Quincey, they are with you, too? Good!'

As I drove to the house I told him of what had passed, and of how my own diary had come to be of some use through Mrs Harker's suggestion; at which the Professor interrupted me:–

'Ah, that wonderful Madam Mina! She has man's brain – a brain that a man should have were he much gifted – and woman's heart. The good God fashioned her for a purpose, believe me, when He made that so good combination. Friend John, up to now fortune has made that woman of help to us; after to-night she must not have to do with this so terrible affair. It is not good that she run a risk so great. We men are determined – nay, are we not pledged? – to destroy this monster; but it is no part for a woman. Even if she be not harmed, her heart may fail her in so much and so many horrors; and hereafter she may suffer – both in waking, from her nerves, and in sleep, from her dreams. And, besides, she is a young woman and not so long married; there may be other things to think of some time, if not now. You tell me she has wrote all, then she must consult with us; but to-morrow she say good-bye to this work, and we go alone.' I agreed heartily with him, and then I told him what we had found in his absence: that the house which Dracula had bought was the very next one to my own. He was amazed, and a great concern seemed to come on him. 'O that we had known it before!' he said, 'for then we might have reached him in time to save poor Lucy. However, "the milk that is spilt cries not out afterwards", as you say. We shall not think of that, but go on our way to the end.'

Then he fell into a silence that lasted till we entered my own gateway. Before we went to prepare for dinner he said to Mrs Harker:—

'I am told, Madam Mina, by my friend John that you and your husband have put up in exact order all things that have been, up to this moment.'

'Not up to this moment, Professor,' she said impulsively, 'but up to this morning.'

'But why not up to now? We have seen hitherto how good light all the little things have made. We have told our secrets, and yet no one who has told is the worse for it.'

Mrs Harker began to blush, and taking a paper from her pocket, she said:—

'Dr Van Helsing, will you read this, and tell me if it must go in. It is my record of to-day. I too have seen the need of putting down at present everything, however trivial; but there is little in this except what is personal. Must it go in?' The Professor read it over gravely, and handed it back, saying:—

'It need not go in if you do not wish it; but pray that it may. It can but make your husband love you the more, and all us, your friends, more honour you – as well as more esteem and love.' She took it back with another blush and a bright smile.

And so now, up to this very hour, all the records we have are complete and in order. The Professor took away one copy to study after dinner, and before our meeting, which is fixed for nine o'clock. The rest of us have already read everything; so when we meet in the study we shall all be informed as to facts, and can arrange our plan of battle with this terrible and mysterious enemy.

MINA HARKER'S JOURNAL

30 September.– When we met in Dr Seward's study two hours after dinner, which had been at six o'clock, we unconsciously formed a sort of board or committee. Professor Van Helsing took the head of the table, to which Dr Seward motioned him as he came into the room. He made me sit next to him on his right, and asked me to act as secretary; Jonathan sat next to me. Opposite us were Lord Godalming, Dr Seward, and Mr Morris – Lord Godalming being next to the Professor, and Dr Seward in the centre. The Professor said:—

'I may, I suppose, take it that we are all acquainted with the facts that are in these papers.' We all expressed assent, and he went on:—

'Then it were, I think, good that I tell you something of the kind of enemy with which we have to deal. I shall then make known to you something of the history of this man, which has been ascertained for me. So we then can discuss how we shall act, and can take our measure according.

'There are such beings as vampires; some of us have evidence that they exist. Even had we not the proof of our own unhappy experience, the teachings and the records of the past give proof enough for sane peoples. I admit that at the first I was sceptic. Were it not that through long years I have trained myself to keep an open mind, I could not have believed until such time as that fact thunder on my ear: "See! see! I prove; I prove." Alas! Had I known at the first what now I know – nay, had I even guess at him – one so precious life had been spared to many of us who did love her. But that is gone; and we must so work that other poor souls perish not, whilst we can save. The *nosferatu* do not die like the bee when he sting once. He is only stronger; and being stronger, have yet more power to work evil. This vampire which is amongst us is of himself so strong in person as twenty men; he is of cunning more than mortal, for his cunning be the growth of ages; he have still the aids of necromancy, which is, as his etymology imply, the divination by the dead, and all the dead that he can come nigh to are for him at command; he is brute, and more than brute; he is devil in callous, and the heart of him is not; he can, within limitations, appear at will when, and where, and in any of the forms that are to him; he can, within his range, direct the elements: the storm, the fog, the thunder; he can command all the meaner things: the rat, and the owl, and the bat – the moth, and the fox, and the wolf; he can grow and become small; and he can at times vanish and come unknown. How then are we to begin our strife to destroy him? How shall we find his where; and having found it, how can we destroy? My friends, this is much; it is a terrible task that we undertake, and there may be consequence to make the brave shudder. For if we fail in this our fight he must surely win: and then where end we? Life is nothings! I heed him not. But to fail here is not mere life or death. It is that we become as him; that we henceforward become foul things of the night like him – without heart or conscience, preying on the bodies and the souls of those we love best. To us for ever are the gates of heaven shut; for who shall open them to us again? We go on for all time abhorred by all; a blot on the face of God's sunshine; an arrow in the side of Him who died for man. But we are face to face with duty; and in such case must we shrink? For me, I say, no; but then I am old, and life, with his sunshine, his fair places, his song of birds, his music, and his love, lie far behind. You others are young. Some have seen sorrow; but there are fair days yet in store. What say you?'

Whilst he was speaking Jonathan had taken my hand. I feared, oh so much, that the appalling nature of our danger was overcoming him when I saw his hand stretch out; but it was life to me to feel its touch – so strong, so self-reliant, so resolute. A brave man's hand can speak for itself; it does not even need a woman's love to hear its music.

When the Professor had done speaking my husband looked in my eyes, and I in his; there was no need for speaking between us.

'I answer for Mina and myself,' he said.

'Count me in, Professor,' said Mr Quincey Morris, laconically as usual.

'I am with you,' said Lord Godalming, 'for Lucy's sake, if for no other reason.'

Dr Seward simply nodded. The Professor stood up, and, after laying his golden crucifix on the table, held out his hand on either side. I took his right hand, and Lord Godalming his left; Jonathan held my right with his left and stretched across to Mr Morris. So as we all took hands our solemn compact was made. I felt my heart icy cold, but it did not even occur to me to draw back. We resumed our places, and Dr Van Helsing went on with a sort of cheerfulness which showed that the serious work had begun. It was to be taken as gravely, and in as businesslike a way, as any other transaction of life:–

'Well, you know what we have to contend against; but we, too, are not without strength. We have on our side power of combination – a power denied to the vampire kind; we have resources of science; we are free to act and think; and the hours of the day and the night are ours equally. In fact, so far as our powers extend, they are unfettered, and we are free to use them. We have self-devotion in a cause, and an end to achieve which is not a selfish one. These things are much.

'Now let us see how far the general powers arrayed against us are restrict, and how the individual cannot. In fine, let us consider the limitations of the vampire in general, and of this one in particular.

'All we have to go upon are traditions and superstitions. These do not at the first appear much, when the matter is one of life and death – nay, of more than either life or death. Yet must we be satisfied; in the first place because we have to be – no other means is at our control – and secondly, because, after all, these things – tradition and superstition – are everything. Does not the belief in vampires rest for others – though not, alas! for us – on them? A year ago which of us would have received such a possibility, in the midst of our scientific, sceptical, matter-of-fact nineteenth century? We even scouted a belief that we saw justified under our very eyes. Take it, then, that the vampire, and the belief in his limitations and his cure, rest for the moment on the same base. For, let me tell you, he is known everywhere that men have been. In old Greece, in old Rome; he flourish in Germany all over, in France, in India, even in the Chersonese; and in China, so far from us in all ways, there even is he, and the peoples fear him at this day. He have follow the wake of the berserker Icelander, the devil-begotten Hun, the Slav, the Saxon, the Magyar. So far, then, we have all we may act upon; and let me tell you that very much of the beliefs are justified by what we have seen in our own so unhappy experience. The vampire live on, and cannot die by mere passing of the time; he can flourish when that he can fatten on the blood of the living. Even more, we have seen amongst us that he can grow even younger; that his vital faculties grow strenuous, and seem as though they refresh themselves when his special pabulum is plenty. But he cannot flourish without this diet; he eat not as others. Even friend Jonathan, who lived with him for weeks, did never see him to eat, never! He throws no shadow; he make in the mirror no reflect, as again Jonathan observe. He has the strength of many in his hand – witness again Jonathan when he shut the door against the wolfs, and when he help him from the diligence too. He can transform himself to wolf, as we gather from the ship arrival in Whitby, when he tear open the dog; he can be as bat, as Madam Mina saw him on the window at Whitby, and as friend John saw him fly from this so near house, and as my friend Quincey saw him at the window of Miss Lucy. He can come in mist which he create – that noble ship's captain proved him of this; but, from what we know, the distance he can make this mist is limited, and it can only be round himself. He come on moonlight rays as elemental dust – as again Jonathan saw those sister in the castle of Dracula. He become so small – we ourselves saw Miss Lucy, ere she was at peace, slip through a hair-breadth space at the tomb door. He can, when once he find his way, come out from anything or into anything, no matter how close it be bound or even fused up with fire – solder you call it. He can see in the dark – no small power this, in a world which is one half shut from the light. Ah, but hear me through. He can do all these things, yet he is not free. Nay, he is even more prisoner than the slave of the galley, than the madman in his cell. He cannot go where he lists; he who is not of nature has yet to obey some of nature's laws – why we know not. He may not enter anywhere at the first, unless there be someone of the household who bid him to come; though afterwards he can come as he please. His power ceases, as does that of all evil things, at the coming of the day. Only at certain times can he have limited freedom. If he be not at the place whither he is bound, he can only change himself at noon or at exact sunrise or sunset. These things are we told, and in this record of ours we have proof by inference. Thus, whereas he can do as he will within his limit, when he have his earth-home, his coffin-home, his hell-home, the place unhallowed, as we saw when he went to the grave of the suicide at Whitby; still at other time he can only change when the time come. It is said, too, that he can only pass running water at the slack or the flood of the tide. Then there are things which so afflict him that he has no power, as the garlic that we know of, and as for things sacred, as this symbol, my crucifix, that was amongst us even now when we resolve, to them he is nothing, but in their presence he take his place far off and silent with respect. There are others, too, which I shall tell you of, lest in our seeking we may need them. The branch of wild rose on his coffin keep him that he move not from it; a sacred bullet fired into the coffin kill him so that he be true dead; and as for the stake through him, we know already of its peace; or the cut-off head that giveth rest. We have seen it with our eyes.

'Thus when we find the habitation of this man-that-was, we can confine him to his coffin and destroy him, if we obey what we know. But he is clever. I have asked my friend Arminius, of Buda-Pesth University, to make his record; and, from all the means that are, he tell me of what he has been. He must, indeed, have been that Voivode Dracula who won his name against the Turk, over the great river on the very frontier of Turkey-land. If it be so, then was he no common man; for in that time, and for centuries after, he was spoken of as the cleverest and the most cunning, as well as the bravest of the sons of the "land beyond the forest". That mighty brain and that iron resolution went with him to his grave, and are even now arrayed against us. The Draculas were, says Arminius, a great and noble race, though now and again were scions who were held by their coevals to have had dealings with the Evil One. They learned his secrets in the Scholomance, amongst the mountains over Lake Hermanstadt, where the devil claims the tenth scholar as his due. In the records are such words as "stregoica" – witch; "ordog" and "pokol" – Satan and hell; and in one manuscript this very Dracula is spoken of as "wampyr", which we all understand too well. There have been from the loins of this very one great men and good women, and their graves make sacred the earth where alone this foulness can dwell. For it is not the least of its terrors that this evil thing is rooted deep in all good; in soil barren of holy memories it cannot rest.'

Whilst they were talking Mr Morris was looking steadily at the window, and he now got up quietly, and went out of the room. There was a little pause, and then the Professor went on:–

'And now we must settle what we do. We have here much data, and we must proceed to lay out our campaign. We know from the inquiry of Jonathan that from the castle to Whitby came fifty boxes of earth, all of which were delivered at Carfax; we also know that at least some of these boxes have been removed. It seems to me, that our first step should be to ascertain whether all the rest remain in the house beyond that wall where we look to-day; or whether any more have been removed. If the latter, we must trace – '

Here we were interrupted in a very startling way. Outside the house came the sound of a pistol-shot; the glass of the window was shattered with a bullet, which, ricochetting from the top of the embrasure, struck the far wall of the room. I am afraid I am at heart a coward, for I shrieked out. The men all jumped to their feet; Lord Godalming flew over to the window and threw up the sash. As he did so we heard Mr Morris's voice without:–

'Sorry! I fear I have alarmed you. I shall come in and tell you about it.' A minute later he came in and said:–

'It was an idiotic thing of me to do, and I ask your pardon, Mrs Harker, most sincerely; I fear I must have frightened you terribly. But the fact is that while the Professor was talking there came a big bat and sat on the window-sill. I have got such a horror of the damned brutes from recent events that I cannot stand them, and I went out to have a shot, as I have been doing of late of evenings whenever I have seen one. You used to laugh at me for it then, Art.'

'Did you hit it?' asked Dr Van Helsing.

'I don't know; I fancy not, for it flew away into the wood.' Without saying any more he took his seat, and the Professor began to resume his statement:–

'We must trace each of these boxes; and when we are ready, we must either capture or kill this monster in his lair; or we must, so to speak, sterilize the earth, so that no more can he seek safety in it. Thus in the end we may find him in his form of man between the hours of noon and sunset, and so engage with him when he is at his most weak.

'And now for you, Madam Mina, this night is the end until all be well. You are too precious to us to have such risk. When we part to-night, you no more must question. We shall tell you all in good time. We are men, and are able to bear; but you must be our star and our hope, and we shall act all the more free that you are not in the danger, such as we are.'

All the men, even Jonathan, seemed relieved; but it did not seem to me good that they should brave danger and, perhaps, lessen their safety – strength being the best safety – through care of me; but their minds were made up, and, though it was a bitter pill for me to swallow, I could say nothing, save to accept their chivalrous care of me.

Mr Morris resumed the discussion:–

'As there is no time to lose, I vote we have a look at his house right now. Time is everything with him; and swift action on our part may save another victim.'

I own that my heart began to fail me when the time for action came so close, but I did not say anything, for I had a greater fear that if I appeared as a drag or a hindrance to their work, they might even leave me out of their counsels altogether. They have now gone off to Carfax, with means to get into the house.

Manlike, they have told me to go to bed and sleep; as if a woman can sleep when those she loves are in danger! I shall lie down and pretend to sleep, lest Jonathan have added anxiety about me when he returns.

DR SEWARD'S DIARY

1 October, 4 a.m.– Just as we were about to leave the house, an urgent message was brought to me from Renfield to know if I would see him at once, as he had something of the utmost importance to say to me. I told the messenger to say that I would attend to his wishes in the morning; I was busy just at the moment. The attendant added:–

'He seems very importunate, sir. I have never seen him so eager. I don't know but what, if you don't see him soon, he will have one of his violent fits.' I knew the man would not have said this without some cause, so I said: 'All right, I'll go now'; and I asked the others to wait a few minutes for me, as I had to go and see my patient.

'Take me with you, friend John,' said the Professor. 'His case in your diary interested me much, and it had bearing, too, now and again on *our* case. I should much like to see him, and especially when his mind is disturbed.'

'May I come also?' asked Lord Godalming.

'Me too?' said Quincey Morris. I nodded, and we all went down the passage together.

We found him in a state of considerable excitement, but far more rational in his speech and manner than I had ever seen him. There was an unusual understanding of himself, which was unlike anything I had ever met with in a lunatic; and he took it for granted that his reasons would prevail with others entirely sane. We all four went into the room, but none of the others at first said anything. His request was that I would at once release him from the asylum and send him home. This he backed up with arguments regarding his complete recovery, and adduced his own existing sanity. 'I appeal to your friends,' he said; 'they will, perhaps, not mind sitting in judgment on my case. By the way, you have not introduced me.' I was so much astonished, that the oddness of introducing a madman in an asylum did not strike me at the moment; and, besides, there was a certain dignity in the man's manner, so much of the habit of equality, that I at once made the introduction: 'Lord Godalming; Professor Van

Helsing; Mr Quincey Morris, of Texas; Mr Renfield.' He shook hands with each of them, saying in turn:–

'Lord Godalming, I had the honour of seconding your father at the Windham; I grieve to know, by your holding the title, that he is no more. He was a man loved and honoured by all who knew him; and in his youth was, I have heard, the inventor of a burnt rum punch, much patronized on Derby night. Mr Morris, you should be proud of your great state. Its reception into the Union was a precedent which may have far-reaching effects hereafter, when the Pole and the Tropics may hold allegiance to the Stars and Stripes. The power of Treaty may yet prove a vast engine of enlargement, when the Monroe doctrine takes its true place as a political fable. What shall any man say of his pleasure at meeting Van Helsing? Sir, I make no apology for dropping all forms of conventional prefix. When an individual has revolutionized therapeutics by his discovery of the continuous evolution of brain-matter, conventional forms are unfitting, since they would seem to limit him to one of a class. You gentlemen, who by nationality, by heredity, or by the possession of natural gifts, are fitted to hold your respective places in the moving world, I take to witness that I am as sane as at least the majority of men who are in full possession of their liberties. And I am sure that you, Dr Seward, humanitarian and medico-jurist as well as scientist, will deem it a moral duty to deal with me as one to be considered as under exceptional circumstances.' He made this last appeal with a courtly air of conviction which was not without its own charm.

I think we were all staggered. For my own part, I was under the conviction, despite my knowledge of the man's character and history, that his reason had been restored; and I felt under a strong impulse to tell him that I was satisfied as to his sanity, and would see about the necessary formalities for his release in the morning. I thought it better to wait, however, before making so grave a statement, for of old I knew the sudden changes to which this particular patient was liable. So I contented myself with making a general statement that he appeared to be improving very rapidly; that I would have a longer chat with him in the morning, and would then see what I could do in the direction of meeting his wishes. This did not all satisfy him, for he said quickly:–

'But I fear, Dr Seward, that you hardly apprehend my wish. I desire to go at once – here – now – this very hour – this very moment, if I may. Time presses, and in our implied agreement with the old scytheman it is of the essence of the contract. I am sure it is only necessary to put before so admirable a practitioner as Dr Seward so simple, yet so momentous a wish, to ensure its fulfilment.' He looked at me keenly, and seeing the negative in my face, turned to the others, and scrutinized them closely. Not meeting any sufficient response, he went on:–

'Is it possible that I have erred in my supposition?'

'You have,' I said frankly, but at the same time, as I felt, brutally. There was a considerable pause, and then he said slowly:—

'Then I suppose I must only shift my ground of request. Let me ask for this concession – boon, privilege, what you will. I am content to implore in such a case, not on personal grounds, but for the sake of others. I am not at liberty to give you the whole of my reasons; but you may, I assure you, take it from me that they are good ones, sound and unselfish, and springing from the highest sense of duty. Could you look, sir, into my heart, you would approve to the full the sentiments which animate me. Nay, more, you would count me amongst the best and truest of your friends.' Again he looked at us all keenly. I had a growing conviction that this sudden change of his entire intellectual method was but yet another form or phase of his madness, and so determined to let him go on a little longer, knowing from experience that he would, like all lunatics, give himself away in the end. Van Helsing was gazing at him with a look of the utmost intensity, his busy eyebrows almost meeting with the fixed concentration of his look. He said to Renfield in a tone which did not surprise me at the time, but only when I thought of it afterwards – for it was as of one addressing an equal:—

'Can you not tell frankly your real reason for wishing to be free to-night? I will undertake that if you satisfy even me – a stranger, without prejudice, and with the habit of keeping an open mind – Dr Seward will give you, at his own risk and on his own responsibility, the privilege you seek.' He shook his head sadly, and with a look of poignant regret on his face. The Professor went on:—

'Come sir, bethink yourself. You claim the privilege of reason in the highest degree, since you seek to impress us with your complete reasonableness. You do this, whose sanity we have reason to doubt, since you are not yet released from medical treatment for this very defect. If you will not help us in our effort to choose the wisest course, how can we perform the duty which you yourself put upon us? Be wise, and help us; and if we can we shall aid you to achieve your wish.' He still shook his head as he said:—

'Dr Van Helsing, I have nothing to say. Your argument is complete, and if I were free to speak I should not hesitate a moment; but I am not my own master in the matter. I can only ask you to trust me. If I am refused, the responsibility does not rest with me.' I thought it was now time to end the scene, which was becoming too comically grave, so I went towards the door, simply saying:—

'Come, my friends, we have work to do. Good night.'

As, however, I got near the door, a new change came over the patient.

He moved towards me so quickly that for the moment I feared that he was about to make another homicidal attack. My fears, however, were groundless, for he held up his two hands imploringly, and made his petition in a moving manner. As he saw that the very excess of his emotion was militating against him, by restoring us more to our old relations, he became still more demonstrative. I glanced at Van Helsing, and saw my conviction reflected in his eyes; so I became a little more fixed in my manner, if not more stern, and motioned to him that his efforts were unavailing. I had previously seen something of the same constantly growing excitement in him when he had to make some request of which at the time he had thought much, such, for instance, as when he wanted a cat; and I was prepared to see the collapse into the same sullen acquiescence on this occasion. My expectation was not realized, for, when he found that this appeal would not be successful, he got into quite a frantic condition. He threw himself on his knees, and held up his hands, wringing them in plaintive supplication, and poured forth a torrent of entreaty, with the tears rolling down his cheeks and his whole face and form expressive of the deepest emotion:—

'Let me entreat you, Dr Seward, oh, let me implore you, to let me out of this house at once. Send me away how you will and where you will; send keepers with me with whips and chains; let them take me in a strait-waistcoat, manacled and leg-ironed, even to a gaol; but let me go out of this. You don't know what you do by keeping me here. I am speaking from the depths of my heart – of my very soul. You don't know whom you wrong, or how; and I may not tell. Woe is me! I may not tell. By all you hold sacred – by all you hold dear – by your love that is lost – by your hope that lives – for the sake of the Almighty, take me out of this and save my soul from guilt! Can't you hear me, man? Can't you understand? Will you never learn? Don't you know that I am sane and earnest now; that I am no lunatic in a mad fit, but a sane man fighting for his soul? Oh, hear me! hear me! Let me go! let me go! let me go!'

I thought that the longer this went on the wilder he would get, and so would bring on a fit; so I took him by the hand and raised him up.

'Come,' I said sternly, 'no more of this; we have had quite enough already. Get to your bed and try to behave more discreetly.'

He suddenly stopped and looked at me intently for several moments. Then without a word he rose, and moving over, sat down on the side of the bed. The collapse had come, as on former occasions, just as I had expected.

When I was leaving the room, last of our party, he said to me in a quiet, well-bred voice:—

'You will, I trust, Dr Seward, do me the justice to bear in mind, later on, that I did what I could to convince you to-night.'

19

JONATHAN HARKER'S JOURNAL

1 October, 5 a.m. – I went with the party to the search with an easy mind, for I think I never saw Mina so absolutely strong and well. I am so glad that she consented to hold back and let us men do the work. Somehow, it was a dread to me that she was in this fearful business at all; but now that her work is done, and that it is due to her energy and brains and foresight that the whole story is put together in such a way that every point tells, she may well feel that her part is finished, and that she can henceforth leave the rest to us. We were, I think, all a little upset by the scene with Mr Renfield. When we came away from his room we were still silent till we got back to the study. Then Mr Morris said to Dr Seward:–

'Say, Jack, if that man wasn't attempting a bluff, he is about the sanest lunatic I ever saw. I'm not sure, but I believe that he had some serious purpose, and if he had, it was pretty rough on him not to get a chance.' Lord Godalming and I were silent, but Dr Van Helsing added:–

'Friend John, you know more of lunatics than I do, and I'm glad of it, for I fear that if it had been to me to decide I would before that last hysterical outburst have given him free. But we live and learn, and in our present task we must take no chance, as my friend Quincey would say. All is best as they are.' Dr Seward to answer them both in a dreamy kind of way:–

'I don't know but that I agree with you. If that man had been an ordinary lunatic I would have taken my chance of trusting him; but he seems so mixed up with the Count in an indexy kind of way that I am afraid of doing anything wrong by helping his fads. I can't forget how he prayed with almost equal fervour for a cat, and then tried to tear my throat out with his teeth. Besides, he called the Count "lord and master", and he may want to get out to help him in some diabolical way. That horrid thing has the wolves and the rats and his own kind to help him, so I suppose he isn't above trying to use a respectable lunatic. He certainly did seem earnest, though. I only hope we have done what is best. These things, in conjunction with the work we have in hand, help to unnerve a man.' The Professor stepped over, and laying a hand on his shoulder, said in his grave, kindly way:–

'Friend John, have no fear. We are trying to do our duty in a very sad and terrible case; we can only do as we deem best. What else have we to hope for, except the pity of the good God?' Lord Godalming had slipped away for a few minutes, but he now returned. He held up a little silver whistle as he remarked:–

'That old place may be full of rats, and if so, I've got an antidote on call.' Having passed the wall, we took our way to the house, taking care to keep in the shadows of the trees on the lawn when the moonlight shone out. When we got to the porch the Professor opened his bag and took out a lot of things, which he laid on the step, sorting them into four little groups, evidently one for each. Then he spoke:–

'My friends, we are going into a terrible danger, and we need arms of many kinds. Our enemy is not merely spiritual. Remember that he has the strength of twenty men, and that, though our necks or our windpipes are of the common kind – and therefore breakable or crushable – he is not amenable to mere strength. A stronger man, or a body of men more strong in all than him, can at certain times hold him; but yet they cannot hurt him as we can be hurt by him. We must, therefore, guard ourselves from his touch. Keep this near your heart' – as he spoke he lifted a little silver crucifix and held it out to me, I being nearest to him – 'put these flowers round your neck' – here he handed to me a wreath of withered garlic blossoms – 'for other enemies more mundane, this revolver and this knife; and for aid in all, these so small electric lamps, which you can fasten to your breast; and for all, and above all the last, this, which we must not desecrate needless.' This was a portion of sacred wafer, which he put in an envelope and handed to me. Each of the others was similarly equipped. 'Now,' he said, 'friend John, where are the skeleton keys? If so that we can open the door, we need not break house by the window, as before at Miss Lucy's.'

Dr Seward tried one or two skeleton keys, his mechanical dexterity as a surgeon standing him in good stead. Presently he got one to suit; after a little play back and forward the bolt yielded, and, with a rusty clang, shot back. We pressed on the door, the rusty hinges creaked, and it slowly opened. It was startlingly like the image conveyed to me in Dr Seward's diary of the opening of Miss Westenra's tomb; I fancy that the same idea seemed to strike the others, for with one accord they shrank back. The Professor was the first to move forward, and stepped into the open door.

'*In manus tuas, Domine!*' he said, crossing himself as he passed over the threshold. We closed the door behind us, lest when we should have lit our lamps we might possibly attract attention from the road. The Professor carefully tried the lock, in case we might not be able to open it from within should we be in a hurry to make our exit. Then we all lit our lamps and proceeded on our search.

The light from the tiny lamps fell in all sorts of odd forms, as the rays crossed each other, or the opacity of our bodies threw great shadows. I could not for my life get away from the feeling that there was someone else amongst us. I suppose it was the recollection, so powerfully brought home to me by the grim surroundings, of that terrible experience in Transylvania. I think the feeling was common to us all, for I noticed that the others kept looking over their shoulders at every sound and every new shadow, just as I felt myself doing.

The whole place was thick with dust. The floor was seemingly inches deep, except where there were recent footsteps, in which on holding down my lamp I could see marks of hobnails where the dust was caked. The walls were fluffy and heavy with dust, and in the corners were masses of spiders' webs, whereon the dust had gathered till they looked like old tattered rags as the weight had torn them partly down. On a table in the hall was a great bunch of keys, with a time-yellowed label on each. They had been used several times, for on the table were several similar rents in the blanket of dust, like that exposed when the Professor lifted the keys. He turned to me and said:—

'You know this place, Jonathan. You have copied maps of it, and you know at least more than we do. Which is the way to the chapel?' I had an idea of its direction, though on my former visit I had not been able to get admission to it; so I led the way, and after a few wrong turnings found myself opposite a low, arched oaken door, ribbed with iron bands. 'This is the spot,' said the Professor, as he turned his lamp on a small map of the house, copied from the file of my original correspondence regarding the purchase. With a little trouble we found the key on the bunch and opened the door. We were prepared for some unpleasantness, for as we were opening the door a faint, malodorous air seemed to exhale through the gaps, but none of us ever expected such an odour as we encountered. None of the others had met the Count at all at close quarters, and when I had seen him he was either in the fasting stage of his existence in his rooms or, when he was glutted with fresh blood, in a ruined building open to the air; but here the place was small and close, and the long disuse had made the air stagnant and foul. There was an earthy smell, as of some dry miasma, which came through the fouler air. But as to the odour itself, how shall I describe it? It was not alone that it was composed of all the ills of mortality and with the pungent, acrid smell of blood, but it seemed as though corruption had become itself corrupt. Faugh! it sickens me to think of it. Every breath exhaled by that monster seemed to have clung to the place and intensified its loathsomeness.

Under ordinary circumstances such a stench would have brought our enterprise to an end; but this was no ordinary case, and the high and terrible purpose in which we were involved gave us a strength which rose above merely physical considerations. After the involuntary shrinking consequent on the first nauseous whiff, we one and all set about our work as though that loathsome place were a garden of roses.

We made an accurate examination of the place, the Professor saying as we began:–

'The first thing is to see how many of the boxes are left; we must then examine every hole and corner and cranny, and see if we cannot get some clue as to what has become of the rest.' A glance was sufficient to show how many remained, for the great earth chests were bulky, and there was no mistaking them.

There were only twenty-nine left out of the fifty! Once I got a fright, for, seeing Lord Godalming suddenly turn and look out of the vaulted door into the dark passage beyond, I looked too, and for an instant my heart stood still. Somewhere, looking out from the shadow, I seemed to see the high lights of the Count's evil face, the ridge of the nose, the red eyes, the red lips, the awful pallor. It was only for a moment, for as Lord Godalming said, 'I thought I saw a face, but it was only the shadows,' and resumed his inquiry, I turned my lamp in the direction, and stepped into the passage. There was no sign of anyone; and as there were no corners, no doors, no aperture of any kind, but only the solid walls of the passage, there could be no hiding-place, even for *him*. I took it that fear had helped imagination, and said nothing.

A few minutes later I saw Morris step suddenly back from a corner, which he was examining. We all followed his movements with our eyes, for undoubtedly some nervousness was growing on us, and we saw a whole mass of phosphorescence, which twinkled like stars. We all instinctively drew back. The whole place was becoming alive with rats.

For a moment or two we stood appalled, all save Lord Godalming, who was seemingly prepared for such an emergency. Rushing over to the great iron-bound oaken door, which Dr Seward had described from the outside, and which I had seen myself, he turned the key in the lock, drew the huge bolts, and swung the door open. Then, taking his little silver whistle from his pocket, he blew a low, shrill call. It was answered from behind Dr Seward's house by the yelping of dogs, and after about a minute three terriers came dashing round the corner of the house. Unconsciously we had all moved towards the door, and as we moved I noticed that the dust had been much disturbed: the boxes which had been taken out had been brought this way. But even in the minute that had elapsed the number of the rats had vastly increased. They seemed to swarm over the place all at once, till the lamplight, shining on their moving dark bodies and glittering, baleful eyes, made the place look like a bank of earth set with fireflies. The dogs dashed on, but at the threshold suddenly stopped and snarled, and then, simultaneously lifting their noses, began to howl in most lugubrious fashion. The rats were multiplying in thousands, and moved out.

Lord Godalming lifted one of the dogs, and carrying him in, placed him on the floor. The instant his feet touched the ground he seemed to recover his courage, and rushed at his natural enemies. They fled before him so fast that, before he had shaken the life out of a score, the other dogs, who had by now been lifted in in the same manner, had but small prey ere the whole mass had vanished.

With their going it seemed as if some evil presence had departed, for the dogs frisked about and barked merrily as they made sudden darts at their prostrate foes, and turned them over and over and tossed them in the air with vicious shakes. We all seemed to find our spirits rise. Whether it was the purifying of the deadly atmosphere by the opening of the chapel door, or the relief which we experienced by finding ourselves in the open, I know not; but most certainly the shadow of dread seemed to slip from us like a robe, and the occasion of our coming lost something of its grim significance, though we did not slacken a whit in our resolution. We closed the outer door and barred and locked it, and bringing the dogs with us, began our search of the house. We found nothing throughout except dust in extraordinary proportions, and all untouched save for my own footsteps when I had made my first visit. Never once did the dogs exhibit any symptom of uneasiness, and even when we returned to the chapel they frisked about as though they had been rabbit-hunting in a summer wood.

The morning was quickening in the east when we emerged from the front. Dr Van Helsing had taken the key of the hall-door from the bunch, and locked the door in orthodox fashion, putting the key into his pocket when he had done.

'So far,' he said, 'our night has been eminently successful. No harm has come to us such as I feared might be, and yet we have ascertained how many boxes are missing. More than all do I rejoice that this, our first – and perhaps our most difficult and dangerous – step has been accomplished without the bringing thereinto our most sweet Madam Mina or troubling her waking or sleeping thoughts with sights and sounds and smells of horror which she might never forget. One lesson, too, we have learned, if it be allowable to argue *a particulari*: that the brute beasts which are to the Count's command are yet themselves not amenable to his spiritual power; for look, these rats that would come to his call, just as from his castle top he summon the wolves to your going and to that poor mother's cry, though they come to him, they run pell-mell from the so little dogs of my friend Arthur. We have other matters before us, other dangers, other fears; and that monster – he has not used his power over the brute world for the only or the last time to-night. So be it that he has gone elsewhere. Good! It has given us opportunity to cry "check" in some way in this chess game, which we play for the stake of human souls. And now let us go home. The dawn is close at hand, and we have reason to be content with our first night's work. It may be ordained that we have many nights and days to follow, if full of peril; but we must go on, and from no danger shall we shrink.'

The house was silent when we got back, save for some poor creature who was screaming away in one of the distant wards, and a low, moaning sound from Renfield's room. The poor wretch was doubtless torturing himself, after the manner of the insane, with needless thoughts of pain.

I came tiptoe into our own room, and found Mina asleep, breathing so softly that I had to put my ear down to hear it. She looks paler than usual. I hope the meeting to-night has not upset her. I am truly thankful that she is to be left out of our future work, and even of our deliberations. It is too great a strain for a woman to bear. I did not think so at first, but I know better now. Therefore I am glad that it is settled. There may be things which would frighten her to hear; and yet to conceal them from her might be worse than to tell her if once she suspected that there was any concealment. Henceforth our work is to be a sealed book to her, till at least such time as we can tell her that all is finished, and the earth free from a monster of the nether world. I daresay it will be difficult to begin to keep silence after such confidence as ours; but I must be resolute, and to-morrow I shall keep dark over to-night's doings, and shall refuse to speak of anything that has happened. I rest on the sofa, so as not to disturb her.

1 October, later. — I suppose it was natural that we should have all overslept ourselves, for the day was a busy one, and the night had no rest at all. Even Mina must have felt its exhaustion, for though I slept till the sun was high, I was awake before her, and had to call two or three times before she awoke. Indeed, she was so sound asleep that for a few seconds she did not recognize me, but looked at me with a sort of blank terror, as one looks who has been waked out of a bad dream. She complained a little of being tired, and I let her rest till later in the day. We now know of twenty-one boxes having been removed, and if it be that several were taken in any of these removals we may be able to trace them all. Such will, of course, immensely simplify our labour, and the sooner the matter is attended to the better. I shall look up Thomas Snelling today.

DR SEWARD'S DIARY

1 October. — It was towards noon when I was awakened by the Professor walking into my room. He was more jolly and cheerful than usual, and it is quite evident that last night's work has helped to take some of the brooding weight off his mind. After going over the adventure of the night he suddenly said:—

'Your patient interests me much. May it be that with you I visit him this morning? Or if that you are too occupy, I can go alone if it may be. It is a new experience to me to find a lunatic who talk philosophy, and reason so sound.' I had some work to do which pressed, so I told him that if he would go alone I would be glad, as then I should not have to keep him waiting; so I called an attendant and gave him the necessary instructions. Before the Professor left the room I cautioned him against getting any false impression from my patient. 'But,' he answered, 'I want him to talk of himself and of his delusion as to consuming live things. He said to Madam Mina, as I see in your diary of yesterday, that he had once had such a belief. Why do you smile, friend John?'

'Excuse me,' I said, 'but the answer is here.' I laid my hand on the typewritten matter. 'When our sane and learned lunatic made that very statement of how he *used* to consume life, his mouth was actually nauseous with the flies and spiders which he had eaten just before Mrs Harker entered the room.' Van Helsing smiled in turn. 'Good!' he said. 'Your memory is true, friend John. I should have remembered. And yet it is this very obliquity of thought and memory which makes mental disease such a fascinating study. Perhaps I may gain more knowledge out of the folly of this madman than I shall from the teaching of the most wise. Who knows?' I went on with my work, and before long was through that in hand. It seemed that the time had been very short indeed, but there was Van Helsing back in the study. 'Do I interrupt?' he asked politely as he stood at the door.

'Not at all,' I answered. 'Come in. My work is finished, and I am free. I can go with you now, if you like.'

'It is needless; I have seen him!'

'Well?'

'I fear that he does not appraise me at much. Our interview was short. When I entered the room he was sitting on a stool in the centre, with his elbows on his knees, and his face was the picture of sullen discontent. I spoke to him as cheerfully as I could, and with such a measure of respect as I could assume. He made no reply whatever. "Don't you know me?" I asked. His answer was not reassuring: "I know you well enough; you are the old fool Van Helsing. I wish you would take yourself and your idiotic brain theories somewhere else. Damn all thick-headed Dutchmen!" Not a word more would he say, but sat in his implacable sullenness as indifferent to me as though I had not been in the room at all. Thus departed for this time my chance of much learning from this so clever lunatic; so I shall go, if I may, and cheer myself with a few happy words with that sweet soul Madam Mina. Friend John, it does rejoice me unspeakable that she is no more to be pained, no more to be worried, with our terrible things. Though we shall much miss her help, it is better so.'

'I agree with you with all my heart,' I answered earnestly, for I did not want him to weaken in this matter. 'Mrs Harker is better out of it. Things are quite bad enough for us, all men of the world, and who have been in many tight places in our time; but it is no place for a woman, and if she had remained in touch with the affair, it would in time infallibly have wrecked her.'

So Van Helsing has gone to confer with Mrs Harker and Harker; Quincey and Art are both out following up the clues as to the earth-boxes. I shall finish my round of work, and we shall meet to-night.

MINA HARKER'S JOURNAL

1 October. – It is strange to me to be kept in the dark as I am to-day; after Jonathan's full confidence for so many years, to see him manifestly avoid certain matters, and those the most vital of all. This morning I slept late after the fatigues of yesterday, and though Jonathan was late too, he was the earlier. He spoke to me before he went out, never more sweetly or tenderly, but he never mentioned a word of what had happened in the visit to the Count's house. And yet he must have known how terribly anxious I was. Poor dear fellow! I suppose it must have distressed him even more than it did me. They all agreed that it was best that I should not be drawn further into this awful work, and I acquiesced. But to think that he keeps anything from me! And now I am crying like a silly fool, when I *know* it comes from my husband's great love and from the good, good wishes of those other strong men. . . .

That has done me good. Well, some day Jonathan will tell me all; and lest it should ever be that he should think for a moment that I kept anything from him, I still keep my journal as usual. Then if he has doubted of my trust I shall show it to him, with every thought of my heart put down for his dear eyes to read. I feel strangely sad and low-spirited to-day. I suppose it is the reaction from the terrible excitement.

Last night I went to bed when the man had gone, simply because they told me to. I didn't feel sleepy, and I did feel full of devouring anxiety. I kept thinking over everything that has been ever since Jonathan came to see me in London, and it all seems like a horrible tragedy, with fate pressing on relentlessly to some destined end. Everything that one does seems, no matter how right it may be, to bring on the very thing which is

209

most to be deplored. If I hadn't gone to Whitby, perhaps poor dear Lucy would be with us now. She hadn't taken to visiting the churchyard till I came, and if she hadn't come there in the daytime with me she wouldn't have walked there in her sleep; and if she hadn't gone there at night and asleep, that monster couldn't have destroyed her as he did. Oh, why did I ever go to Whitby. There now, crying again! I wonder what has come over me to-day. I must hide it from Jonathan, for if he knew that I had been crying twice in one morning – I, who never cried on my own account, and whom he has never caused to shed a tear – the dear fellow would fret his heart out. I shall put a bold face on, and if I do feel weepy, he shall never see it. I suppose it is one of the lessons that we poor women have to learn. . . .

I can't quite remember how I fell asleep last night. I remember hearing the sudden barking of the dogs and a lot of queer sounds, like braying on a very tumultuous scale, from Mr Renfield's room, which is somewhere under this. And then there was silence over everything, silence so profound that it startled me, and I got up and looked out of the window. All was dark and silent, the black shadows thrown by the moonlight seeming full of a silent mystery of their own. Not a thing seemed to be stirring, but all to be grim and fixed as death or fate; so that a thin streak of white mist, that crept with almost imperceptible slowness across the grass towards the house, seemed to have a sentience and a vitality of its own. I think that the digression of my thoughts must have done me good, for when I got back to bed I found a lethargy creeping over me. I lay a while, but could not quite sleep, so I got out and looked out of the window again. The mist spreading, and was now close up to the house, so that I could see it lying thick against the wall, as though it were stealing up to the windows. The poor man was more loud than ever, and though I could not distinguish a word he said, I could in some way recognize in his tones some passionate entreaty on his part. Then there was the sound of a struggle, and I knew that the attendants were dealing with him. I was so frightened that I crept into bed, and pulled the clothes over my head, putting my fingers in my ears. I was not then a bit sleepy, at least so I thought; but I must have fallen asleep, for, except dreams, I do not remember anything until the morning, when Jonathan woke me. I think that it took me an effort and a little time to realize where I was, and that it was Jonathan who was bending over me. My dream was very peculiar, and was almost typical of the way that waking thoughts become merged in, or continued in, dreams.

I thought that I was asleep, and waiting for Jonathan to come back. I was very anxious about him, and I was powerless to act; my feet, and my hands, and my brain were weighted, so that nothing could proceed at the usual pace. And so I slept uneasily and thought. Then it began to dawn upon me that the air was heavy, and dank, and cold. I put back the clothes from my face, and found, to my surprise, that all was dim around me. The gas-light which I had left lit for Jonathan, but turned down, came only like a tiny red spark through the fog, which had evidently grown thicker and poured into the room. Then it occurred to me that I had shut the window before I had come to bed. I would have got out to make certain on the point, but some leaden lethargy seemed to chain my limbs and even my will. I lay still and endured; that was all. I closed my eyes, but could still see through my eyelids. (It is wonderful what tricks our dreams play us, and how conveniently we can imagine.) The mist grew thicker and thicker, and I could see now how it came in, for I could see it like smoke – or with the white energy of boiling water – pouring in, not through the window, but through the joinings of the door. It got thicker and thicker, till it seemed as if it became concentrated into a sort of pillar of cloud in the room, through the top of which I could see the light of the gas shining like a red eye. Things began to whirl through my brain just as the cloudy column was now whirling in the room, and through it all came the scriptural words 'a pillar of cloud by day and of fire by night'. Was it indeed some spiritual guidance that was coming to me in my sleep? But the pillar was composed of both the day and the night guiding, for the fire was in the red eye, which at the thought got a new fascination for me; till, as I looked, the fire divided, and seemed to shine on me through the fog like two red eyes, such as Lucy told me of in her momentary mental wandering when, on the cliff, the dying sunlight struck the windows of St Mary's Church. Suddenly the horror burst open upon me that it was thus that Jonathan had seen those awful women growing into reality through the whirling mist in the moonlight, and in my dream I must have fainted, for all became black darkness. The last conscious effort which imagination made was to show me a livid white face bending over me out of the mist. I must be careful of such dreams, for they would unseat one's reason if there was too much of them. I would get Dr Van Helsing or Dr Seward to prescribe something for me which would make me sleep, only that I fear to alarm them. Such a dream at the present time would become woven into their fears for me. To-night I shall strive hard to sleep naturally. If I do not, I shall to-morrow night get them to give me a dose of chloral; that cannot hurt me for once, and it will give me a good night's sleep. Last night tired me more than if I had not slept at all.

2 October, 10 p.m.. – Last night I slept, but did not dream. I must have slept soundly, for I was not waked by Jonathan coming to bed; but the sleep has not refreshed me, for to-day I feel terribly weak and spiritless. I spent all yesterday trying to read, or lying down dozing. In the afternoon

Mr Renfield asked if he might see me. Poor man, he was very gentle, and when I came away he kissed my hand and bade God bless me. Some way it affected me much; I am crying when I think of him. This is a new weakness, of which I must be careful. Jonathan would be miserable if he knew I had been crying. He and the others were out until dinner-time, and they all came in tired. I did what I could to brighten them up, and I suppose that the effort did me good, for I forgot how tired I was. After dinner they sent me to bed, and all went off to smoke together, as they said, but I knew that they wanted to tell each other of what had occurred to each during the day; I could see from Jonathan's manner that he had something important to communicate. I was not so sleepy as I should have been; so before they went I asked Dr Seward to give me a little opiate of some kind, as I had not slept well the night before. He very kindly made me up a sleeping draught, which he gave to me, telling me that it would do me no harm, as it was very mild. . . . I have taken it, and am waiting for sleep, which still keeps aloof. I hope I have not done wrong, for as sleep begins to flirt with me, a new fear comes: that I may have been foolish in thus depriving myself of the power of waking. I might want it. Here comes sleep. Good-night.

20

JONATHAN HARKER'S JOURNAL

1 October, evening. – I found Thomas Snelling in his house at Bethnal Green, but unhappily he was not in a condition to remember anything. The very prospect of beer which my expected coming had opened to him had proved too much, and he had begun too early on his expected debauch. I learned, however, from his wife, who seemed a decent, poor soul, that he was only the assistant to Smollet, who of the two mates was the responsible person. So off I drove to Walworth, and found Mr Joseph Smollet at home and in his shirt-sleeves, taking a late tea out of a saucer. He is a decent, intelligent fellow, distinctly a good, reliable type of workman, and with a head-piece of his own. He remembered all about the incident of the boxes, and from a wonderful dog's-eared notebook, which he produced from some mysterious receptacle about the seat of his trousers, and which had hieroglyphical entries in thick, half-obliterated pencil, he gave me the destinations of the boxes. There were, he said, six in the cartload which he took from Carfax and left at 197 Chicksand Street,

Mile End New Town, and another six which he deposited at Jamaica Lane, Bermondsey. If then the Count meant to scatter these ghastly refuges of his over London, these places were chosen as the first of delivery, so that later he might distribute more fully. The systematic manner in which this was done made me think that he could not mean to confine himself to two sides of London. He was now fixed on the far east of the northern shore, on the east of the southern shore, and on the south. The north and west were surely never meant to be left out of his diabolical scheme – let alone the City itself and the very heart of fashionable London in the south-west and west. I went back to Smollet and asked him if he could tell us if any other boxes had been taken from Carfax.

He replied:–

'Well, guv'nor, you've treated me wery 'an'some' – I had given him half a sovereign – 'an' I'll tell yer all I know. I heeard a man by the name of Bloxam say four nights ago in the " 'Are an' 'Ounds'', in Pincher's Alley, as 'ow he an' his mate 'ad 'ad a rare dusty job in a old 'ouse at Purfleet. There ain't a-many such jobs as this 'ere, an' I'm thinkin' that maybe Sam Bloxam could tell ye summut.' I asked if he could tell me where to find him. I told him that if he could get me the address it would be worth another half-sovereign to him. So he gulped down the rest of his tea and stood up, saying that he was going to begin the search then and there. At the door he stopped, and said:–

'Look, 'ere, guv'nor, there ain't no sense in me a-keepin' you 'ere. I may find Sam soon, or I mayn't; but anyhow he ain't like to be in a way to tell ye much to-night. Sam is a rare one when he starts on the booze. If you can give me a envelope with a stamp on it, and put yer address on it, I'll find out where Sam is to be found and post it ye to-night. But ye'd better be up arter 'im soon in the mornin', or maybe ye won't ketch 'im; for Sam gets off main early, never mind the booze the night afore.'

This was all practical, so one of the children went off with a penny to buy an envelope and a sheet of paper, and to keep the change. When she came back I addressed the envelope and stamped it, and when Smollet had again faithfully promised to post the address when found, I took my way to home. We're on the track anyhow. I am tired to-night, and want sleep. Mina is fast asleep, and looks a little too pale; her eyes look as though she had been crying. Poor dear, I've no doubt it frets her to be kept in the dark, and it may make her doubly anxious about me and the others. But it is best as it is. It is better to be disappointed and worried in such a way now than to have her nerve broken. The doctors were quite right to insist on her being kept out of this dreadful business. I must be firm, for on me this particular burden of silence must rest. I shall not ever enter on the subject with her under any circumstances. Indeed, it may not be a hard

213

task after all, she herself has become reticent on the subject, and has not spoken of the Count or his doings ever since we told her of our decision.

2 October, evening. – A long and trying and exciting day. By the first post I got my directed envelope with a dirty scrap of paper enclosed, on which was written with a carpenter's pencil in a sprawling hand:–

'Sam Bloxam, Korkrans, 4 Poters Cort,
Bartel Street, Walworth. Arsk for the depite.'

I got the letter in bed, and rose without waking Mina. She looked heavy and sleepy and pale, and far from well. I determined not to wake her, but that, when I should return from this new search, I would arrange for her going back to Exeter. I think she would be happier in our own home, with her daily tasks to interest her, than in being here amongst us and in ignorance. I only saw Dr Seward for a moment, and told him where I was off to, promising to come back and tell the rest so soon as I should have found out anything. I drove to Walworth and found, with some difficulty, Potter's Court. Mr Smollet's spelling misled me, as I asked for Poter's Court instead of Potter's Court. However, when I had found the court I had no difficulty in discovering Corcoran's lodging-house. When I asked the man who came to the door for the 'depite', he shook his head, and said: 'I dunno 'im. There ain't no such person 'ere; I never 'eard of 'im in all my bloomin' days. Don't believe there ain't nobody of that kind livin' 'ere or anywheres.' I took out Smollet's letter, and as I read it it seemed to me that the lesson of the spelling of the name of the court might guide me. 'What are you?' I asked.

'I'm the depity,' he answered. I saw at once that I was on the right track; phonetic spelling had again misled me. A half-crown tip put the deputy's knowledge at my disposal, and I learned that Mr Bloxam, who had slept off the remains of his beer on the previous night at Corcoran's, had left for work at Poplar at five o'clock that morning. He could not tell me where the place of work was situated, but he had a vague idea that it was some kind of a 'new-fangled ware'us'; and with this slender clue I had to start for Poplar. I was twelve o'clock before I got any satisfactory hint of such a building, and this I got at a coffee-shop, where some workmen were having their dinner. One of these suggested that there was being erected at Cross Angel Street a new 'cold storage' building; and as this suited the condition of a 'new fangled ware'us', I at once drove to it. An interview with a surly gate-keeper and a surlier foreman, both of whom were appeased with coin of the realm, put me on the track of Bloxam; he was sent for on my suggesting that I was willing to pay his day's wages to his foreman for the privilege of asking him a few questions on a private matter. He was a smart enough fellow, though rough of speech and bearing. When I had promised to pay for his information and given him an earnest, he told me that he had made two journeys between Carfax and a house in Piccadilly, and had taken from this house to the latter nine great boxes – 'main heavy ones' – with a horse and cart hired by him for this purpose. I asked him if he could tell me the number of the house in Piccadilly, to which he replied:–

'Well, guv'nor, I forgits the number, but it was only a few doors from a big white church or somethink of the kind, not long built. It was a dusty old 'ouse, too, though nothin' to the dustiness of the 'ouse we tooked the bloomin' boxes from.'

'How did you get into the house if they were both empty?'

'There was the old party what engaged me a-waitin' in the 'ouse at Purfleet. He 'elped me to lift the boxes and put them in the dray. Curse me, but he was the strongest chap I ever struck, an' him a old feller, with a white moustache, one that thin you would think he couldn't throw a shadder.'

How this phrase thrilled through me!

'Why, 'e took up 'is end o' the boxes like they was pounds of tea, and me a-puffin' an' a-blowin' afore I could up-end mine anyhow – an' I'm no chicken, neither.'

'How did you get into the house in Piccadilly?' I asked.

'He was there too. He must 'a' started off and got there afore me, for when I rung of the bell he kem an' opened the door 'isself an' 'elped me to carry the boxes into the 'all.'

'The whole nine?' I asked.

'Yus; there was five in the first load 'an four in the second. It was main dry work, an' I don't so well remember 'ow I got 'ome.' I interrupted him:–

'Were the boxes left in the hall?'

'Yus; it was a big 'all, an' there was nothin' else in it.' I made one more attempt to further matters:–

'You didn't have any key?'

'Never used no key nor nothink. The old gent, he opened the door 'isself an' shut it again when I druv off. I don't remember the last time – but that was the beer.'

'And you can't remember the number of the house?'

'No, sir. But ye needn't have no difficulty about that. It's a 'igh 'un with a stone front with a bow in it, and 'igh steps up to the door. I know them steps, 'avin' 'ad to carry the boxes up with three loafers what come round to earn a copper. The old gent give them shillin's, an' they seein' they got so much, they wanted more; but 'e took one of them by the shoulder and was like to throw 'im down the steps, till the lot of them went away cussin'.' I thought that with this description I could find the house, so having paid my friend for his information, I started off for Piccadilly. I had gained a new painful experience: the Count could, it was evident, handle the earth-boxes himself. If so, time was precious; for, now he had achieved a certain amount of distribution, he could, by choosing his own time, complete the task unobserved. At Piccadilly Circus I discharged my cab, and walked westward; beyond the Junior Constitutional I came across the house described, and was satisfied that this was the next of the lairs arranged by Dracula. The house looked as though it had been long untenanted. The windows were encrusted with dust, and the shutters were up. All the framework was black with time, and from the iron the paint had mostly scaled away. It was evident that up to lately there had been a large noticeboard in front of the balcony; it had, however, been roughly torn away, the uprights which had supported it still remaining. Behind the rails of the balcony I saw there were some loose boards, whose raw edges looked white. I would have given a good deal to have been able to see the noticeboard intact, as it would, perhaps, have given some clue to the ownership of the house. I remembered my experience of the investigation and purchase of Carfax, and I could not but feel that if I could find the former owner there might be some means of gaining access to the house.

There was at present nothing to be learned from the Piccadilly side, and nothing could be done; so I went round to the back to see if anything could be gathered from this quarter. The mews were active, the Piccadilly houses being mostly in occupation. I asked one or two of the grooms and helpers whom I saw around if they could tell me anything about the empty house. One of them said he had heard it had lately been taken, but he couldn't say from whom. He told me, however, that up to very lately there had been a noticeboard of 'For Sale' up, and that perhaps Mitchell, Sons & Candy, the house agents, could tell me something, as he thought he remembered seeing the name of that firm on the board. I did not wish to seem too eager, or to let my informant know or guess too much, so, thanking him in the usual manner, I strolled away. It was now growing dusk, and the autumn night was closing in, so I did not lose any time. Having learned the address of Mitchell, Sons & Candy from a directory at the Berkeley, I was soon at their office in Sackville Street.

The gentleman who saw me was particularly suave in manner, but uncommunicative in equal proportion. Having once told me that the Piccadilly house – which throughout our interview he called a 'mansion' – was sold, he considered my business as concluded. When I asked who had purchased it, he opened his eyes a thought wider, and paused a few seconds before replying:–

'It is sold, sir.'

'Pardon me,' I said, with equal politeness, 'but I have a special reason for wishing to know who purchased it.'

Again he paused longer, and raised his eyebrows still more. 'It is sold, sir,' was again his laconic reply.

'Surely,' I said, 'you do not mind letting me know so much.'

'But I do mind,' he answered. 'The affairs of their clients are absolutely safe in the hands of Mitchell, Sons & Candy.' This was manifestly a prig of the first water, and there was no use arguing with him. I thought I had best meet him on his own ground, so I said:—

'Your clients, sir, are happy in having so resolute a guardian of their confidence. I am myself a professional man.' Here I handed him my card. 'In this instance I am not prompted by curiosity; I act on the part of Lord Godalming, who wishes to know something of the property which was, he understood, lately for sale.' These words put a different complexion on affairs. He said:—

'I would like to oblige you if I could, Mr Harker, and especially would I like to oblige his lordship. We once carried out a small matter of renting some chambers for him when he was the Honourable Arthur Holmwood. If you will let me have his lordship's address I will consult the House on the subject, and will, in any case, communicate with his lordship by to-night's post. It will be a pleasure if we can so far deviate from our rules as to give the required information to his lordship.'

I wanted to secure a friend, and not to make an enemy, so I thanked him, gave the address at Dr Seward's, and came away. It was now dark, and I was tired and hungry. I got a cup of tea at the Aerated Bread Company and came down to Purfleet by the next train.

I found all the others at home. Mina was looking tired and pale, but she made a gallant effort to be bright and cheerful; it wrung my heart to think that I had had to keep anything from her and so caused her disquietude. Thank God, this will be the last night of her looking on at our conferences, and feeling the sting of our not showing our confidence. It took all my courage to hold the wise resolution of keeping her out of our grim task. She seems somehow more reconciled; or else the very subject seems to have become repugnant to her, for when any accidental allusion is made she actually shudders. I am glad we made our resolution in time, as with such a feeling as this our growing knowledge would be torture to her.

I could not tell the others of the day's discovery till we were alone; so after dinner – followed by a little music to save appearances even amongst ourselves – I took Mina to her room and left her to go to bed. The dear girl was more affectionate with me than ever, and clung to me as though she would detain me; but there was much to be talked of and I came away.

217

Thank God, the ceasing of telling things has made no difference between us.

When I came down again I found the others all gathered round the fire in the study. In the train I had written my diary so far, and simply read it off to them as the best means of letting them get abreast of my own information; when I had finished Van Helsing said:–

'This has been a great day's work, friend Jonathan. Doubtless we are on the track of the missing boxes. If we find them all in that house, then our work is near the end. But if there be some missing, we must search until we find them. Then shall we make our final *coup*, and hunt the wretch to his real death.' We all sat silent awhile, and all at once Mr Morris spoke:–

'Say! how are we going to get into that house?'

'We got into the other,' answered Lord Godalming quickly.

'But, Art, this is different. We broke house at Carfax, but we had night and a walled park to protect us. It will be a mighty different thing to commit burglary in Piccadilly, either by day or night. I confess I don't see how we are going to get in unless that agency duck can find us a key of some sort; perhaps we shall know when you get his letter in the morning.' Lord Godalming's brows contracted, and he stood up and walked about the room. By-and-by he stopped and said, turning from one to another of us:–

'Quincey's head is level. This burglary business is getting serious; we got off once all right; but we have now a rare job on hand – unless we can find the Count's key basket.'

As nothing could well be done before morning, and as it would be at least advisable to wait till Lord Godalming should hear from Mitchell's, we decided not to take any active step before breakfast time. For a good while we sat and smoked, discussing the matter in its various bearings; I took the opportunity of bringing this diary right up to the moment. I am very sleepy and shall go to bed. . . .

Just a line. Mina sleeps soundly and her breathing is regular. Her forehead is puckered up into little wrinkles, as though she thinks even in her sleep. She is still too pale, but does not look so haggard as she did this morning. To-morrow will, I hope, mend all this; she will be herself at home in Exeter. Oh, but I am sleepy!

DR SEWARD'S DIARY

1 October. – I am puzzled afresh about Renfield. His moods change so rapidly that I find it difficult to keep touch with them, and as they always mean something more than his own well-being, they form a more than interesting study. This morning, when I went to see him after his repulse of Van Helsing, his manner was that of a man commanding destiny. He was, in fact, commanding destiny – subjectively. He did not really care for any of the things of mere earth; he was in the clouds and looked down on all the weaknesses and wants of us poor mortals. I thought I would improve the occasion and learn something, so I asked him:–

'What about the flies these times?' He smiled on me in quite a superior sort of way – such a smile as would have become the face of Malvolio – as he answered me:–

'The fly, my dear sir, has one striking feature: its wings are typical of the aerial powers of the psychic faculties. The ancients did well when they typified the soul as a butterfly!'

I thought I would push his analogy to its utmost logically, so I said quickly:–

'Oh, it is a soul you are after now, is it?' His madness foiled his reason, and a puzzled look spread over his face as, shaking his head with a decision which I had but seldom seen in him, he said:–

'Oh no, oh no! I want no souls. Life is all I want.' Here he brightened up: 'I am pretty indifferent about it at present. Life is all right; I have all I want. You must get a new patient, doctor, if you wish to study zoophagy!'

This puzzled me a little, so I drew him on:–

'Then you command life; you are a god, I suppose?' He smiled with an ineffably benign superiority.

'Oh no! Far be it from me to arrogate to myself the attributes of the Deity. I am not even concerned in His especially spiritual doings. If I may state my intellectual position I am, so far as concerns things purely terrestrial, somewhat in the position which Enoch occupied spiritually!' This was a poser to me. I could not at the moment recall Enoch's appositeness; so I had to ask a simple question, though I felt that by doing so I was lowering myself in the eyes of the lunatic:–

'And why Enoch?'

'Because he walked with God.' I could not see the analogy, but did not like to admit it; so I harked back to what he had denied:–

'So you don't care about life and you don't want souls. Why not?' I put my question quickly and somewhat sternly, on purpose to disconcert him. The effort succeeded; for an instant he unconsciously relapsed into his old servile manner, bent low before me, and actually fawned upon me as he replied:–

'I don't want any souls, indeed, indeed! I don't. I couldn't use them if I had them! they would be no manner of use to me. I couldn't eat them or –' He suddenly stopped and the old cunning look spread over his face, like a wind-sweep on the surface of the water. 'And, doctor, as to life, what is it after all? When you've got all you require, and you know that you will never want, that is all. I have friends – good friends – like you, Dr Seward,' he said with a leer of inexpressible cunning; 'I know that I shall never lack the means of life!'

I think that through the cloudiness of his insanity he saw some antagonism in me, for he at once fell back on the last refuge of such as he – a dogged silence. After a short time I saw that for the present it was useless to speak to him. He was sulky, and so I came away.

Later in the day he sent for me. Ordinarily I would not have come without special reason, but just at present I am so interested in him that I would gladly make an effort. Besides, I am glad to have anything to help to pass the time. Harker is out, following up clues; and so are Lord Godalming and Quincey. Van Helsing sits in my study poring over the record prepared by the Harkers; he seems to think that by accurate knowledge of all details he will light upon some clue. He does not wish to be disturbed in the work, without cause. I would have taken him with me to see the patient, only I thought that after his last repulse he might not care to go again. There was also another reason: Renfield might not speak so freely before a third person as when he and I were alone.

I found him sitting out in the middle of the floor on his stool, a pose which is generally indicative of some mental energy on his part. When I came in, he said at once, as though the question had been waiting on his lips:–

'What about souls?' It was evident then that my surmise had been correct. Unconscious cerebration was doing its work, even with the lunatic. I determined to have the matter out. 'What about them yourself?' I asked. He did not reply for a moment but looked all round him, and up and down, as though he expected to find some inspiration for an anwer.

'I don't want any souls!' he said in a feeble, apologetic way. The matter seemed preying on his mind, and so I determined to use it – to 'be cruel only to be kind'. So I said:–

'You like life, and you want life?'

'Oh yes! but that is all right; you needn't worry about that!'

'But,' I asked, 'how are we to get the life without getting the soul also?' This seemed to puzzle him, so I followed it up:–

'A nice time you'll have some time when you're flying out there, with the souls of thousands of flies and spiders and birds and cats buzzing and twittering and miauing all round you. You've got their lives, you know, and you must put up with their souls!' Something seemed to affect his imagination, for he put his fingers to his ears and shut his eyes, screwing them up tightly just as a small boy does when his face is being soaped. There was something pathetic in it that touched me; it also gave me a lesson, for it seemed that before me was a child – only a child, though the features were worn, and the stubble on the jaws was white. It was evident that he was undergoing some process of mental disturbance, and, knowing how his past moods had interpreted things seemingly foreign to himself, I thought I would enter into his mind as well as I could and go with him. The first step was to restore confidence, so I asked him, speaking pretty loud so that he would hear me through his closed ears:—

'Would you like some sugar to get your flies round again?' He seemed to wake up all at once, and shook his head. With a laugh he replied:—

'Not much! flies are poor things, after all!' after a pause he added, 'But I don't want their souls buzzing round me all the same.'

'Or spiders?' I went on.

'Blow spiders! What's the use of spiders? There isn't anything in them to eat or – ' He stopped suddenly, as though reminded of a forbidden topic.

'So, so!' I thought to myself, 'this is the second time he has suddenly stopped at the word "drink"; what does it mean?' Renfield seemed himself aware of having made a lapse, for he hurried on, as though to distract my attention from it:—

'I don't take any stock at all in such matters. "Rats and mice and such small deer" as Shakespeare has it; "chicken-feed of the larder" they might be called. I'm past all that sort of nonsense. You might as well ask a man to eat molecules with a pair of chop-sticks, as to try to interest me about the lesser carnivora, when I know of what is before me.'

'I see,' I said. 'You want big things that you can make your teeth meet in? How would you like to breakfast on elephant?'

'What ridiculous nonsense you are talking!' He was getting too wide awake, so I thought I would press him hard. 'I wonder,' I said reflectively, 'what an elephant's soul is like!' The effect I desired was obtained, for he at once fell from his high-horse and became a child again.

'I don't want an elephant's soul, or any soul at all!' he said. For a few moments he sat despondently. Suddenly he jumped to his feet, with his eyes blazing and all the signs of intense cerebral excitement. 'To hell with you and your souls!' he shouted. 'Why do you plague me about souls? Haven't I got enough to worry, and pain, and distract me already, without thinking of souls?' He looked so hostile that I thought he was in for another homicidal fit, so I blew my whistle. The instant, however, that I did so he became calm, and said apologetically:—

'Forgive me, doctor; I forgot myself. You do not need any help. I am so worried in my mind that I am apt to be irritable. If you only knew the problem I have to face, and that I am working out, you would pity, and tolerate, and pardon me. Pray do not put me in a strait-waistcoat. I want to think, and I cannot think freely when my body is confined. I am sure

221

you will understand!' He had evidently self-control; so when the attendants came I told them not to mind, and they withdrew. Renfield watched them go; when the door was closed he said, with considerable dignity and sweetness:—

'Dr Seward, you have been very considerate towards me. Believe me that I am very very grateful to you!' I thought it well to leave him in this mood, and so I came away. There is certainly something to ponder over in this man's state. Several points seem to make what the American interviewer calls 'a story', if one could only get them in proper order. Here they are:—

Will not mention 'drinking'.

Fears the thought of being burdened with the 'soul' of anything.

Has no dread of wanting 'life' in the future.

Despises the meaner forms of life altogether, though he dreads being haunted by their souls.

Logically all these things point one way! he has assurance of some kind that he will acquire some higher life. He dreads the consequence – the burden of a soul. Then it is a human life he looks to!

And the assurance – ?

Merciful God! the Count has been to him, and there is some new scheme of terror afoot!

Later. – I went after my round to Van Helsing and told him my suspicion. He grew very grave; and, after thinking the matter over for a while, asked me to take him to Renfield. I did so. As we came to the door we heard the lunatic within singing gaily, as he used to do in the time which now seems so long ago. When he entered we saw with amazement that he had spread out his sugar as of old; the flies, lethargic with the autumn, were beginning to buzz into the room. We tried to make him talk of the subject of our previous conversation, but he would not attend. He went on with his singing, just as though we had not been present. He had got a scrap of paper and was folding it into a note-book. We had to come away as ignorant as we went in.

His is a curious case indeed; we must watch him to-night.

Letter, Mitchell, Sons & Candy to Lord Godalming.

'*1 October.*

'My Lord,–

'We are at all times only too happy to meet your wishes. We beg, with regard to the desire of your Lordship, expressed by Mr Harker on your behalf, to supply the following information concerning the sale and purchase of No. 347 Piccadilly. The originial vendors are the executors of the late Mr Archibald Winter-Suffield. The purchaser is a foreign nobleman, Count de Ville, who effected the purchase himself, paying the purchase money in notes "over the counter", if your Lordship will pardon us using so vulgar an expression. Beyond this we know nothing whatever of him. We are, my Lord,

'Your Lordship's humble servants,

'MITCHELL, SONS & CANDY.'

DR SEWARD'S DIARY

2 October. – I placed a man in the corridor last night, and told him to make an accurate note of any sound he might hear from Renfield's room, and gave him instructions that if there should be anything strange he was to call me. After dinner, when we had all gathered round the fire in the study – Mrs Harker having gone to bed – we discussed the attempts and discoveries of the day. Harker was the only one who had any result, and we are in great hopes that his clue may be an important one.

Before going to bed I went round to the patient's room and looked in through the observation trap. He was sleeping soundly, and his chest rose and fell with regular respiration.

This morning the man on duty reported to me that a little after midnight he was restless and kept saying his prayers somewhat loudly. I asked him if that was all; he replied that it was all he heard. There was something about his manner so suspicious that I asked point-blank if he had been asleep. He denied sleep, but admitted to having 'dozed' for a while. It is too bad that men cannot be trusted unless they are watched.

To-day Harker is out following up his clue, and Art and Quincey are looking after horses. Godalming thinks that it will be well to have horses always in readiness, for when we get the information which we seek there will be no time to lose. We must sterilize all the imported earth between sunrise and sunset; we shall thus catch the Count at his weakest, and without a refuge to fly to. Van Helsing is off to the British Museum, looking up some authorities on ancient medicine. The old physicians took account of things which their followers do not accept, and the Professor is searching for witch and demon cures which may be useful later.

I sometimes think we must all be mad and that we shall wake to sanity in strait-waistcoats.

Later. – We have met again. We seem at last to be on the track, and our work of to-morrow may be the beginning of the end. I wonder if Renfield's quiet has anything to do with this. His moods have so followed the doings of the Count, that the coming destruction of the monster may be carried to him in some subtle way. If we could only get some hint as to what passed in his mind between the time of my argument with him yesterday and his resumption of fly-catching, it might afford us a valuable clue. He is now seemingly quiet for a spell. . . . Is he? – that wild yell seemed to come from his room. . . .

The attendent came bursting into my room and told me that Renfield had somehow met with some accident. He had heard him yell; and when he went to him found him lying on his face on the floor, all covered in blood. I must go at once. . . .

21

DR SEWARD'S DIARY

3 October. – Let me put down with exactness all that happened, as well as I can remember it, since last I made an entry. Not a detail that I can recall must be forgotten; in all calmness I must proceed.

When I came to Renfield's room I found him lying on the floor on his left side in a glittering pool of blood. When I went to move him, it became at once apparent that he had received some terrible injuries; there seemed none of that unity of purpose between the parts of the body which marks even lethargic sanity. As the face was exposed I could see that it was horribly bruised, as though it had been beaten against the floor – indeed it was from the face wounds that the pool of blood originated. The attendant who was kneeling beside the body said to me as we turned him over:–

'I think, sir, his back is broken. See, both his right arm and leg and the whole side of his face are paralysed.' How such a thing could have happened puzzled the attendant beyond measure. He seemed quite bewildered, and his brows were gathered in as he said:–

'I can't understand the two things. He could mark his face like that by beating his own head on the ground. I saw a young woman do it once at the Eversfield Asylum before anyone could lay hands on her. And I suppose he might have broke his back by falling out of bed, if he got in an awkward kink. But for the life of me I can't imagine how the two things occurred. If his back was broken, he couldn't beat his head; and if his face was like that before the fall out of bed, there would be marks of it.' I said to him:–

'Go to Dr Van Helsing, and ask him to kindly come here at once. I want him without an instant's delay.' The man ran off, and within a very few minutes the Professor, in his dressing-gown and slippers appeared. When he saw Renfield on the ground, he looked keenly at him a moment and then turned to me. I think he recognized my thought in my eyes, for he said very quietly, manifestly for the ears of the attendant:–

'Ah, a sad accident! He will need very careful watching, and much attention. I shall stay with you myself; but I shall first dress myself. If you will remain I shall in a few minutes join you.'

The patient was now breathing stertorously, and it was easy to see that he had suffered some terrible injury. Van Helsing returned with extraordinary celerity, bearing with him a surgical case. He had evidently been thinking and had his mind made up; for, almost before he looked at the patient, he whispered to me:–

'Send the attendant away. We must be alone with him when he becomes conscious, after the operation.' So I said:–

'I think that will do now, Simmons. We have done all that we can at present. You had better go your round, and Dr Van Helsing will operate. Let me know instantly if there be anything unusual anywhere.'

The man withdrew, and we went into a strict examination of the patient. The wounds of the face were superficial; the real injury was a depressed fracture of the skull, extending right up through the motor area. The Professor thought a moment and said:–

'We must reduce the pressure and get back to normal conditions, as far as can be; the rapidity of the suffusion shows the terrible nature of his injury. The whole motor area seems affected. The suffusion of the brain will increase quickly, so we must trephine at once or it may be too late.' As he was speaking there was a soft tapping at the door. I went over and opened it and found in the corridor without, Arthur and Quincey in pyjamas and slippers: the former spoke:–

'I heard your man call up Dr Van Helsing and tell him of an accident. So I woke Quincey, or rather called for him as he was not asleep. Things are moving too quickly and too strangely for sound sleep for any of us these times. I've been thinking that to-morrow night will not see things as they have been. We'll have to look back – and forward a little more than we have done. May we come in?' I nodded, and held the door open till they had entered; then I closed it again. When Quincey saw the attitude and state of the patient, and noted the horrible pool on the floor, he said softly:–

'My God! what has happened to him! Poor, poor devil!' I told him briefly, and added that we expected he would recover consciousness after the operation – for a short time at all events. He went at once and sat down on the edge of the bed, with Godalming beside him; we all watched in patience.

225

'We shall wait,' said Van Helsing, 'just long enough to fix the best spot for trephining, so that we may most quickly and perfectly remove the blood clot; for it is evident that the haemorrhage is increasing.'

The minutes during which we waited passed with fearful slowness. I had a horrible sinking in my heart, and from Van Helsing's face I gathered that he felt some fear or apprehension as to what was to come. I dreaded the words that Renfield might speak. I was positively afraid to think; but the conviction of what was coming was on me, as I have read of men who have heard the death-watch. The poor man's breathing came in uncertain gasps. Each instant he seemed as though he would open his eyes and speak; but then would follow a prolonged stertorous breath, and he would relapse into a more fixed insensibility. Inured as I was to sick-beds and death, this suspense grew and grew upon me. I could almost hear the beating of my own heart; and the blood surging through my temples sounded like blows from a hammer. The silence finally became agonizing. I looked at my companions, one after another, and saw from their flushed faces and damp brows that they were enduring equal torture. There was a nervous suspense over us all, as though overhead some dread bell would peal out powerfully when we should least expect it.

At last there came a time when it was evident that the patient was sinking fast; he might die at any moment. I looked up at the Professor and caught his eyes fixed on mine. His face was sternly set as he spoke:—

'There is no time to lose. His words may be worth many lives; I have been thinking so, as I stood here. It may be there is a soul at stake! We shall operate just above the ear.'

Without another word he made the operation. For a few moments the breathing continued to be stertorous. Then there came a breath so prolonged that it seemed as though it would tear open his chest. Suddenly his eyes opened, and became fixed in a wild, helpless stare. This was continued for a few moments; then it softened into a glad surprise, and from the lips came a sigh of relief. He moved convulsively, and as he did so, said:—

'I'll be quiet, doctor. Tell them to take off the strait-waistcoat. I have had a terrible dream, and it has left me so weak that I cannot move. What's wrong with my face? it feels all swollen, and it smarts dreadfully.' He tried to turn his head; but even with the effort his eyes seemed to grow glassy again, so I gently put it back. Then Van Helsing said in a quiet, grave tone:—

'Tell us your dream, Mr Renfield.' As he heard the voice his face brightened through its mutilation, and he said:—

'That is Dr Van Helsing. How good it is of you to be here. Give me some water, my lips are dry; and I shall try to tell you. I dreamed — ' he stopped and seemed fainting. I called quietly to Quincey – 'The brandy – it is in my study – quick!' He flew and returned with a glass, the decanter of brandy and a carafe of water. We moistened the parched lips, and the patient quickly revived. It seemed, however, that his poor injured brain had been working in the interval, for, when he was quite conscious, he looked at me piercingly with an agonized confusion which I shall never forget, and said:–

'I must not deceive myself; it was no dream, but all a grim reality.' Then his eyes roved round the room; as they caught sight of the two figures sitting patiently on the edge of the bed he went on:–

'If I were not sure already, I should know from them.' For an instant his eyes closed – not with pain or sleep but voluntarily, as though he were bringing all his faculties to bear; when he opened them he said, hurriedly, and with more energy than he had yet displayed:–

'Quick, doctor, quick. I am dying! I feel that I have but a few minutes; and then I must go back to death – or worse! Wet my lips with brandy again. I have something that I must say before I die; or before my poor crushed brain dies anyhow. Thank you! It was that night after you left me, when I implored you to let me go away. I couldn't speak then, for I felt my tongue was tied; but I was as sane then, except in that way, as I am now. I was in an agony of despair for a long time after you left me; it seemed hours. Then there came a sudden peace to me. My brain seemed to become cool again, and I realized where I was. I heard the dogs bark behind our house, but not where He was!' As he spoke Van Helsing's eyes never blinked, but his hand came out and met mine and gripped it hard. He did not, however, betray himself; he nodded slightly, and said: 'Go on,' in a low voice. Renfield proceeded:–

'He came up to the window in the mist, as I had seen Him often before; but He was solid then – not a ghost, and His eyes were fierce like a man's when angry. He was laughing with His red mouth; the sharp white teeth glinted in the moonlight when He turned to look back over the belt of trees, to where the dogs were barking. I wouldn't ask Him to come in at first, though I knew He wanted to – just as He had wanted to all along. Then He began promising me things – not in words but by doing them.' He was interrupted by a word from the Professor:–

'How?'

'By making them happen; just as He used to send in the flies when the sun was shining. Great big fat ones with steel and sapphire on their wings; and big moths, in the night, with skull and cross-bones on their backs.' Van Helsing nodded to him as he whispered to me unconsciously:–

'The *Acherontia atropos of the Sphinges* – what you call the "Death's-head moth"!' The patient went on without stopping.

'Then he began to whisper: "Rats, rats, rats! Hundreds, thousands, millions of them, and every one a life; and dogs to eat them, and cats too. All lives! all red blood, with years of life in it; and not merely buzzing flies!" I laughed at Him, for I wanted to see what He could do. Then the dogs howled, away beyond the dark trees in His house. He beckoned me to the window. I got up and looked out, and He raised His hands, and seemed to call out without using any words. A dark mass spread over the grass, coming on like the shape of a flame of fire; and then He moved the mist to the right and left, and I could see that there were thousands of rats with their eyes blazing red – like His, only smaller. He held up His hand, and they all stopped; and I thought He seemed to be saying: "All these lives will I give you, ay, and many more and greater, through countless ages, if you will fall down and worship me!" And then a red cloud, like the colour of blood, seemed to close over my eyes; and before I knew what I was doing, I found myself opening the sash and saying to Him: "Come in, Lord and Master!" The rats were all gone, but He slid into the room through the sash, though it was only open an inch wide – just as the Moon herself has often come in through the tiniest crack, and has stood before me in all her size and splendour.'

His voice was weaker, so I moistened his lips with the brandy again, and he continued; but it seemed as though his memory had gone on working in the interval, for his story was further advanced. I was about to call him back to the point, but Van Helsing whispered to me: 'Let him go on. Do not interrupt him; he cannot go back, and maybe could not proceed at all if once he lost the thread of his thought.' He proceeded:–

'All day I waited to hear from Him, but He did not send me anything, not even a blow-fly, and when the moon got up I was pretty angry with Him. When He slid in through the window, though it was shut, and did not even knock, I got mad with Him. He sneered at me, and His white face looked out of the mist with His red eyes gleaming, and He went on as though he owned the whole place, and I was no one. He didn't even smell the same as He went by me. I couldn't hold Him. I thought that, somehow, Mrs Harker had come into the room.'

The two men sitting on the bed stood up and came over, standing behind him so that he could not see them, but where they could hear better. They were both silent, but the Professor started and quivered; his face, however, grew grimmer and sterner still. Renfield went on without noticing:–

'When Mrs Harker came in to see me this afternoon she wasn't the same; it was like tea after the teapot had been watered.' Here we all moved, but no one said a word; he went on:–

'I didn't know that she was here till she spoke; and she didn't look the same. I don't care for the pale people, I like them with lots of blood in them, and hers had all seemed to have run out. I didn't think of it at the time; but when she went away I began to think, and it made me mad to know that. He had been taking the life out of her.' I could feel that the rest quivered, as I did; but we remained otherwise still. 'So when He came to-night I was ready for Him. I saw the mist stealing in, and I grabbed it tight. I had heard that madmen have unnatural strength; and as I knew I was a madman – at times anyhow – I resolved to use my power. Ay, and He felt it too, for He had to come out of the mist to struggle with me. I held tight; and I thought I was going to win, for I didn't mean Him to take any more life, till I saw His eyes. They burned into me, and my strength became like water. He slipped through it, and when I tried to cling to Him, He raised me up and flung me down. There was a red cloud before me, and a noise like thunder, and the mist seemed to steal away under the door.' His voice was becoming fainter and his breath more stertorous. Van Helsing stood up instinctively.

'We know the worst now,' he said. 'He is here, and we know his purpose. It may not be too late. Let us be armed – the same as we were the other night, but lose no time; there is not an instant to spare.' There was no need to put our fear, nay our conviction, into words – we shared them in common. We all hurried and took from our rooms the same things that we had when we entered the Count's house. The Professor had his ready and as we met in the corridor he pointed to them significantly as he said:–

'They never leave me; and they shall not till this unhappy business is over. Be wise also, my friends. It is no common enemy that we deal with. Alas! alas that the dear Madam Mina should suffer.' He stopped; his voice was breaking, and I do not know if rage or terror predominated in my own heart.

Outside the Harkers' door we paused. Art and Quincey held back, and the latter said:–

'Should we disturb her?'

'We must,' said Van Helsing grimly. 'If the door be locked, I shall break it in.'

'May it not frighten her terribly? It is unusual to break into a lady's room!' Van Helsing said solemnly:–

'You are always right; but this is life and death. All chambers are alike to the doctor; and even were they not they are all as one to me to-night. Friend John, when I turn the handle, if the door does not open, do you put your shoulder down and shove; and you too, my friends. Now!'

He turned the handle as he spoke, but the door did not yield. We threw ourselves against it; with a crash it burst open, and we almost fell headlong into the room. The Professor did actually fall, and I saw across him as he gathered himself up from hands and knees. What I saw appalled me. I felt my hair rise like bristles on the back of my neck, and my heart seemed to stand still.

The moonlight was so bright that through the thick yellow blind the room was light enough to see. On the bed beside the window lay Jonathan Harker, his face flushed, and breathing heavily as though in a stupor. Kneeling on the near edge of the bed facing outwards was the white-clad figure of his wife. By her side stood a tall, thin man, clad in black. His face was turned from us, but the instant we saw it we all recognized the Count – in every way, even to the scar on his forehead. With his left hand he held both Mrs Harker's hands, keeping them away with her arms at full tension; his right hand gripped her by the back of the neck, forcing her face down on his bosom. Her white nightdress was smeared with blood, and a thin stream trickled down the man's bare breast, which was shown by his torn-open dress. The attitude of the two had a terrible resemblance to a child forcing a kitten's nose into a saucer of milk to compel it to drink. As we burst into the room, the Count turned his face, and the hellish look that I had heard described seemed to leap into it. His eyes flamed red with devilish passion; the great nostrils of the white aquiline nose opened wide and quivered at the edges; and the white sharp teeth, behind the full lips of the blood-dripping mouth, champed together like those of a wild beast. With a wrench, which threw his victim back upon the bed as though hurled from a height, he turned and sprang at us. But by this time the Professor had gained his feet, and was holding towards him the envelope which contained the Sacred Wafer. The Count suddenly stopped, just as poor Lucy had done outside the tomb, and cowered back. Further and further back he cowered, as we, lifting our crucifixes, advanced. The moonlight suddenly failed, as a great black cloud sailed across the sky; and when the gaslight sprang up under Quincey's match, we saw nothing but a faint vapour. This, as we looked, trailed under the door, which with the recoil from its bursting open had swung back to its old position. Van Helsing, Art and I moved forward to Mrs Harker, who by this time had drawn her breath and with it had given a scream so wild, so ear-piercing, so despairing that it seems to me now that it will ring in my ears till my dying day. For a few seconds she lay in her helpless attitude and disarray. Her face was ghastly, with a pallor which was accentuated by the blood which smeared her lips and cheeks and chin; from her throat trickled a thin stream of blood. Her eyes were mad with terror. Then she put before her face her poor crushed hands, which bore on their whiteness the red mark of the Count's terrible grip, and from behind them came a low desolate wail which made the terrible scream seem only the quick expression of an endless grief. Van Helsing stepped forward and drew the coverlet gently over her body, whilst Art, after looking at her face for an instant despairingly, ran out of the room. Van Helsing whispered to me:–

'Jonathan is in a stupor such as we know the Vampire can produce. We can do nothing with poor Madam Mina for a few moments till she recovers herself; I must wake him!' He dipped the end of a towel in cold water and with it began to flick him on the face, his wife all the while holding her face between her hands and sobbing in a way that was heart-breaking to hear. I raised the blind, and looked out of the window. There was much moonshine; and as I looked I could see Quincey Morris run across the lawn and hide himself in the shadow of a great yew tree. It puzzled me to think why he was doing this; but at the instant I heard Harker's quick exclamation as he woke to partial consciousness, and turned to the bed. On his face, as there might well be, was a look of wild amazement. He seemed dazed for a few seconds, and then full conscious-ness seemed to burst upon him all at once, and he started up. His wife was aroused by the quick movement, and turned to him with her arms stretched out, as though to embrace him; instantly, however, she drew them in again, and putting her elbows together, held her hands before her face, and shuddered till the bed beneath her shook.

'In God's name what does this mean?' Harker cried out. 'Dr Seward, Dr Van Helsing, what is it? What has happened? What is wrong? Mina, dear, what is it? What does that blood mean? My God, my God! has it come to this!' and, raising himself to his knees, he beat his hands wildly together. 'Good God help us! help her! oh, help her!' With a quick movement he jumped from bed, and began to pull on his clothes – all the man in him awake at the need for instant exertion. 'What has happened? Tell me about it!' he cried without pausing. 'Dr Van Helsing, you love Mina, I know. Oh, do something to save her. It cannot have gone too far yet. Guard her while I look for *him*!' His wife, through her terror and horror and distress, saw some sure danger to him; instantly forgetting her own grief, she seized hold of him and cried out:–

'No! no! Jonathan, you must not leave me. I have suffered enough to-night, God knows, without the dread of his harming you. You must stay with me. Stay with these friends who will watch over you!' Her expression became frantic as she spoke; and as he yielded to her, she pulled him down sitting on the bedside, and clung to him fiercely.

Van Helsing and I tried to calm them both. The Professor held up his little golden crucifix, and said with wonderful calmness:–

'Do not fear, my dear. We are here; and whilst this is close to you no foul thing can approach. You are safe for to-night; and we must be calm and take counsel together.' She shuddered and was silent, holding down her head on her husband's breast. When she raised it, his white night-robe was stained with blood where her lips had touched, and where the thin open wound in her neck had sent forth drops. The instant she saw it she drew back, with a low wail, and whispered, amidst choking sobs:–

'Unclean, unclean! I must touch him or kiss him no more. Oh, that it should be that it is I who am now his worst enemy, and whom he may have most cause to fear.' To this he spoke out resolutely:–

'Nonsense, Mina. It is a shame to me to hear such a word. I would not hear it of you; and I shall not hear it from you. May God judge me by my deserts, and punish me with more bitter suffering than even this hour, if by any act or will of mine anything ever come between us!' He put out his arms and folded her to his breast; and for a while she lay there sobbing. He looked at us over her bowed head, with eyes that blinked damply above his quivering nostrils; his mouth was set as steel. After a while her sobs became less frequent and more faint, and then he said to me, speaking with a studied calmness which I felt tried his nervous power to the utmost:–

'And now, Dr Seward, tell me all about it. Too well I know the broad fact; tell me all that has been.' I told him exactly what had happened, and he listened with seeming impassiveness; but his nostrils twitched and his eyes blazed as I told how the ruthless hands of the Count had held his wife in that terrible and horrid position, with her mouth to the open wound in his breast. It interested me, even at that moment, to see that whilst the face of white set passion worked convulsively over the bowed head, the hands tenderly and lovingly stroked the ruffled hair. Just as I had finished Quincey and Godalming knocked at the door. They entered in obedience to our summons. Van Helsing looked at me questioningly. I understood him to mean we were to take advantage of their coming to divert if possible the thoughts of the unhappy husband and wife from each other and from themselves; so on my nodding acquiescence to him he asked them what they had seen or done. To which Lord Godalming answered:–

'I could not see him anywhere in the passage, or in any of our rooms. I looked in the study, but, though he had been there, he had gone. He had, however – ' He stopped suddenly, looking at the poor drooping figure on the bed. Van Helsing said gravely:– 'Go on, friend Arthur. We want no more concealments. Our hope now is in knowing all. Tell freely!' So Art went on:–

'He had been there, and though it could only have been for a few seconds, he made rare hay of the place. All the manuscript had been burned, and the blue flames were flickering amongst the white ashes; the cylinders of your phonograph too were thrown on the fire, and the wax had helped the flames.' Here I interrupted. 'Thank God there is the other copy in the safe!' His face lit for a moment, but fell again as he went on: 'I ran downstairs then, but could see no sign of him. I looked into Renfield's room; but there was no trace there except – !' Again he paused. 'Go on,' said Harker hoarsely; so he bowed his head, and moistening his lips with his tongue, added: 'except that the poor fellow is dead.' Mrs Harker raised her head, looking from one to the other of us as she said solemnly:–

'God's will be done!' I could not but feel that Art was keeping back something; but, as I took it that it was with a purpose, I said nothing. Van Helsing turned to Morris and asked:–

'And you, friend Quincey, have you any to tell?'

'A little,' he answered. 'It may be much eventually, but at present I can't say. I thought it well to know if possible where the Count would go when he left the house. I did not see him; but I saw a bat rise from Renfield's window, and flap westward. I expected to see him in some shape go back to Carfax; but he evidently sought some other lair. He will not be back to-night; for the sky is reddening in the east, and the dawn is close. We must work to-morrow!'

He said the latter words through his shut teeth. For a space of perhaps a couple of minutes there was silence, and I could fancy that I could hear the sound of our hearts beating; then Van Helsing said, placing his hand very tenderly on Mrs Harker's head:–

'And now, Madam Mina – poor, dear, dear Madam Mina – tell us exactly what happened. God knows that I do not want that you be pained; but it is need that we know all. For now more than ever has all work to be done quick and sharp, and in deadly earnest. The day is close to us that must end all, if it may so be; and now is the chance that we may live and learn.'

The poor, dear lady shivered, and I could see the tension of her nerves as she clasped her husband closer to her and bent her head lower and lower still on his breast. Then she raised her head proudly, and held out one hand to Van Helsing, who took it in his, and, after stooping and kissing it reverently, held it fast. The other hand was locked in that of her husband, who held his other arm thrown round her protectingly. After a pause in which she was evidently ordering her thoughts, she began:–

'I took the sleeping draught which you had so kindly given me, but for a long time it did not act. I seemed to become more wakeful, and myriads of horrible fancies began to crowd in upon my mind – all of them connected with death, and vampires; with blood, and pain, and trouble.' Her husband involuntarily groaned as she turned to him and said lovingly: 'Do not fret, dear. You must be brave and strong, and help me through the horrible task. If you only knew what an effort it is to me to tell of this fearful thing at all, you would understand how much I need your help. Well, I saw I must try to help the medicine do its work with my will, if it

233

was to do me any good, so I resolutely set myself to sleep. Sure enough sleep must soon have come to me, for I remembered no more. Jonathan coming in had not waked me, for he lay by my side when next I remember. There was in the room the same thin white mist that I had before noticed. But I forget now if you know of this; you will find it in my diary which I shall show you later. I felt the same vague terror which had come to me before, and the same sense of some presence. I turned to wake Jonathan, but found that he slept so soundly that it seemed as if it was he who had taken the sleeping draught and not I. I tried, but could not wake him. This caused me a great fear, and I looked around terrified. Then indeed my heart sank within me: beside the bed, as if he had stepped out of the mist – or rather as if the mist had turned into his figure, for it had entirely disappeared – stood a tall, thin man, all in black. I knew him at once from the descriptions of the others. The waxen face; the high aquiline nose, on which the light fell in a thin white line; the parted red lips, with the sharp white teeth showing between; and the red eyes that I had seemed to see in the sunset on the windows of St Mary's Church at Whitby. I knew, too, the red scar on his forehead where Jonathan had struck him. For an instant my heart stood still, and I would have screamed out, only that I was paralysed. In the pause he spoke in a sort of keen, cutting whisper, pointing as he spoke to Jonathan:–

' "Silence! If you make a sound I shall take him and dash his brains out before your very eyes." I was appalled and was too bewildered to do or say anything. With a mocking smile, he placed one hand upon my shoulder and, holding me tight, bared my throat with the other, saying as he did so: "First, a little refreshment to reward my exertions. You may as well be quiet; it is not the first time, or the second, that your veins have appeased my thirst!" I was bewildered, and, strangely enough, I did not want to hinder him. I suppose it is a part of the horrible curse that this happens when his touch is on his victim. And oh, my God, my God, pity me! He placed his reeking lips upon my throat!' Her husband groaned again. She clasped his hand harder, and looked at him pityingly, as if he were the injured one, and went on:–

'I felt my strength fading away, and I was in a half-swoon. How long this horrible thing lasted I know not; but it seemed that a long time must have passed before he took his foul, awful sneering mouth away. I saw it drip with the fresh blood!' The remembrance seemed for a while to overpower her, and she drooped and would have sunk down but for her husband's sustaining arm. With a great effort she recovered herself and went on:–

'Then he spoke to me mockingly: "And so you, like the others, would play your brains against mine. You would help these men to hunt me and frustrate me in my designs! You know now, and they know in part already, and will know in full before long, what it is to cross my path. They should have kept their energies for use closer to home. Whilst they played wits against me – against me who commanded nations, and intrigued for them, and fought for them, hundreds of years before they were born – I was countermining them. And you, their best beloved one, are now to me flesh of my flesh; blood of my blood; kin of my kin; my bountiful wine-press for a while; and shall be later on my companion and my helper. You shall be avenged in turn; for not one of them but shall minister to your needs. But as yet you are to be punished for what you have done. You have aided in thwarting me; now you shall come to my call. When my brain says 'Come!' to you, you shall cross land or sea to do my bidding; and to that end this!" With that he pulled open his shirt, and with his long sharp nails opened a vein in his breast. When the blood began to spurt out, he took my hands in one of his, holding them tight, and with the other seized my neck and pressed my mouth to the wound, so that I must either suffocate or swallow some of the – Oh, my God, my God! what have I done? What have I done to deserve such a fate, I who have tried to walk in meekness and righteousness all my days? God pity me! Look down on a pour soul in worse than mortal peril; and in mercy pity those to whom she is dear!' Then she began to rub her lips as though to cleanse them from pollution.

As she was telling her terrible story, the eastern sky began to quicken, and everything became more and more clear. Harker was still and quiet; but over his face, as the awful narrative went on, came a grey look which deepened and deepened in the morning light, till when the first red streak of the coming dawn shot up, the flesh stood darkly out against the whitening hair.

We have arranged that one of us is to stay within call of the unhappy pair till we can meet together and arrange about taking action.

Of this I am sure: the sun rises to-day on no more miserable house in all the great round of its daily course.

22

JONATHAN HARKER'S JOURNAL

3 October. – As I must do something or go mad, I write this diary. It is now six o'clock, and we are to meet in the study in half an hour and take something to eat; for Dr Van Helsing and Dr Seward are agreed that if we do not eat we cannot work our best. Our best will be, God knows, required to-day. I must keep writing at every chance, for I dare not stop to think. All, big and little, must go down; perhaps at the end the little things may teach us most. The teaching, big or little, could not have landed Mina or me anywhere worse than we are to-day. However, we must trust and hope. Poor Mina told me just now, with the tears running down her dear cheeks, that it is in trouble and trial that our faith is tested – that we must keep on trusting; and that God will aid us up to the end. The end! oh, my God! what end? . . . To work! To work!

When Dr Van Helsing and Dr Seward had come back from seeing poor Renfield, we went gravely into what was to be done. First, Dr Seward told us that when he and Dr Van Helsing had gone down to the room below they had found Renfield lying on the floor, all in a heap. His face was all bruised and crushed in, and the bones of the neck were broken.

Dr Seward asked the attendant who was on duty in the passage if he had heard anything. He said that he had been sitting down – he confessed to half dozing – when he heard loud voices in the room, and then Renfield had called out loudly several times, 'God! God! God!' After that there was a sound of falling, and when he entered the room he found him lying on the floor, face down, just as the doctors had seen him. Van Helsing asked if he had heard 'voices' or 'a voice', and he said he could not say; that at first it had seemed to him as if there were two, but as there was no one in the room it could have been only one. He could swear to it, if required, that the word 'God' was spoken by the patient. Dr Seward said to us, when we were alone, that he did not wish to go into the matter; the question of an inquest had to be considered, and it would never do to put forward the truth, as no one would believe it. As it was, he thought that on the attendant's evidence he could give a certificate of death by misadventure in falling from bed. In case the coroner should demand it, there would be a formal inquest, necessarily to the same result.

When the question began to be discussed as to what should be our next step, the very first thing we decided was that Mina should be in full confidence; that nothing of any sort – no matter how painful – should be kept from her. She herself agreed as to its wisdom, and it was pitiful to see her so brave and yet so sorrowful, and in such a depth of despair. 'There must be no more concealment,' she said. 'Alas! we have had too much already. And besides there is nothing in all the world that can give me more pain than I have already endured – than I suffer now! Whatever may happen, it must be of new hope or of new courage to me!' Van Helsing was looking at her fixedly as she spoke, and said, suddenly but quietly:–

'But, dear Madam Mina, are you not afraid; not for yourself, but for others from yourself, after what has happened?' Her face grew set in its lines, but her eyes shone with the devotion of a martyr as she answered:—

'Ah no! for my mind is made up!'

'To what?' he asked gently, whilst we were all very still; for each in our own way we had a sort of vague idea of what she meant. Her answer came with direct simplicity, as though she were simply stating a fact:—

'Because if I find in myself — and I shall watch keenly for it — a sign of harm to any that I love, I shall die!'

'You would not kill yourself?' he asked hoarsely.

'I would; if there were no friend who loved me, who would save me such a pain, and so desperate an effort!' She looked at him meaningly as she spoke. He was sitting down; but now he rose and came close to her and put his hand on her head as he said solemnly:—

'My child, there is such an one if it were for your good. For myself I could hold it in my account with God to find such an euthanasia for you, even at this moment, if it were best. Nay, were it safe! But, my child —' for a moment he seemed choked, and a great sob rose in his throat; he gulped it down and went on:—

'There are here some who would stand between you and death. You must not die. You must not die by any hand; but least of all by your own. Until the other, who has fouled your sweet life, is true dead you must not die; for if he is still with the quick Un-Dead, your death would make you even as he is. No, you must live! You must struggle and strive to live, though death would seem a boon unspeakable. You must fight Death himself, though he come to you in pain or in joy; by the day, or the night; in safety or in peril! On your living soul I charge you that you do not die — nay, nor think of death — till this great evil be past.' The poor dear grew white as death, and shook and shivered, as I have seen a quicksand shake and shiver at the incoming of the tide. We were all silent; we could do nothing. At length she grew more calm, and turning to him said, sweetly, but oh! so sorrowfully, as she held out her hand:—

'I promise you, my dear friend, that if God will let me live, I shall strive to do so; till, if it may be in His good time, this horror may have passed away from me.' She was so good and brave that we all felt that our hearts were strengthened to work and endure for her, and we began to discuss what we were to do. I told her that she was to have all the papers in the safe, and all the papers or diaries and phonographs we might hereafter use; and was to keep the record as she had done before. She was pleased with the prospect of anything to do — if 'pleased' could be used in connection with so grim an interest.

As usual Van Helsing had thought ahead of everyone else, and was prepared with an exact ordering of our work.

237

'It is perhaps well,' he said, 'that at our meeting after our visit to Carfax we decided not to do anything with the earth-boxes that lay there. Had we done so, the Count must have guessed our purpose, and would doubtless have taken measures in advance to frustrate such an effort with regard to the others; but now he does not know our intentions. Nay more, in all probability he does not know that such a power exists to us as can sterilize his lairs, so that he cannot use them as of old. We are now so much further advanced in our knowledge as to their disposition, that, when we have examined the house in Piccadilly, we may track the very last of them. To-day, then, is ours; and in it rests our hope. The sun that rose on our sorrow this morning guards us in its course. Until it sets to-night, that monster must retain whatever form he now has. He is confined within the limitations of his earthly envelope. He cannot melt into thin air nor disappear through cracks or chinks or crannies. If he go through a doorway, he must open the door like a mortal. And so we have this day to hunt out all his lairs and sterilize them. So we shall, if we have not yet catch him and destroy him, drive him to bay in some place where the catching and the destroying shall be, in time, sure.' Here I started up, for I could not contain myself at the thought that the minutes and seconds so previously laden with Mina's life and happiness were flying from us, since whilst we talked action was possible. But Van Helsing held up his hand warningly. 'Nay, friend Jonathan,' he said, 'in this, the quickest way home is the longest way, so your proverb say. We shall all act, and act with desperate quick, when the time has come. But think, in all probable the key of the situation is in that house in Piccadilly. The Count may have many houses which he has bought. Of them he will have deeds of purchase, keys and other things. He will have paper that he write on; he will have his book of cheques. There are many belongings that he must have somewhere; why not in this place so central, so quiet, where he come and go by the front or the back at all hour, when in the very vast of the traffic there is none to notice? We shall go there and search that house; and when we learn what it holds, then we do what our friend Arthur call, in his phrases of hunt, "stop the earth", and so we run down our old fox – so? is it not?'

'Then let us come at once,' I cried; 'we are wasting the precious, precious time!' The Professor did not move, but simply said:–

'And how are we to get into that house in Piccadilly?'

'Any way!' I cried. 'We shall break in if need be.'

'And your police; where will they be, and what will they say?'

I was staggered; but I knew that if he wished to delay he had a good reason for it. So I said, as quietly as I could:–

'Don't wait more than need be; you know, I am sure, what torture I am in.'

'Ah, my child, that I do; and indeed there is no wish of me to add to your anguish. But just think, what can we do, until all the world be at movement? Then will come our time. I have thought and thought, and it seems to me that the simplest way is the best of all. Now we wish to get into the house, but we have no key; is it not so?' I nodded.

'Now suppose that you were, in truth, the owner of that house, and could not still get it; and think there was to you no conscience of the housebreaker, what would you do?'

'I should get a respectable locksmith, and set him to work to pick the lock for me.'

'And your police, they would interfere, would they not?'

'Oh no! not if they knew the man was properly employed.'

'Then,' he looked at me keenly as he spoke, 'all that is in doubt is the conscience of the employer, and the belief of your policemen as to whether or no that employer has a good conscience or a bad one. Your police must indeed be zealous men and clever – oh, so clever! – in reading the heart, that they trouble themselves in such matter. No, no, my friend Jonathan, you go take the lock off a hundred empty houses in this your London, or of any city in the world; and if you do it as such things are rightly done, and at the time such things are rightly done, no one will interfere. I have read of a gentleman who owned a so fine house in your London, and when he went for months of summer to Zwitzerland and lock up his house, some burglar came and broke window at back and got in. Then he went and made open the shutters in front and walk out and in through the door, before the very eyes of the police. Then he have an auction in that house, and advertise it, and put up big notice; and when the day come he sell off by a great auctioneer all the goods of that other man who own them. Then he go to a builder, and he sell him that house, making an agreement that he pull it down and take all away within a certain time. And your police and other authority help him all they can. And when that owner come back from his holiday in Zwitzerland he find only an empty hole where his house had been. This was all done *en règle*; and in our work we shall be *en règle* too. We shall not go so early that the policeman who have then little to think of, shall deem it strange; but we shall go after ten o'clock when there are many about, and when such things would be done were we indeed owners of the house.'

I could not but see how right he was, and the terrible despair of Mina's face became relaxed a thought; there was hope in such good counsel. Van Helsing went on:–

'When once within that house we may find more clues; at any rate some of us can remain there whilst the rest find the other places where there be more earth-boxes – at Bermondsey and Mile End.'

239

Lord Godalming stood up. 'I can be of some use here,' he said. 'I shall wire to my people to have horses and carriages where they will be most convenient.'

'Look here, old fellow,' said Morris, 'it is a capital idea to have all ready in case we want to go horsebacking; but don't you think that one of your snappy carriages with its heraldic adornments in a byeway at Walworth or Mile End would attract too much attention for our purposes? It seems to me that we ought to take cabs when we go south or east; and even leave them somewhere near the neighbourhood we are going to.'

'Friend Quincey is right!' said the Professor. 'His head is what you call in plane with the horizon. It is a difficult thing that we go to do, and we do not want no peoples to watch us if so it may.'

Mina took a growing interest in everything, and I was rejoiced to see that the exigency of affairs was helping her to forget for a time the terrible experience of the night. She was very, very pale – almost ghastly, and so thin that her lips were drawn away, showing her teeth somewhat prominently. I did not mention this last, lest it should give her needless pain; but it made my blood run cold in my veins to think of what had occurred with poor Lucy when the Count had sucked her blood. As yet there was no sign of the teeth growing sharper; but the time as yet was short, and there was time for fear.

When we came to the discussion of the sequence of our efforts and of the disposition of our forces, there were new sources of doubt. It was finally agreed that before starting for Piccadilly we should destroy the Count's lair close at hand. In case he should find it out too soon, we should thus be still ahead of him in our work of destruction; and his presence in his purely material shape, and at his weakest, might give us some new clue.

As to the disposal of forces, it was suggested by the Professor that, after our visit to Carfax, we should all enter the house in Piccadilly; that the two doctors and I should remain there, whilst Lord Godalming and Quincey found the lairs at Walworth and Mile End and destroyed them. It was possible, if not likely, the Professor urged, that the Count might appear in Piccadilly during the day, and that if so we might be able to cope with him then and there. At any rate we might be able to follow him in force. To this plan I strenuously objected, in so far as my going was concerned, for I said that I intended to stay and protect Mina. I thought that my mind was made up on the subject; but Mina would not listen to my objection. She said that there might be some law matter in which I could be useful; that amongst the Count's papers might be some clue which I could understand out of my experience in Transylvania; and that, as it was, all the strength we could muster was required to cope with the

Count's extraordinary power. I had to give in, for Mina's resolution was fixed; she said that it was the last hope for *her* that we should all work together. 'As for me,' she said, 'I have no fear. Things have been as bad as they can be; and whatever may happen must have in it some element of hope or comfort. Go, my husband! God can, if He wishes it, guard me as well alone as with anyone present.' So I started up, crying out: 'Then in God's name let us come at once, for we are losing time. The Count may come to Piccadilly earlier than we think.'

'Not so!' said Van Helsing, holding up his hand.

'But why?' I asked.

'Do you forget,' he said, with actually a smile, 'that last night he banqueted heavily, and will sleep late?'

Did I forget! shall I ever – can I ever! Can any of us ever forget that terrible scene! Mina struggled hard to keep her brave countenance; but the pain overmastered her and she put her hands before her face, and shuddered whilst she moaned. Van Helsing had not intended to recall her frightful experience. He had simply lost sight of her and her part in the affair in his intellectual effort. When it struck him what he had said, he was horrified at his thoughtlessness and tried to comfort her. 'Oh, Madam Mina,' he said, 'dear, dear Madam Mina, alas! that I, of all who so reverence you, should have said anything so forgetful. These stupid old lips of mine and this stupid old head do not deserve so; but you will forget it, will you not?' He bent low beside her as he spoke; she took his hands, and looking at him through her tears, said hoarsely:–

'No, I shall not forget, for it is well that I remember; and with it I have so much in memory of you that is sweet, that I take it all together. Now, you must all be going soon. Breakfast is ready, and we must all eat that we may be strong.'

Breakfast was a strange meal to us all. We tried to be cheerful and encourage each other, and Mina was the brightest and most cheerful of us. When it was over, Van Helsing stood up and said:–

'Now, my dear friends, we go forth to our terrible enterprise. Are we all armed, as we were on that night when first we visited our enemy's lair; armed against ghostly as well as carnal attack?' We all assured him. 'Then it is well. Now, Madam Mina, you are in any case *quite* safe here until the sunset; and before then we shall return – if – We shall return! But before we go let me see you armed against personal attack. I have myself, since you came down, prepared your chamber by the placing of the things of which we know, so that he may not enter. Now let me guard yourself. On your forehead I touch this piece of Sacred Wafer in the name of the Father, the Son, and –'

There was a fearful scream which almost froze our hearts to hear. As he placed the Wafer on Mina's forehead, it had seared it – had burned into

241

the flesh as though it had been a piece of white-hot metal. My poor darling's brain told her the significance of the fact as quickly as her nerves received the pain of it: and the two so overwhelmed her that her overwrought nature had its voice in that dreadful scream. But the words to her thought came quickly; the echo of the scream had not ceased to ring on the air when there came the reaction, and she sank on her knees on the floor in an agony of abasement. Pulling her beautiful hair over her face, as the leper of old his mantle, she wailed out:—

'Unclean! Unclean! Even the Almighty shuns my polluted flesh! I must bear this mark of shame upon my forehead until the Judgment Day.' They all paused. I had thrown myself beside her in an agony of helpless grief, and putting my arms around held her tight. For a few minutes our sorrowful hearts beat together, whilst the friends around us turned away their eyes that ran tears silently. Then Van Helsing turned and said gravely; so gravely that I could not help feeling that he was in some way inspired and was stating things outside himself:—

'It may be that you may have to bear that mark till God Himself see fit, as He most surely shall, on the Judgment Day to redress all wrongs of the earth and of His children that He has placed thereon. And oh, Madam Mina, my dear, my dear, may we who love you be there to see, when that red scar, the sign of God's knowledge of what has been, shall pass away and leave your forehead as pure as the heart we know. For so surely as we live, that scar shall pass away when God see right to lift the burden that is hard upon us. Till then we bear our Cross, as His Son did in obedience to His will. It may be that we are chosen instruments of His good pleasure, and that we ascend to His bidding as that other through stripes and shame; through tears and blood; through doubts and fears, and all that makes the difference between God and man.'

There was hope in his words, and comfort; and they made for resignation. Mina and I both felt so, and simultaneously we each took one of the old man's hands and bent over and kissed it. Then without a word we all knelt down together, and, all holding hands, swore to be true to each other. We men pledged ourselves to raise the veil of sorrow from the head of her whom, each in his own way, we loved; and we prayed for help and guidance in the terrible task which lay before us.

It was then time to start. So I said farewell to Mina, a parting which neither of us shall forget to our dying day; and we set out.

To one thing I have made up my mind: if we find out that Mina must be a vampire in the end, then she shall not go into that unknown and terrible land alone. I suppose it is thus that in old times one vampire meant many; just as their hideous bodies could only rest in sacred earth, so the holiest love was the recruiting sergeant for their ghastly ranks.

We entered Carfax without trouble and found all things the same as on the first occasion. It was hard to believe that amongst so prosaic surroundings of neglect and dust and decay there was any ground for such fear as we already knew. Had not our minds been made up, and had there not been terrible memories to spur us on, we could hardly have proceeded with our task. We found no papers, nor any sign of use in the house; and in the old chapel the great boxes looked just as we had seen them last. Dr Van Helsing said to us solemnly as we stood before them:–

'And now, my friends, we have a duty here to do. We must sterilize this earth, so sacred of holy memories, that he has brought from a far distant land for such fell use. He has chosen this earth because it has been holy. Thus we defeat him with his own weapon, for we make it more holy still. It was sanctified to such use of man, now we sanctify it to God.' As he spoke he took from his bag a screw-driver and a wrench, and very soon the top of one of the cases was thrown open. The earth smelled musty and close; but we did not somehow seem to mind, for our attention was concentrated on the Professor. Taking from his box a piece of Sacred Wafer he laid it reverently on the earth, and then shutting down the lid began to screw it home, we aiding him as he worked.

One by one we treated in the same way each of the great boxes, and left them as we had found them to all appearance; but in each was a portion of the Host.

When we closed the door behind us, the Professor said solemnly:–

'So much is already done. If it may be that with all the others we can be so successful, then the sunset of this evening may shine on Madam Mina's forehead all white as ivory and with no stain!'

As we passed across the lawn on our way to the station to catch our train we could see the front of the asylum. I looked eagerly, and in the window of my room saw Mina. I waved my hand to her, and nodded to tell that our work there was successfully accomplished. She nodded in reply to show that she understood. The last I saw, she was waving her hand in farewell. It was with a heavy heart that we sought the station and just caught the train, which was steaming in as we reached the platform.

I have written this in the train.

Piccadilly, 12.30 o'clock. – Just before we reached Fenchurch Street Lord Godalming said to me:–

'Quincey and I will find a locksmith. You had better not come with us in case there should be any difficulty; for under the circumstances it wouldn't seem so bad for us to break into an empty house. But you are a solicitor, and the Incorporated Law Society might tell you that you should have known better.' I demurred as to my not sharing any danger even of odium, but he went on: 'Besides, it will attract less attention if there are

243

not too many of us. My title will make it all right with the locksmith, and with any policeman that may come along. You had better go with Jack and the Professor and stay in the Green Park, somewhere in sight of the house; and when you see the door open and the smith has gone away, do you all come across. We shall be on the look-out for you, and will let you in.'

'The advice is good!' said Van Helsing, so we said no more. Godalming and Morris hurried off in a cab, we following in another. At the corner of Arlington Street our contingent got out and strolled into the Green Park. My heart beat as I saw the house on which so much of our hope was centred, looming up grim and silent in its deserted condition amongst its more lively and spruce-looking neighbours. We sat down on a bench within a good view, and began to smoke cigars so as to attract as little attention as possible. The minutes seemed to pass with leaden feet as we waited for the coming of the others.

At length we saw a four-wheeler drive up. Out of it, in leisurely fashion, got Lord Godalming and Morris; and down from the box descended a thick-set working man with his rush-woven basket of tools. Morris paid the cabman, who touched his hat and drove away. Together the two ascended the steps, and Lord Godalming pointed out what he wanted done. The workman took off his coat leisurely and hung it on one of the spikes of the railing, saying something to a policeman who just then sauntered along. The policeman nodded acquiescence, and the man kneeling down placed his bag beside him. After searching through it, he took out a selection of tools which he proceeded to lay beside him in orderly fashion. Then he stood up, looked into the keyhole, blew into it, and turning to his employers, made some remark. Lord Godalming smiled, and the man lifted a good-sized bunch of keys; selecting one of them, he began to probe the lock, as if feeling his way with it. After fumbling about for a bit he tried a second, and then a third. All at once the door opened under a slight push from him, and he and the two others entered the hall. We sat still; my own cigar burnt furiously, but Van Helsing's went cold altogether. We waited patiently as we saw the workman come out and take in his bag. Then he held the door partly open, steadying it with his knees, whilst he fitted a key to the lock. This he finally handed to Lord Godalming, who took out his purse and gave him something. The man touched his hat, took his bag, put on his coat and departed; not a soul took the slightest notice of the whole transaction.

When the man had fairly gone, we three crossed the street and knocked at the door. It was immediately opened by Quincey Morris, beside whom stood Lord Godalming lighting a cigar.

'The place smells so vilely,' said the latter as we came in. It did indeed smell vilely – like the old chapel at Carfax – and with our previous experience it was plain to us that the Count had been using the place pretty freely. We moved to explore the house, all keeping together in case of attack; for we knew we had a strong and wily enemy to deal with, and as yet we did not know whether the Count might not be in the house. In the dining-room, which lay at the back of the hall, we found eight boxes of earth. Eight boxes only out of the nine which we sought! Our work was not over, and would never be until we should have found the missing box. First we opened the shutters of the window which looked out across a narrow stone-flagged yard at the blank face of a stable, pointed to look like the front of a miniature house. There were no windows in it, so we were not afraid of being overlooked. We did not lose any time in examining the chests. With the tools which we had brought with us we opened them, one by one, and treated them as we had treated those others in the chapel. It was evident to us that the Count was not at present in the house, and we proceeded to search for any of his effects.

After a cursory glance at the rest of the rooms from basement to attic, we came to the conclusion that the dining-room contained any effects which might belong to the Count; and so we proceeded to minutely examine them. They lay in a sort of orderly disorder on the great dining-room table. There were title-deeds of the Piccadilly house in a great bundle; deeds of the purchase of the houses at Mile End and Bermondsey; note-paper, envelopes, and pens and ink. All were covered up in thin wrapping paper to keep them from the dust. There were also a clothes brush, a brush and comb, and a jug and basin – the latter containing dirty water which was reddened as if with blood. Last of all was a little heap of keys of all sorts and sizes, probably those belonging to the other houses. When we had examined this last find, Lord Godalming and Quincey Morris, taking accurate notes of the various addresses of the houses in the East and the South, took with them the keys in a great bunch, and set out to destroy the boxes in these places. The rest of us are, with what patience we can, awaiting their return – or the coming of the Count.

23

DR SEWARD'S DIARY

3 October. – The time seemed terribly long whilst we were waiting for the coming of Godalming and Quincey Morris. The Professor tried to keep our minds active by using them all the time. I could see his beneficent purpose, by the side glances which he threw from time to time at Harker. The poor fellow is overwhelmed in a misery that is appalling to see. Last night he was a frank, happy-looking man, with strong youthful face, full of energy, and with dark brown hair. To-day he is a drawn, haggard old man, whose white hair matches well with the hollow burning eyes and grief-written lines of his face. His energy is still intact; in fact he is like a living flame. This may yet be his salvation, for, if all goes well, it will tide him over the despairing period; he will then, in a kind of way, wake again to the realities of life. Poor fellow, I thought my own trouble was bad enough, but his – ! The Professor knows this well enough, and is doing his best to keep his mind active. What he has been saying was, under the circumstances, of absorbing interest. As well as I can remember, here it is:–

'I have studied, over and over again since they came into my hands, all the papers relating to this monster; and the more I have studied, the greater seems the necessity to utterly stamp him out. All through there are signs of his advance; not only of his power, but of his knowledge of it. As I learned from the researches of my friend Aminius of Buda-Pesth, he was in life a most wonderful man. Soldier, statesman, and alchemist – which latter was the highest development of the science-knowledge of his time. He had a mighty brain, a learning beyond compare, and a heart that knew no fear and no remorse. He dared even to attend the Scholomance, and there was no branch of knowledge of his time that he did not essay. Well, in him the brain powers survived the physical death; though it would seem that memory was not all complete. In some faculties of mind he has been, and is, only a child; but he is growing, and some things that were childish at the first are now of man's stature. He is experimenting, and doing it well; and if it had not been that we have crossed his path he would be yet – he may be yet if we fail – the father or furtherer of a new order of beings, whose road must lead through Death, not Life.'

Harker groaned and said: 'And this is all arrayed against my darling! But how is he experimenting? The knowledge may help us to defeat him!'

'He has all along, since his coming, been trying his power, slowly but surely; that big child-brain of his is working. Well for us, it is, as yet, a child-brain; for had he dared, at the first, to attempt certain things he would long ago have been beyond our power. However, he means to succeed, and a man who has centuries before him can afford to wait and to go slow. *Festina lente* may well be his motto.'

'I fail to understand,' said Harker wearily. 'Oh, do be more plain to me! Perhaps grief and trouble are dulling my brain.' The Professor laid his hand tenderly on his shoulder as he spoke:–

'Ah, my child, I will be plain. Do you not see how, of late, this monster has been creeping into knowledge experimentally. How he has been making use of the zoophagous patient to effect his entry into friend John's home; for your Vampire, though in all afterwards he can come when and how he will, must at the first make entry only when asked thereto by an inmate. But these are not his most important experiments. Do we not see how at the first all these so great boxes were moved by others. He knew not then but that must be so. But all the time that so great child-brain of his was growing, and he began to consider whether he might not himself move the box. So he begin to help; and then, when he found that this be all right, he try to move them all alone. And so he progress, and he scatter these graves of him; and none but he know where they are hidden. He may have intend to bury them deep in the ground. So that he only use them in the night, or at such time as he can change his form, they do him equal well; and none may know these are his hiding place! But, my child, do not despair; this knowledge come to him just too late! Already all of his lairs but one be sterilize as for him; and before the sunset this shall be so. Then he have no place where he can move and hide. I delayed this morning that so we might be sure. Is there not more at stake for us than for him? By my clock it is one hour, and already, if all be well, friend Arthur and Quincey are on their way to us. To-day is our day, and we must go sure, if slow, and lose no chance. See! There are five of us when those absent ones return.'

Whilst he was speaking we were startled by a knock at the hall door, the double postman's knock of the telegraph boy. We all moved out to the hall with one impulse, and Van Helsing, holding up his hand to us to keep silence, stepped to the door and opened it. The boy handed in a despatch. The Professor closed the door again and, after looking at the direction, opened it and read it aloud:—

' "Look out for D. He has just now, 12.45, come from Carfax hurriedly and hastened towards the south. He seems to be going the round and may want to see you – MINA." '

There was a pause, broken by Jonathan Harker's voice:—

'Now, God be thanked, we shall soon meet!' Van Helsing turned to him quickly and said:—

'God will act in His own way and time. Do not fear, and do not rejoice as yet; for what we wish for at the moment may be our undoings.'

'I care for nothing now,' he answered hotly, 'except to wipe out this brute from the face of creation. I would sell my soul to do it!'

'Oh, hush, hush, my child!' said Van Helsing, 'God does not purchase souls in this wise; and the Devil, though he may purchase, does not keep faith. But God is merciful and just, and knows your pain and your

247

devotion to that dear Madam Mina. Think you, how her pain would be doubled, did she but hear your wild words. Do not fear any of us; we are all devoted to this cause, and to-day shall see the end. The time is coming for action; to-day this Vampire is limit to the powers of man, and till sunset he may not change. It will take him time to arrive here – see, it is twenty minutes past one – and there are yet some times before he can hither come, be he never so quick . What we must hope for is that my Lord Arthur and Quincey arrive first.'

About half an hour after we had received Mrs Harker's telegram, there came a quiet resolute knock at the hall door. It was just an ordinary knock, such as is given hourly by thousands of gentlemen, but it made the Professor's heart and mine beat loudly. We looked at each other, and together moved out into the hall; we each held ready to use our various armaments – the spiritual in the left hand, the moral in the right. Van Helsing pulled back the latch, and, holding the door half open, stood back, having both hands ready for action. The gladness of our hearts must have shown upon our faces when on the step, close to the door, we saw Lord Godalming and Quincey Morris. They came quickly in and closed the door behind them, the former saying, as they moved along the hall:–

'It is all right. We found both places; six boxes in each, and we destroyed them all!'

'Destroyed?' asked the Professor.

'For him!' We were silent for a minute, and then Quincey said:–

'There's nothing to do but to wait here. If, however, he doesn't turn up by five o'clock, we must start off; for it won't do to leave Mrs Harker alone after sunset.'

'He will be here before long now,' said Van Helsing, who had been consulting his pocket-book. '*Nota bene*, in Madam's telegram he went south from Carfax, that means he went to cross the river, and he could only do so at slack of tide, which should be something before one o'clock. That he went south has a meaning for us. He is as yet only suspicious; and he went from Carfax first to the place where he would suspect interference least. You must have been at Bermondsey only a short time before him. That he is not here already shows that he went to Mile End next. This took him some time; for he would have to be carried over the river in some way. Believe me, my friends, we shall not have long to wait now. We should have ready some plan of attack, so that we may throw away no chance. Hush, there is no time now. Have all your arms! Be ready!' He held up a warning hand as he spoke, for we all could hear a key softly inserted in the lock of the hall-door.

I could not but admire, even at such a moment, the way in which a dominant spirit asserted itself. In all our hunting parties and adventures on different parts of the world, Quincey Morris had always been the one to arrange the plan of action, and Arthur and I had been accustomed to obey him implicitly. Now, the old habit seemed to be renewed instinctively. With a swift glance round the room, he at once laid out our plan of attack, and, without speaking a word, with a gesture, placed us each in position. Van Helsing, Harker, and I were just behind the door so that when it was opened the Professor could guard it whilst we two stepped between the incomer and the door. Godalming behind and Quincey in front stood just out of sight ready to move in front of the window. We waited in a suspense that made the seconds pass with nightmare slowness. The slow, careful steps came along the hall; the Count was evidently prepared for some surprise – at least he feared it.

Suddenly with a single bound he leaped into the room, winning a way past us before any of us could raise a hand to stay him. There was something so panther-like in the movement – something so unhuman, that it seemed to sober us all from the shock of his coming. The first to act was Harker, who, with a quick movement, threw himself before the door leading into the room in the front of the house. As the Count saw us, a horrible sort of snarl passed over his face, showing the eye-teeth long and pointed; but the evil smile as quickly passed into a cold stare of lion-like disdain. His expression again changed, as with a single impulse, we all advanced upon him. It was a pity that we had not some better organized plan of attack, for even at the moment I wondered what we were to do. I did not myself know whether our lethal weapons would avail us anything. Harker evidently meant to try the matter, for he had ready his great Kukri knife, and made a fierce and sudden cut at him. The blow was a powerful one; only the diabolical quickness of the Count's leap back saved him. A second less and the trenchant blade had shorn through his heart. As it was, the point just cut the cloth of his coat, making a wide gap whence a bundle of bank-notes and a stream of gold fell out. The expression of the Count's face was so hellish, that for a moment I feared for Harker, though I saw him throw the terrible knife aloft again for another stroke. Instinctively I moved forward with a protective impulse, holding the crucifix and wafer in my hand. I felt a mighty power fly along my arm; and it was without surprise that I saw the monster cower back before a similar movement made spontaneously by each one of us. It would be impossible to describe the expression of hate and baffled malignity – of anger and hellish rage – which came over the Count's face. His waxen hue became greenish-yellow by the contrast of his burning eyes, and the red scar on the forehead showed on the pallid skin like a palpitating wound. The next instant, with a sinuous dive he swept under Harker's arm ere his blow could fall, and, grasping a handful of the money from the floor, dashed across the room, and threw himself at the window. Amid the crash and glitter of the falling glass, he tumbled into the flagged area below. Through the sound of the shivering glass I could hear the 'ting' of the gold, as some of the sovereigns fell on the flagging.

We ran over and saw him spring unhurt from the ground. He, rushing up the steps, crossed the flagged yard, and pushed open the stable door. There he turned and spoke to us:–

'You think to baffle me, you – with your pale faces all in a row, like sheep in a butcher's. You shall be sorry yet, each one of you! You think you have left me without a place to rest; but I have more. My revenge is just begun! I spread it over centuries, and time is on my side. Your girls that you all love are mine already; and through them you and others shall yet be mine – my creatures, to do my bidding and to be my jackals when I want to feed. Bah!' With a contemptuous sneer, he passed quickly through the door, and we heard the rusty bolt creak as he fastened it behind him. A door beyond opened and shut. The first of us to speak was the Professor, as, realizing the difficulty of following him through the stable, we moved towards the hall.

'We have learnt something – much! Notwithstanding his brave words, he fears us; he fear time, he fear want! For if not, why he hurry so? His very tone betray him, or my ears deceive. Why take that money? You follow quick. You are hunters of wild beasts, and understand it so. For me, I make sure that nothing here may be of use to him, if so that he return.' As he spoke he put the money remaining into his pocket; took the title-deeds in the bundle as Harker had left them, and swept the remaining things into the open fireplace, where he set fire to them with a match.

Godalming and Morris had rushed out into the yard, and Harker had lowered himself from the window to follow the Count. He had, however, bolted the stable door; and by the time they had forced it open there was no sign of him. Van Helsing and I tried to make inquiry at the back of the house; but the mews was deserted and no one had seen him depart.

It was now late in the afternoon, and sunset was not far off. We had to recognize that our game was up; with heavy hearts we agreed with the Professor when he said:–

'Let us go back to Madam Mina – poor, poor, dear Madam Mina. All we can do just now is done; and we can there, at least, protect her. But we need not despair. There is but one more earth-box, and we must try to find it; when that is done all may yet be well.' I could see that he spoke as bravely as he could to comfort Harker. The poor fellow was quite broken down; now and again he gave a low groan which he could not suppress – he was thinking of his wife.

With sad hearts we came back to my house, where we found Mrs

Harker awaiting us, with an appearance of cheerfulness which did honour to her bravery and unselfishness. When she saw our faces, her own became as pale as death; for a second or two her eyes were closed as if she were in secret prayer; and then she said cheerfully:–

'I can never thank you all enough. Oh, my poor darling!' As she spoke she took her husband's grey head in her hands and kissed it – 'Lay your poor head here and rest it. All will yet be well, dear! God will protect us if He so will it in His good intent.' The poor fellow only groaned. There was no place for words in his sublime misery.

We had a sort of perfunctory supper together, and I think it cheered us all up somewhat. It was, perhaps, the mere animal heat of food to hungry people – for none of us had eaten anything since breakfast – or the sense of companionship may have helped us; but anyhow we were all less miserable, and saw the morrow as not altogether without hope. True to our promise, we told Mrs Harker everything which had passed; and although she grew snowy white at times when danger had seemed to threaten her husband, and red at others when his devotion to her was manifested, she listened bravely and with calmness. When we came to the part where Harker had rushed at the Count so recklessly, she clung to her husband's arm, and held it tight as though her clinging could protect him from any harm that might come. She said nothing, however, till the narration was all done, and matters had been brought right up to the present time. Then without letting go her husband's hand she stood up amongst us and spoke. Oh! that I could give any idea of the scene; of that sweet, sweet, good, good woman in all the radiant beauty of her youth and animation, with the red scar on her forehead of which she was conscious, and which we saw with grinding of our teeth – remembering whence and how it came; her loving kindness against our grim hate; her tender faith against all our fears and doubting; and we, knowing that, so far as symbols went, she with all her goodness and purity and faith was outcast from God.

'Jonathan,' she said, and the word sounded like music on her lips, it was so full of love and tenderness, 'Jonathan dear, and you all, my true, true friends, I want you to bear something in mind through all this dreadful time. I know that you must fight – that you must destroy even as you destroyed the false Lucy so that the true Lucy might live hereafter; but it is not a work of hate. That poor soul who has wrought all this misery is the saddest case of all. Just think what will be his joy when he too is destroyed in his worser part that this better part may have spiritual immortality. You must be pitiful to him too, though it may not hold your hands from his destruction.'

As she spoke I could see her husband's face darken and draw together, as though the passion in him were shrivelling his being to its core. Instinctively the clasp on his wife's hand grew closer, till his knuckles looked white. She did not flinch from the pain which I knew she must have suffered, but looked at him with eyes that were more appealing than ever. As she stopped speaking he leaped to his feet, almost tearing his hand from hers as he spoke:–

'May God give him into my hand just for long enough to destroy that earthly life of him which we were aiming at. If beyond it I could send his soul for ever and ever to burning hell I would do it!'

'Oh, hush! oh, hush! in the name of the good God. Don't say such things, Jonathan, my husband; or you will crush me with fear and horror. Just think, my dear – I have been thinking all this long, long day of it – that ... perhaps ... some day ... I too may need such pity; and that some other like you – and with equal cause for anger – may deny it to me! Oh, my husband! my husband, indeed I would have spared you such a thought had there been another way; but I pray that God may not have treasured your wild words, except as the heart-broken wail of a very loving and sorely stricken man. O God, let these poor white hairs go in evidence of what he has suffered, who all his life has done no wrong, and on whom so many sorrows have come.'

We men were all in tears now. There was no resisting them, and we wept openly. She wept too, to see that her sweeter counsels had prevailed. Her husband flung himself on his knees beside her, and putting his arms round her, hid his face in the folds of her dress. Van Helsing beckoned to us and we stole out of the room, leaving the two loving hearts alone with God.

Before they retired the Professor fixed up the room against any coming of the Vampire, and assured Mrs Harker that she might rest in peace. She tried to school herself to the belief, and, manifestly for her husband's sake, tried to seem content. It was a brave struggle; and was, I think and believe, not without its reward. Van Helsing had placed at hand a bell which either of them was to sound in case of any emergency. When they had retired, Quincey, Godalming, and I arranged that we should sit up, dividing the night between us, and watch over the safety of the poor stricken lady. The first watch falls to Quincey, so the rest of us will be off to bed as soon as we can. Godalming has already turned in, for his is the second watch. Now that my work is done, I, too, shall go to bed.

JONATHAN HARKER'S JOURNAL

3–4 October close to midnight. – I thought yesterday would never end. There was over me a yearning for sleep in some sort of blind belief that to wake would be to find things changed, and that any change must now be for the better. Before we parted, we discussed what our next step was to be, but we could arrive at no result. All we knew was that one earth-box remained, and that the Count alone knew where it was. If he chooses to lie hidden, he may baffle us for years; and in the meantime! – the thought is too horrible, I dare not think of it even now. This I know: that if ever there was a woman who was all perfection, that one is my poor wronged darling. I love her a thousand times more for her sweet pity of last night, a pity that made my own hate of the moster seem despicable. Surely God will not permit the world to be the poorer by the loss of such a creature. This is hope to me. We are all drifting reefwards now, and faith is our only anchor. Thank God! Mina is sleeping, and sleeping without dreams. I fear what her dreams might be like, with such terrible memories to ground them on. She has not been so calm, within my seeing, since the sunset. Then, for a while, there came over her face a repose which was like spring after the blasts of March. I thought at the time that it was the softness of the red sunset on her face, but somehow now I think it had a deeper meaning. I am not sleepy myself, though I am weary – weary to death. However, I must try to sleep; for there is to-morrow to think of, and there is no rest for me until . . . .

Later. – I must have fallen asleep, for I was awakened by Mina, who was sitting up in bed, with a startled look on her face. I could see easily, for we did not leave the room in darkness; she had placed a warning hand over my mouth, and now she whispered in my ear:–

'Hush! there is someone in the corridor!' I got up softly, and crossing the room, gently opened the door.

Just outside, stretched on a mattress, lay Mr Morris, wide awake. He raised a warning hand for silence as he whispered to me:–

'Hush! go back to bed; it is all right. One of us will be here all night. We don't mean to take any chances!'

His look and gesture forbade discussion, so I came back and told Mina. She sighed, and positively a shadow of a smile stole over her poor, pale face as she put her arms round me and said softly:–

'Oh, thank God for brave men!' With a sigh she sank back again to sleep. I write this as I am not sleepy, though I must try again.

4 October, morning. – Once again during the night I was wakened by Mina. This time we had all had a good sleep, for the grey of the coming dawn was making the windows into sharp oblongs, and the gas flame was like a speck rather than a disc of light. She said to me hurriedly:–

'Go call the Professor. I want to see him at once.'

'Why?' I asked.

'I have an idea. I suppose it must have come in the night, and matured without my knowing it. He must hypnotize me before the dawn, and then I shall be able to speak. Go quick, dearest; the time is getting close.' I went to the door. Dr Seward was resting on the mattress, and, seeing me, he sprang to his feet.

'Is anything wrong?' he asked, in alarm.

'No,' I replied; 'but Mina wants to see Dr Van Helsing at once.'

'I will go,' he said, and hurried into the Professor's room.

Two or three minutes later Van Helsing was in the room in his dressing-gown, and Mr Morris and Lord Godalming were with Dr Seward at the door asking questions. When the Professor saw Mina a smile – a positive smile – ousted the anxiety of his face; he rubbed his hands as he said:–

'Oh, my dear Madam Mina, this is indeed a change. See! friend Jonathan, we have got our dear Madam Mina, as of old, back to us to-day!' Then turning to her, he said cheerfully: 'And what am I do for you? For at this hour you do not want me for nothings.'

'I want you to hypnotize me!' she said. 'Do it before the dawn, for I feel that then I can speak, and speak freely. Be quick, for the time is short!' Without a word he motioned her to sit up in bed.

Looking fixedly at her, he commenced to make passes in front of her, from over the top of her head downward, with each hand in turn. Mina gazed at him fixedly for a few minutes, during which my own heart beat like a trip hammer, for I felt that some crisis was at hand. Gradually her eyes closed, and she sat stock still; only by the gentle heaving of her bosom could one know that she was alive. The Professor made a few more passes and then stopped, and I could see that his forehead was covered with great beads of perspiration. Mina opened her eyes; but she did not seem the same woman. There was a faraway look in her eyes, and her voice had a sad dreaminess which was new to me. Raising his hand to impose silence, the Professor motioned to me to bring the others in. They came on tip-toe, closing the door behind them, and stood at the foot of the bed, looking on. Mina appeared not to see them. The stillness was broken by Van Helsing's voice speaking in a low level tone which would not break the current of her thoughts:–

'Where are you!' The answer came in a neutral way:–

'I do not know. Sleep has no place it can call its own.' For several minutes there was silence. Mina sat rigid, and the Professor stood staring at her fixedly; the rest of us hardly dared to breathe. The room was growing lighter; without taking his eyes from Mina's face, Dr Van Helsing motioned me to pull up the blind. I did so, and the day seemed just upon us. A red streak shot up, and a rosy light seemed to diffuse itself through the room. On the instant the Professor spoke again:–

'Where are you now?' The answer came dreamily, but with intention; it was as though she were interpreting something. I have heard her use the same tone when reading her notes.

'I do not know. It is all strange to me!'

'What do you see?'

'I can see nothing; it is all dark.'

'What do you hear?' I could detect the strain in the Professor's patient voice.

'The lapping of water. It is gurgling by, and little waves leap. I can hear them on the outside.'

'Then you are on a ship?' We all looked at each other, trying to glean something each from the other. We were afraid to think. The answer came quick:–

'Oh, yes!'

'What else do you hear?'

'The sound of men stamping overhead as they run about. There is the creaking of a chain, and the loud tinkle as the check of the capstan falls into the ratchet.'

'What are you doing?'

'I am still – oh, so still. It is like death!' The voice faded away into a deep breath as of one sleeping, and the open eyes closed again.

By this time the sun had risen, and we were all in the full light of day. Dr Van Helsing placed his hands on Mina's shoulders, and laid her head down softly on her pillow. She lay like a sleeping child for a few moments, and then, with a long sigh, awoke and stared in wonder to see us all around her. 'Have I been talking in my sleep?' was all she said. She seemed, however, to know the situation without telling; though she was eager to know what she had told. The Professor repeated the conversation, and she said:

'Then there is not a moment to lose: it may not be yet too late!' Mr Morris and Lord Godalming started for the door, but the Professor's calm voice called them back:

'Stay, my friends. That ship, wherever it was, was weighing anchor whilst she spoke. There are many ships weighing anchor at the moment in your so great Port of London. Which of them is it that you seek? God be thanked that we have once again a clue, though whither it may lead us we know not. We have been blind somewhat; blind after the manner of men, since when we can look back we see what we might have seen looking forward if we had been able to see what we might have seen! Alas! but that sentence is a puddle; is it not? We can know now what was in the Count's mind when he seize that money, though Jonathan's so fierce knife put him in the danger that even he dread. He meant escape. Hear, me,

255

ESCAPE! He saw that with but one earth-box left, and a pack of men following like dogs after a fox, this London was no place for him. He have take his last earth-box on board a ship, and he leave the land. He think to escape, but no! we follow him. Tally ho! as friend Arthur would say when he put on his red frock! Our old fox is wily; oh; so wily, and we must follow with wile. I too am wily and I think his mind in a little while. In meantime we may rest and in peace, for there are waters between us which he do not want to pass, and which he could not if he would – unless the ship were to touch the land, and then only at full or slack tide. See, and the sun is just rose, and all day to sunset is to us. Let us take bath, and dress, and have breakfast which we all need, and which we can eat comfortable since he be not in the same land with us.' Mina looked at him appealingly as she asked:

'But why need we seek him further, when he is gone away from us?' He took her hand and patted it as he replied:–

'Ask me nothing as yet. When we have breakfast, then I answer all questions.' He would say no more, and we separated to dress.

After breakfast Mina repeated her question. He looked at her gravely for a minute and then said sorrowfully:–

'Because, my dear, dear Madam Mina, now more than ever must we find him even if we have to follow him to the jaws of Hell.' She grew paler as she asked faintly:–

'Why?'

'Because,' he answered solemnly, 'he can live for centuries, and you are but mortal woman. Time is now to be dreaded – since once he put that mark upon your throat.'

I was just in time to catch her as she fell forward in a faint.

24

DR SEWARD'S PHONOGRAPH DIARY, SPOKEN BY
VAN HELSING

This to Jonathan Harker.

You are to stay with your dear Madam Mina. We shall go to make our search – if I can call it so, for it is not search but knowing, and we seek confirmation only. But do you stay and take care of her to-day. This is your best and most holiest office. This day nothing can find him here. Let me tell you that so you will know what we four know already, for I have tell them. He, our enemy, have gone away; he have gone back to his Castle in Transylvania. I know it so well, as if a great hand of fire wrote in on the wall. He have prepared for this in some way, and that last earth-box was ready to ship somewheres. For this he took the money; for this he hurried at the last, lest we catch him before the sun go down. It was his last hope, save that he might hide in the tomb, that he think poor Miss Lucy, being as he thought like him, keep open to him. But there was not of time. When that fail he make straight for his last resource – his last earthwork I might say did I wish *double entente*. He is clever, oh, so clever! he know that his game here was finish; and so he decide he go back home. He find ship going by the route he came, and he go in it. We go off now to find what ship, and whither bound; when we have discovered that, we come back and tell you all. Then we will comfort you and poor dear Madam Mina with new hope. For it will be hope when you think it over: that all is not lost. This very creature that we pursue, he take hundreds of years to get so far as London; and yet in one day, when we know of the disposal of him, we drive him out. He is finite, though he is powerful to do much harm and suffers not as we do. But we are strong, each in our purpose; and we are all more strong together. Take heart afresh, dear husband of Madam Mina. This battle is but begun, and in the end we shall win – so sure as that God sits on high to watch over His children. Therefore be of much comfort till we return.

Van Helsing

JONATHAN HARKER'S JOURNAL

4 October. – When I read to Mina Van Helsing's message in the phonograph, the poor girl brightened up considerably. Already the certainty that the Count is out of the country has given her comfort; and comfort is strength to her. For my own part, now that this horrible danger is not face to face with us, it seems almost impossible to believe in it. Even my own terrible experiences in Castle Dracula seem like a long-forgotten dream. Here in the crisp autumn air, in the bright sunlight –

Alas! how can I disbelieve! In the midst of my thought my eye fell on the red scar on my poor darling's white forehead. Whilst that lasts, there can be no disbelief. And afterwards the very memory of it will keep faith crystal clear. Mina and I fear to be idle, so we have been over all the diaries again and again. Somehow, although the reality seems greater each time, the pain and the fear seem less. There is something of a guiding purpose manifest throughout, which is comforting. Mina says that perhaps we are the instruments of ultimate good. It may be! I shall try to think as she does. We have never spoken to each other yet of the future. It is better to wait till we see the Professor and the others after their investigations.

The day is running by more quickly than I ever thought a day could run for me again. It is now three o'clock.

MINA HARKER'S JOURNAL

5 October, 5 p.m. – Our meeting for report. Present: Professor Van Helsing, Lord Godalming, Dr Seward, Mr Quincey Morris, Jonathan Harker, Mina Harker.

Dr Van Helsing described what steps were taken during the day to discover on what boat and whither bound Count Dracula made his escape:–

'As I knew that he wanted to get back to Transylvania, I felt sure that he must go by the Danube mouth; or by somewhere in the Black Sea, since by that way he come. It was a dreary blank that was before us. *Omne ignotum pro magnifico*; and so with heavy hearts we start to find what ships leave for the Black Sea last night. He was in sailing ship, since Madam Mina tells of sails being set. These not so important as to go in your list of the shipping in *The Times*, and so we go, by suggestion of my Lord Godalming, to your Lloyd's, where are note of all ships that sail, however so small. There we find that only one Black Sea bound ship go out with the tide. She is the *Czarina Catherine*, and she sail from Doolittle's Wharf for Varna, and thence on to other parts and up the Danube. "Soh!" said I, "this is the ship whereon is the Count." So off we go to Doolittle's Wharf, and there we find a man in an office of wood so small that the man look bigger than the office. From him we inquire of the goings of the *Czarina Catherine*. He swear much, and he red face and loud of voice, but he good fellow all the same; and when Quincey give him something from his pocket which crackle as he roll it up, and put it in a so small bag which he have hid deep in his clothing, he still better fellow and humble servant to us. He come with us, and ask many men who are rough and hot; these be better fellows too when they have been no more thirsty. They say much of blood and bloom and of others which I comprehend not, though I guess what they mean; but nevertheless they tell us all things which we want to know.

'They make known to us among them how last afternoon at about five o'clock comes a man so hurry. A tall man, thin and pale, with high nose and teeth so white, and eyes that seem to be burning. That he be all in black, except that he have a hat of straw which suit not him or the time. That he scatter his money in making quick inquiry as to what ship sails for the Black Sea and for where. Some took him to the office and then to the ship, where he will not go aboard but halt at shore end of gangplank, and ask that the captain come to him. The captain come, when told that he will be pay well; and though he swear much at the first he agree to term. Then the thin man go and someone tell him where horse and cart can be hired. He go there, and soon he come again, himself driving cart on which is a great box; this he himself lift down, though it take several to put it on truck for the ship. He give much talk to captain as to how and where his box is to be placed; but the captain like it not and swear at him in many tongues, and tell him that if he like he can come and see where it shall be. But he say "no"; that he come not yet, for that he have much to do. Whereupon the captain tell him that he had better be quick – with blood – for that his ship will leave the place – of blood – before the turn of the tide – with blood. Then the thin man smile, and say that of course he must go when he think fit; but he will be surprise if he go quite so soon. The captain swear again, polyglot, and then the thin man make him bow, and thank him, and say that he will so far intrude on his kindness as to come aboard before the sailing. Final the captain, more red than ever, and in more tongues, tell him that he doesn't want no Frenchmen – with bloom upon them and also with blood – in his ship – with blood on her also. And so, after asking where there might be close at hand a ship where he might purchase ships forms, he departed.

'No one knew where he went "or bloomin' well cared", as they said, for they had something else to think of – well with blood again; for it soon became apparent to all that the *Czarina Catherine* would not sail as was expected. A thin mist began to creep up from the river, and it grew, and grew; till soon a dense fog. He must have come off by himself, for none notice him. Polyglot – very polyglot – polyglot with bloom and blood; but he could do nothing. The water rose and rose; and he began to fear that he would lose the tide altogether. He was in no friendly mood when, just at full tide, the thin man came up the gangplank again and asked to see where his box had been stowed. Then the captain replied that he wished that he and his box – old and with much bloom and blood – were in hell. But the thin man did not be offend, and went down with the mate and saw where it was place, and came up and stood awhile on deck in fog. He must have come off by himself, for none notice him. Indeed they thought not of him; for soon the fog begin to melt away, and all was clear again. My friends of the thirst and the language that was of bloom and blood laughed, as they told how the captain's swears exceeded even his usual polyglot, and was more than ever full of picturesque, when on questioning other mariners who were in movement up and down the river that hour, he found that few of them had seen any of fog at all, except where it lay round the wharf. However the ship went out on the ebb tide; and was doubtless by morning far down the river mouth. She was by then, when they told us, well out to sea.

'And so, my dear Madam Mina, it is that we have to rest for a time, for our enemy is on the sea, with the fog at his command, on his way to the Danube mouth. To sail a ship takes time, go she never so quick; and when we start we go on land more quick, and we meet him there. Our best hope is to come on him when in the box between sunrise and sunset; for then he can make no struggle, and we may deal with him as we should. There are days for us in which we can make ready our plan. We know all about where he go; for we have seen the owner of the ship, who have shown us invoices and all papers that can be. The box we seek is to be landed in Varna, and to be given to an agent, one Ristics, who will there present his credentials; and so our merchant friend will have done his part. When he ask if there be any wrong, for that so, he can telegraph and have inquiry made at Varna, we say "no"; for what is to be done is not for police or of the customs. It must be done by us alone and in our own way.'

When Dr Van Helsing had done speaking, I asked him if it were certain that the Count had remained on board the ship. He replied: 'We have the best proof of that: your own evidence, when in the hypnotic trance this morning.' I asked him again if it were really necessary that they should pursue the Count, for oh! I dread Jonathan leaving me, and I know that he would surely go if the others went. He answered in growing passion, at first quietly. As he went on, however, he grew more angry and more forceful, till in the end we could not but see wherein was at least some of that personal dominance which made him so long a master amongst men:—

'Yes, it is necessary — necessary — necessary! For your sake in the first, and then for the sake of humanity. This monster has done much harm already, in the narrow scope where he find himself, and in the short time when as yet he was only as a body groping his so small measure in darkness and not knowing. All this have I told these others; you, my dear Madam Mina, will learn it in the phonograph of my friend John, or in that of your husband. I have told them how the measure of leaving his own barren land — barren of people — and coming to a new land where life of man teems till they are like the multitude of standing corn, was the work of centuries. Were another of the Un-Dead, like him, try to do what he has done, perhaps not all the centuries of the world that have been, or that will be, could aid him. With this one, all the forces of nature that are occult and deep and strong must have worked together in some wondrous way. The very place where he have been alive, Un-Dead for all these centuries, is full of strangeness of the geologic and chemical world. There are deep caverns and fissures that reach none know whither. There have

been volcanoes, some of whose openings still send out waters of strange properties, and gases that kill or make to vivify. Doubtless, there is something magnetic or electric in some of these combinations of occult forces which work for physical life in strange way; and in himself were from the first some great qualities. In a hard and warlike time he was celebrate that he have more iron nerve, more subtle brain, more braver heart, than any man. In him some vital principle have in strange way found their utmost; and as his body keep strong and grow and thrive, so his brain grow too. All this without that diabolic aid which is surely to him; for it have to yield to the powers that come from, and are, symbolic of good. And now this is what he is to us. He have infect you – oh, forgive me, my dear, that I must say such; but it is for good of you that I speak. He infect you in such wise, that even if he do no more, you have only to live – to live in your old, sweet way; and so in time, death, which is of man's common lot and with God's sanction, shall make you like to him. This must not be! We have sworn together that it must not. Thus are we ministers of God's own wish: that the world, and men for whom His Son die, will not be given over to monsters, whose very existence would defame Him. He have allowed us to redeem one soul already, and we go out as the old knights of the Cross to redeem more. Like them we shall travel towards the sunrise; and like them, if we fall, we fall in good cause.'
He paused and I said:–

'But will not the Count take his rebuff wisely? Since he has been driven from England, will he not avoid it, as a tiger does the village from which he has been hunted?'

'Aha!' he said, 'your simile of the tiger good, for me, and I shall adopt him. Your man-eater, as they of India call the tiger who has once taste blood of the human, care no more for other prey, but prowl unceasing till he get him. This that we hunt from our village is a tiger, too, a man-eater, and he never cease to prowl. Nay, in himself he is not one to retire and stay afar. In his life, his living life, he go over the Turkey frontier and attack his enemy on his own ground; he be beaten back, but did he stay? No? He come again, and again, and again. Look at his persistence and endurance. With the child-brain that was to him he have long since conceive the idea of coming to a great city. What does he do? He find out the place of all the world most of promise for him. Then he deliberately set himself down to prepare for the task. He find in patience just how is his strength, and what are his powers. He study new tongues. He learn new social life; new environment of old ways, the politic, the law, the finance, the science, the habit of a new land and a new people who have come to be since he was. His glimpse that he have had whet his appetite only and enkeen his desire. Nay, it help him to grow as to his brain; for it all prove to him how right he was at the first in his surmises. He have done this alone; all alone! from

261

a ruin tomb in a forgotten land. What more may he not do when the greater world of thought is open to him? He that can smile at death, as we know him; who can flourish in the midst of diseases that kill off whole peoples. Oh! if such an one was to come from God, and not the Devil, what a force for good might he not be in this old world of ours! But we are pledged to set the world free. Our toil must be in silence, and our efforts all in secret; for this enlightened age, when men believe not even what they see, the doubting of wise men would be his greatest strength. It would be at once his sheath and his armour, and his weapons to destroy us, his enemies, who are willing to peril even our own souls for the safety of one we love – for the good of mankind, and for the honour and glory of God.'

After a general discussion it was determined that for to-night nothing be definitely settled; that we should all sleep on the facts, and try to think out the proper conclusions. To-morrow at breakfast we are to meet again, and, after making our conclusions known to one another, we shall decide on some course of action.

* * *

I feel a wonderful peace and rest to-night. It is as if some haunting presence were removed from me. Perhaps . . . .

My surmise was not finished, could not be; for I caught sight in the mirror of the red mark upon my forehead; and I knew that I was still unclean.

DR SEWARD'S DIARY

5 October. – We all rose early, and I think that sleep did much for each and all of us. When we met at early breakfast there was more general cheerfulness than any of us had ever expected to experience again.

It is really wonderful how much resilience there is in human nature. Let any obstructing cause, no matter what, be removed in any way – even by death – and we fly back to first principles of hope and enjoyment. More than once, as we sat around the table, my eyes opened in wonder whether the whole of the past days had not been a dream. It was only when I caught sight of the red blotch on Mrs Harker's forehead that I was brought back to reality. Even now, when I am gravely resolving the matter, it is almost impossible to realize that the cause of all our trouble is still existent. Even Mrs Harker seems to lose sight of her trouble for whole spells; it is only now and again, when something recalls it to her mind, that she thinks of her terrible scar. We are to meet here in my study in half an hour and decide on our course of action. I see only one immediate difficulty, I know it by instinct rather than reason: we shall all have to speak frankly; and yet I fear that in some mysterious way poor Mrs Harker's tongue is tied. I *know* that she forms conclusions of her own, and from all that has been I can guess how brilliant and how true they must be; but she will not, or cannot, give them utterance. I have mentioned this to Van Helsing, and he and I are to talk it over when we are alone. I suppose it is some of that horrid poison which has got into her veins beginning to work. The Count had his own purposes when he gave her what Van Helsing called 'the Vampire's baptism of blood'. Well, there may be a poison that distils itself out of good things; in an age when the existence of ptomaines is a mystery we should not wonder at anything! One thing I know: that if my instinct be true regarding poor Mrs Harker's silences, then there is a terrible difficulty – an unknown danger – in the work before us. The same power that compels her silence may compel her speech. I dare not think further; for so I should in my thoughts dishonour a noble woman!

Van Helsing is coming to my study a little before the others. I shall try to open the subject with him.

Later. – When the Professor came in, we talked over the state of things. I could see that he had something on his mind which he wanted to say, but felt some hesitancy about broaching the subject. After beating about the bush a little, he said suddenly:–

'Friend John, there is something that you and I must talk of alone, just at the first at any rate. Later, we may have to take the others into our confidence'; then he stopped, so I waited; he went on:–

'Madam Mina, our poor, dear Madam Mina, is changing.' A cold shiver ran through me to find my worst fears thus endorsed. Van Helsing continued:–

'With the sad experience of Miss Lucy, we must this time be warned before things go too far. Our task is now in reality more difficult than ever, and this new trouble makes every hour of the direst importance. I can see the characteristics of the vampire coming in her face. It is now but very, very slight; but it is to be seen if we have eyes to notice without to prejudge. Her teeth are some sharper, and at times her eyes are more hard. But these are not all, there is to her the silence now often; as so it was with Miss Lucy. She did not speak, even when she wrote that which she wished to be known later. Now my fear is this. If it be that she can, by our hypnotic trance, tell what the Count see and hear, is it not more true that he who have hypnotize her first, and who have drink of her very blood and make her drink of his, should, if he will, compel her mind to disclose to him that which she know?' I nodded acquiescence; he went on:–

'Then what we must do is to prevent this; we must keep her ignorant of our intent, and so she cannot tell what she know not. This is a painful task! Oh! so painful that it heartbreak me to think of; but it must be. When to-day we meet, I must tell her that for reason which we will not to speak she must not more be of our council, but be simply guarded by us.' He wiped his forehead, which had broken out in profuse perspiration at the thought of the pain which he might have to inflict upon the poor soul already so tortured. I knew that it would be some sort of comfort to him if I told him that I also had come to the same conclusion; for at any rate it would take away the pain of doubt. I told him and the effect was as I expected.

It is now close to the time of our general gathering. Van Helsing has gone away to prepare for the meeting, and his painful part of it. I really believe his purpose is to be able to pray alone.

Later. – At the very outset of our meeting a great personal relief was experienced by both Van Helsing and myself. Mrs Harker had sent a message by her husband to say that she would not join us at present, as she thought it better that we should be free to discuss our movements without her presence to embarrass us. The Professor and I looked at each other for an instant, and somehow we both seemed relieved. For my own part, I thought that if Mrs Harker realized the danger herself, it was much pain as well as much danger averted. Under the circumstances we agreed, by a questioning look and answer, with finger on lip, to preserve silence of our suspicions, until we should have been able to confer alone again. We went at once into our Plan of Campaign. Van Helsing roughly put the facts before us first:–

'The *Czarina Catherine* left the Thames yesterday morning. It will take her at the quickest speed she has ever made at least three weeks to reach Varna; but we can travel overland to the same place in three days. Now, if we allow for two days less for the ship's voyage, owing to such weather influences as we know that the Count can bring to bear; and if we allow a whole day and night for any delays which may occur to us, then we have a margin of nearly two weeks. Thus, in order to be quite safe, we must leave here on 17th at latest. Then we shall at any rate be in Varna a day before the ship arrives, and able to make such preparations as may be necessary. Of course we shall all go armed – armed against evil things, spiritual as well as physical.' Here Quincey Morris added:–

'I understand that the Count comes from a wolf country, and it may be that he will get there before us. I propose that we add Winchesters to our armament. I have a kind of belief in a Winchester when there is any trouble of that sort around. Do you remember, Art, when we had the pack after us at Tobolsk? What wouldn't we have given then for a repeater apiece!'

'Good!' said Van Helsing. 'Winchesters it shall be. Quincey's head is level at all times, but most so when there is to hunt, though my metaphor be more dishonour to science than wolves be of danger to man. In the meantime we can do nothing here; and as I think that Varna is not familiar to any of us, why not go there more soon? It is as long to wait here as there. To-night and to-morrow we can get ready, and then, if all be well, we four can set out on our journey.'

'We four?' said Harker interrogatively, looking from one to another of us.

'Of course!' answered the Professor quickly. 'You must remain to take care of your so sweet wife!' Harker was silent for a while and then said in a hollow voice:—

'Let us talk of that part of it in the morning. I want to consult with Mina.' I thought that now was the time for Van Helsing to warn him not to disclose our plans to her; but he took no notice. I looked at him significantly and coughed. For answer he put his finger on his lip and turned away.

JONATHAN HARKER'S JOURNAL

5 October, afternoon. – For some time after our meeting this morning I could not think. The new phases of things leave my mind in a state of wonder which allows no room for active thought. Mina's determination not to take any part in the discussion set me thinking; and as I could not argue the matter with her, I could only guess. I am as far as ever from a solution now. The way the others received it, too, puzzled me; the last time we talked of the subject we agreed that there was to be no more concealment of anything amongst us. Mina is sleeping now, calmly and sweetly like a little child. Her lips are curved and her face beams with happiness. Thank God there are such moments still for her.

Later. – How strange it all is! I sat watching Mina's happy sleep, and came as near to being happy myself as I suppose I shall ever be. As the evening drew on, and the earth took its shadows from the sun sinking lower, the silence of the room grew more and more solemn to me. All at once Mina opened her eyes, and looking at me tenderly said:—

'Jonathan, I want you to promise me something on your word of honour. A promise made to me, but made holily in God's hearing, and not to be broken though I should go down on my knees and implore you with bitter tears. Quick, you must make it to me at once.'

'Mina,' I said, 'a promise like that, I cannot make at once. I may have no right to make it.'

'But, dear one,' she said, with such spiritual intensity that her eyes were like pole stars, 'it is I who wish it; and it is not for myself. You can ask Dr Van Helsing if I am right; if he disagrees you may do as you will. Nay, more, if you all agree, later, you are absolved from the promise.'

'I promise!' I said, and for a moment she looked supremely happy; though to me all happiness for her was denied by the red scar on her forehead. She said:–

'Promise me that you will not tell me anything of the plans formed for the campaign against the Count. Not by word, or inference, or implication; not at any time whilst this remains to me!' and she solemnly pointed to the scar. I saw that she was in earnest, and said solemnly:–

'I promise!' and as I said it I felt from that instant a door had been shut between us.

Later, midnight. – Mina has been bright and cheerful all the evening. So much so that all the rest seemed to take courage, as if infected somewhat with her gaiety; as a result even I myself felt as if the pall of gloom which weighs us down were somewhat lifted. We all retired early. Mina is now sleeping like a child; it is a wonderful thing that her faculty of sleep remains to her in the midst of her terrible trouble. Thank God for it, for then at least she can forget her care. Perhaps her example may affect me as her gaiety did to-night. I shall try it. Oh! for a dreamless sleep.

6 *October, morning.* – Another surprise. Mina woke me early, about the same time as yesterday, and asked me to bring Dr Van Helsing. I thought that it was another occasion for hypnotism, and without question went for the Professor. He had evidently expected some such call, for I found him dressed in his room. His door was ajar, so that he could hear the opening of the door of our room. He came at once; as he passed into the room, he asked Mina if the others might come too.

'No,' she said quite simply, 'it will not be necessary. You can tell them just as well. I must go with you on your journey.'

Dr Van Helsing was as startled as I was. After a moment's pause he asked:–

'But why?'

'You must take me with you. I am safer with you, and you shall be safer too.'

'But why, dear Madam Mina? You know that your safety is our solemnest duty. We got into danger, to which you are, or may be, more liable than any of us from – from circumstances – things that have been.' He paused embarrassed.

As she replied, she raised her finger and pointed to her forehead:–

'I know. That is why I must go. I can tell you now, whilst the sun is coming up; I may not be able again. I know that when the Count wills me I must go. I know that if he tells me to come in secret, I must come by wile; by any device to hoodwink – even Jonathan.' God saw the look that she turned on me as she spoke, and if there be indeed a Recording Angel that look is noted to her everlasting honour. I could only clasp her hand. I could not speak; my emotion was too great for even the relief of tears. She went on:–

'You men are brave and strong. You are strong in your numbers, for you can defy that which would break down the human endurance of one who had to guard alone. Besides, I may be of service, since you can hypnotize me and so learn that which even I myself do not know.' Dr Van Helsing said very gravely:–

'Madam Mina, you are, as always, most wise. You shall with us come; and together we shall do that which we go forth to achieve.' When he had spoken, Mina's long spell of silence made me look at her. She had fallen back on her pillow asleep; she did not even wake when I had pulled up the blind and let in the sunlight which flooded the room. Van Helsing motioned to me to come with him quietly. We went to his room, and within a minute Lord Godalming, Dr Seward, and Mr Morris were with us also. He told them what Mina had said, and went on:–

'In the morning we shall leave for Varna. We have now to deal with a new factor: Madam Mina. Oh, but her soul is true. It is to her an agony to tell us so much as she has done; but it is most right, and we are warned in time. There must be no chance lost, and in Varna we must be ready to act the instant when that ship arrives.'

'What shall we do exactly?' asked Mr Morris laconically. The Professor paused before replying:–

'We shall at the first board that ship; then, when we have identified the box, we shall place a branch of wild rose on it. This we shall fasten, for when it is there none can emerge; so at least says the superstition. And to superstition must we trust at the first; it was man's faith in the early, and it have its root in faith still. Then, when we get the opportunity that we seek, when none are near to see, we shall open the box, and – and all will be well.'

'I shall not wait for any opportunity,' said Morris. 'When I see the box I shall open it and destroy the monster, though there were a thousand men looking on, and if I am to be wiped out for it the next moment!' I grasped his hand instinctively and found it as firm as a piece of steel. I think he understood my look; I hope he did.

'Good boy,' said Dr Van Helsing. 'Brave boy. Quincey is all man, God bless him for it. My child, believe me, none of us shall lag behind or pause from any fear. I do but say what we may do – what we must do. But, indeed, indeed we cannot say what we shall do. There are so many things which may happen, and their ways and their ends are so various that until the moment we may not say. We shall all be armed, in all ways; and when

267

the time for the end has come, our effort shall not be lack. Now let us to-day put all our affairs in order. Let all things which touch on others dear to us, and who on us depend, be complete; for none of us can tell what, or when, or how, the end may be. As for me, my own affairs are regulate; and as I have nothing else to do, I shall go make arrangment for the travel. I shall have all tickets and so forth for our journey.'

There was nothing further to be said, and we parted. I shall now settle up all my affairs of earth, and be ready for whatever may come. . . .

Later. – It is all done; my will is made, and all complete. Mina if she survive is my sole heir. If it should not be so, then the others who have been so good to us will have the remainder.

It is now drawing towards the sunset; Mina's uneasiness calls my attention to it. I am sure that there is something on her mind which the time of exact sunset will reveal. These occasions are becoming harrowing times for us all, for each sunrise and sunset opens up some new danger – some new pain, which, however, may in God's will be means to a good end. I write all these things in the diary since my darling must not hear them now; but if it may be that she can see them again, they shall be ready.

She is calling to me.

25

DR SEWARD'S DIARY

11 October, evening – Jonathan Harker has asked me to note this, as he says he is hardly equal to the task, and he wants an exact record kept.

I think that none of us were surprised when we were asked to see Mrs Harker a little before the time of sunset. We have of late come to understand that sunrise and sunset are to her times of peculiar freedom, when her old self can be manifested without any controlling force subduing or restraining her, or inciting her to action. This mood or condition begins some half-hour or more before actual sunrise or sunset, and lasts till either the sun is high, or whilst the clouds are still aglow with the rays streaming above the horizon. At first there is a sort of negative condition, as if some tie were loosened, and then the absolute freedom quickly follows; when, however, the freedom ceases the change-back or relapse comes quickly, preceded only by a spell of warning silence.

To-night, when we met she was somewhat constrained, and bore all the signs of an internal struggle. I put it down myself to her making a violent effort at the earliest instant she could do so. A very few minutes, however, gave her complete control of herself; then, motioning her husband to sit beside her on the sofa where she was half reclining, she made the rest of us bring chairs up close. Taking her husband's hand in hers she began:—

'We are all here together in freedom, for perhaps the last time! I know, dear; I know that you will always be with me to the end.' This was to her husband, whose hand had, as we could see, tightened upon hers. 'In the morning we go out upon our task, and God alone knows what may be in store for any of us. You are going to be so good to me as to take me with you. I know that all that brave earnest men can do for a poor weak woman, whose soul is perhaps lost — no, no, not yet, but is as any any rate at stake — you will do. But you must remember that I am not as you are. There is a poison in my blood, in my soul, which may destroy me; which must destroy me, unless some relief comes to us. Oh, my friends, you know as well as I do, that my soul is at stake; and though I know there is one way out for me, you must not and I must not take it!' She looked appealingly at us all in turn, beginning and ending with her husband.

'What is that way?' asked Van Helsing in a hoarse voice. 'What is that way, which we must not — may not — take?'

'That I may die now, either by my own hand or that of another, before the greater evil is entirely wrought. I know, and you know, that were I once dead you could and would set free my immortal spirit, even as you did my poor Lucy's. Were death, or the fear of death, the only thing that stood in the way, I would not shrink to die here, now, amidst the friends who love me. But death is not all. I cannot believe that to die in such a case, when there is hope before us and a better task to be done, is God's will. Therefore, I on my part give up here the certainty of eternal rest, and go out into the dark where may be the blackest things that the world or the nether world holds!' We were all silent, for we knew instinctively that this was only a prelude. The faces of the others were set, and Harker's grew ashen grey; perhaps he guessed better than any of us what was coming. She continued:—

'This is what I can give into the hotch-pot.' I could not but note the quaint legal phrase which she used in such a place, and with all seriousness. 'What will each of you give? Your lives, I know,' she went on quickly; 'that is easy for brave men. Your lives are God's and you can give them back to Him; but what will you give me?' She looked again questioningly, but this time avoided her husband's face. Quincey seemed to understand; he nodded, and her face lit up. 'Then I shall tell you plainly what I want, for there must be no doubtful matter in this connection between us now. You must promise me, one and all — even you, my beloved husband — that, should the time come, you will kill me.'

'What is that time?' The voice was Quincey's but it was low and strained.

'When you shall be convinced that I am so changed that it is better that I die that I may live. When I am thus dead in the flesh, then you will, without a moment's delay, drive a stake through me and cut off my head; or do whatever else may be wanting to give me rest!'

Quincey was the first to rise after the pause. He knelt down before her and taking her hand in his said solemnly:—

'I'm only a rough fellow, who hasn't, perhaps, lived as a man should to win such a distinction, but I swear to you by all that I hold sacred and dear that, should the time ever come, I shall not flinch from the duty that you have set us. And I promise you, too, that I shall make all certain, for if I am only doubtful I shall take it that the time has come!'

'My true friend!' was all she could say amid her fast-falling tears, as bending over, she kissed his hand.

'I swear the same, my dear Madam Mina!' said Van Helsing.

'And I!' said Lord Godalming, each of them in turn kneeling to her to take the oath. I followed, myself. Then her husband turned to her, wan-eyed and with a greenish pallor which subdued the snowy whiteness of his hair, and asked:—

'And must I, too, make such a promise, oh, my wife?'

'You too, my dearest,' she said, with infinite yearning of pity in her voice and eyes. 'You must not shrink. You are nearest and dearest and all the world to me; our souls are knit into one, for all life and all time. Think, dear, that there have been times when brave men killed their wives and their womenkind, to keep them from falling into the hands of the enemy. Their hands did not falter any the more because those that they loved implored them to slay them. It is men's duty towards those whom they love, in such times of sore trial! And oh, my dear, if it is to be that I must meet death at any hand, let it be at the hand of him that loves me best. Dr Van Helsing, I have not forgotten your mercy in poor Lucy's case to him who loved' – she stopped with a flying blush, and changed her phrase – 'to him who had best right to give her peace. If that time shall come again, I look to you to make it a happy memory of my husband's life that it was his loving hand which set me free from the awful thrall upon me.'

'Again I swear!' came the Professor's resonant voice. Mrs Harker smiled, positively smiled, as with a sigh of relief she leaned back and said:—

'And now one word of warning, a warning which you must never forget: this time, if it ever come, may come quickly and unexpectedly, and in such case you must lose no time in using your opportunity. At such a time I myself might be – nay! if the time ever comes, *shall* be – leagued with your enemy against you.

'One more request'; she became very solemn as she said this, 'it is not vital and necessary like the other, but I want you to do one thing for me, if you will.' We all acquiesced, but no one spoke; there was no need to speak:—

'I want you to read the Burial Service.' She was interrupted by a deep groan from her husband; taking his hand in hers, she held it over her heart, and continued: 'You must read it over me some day. Whatever may be the issue of all this fearful state of things, it will be a sweet thought to all or some of us. You, my dearest, will, I hope, read it, for then it will be in your voice in my memory for ever – come what may!'

'But oh, my dear one,' he pleaded, 'death is afar off from you.'

'Nay,' she said, holding up a warning hand. 'I am deeper in death at this moment than if the weight of an earthly grave lay heavy upon me!'

'Oh, my wife, must I read it?' he said, before he began.

'It would comfort me, my husband!' was all she said; and he began to read when she had got the book ready.

How can I – how could anyone – tell of that strange scene, its solemnity, its gloom, its sadness, its horror; and, withal, its sweetness? Even a sceptic, who can see nothing but a travesty of bitter truth in anything holy or emotional, would have been melted to the heart had he seen that little group of loving and devoted friends kneeling round that stricken and sorrowing lady; or heard the tender passion of her husband's voice, as in tones so broken with emotion that often he had to pause, he read the simple and beautiful service for the Burial of the Dead. 'I – I cannot go on – words – and v-voice – f-fail m-me!'

She was right in her instinct. Strange as it all was, bizarre as it may hereafter seem even to us who felt its potent influence at the time, it comforted us much; and the silence, which showed Mrs Harker's coming relapse from her freedom of soul, did not seem so full of despair to any of us as we had dreaded.

JONATHAN HARKER'S JOURNAL

15 October. Varna. – We left Charing Cross on the morning of the 12th, got to Paris the same night, and took the places secured for us in the Orient Express. We travelled night and day, arriving here at about five o'clock. Lord Godalming went to the Consulate to see if any telegram had arrived for him, whilst the rest of us came on to this hotel – the Odessus. The journey may have had incidents; I was, however, too eager to get on, to care of them. Until the *Czarina Catherine* comes into port there will be no interest for me in anything in the wide world. Thank God! Mina is well, and looks to be getting stronger; her colour is coming back. She sleeps a great deal; throughout the journey she slept nearly all the time. Before sunrise and sunset, however, she is very wakeful and alert; and it has become a habit for Van Helsing to hypnotize her at such times. At first, some effort was needed, and he had to make many passes; but now, she seems to yield once, as if by habit, and scarcely any action is need. He seems to have power at these particular moments to simply will, and her thoughts obey him. He always asks her what she can see and hear. She answers to the first:—

'Nothing; all is dark.' And to the second:—

'I can hear the waves lapping against the ship, and the water rushing by. Canvas and cordage strain and masts and yards creak. The wind is high – I can hear it in the shrouds, and the bow throws back the foam.' It is evident that the *Czarina Catherine* is still at sea, hastening on her way to Varna. Lord Godalming has just returned. He had four telegrams, one each day since we started, and all to the same effect: that the *Czarina Catherine* had not been reported to Lloyd's from anywhere. He had arranged before leaving London that his agent should send him every day a telegram saying if the ship had been reported. He was to have a message even if she were not reported, so that he might be sure that there was a watch being kept at the other end of the wire.

We had dinner and went to bed early. To-morrow we are to see the Vice-Consul, and to arrange, if we can, about getting on board the ship as soon as she arrives. Van Helsing says that our chance will be to get on board between sunrise and sunset. The Count, even if he takes the form of a bat, cannot cross the running water of his own volition, and so cannot leave the ship. As he dare not change to man's form without suspicion – which he evidently wishes to avoid – he must remain in the box. If, then, we can come on board after sunrise, he is at our mercy; for we can open the box and make sure of him, as we did of poor Lucy, before he wakes. What mercy he will get from us will not count for much. We think that we shall not have much trouble with officials or the seamen. Thank God! this is the country where bribery can do anything, and we are well supplied with money. We have only to make sure that the ship cannot come into port between sunset and sunrise without our being warned, and we shall be safe. Judge Moneybag will settle this case, I think!

16 October. – Mina's report still the same: lapping waves and rushing water, darkness and favouring winds. We are evidently in good time, and when we hear of the *Czarina Catherine* we shall be ready. As she must pass the Dardanelles we are sure to have some report.

*   *   *

17 October. – Everything is pretty well fixed now, I think, to welcome the

272

Count on his return from his tour. Godalming told the shippers that he fancied that the box sent aboard might contain something stolen from a friend of his, and got a half consent that he might open it at his own risk. The owner gave him a paper telling the captain to give him every facility in doing whatever he chose on board the ship, and also a similar authorization to his agent at Varna. We have seen the agent, who was much impressed with Godalming's kindly manner to him, and we are all satisfied that whatever he can do to aid our wishes will be done. We have already arranged what to do in case we get the box open. If the Count is there, Van Helsing and Seward will cut off his head at once and drive a stake through his heart. Morris and Godalming and I shall prevent interference, even if we have to use the arms which we shall have ready. The Professor says that if we can so treat the Count's body, it will soon after fall into dust. In such case there would be no evidence against us, in case any suspicion of murder were aroused. But even if it did not, we should stand or fall by our act, and perhaps some day this very script may be evidence to come between some of us and a rope. For myself, I should take the chance only too thankfully if it were to come. We mean to leave no stone unturned to carry out our intent. We have arranged with certain officials that the instant the *Czarina Catherine* is seen, we are to be informed by a special messenger.

24 October. – A whole week of waiting. Daily telegrams to Godalming, but only the same story: 'Not yet reported.' Mina's hypnotic answer is unvaried: 'Lapping waves, rushing water, and creaking masts.'

Telegram, October 24th.
Rufus Smith, Lloyd's, London, to Lord Godalming, care of H.B.M.
Vice-Consul, Varna

'*Czarina Catherine* reported this morning from Dardanelles.'

DR SEWARD'S DIARY

24 October. – How I miss my phonograph! To write diary with a pen is irksome to me; but Van Helsing says I must. We were all wild with excitement to-day when Godalming got his telegram from Lloyd's. I know now what men feel in battle when the call to action is heard. Mrs Harker, alone of our party, did not show any signs of emotion. After all, it is not strange that she did not; for we took special care not to let her know anything about it, and we all tried not to show any excitement when we

273

were in her presence. In old days she would, I am sure, have noticed, no matter how we might have tried to conceal it; but in this way she is greatly changed during the past three weeks. The lethargy grows upon her, and though she seems strong and well, and is getting back some of her colour, Van Helsing and I are not satisfied. We talk of her often; we have not, however, said a word to the others. It would break poor Harker's heart – certainly his nerve – if he knew that we had even a suspicion of the subject. Van Helsing examines, he tells me, her teeth very carefully, whilst she is in the hypnotic condition, for he says that so long as they do not begin to sharpen there is no active danger of a change in her. If this should come, it would be necessary to take steps! . . . We both know what those steps would have to be, though we do not mention our thoughts to each other. We should neither of us shrink from the task – awful though it be to contemplate. 'Euthanasia' is an excellent and a comforting word! I am grateful to whoever invented it.

It is only about 24 hours' sail from the Dardanelles to here, at the rate the *Czarina Catherine* has come from London. She should therefore arrive some time in the morning; but as she cannot possibly get in before then, we are all about to retire early. We shall get up at one o'clock, so as to be ready.

25 October, Noon. – No news yet of the ship's arrival. Mrs Harker's hypnotic report this morning was the same as usual, so it is possible that we may get news at any moment. We men are all in a fever of excitement, except Harker, who is calm; his hands are as cold as ice, and an hour ago I found him whetting the edge of the great Ghoorka knife which he now always carries with him. It will be a bad look-out for the Count if the edge of that 'Kukri' ever touches his throat, driven by that stern, ice-cold hand!

Van Helsing and I were a little alarmed about Mrs Harker to-day. About noon she got into a sort of lethargy which we did not like; although we kept silent to the others, we were neither of us happy about it. She had been restless all the morning, so that we were at first glad to know that she was sleeping. When, however, her husband mentioned casually that she was sleeping so soundly that he could not wake her, we went to her room to see for ourselves. She was breathing naturally and looked so well and peaceful that we agreed that the sleep was better for her than anything else. Poor girl, she has so much to forget that it is no wonder that sleep, if it brings oblivion to her, does her good.

Later. – Our opinion was justified, for when after a refreshing sleep of some hours she woke up, she seemed brighter and better than she has been for days. At sunset she made the usual hypnotic report. Wherever he may be in the Black Sea, the Count is hurrying to his destination. To his doom, I trust!

26 October. – Another day and no tidings of the *Czarina Catherine*. She ought to be here by now. That she is still journeying *somewhere* is apparent, for Mrs Harker's hypnotic report at sunrise was still the same. It is possible that the vessel may be lying by, at times, for fog; some of the steamers which came in last evening reported patches of fog both to north and south of the port. We must continue our watching, as the ship may now be signalled any moment.

27 October. – Most strange; no news yet of the ship we wait for. Mrs Harker reported last night and this morning as usual: 'Lapping waves and rushing water,' though she added that 'the waves were very faint.' The telegrams from London have been the same: 'No further report.' Van Helsing is terribly anxious, and told me just now that he fears the Count is escaping us. He added significantly:–

'I did not like that lethargy of Madam Mina's. Souls and memories can do strange things during trance.' I was about to ask him more, but Harker just then came in, and he held up a warning hand. We must try to-night, at sunset, to make her speak more fully when in her hypnotic state.

28 October. – Telegram. *Rufus Smith, London, to Lord Godalming, care of H.B.M. Vice-Consul, Varna*

'*Czarina Catherine* reported entering Galatz at one o'clock to-day.'

DR SEWARD'S DIARY

28 October. – When the telegram came announcing the arrival in Galatz I do not think it was such a shock to any of us as might have been expected. True, we did not know whence, or how, or when, the bolt would come; but I think we all expected that something strange would happen. The delay of arrival at Varna made us individually satisfied that things would not be just as we had expected; we only waited to learn where the change would occur. None the less, however, was it a surprise. I suppose that nature works on such a hopeful basis that we believe against ourselves that things will be as they ought to be, not as we should know that they will be. Transcendentalism is a beacon to the angels, even if it be a will-o'-the-wisp to man. It was an odd experience, and we all took it differently. Van Helsing raised his hands over his head for a moment, as though in remonstrance with the Almighty; but he said not a word, and in a few seconds stood up with his face sternly set. Lord Godalming grew very pale, and sat breathing heavily. I was myself half stunned and looked in wonder at one after another. Quincey Morris tightened his belt with that quick movement which I knew so well; in our old wandering days it meant 'action'. Mrs Harker grew ghastly white, so that the scar on her forehead seemed to burn, but she folded her hands meekly and looked up in prayer. Harker smiled – actually smiled – the dark bitter smile of one who is without hope; but at the same time his action belied his words, for his hands instinctively sought the hilt of the great Kukri knife and rested there. 'When does the next train start for Galatz?' said Van Helsing to us generally.

'At 6.30 to-morrow morning!' We all stared, for the answer came from Mrs Harker.

'How on earth do you know?' said Art.

'You forget – or perhaps you do not know, though Jonathan does and so does Dr Van Helsing – that I am a train fiend. At home in Exeter I always used to make up the time-tables, so as to be helpful to my husband. I found it so useful sometimes, that I always make a study of the time-tables now. I knew that if anything were to take us to Castle Dracula we should go by Galatz, or at any rate through Bucharest, so I learned the times very carefully. Unhappily there are not many to learn, as the only train to-morrow leaves as I say.'

'Wonderful woman!' murmured the Professor.

'Can't we get a special?' asked Lord Godalming.

Van Helsing shook his head: 'I fear not. This land is very different from yours or mine; even if we did have a special, it would probably not arrive as soon as our regular train. Moreover, we have something to prepare. We must think. Now let us organize. You, friend Arthur, go to the train and get the tickets and arrange that all be ready for us to go in the morning. Do you, friend Jonathan, go to the agent of the ship and get from him letters to the agent in Galatz, with authority to make search the ship just as it was here. Quincey Morris, you see the Vice-Consul, and get his aid with his fellow in Galatz and all he can do to make our way smooth, so that no times be lost when over the Danube. John will stay with Madam Mina and me, and we shall consult. For so if time be long you may be delayed; and it will not matter when the sun set, since I am here with Madam to make report.'

'And I,' said Mrs Harker brightly, and more like her old self than she had been for many a long day, 'shall try to be of use in all ways, and shall think and write for you as I used to do. Something is shifting from me in some strange way, and I feel freer than I have been of late!' The three younger men looked happier at the moment as they seemed to realize the significance of her words; but Van Helsing and I, turning to each other, met each a grave and troubled glance. We said nothing at the time, however.

When the three men had gone out to their tasks Van Helsing asked Mrs Harker to look up the copy of the diaries and find him the part of Harker's journal at the castle. She went away to get it; when the door shut upon her he said to me:–

'We mean the same! speak out!'

'There is some change. It is a hope that makes me sick, for it may deceive us.'

'Quite so. Do you know why I asked her to get the manuscript?'

'No!' said I, 'unless it was to get an opportunity of seeing me alone.'

'You are in part right, friend John, but only in part. I want to tell you something. And oh, my friend, I am taking a great – a terrible – risk; but I believe it is right. In the moment when Madam said those words that arrest both our understanding, an inspiration come to me. In the trance of three days ago the Count sent her his spirit to read her mind; or more like he took her to see him in his earth-box in the ship with water rushing, just as it go free at rise and set of sun. He learn then that we are here; for she have more to tell in her open life with eyes to see and ears to hear than he, shut, as he is, in his coffin-box. Now he make his most effort to escape us. At present he want her not. He is sure with his so great knowledge that she will come at his call; but he cut her off – take her, as he can do, out of his own power, that so she come not to him. Ah! there I have hope that our man-brains, that have been of man so long and that have not lost the grace of God, will come higher than his child-brain that lie in his tomb for centuries, that grow not yet to our stature, and that do only work selfish and therefore small. Here comes Madam Mina; not a word to her of her trance! She know it not; and it would overwhelm her and make despair just when we want all her hope, all her courage; when most we want all her great brain which is trained like man's brain, but is of sweet woman and have a special power which the Count give her, and which he may not take away altogether – though he think not so. Hush! let me speak, and you shall learn. Oh, John, my friend, we are in awful straits. I fear, as I never feared before. We can only trust the good God, Silence! here she comes!'

I thought that the Professor was going to break down and have hysterics, just as he had when Lucy died, but with a great effort he controlled himself and was at perfect nervous poise when Mrs Harker tripped into the room, bright and happy-looking and, in the doing of work, seemingly forgetful of her misery. As she came in, she handed a number of sheets of typewriting to Van Helsing. He looked over them gravely, his face brightening up as he read. Then, holding the pages between his finger and thumb, he said:–

'Friend John, to you with so much of experience already – and you too, dear Madam Mina, that are young – here is a lesson: do not fear ever to think. A half-thought has been buzzing often in my brain, but I fear to let him loose his wings. Here now, with more knowledge, I go back to where that half-thought come from, and I find that he be no half-thought at all; that he be a whole thought, though so young that he is not yet strong to use his little wings. Nay, like the "Ugly Duck" of my friend Hans Andersen, he be no duck-thought at all, but a big swan-thought that sail nobly on big wings, when the time come for him to try them. See I read here what Jonathan have written:–

' "That other of his race who, in a later age, again and again, brought his forces over the The Great River into Turkey land; who, when he was beaten back, came again, and again, and again, though he had to come alone from the bloody field where his troops were being slaughtered, since he knew that he alone could ultimately triumph."

'What does this tell us? Not much! no! The Count's child-thought see nothing; therefore he speak so free. Your man-thought see nothing, till just now. No! But there comes another word from someone who speak without thought because she too know not what it mean – what it *might* mean. Just as there are elements which rest, yet when in nature's course they move on their way and they touch – then pouf! and there comes a flash of light, heaven's wide, that blind and kill and destroy some; but that show up all earth below for leagues and leagues. Is it not so? Well, I shall explain. To begin, have you ever study the philosophy of crime? "Yes" and "No". You, John, yes; for it is a study of insanity. You, no, Madam Mina; for crime touch you not – not but once. Still, your mind works true, and argues not *a particulari ad universale*. There is this peculiarity in criminals. It is so constant, in all countries and at all times, that even police, who know not much from philosophy, come to know it empirically, that *it is*. That is to be empiric. The criminal always work at one crime – that is the true criminal who seems predestinate to crime, and who will of none other. This criminal has not full man-brain. He is clever and cunning and resourceful; but he be not of man-stature as to brain. He be of child-brain in much. Now this criminal of ours is predestinate to crime also; he too have child-brain, and it is of the child to do what he have done. The little bird, the little fish, the little animal learn not by principle, but empirically; and when he learn to do, then there is to him the ground to start from to do more. "*Dos pou sto,*" said Archimedes. "Give me a fulcrum, and I shall move the world!" To do once, is the fulcrum whereby the child-brain become man-brain; and until he have the purpose to do more, he continue to do the same again every time, just as he have done before! Oh, my dear, I see that your eyes are opened, and that to you the lightning flash show all the leagues,' for Mrs Harker began to clap her hands, and her eyes sparkled. He went on:—

'Now you shall speak. Tell us two dry men of science what you see with those so bright eyes.' He took her hand and held it whilst she spoke. His finger and thumb closed on her pulse, as I thought instinctively and unconsciously, as she spoke:—

'The Count is a criminal and of criminal type. Nordau and Lombroso would so classify him, and *qua* criminal he is of imperfectly formed mind. Thus, in a difficulty he has to seek resource in habit. His past is a clue, and the one page of it that we know — and that from his own lips — tells that once before when in what Mr Morris would call a "tight place", he went back to his own country from the land he had tried to invade, and thence, without losing purpose, prepared himself for a new effort. He came again, better equipped for his work; and won. So he came to London to invade a new land. He was beaten, and when all hope of success was lost, and his existence in danger, he fled back over the sea to his home; just as formerly he had fled back over the Danube from Turkey land.'

'Good, good! oh, you so clever lady!' said Van Helsing, enthusiastically, as he stooped and kissed her hand. A moment later he said to me, as calmly as though we had been having a sick-room consultation:—

'Seventy-two only; and in all this excitement. I have hope.' Turning to her again, he said with keen expectation:—

'But go on. Go on! there is more to tell if you will. Be not afraid; John and I know. I do in any case, and shall tell you if you are right. Speak, without fear!'

'I will try to; but you will forgive me if I seem egotistical.'

'Nay! fear not, you must be egotist, for it is of you that we think.'

'Then, as he is criminal he is selfish; and as his intellect is small and his action is based on selfishness, he confines himself to one purpose. That purpose is remorseless. As he fled back over the Danube, leaving his forces to be cut to pieces, so now he is intent on being safe, careless of all. So, his own selfishness frees my soul somewhat of the terrible power which he acquired over me on that dreadful night. I felt it, oh! I felt it. Thank God for His great mercy! My soul is freer than it has been since that awful hour; and all that haunts me is a fear lest in some trance or dream he may have used my knowledge for his ends.' The Professor stood up:—

'He has so used your mind; and by it he has left us here in Varna, whilst the ship that carried him rushed through enveloping fog up to Galatz, where, doubtless, he had made preparation for escaping from us. But his child-mind only saw so far; and it may be that, as ever is in God's Providence, the very thing that the evil doer most reckoned on for his selfish good, turns out to be his chiefest harm. The hunter is taken in his own snare, as the great Psalmist says. For now that he think he is free from every trace of us all, and that he has escaped us with so many hours to him, then his selfish child-brain will whisper him to sleep. He think, too, that as he cut himself off from knowing your mind, there can be no knowledge of him to you; there is where he fail! That terrible baptism of blood which he give you makes you free to go to him in spirit, as you have as yet done in your times of freedom, when the sun rise and set. At such times you go by my volition and not by his; and this power to good of you and others, you have won from your suffering at his hands. This is now all more precious that he know it not, and to guard himself have even cut himself off from his knowledge of our where. We, however, are not all selfish, and we believe that God is with us through all this blackness, and these many dark hours. We shall follow him; and we shall not flinch; even if we peril ourselves that we become like him. Friend John, this has been a great hour; and it have done much to advance us on our way. You must be scribe and write him all down, so that when the others return from their work you can give it to them; then they shall know as we do.'

And so I have written it whilst we wait their return, and Mrs Harker has written with her typewriter all since she brought the MS. to us.

26

DR SEWARD'S DIARY

29 October. – This is written in the train from Varna to Galatz. Last night we all assembled a little before the time of sunset. Each of us had done his work as well as he could; so far as thought, and endeavour, and opportunity go, we are prepared for the whole of our journey, and for our work when we get to Galatz. When the usual time came round Mrs Harker prepared herself for her hypnotic effort; and after a longer and more strenuous effort on the part of Van Helsing than has been usually necessary, she sank into the trance. Usually she speaks on a hint; but this time the Professor had to ask her questions, and to ask them pretty resolutely, before we could learn anything; at last her answer came:–

'I can see nothing; we are still; there are no waves lapping, but only a steady swirl of water softly running against the hawser. I can hear men's voices calling, near and far, and the roll and creak of oars in the rowlocks. A gun is fired somewhere; the echo of it seems far away. There is tramping of feet overhead, and ropes and chains are dragged along. What is this? There is a gleam of light; I can feel the air blowing upon me.'

Here she stopped. She had risen, as if impulsively, from where she lay on the sofa, and raised both her hands, palms upwards, as if lifting a weight. Van Helsing and I looked at each other with understanding, whilst Harker's hand instinctively closed round the hilt of his Kukri. There was a long pause. We all knew that the time when she could speak was passing; but we felt that it was useless to say anything. Suddenly she sat up, and, as she opened her eyes, said sweetly:–

'Would none of you like a cup of tea? You must all be so tired!' We could only make her happy, and so acquiesced. She bustled off to get tea; when she had gone Van Helsing said:–

'You see, my friends. *He* is close to land; he has left his earth-chest. But he has yet to get on shore. In the night he may lie hidden somewhere; but if he be not carried on shore, or if the ship do not touch it, he cannot achieve the land. In such case he can, if it be in the night, change his form and can jump or fly on shore, as he did at Whitby. But if the day come before he get on shore, then, unless he be carried he cannot escape. And if he be carried, then the customs men may discover what the box contains. Thus, in fine, if he escape not on shore to-night, or before dawn, there will be the whole day lost to him. We may then arrive in time: for if he escape not at night we shall come on him in daytime, boxed up and at our mercy; for he dare not be his true self, awake and visible, lest he be discovered.'

There was no more to be said, so we waited in patience until the dawn; at which time we might learn more from Mrs Harker.

Early this morning we listened, with breathless anxiety, for her response in her trance. The hypnotic stage was even longer in coming than before; and when it came the time remaining until full sunrise was so short that we began to despair. Van Helsing seemed to throw his whole soul into the effort; at last, in obedience to his will she made reply:–

'All is dark. I hear lapping water, level with me, and some creaking as of wood on wood.' She paused, and the red sun shot up. We must wait till to-night.

And so it is that we are travelling towards Galatz in an agony of expectation. We are due to arrive between two and three in the morning; but already, at Bucharest, we are three hours late, so we cannot possibly get in till well after sun-up. Thus we shall have two more hypnotic messages from Mrs Harker; either or both may possibly throw more light on what is happening.

Later. – Sunset has come and gone. Fortunately it came at a time when there was no distraction; for had it occurred whilst we were at a station, we might not have secured the necessary calm and isolation. Mrs Harker yielded to the hypnotic influence even less readily than this morning. I am in fear that her power of reading the Count's sensations may die away, just when we want it most. It seems to me that her imagination is beginning to work. Whilst she has been in the trance hitherto she has confined herself to the simplest of facts. If this goes on it may ultimately mislead us. If I thought that the Count's power over her would die away equally with her power of knowledge it would be a happy thought; but I am afraid that it may not be so. When she did speak, her words were enigmatical:–

'Something is going out; I can feel it pass me like a cold wind. I can hear, far off, confused sounds – as of men talking in strange tongues, fierce-falling water, and the howling of wolves.' She stopped, and a shudder ran through her, increasing in intensity for a few seconds, till, at the end, she shook as though in a palsy. She said no more, even in answer to the Professor's imperative questioning. When she woke from the trance, she was cold, and exhausted, and languid; but her mind was all alert. She could not remember anything, but asked what she had said; when she was told, she pondered over it deeply for a long time and in silence.

30 October, 7 a.m. – We are near Galatz now, and I may not have time to write later. Sunrise this morning was anxiously looked for by us all. Knowing of the increasing difficulty of procuring the hypnotic trance, Van Helsing began his passes earlier than usual. They produced no effect, however, until the regular time, when she yielded with a still greater difficulty, only a minute before the sun rose. The Professor lost no time in his questioning; her answer came with equal quickness:–

'All is dark. I hear the water swirling by, level with my ears, and the creaking of wood on wood. Cattle low far off. There is another sound, a queer one like – ' She stopped and grew white, and whiter still.

'Go on! Go on! Speak, I command you!' said Van Helsing in an agonized voice. At the same time there was despair in his eyes, for the risen sun was reddening even Mrs Harker's pale face. She opened her eyes, and we all stared as she said, sweetly and seemingly with the utmost concern:–

'Oh, Professor, why ask me to do what you know I can't? I don't remember anything.' Then, seeing the look of amazement on our faces, she said, turning from one to the other:–

'What have I said? What have I done? I know nothing, only that I was lying here, half asleep, and I heard you say "Go on! speak, I command you!" It seemed so funny to hear you order me about, as if I were a bad child!'

'Oh, Madam Mina,' he said sadly, 'it is proof, if proof be needed, of how I love and honour you, when a word for your good, spoken more earnest than ever, can seem so strange because it is to order her whom I am proud to obey!'

The whistles are sounding; we are nearing Galatz. We are on fire with anxiety and eagerness.

MINA HARKER'S JOURNAL

30 October. – Mr Morris took me to the hotel where our rooms had been ordered by telegraph, he being the one who could best be spared, since he does not speak any foreign language. The forces were distributed much as they had been at Varna, except that Lord Godalming went to the Vice-Consul, as his rank might serve as an immediate guarantee of some sort to the official, we being in extreme hurry. Jonathon and the two doctors went to the shipping agent to learn particulars of the arrival of the *Czarina Catherine.*

Later. – Lord Godalming has returned. The Consul is away, and the Vice-Consul sick; so the routine work has been attended to by a clerk. He was very obliging, and offered to do anything in his power.

JONATHAN HARKER'S JOURNAL

30 October. – At nine o'clock Dr Van Helsing, Dr Seward, and I called on Messrs Mackenzie & Steinkoff, the agents of the London firm of Hapgood. They had received a wire from London, in answer to Lord Godalming's telegraphed request, asking them to show us any civility in their power. They were more than kind and courteous, and took us at once on board the *Czarina Catherine*, which lay at anchor out in the river harbour. There we saw the captain, Donelson by name, who told us of his voyage. He said that in all his life he had never had so favourable a run.

'Man!' he said, 'but it made us afeared, for we expeckit that we should have to pay for it wi' some rare piece o' ill luck, so as to keep up the average. It's no canny to run frae London to the Black Sea wi' a wind ahint ye, as though the Deil himself were blawin' on yer sail for his ain purpose. An' a' the time we could no' speer a thing. Gin we were nigh a ship, or a port, or a headland, a fog fell on us and travelled wi' us, till when after it had lifted and we looked out, the deil a thing could we see. We ran by Gibraltar wi'oot bein' able to signal; an' till we came to the Dardanelles and had to wait to get our permit to pass, we never were within hail o' aught. At first I inclined to slack off sail and beat about till the fog was lifted; but whiles, I thocht that if the Deil was minded to get us into the Black Sea quick, he was like to do it whether we would or no. If we had a quick voyage it would be no' to our miscredit wi' the owners, or no hurt to our traffic; an' the Old Mon who had served his ain purpose wad be decently grateful to us for no hinderin' him.' This mixture of simplicity and cunning, of superstition and commercial reasoning, aroused Van Helsing, who said: 'Mine friend, that Devil is more clever than he is thought by some; and he know when he meet his match!' The skipper was not displeased with the compliment, and went on:–

'When we got past the Bosphorus the men began to grumble; some o' them, the Roumanians, came and asked me to heave overboard a big box which had been put on board by a queer-lookin' old man just before we had started frae London. I had seen them speer at the fellow, and put out their twa fingers when they saw him, to guard against the evil eye. Man! but the supersteetion of foreigners is pairfectly rideeculous! I sent them aboot their business pretty quick; but as just after a fog closed in on us, I felt a wee bit as they did anent something, though I wouldn't say it was agin the bit box. Well, on we went, and as the fog didn't let up for five days I joost let the wind carry us; for if the Deil wanted to get somewheres – well, he would fetch it up a' reet. An' if he didn't, well, we'd keep a sharp look-out anyhow. Sure enuch, we had a fair way and deep water all the time; and two days ago, when the mornin' sun came through the fog, we found ourselves just in the river opposite Galatz. The Roumanians were wild, and wanted me right or wrong to take out the box and fling it in the river. I had to argy wi' them aboot it wi' a handspike; an' when the last o' them rose off the deck, wi' his head in his hand, I had convinced them that, evil eye or no evil eye, the property and the trust of my owners were better in my hands than in the river Danube. They had, mind ye, taken the box on the deck ready to fling in, and as it was marked Galatz *via* Varna, I thocht I'd let it lie till we discharged in the port an' get rid o't athegither. We didn't do much clearin' that day, an' had to remain the nicht at anchor; but in the mornin', braw an' airly, an hour before sun-up, a man came aboord wi' an order, written to him from England, to receive a box marked for one Count Dracula. Sure enuch the matter was one ready to his hand. He had his papers a' reet, an' glad I was to be rid o' the dam' thing, for I was beginnin' masel' to feel uneasy at it. If the Deil did have any luggage aboord the ship, I'm thinkin' it was nane ither than that same!'

'What was the name of the man who took it?' asked Dr Van Helsing, with restrained eagerness.

'I'll be tellin' ye quick!' he answered, and, stepping down to his cabin, produced a receipt signed 'Immanuel Hildesheim'. Burgen-strasse 16 was the address. We found out that this was all the captain knew; so with thanks we came away.

We found Hildesheim in his office, a Hebrew of rather the Adelphi type, with a nose like a sheep, and a fez. His arguments were pointed with specie – we doing the punctuation – and with a little bargaining he told us what he knew. This turned out to be simple but important. He had received a letter from Mr de Ville of London, telling him to receive, if possible before sunrise, so as to avoid customs, a box which would arrive at Galatz in the *Czarina Catherine*. This he was to give in charge to a certain Petrof Skinsky, who dealt with Slovaks who traded down the river to the port. He had been paid for his work by an English bank-note, which had been duly cashed for gold at the Danube International Bank. When Skinsky had come to him, he had taken him to the ship and handed over the box, so as to save porterage. That was all he knew.

We then sought for Skinsky, but were unable to find him. One of his neighbours, who did not seem to bear him any affection, said that he had gone away two days before, no one knew whither. This was corroborated by his landlord, who had received by messenger the key of the house together with the rent due, in English money. This had been between ten and eleven o'clock last night. We were at a standstill again.

Whilst we were talking, one came running and breathlessly gasped out that the body of Skinsky had been found inside the wall of the churchyard of St Peter, and that the throat had been torn open as if by some wild animal. Those we had been speaking with ran off to see the horror, the women crying out, 'This is the work of a Slovak!' We hurried away lest we should have been in some way drawn into the affair, and so detained.

As we came home we could arrive at no definite conclusion. We were all convinced that the box was on its way, by water, to somewhere; but where that might be we would have to discover. With heavy hearts we came home to the hotel to Mina.

When we met together, the first thing was to consult as to taking Mina again into our confidence. Things are getting desperate, and it is at least a chance, though a hazardous one. As a preliminary step, I was released from my promise to her.

MINA HARKER'S JOURNAL

30 October, evening. – They were so tired and worn-out and dispirited that there was nothing to be done till they had some rest; so I asked them all to lie down for half an hour whilst I should enter everything up to the moment. I feel so grateful to the man who invented the 'Traveller's' typewriter, and to Mr Morris for getting this one for me. I should have felt quite astray doing the work if I had to write with a pen. . . .

It is all done; poor dear, dear Jonathan, what he must have suffered, what must he be suffering now! He lies on the sofa hardly seeming to breathe, and his whole body appears in collapse. His brows are knit; his face is drawn with pain. Poor fellow, maybe he is thinking, and I can see his face all wrinkled up with the concentration of his thoughts. Oh! If I could only help at all. . . . I shall do what I can. . . .

I have asked Dr Van Helsing, and he has got me all the papers that I have not yet seen. . . . Whilst they are resting, I shall go over all carefully, and perhaps I may arrive at some conclusion. I shall try to follow the Professor's example, and think without prejudice on the facts before me. . . .

I do believe that under God's Providence I have made a discovery. I shall get the maps and look over them. . . .

I am more than ever sure that I am right. My new conclusion is ready, so I shall get our party together and read it. They can judge it; it is well to be accurate, and every minute is precious.

MINA HARKER'S MEMORANDUM
(Entered in her Journal)

Ground of inquiry. – Count Dracula's problem is to get back to his own place.

(*a*) He must be *brought back* by someone. This is evident; for, had he power to move himself as he wished, he could go either as man, or wolf, or bat, or in some other way. He evidently fears discovery or interference, in the state of helplessness in which he must be – confined as he is between dawn and sunset in his wooden box.

(*b*) *How is he to be taken?* – Here a process of exclusion may help us. By road, by rail, by water?

1. *By Road.* – There are endless difficulties, especially in leaving a city.

(*a*) There are people; and people are curious, and investigate. A hint, a surmise, a doubt as to what might be in the box would destroy him.

(*b*) There are, or there might be, customs and octroi officers to pass.

(*c*) His pursuers might follow. This is his greatest fear; and in order to prevent his being betrayed he has repelled, so far as he can, even his victim – me!

2. *By rail.* There is no one in charge of the box. It would have to take its chance of being delayed; and delay would be fatal, with enemies on the track. True, he might escape at night; but where would he be if left in a strange place with no refuge that he could fly to? This is not what he intends; and he does not mean to risk it.

3. *By Water.* – Here is the safest way, in one respect, but with most danger in another. On the water he is powerless except at night; even then he can only summon fog and storm and snow and his wolves. But were he wrecked, the living water would engulf him, helpless; and he would

indeed be lost. He could have the vessel drive to land; but if it were unfriendly land, wherein he was not free to move, his position would still be desperate.

We know from the record that he was on the water; so what we have to do is to ascertain *what* water.

The first thing is to realize exactly what he has done as yet; we may, then, get a light on what his later task is to be.

Firstly, we must consider what he did in London as part of his general plan of action, when he was pressed for moments and had to arrange as best he could.

Secondly, we must see, as well as we can surmise it from the facts we know of, what he has done here.

As to the first, he evidently intended to arrive at Galatz, and sent invoice to Varna to deceive us lest we should ascertain his means of exit from England; his immediate and sole purpose then was to escape. The proof of this is the letter of instructions sent to Immanuel Hildesheim to clear and take away the box *before sunrise*. There is also the instruction to Petrof Skinsky. This we must only guess at; but there must have been some letter or message, since Skinsky came to Hildesheim.

That, so far, his plans were successful, we know. The *Czarina Catherine* made a phenomenally quick journey – so much so that Captain Donelson's suspicions were aroused; but his superstition united with his canniness played the Count's game for him, and he ran with his favouring wind through fogs and all till he brought up blindfold at Galatz. That the Count's arrangements were well made has been proved. Hildesheim cleared the box, took it off, and gave it to Skinsky. Skinsky took it – and here we lose the trail. We only know that the box is somewhere on the water, moving along. The customs and the octroi, if there be any, have been avoided.

Now we come to what the Count must have done after his arrival – *on land*, at Galatz.

The box was given to Skinsky before sunrise. At sunrise the Count could appear in his own form. Here, we ask why Skinsky was chosen at all to aid in the work? In my husband's diary, Skinsky is mentioned as dealing with the Slovaks who trade down the river to the port; and the man's remark, that the murder was the work of a Slovak, showed the general feeling against his class. The Count wanted isolation.

My surprise is this: that in London the Count decided to get back to his castle by water, as the most safe and secret way. He was brought from the castle by Szgany, and probably they delivered their cargo to Slovaks who took the boxes to Varna, for there they were shipped for London. Thus the Count had knowledge of the persons who could arrange this service.

287

When the box was on land, before sunrise or after sunset, he came out from his box, met Skinsky and instructed him what to do as to arranging the carriage of the box up some river. When this was done, and he knew that all was in train, he blotted out his traces, as he thought, by murdering his agent.

I have examined the map, and find that the river most unsuitable for the Slovaks to have ascended is either the Pruth or the Sereth. I read in the typescript that in my trance I heard cows low and water swirling level with my ears and the creaking of wood. The Count in his box, then, was on a river in an open boat – propelled probably either by oars or poles, for the banks are near and it is working against stream. There would be no such sound if floating down stream.

Of course it may not be either the Sereth or the Pruth, but we may possibly investigate further. Now of these two, the Pruth is the more easily navigated, but the Sereth is, at Fundu, joined by the Bistritza, which runs up round the Borgo Pass. The loop it makes is manifestly as close to Dracula's Castle as can be got by water.

MINA HARKER'S JOURNAL (continued)

When I had done reading, Jonathan took me in his arms and kissed me. The others kept shaking me by both hands, and Dr Van Helsing said:–

'Our dear Madam Mina is once more our teacher. Her eyes have seen where we were blinded. Now we are on the track once again, and this time we may succeed. Our enemy is at his most helpless; and if we can come on him by day, on the water, our task will be over. He has a start, but he is powerless to hasten, as he may not leave his box lest those who carry him may suspect; for them to suspect would be to prompt them to throw him in the stream, where he perish. This he knows, and will not. Now, men, to our Council of War; for, here and now, we must plan what each and all shall do.'

'I shall get a steam launch and follow him,' said Lord Godalming.

'And I, horses to follow on the bank lest by chance he land,' said Mr Morris.

'Good!' said the Professor. 'Both good. But neither must go alone. There must be force to overcome force if need be; the Slovak is strong and rough, and he carries rude arms.' All the men smiled, for amongst them they carried a small arsenal. Said Mr Morris:–

'I have brought some Winchesters; they are pretty handy in a crowd, and there may be wolves. The Count, if you remember, took some other precautions; he made some requisitions on others that Mrs Harker could not quite hear or understand. We must be ready at all points.' Dr Seward said:–

'I think I had better go with Quincey. We have been accustomed to hunt together, and we two, well armed, will be a match for whatever may come along. You must not be alone, Art. It may be necessary to fight the Slovaks, and a chance thrust – for I don't suppose these fellows carry guns – would undo all our plans. There must be no chances, this time; we shall not rest until the Count's head and body have been separated, and we are sure that he cannot reincarnate.' He looked at Jonathan as he spoke, and Jonathan looked at me. I could see that the poor dear was torn about in his mind. Of course he wanted to be with me; but then the boat service would, most likely, be the one which would destroy the . . . the . . . the . . . Vampire. (Why did I hesitate to write the word?) He was silent awhile, and during his silence Dr Van Helsing spoke:–

'Friend Jonathan, this is to you for twice reasons. First, because you are young and brave and can fight, and all energies may be needed at the last; and again that it is your right to destroy him – that – which has wrought such woe to you and yours. Be not afraid for Madam Mina; she will be my care, if I may. I am old. My legs are not so quick to run as once; and I am not used to ride so long or to pursue as need be; or to fight with lethal weapons. But I can be of other service; I can fight in other way. And I can die, if need be, as well as younger men. Now let me say that what I would is this; while you, my Lord Goldalming, and friend Jonathan go in your so swift little steamboat up the river, and whilst John and Quincey guard the bank where perchance he might be landed, I will take Madam Mina right into the heart of the enemy's country. Whilst the old fox is tied in his box, floating on the running stream whence he cannot escape to land – where he dares not raise the lid of his coffin-box lest his Slovak carriers should in fear leave him to perish – we shall go in the track where Jonathan went – from Bistritz over the Borgo – and find our way to the Castle of Dracula. Here, Madam Mina's hypnotic power will surely help, and we shall find our way – all dark and unknown otherwise – after the first sunrise when we near that fateful place. There is much to be done, and other places to be made sanctify, so that that nest of vipers be obliterated.' Here Jonathan interrupted him hotly:–

'Do you mean to say, Professor Van Helsing, that you would bring Mina, in her sad case and tainted as she is with that devil's illness, right into the jaws of his death-trap? Not for the world! Not for Heaven or Hell!' He became almost speechless for a minute, and then went on:–

'Do you know what the place is? Have you seen that awful den of hellish infamy – with the very moonlight alive with grisly shapes, and every speck of dust that whirls in the wind a devouring monster in embryo? Have you felt the Vampire's lips upon your throat?' Here he turned to me, and as his eyes lit on my forehead, he threw up his arms with a cry: 'Oh, my God, what have we done to have this terror upon us!' and he sank down on the sofa in a collapse of misery. The Professor's voice, as he spoke in clear, sweet tones, which seemed to vibrate in the air, calmed us all:—

'Oh, my friend, it is because I would save Madam Mina from that awful place that I would go. God forbid that I should take her into that place! There is work – wild work – to be done there, that her eyes may not see. We men here, all save Jonathan, have seen with our own eyes what is to be done before that place can be purify. Remember that we are in terrible straits. If the Count escape us this time – and he is strong and subtle and cunning – he may choose to sleep him for a century; and then in time our dear one' – he took my hand – 'would come to him to keep him company, and would be as those others that you, Jonathan, saw. You have told us of their gloating lips; you heard their ribald laugh as they clutched the moving bag that the Count threw to them. You shudder; and well may it be. Forgive me that I make you so much pain, but it is necessary. My friend, is it not a dire need for the which I am giving, if need be, my life? If it were that anyone went into that place to stay, it is I who would have to go, to keep them company.'

'Do as you will,' said Jonathan, with a sob that shook him all over; 'we are in the hands of God!'

Later. – Oh, it did me good to see the way that these brave men worked. How can women help loving men when they are so earnest, and so true, and so brave! And, too, it made me think of the wonderful power of money! What can it not do when it is properly applied; and what might it do when basely used! I felt so thankful that Lord Godalming is rich, and that both he and Mr Morris, who also has plenty of money, are willing to spend it so freely. For if they did not, our little expedition could not start, either so promptly or so well equipped, as it will within another hour. It is not three hours since it was arranged what part each of us was to do; now Lord Godalming and Jonathan have a lovely steam launch, with steam up, ready to start at a moment's notice. Dr Seward and Mr Morris have half a dozen beautiful horses, well appointed. We have all the maps and appliances of various kinds that can be had. Professor Van Helsing and I are to leave by the 11.40 train to-night for Veresti, where we are to get a carriage to drive to the Borgo Pass. We are bringing a good deal of ready money, as we are to buy a carriage and horses. We shall drive ourselves, for we have no one whom we can trust in this matter. The Professor knows something of a great many languages, so we shall get on all right. We have all got arms, even for me a large-bore revolver; Jonathan would not be happy unless I was armed like the rest. Alas! I cannot carry one arm that the rest do; the scar on my forehead forbids that. Dear Dr Van

Helsing comforts me by telling me that I am fully armed as there may be wolves; the weather is getting colder every hour, and there are snow-flurries which come and go as warnings.

Later. – It took all my courage to say good-bye to my darling. We may never meet again. Courage, Mina! the Professor is looking at you keenly; his look is a warning. There must be no tears now – unless it may be that God will let them fall in gladness.

JONATHAN HARKER'S JOURNAL

October 30, night. – I am writing this in the light from the furnace door of the steam launch; Lord Godalming is firing up. He is an experienced hand at the work, as he has had for years a launch of his own on the Thames, and another on the Norfolk Broads. Regarding our plans, we finally decided that Mina's guess was correct, and that if any waterway was chosen for the Count's escape back to his castle, the Sereth, and then the Bistritza at its junction, would be the one. We took it that somewhere about the 47th degree, north latitude, would be the place chosen for crossing the country between the river and the Carpathians. We have no fear in running at good speed up the river at night; there is plenty of water, and the banks are wide enough apart to make steaming, even in the dark, easy enough. Lord Goldalming tells me to sleep for a while, as it is enough for the present for one to be on watch. But I cannot sleep – how can I with the terrible danger hanging over my darling, and her going out into that awful place? . . . My only comfort is that we are in the hands of God. Only for that faith it would be easier to die than to live, and so be quit of all the trouble. Mr Morris and Dr Seward were off on their long ride before we started; they are to keep up the right bank, far enough off to get on higher lands, where they can see a good stretch of river and avoid the following of its curves. They have, for the first stages, two men to ride and lead their spare horses – four in all, so as not to excite curiosity. When they dismiss the men, which will be shortly, they will themselves look after the horses. It may be necessary for us to join forces; if so they can mount our whole party. One of the saddles has a movable horn, and can be easily adapted for Mina, if required.

It is a wild adventure we are on. Here, as we are rushing along through the darkness, with the cold from the river seeming to rise up and strike us; with all the mysterious voices of the night around us, it all comes home. We seem to be drifting into unknown places and unknown ways; into a whole world of dark and dreadful things. Godalming is shutting the furnace door. . . .

31 October. – Still hurrying along. The day has come, and Godalming is sleeping. I am on watch. The morning is bitterly cold; the furnace heat is grateful, though we have heavy fur coats. As yet we have passed only a few open boats, but none of them had on board any box or package of anything like the size of the one we seek. The men were scared every time we turned our electric lamp on them, and fell on their knees and prayed.

1 November, evening. – No news all day; we have found nothing of the kind we seek. We have now passed into the Bistritza; and if we are wrong in our surmise our chance is gone. We have overhauled every boat, big and little. Early this morning, one crew took us for a Government boat, and treated us accordingly. We saw in this a way of smoothing matters, so at Fundu, where the Bistritza runs into the Sereth, we got a Roumanian flag, which we now fly conspicuously. With every boat which we have overhauled since then this trick has succeeded; we have had every deference shown to us, and not once any objection to whatever we chose to ask or do. Some of the Slovaks tell us that a big boat passed them, going at more than usual speed as she had a double crew on board. This was before they came to Fundu, so they could not tell us whether the boat turned into the Bistritza or continued on up the Sereth. At Fundu we could not hear of any such boat, so she must have passed there in the night. I am feeling very sleepy; the cold is perhaps beginning to tell upon me, and nature must have rest some time. Godalming insists that he shall keep the first watch. God bless him for all his goodness to poor dear Mina and me.

2 November, morning. – It is broad daylight. That good fellow would not wake me. He says it would have been a sin to, for I slept so peacefully and was forgetting my trouble. It seems brutally selfish of me to have slept so long, and let him watch all night; but he was quite right. I am a new man this morning; and, as I sit here and watch him sleeping, I can do all that is necessary both as to minding the engine, steering, and keeping watch. I can feel that my strength and energy are coming back to me. I wonder where Mina is now, and Van Helsing. They should have got to Veresti about noon on Wednesday. It would take them some time to get the carriage and horses; so if they had started and travelled hard, they would be about now at the Borgo Pass. God guide and help them! I am afraid to think what may happen. If we could only go faster! but we cannot; the engines are throbbing and doing their utmost. I wonder how Dr Seward and Mr Morris are getting on. There seem to be endless streams running down from the mountains into this river, but as none of them are very large – at present, at all events, though they are terrible doubtless in winter and when the snow melts – the horsemen may not have met much obstruction. I hope that before we get to Strasba we may see them; for if by that time we have not overtaken the Count, it may be necessary to take counsel together on what to do next.

DR SEWARD'S DIARY

2 November. – Three days on the road. No news, and no time to write it if there had been, for every moment is precious. We have had only the rest needful for the horses; but we are both bearing it wonderfully. Those adventurous days of ours are turning up useful. We must push on; we shall never feel happy till we get the launch in sight again.

3 November. – We heard at Fundu that the launch had gone up the Bistritza. I wish it wasn't so cold. There are signs of snow coming; and if it falls heavy it will stop us. In such case we must get a sledge and go on, Russian fashion.

4 November. – Today we heard of the launch having been detained by an accident when trying to force a way up the rapids. The Slovak boats get up all right, by aid of a rope, and steering with knowledge. Some went up only a few hours before. Godalming is an amateur fitter himself, and evidently it was he who put the launch in trim again. Finally, they got up the rapids all right, with local help, and are off on the chase afresh. I fear that the boat is not any better for the accident; the peasantry tell us that after she got upon the smooth water again, she kept stopping every now and again so long as she was in sight. We must push on harder than ever; our help may be wanted soon.

MINA HARKER'S JOURNAL

31 October. – Arrived at Veresti at noon. The Professor tells me that this morning at dawn he could hardly hypnotize me at all, and that all I could say was, 'Dark and quiet.' He is off now buying a carriage and horses. He says that he will later on try to buy additional horses, so that we may be able to change them on the way. We have something more than seventy miles before us. The country is lovely, and most interesting; if only it were under different conditions, how delightful it would be to see it all! If Jonathan and I were driving through it alone what a pleasure it would be! To stop and see people, and learn something of their life, and to fill our minds and memories with all the colour and picturesqueness of the whole wild, beautiful country and the quaint people! But, alas! . . .

Later. – Dr Van Helsing has returned. He has got the carriage and horses; we are to have some dinner, and to start in an hour. The landlady is putting us up a huge basket of provision; it seems enough for a company of soldiers. The Professor encourages her, and whispers to me that it may be a week before we can get any good food again. He has been shopping too, and has sent home such a wonderful lot of fur coats and wraps, and all sorts of warm things. There will not be any chance of our being cold.

* * *

We shall soon be off. I am afraid to think what may happen to us. We are truly in the hands of God. He alone knows what may be, and I pray Him, with all the strength of my sad and humble soul, that He will watch over my beloved husband; that whatever may happen, Jonathan may know that I loved him and honoured him more than I can say, and that my latest and truest thought will be always for him.

27

MINA HARKER'S JOURNAL

1 November. – All day long we have travelled, and at a good speed. The horses seem to know that they are being kindly treated, for they go willingly their full stage at best speed. We have now had so many changes and find the same thing so constantly that we are encouraged to think that the journey will be an easy one. Dr Van Helsing is laconic; he tells the farmers that he is hurrying to Bistritz, and pays them well to make the exchange of horses. We get hot soup, or coffee, or tea; and off we go. It is a lovely country; full of beauties of all imaginable kinds, and the people are brave, and strong, and simple, and seem full of nice qualities. They are *very, very* superstitious. In the first house where we stopped, when the woman who served us saw the scar on my forehead, she crossed herself and put out two fingers towards me, to keep off the evil eye. I believe they went to the trouble of putting an extra amount of garlic into our food; and I can't abide garlic. Ever since then I have taken care not to take off my hat or veil, and so have escaped their suspicions. We are travelling fast, and as we have no driver with us to carry tales, we go ahead of scandal; but I daresay that fear of the evil eye will follow hard behind us all the way. The Professor seems tireless; all day he would not take any rest, though he made me sleep for a long spell. At sunset time he hypnotized me, and he says that I answered as usual 'Darkness, lapping water and creaking wood'; so our enemy is still on the river. I am afraid to think of Jonathan, but somehow I have now no fear for him, or for myself. I write this whilst we wait in a farmhouse for the horses to be got ready. Dr Van Helsing is sleeping. Poor dear, he looks very tired and old and grey, but his mouth is set as firmly as a conqueror's; even in his sleep he is instinct with resolution. When we have well started I must make him rest whilst I drive. I shall tell him that we have days before us, and he must not break down when most of all his strength will be needed. . . . All is ready; we are off shortly.

2 November, morning. – I was successful, and we took turns driving all night; now the day is on us, bright though cold. There is a strange heaviness in the air – I say heaviness for want of a better word; I mean that it oppresses us both. It is very cold, and only our warm furs keep us comfortable. At dawn Van Helsing hypnotized me; he says I answered 'Darkness, creaking wood and roaring water', so the river is changing as they ascend. I do hope that my darling will not run any chance of danger – more than need be; but we are in God's hands.

2 November, night. – All day long driving. The country gets wilder as we go, and the great spurs of the Carpathians, which at Veresti seemed so far from us and so low on the horizon, now seem to gather round us and tower in front. We both seem in good spirits; I think we make an effort each to cheer the other; in the doing so we cheer ourselves. Dr Van Helsing says that by morning we shall reach the Borgo Pass. The houses are very few here now, and the Professor says that the last horses we got will have to go on with us, as we may not be able to change. He got two in addition to the two we changed, so that now we have a rude four-in-hand. The dear horses are patient and good, and they give us no trouble. We are not worried with other travellers, and so even I can drive. We shall get to the Pass in daylight; we do not want to arrive before. So we take it easy and have each a long rest in turn. Oh, what will to-morrow bring to us? We go to seek the place where my poor darling suffered so much. God grant that we may be guided aright, and that He will deign to watch over my husband and those dear to us both, and who are in such deadly peril. As for me, I am not worthy in His sight. Alas! I am unclean to His eyes, and shall be until He may deign to let me stand forth in His sight as one of those who have not incurred His wrath.

MEMORANDUM BY ABRAHAM VAN HELSING

4 November. – This to my old and true friend John Seward, M.D., of Purfleet, London, in case I may not see him. It may explain. It is morning, and I write by a fire which all the night I have kept alive – Madam Mina aiding me. It is cold, cold; so cold that the grey heavy sky is full of snow, which when it falls will settle for all winter as the ground is hardening to receive it. It seems to have affected Madam Mina; she has been so heavy of head all day that she was not like herself. She sleeps, and sleeps, and sleeps! She, who is usual so alert, have done literally nothing all the day; she even have lost her appetite. She make no entry into her little diary, she who write so faithful at every pause. Something whisper to me that all is not well. However, to-night she is more *vif*. Her long sleep all day have refresh and restore her, for now she is all sweet and bright as ever. At sunset I try to hypnotize her, but alas! with no effect; the power has grown less and less with each day, and to-night it fail me altogether. Well, God's will be done – whatever it may be, and whithersoever it may lead!

Now to the historical, for as Madam Mina write not in her stenography, I must, in my cumbrous old fashion, that so each day of us may not go unrecorded.

We got to the Borgo Pass just after sunrise yesterday morning. When I saw the signs of the dawn I got ready for the hypnotism. We stopped our carriage, and got down so that there might be no disturbance. I made a couch with furs, and Madam Mina, lying down, yield herself as usual, but more slow and more short time than ever, to the hypnotic sleep. As before, came the answer: 'Darkness and the swirling of water.' Then she woke, bright and radiant, and we go on our way and soon reach the Pass. At this time and place she become all on fire with zeal; some new guiding power be in her manifested, for she point to a road and say:–

'This is the way.'

'How know you it?' I ask.

'Of course I know it,' she answer, and with a pause, add: 'Have not my Jonathan travel it and wrote of his travel?'

At first I think somewhat strange, but soon I see that there be only one such by-road. It is used but little, and very different from the coach road from Bukovina to Bistritz, which is more wide and hard, and more of use.

So we came down this road; when we meet other ways – not always were we sure that they were roads at all, for they be neglect and light snow have fallen – the horses know and they only. I give rein to them, and they go on so patient. By-and-by we find all the things which Jonathan have note in that wonderful diary of him. Then we go on for long, long hours and hours. At the first, I tell Madam Mina to sleep; she try, and she succeed. She sleep all the time; till at the last, I feel myself to suspicious grow, and attempt to wake her. But she sleep on, and I may not wake her though I try. I do not wish to try too hard lest I harm her; for I know that she have suffer much, and sleep at times be all-in-all to her. I think I drowse myself, for all of sudden I feel guilt, as though I have done something; I find myself bolt up, with the reins in my hand, and the good horses go along jog, jog, just as ever. I look down and find Madam Mina still sleep. It is now not far off sunset time, and over the snow the light of the sun flow in big yellow flood, so that we throw great long shadow on where the mountain rise so steep. For we are going up, and up; and all is oh! so wild and rocky, as though it were the end of the world.

Then I arouse Madam Mina. This time she wake with not much trouble, and then I try to put her to hypnotic sleep. But she sleep not, being as though I were not. Still I try and try, till all at once I find her and myself in dark; so I look round, and find that the sun have gone down. Madam Mina laugh, and I turn and look at her. She is now quite awake, and look so well as I never saw her since that night at Carfax when we first enter the Count's house. I am amaze, and not at ease then; but she is so bright and tender and thoughtful for me that I forget all fear. I light a fire, for we have brought supply of wood with us, and she prepare food while I undo the horses and set them tethered in shelter, to feed. Then when I return to the fire she have my supper ready. I go to help her; but she smile, and tell me that she have eat already – that she was so hungry that she would not wait. I like it not, and I have grave doubts; but I fear to affright her, and so I am silent of it. She help me and I eat alone; and then we wrap in fur and lie beside the fire, and I tell her to sleep while I watch. But presently I forget all of watching; and when I sudden remember that I watch, I find her lying quiet, but awake, and looking at me with so bright eyes. Once, twice more the same occur, and I get much sleep till before morning. When I wake I try to hypnotize her; but alas! though she shut her eyes obedient, she may not sleep. The run rise up, and up, and up; and then sleep come to her too late, but so heavy that she will not wake. I have to lift her up and place her sleeping in the carriage when I have harnessed the horses and made all ready. Madam still sleep, and sleep; and she look in her sleep more healthy and more redder than before. And I like it not. And I am afraid, afraid, afraid! – I am afraid of all things – even to think; but I must go on my way. The stake we play for is life and death, or more than these, and we must not flinch.

5 November, morning. – Let me be accurate in everything, for though you and I have seen some strange things together, you may at the first think that I, Van Helsing, am mad – that the many horrors and the so long strain on nerves has at the last turn my brain.

All yesterday we travel, ever getting closer to the mountains, and moving into a more and more wild and desert land. There are great, frowning precipices and much falling water, and Nature seemed to have held sometime her carnival. Madam Mina will sleep and sleep; and though I did have hunger and appeased it, I could not waken her – even for food. I began to fear that the fatal spell of the place was upon her, tainted as she is with that Vampire baptism. 'Well,' said I to myself, 'if it be that she sleep all the day, it shall also be that I do not sleep at night.' As we travel on the rough road, for a road of an ancient and imperfect kind there was, I held down my head and slept. Again I waked with a sense of guilt and of time passed, and found Madam Mina still sleeping, and the sun low down. But all was indeed changed; the frowning mountains seemed further away, and we were near the top of a steep-rising hill, on summit of which was such a castle as Jonathan tell of in his diary. At once I exulted and feared; for now, for good or ill, the end was near. I woke Madam Mina, and again tried to hypnotize her; but alas! unavailing till too late. Then, ere the great dark came upon us – for even after down-sun the heavens reflected the gone sun on the snow, and all was for a time in a great twilight – I took out the horses and fed them in what shelter I could. Then I make a fire; and near it I made Madam Mina, now wake and more charming than ever, sit comfortable amid her rugs. I got ready food; but she would not eat, simply saying that she had not hunger. I did not press her, knowing her unavailingness. But I myself eat, for I must needs now be strong for all. Then, with the fear on me of what might be, I drew a ring, so big for her comfort, round where Madam Mina sat; and over the ring I passed some of the Wafer, and I broke it fine so that all was well guarded. She sat still all the time – so still as one dead; and she grew whiter and ever whiter till the snow was not more pale; and no word she said. But when I drew near, she clung to me, and I could know that the poor soul shook her from head to feet with a tremor that was pain to feel. I said to her presently, when she had grown more quiet:–

'Will you not come over to the fire?' for I wished to make a test of what she could. She rose obedient, but when she have made a step she stopped, and stood as one stricken.

'Why not go on?' I asked. She shook her head, and, coming back, sat down in her place. Then, looking at me with open eyes, as of one waked from sleep, she said simply:–

'I cannot!' and remained silent. I rejoiced, for I knew that what she could not, none of those that we dreaded could. Though there might be danger to her body, yet her soul was safe!

Presently the horses began to scream, and tore at their tethers till I came to them and quieted them. When they did feel my hands on them, they whinnied low as in joy, and licked at my hands and were quiet for a time. Many times through the night did I come to them, till it arrive to the cold hour when all nature is at lowest; and every time my coming was with quiet of them. In the cold hour the fire began to die, and I was about stepping forth to replenish it, for now the snow came in flying sweeps and with it a chill mist. Even in the dark there was a light of some kind, as there ever is over snow; and it seemed as though the snow-flurries and the wreaths of mist took shape as of women with trailing garments. All was in dead, grim silence, only that the horses whinnied and cowered, as if in terror of the worst. I began to fear – horrible fears; but then came to me the sense of safety in that ring wherein I stood. I began, too, to think that my imaginings were of the night, and the gloom, and the unrest that I have gone through, and all the terrible anxiety. It was as though my memories of all Jonathan's horrid experience were befooling me; for the snowflakes and the mist began to wheel and circle round, till I could get as though a shadowy glimpse of those women that would have kissed him. And then the horses cowered lower and lower, and moaned in terror as men do in pain. Even the madness of fright was not to them, so that they could break away. I feared for my dear Madam Mina when these weird figures drew near and circled round. I looked at her, but she sat calm, and smiled at me; when I would have stepped to the fire to replenish it, she caught me and held me back, and whispered, like a voice that one hears in a dream, so low it was:–

'No! no! Do not go without. Here you are safe!' I turned to her, and looking in her eyes, said:–

'But you? It is for you that I fear!' whereat she laughed – a laugh low and unreal, and said:–

'Fear for *me*! Why fear for me? None safer in all the world from them than I am,' and as I wondered at the meaning of her words, a puff of wind made the flame leap up, and I see the red scar on her forehead. Then, alas! I knew. Did I not, I would soon have learned, for the wheeling figures of mist and snow came closer, but keeping ever without the Holy circle. Then they began to materialize, till – if God have not take away my reason, for I saw it through my eyes – there were before me in actual flesh the same three women that Jonathan saw in the room, when they would have kissed his throat. I knew the swaying round forms, the bright hard eyes, the white teeth, the ruddy colour, the voluptuous lips. They smiled ever at poor dear Madam Mina; and as their laugh came through the silence of the night, they twined their arms and pointed to her, and said in those so sweet tingling tones that Jonathan said were of the intolerable sweetness of the water-glasses:–

'Come, sister. Come to us. Come! Come!' In fear I turned to my poor Madam Mina, and my heart with gladness leapt like flame; for oh! the terror in her sweet eyes, the repulsion, the horror, told a story to my heart that was all of hope. God be thanked she was not, yet, of them. I seized some of the firewood which was by me, and holding out some of the Wafer, advanced on them towards the fire. They drew back before me, and laughed their low horrid laugh. I fed the fire, and feared them not; for I knew that we were safe within our protections. They could not approach me, whilst so armed, nor Madam Mina whilst she remained within the ring, which she could not leave no more than they could enter. The horses had ceased to moan, and lay still on the ground; the snow fell on them softly, and they grew whiter. I knew that there was for the poor beasts no more of terror.

And so we remained till the red of the dawn began to fall through the snow-gloom. I was desolate and afraid, and full of woe and terror; but when that beautiful sun began to climb the horizon life was to me again. At the first coming of the dawn the horrid figures melted in the whirling mist and snow; the wreaths of transparent gloom moved away towards the castle, and were lost.

Instinctively, with the dawn coming, I turned to Madam Mina, intending to hypnotize her; but she lay in a deep and sudden sleep, from which I could not wake her. I tried to hypnotize through her sleep, but she made no response, none at all; and the day broke. I fear yet to stir. I have made my fire and have seen the horses; they are all dead. To-day I have much to do here, and I keep waiting till the sun is up high; for there may be places where I must go, where that sunlight, though snow and mist obscure it, will be to me a safety.

I will strengthen me with breakfast, and then I will to my terrible work. Madam Mina still sleeps; and, God be thanked! she is calm in her sleep. . . .

JONATHAN HARKER'S JOURNAL

4 November, evening. – The accident to the launch has been a terrible thing for us. Only for it we should have overtaken the boat long ago; and by now my dear Mina would have been free. I fear to think of her, off on the wolds near that horrid place. We have got horses, and we follow on the track. I note this whilst Godalming is getting ready. We have our arms. The Szgany must look out if they mean fight. Oh, if only Morris and Seward were with us! We must only hope! If I write no more, Good-bye, Mina! God bless and keep you.

DR SEWARD'S DIARY

5 November. – With the dawn we saw the body of Szgany before us dashing away from the river with their leiter-waggon. They surrounded it in a cluster, and hurried along as though beset. The snow is falling lightly and there is a strange excitement in the air. It may be our own excited feelings, but the depression is strange. Far off I hear the howling of wolves; the snow brings them down from the mountains, and there are dangers to all of us, and from all sides. The horses are nearly ready, and we are soon off. We ride to death of someone. God alone knows who, or where, or what, or when, or how it may be. . . .

DR VAN HELSING'S MEMORANDUM

5 November, afternoon. – I am at least sane. Thank God for that mercy at all events, though the proving it has been dreadful. When I left Madam Mina sleeping within the Holy circle, I took my way to the castle. The blacksmith hammer which I took in the carriage from Veresti was useful; though the doors were all open I broke them off the rusty hinges, lest some ill-intent or ill-chance should close them, so that being entered I might not get out. Jonathan's bitter experience served me here. By memory of his diary I found my way to the old chapel, for I knew that here my work lay. The air was oppressive; it seemed as if there was some sulphurous fume, which at times made me dizzy. Either there was a roaring in my ears or I heard afar off the howl of wolves. Then I bethought me of my dear Madam Mina, and I was in terrible plight. The dilemma had me between his horns. Her, I had not dare to take into this place, but left safe from the Vampire in that Holy circle; and yet even there would be the wolf! I resolve me that my work lay here, and that as to the wolves we must submit, if it were God's will. At any rate it was only death and freedom beyond. So did I choose for her. Had it but been for myself the choice had been easy; the maw of the wolf were better to rest in than the grave of the Vampire! So I make my choice to go on with my work.

I knew that there were at least three graves to find – graves that are inhabit; so I search, and search, and I find one of them. She lay in her Vampire sleep, so full of life and voluptuous beauty that I shudder as though I have come to do murder. Ah, I doubt not that in old time, when such things were, many a man who set forth to do such a task as mine, found at the last his heart fail him, and then his nerve. So he delay, and delay, and delay, till the mere beauty and the fascination of the wanton Un-Dead have hypnotize him; and he remain on, and on, till sunset come, and the Vampire sleep be over. Then the beautiful eyes of the fair woman open and look love, and the voluptuous mouth present to a kiss – and man is weak. And there remain one more victim in the Vampire fold; one more to swell the grim and grisly ranks of the Un-Dead! . . .

There is some fascination, surely, when I am moved by the mere presence of such an one, even lying as she lay in a tomb fretted with age and heavy with the dust of centuries, though there be that horrid odour such as the lairs of the Count have had. Yes, I was moved – I, Van Helsing, with all my purpose and with my motive for hate – I was moved to a yearning for delay which seemed to paralyse my faculties and to clog my very soul. It may have been that the need of natural sleep, and the strange oppression of the air, were beginning to overcome me. Certain it was that I was lapsing into sleep, the open-eyed sleep of one who yields to a sweet fascination, when there came through the snow-stilled air a long, low wail, so full of woe and pity that it woke me like the sound of a clarion. For it was the voice of my dear Madam Mina that I heard.

Then I braced myself again to my horrid task, and found by wrenching away tomb-tops one other of the sisters, the other dark one. I dared not pause to look on her as I had on her sister, lest once more I should begin to be enthral; but I go on searching until, presently, I find in a high great tomb as if made to one much beloved that other fair sister which, like Jonathan, I had seen to gather herself out of the atoms of the mist. She was so fair to look on, so radiantly beautiful, so exquisitely voluptuous, that the very instinct of man in me, which calls some of my sex to love and to protect one of hers, made my head whirl with new emotion. But, God be thanked, that soul-wail of my dear Madam Mina had not died out of my ears; and, before the spell could be wrought further upon me, I had nerved myself to my wild work. By this time I had searched all the tombs in the chapel, so far as I could tell; and as there had been only three of these Un-Dead phantoms around us in the night, I took it that there were no more of active Un-Dead existent. There was one great tomb more lordly than all the rest; huge it was, and nobly proportioned. On it was but one word,

DRACULA

This then was the Un-Dead home of the King-Vampire, to whom so many more were due. Its emptiness spoke eloquent to make certain what I knew. Before I began to restore these women to their dead selves through my awful work, I laid in Dracula's tomb some of the Wafer, and so banished him from it, Un-Dead, for ever.

Then began my terrible task, and I dreaded it. Had it been but one, it had been easy, comparative. But three! To begin twice more after I had been through a deed of horror; for if it was terrible with the sweet Miss Lucy, what would it not be with these strange ones who had survived through centuries, and who had been strengthened by the passing of the years; who would, if they could, have fought for their foul lives? . . .

Oh, my friend John, but it was butcher work; had I not been nerved by thoughts of other dead, and of the living over whom hung such a pall of fear, I could not have gone on. I tremble and tremble even yet, though till all was over, God be thanked, my nerve did stand. Had I not seen the repose in the first face, and the gladness that stole over it just ere the final dissolution came, as realization that the soul had been won, I could not have gone further with my butchery. I could not have endured the horrid screeching as the stake drove home; the plunging of writhing form, and lips of bloody foam. I should have fled in terror and left my work undone. But it is over! And the poor souls, I can pity them now and weep, as I think of them placid each in her full sleep of death, for a short moment ere fading. For, friend John, hardly had my knife severed the head of each, before the whole body began to melt away and crumble into its native dust, as though the death that should have come centuries agone had at last assert himself and say at once and loud 'I am here!'

Before I left the castle I so fixed its entrances that never more can the Count enter there Un-Dead.

When I stepped into the circle where Madam Mina slept, she woke from her sleep, and seeing me, cried out in pain that I had endured too much.

'Come!' she said, 'come away from this awful place! Let us go to meet my husband, who is, I know, coming towards us.' She was looking thin and pale and weak; but her eyes were pure and glowed with fervour. I was glad to see her paleness and her illness, for my mind was full of the fresh horror of that ruddy Vampire sleep.

And so with trust and hope, and yet full of fear, we go eastward to meet our friends – and *him* – whom Madam Mina tell me that she *know* are coming to meet us.

MINA HARKER'S JOURNAL

6 November. – It was late in the afternoon when the Professor and I took our way towards the east whence I knew Jonathan was coming. We did not go fast, though the way was steeply downhill, for we had to take heavy rugs and wraps with us; we dared not face the possibility of being left without warmth in the cold and the snow. We had to take some of our provisions too, for we were in a perfect desolation, and, so far as we could see through the snowfall, there was not even the sign of a habitation. When we had gone about a mile, I was tired with the heavy walking and sat down to rest. Then we looked back and saw where the clear line of Dracula's Castle cut the sky; for we were so deep under the hill whereon it was set that the angle of perspective of the Carpathian mountains was far below it. We saw it in all its grandeur, perched a thousand feet on the summit of a sheer precipice, and with seemingly a great gap between it and the steep of the adjacent mountain on any side. There was something wild and uncanny about the place. We could hear the distant howling of wolves. They were far off, but the sound, even though coming muffled through the deadening snowfall, was full of terror. I knew from the way Dr Van Helsing was searching about that he was trying to seek some strategic point, where we would be less exposed in case of attack. The rough roadway still led downwards; we could trace it through the drifted snow.

In a little while the Professor signalled to me, so I got up and joined him. He had found a wonderful spot, a sort of natural hollow in a rock, with an entrance like a doorway between two boulders. He took me by the hand and drew me in: 'See!' he said, 'here you will be in shelter; and if the wolves do come I can meet them one by one.' He brought in our furs, and made a snug nest for me, and got out some provisions and forced them upon me. But I could not eat; to even try to do so was repulsive to me, and, much as I would have liked to please him, I could not bring myself to the attempt. He looked very sad, but did not reproach me. Taking his field-glasses from the case, he stood on the top of the rock, and began to search the horizon. Suddenly he called out:—

'Look Madam Mina, look! look!' I sprang up and stood beside him on the rock; he handed me his glasses and pointed. The snow was now falling more heavily, and swirled about fiercely, for a high wind was beginning to blow. However, there were times when there were pauses between the snow-flurries, and I could see a long way round. From the height where we were it was possible to see a great distance; and far off, beyond the white waste of snow, I could see the river lying like a black ribbon in kinks and curls as it wound its way. Straight in front of us and not far off – in fact so near that I wondered we had not noticed before – came a group of mounted men hurrying along. In the midst of them was a cart, a long leiter-waggon, which swept from side to side, like a dog's tail wagging, with each stern inequality of the road. Outlined against the snow as they were, I could see from the men's clothes that they were peasants or gipsies of some kind.

On the cart was a great square chest. My heart leaped as I saw it, for I felt that the end was coming. The evening was now drawing close, and well I knew that at sunset the Thing, which was till then imprisoned there, would take new freedom and could in any of many forms elude all pursuit. In fear I turned to the Professor; to my consternation, however, he was not there. An instant later, I saw him below me. Round the rock he had drawn a circle, such as we had found shelter in last night. When he had completed it he stood beside me again, saying:—

'At least you shall be safe here from *him*!' He took the glasses from me, and at the next lull of the snow swept the whole space below us. 'See,' he said, 'they come quickly; they are flogging the horses, and galloping as hard as they can.' He paused and went on in a hollow voice:—

'They are racing for the sunset. We may be too late. God's will be done!' Down came another blinding rush of driving snow, and the whole landscape was blotted out. It soon passed, however, and once more his glasses were fixed on the plain. Then came a sudden cry:–

'Look! Look! Look! See, two horsemen follow fast, coming up from the south. It must be Quincey and John. Take the glass. Look, before the snow blots it all out!' I took it and looked. The two men might be Dr Seward and Mr Morris. I knew at all events that neither of them was Jonathan. At the same time I *knew* that Jonathan was not far off; looking around I saw on the north side of the coming party two other men, riding at break-neck speed. One of them I knew was Jonathan, and the other I took, of course, to be Lord Godalming. They, too, were pursuing the party with the cart. When I told the Professor he shouted in glee like a schoolboy, and, after looking intently till snowfall made sight impossible, he laid his Winchester rifle ready for use against the boulder at the opening of our shelter. 'They are all converging,' he said. 'When the time comes we shall have the gipsies on all sides.' I got out my revolver ready to hand, for whilst we were speaking the howling of wolves came louder and closer. When the snowstorm abated a moment we looked again. It was strange to see the snow falling in such heavy flakes close to us, and beyond, the sun shining more and more brightly as it sank down towards the far mountain tops. Sweeping the glass all around us I could see here and there dots moving singly and in twos and threes and larger numbers – the wolves were gathering for their prey.

Every instant seemed an age whilst we waited. The wind came now in fierce bursts, and the snow was driven with fury as it swept upon us in circling eddies. At times we could not see an arm's length before us; but at others as the hollow-sounding wind swept by us, it seemed to clear the air-space around us so that we could see far off. We had of late been so accustomed to watch for sunrise and sunset, that we knew with fair accuracy when it would be; and we knew that before long the sun would set.

It was hard to believe that by our watches it was less than an hour that we waited in that rocky shelter before the various bodies began to converge close upon us. The wind came now with fiercer and more bitter sweeps, and more steadily from the north. It seemingly had driven the snow-clouds from us, for, with only occasional bursts, the snow fell. We could distinguish clearly the individuals of each party, the pursued and the pursuers. Strangely enough those pursued did not seem to realize, or at least to care, that they were pursued; they seemed, however, to hasten with redoubled speed as the sun dropped lower and lower on the mountain tops.

Closer and closer they drew. The Professor and I crouched down behind our rock, and held our weapons ready: I could see that he was determined that they should not pass. One and all were quite unaware of our presence.

All at once two voices shouted out to 'Halt!' One was my Jonathan's, raised in a high key of passion; the other, Mr Morris's strong resolute tone of quiet command. The gipsies may not have known the language, but there was no mistaking the tone, in whatever tongue the words were spoken. Instinctively they reined in, and at the instant Lord Godalming and Jonathan dashed up at one side and Dr Seward and Mr Morris on the other. The leader of the gipsies, a splendid-looking fellow, who sat his horse like a centaur, waved them back, and in a fierce voice gave to his companions some word to proceed. They lashed the horses, which sprang forward; but the four men raised their Winchester rifles, and in an unmistakable way commanded them to stop. At the same moment Dr Van Helsing and I rose behind the rock and pointed our weapons at them. Seeing that they were surrounded, the men tightened their reins and drew up. The leader turned to them and gave a word, at which every man of the gipsy party drew what weapon he carried, knife or pistol, and held himself in readiness to attack. Issue was joined in an instant.

The leader, with a quick movement of his rein, threw his horse out in front, and pointing first to the sun – now close down on the hill-tops – and then to the castle, said something which I did not understand. For answer all four men of our party threw themselves from their horses and dashed towards the cart. I should have felt terrible fear at seeing Jonathan in such danger, but that the ardour of battle must have been upon me as well as the rest of them; I felt no fear, but only a wild, surging desire to do something. Seeing a quick movement of our parties, the leader of the gipsies gave a command; his men instantly formed round the cart in a sort of undisciplined endeavour, each one shouldering and pushing the other in his eagerness to carry out the order.

In the midst of this I could see that Jonathan on one side of the ring of men, and Quincey on the other, were forcing a way to the cart; it was evident that they were bent on finishing their task before the sun should set. Nothing seemed to stop or even to hinder them. Neither the levelled weapons or the flashing knives of the gipsies in front, or the howling of the wolves behind, appeared to even attract their attention. Jonathan's impetuosity, and the manifest singleness of his purpose, seemed to overawe those in front of him; instinctively they cowered aside and let him pass. In an instant he had jumped upon the cart, and, with a strength which seemed incredible, raised the great box, and flung it over the wheel to the ground. In the meantime, Mr Morris had had to use force to pass through his side of the ring of Szgany. All the time I had been breathlessly watching Jonathan I had, with the tail of my eye, seen him pressing desperately forward, and had seen the knives of the gipsies flash as he won a way through them, and they cut at him. He parried with his great bowie knife, and at first I thought that he too had come through in safety; but as he sprang beside Jonathan, who had by now jumped from the cart, I could see that with his left hand he was clutching at his side, and that the blood was spurting through his fingers. He did not delay notwithstanding this, for as Jonathan, with desperate energy, attacked one end of the chest, attempting to prise off the lid with his great Kukri knife, he attacked the other frantically with his bowie. Under the efforts of both men the lid began to yield; the nails grew with a quick screeching sound, and the top of the box was thrown back.

By this time the gipsies, seeing themselves covered by the Winchesters, and at the mercy of Lord Godalming and Dr Seward, had given in and made no further resistance. The sun was almost down on the mountain tops, and the shadows of the whole group fell long upon the snow. I saw the Count lying within the box upon the earth, some of which the rude falling from the cart had scattered over him. He was deathly pale, just like a waxen image, and the red eyes glared with the horrible vindictive look which I knew too well.

As I looked, the eyes saw the sinking sun, and the look of hate in them turned to triumph.

But, on the instant, came the sweep and flash of Jonathan's great knife. I shrieked as I saw it shear through the throat; whilst at the same moment Mr Morris' bowie knife plunged in the heart.

It was like a miracle; but before our very eyes, and almost in the drawing of a breath, the whole body crumbled into dust and passed from our sight.

I shall be glad as long as I live that even in that moment of final dissolution there was in the face a look of peace, such as I never could have imagined might have rested there.

The Castle of Dracula now stood out against the red sky, and every stone of its broken battlements was articulated against the light of the setting sun.

The gipsies, taking us as in some way the cause of the extraordinary disappearance of the dead man, turned, without a word, and rode away as if for their lives. Those who were unmounted jumped upon the leiter-waggon and shouted to the horsemen not to desert them. The wolves, which had withdrawn to a safe distance, followed in their wake, leaving us alone.

Mr Morris, who had sunk to the ground, leaned on his elbow, holding his hand pressed to his side; the blood still gushed through his fingers. I flew to him, for the Holy circle did not now keep me back; so did the two doctors. Jonathan knelt behind him and the wounded man laid back his head on his shoulder. With a sigh he took, with a feeble effort, my hand in that of his own which was unstained. He must have seen the anguish of my heart in his face, for he smiled at me and said:–

'I am only too happy to have been of any service! Oh, God!' he cried suddenly, struggling up to a sitting posture and pointing to me, 'it was worth this to die! Look! look!'

The sun was now right down upon the mountain top, and the red gleams fell upon my face, so that it was bathed in rosy light. With one impulse the men sank on their knees, and a deep and earnest 'Amen' broke from all as their eyes followed the pointing of his finger as the dying man spoke:–

'Now God be thanked that all has not been in vain! See! the snow is not more stainless than her forehead! The curse has passed away!'

And, to our bitter grief, with a smile and silence, he died, a gallant gentleman.

NOTE

Seven years ago we all went through the flames; and the happiness of some of us since then is, we think, well worth the pain we endured. It is an added joy to Mina and to me that our boy's birthday is the same day as that on which Quincey Morris died. His mother holds, I know, the secret belief that some of our brave friend's spirit has passed into him. His bundle of names links all our little band of men together; but we call him Quincey.

In the summer of this year we made a journey to Transylvania, and went over the old ground which was, and is, to us so full of vivid and terrible memories. It was almost impossible to believe that the things which we had seen with our own eyes and heard with our own ears were living truths. Every trace of all that had been was blotted out. The Castle stood as before, reared high above a waste of desolation.

When we got home we got to talking of the old time – which we could all look back on without despair, for Godalming and Seward are both happily married. I took the papers from the safe where they have been ever since our return so long ago. We were struck with the fact that, in all the mass of material of which the record is composed, there is hardly one authentic document! nothing but a mass of type-writing, except the later note-books of Mina and Seward and myself, and Van Helsing's memorandum. We could hardly ask anyone, even did we wish to, to accept these as proofs of so wild a story. Van Helsing summed it all up as he said, with our boy on his knee:–

'We want no proofs; we ask none to believe us! This boy will some day know what a brave and gallant woman his mother is. Already he knows her sweetness and loving care; later on he will understand how some men so loved her, that they did dare much for her sake.'

JONATHAN HARKER

The Lair
of the
White Worm

To my friend
BERTHA NICOLL
with affectionate esteem

1

ADAM SALTON ARRIVES

Adam Salton sauntered into the Empire Club, Sydney, and found awaiting him a letter from his grand-uncle. He had first heard from the old gentleman less than a year before, when Richard Salton had claimed kinship, stating that he had been unable to write earlier, as he had found it very difficult to trace his grand-nephew's address. Adam was delighted and replied cordially; he had often heard his father speak of the older branch of the family with whom his people had long lost touch. Some interesting correspondence had ensued. Adam eagerly opened the letter which had only just arrived, and conveyed a cordial invitation to stop with his grand-uncle at Lesser Hill, for as long a time as he could spare.

'Indeed,' Richard Salton went on, 'I am in hopes that you will make your permanent home here. You see, my dear boy, you and I are all that remain of our race, and it but fitting that you should succeed me when the time comes. In this year of grace, 1860, I am close on eighty years of age, and though we have been a long-lived race, the span of life cannot be prolonged beyond reasonable bounds. I am prepared to like you, and to make your home with me as happy as you could wish. So do come at once on receipt of this, and find the welcome I am waiting to give you. I send, in case such may make matters easy for you, a banker's draft for £200. Come soon, so that we may both of us enjoy many happy days together. If you are able to give me the pleasure of seeing you, send me as soon as you can a letter telling me when to expect you. Then when you arrive at Plymouth or Southampton or whatever port you are bound for, wait on board, and I will meet you at the earliest hour possible.'

* * *

Old Mr Salton was delighted when Adam's reply arrived and sent a groom hot-foot to his crony, Sir Nathaniel de Salis, to inform him that his grand-nephew was due at Southampton on the twelfth of June.

Mr Salton gave instructions to have ready a carriage early on the

311

important day, to start for Stafford, where he would catch the 11.40 a.m. train. He would stay that night with his grand-nephew, either on the ship, which would be a new experience for him, or, if his guest should prefer it, at a hotel. In either case they would start in the early morning for home. He had given instructions to his bailiff to send the postilion carriage on to Southampton, to be ready for their journey home, and to arrange for relays of his own horses to be sent on at once. He intended that his grand-nephew, who had been all his life in Australia, should see something of rural England on the drive. He had plenty of young horses of his own breeding and breaking, and could depend on a journey memorable to the young man. The luggage would be sent on by rail to Stafford, where one of his carts would meet it. Mr Salton, during the journey to Southampton, often wondered if his grand-nephew was as much excited as he was at the idea of meeting so near a relation for the first time; and it was with an effort that he controlled himself. The endless railway lines and switches round the Southampton docks fired his anxiety afresh.

As the train drew up on the dockside, he was getting his hand traps together, when the carriage door was wrenched open and a young man jumped in.

'How are you, uncle? I recognized you from the photo you sent me! I wanted to meet you as soon as I could, but everything is so strange to me that I didn't quite know what to do. However, here I am. I am glad to see you, sir. I have been dreaming of this happiness for thousands of miles; now I find that the reality beats all the dreaming!' As he spoke the old man and the young one were heartily wringing each other's hands.

The meeting so auspiciously begun proceeded well. Adam, seeing that the old man was interested in the novelty of the ship, suggested that he should stay the night on board, and that he would himself be ready to start at any hour and go anywhere that the other suggested. This affectionate willingness to fall in with his own plans quite won the old man's heart. He warmly accepted the invitation, and at once they became not only on terms of affectionate relationship, but almost like old friends. The heart of the old man, which had been empty for so long, found a new delight. The young man found, on landing in the old country, a welcome and a surrounding in full harmony with all his dreams throughout his wanderings and solitude, and the promise of a fresh and adventurous life. It was not long before the old man accepted him to full relationship by calling him by his Christian name. After a long talk on affairs of interest, they retired to the cabin, which the elder was to share. Richard Salton put his hands affectionately on the boy's shoulders – though Adam was in his twenty-seventh year, he was a boy, and always would be to his grand-uncle.

'I am so glad to find you as you are, my dear boy – just such a young man as I had always hoped for as a son, in the days when I still had such hopes. However, that is all past. But, thank God, there is a new life to begin for both of us. To you must be the larger part – but there is still time for some of it to be shared in common. I have waited till we should have seen each other to enter upon the subject; for I thought it better not to tie up your young life to my old one till we should have sufficient personal knowledge to justify such a venture. Now I can, so far as I am concerned, enter into it freely, since from the moment my eyes rested on you I saw my son – as he shall be, God willing – if he chooses such a course himself.'

'Indeed I do, sir – with all my heart!'

'Thank you, Adam, for that.' The old man's eyes filled and his voice trembled. Then, after a long silence between them, he went on: 'When I heard you were coming I made my will. It was well that your interests should be protected from that moment on. Here is the deed – keep it, Adam. All I have shall belong to you; and if love and good wishes, or the memory of them, can make life sweeter, yours shall be a happy one. Now, my dear boy, let us turn in. We start early in the morning and have a long drive before us. I hope you don't mind driving? I was going to have the old travelling carriage in which my grandfather, your great-grand-uncle, went to Court when William IV was king. It is all right – they built well in those days – and it has been kept in perfect order. But I think I have done better: I have sent the carriage in which I travel myself. The horses are of my own breeding, and relays of them shall take us all the way. I hope you like horses? They have long been one of my greatest interests in life.'

'I love them, sir, and I am happy to say I have many of my own. My father gave me a horse farm for myself when I was eighteen. I devoted myself to it, and it has gone on. Before I came away, my steward gave me a memorandum that we have in my own place more than a thousand, nearly all good.'

'I am glad, my boy. Another link between us.'

'Just fancy what a delight it will be, sir, to see so much of England – and with you!'

'Thank you again, my boy. I will tell you all about your future home and its surroundings as we go. We shall travel in old-fashioned state, I tell you. My grandfather always drove four-in-hand; and so shall you.'

'Oh, thanks, sir, thanks. May I take the ribbons sometimes?'

'Whenever you choose, Adam. The team is your own. Every horse we use to-day is to be your own.'

'You are too generous, uncle!'

'Not at all. Only an old man's selfish pleasure. It is not every day that an heir to the old home comes back. And – oh, by the way. . . . No, we had better turn in now – I shall tell you the rest in the morning.'

2

THE CASWALLS OF CASTRA REGIS

Mr Salton had all his life been an early riser, and necessarily an early waker. But early as he woke on the next morning – and although there was an excuse for not prolonging sleep in the constant whirr and rattle of the 'donkey' engine winches of the great ship – he met the eyes of Adam fixed on him from his berth. His grand-nephew had given him the sofa, occupying the lower berth himself. The old man, despite his great strength and normal activity, was somewhat tired by his long journey of the day before, and the prolonged and exciting interview which followed it. So he was glad to lie still and rest his body, whilst his mind was actively exercised in taking in all he could of his strange surrounding. Adam, too, after the pastoral habit to which he had been bred, woke with the dawn, and was ready to enter on the experiences of the new day whenever it might suit his elderly companion. It was little wonder, then, that, so soon as each realized the other's readiness, they simultaneously jumped up and began to dress. The steward had by previous instructions early breakfast prepared, and it was not long before they went down the gangway on shore in search of the carriage.

They found Mr Salton's bailiff looking out for them on the dock, and he brought them at once to where the carriage was waiting in the street. Richard Salton pointed out with pride to his young companion the suitability of the vehicle for every need of travel. To it were harnessed four useful horses, with a postilion to each pair.

'See,' said the old man proudly, 'how it has all the luxuries of useful travel – silence and isolation as well as speed. There is nothing to obstruct the view of those travelling and no one to overhear what they may say. I have used that trap for a quarter of a century, and I never saw one more suitable for travel. You shall test it shortly. We are going to drive through the heart of England; and as we go I'll tell you what I was speaking of last night. Our route is to be by Salisbury, Bath, Bristol, Cheltenham, Worcester, Stafford; and so home.'

Adam remained silent a few minutes, during which he seemed all eyes, for he perpetually ranged the whole circle of the horizon.

'Has our journey to-day, sir,' he asked, 'any special relation to what you said last night that you wanted to tell me?'

'Not directly; but indirectly, everything.'

'Won't you tell me now – I see we cannot be overheard – and if anything strikes you as we go along, just run it in. I shall understand.'

So old Salton spoke:

'To begin at the beginning, Adam. That lecture of yours on "The Romans in Britain", a report of which you posted to me, set me thinking – in addition to telling me your tastes. I wrote to you at once and asked you to come home, for it struck me that if you were fond of historical research – as seemed a fact – this was exactly the place for you, in addition to its being the home of your own forebears. If you could learn so much of the British Romans so far away in New South Wales, where there cannot be even a tradition of them, what might you not make of the same amount of study on the very spot. Where we are going is in the real heart of the old kingdom of Mercia, where there are traces of all the various nationalities which made up the conglomerate which became Britain.'

'I rather gathered that you had some more definite – more personal reason for my hurrying. After all, history can keep – except in the making!'

'Quite right, my boy. I had a reason such as you very wisely guessed. I was anxious for you to be here when a rather important phase of our local history occurred.'

'What is that, if I may ask, sir?'

'Certainly. The principal land-owner of our part of the county is on his way home, and there will be a great home-coming, which you may care to see. The fact is, for more than a century the various owners in the succession here, with the exception of a short time, have lived abroad.'

'How is that, sir, if I may ask?'

'The great house and estate in our part of the world is Castra Regis, the family seat of the Caswall family. The last owner who lived here was Edgar Caswall, grandfather of the man who is coming here – and he was the only one who stayed even a short time. This man's grandfather, also named Edgar – they keep the tradition of the family Christian name – quarrelled with his family and went to live abroad, not keeping up any intercourse, good or bad, with his relatives, although this particular Edgar, as I told you, did visit his family estate, yet his son was born and lived and died abroad, while his grandson, the latest inheritor, was also born and lived abroad till he was over thirty – his present age. This was the second line of absentees. The great estate of Castra Regis has had no knowledge of its owner for five generations – covering more than a hundred and twenty years. It has been well administered, however, and no tenant or other connected with it has had anything of which to complain. All the same, there has been much natural anxiety to see the new owner, and we are all excited about the event of his coming. Even I

315

am, though I own my own estate, which, though adjacent, is quite apart from Castra Regis. – Here we are now in new ground for you. That is the spire of Salisbury Cathedral, and when we leave that we shall be getting close to the old Roman county, and you will naturally want your eyes. So we shall shortly have to keep our minds on old Mercia. However, you need not be disappointed. My old friend, Sir Nathaniel de Salis, who, like myself, is a freeholder near Castra Regis – his estate, Doom Tower, is over the border of Derbyshire, on the Peak – is coming to stay with me for the festivities to welcome Edgar Caswall. He is just the sort of man you will like. He is devoted to history, and is President of the Mercian Archæological Society. He knows more of our own part of the country, with its history and its people, than anyone else. I expect he will have arrived before us, and we three can have a long chat after dinner. He is also our local geologist and natural historian. So you and he will have many interests in common. Amongst other things, he has a special knowledge of the Peak and its caverns, and knows all the old legends of prehistoric times.'

They spent the night at Cheltenham, and on the following morning resumed their journey to Stafford. Adam's eyes were in constant employment, and it was not till Salton declared that they had now entered on the last stage of their journey, that he referred to Sir Nathaniel's coming.

As the dusk was closing down, they drove on to Lesser Hill, Mr Salton's house. It was now too dark to see any details of their surroundings. Adam could just see that it was on the top of a hill, not quite so high as that which was covered by the Castle, on whose tower flew the flag, and which was all ablaze with moving lights, manifestly used in the preparations for the festivities on the morrow. So Adam deferred his curiosity till daylight. His grand-uncle was met at the door by a fine old man, who greeted him warmly.

'I came over early as you wished. I suppose this is your grand-nephew – I am glad to meet you, Mr Adam Salton. I am Nathaniel de Salis, and your uncle is one of my oldest friends.'

Adam, from the moment of their eyes meeting, felt as if they were already friends. The meeting was a new note of welcome to those that had already sounded in his ears.

The cordiality with which Sir Nathaniel and Adam met, made the imparting of information easy. Sir Nathaniel was a clever man of the world, who had travelled much, and within a certain area studied deeply. He was a brilliant conversationalist, as was to be expected from a successful diplomatist, even under unstimulating conditions. But he had been touched and to a certain extent fired by the younger man's evident admiration and willingness to learn from him. Accordingly the conversation, which began on the most friendly terms, soon warmed to an interest above proof, as the old man spoke of it next day to Richard Salton. He knew already that his old friend wanted his grand-nephew to learn all he could of the subject in hand, and so had during his journey from the Peak put his thoughts in sequence for narration and explanation. Accordingly, Adam had only to listen and he must learn much that he wanted to know. When dinner was over and the servants had withdrawn, leaving the three men at their wine, Sir Nathaniel began.

'I gather from your uncle – by the way, I suppose we had better speak of you as uncle and nephew, instead of going into exact relationship? In fact, your uncle is so old and dear a friend, that, with your permission, I shall drop formality with you altogether and speak of you and to you as Adam, as though you were his son.'

'I should like,' answered the young man, 'nothing better!'

The answer warmed the hearts of both the old men, but, with the usual avoidance of Englishmen of emotional subjects personal to themselves, they instinctively returned to the previous question. Sir Nathaniel took the lead.

'I understand, Adam, that your uncle has posted you regarding the relationships of the Caswall family?'

'Partly, sir; but I understood that I was to hear minuter details from you – if you would be so good.'

'I shall be delighted to tell you anything so far as my knowledge goes. Well, the first Caswall in our immediate record is Edgar, head of the family and owner of the estate, who came into his kingdom just about the time that George III died. He had one son of about twenty-four. There was a violent quarrel between the two. No one of this generation has any idea of the cause; but, considering the family characteristics, we may take it for granted that though it was deep and violent, it was on the surface trivial.

'The result of the quarrel was that the son left the house without a reconciliation or without even telling his father where he was going. He never came back again. A few years after, he died, without having in the meantime exchanged a word or a letter with his father. He married abroad and left one son, who seems to have been brought up in ignorance of all belonging to him. The gulf between them appears to have been unbridgeable; for in time this son married and in turn had a son, but neither joy nor sorrow brought the sundered together. Under such conditions no *rapprochement* was to be looked for, and an utter indifference, founded at best on ignorance, took the place of family affection – even on community of interests. It was only due to the

317

watchfulness of the lawyers that the birth of this new heir was ever made known. He actually spent a few months in the ancestral home.

'After this the family interest merely rested on heirship of the estate. As no other children have been born to any of the newer generations in the intervening years, all hopes of heritage are now centred in the grandson of this man.

'Now, it will be well for you to bear in mind the prevailing characteristics of this race. These were well preserved and unchanging; one and all they are the same: cold, selfish, dominant, reckless of consequences in pursuit of their own will. It was not that they did not keep faith, though that was a matter which gave them little concern, but that they took care to think beforehand of what they should do in order to gain their own ends. If they should make a mistake, someone else should bear the burthen of it. This was so perpetually recurrent that it seemed to be a part of a fixed policy. It was no wonder that, whatever changes took place, they were always ensured in their own possessions. They were absolutely cold and hard by nature. Not one of them – so far as we have any knowledge – was ever known to be touched by the softer sentiments, to swerve from his purpose, or hold his hand in obedience to the dictates of his heart. The pictures and effigies of them all show their adherence to the early Roman type. Their eyes were full; their hair, of raven blackness, grew thick and close and curly. Their figures were massive and typical of strength.

'The thick black hair, growing low down on the neck, told of vast physical strength and endurance. But the most remarkable characteristic is the eyes. Black, piercing, almost unendurable, they seem to contain in themselves a remarkable will power which there is no gainsaying. It is a power that is partly racial and partly individual: a power impregnated with some mysterious quality, partly hypnotic, partly mesmeric, which seems to take away from eyes that meet them all power of resistance – nay, all power of wishing to resist. With eyes like those, set in that all-commanding face, one would need to be strong indeed to think of resisting the inflexible will that lay behind.

'You may think, Adam, that all this is imagination on my part, especially as I have never seen any of them. So it is, but imagination based on deep study. I have made use of all I know or can surmise logically regarding this strange race. With such strange compelling qualities, is it any wonder that there is abroad an idea that in the race there is some demoniac possession, which tends to a more definite belief that certain individuals have in the past sold themselves to the Devil?

'But I think we had better go to bed now. We have a lot to get through to-morrow, and I want you to have your brain clear, and all your susceptibilities fresh. Moreover, I want you to come with me for an early walk, during which we may notice, whilst the matter is fresh in our minds, the peculiar disposition of this place – not merely your grand-uncle's estate, but the lie of the country around it. There are many things on which we may seek – and perhaps find – enlightenment. The more we know at the start, the more things which may come into our view will develop themselves.'

3

DIANA'S GROVE

Curiosity took Adam Salton out of bed in the early morning, but when he had dressed and gone downstairs, he found that, early as he was, Sir Nathaniel was ahead of him. The old gentleman was quite prepared for a long walk, and they started at once.

Sir Nathaniel, without speaking, led the way to the east, down the hill. When they had descended and risen again, they found themselves on the eastern brink of a steep hill. It was of lesser height than that on which the Castle was situated; but it was so placed that it commanded the various hills that crowned the ridge. All along the ridge the rock cropped out, bare and bleak, but broken in rough natural castellation. The form of the ridge was a segment of a circle, with the higher points inland to the west. In the centre rose the Castle, on the highest point of all. Between the various rocky excrescences were groups of trees of various sizes and heights, amongst some of which were what, in the early morning light, looked like ruins. These – whatever they were – were of massive grey stone, probably limestone rudely cut – if indeed they were not shaped naturally. The fall of the ground was steep all along the ridge, so steep that here and there both trees and rocks and buildings seemed to overhang the plain far below, through which ran many streams.

Sir Nathaniel stopped and looked around, as though to lose nothing of the effect. The sun had climbed the eastern sky and was making all details clear. He pointed with a sweeping gesture, as though calling Adam's attention to the extent of the view. Having done so, he covered the ground more slowly, as though inviting attention to detail. Adam was a willing and attentive pupil, and followed his motions exactly, missing – or trying to miss – nothing.

'I have brought you here, Adam, because it seems to me that this is the spot on which to begin our investigations. You have now in front of you almost the whole of the ancient kingdom of Mercia. In fact, we see the whole of it except that furthest part, which is covered by the Welsh Marches and those parts which are hidden from where we stand by the high ground of the immediate west. We can see – theoretically – the whole of the eastern bound of the kingdom, which ran south from the Humber to the Wash. I want you to bear in mind the trend of the ground, for some time, sooner or later, we shall do well to have it in our mind's eye when we are considering the ancient traditions and superstitions, and are trying to find the *rationale* of them. Each legend, each superstition which we receive, will help in the understanding and possible elucidation of the others. And as all such have a local basis, we can come closer to the truth – or the probability – by knowing the local conditions as we go along. It will help us to bring to our aid such geological truth as we may have between us. For instance, the building materials used in various ages can afford their own lessons to understanding eyes. The very heights and shapes and materials of these hills – nay, even of the wide plain that lies between us and the sea – have in themselves the materials of enlightening books.'

'For instance, sir?' said Adam, venturing a question.

'Well, look at those hills which surround the main one where the site for the Castle was wisely chosen – on the highest ground. Take the others. There is something ostensible in each of them, and in all probability something unseen and unproved, but to be imagined, also.'

'For instance?' continued Adam.

'Let us take them *seriatim*. That to the east, where the trees are, lower down – that was once the location of a Roman temple, possibly founded on a pre-existing Druidical one. Its name implies the former, and the grove of ancient oaks suggests the latter.'

'Please explain.'

'The old name translated means "Diana's Grove". Then the next one higher than it, but just beyond it, is called "*Mercy*" – in all probability a corruption or familiarization of the word *Mercia*, with a Roman pun included. We learn from early manuscripts that the place was called *Vilula Misericordi*. It was originally a nunnery, founded by Queen Bertha, but done away with by King Penda, the reactionary to Paganism after St Augustine. Then comes your uncle's place – Lesser Hill. Though it is so close to the Castle, it is not connected with it. It is a freehold, and, so far as we know, of equal age. It has always belonged to your family.'

'Then there only remains the Castle!'

'That is all; but its history contains the histories of all the others – in fact, the whole history of early England.' Sir Nathaniel, seeing the expectant look on Adam's face, went on:

'The history of the Castle has no beginning so far as we know. The furthest records or surmises or inferences simply accept it as existing. Some of these – guesses, let us call them – seem to show that there was some sort of structure there when the Romans came, therefore, it must have been a place of importance in Druid times – if indeed that was the beginning. Naturally the Romans accepted it, as they did everything of the kind that was, or might be, useful. The change is shown or inferred in the name Castra. It was the highest protected ground, and so naturally became the most important of their camps. A study of the map will show you that it must have been a most important centre. It both protected the advances already made to the north, and helped to dominate the sea coast. It sheltered the western marches, beyond which lay savage Wales – and danger. It provided a means of getting to the Severn, round which lay the great Roman roads then coming into existence, and made possible the great waterway to the heart of England – through the Severn and its tributaries. It brought the east and the west together by the swiftest and easiest ways known to those times. And, finally, it provided means of descent on London and all the expanse of country watered by the Thames.

'With such a centre, already known and organized, we can easily see that each fresh wave of invasion – the Angles, the Saxons, the Danes, and the Normans – found it a desirable possession and so ensured its upholding. In the earlier centuries it was merely a vantage ground. But when the victorious Romans brought with them the heavy solid fortifications impregnable to the weapons of the time, its commanding position alone ensured its adequate building and equipment. Then it was that the fortified camp of the Cæsars developed into the castle of the king. As we are as yet ignorant of the names of the first kings of Mercia, no historian has been able to guess which of them made it his ultimate defence; and I suppose we shall never know now. In process of time, as the arts of war developed, it increased in size and strength, and although recorded details are lacking, the history is written not merely in the stone of its building, but is inferred in the changes of structure. Then the sweeping changes which followed the Norman Conquest wiped out all lesser records than its own. To-day we must accept it as one of the earliest castles of the Conquest, probably not later than the time of Henry I. Roman and Norman were both wise in their retention of places of approved strength or utility. So it was that these surrounding heights, already established and to a certain extent proved, were retained. Indeed, such characteristics as already pertained to them were preserved, and to-day afford to us lessons regarding things which have themselves long since passed away.

'So much for the fortified heights; but the hollows too have their own story. But how the time passes! We must hurry home, or your uncle will wonder what has become of us.'

He started with long steps towards Lesser Hill, and Adam was soon furtively running in order to keep up with him.

4

THE LADY ARABELLA MARCH

'Now, there is no hurry, but so soon as you are both ready we shall start,' Mr Salton said when breakfast had begun. 'I want to take you first to see a remarkable relic of Mercia, and then we'll go to Liverpool through what is called "The Great Vale of Cheshire". You may be disappointed, but take care not to prepare your mind' – this to Adam – 'for anything stupendous or heroic. You would not think the place a vale at all, unless you were told so beforehand, and had confidence in the veracity of the teller. We should get to the Landing Stage in time to meet the *West African*, and catch Mr Caswall as he comes ashore. We want to do him honour – and, besides, it will be more pleasant to have the introductions over before we go to his *fête* at the Castle.'

The carriage was ready, the same as had been used the previous day, but there were different horses – magnificent animals, and keen for work. Breakfast was soon over, and they shortly took their places. The postilions had their orders, and were quickly on their way at an exhilarating pace.

Presently, in obedience to Mr Salton's signal, the carriage drew up opposite a great heap of stones by the wayside.

'Here, Adam,' he said, 'is something that you of all men should not pass by unnoticed. That heap of stones brings us at once to the dawn of the Anglian kingdom. It was begun more than a thousand years ago – in the latter part of the seventh century – in memory of a murder. Wulfere, King of Mercia, nephew of Penda, here murdered his two sons for embracing Christianity. As was the custom of the time, each passer-by added a stone to the memorial heap. Penda represented heathen reaction after St Augustine's mission. Sir Nathaniel can tell you as much as you want about this, and put you, if you wish, on the track of such accurate knowledge as there is.'

Whilst they were looking at the heap of stones, they noticed that another carriage had drawn up beside them, and the passenger – there was only one – was regarding them curiously. The carriage was an old heavy travelling one, with arms blazoned on it gorgeously. The men took off their hats, as the occupant, a lady, addressed them.

'How do you do, Sir Nathaniel? How do you do, Mr Salton? I hope you have not met with any accident. Look at me!'

As she spoke she pointed to where one of the heavy springs was broken across, the broken metal showing bright. Adam spoke up at once:

'Oh, that can soon be put right.'

'Soon? There is no one near who can mend a break like that.'

'I can.'

'You!' She looked incredulously at the dapper young gentleman who spoke. 'You – why, it's a workman's job.'

'All right, I am a workman – though that is not the only sort of work I do. I am an Australian, and, as we have to move about fast, we are all trained to farriery and such mechanics as come into travel – I am quite at your service.'

'I hardly know how to thank you for your kindness, of which I gladly avail myself. I don't know what else I can do, as I wish to meet Mr Caswall of Castra Regis, who arrives home from Africa to-day. It is a notable home-coming; all the countryside want to do him honour.' She looked at the old men and quickly made up her mind as to the identity of the stranger. 'You must be Mr Adam Salton of Lesser Hill. I am Lady Arabella March of Diana's Grove.' As she spoke she turned slightly to Mr Salton, who took the hint and made a formal introduction.

So soon as this was done, Adam took some tools from his uncle's carriage, and at once began work on the broken spring. He was an expert workman, and the breach was soon made good. Adam was gathering the tools which he had been using – which, after the manner of all workmen, had been scattered about – when he noticed that several black snakes had crawled out from the heap of stones and were gathering round him. This naturally occupied his mind, and he was not thinking of anything else when he noticed Lady Arabella, who had opened the door of the carriage, slip from it with a quick gliding motion. She was already among the snakes when he called out to warn her. But there seemed to be no need of warning. The snakes had turned and were wriggling back to the mound as quickly as they could. He laughed to himself behind his teeth as he whispered, 'No need to fear there. They seem much more afraid of her than she of them.' All the same he began to beat on the ground with a stick which was lying close to him, with the instinct of one used to such vermin. In an instant he was alone beside the mound with Lady Arabella, who appeared quite unconcerned at the incident. Then he took a long look at

323

her, and her dress alone was sufficient to attract attention. She was clad in some kind of soft white stuff, which clung close to her form, showing to the full every movement of her sinuous figure. She wore a close-fitting cap of some fine fur of dazzling white. Coiled round her white throat was a large necklace of emeralds, whose profusion of colour dazzled when the sun shone on them. Her voice was peculiar, very low and sweet, and so soft that the dominant note was of sibilation. Her hands, too, were peculiar – long, flexible, white, with a strange movement as of waving gently to and fro.

She appeared quite at ease, and, after thanking Adam, said that if any of his uncle's party were going to Liverpool she would be most happy to join forces.

'Whilst you are staying here, Mr Salton, you must look on the grounds of Diana's Grove as your own, so that you may come and go just as you do in Lesser Hill. There are some fine views, and not a few natural curiosities which are sure to interest you, if you are a student of natural history – especially of an earlier kind, when the world was younger.'

The heartiness with which she spoke, and the warmth of her words – not of her manner, which was cold and distant – made him suspicious. In the meantime both his uncle and Sir Nathaniel had thanked her for the invitation – of which, however, they said they were unable to avail themselves. Adam had a suspicion that, though she answered regretfully, she was in reality relieved. When he had got into the carriage with the two old men, and they had driven off, he was not surprised when Sir Nathaniel spoke.

'I could not but feel that she was glad to be rid of us. She can play her game better alone!'

'What is her game?' asked Adam unthinkingly.

'All the county knows it, my boy. Caswall is a very rich man. Her husband was rich when she married him – or seemed to be. When he committed suicide, it was found that he had nothing left, and the estate was mortgaged up to the hilt. Her only hope is in a rich marriage. I suppose I need not draw any conclusion; you can do that as well as I can.'

Adam remained silent nearly all the time they were travelling through the alleged Vale of Cheshire. He thought much during that journey and came to several conclusions, though his lips were unmoved. One of these conclusions was that he would be very careful about paying any attention to Lady Arabella. He was himself a rich man, how rich not even his uncle had the least idea, and would have been surprised had he known.

The remainder of the journey was uneventful, and upon arrival at Liverpool they went aboard the *West African*, which had just come to the landing-stage. There his uncle introduced himself to Mr Caswall, and followed this up by introducing Sir Nathaniel and then Adam.

The newcomer received them graciously, and said what a pleasure it was to be coming home after so long an absence of his family from their old seat. Adam was pleased at the warmth of the reception; but he could not avoid a feeling of repugnance at the man's face. He was trying hard to overcome this when a diversion was caused by the arrival of Lady Arabella. The diversion was welcome to all; the two Saltons and Sir Nathaniel were shocked at Caswall's face – so hard, so ruthless, so selfish, so dominant. 'God help any,' was the common thought, 'who is under the domination of such a man!'

Presently his African servant approached him, and at once their thoughts changed to a larger toleration. Caswall looked indeed a savage – but a cultured savage. In him were traces of the softening civilization of ages – of some of the higher instincts and education of man, no matter how rudimentary these might be. But the face of Oolanga, as his master called him, was unreformed, unsoftened savage, and inherent in it were all the hideous possibilities of a lost, devil-ridden child of the forest and the swamp. Lady Arabella and Oolanga arrived almost simultaneously, and Adam was surprised to notice what effect their appearance had on each other. The woman seemed as if she would not – could not – condescend to exhibit any concern or interest in such a creature. On the other hand, the negro's bearing was such as in itself to justify her pride. He treated her not merely as a slave treats his master, but as a worshipper would treat a deity. He knelt before her with his hands outstretched and his forehead in the dust. So long as she remained he did not move; it was only when she went over to Caswall that he relaxed his attitude of devotion and stood by respectfully.

Adam spoke to his own man, Davenport, who was standing by, having arrived with the bailiff of Lesser Hill, who had followed Mr Salton in a pony trap. As he spoke, he pointed to an attentive ship's steward, and presently the two men were conversing.

'I think we ought to be moving,' Mr Salton said to Adam. 'I have some things to do in Liverpool, and I am sure that both Mr Caswall and Lady Arabella would like to get under way for Castra Regis.'

'I too, sir, would like to do something,' replied Adam. 'I want to find out where Ross, the animal merchant, lives – I want to take a small animal home with me, if you don't mind. He is only a little thing, and will be no trouble.'

'Of course not, my boy. What kind of animal is it that you want?'

'A mongoose.'

'A mongoose! What on earth do you want it for?'

'To kill snakes.'

'Good!' The old man remembered the mound of stones. No explanation was needed.

When Ross heard what was wanted, he asked:

'Do you want something special, or will an ordinary mongoose do?'

'Well, of course I want a good one. But I see no need for anything special. It is for ordinary use.'

'I can let you have a choice of ordinary ones. I only asked, because I have in stock a very special one which I got lately from Nepal. He has a record of his own. He killed a king cobra that had been seen in the Rajah's garden. But I don't suppose we have any snakes of the kind in this cold climate – I daresay an ordinary one will do.'

When Adam got back to the carriage, carefully carrying the box with the mongoose, Sir Nathaniel said: 'Hullo! what have you got there?'

'A mongoose.'

'What for?'

'To kill snakes!'

Sir Nathaniel laughed.

'I heard Lady Arabella's invitation to you to come to Diana's Grove.'

'Well, what on earth has that got to do with it?'

'Nothing directly that I know of. But we shall see.' Adam waited, and the old man went on: 'Have you by any chance heard the other name which was given long ago to that place?'

'No, sir.'

'It was called – Look here, this subject wants a lot of talking over. Suppose we wait till we are alone and have lots of time before us.'

'All right, sir.' Adam was filled with curiosity, but he thought it better not to hurry matters. All would come in good time. Then the three men returned home, leaving Mr Caswall to spend the night in Liverpool.

The following day the Lesser Hill party set out for Castra Regis, and for the time Adam thought no more of Diana's Grove or of what mysteries it had contained – or might still contain.

The guests were crowding in, and special places were marked for important people. Adam, seeing so many persons of varied degree, looked round for Lady Arabella, but could not locate her. It was only when he saw the old-fashioned travelling carriage approach and heard the sound of cheering which went with it, that he realized that Edgar Caswall had arrived. Then, on looking more closely, he saw that Lady Arabella, dressed as he had seen her last, was seated beside him. When her carriage drew up at the great flight of steps, the host jumped down and gave her his hand.

It was evident to all that she was the chief guest at the festivities. It was not long before the seats on the dais were filled, while the tenants and guests of lesser importance had occupied all the coigns of vantage not reserved. The order of the day had been carefully arranged by a committee. There were some speeches, happily neither many nor long; and then festivities were suspended till the time for feasting arrived. In the interval Caswall walked among his guests, speaking to all in a friendly manner and expressing a general welcome. The other guests came down from the dais and followed his example, so there was unceremonious meeting and greeting between gentle and simple.

Adam Salton naturally followed with his eyes all that went on within their scope, taking note of all who seemed to afford any interest. He was young and a man and a stranger from a far distance; so on all these accounts he naturally took stock rather of the women than of the men, and of these, those who were young and attractive. There were lots of pretty girls among the crowd, and Adam, who was a handsome young man and well set up, got his full share of admiring glances. These did not concern him much, and he remained unmoved until there came along a group of three, by their dress and bearing, of the farmer class. One was a sturdy old man; the other two were good-looking girls, one of a little over twenty, the other not quite so old. So soon as Adam's eyes met those of the younger girl, who stood nearest to him, some sort of electricity flashed – that divine spark which begins by recognition, and ends in obedience. Men call it 'Love'.

Both his companions noticed now much Adam was taken by the pretty girl, and spoke of her to him in a way which made his heart warm to them.

'Did you notice that party that passed? The old man is Michael Watford, one of the tenants of Mr Caswall. He occupies Mercy Farm, which Sir Nathaniel pointed out to you to-day. The girls are his grand-daughters, the elder, Lilla, being the only child of his elder son, who died when she was less than a year old. His wife died on the same day. She is a good girl – as good as she is pretty. The other is her first cousin, the daughter of Watford's second son. He went for a soldier when he was just over twenty, and was drafted abroad. He was not a good correspondent, though he was a good enough son. A few letters came, and then his father heard from the colonel of his regiment that he had been killed by dacoits in Burma. He heard from the same source that his boy had been married to a Burmese, and that there was a daughter only a year old. Watford had the child brought home, and she grew up beside Lilla. The only thing that they heard of her birth was that her name was Mimi. The two children adored each other, and do so to this day. Strange how different they are! Lilla all fair, like the old Saxon stock from which she is sprung; Mimi showing a trace of her mother's race. Lilla is as gentle as a dove, but Mimi's black eyes can glow whenever she is upset. The only thing that upsets her is when anything happens to injure or threaten to annoy Lilla. Then her eyes glow as do the eyes of a bird when her young are menaced.'

5

THE WHITE WORM

Mr Salton introduced Adam to Mr Watford and his grand-daughters, and they all moved on together. Of course neighbours in the position of the Watfords knew all about Adam Salton, his relationship, circumstances and prospects. So it would have been strange indeed if both girls did not dream of possibilities of the future. In agricultural England, eligible men of any class are rare. This particular man was especially eligible, for he did not belong to a class in which barriers of caste were strong. So when it began to be noticed that he walked beside Mimi Watford and seemed to desire her society, all their friends were endeavoured to give the promising affair a helping hand. When the gongs sounded for the banquet, he went with her into the tent where her grandfather had seats. Mr Salton and Sir Nathaniel noticed that the young man did not come to claim his appointed place at the dais table; but they understood and made no remark, or indeed did not seem to notice his absence.

Lady Arabella sat as before at Edgar Caswall's right hand. She was certainly a striking and unusual woman, and to all it seemed fitting from her rank and personal qualities that she should be the chosen partner of the heir on his first appearance. Of course nothing was said openly by those of her own class who were present; but words were not necessary when so much could be expressed by nods and smiles. It seemed to be an accepted thing that at last there was to be a mistress of Castra Regis, and that she was present amongst them. There were not lacking some who, whilst admitting all her charm and beauty, placed her in the second rank, Lilla Watford being marked as first. There was sufficient divergence of type, as well as of individual beauty, to allow of fair comment; Lady Arabella represented the aristocratic type, and Lilla that of the commonality.

When the dusk began to thicken, Mr Salton and Sir Nathaniel walked home – the trap had been sent away early in the day – leaving Adam to follow in his own time. He came in earlier than was expected, and seemed upset about something. Neither of the elders made any comment. They all lit cigarettes, and, as dinner-time was close at hand, went to their rooms to get ready.

Adam had evidently been thinking in the interval. He joined the others in the drawing-room, looking ruffled and impatient – a condition of things seen for the first time. The others, with the patience – or the experience – of age, trusted to time to unfold and explain things. They had not long to wait. After sitting down and standing up several times, Adam suddenly burst out.

'That fellow seems to think he owns the earth. Can't he let people alone! He seems to think that he has only to throw his handkerchief to any woman, and be her master.'

This outburst was in itself enlightening. Only thwarted affection in some guise could produce this feeling in an amiable young man. Sir Nathaniel, as an old diplomatist, had a way of understanding, as if by foreknowledge, the true inwardness of things, and asked suddenly, but in a matter-of-fact, indifferent voice:

'Was he after Lilla?'

'Yes, and the fellow didn't lose any time either. Almost as soon as they met, he began to butter her up, and tell her how beautiful she was. Why, before he left her side, he had asked himself to tea to-morrow at Mercy Farm. Stupid ass! He might see that the girl isn't his sort! I never saw anything like it. It was just like a hawk and a pigeon.'

As he spoke, Sir Nathaniel turned and looked at Mr Salton – a keen look which implied a full understanding.

'Tell us all about it, Adam. There are still a few minutes before dinner, and we shall all have better appetites when we have come to some conclusion on this matter.'

'There is nothing to tell, sir; that is the worst of it. I am bound to say that there was not a word said that a human being could object to. He was very civil, and all that was proper – just what a landlord might be to a tenant's daughter. . . . Yet – yet – well, I don't know how it was, but it made my blood boil.'

'How did the hawk and the pigeon come in?' Sir Nathaniel's voice was soft and soothing, nothing of contradiction or overdone curiosity in it – a tone eminently suited to win confidence.

'I can hardly explain. I can only say that he looked like a hawk and she like a dove – and, now that I think of it, that is what they each did look like; and do look like in their normal condition.'

'That is so!' came the soft voice of Sir Nathaniel.

Adam went on:

'Perhaps that early Roman look of his set me off. But I wanted to protect her; she seemed in danger.'

'She seems in danger, in a way, from all you young men. I couldn't help noticing the way that even you looked – as if you wished to absorb her!'

'I hope both you young men will keep your heads cool,' put in Mr Salton. 'You know, Adam, it won't do to have any quarrel between you, especially as soon after his home-coming and your arrival here. We must think of the feelings and happiness of our neighbours; mustn't we?'

'I hope so, sir. I assure you, that, whatever may happen, or even threaten, I shall obey your wishes in this as in all things.'

'Hush!' whispered Sir Nathaniel, who heard the servants in the passage bringing dinner.

After dinner, over the walnuts and the wine, Sir Nathaniel returned to the subject of the local legends.

'It will perhaps be a less dangerous topic for us to discuss than more recent ones.'

'All right, sir,' said Adam heartily. 'I think you may depend on me now with regard to any topic. I can even discuss Mr Caswall. Indeed, I may meet him to-morrow. He is going, as I said, to call at Mercy Farm at three o'clock – but I have an appointment at two.'

'I notice,' said Mr Salton, 'that you do not lose any time.'

The two old men once more looked at each other steadily. Then, lest the mood of his listener should change with delay, Sir Nathaniel began at once:

'I don't propose to tell you all the legends of Mercia, or even to make a selection of them. It will be better, I think, for our purpose if we consider a few facts – recorded or unrecorded – about this neighbourhood. I think we might begin with Diana's Grove. It has roots in the different epochs of our history, and each has its special crop of legend. The Druid and the Roman are too far off for matters of details; but it seems to me the Saxon and the Angles are near enough to yield material for legendary lore. We find that this particular place had another name besides Diana's Grove. This was manifestly of Roman origin, or of Grecian accepted as Roman. The other is more pregnant of adventure and romance than the Roman name. In Mercian tongue it was "The Lair of the White Worm". This needs a word of explanation at the beginning.

'In the dawn of the language, the word "worm" had a somewhat different meaning from that in use to-day. It was an adaptation of the Anglo-Saxon "wyrm", meaning a dragon or snake; or from the Gothic "waurms", a serpent; or the Icelandic "ormur", or the German "wurm". We gather that it conveyed originally an idea of size and power, not as now in the diminutive of both these meanings. Here legendary history helps us. We have the well-known legend of the "Worm Well" of Lambton Castle, and that of the "Laidly Worm of Spindleston Heugh" near Bamborough. In both these legends the "worm" was a monster of vast size and power – a veritable dragon or serpent, such as legend attributes to vast fens or quags where there was illimitable room for expansion. A glance at a geological map will show that whatever truth there may have been of the actuality of such monsters in the early geologic periods, at least there was plenty of possibility. In England there were originally vast plains where the plentiful supply of water could gather. The streams were deep and slow, and there were holes of abysmal depth, where any kind and size of antediluvian monster could find a habitat. In places, which now we can see from our windows, were mud-holes a hundred or more feet deep. Who can tell us when the age of the monsters which flourished in slime came to an end? There must have been places and conditions which made for greater longevity, greater size, greater strength than was usual. Such over-lappings may have come down even to our earlier centuries. Nay, are there not now creatures of a vastness of bulk regarded by the generality of men as impossible? Even in our own day there are seen the traces of animals, if not the animals themselves, of stupendous size – veritable survivals from earlier ages, preserved by some special qualities in their habitats. I remember meeting a distinguished man in India, who had the reputation of being a great shikaree, who told me that the greatest temptation he had ever had in his life was to shoot a giant snake which he had come across in the Terai of Upper India. He was on a tiger-shooting expedition, and as his elephant was crossing a nullah, it squealed. He looked down from his howdah and saw that the elephant had stepped across the body of a snake which was dragging itself through the jungle. "So far as I could see," he said, "it must have been eighty or one hundred feet in length. Fully forty or fifty feet on each side of the track, and though the weight which it dragged had thinned it, it was as thick round as a man's body. I suppose you know that when you are after tiger, it is a point of honour not to shoot at anything else, as life may depend on it. I could easily have spined this monster, but I felt that I must not – so, with regret, I had to let it go."

'Just imagine such a monster anywhere in this country, and at once we could get a sort of idea of the "worms", which possibly did frequent the great morasses which spread round the mouths of many of the great European rivers.'

'I haven't the least doubt, sir, that there may have been such monsters as you have spoken of still existing at a much later period than is generally accepted,' replied Adam. 'Also, if there were such things, that this was the very place for them. I have tried to think over the matter since you pointed out the configuration of the ground. But it seems to me that there is a hiatus somewhere. Are there not mechanical difficulties?'

'In that way?'

'Well, our antique monster must have been mighty heavy, and the distances he had to travel were long and the ways difficult. From where we are now sitting down to the level of mud-holes is a distance of several hundred feet – I am leaving out of consideration altogether any lateral distance. Is it possible that there was a way by which a monster could travel up and down, and yet no chance recorder have ever seen him? Of course we have the legends; but is not some more exact evidence necessary in a scientific investigation?'

'My dear Adam, all you say is perfectly right, and, were we starting on such an investigation, we could not do better than follow your reasoning. But, my dear boy, you must remember that all this took place thousands of years ago. You must remember, too, that all records of the kind that would help us are lacking. Also, that the places to be considered were desert, so far as human habitation or population are considered. In the vast desolation of such a place as complied with the necessary conditions, there must have been such profusion of natural growth as would bar the progress of men formed as we are. The lair of such a monster would not have been disturbed for hundreds – or thousands – of years. Moreover, these creatures must have occupied places quite inaccessible to man. A snake who could make himself comfortable in a quagmire, a hundred feet deep, would be protected on the outskirts by such stupendous morasses as now no longer exist, or which, if they exist anywhere at all, can be on very few places on the earth's surface. Far be it from me to say that in more elemental times such things could not have been. The condition belongs to the geologic age – the great birth and growth of the world, for existence was so savage that no vitality which was not founded in a gigantic form could have even a possibility of survival. That such a time existed, we have evidences in geology, but there only; we can never expect proofs such as this age demands. We can only imagine or surmise such things – or such conditions and such forces as overcame them.'

6

HAWK AND PIGEON

At breakfast-time next morning Sir Nathaniel and Mr Salton were seated when Adam came hurriedly into the room.

'Any news?' asked his uncle mechanically.

'Four.'

'Four what?' asked Sir Nathaniel.

'Snakes, ' said Adam, helping himself to a grilled kidney.

'Four snakes. I don't understand.'

'Mongoose,' said Adam, and then added explanatorily: 'I was out with the mongoose just after three.'

'Four snakes in one morning! Why, I didn't know there were so many on the Brow' – the local name for the western cliff. 'I hope that wasn't the consequence of our talk of last night?'

'It was, sir. But not directly.'

'But, God bless my soul, you didn't expect to get a snake like the Lambton worm, did you? Why, a mongoose, to tackle a monster like that – if there were one – would have to be bigger than a haystack.'

'These were ordinary snakes, about as big as a walking-stick.'

'Well, it's pleasant to be rid of them, big or little. That is a good mongoose, I am sure; he'll clear out all such vermin round here,' said Mr Salton.

Adam went on quietly with his breakfast. Killing a few snakes in a morning was no new experience to him. He left the room the moment breakfast was finished and went to the study that his uncle had arranged for him. Both Sir Nathaniel and Mr Salton took it that he wanted to be by himself, so as to avoid any questioning or talk of the visit that he was to make that afternoon. They saw nothing further of him till about half an hour before dinner-time. Then he came quietly into the smoking-room, where Mr Salton and Sir Nathaniel were sitting together, ready dressed.

'I supposed there is no use waiting. We had better get it over at once,' remarked Adam.

His uncle, thinking to make things easier for him, said: 'Get what over?'

There was a sign of shyness about him at this. He stammered a little at first, but his voice became more even as he went on.

'My visit to Mercy Farm.'

Mr Salton waited eagerly. The old diplomatist simply smiled.

'I suppose you both know that I was much interested yesterday in the Watfords?' There was no denial or fending off the question. Both the old men smiled acquiescence. Adam went on: 'I meant you to see it – both of you. You, uncle, because you are my uncle and the nearest of my own kin, and, moreover, you couldn't have been more kind to me or made me more welcome if you had been my own father.' Mr Salton said nothing. He simply held out his hand, and the other took it and held it for a few seconds. 'And you, sir, because you have shown me something of the same affection which in my wildest dreams of home I had no right to expect.' He stopped for an instant, much moved.

Sir Nathaniel answered softly, laying his hand on the youth's shoulder.

'You are right, my boy; quite right. That is the proper way to look at it. And I may tell you that we old men, who have no children of our own, feel our hearts growing warm when we hear words like those.'

Then Adam hurried on, speaking with a rush, as if he wanted to come to the crucial point.

'Mr Watford had not come in, but Lilla and Mimi were at home, and they made me feel very welcome. They have all a great regard for my uncle. I am glad of that anyway, for I like them all – very much. We were having tea, when Mr Caswall came to the door, attended by the negro. Lilla opened the door herself. The window of the living-room at the farm is a large one, and from within you cannot help seeing anyone coming. Mr Caswall said he had ventured to call, as he wished to make the acquaintance of all his tenants, in a less formal way, and more individually, than had been possible to him on the previous day. The girls made him welcome – they are very sweet girls those, sir; someone will be very happy some day there – with either of them.'

'And that man may be you, Adam,' said Mr Salton heartily.

A sad look came over the young man's eyes, and the fire his uncle had seen there died out. Likewise the timbre left his voice, making it sound lonely.

'Such might crown my life. But that happiness, I fear, is not for me – or not without pain and loss and woe.'

'Well, it's early days yet!' cried Sir Nathaniel heartily.

The young man turned on him his eyes, which had now grown excessively sad.

'Yesterday – a few hours ago – that remark would have given me new hope – new courage; but since then I have learned too much.'

The old man, skilled in the human heart, did not attempt to argue in such a matter.

'Too early to give in, my boy.'

'I am not of a giving-in kind,' replied the young man earnestly. 'But, after all, it is wise to realize a truth. And when a man, though he is young, feels as I do – as I have felt ever since yesterday, when I first saw Mimi's eyes – his heart jumps. He does not need to learn things. He knows.'

There was silence in the room, during which the twilight stole on imperceptibly. It was Adam who again broke the silence.

'Do you know, uncle, if we have any second sight in our family?'

'No, not that I ever heard about. Why?'

'Because,' he answered slowly, 'I have a conviction which seems to answer all the conditions of second sight.'

'And then?' asked the old man, much perturbed.

'And then the usual inevitable. What in the Hebrides and other places, where the Sight is a cult – a belief – is called "the Doom" – the court from which there is no appeal. I have often heard of second sight – we have many western Scots in Australia; but I have realized more of its true inwardness in an instant of this afternoon than I did in the whole of my life previously – a granite wall stretching up to the very heavens, so high and so dark that the eye of God Himself cannot see beyond. Well, if the Doom must come, it must. That is all.'

The voice of Sir Nathaniel broke in, smooth and sweet and grave.

'Can there not be a fight for it? There can for most things.'

'For most things, yes, but for the Doom, no. What a man can do I shall do. There will be – must be – a fight. When and where and how I know not, but a fight there will be. But, after all, what is a man in such a case?'

'Adam, there are three of us.' Salton looked at his old friend as he spoke, and that old friend's eyes blazed.

'Ay, three of us,' he said, and his voice rang.

There was again a pause, and Sir Nathaniel endeavoured to get back to less emotional and more neutral ground.

'Tell us of the rest of the meeting. Remember we are all pledged to this. It is a fight *à l'outrance*, and we can afford to throw away or forgo no chance.'

'We shall throw away or lose nothing that we can help. We fight to win, and the stake is life – perhaps more than one – we shall see.' Then he went on in a conversational tone, such as he had used when he spoke of the coming to the farm of Edgar Caswall: 'When Mr Caswall came in, the negro went a short distance away and there remained. It gave me the idea that he expected to be called, and intended to remain in sight, or within hail. Then Mimi got another cup and made fresh tea, and we all went on together.'

'Was there anything uncommon – were you all quite friendly?' asked Sir Nathaniel quickly.

'Quite friendly. There was nothing that I could notice out of the common – except,' he went on, with a slight hardening of the voice, 'except that he kept his eyes fixed on Lilla, in a way which was quite intolerable to any man who might hold her dear.'

'Now, in what way did he look?' asked Sir Nathaniel.

'There was nothing in itself offensive; but no one could help noticing it.'

'You did. Miss Watford herself, who was the victim, and Mr Caswall, who was the offender, are out of range as witnesses. Was there anyone else who noticed?'

'Mimi did. Her face flamed with anger as she saw the look.'

'What kind of look was it? Over-ardent or too admiring, or what? Was it the look of a lover, or one who fain would be? You understand?'

'Yes, sir, I quite understand. Anything of that sort I should of course notice. It would be part of my preparation for keeping my self-control – to which I am pledged.'

'If it were not amatory, was it threatening? Where was the offence?'

335

Adam smiled kindly at the old man.

'It was not amatory. Even if it was, such was to be expected. I should be the last man in the world to object, since I am myself an offender in that respect. Moreover, not only have I been taught to fight fair, but by nature I believe I am just. I would be as tolerant of and as liberal to a rival as I should expect him to be to me. No, the look I mean was nothing of that kind. And so long as it did not lack proper respect, I should not of my own part condescend to notice it. Did you ever study the eyes of a hound?'

'At rest?'

'No, when he is following his instincts! Or, better still,' Adam went on, 'the eyes of a bird of prey when he is following his instincts. Not when he is swooping, but merely when he is watching his quarry?'

'No,' said Sir Nathaniel, 'I don't know that I ever did. Why, may I ask?'

'That was the look. Certainly not amatory or anything of that kind – yet it was, it struck me, more dangerous, if not so deadly as an actual threatening.'

Again there was a silence, which Sir Nathaniel broke as he stood up:

'I think it would be well if we all thought over this by ourselves. Then we can renew the subject.'

7

OOLANGA

Mr Salton had an appointment for six o'clock at Liverpool. When he had driven off, Sir Nathaniel took Adam by the arm.

'May I come with you for a while to your study? I want to speak to you privately without your uncle knowing about it, or even what the subject is. You don't mind, do you? It is not idle curiosity. No, no. It is on the subject to which we are all committed.'

'Is it necessary to keep my uncle in the dark about it? He might be offended.'

'It is not necessary; but it is advisable. It is for his sake that I asked. My friend is an old man, and it might concern him unduly – even alarm him. I promise you there shall be nothing that could cause him anxiety in our silence, or at which he could take umbrage.'

'Go on, sir!' said Adam simply.

'You see, your uncle is now an old man. I know it, for we were boys together. He has led an uneventful and somewhat self-contained life, so that any such condition of things as has now arisen is apt to perplex him from its very strangeness. In fact, any new matter is trying to old people. It has its own disturbances and its own anxieties, and neither of these things are good for lives that should be restful. Your uncle is a strong man, with a very happy and placid nature. Given health and ordinary conditions of life, there is no reason why he should not live to be a hundred. You and I, therefore, who both love him, though in different ways, should make it our business to protect him from all disturbing influences. I am sure you will agree with me that any labour to this end would be well spent. All right, my boy! I see your answer in your eyes; so we need say no more of that. And now,' here his voice changed, 'tell me all that took place at that interview. There are strange things in front of us – how strange we cannot at present even guess. Doubtless some of the difficult things to understand which lie behind the veil will in time be shown to us to see and to understand. In the meantime, all we can do is to work patiently, fearlessly, and unselfishly, to an end that we think is right. You had got so far as where Lilla opened the door to Mr Caswall and the negro. You also observed that Mimi was disturbed in her mind at the way Mr Caswall looked at her cousin.'

'Certainly – though "disturbed" is a poor way of expressing her objection.'

'Can you remember well enough to describe Caswall's eyes, and how Lilla looked, and what Mimi said and did? Also Oolanga, Caswall's African servant.'

'I'll do what I can, sir. All the time Mr Caswall was staring, he kept his eyes fixed and motionless – but not as if he was in a trance. His forehead was wrinkled up, as it is when one is trying to see through or into something. At the best of times his face has not a gentle expression; but when it was screwed up like that it was almost diabolical. It frightened poor Lilla so that she trembled, and after a bit got so pale that I thought she had fainted. However, she held up and tried to stare back, but in a feeble kind of way. Then Mimi came close and held her hand. That braced her up, and – still, never ceasing her return stare – she got colour again and seemed more like herself.'

'Did he stare too?'

'More than ever. The weaker Lilla seemed, the stronger he became, just as if he were feeding on her strength. All at once she turned round, threw up her hands, and fell down in a faint. I could not see what else happened just then, for Mimi had thrown herself on her knees beside her and hid her from me. Then there was something like a black shadow between us, and there was the negro, looking more like a malignant devil than ever. I am not usually a patient man, and the sight of that ugly devil is enough to

337

make one's blood boil. When he saw my face, he seemed to realize danger – immediate danger – and slunk out of the room as noiselessly as if he had been blown out. I learned one thing, however – he is an enemy, if ever a man had one.'

'That still leaves us three to two!' put in Sir Nathaniel.

'Then Caswall slunk out, much as the negro had done. When he had gone, Lilla recovered at once.'

'Now,' said Sir Nathaniel, anxious to restore peace, 'have you found out anything yet regarding the negro? I am anxious to be posted regarding him. I fear there will be, or may be, grave trouble with him.'

'Yes, sir, I've heard a good deal about him – of course it is not official; but hearsay must guide us at first. You know my man Davenport – private secretary, confidential man of business, and general factotum. He is devoted to me, and has my full confidence. I asked him to stay on board the *West African* and have a good look round, and find out what he could about Mr Caswall. Naturally, he was struck with the savage. He found one of the ship's stewards, who had been on the regular voyages to South Africa. He knew Oolanga and had made a study of him. He is a man who gets on well with negroes, and they open their hearts to him. It seems that this Oolanga is quite a great person in the world of his origin. He has the two things which men of his own colour respect; he can make them afraid, and he is lavish with money. I don't know whose money – but that does not matter. They are always ready to trumpet his greatness. Evil greatness it is – but neither does that matter. Briefly, this is his history. He was originally a witch-finder – about as low an occupation as exists amongst aboriginal savages. Then he got up in the world and became an Obi-man, which gives an opportunity to wealth *via* blackmail. Finally, he reached the highest honour in hellish service. He became a user of Voodoo, which seems to be a service of the utmost baseness and cruelty. I was told some of his deeds of cruelty, which are simply sickening. They made me long for an opportunity of helping to drive him back to hell. You might think to look at him that you could measure in some way the extent of his vileness; but it would be a vain hope. Monsters such as he is belong to an earlier and more rudimentary stage of barbarism. He is in his way a clever fellow; but is none the less dangerous or the less hateful for that. The men in the ship told me that he was a collector: some of them had seen his collections. Such collections! All that was potent for evil in bird or beast, or even in fish. Beaks that could break and rend and tear – all the birds represented were of a predatory kind. Even the fishes are those which are born to destroy, to wound, to torture. The collection, I assure you, was an object lesson in human malignity. This being has enough evil in his face to frighten even a strong man. It is little wonder that the sight of it put that poor girl into a dead faint!'

Nothing more could be done at the moment, so they separated.

Adam was up in the early morning and took a smart walk round the Brow. As he was passing Diana's Grove, he looked in on the short avenue of trees, and noticed the snakes killed on the previous morning by the mongoose. They all lay in a row, straight and rigid, as if they had been placed by hands. Their skins seemed damp and sticky, and they were covered all over with ants and other insects. They looked loathsome, so after a glance, he passed on.

A little later, when his steps took him, naturally enough, past the entrance to Mercy Farm, he was passed by the negro, moving quickly under the trees wherever there was shadow. Laid across one extended arm, looking like dirty towels across a rail, he had the horrid-looking snakes. He did not seem to see Adam. No one was to be seen at Mercy except a few workmen in the farmyard, so, after waiting on the chance of seeing Mimi, Adam began to go slowly home.

Once more he was passed on the way. This time it was by Lady Arabella, walking hurriedly and so furiously angry that she did not recognize him, even to the extent of acknowledging his bow.

When Adam got back to Lesser Hill, he went to the coach-house where the box with the mongoose was kept, and took it with him, intending to finish at the Mound of Stone what he had begun the previous morning with regard to the extermination. He found that the snakes were even more easily attacked than on the previous day; no less than six were killed in the first half-hour. As no more appeared, he took it for granted that the morning's work was over, and went towards home. The mongoose had by this time become accustomed to him, and was willing to let himself be handled freely. Adam lifted him up and put him on his shoulder and walked on. Presently he saw a lady advancing towards him, and recognized Lady Arabella.

Hitherto the mongoose had been quiet, like a playful affectionate kitten; but when the two got close, Adam was horrified to see the mongoose, in a state of the wildest fury, with every hair standing on end, jump from his shoulder and run towards Lady Arabella. It looked so furious and so intent on attack that he called a warning.

'Look out – look out! The animal is furious and means to attack.'

Lady Arabella looked more than ever disdainful and was passing on; the mongoose jumped at her in a furious attack. Adam rushed forward with his stick, the only weapon he had. But just as he got within striking distance, the lady drew out a revolver and shot the animal, breaking his backbone. Not satisfied with this, she poured shot after shot into him till the magazine was exhausted. There was no coolness or hauteur about her now; she seemed more furious even than the animal, her face transformed

339

with hate, and as determined to kill as he had appeared to be. Adam, not knowing exactly what to do, lifted his hat in apology and hurried on to Lesser Hill.

8

SURVIVALS

At breakfast Sir Nathaniel noticed that Adam was put out about something, but he said nothing. The lesson of silence is better remembered in age than in youth. When they were both in the study, where Sir Nathaniel followed him, Adam at once began to tell his companion of what had happened. Sir Nathaniel looked graver and graver as the narration proceeded, and when Adam had stopped he remained silent for several minutes, before speaking.

'This is very grave. I have not formed any opinion yet; but it seems to me at first impression that this is worse than anything I had expected.'

'Why, sir!' said Adam. 'Is the killing of a mongoose – no matter by whom – so serious a thing as all that?'

His companion smoked on quietly for quite another few minutes before he spoke.

'When I have properly thought it over I may moderate my opinion, but in the meantime it seems to me that there is something dreadful behind all this – something that may affect all our lives – that may mean the issue of life or death to any of us.'

Adam sat up quickly.

'Do tell me, sir, what is in your mind – if, of course, you have no objection, or do not think it better to withhold it.'

'I have no objection, Adam – in fact, if I had, I should have to overcome it. I fear there can be no more reserved thoughts between us.'

'Indeed, sir, that sounds serious, worse than serious!'

'Adam, I greatly fear that the time has come for us – for you and me, at all events – to speak out plainly to one another. Does not there seem something very mysterious about this?'

'I have thought so, sir, all along. The only difficulty one has is what one is to think and where to begin.'

'Let us begin with what you have told me. First take the conduct of the mongoose. He was quiet, even friendly and affectionate with you. He only attacked the snakes, which is, after all, his business in life.'

'That is so!'

'Then we must try to find some reason why he attacked Lady Arabella.'

'May it not be that a mongoose may have merely the instinct to attack, that nature does not allow or provide him with the fine reasoning powers to discriminate who he is to attack?'

'Of course that may be so. But, on the other hand, should we not satisfy ourselves why he does wish to attack anything? If for centuries, this particular animal is known to attack only one kind of other animal, are we not justified in assuming that when one of them attacks a hitherto unclassed animal, he recognizes in that animal some quality which it has in common with the hereditary enemy?'

'That is a good argument, sir,' Adam went on, 'but a dangerous one. If we followed it out, it would lead us to believe that Lady Arabella is a snake.'

'We must be sure, before going to such an end, that there is no point as yet unconsidered which would account for the unknown thing which puzzles us.'

'In what way?'

'Well, suppose the instinct works on some physical basis – for instance, smell. If there were anything in recent juxtaposition to the attacked which would carry the scent, surely that would supply the missing cause.'

'Of course!' Adam spoke with conviction.

'Now, from what you tell me, the negro had just come from the direction of Diana's Grove, carrying the dead snakes which the mongoose had killed the previous morning. Might not the scent have been carried that way?'

'Of course it might, and probably was. I never thought of that. Is there any possible way of guessing approximately how long a scent will remain? You see, this is a natural scent, and may derive from a place where it has been effective for thousand of years. Then, does a scent of any kind carry with it any form or quality of another kind, either good or evil? I ask you because one ancient name of the house lived in by the lady who was attacked by the mongoose was "The Lair of the White Worm". If any of these things be so, our difficulties have multiplied indefinitely. They may even change in kind. We may get into moral entanglements; before we know it, we may be in the midst of a struggle between good and evil.'

Sir Nathaniel smiled gravely.

'With regard to the first question – so far as I know, there are no fixed periods for which a scent may be active – I think we may take it that that period does not run into thousands of years. As to whether any moral change accompanies a physical one, I can only say that I have met no proof of the fact. At the same time, we must remember that "good" and

341

"evil" are terms so wide as to take in the whole scheme of creation, and all that is implied by them and by their mutual action and reaction. Generally, I would say that in the scheme of a First Cause anything is possible. So long as the inherent forces or tendencies of any one thing are veiled from us we must expect mystery.'

'There is one other question on which I should like to ask your opinion. Suppose that there are any permanent forces appertaining to the past, what we may call "survivals", do these belong to good as well as to evil? For instance, if the scent of the primæval monster can so remain in proportion to the original strength, can the same be true of things of good import?'

Sir Nathaniel thought for a while before he answered.

'We must be careful not to confuse the physical and the moral. I can see that already you have switched on the moral entirely, so perhaps we had better follow it up first. On the side of the moral, we have certain justification for belief in the utterances of revealed religion. For instance, "the effectual fervent prayer of a righteous man availeth much" is altogether for good. We have nothing of a similar kind on the side of evil. But if we accept this dictum we need have no more fear of "mysteries": these become thenceforth merely obstacles.'

Adam suddenly changed to another phase of the subject.

'And now, sir, may I turn for a few minutes to purely practical things, or rather to matters of historical fact.'

Sir Nathaniel bowed acquiescence.

'We have already spoken of the history, so far as it is known, of some of the places round us – "Castra Regis", "Diana's Grove", and "The Lair of the White Worm". I would like to ask if there is anything not necessarily of evil import about any of the places?'

'Which?' asked Sir Nathaniel shrewdly.

'Well, for instance, this house and Mercy Farm?'

'Here we turn,' said Sir Nathaniel, 'to the other side, the light side of things. Let us take Mercy Farm first. When Augustine was sent by Pope Gregory to Christianize England, in the time of the Romans, he was received and protected by Ethelbert, King of Kent, whose wife, daughter of Charibert, King of Paris, was a Christian, and did much for Augustine. She founded a nunnery in memory of Columba, which was named *Sedes misericordia*, the House of Mercy, and, as the region was Mercian, the two names became involved. As Columba is the Latin for dove, the dove became a sort of signification of the nunnery. She seized on the idea and made the newly-founded nunnery a house of doves. Someone sent her a freshly-discovered dove, a sort of carrier, but which had in the white feathers of its head and neck the form of a religious cowl. The nunnery flourished for more than a century, when, in the time of Penda, who was the reactionary of heathendom, it fell into decay. In the meantime the doves, protected by religious feeling, had increased mightily, and were known in all Catholic communities. When King Offa ruled in Mercia, about a hundred and fifty years later, he restored Christianity, and under its protection the nunnery of St Columba was restored and its doves flourished again. In process of time this religious house again fell into desuetude; but before it disappeared it had achieved a great name for good works, and in especial for the piety of its members. If deeds and prayers and hopes and earnest thinking leave anywhere any moral effect, Mercy Farm and all around it have almost the right to be considered holy ground.'

'Thank you, sir,' said Adam earnestly, and was silent. Sir Nathaniel understood.

After lunch that day, Adam casually asked Sir Nathaniel to come for a walk with him. The keen-witted old diplomatist guessed that there must be some motive behind the suggestion, and he at once agreed.

As soon as they were free from observation, Adam began.

'I am afraid, sir, that there is more going on in this neighbourhood than most people imagine. I was out this morning, and on the edge of the small wood, I came upon the body of a child by the roadside. At first, I thought she was dead, and while examining her, I noticed on her neck some marks that looked like those of teeth.'

'Some wild dog, perhaps?' put in Sir Nathaniel.

'Possibly, sir, though I think not – but listen to the rest of my news. I glanced round, and to my surprise, I noticed something white moving among the trees. I placed the child down carefully, and followed, but I could not find any further traces. So I returned to the child and resumed my examination, and, to my delight, I discovered that she was still alive. I chafed her hands and gradually she revived, but to my disappointment she remembered nothing – except that something had crept up quietly from behind, and had gripped her round the throat. Then, apparently, she fainted.'

'Gripped her round the throat! Then it cannot have been a dog.'

'No, sir, that is my difficulty, and explains why I brought you out here, where we cannot possibly be overheard. You have noticed, of course, the peculiar sinuous way in which Lady Arabella moves – well, I feel certain that the white thing that I saw in the wood was the mistress of Diana's Grove!'

'Good God, boy, be careful what you say.'

'Yes, sir, I fully realize the gravity of my accusation, but I feel convinced that the marks on the child's throat were human – and made by a woman.'

343

Adam's companion remained silent for some time, deep in thought.

'Adam, my boy,' he said at last, 'this matter appears to me to be far more serious even than you think. It forces me to break confidence with my old friend, your uncle – but, in order to spare him, I must do so. For some time now, things have been happening in this district that have been worrying him dreadfully – several people have disappeared, without leaving the slightest trace; a dead child was found by the roadside, with no visible or ascertainable cause of death – sheep and other animals have been found in the fields, bleeding from open wounds. There have been other matters – many of them apparently trivial in themselves. Some sinister influence has been at work, and I admit that I have suspected Lady Arabella – that is why I questioned you so closely about the mongoose and its strange attack upon Lady Arabella. You will think it strange that I should suspect the mistress of Diana's Grove, a beautiful woman of aristocratic birth. Let me explain – the family seat is near my own place, Doom Tower, and at one time I knew the family well. When still a young girl, Lady Arabella wandered into a small wood near her home, and did not return. She was found unconscious and in a high fever – the doctor said that she had received a poisonous bite, and the girl being at a delicate and critical age, the result was serious – so much so that she was not expected to recover. A great London physician came down but could do nothing – indeed, he said that the girl would not survive the night. All hope had been abandoned, when, to everyone's surprise, Lady Arabella made a sudden and startling recovery. Within a couple of days she was going about as usual! But to the horror of her people, she developed a terrible craving for cruelty, maiming and injuring birds and small animals – even killing them. This was put down to a nervous disturbance due to her age, and it was hoped that her marriage to Captain March would put this right. However, it was not a happy marriage, and eventually her husband was found shot through the head. I have always suspected suicide, though no pistol was found near the body. He may have discovered something – God knows what! – so possibly Lady Arabella may herself have killed him. Putting together many small matters that have come to my knowledge, I have come to the conclusion that the foul White Worm obtained control of her body, just as her soul was leaving its earthly tenement – that would explain that sudden revival of energy, the strange and inexplicable craving for maiming and killing, as well as many other matters with which I need not trouble you now, Adam. As I said just now, God alone knows what poor Captain March discovered – it must have been something too ghastly for human endurance, if my theory is correct that the once beautiful human body of Lady Arabella is under the control of this ghastly White Worm.'

Adam nodded.

'But what can we do, sir – it seems a most difficult problem.'

'We can do nothing, my boy – that is the important part of it. It would be impossible to take action – all we can do is keep careful watch, especially as regards Lady Arabella, and be ready to act, promptly and decisively, if the opportunity occurs.'

Adam agreed, and the two men returned to Lesser Hill.

9

SMELLING DEATH

Adam Salton, though he talked little, did not let the grass grow under his feet in any matter which he had undertaken, or in which he was interested. He had agreed with Sir Nathaniel that they should not *do* anything with regard to the mystery of Lady Arabella's fear of the mongoose, but he steadily pursued his course in being *prepared* to act whenever the opportunity might come. He was in his own mind perpetually casting about for information or clues which might lead to possible lines of action. Baffled by the killing of the mongoose, he looked around for another line to follow. He was fascinated by the idea of there being a mysterious link between the woman and the animal, but he was already preparing a second string to his bow. His new idea was to use the faculties of Oolanga, so far as he could, in the service of discovery. His first move was to send Davenport to Liverpool to try to find the steward of the *West African*, who had told him about Oolanga, and if possible secure any further information, and then try to induce (by bribery or other means) the negro to come to the Brow. So soon as he himself could have speech of the Voodoo-man he would be able to learn from him something useful. Davenport was successful in his missions, for he had to get another moongose, and he was able to tell Adam that he had seen the steward, who told him much that he wanted to know, and had also arranged for Oolanga to come to Lesser Hill the following day. At this point Adam saw his way sufficiently clear to admit Davenport to some extent into his confidence. He had come to the conclusion that it would be better – certainly at first – not himself to appear in the matter with which Davenport was fully competent to deal. It would be time for himself to take a personal part when matters had advanced a little further.

If what the negro said was in any wise true, the man had a rare gift which might be useful in the quest they were after. He could, as it were, 'smell death'. If any one was dead, if any one had died, or if a place had been used in connection with death, he seemed to know the broad fact by intuition. Adam made up his mind that to test this faculty with regard to several places would be his first task. Naturally he was anxious, and the time passed slowly. The only comfort was the arrival the next morning of a strong packing case, locked, from Ross, the key being in the custody of Davenport. In the case were two smaller boxes, both locked. One of them contained a mongoose to replace that killed by Lady Arabella; the other was the special mongoose which had already killed the king-cobra in Nepal. When both the animals had been safely put under lock and key, he felt that he might breathe more freely. No one was allowed to know the secret of their existence in the house, except himself and Davenport. He arranged that Davenport should take Oolanga round the neighbourhood for a walk, stopping at each of the places which he designated. Having gone all along the Brow, he was to return the same way and induce him to touch on the same subjects in talking with Adam, who was to meet them as if by chance at the farthest part – that beyond Mercy Farm.

The incidents of the day proved much as Adam expected. At Mercy Farm, at Diana's Grove, at Castra Regis, and a few other spots, the negro stopped and, opening his wide nostrils as if to sniff boldly, said that he smelled death. It was not always in the same form. At Mercy Farm he said there were many small deaths. At Diana's Grove his bearing was different. There was a distinct sense of enjoyment about him, especially when he spoke of many great deaths. Here, too, he sniffed in a strange way, like a bloodhound at check, and looked puzzled. He said no word in either praise or disparagement, but in the centre of the Grove, where, hidden amongst ancient oak stumps, was a block of granite slightly hollowed on the top, he bent low and placed his forehead on the ground. This was the only place where he showed distinct reverence. At the Castle, though he spoke of much death, he showed no sign of respect.

There was evidently something about Diana's Grove which both interested and baffled him. Before leaving, he moved all over the place unsatisfied, and in one spot, close to the edge of the Brow, where there was a deep hollow, he appeared to be afraid. After returning several times to this place, he suddenly turned and ran in a panic of fear to the higher ground, crossing as he did so, the outcropping rock. Then he seemed to breathe more freely, and recovered some of his jaunty impudence.

All this seemed to satisfy Adam's expectations. He went back to Lesser Hill with a serene and settled calm upon him. Sir Nathaniel followed him into his study.

'By the way, I forgot to ask you details about one thing. When that extraordinary staring episode of Mr Caswall went on, how did Lilla take it – how did she bear herself?'

'She looked frightened and trembled just as I have seen a pigeon with a hawk, or a bird with a serpent.'

'Thanks. It is just as I expected. There have been circumstances in the Caswall family which lead one to believe that they have had from the earliest times some extraordinary mesmeric or hypnotic faculty. Indeed, a skilled eye could read so much in their physiognomy. That shot of yours, whether by instinct or intention, of the hawk and the pigeon was peculiarly apposite. I think we may settle on that as a fixed trait to be accepted throughout our investigation.'

When dusk had fallen, Adam took the new mongoose – not the one from Nepal – and, carrying the box slung over his shoulder, strolled towards Diana's Grove. Close to the gateway he met Lady Arabella, clad as usual in tightly fitting white, which showed off her slim figure.

To this intense astonishment the mongoose allowed her to pet him, take him up in her arms, and fondle him. As she was going in his direction, they walked on together.

Round the roadway between the entrances of Diana's Grove and Lesser Hill were many trees, with not much foliage except at the top. In the dusk this place was shadowy, and the view was hampered by the clustering trunks. In the uncertain tremulous light which fell through the tree-tops, it was hard to distinguish anything clearly, and at last, somehow, he lost sight of her altogether, and turned back on his track to find her. Presently he came across her close to her own gate. She was leaning over the paling of split oak branches which formed the paling of the avenue. He could not see the mongoose, so he asked her where it had gone.

'He slipped out of my arms while I was petting him,' she answered, 'and disappeared under the hedges.'

They found him at a place where the avenue widened so as to let carriages pass each other. The little creature seemed quite changed. He had been ebulliently active; now he was dull and spiritless – seemed to be dazed. He allowed himself to be lifted by either of the pair; but when he was alone with Lady Arabella he kept looking round him in a strange way as though trying to escape. When they had come out on the roadway Adam held the mongoose tight to him, and, lifting his hat to his companion, moved quickly towards Lesser Hill; he and Lady Arabella lost sight of each other in the thickening gloom.

When Adam got home, he put the mongoose in his box, and locked the door of the room. The other mongoose – the one from Nepal – was safely locked in his own box, but he lay quiet and did not stir. When he got to his study Sir Nathaniel came in, shutting the door behind him.

'I have come,' he said, 'while we have an opportunity of being alone, to tell you something of the Caswall family which I think will interest you. There is, or used to be, a belief in this part of the world that the Caswall family had some strange power of making the wills of other persons subservient to their own. There are many allusions to the subject in memoirs and other unimportant works, but I only know of one where the subject is spoken of definitely. It is *Mercia and its Worthies*, written by Ezra Toms more than a hundred years ago. The author goes into the question of the close association of the then Edgar Caswall with Mesmer in Paris. He speaks of Caswall being a pupil and the fellow-worker of Mesmer, and states that though, when the latter left France, he took away with him a vast quantity of philosophical and electric instruments, he was never known to use them again. He once made it known to a friend that he had given them to his old pupil. The term he used was odd, for it was "bequeathed", but no such bequest of Mesmer was ever made known. At any rate the instruments were missing, and never turned up.'

A servant came into the room to tell Adam that there was some strange noise coming from the locked room into which he had gone when he came in. He hurried off to the place at once, Sir Nathaniel going with them. Having locked the door behind them, Adam opened the packing-case where the boxes of the two mongooses were locked up. There was no sound from one of them, but from the other a queer restless struggling. Having opened both boxes, he found that the noise was from the Nepal animal, which, however, became quiet at once. In the other box the new mongoose lay dead, with every appearance of having being strangled!

10

THE KITE

On the following day, a little after four o'clock, Adam set out for Mercy.

He was home just as the clocks were striking six. He was pale and upset, but otherwise looked strong and alert. The old man summed up his appearance and manner thus: 'Braced up for battle.'

'Now!' said Sir Nathaniel, and settled down to listen, looking at Adam steadily and listening attentively that he might miss nothing – even the inflection of a word.

'I found Lilla and Mimi at home. Watford had been detained by business on the farm. Miss Watford received me as kindly as before;

Mimi, too, seemed glad to see me. Mr Caswall came so soon after I arrived, that he, or someone on his behalf, must have been watching for me. He was followed closely by the negro, who was puffing hard as if he had been running – so it was probably he who watched. Mr Caswall was very cool and collected, but there was a more than usually iron look about his face that I did not like. However, we got on very well. He talked pleasantly on all sorts of questions. The negro waited a while and then disappeared as on the other occasion. Mr Caswall's eyes were as usual fixed on Lilla. True, they seemed to be very deep and earnest, but there was no offence in them. Had it not been for the drawing down of the brows and the stern set of the jaws, I should not at first have noticed anything. But the stare, when presently it began, increased in intensity. I could see that Lilla began to suffer from nervousness, as on the first occasion; but she carried herself bravely. However, the more nervous she grew, the harder Mr Caswall stared. It was evident to me that he had come prepared for some sort of mesmeric or hypnotic battle. After a while he began to throw glances round him and then raised his hand, without letting either Lilla or Mimi see the action. It was evidently intended to give some sign to the negro, for he came, in his usual stealthy way, quietly in by the hall door, which was open. Then Mr Caswall's efforts at staring became intensified, and poor Lilla's nervousness grew greater. Mimi, seeing that her cousin was distressed, came close to her, as if to comfort or strengthen her with the consciousness of her presence. This evidently made a difficulty for Mr Caswall, for his efforts, without appearing to get feebler, seemed less effective. This continued for a little while, to the gain of both Lilla and Mimi. Then there was a diversion. Without word or apology the door opened, and Lady Arabella March entered the room. I had seen her coming through the great window. Without a word she crossed the room and stood beside Mr Caswall. It really was very like a fight of a peculiar kind; and the longer it was sustained the more earnest – the fiercer – it grew. That combination of forces – the over-lord, the white woman, and the black man – would have cost some – probably all of them – their lives in the Southern States of America. To us it was simply horrible. But all that you can understand. This time, to go on in sporting phrase, it was understood by all to be a "fight to a finish", and the mixed group did not slacken a moment to relax their efforts. On Lilla the strain began to tell disastrously. She grew pale – a patchy pallor, which meant that her nerves were out of order. She trembled like an aspen, and though she struggled bravely, I noticed that her legs would hardly support her. A dozen times she seemed about to collapse in a faint, but each time, on catching sight of Mimi's eyes, she made a fresh struggle and pulled through.

349

'By now Mr Caswall's face had lost its appearance of passivity. His eyes glowed with a fiery light. He was still the old Roman in inflexibility of purpose; but grafted on to the Roman was a new Berserker fury. His companions in the baleful work seemed to have taken on something of his feeling. Lady Arabella looked like a soulless, pitiless being, not human, unless it revived old legends of transformed human beings who had lost their humanity in some transformation or in the sweep of natural savagery. As for the negro – well, I can only say that it was solely due to the self-restraint which you impressed on me that I did not wipe him out as he stood – without warning, without fair play – without a single one of the graces of life and death. Lilla was silent in the helpless concentration of deadly fear; Mimi was all resolve and self-forgetfulness, so intent on the soul-struggle in which she was engaged that there was no possibility of any other thought. As for myself, the bonds of will which held me inactive seemed like bands of steel which numbed all my faculties, except sight and hearing. We seemed fixed in an *impasse*. Something must happen, though the power of guessing was inactive. As in a dream, I saw Mimi's hand move restlessly, as if groping for something. Mechanically, it touched that of Lilla, and in that instant she was transformed. It was as if youth and strength entered afresh into something already dead to sensibility and intention. As if by inspiration, she grasped the other's hand with a force which blenched the knuckles. Her face suddenly flamed, as if some divine light shone through it. Her form expanded till it stood out majestically. Lifting her right hand, she stepped forward towards Caswall, and with a bold sweep of her arm seemed to drive some strange force towards him. Again and again was the gesture repeated, the man falling back from her at each movement. Towards the door he retreated, she following. There was a sound as of the cooing sob of doves, which seemed to multiply and intensify with each second. The sound from the unseen source rose and rose as he retreated, till finally it swelled out in a triumphant peal, as she, with a fierce sweep of her arm, seemed to hurl something at her foe, and he, moving his hands blindly before his face, appeared to be swept through the doorway and out into the open sunlight.

'All at once my own faculties were fully restored; I could see and hear everything, and be fully conscious of what was going on. Even the figures of the baleful group were there, though dimly seen as through a veil – a shadowy veil. I saw Lilla sink down in a swoon, and Mimi throw up her arms in a gesture of triumph. As I saw her through the great window, the sunshine flooded the landscape, which, however, was momentarily becoming eclipsed by an onrush of a myriad birds.'

By the next morning, daylight showed the actual danger which threatened. From every part of the eastern counties reports were received concerning the enormous immigration of birds. Experts were sending – on their own account, on behalf of learned societies, and through local and imperial governing bodies – reports dealing with the matter, and suggesting remedies.

The reports closer to home were even more disturbing. All day long it would seem that the birds were coming thicker from all quarters. Doubtless many were going as well as coming, but the mass seemed never to get less. Each bird seemed to sound some note of fear or anger or seeking, and the whirring of wings never ceased nor lessened. The air was full of a muttered throb. No window or barrier could shut out the sound, till the ears of any listener became dulled by the ceaseless murmur. So monotonous it was, so cheerless, so disheartening, so melancholy, that all longed, but in vain, for any variety, no matter how terrible it might be.

The second morning the reports from all the districts round were more alarming than ever. Farmers began to dread the coming of winter as they saw the dwindling of the timely fruitfulness of the earth. And as yet it was only a warning of evil, not the evil accomplished; the ground began to look bare whenever some passing sound temporarily frightened the birds.

Edgar Caswall tortured his brain for a long time unavailingly, to think of some means of getting rid of what he, as well as his neighbours, had come to regard as a plague of birds. At last he recalled a circumstance which promised a solution of the difficulty. The experience was of some years ago in China, far up-country, towards the head-waters of the Yang-tze-Kiang, where the smaller tributaries spread out in a sort of natural irrigation scheme to supply the wilderness of paddy-fields. It was at the time of the ripening rice, and the myriads of birds which came to feed on the coming crop was a serious menace, not only to the district, but to the country at large. The farmers, who were more or less afflicted with the same trouble every season, knew how to deal with it. They made a vast kite, which they caused to be flown over the centre spot of the incursion. The kite was shaped like a great hawk; and the moment it rose into the air the birds began to cower and seek protection – and then to disappear. So long as that kite was flying overhead the birds lay low and the crop was saved. Accordingly Caswall ordered his men to construct an immense kite, adhering as well as they could to the lines of a hawk. Then he and his men, with a sufficiency of cord, began to fly it high overhead. The experience of China was repeated. The moment the kite rose, the birds hid or sought shelter. The following morning, the kite was still flying high, no bird was to be seen as far as the eye could reach from Castra Regis. But there followed in turn what proved even a worse evil. All the birds were cowed; their sounds stopped. Neither song nor chirp was heard – silence seemed to have taken the place of the normal voices of bird life. But that was not all. The silence spread to all animals.

351

The fear and restraint which brooded amongst the denizens of the air began to affect all life. Not only did the birds cease song or chirp, but the lowing of the cattle ceased in the fields and the varied sounds of life died away. In place of these things was only a soundless gloom, more dreadful, more disheartening, more soul-killing than any concourse of sounds, no matter how full of fear and dread. Pious individuals put up constant prayers for relief from the intolerable solitude. After a little there were signs of universal depression which those who ran might read. One and all, the faces of men and women seemed bereft of vitality, of interest, of thought, and, most of all, of hope. Men seemed to have lost the power of expression of their thoughts. The soundless air seemed to have the same effect as the universal darkness when men gnawed their tongues with pain.

From this infliction of silence there was no relief. Everything was affected; gloom was the predominant note. Joy appeared to have passed away as a factor of life, and this creative impulse had nothing to take its place. That giant spot in high air was a plague of evil influence. It seemed like a new misanthropic belief which had fallen on human beings, carrying with it the negation of all hope.

After a few days, men began to grow desperate; their very words as well as their senses seemed to be in chains. Edgar Caswall again tortured his brain to find any antidote or palliative of this greater evil than before. He would gladly have destroyed the kite, or caused its flying to cease; but the instant it was pulled down, the birds rose up in even greater numbers; all those who depended in any way on agriculture sent pitiful protests to Castra Regis.

It was strange indeed what influence that weird kite seemed to exercise. Even human beings were affected by it, as if both it and they were realities. As for the people at Mercy Farm, it was like a taste of actual death. Lilla felt it most. If she had been indeed a real dove, with a real kite hanging over her in the air, she could not have been more frightened or more affected by the terror this created.

Of course, some of those already drawn into the vortex noticed the effect on individuals. Those who were interested took care to compare their information. Strangely enough, as it seemed to the others, the person who took the ghastly silence least to heart was the negro. By nature he was not sensitive to, or afflicted by nerves. This alone would not have produced the seeming indifference, so they set their minds to discover the real cause. Adam came quickly to the conclusion that there was for him some compensation that the others did not share; and he soon believed that that compensation was in one form or another the enjoyment of the sufferings of others. Thus the black had a never-failing source of amusement.

Lady Arabella's cold nature rendered her immune to anything in the way of pain or trouble concerning others. Edgar Caswall was far too haughty a person, and too stern of nature, to concern himself about poor or helpless people, much less the lower order of mere animals. Mr Watford, Mr Salton, and Sir Nathaniel were all concerned in the issue, partly from kindness of heart – for none of them could see suffering, even of wild birds, unmoved – and partly on account of their property, which had to be protected, or ruin would stare them in the face before long.

Lilla suffered acutely. As time went on, her face became pinched, and her eyes dull with watching and crying. Mimi suffered too on account of her cousin's suffering. But as she could do nothing, she resolutely made up her mind to self-restraint and patience. Adam's frequent visits comforted her.

11

MESMER'S CHEST

After a couple of weeks had passed, the kite seemed to give Edgar Caswall a new zest for life. He was never tired of looking at its movements. He had a comfortable armchair put out on the tower, wherein he sat sometimes all day long, watching as though the kite was a new toy, and he a child lately come into the possession of it. He did not seem to have lost interest in Lilli, for he still paid an occasional visit at Mercy Farm.

Indeed, his feeling towards her, whatever it had been at first, had now so far changed that it had become a distinct affection of a purely animal kind. Indeed, it seemed as though the man's nature had become corrupted, and that all the baser and more selfish and more reckless qualities had become more conspicuous. There was not so much sternness apparent in his nature, because there was less self-restraint. Determination had become indifference.

The visible change in Edgar was that he grew morbid, sad, silent; the neighbours thought he was going mad. He became absorbed in the kite, and watched it not only by day, but often all night long. It became an obsession to him.

Caswall took a personal interest in the keeping of the great kite flying. He had a vast coil of cord efficient for the purpose, which worked on a roller fixed on the parapet of the tower. There was a winch for the pulling in of the slack; the outgoing line being controlled by a racket. There was invariably one man at least, day and night, on the tower to attend to it. At such an elevation there was always a strong wind, and at times the kite rose to an enormous height, as well as travelling for great distances laterally. In fact, the kite became, in a short time, one of the curiosities of Castra Regis and all around it. Edgar began to attribute to it, in his own mind, almost human qualities. It became to him a separate entity, with a mind and a soul of its own. Being idle-handed all day, he began to apply to what he considered the service of the kite some of his spare time, and found a new pleasure – a new object in life – in the old schoolboy game of sending up 'runners' to the kite. The way this is done is to get round pieces of paper so cut that there is a hole in the centre, through which the string of the kite passes. The natural action of the wind-pressure takes the paper along the string, and so up to the kite itself, no matter how high or how far away it may have gone.

In the early days of this amusement Edgar Caswall spent hours. Hundreds of such messengers flew along the string, until soon he bethought him of writing messages on these papers so that he could make known his ideas to the kite. It may be that his brain gave way under the opportunities given by his illusion of the entity of the toy and its power of separate thought. From sending messages he came to making direct speech to the kite – without, however, ceasing to send the runners. Doubtless, the height of the tower, seated as it was on the hilltop, the rushing of the ceaseless wind, the hypnotic effect of the lofty altitude of the speck in the sky at which he gazed, and the rushing of the paper messengers up the string till sight of them was lost in distance, all helped to further affect his brain, undoubtedly giving way under the strain of beliefs and cirumstances which were at once stimulating to the imagination, occupative of his mind, and absorbing.

The next step of intellectual decline was to bring to bear on the main idea of the conscious identity of the kite all sorts of subjects which had imaginative force or tendency of their own. He had, in Castra Regis, a large collection of curios and interesting things formed in the past by his forbears, of similar tastes to his own. There were all sorts of strange anthropological specimens, both old and new, which had been collected through various travels in strange places: ancient Egyptian relics from tombs and mummies; curios from Australia, New Zealand, and the South Seas; idols and images – from Tartar ikons to ancient Egyptian, Persian, and Indian objects of worship; objects of death and torture of American Indians; and, above all, a vast collection of lethal weapons of every kind and from every place – Chinese 'high pinders', double knives, Afghan double-edged scimitars made to cut a body in two, heavy knives from all the Eastern countries, ghost daggers from Thibet, the terrible kukri of the

Gurka and other hill tribes of India, assassins' weapons from Italy and Spain, even the knife which was formerly carried by the slavedrivers of the Mississippi region. Death and pain of every kind were fully represented in that gruesome collection.

That it had a fascination for Oolanga goes without saying. He was never tired of visiting the museum in the tower, and spent endless hours in inspecting the exhibits, till he was thoroughly familiar with every detail of all of them. He asked permission to clean and polish and sharpen them – a favour which was readily granted. In addition to the above objects, there were many things of a kind to awaken human fear. Stuffed serpents of the most objectionable and horrid kind; giant insects from the tropics, fearsome in every detail; fishes and crustaceans covered with weird spikes; dried octopuses of great size. Other things, too, there were, not less deadly though seemingly innocuous – dried fungi, traps intended for birds, beasts, fishes, reptiles, and insects; machines which could produce pain of any kind and degree, and the only mercy of which was the power of producing speedy death.

Caswall, who had never before seen any of these things, except those which he had collected himself, found a constant amusement and interest in them. He studied them, their uses, their mechanism – where there was such – and their places of origin, until he had an ample and real knowledge of all concerning them. Many were secret and intricate, but he never rested till he found out all the secrets. When once he had become interested in strange objects, and the way to use them, he began to explore various likely places for similar finds. He began to inquire of his household where strange lumber was kept. Several of the men spoke of old Simon Chester as one who knew everything in and about the house. Accordingly, he sent for the old man, who came at once. He was very old, nearly ninety years of age, and very infirm. He had been born in the Castle, and had served its succession of masters – present or absent – ever since. When Edgar began to question him on the subject regarding which he had sent for him, old Simon exhibited much perturbation. In fact, he became so frightened that his master, fully believing that he was concealing something, ordered him to tell at once what remained unseen, and where it was hidden away. Face to face with discovery of his secret, the old man, in a pitiable state of concern, spoke out even more fully than Mr Caswall had expected.

'Indeed, indeed, sir, everything is here in the tower that has ever been put away in my time – except – except – ' here he began to shake and tremble – 'except the chest which Mr Edgar – he who was Mr Edgar when I first took service – brought back from France, after he had been with Dr Mesmer. The trunk has been kept in my room for safety; but I shall send it down here now.'

'What is in it?' asked Edgar sharply.

'That I do not know. Moreover, it is a peculiar trunk, without any visible means of opening.'

'Is there no lock?'

'I suppose so sir; but I do not know. There is no keyhole.'

'Send it here; and then come to me yourself.'

The trunk, a heavy one with steel bands round it, but no lock or keyhole, was carried in by two men. Shortly afterwards old Simon attended his master. When he came into the room, Mr Caswall himself went and closed the door; then he asked:

'How do you open it?'

'I do not know, sir.'

'Do you mean to say that you never opened it?'

'Most certainly I say so, your honour. How could I? It was entrusted to me with the other things by my master. To open it, would have been a breach of trust.'

Caswall sneered.

'Quite remarkable! Leave it with me. Close the door behind you. Stay – did no one ever tell you about it – say anything regarding it – make any remark?'

Old Simon turned pale, and put his trembling hands together.

'Oh, sir, I entreat you not to touch it. That trunk probably contains secrets which Dr Mesmer told my master. Told them to his ruin!'

'How do you mean? What ruin?'

'Sir, he it was who, men said, sold his soul to the Evil One; I had thought that that time and the evil of it had all passed away.'

'That will do. Go away; but remain in your own room, or within call. I may want you.'

The old man bowed deeply and went out trembling, but without speaking a word.

12

THE CHEST OPENED

Left alone in the turret-room, Edgar Caswall carefully locked the door and hung a handkerchief over the keyhole. Next, he inspected the windows, and saw that they were not overlooked from any angle of the main building. Then he carefully examined the trunk, going over it with a magnifying glass. He found it intact: the steel bands were flawless; the whole trunk was compact. After sitting opposite to it for some time, and the shades of evening beginning to melt into darkness, he gave up the task and went to his bedroom, after locking the door of the turret-room behind him and taking away the key.

He woke in the morning at daylight, and resumed his patient but unavailing study of the metal trunk. This he continued during the whole day with the same result – humiliating disappointment, which over-wrought his nerves and made his head ache. The result of the long strain was seen later in the afternoon, when he sat locked within the turret-room before the still baffling trunk, distrait, listless and yet agitated, sunk in a settled gloom. As the dusk was falling he told the steward to send him two men, strong ones. These he ordered to take the trunk to his bedroom. In that room he then sat on into the night, without pausing even to take any food. His mind was in a whirl, a fever of excitement. The result was that when, late in the night, he locked himself in his room his brain was full of odd fancies: he was on the high road to mental disturbance. He lay down on his bed in the dark, still brooding over the mystery of the closed trunk.

Gradually he yielded to the influences of silence and darkness. After lying there quietly for some time, his mind became active again. But this time there were round him no disturbing influences; his brain was active and able to work freely and to deal with memory. A thousand forgotten – or only half-known – incidents, fragments of conversations or theories long ago guessed at and long forgotten, crowded on his mind. He seemed to hear again around him the legions of whirring wings to which he had been so lately accustomed. Even to himself he knew that that was an effort of imagination founded on imperfect memory. But he was content that imagination should work, for out of it might come some solution of the mystery which surrounded him. And in this frame of mind, sleep made another and more successful essay. This time he enjoyed peaceful slumber, restful alike to his wearied body and his overwrought brain.

In his sleep he arose, and, as if in obedience to some influence beyond and greater than himself, lifted the great trunk and set it on a strong table at one side of the room, from which he had previously removed a quantity of books. To do this, he had to use an amount of strength which was, he knew, far beyond him in his normal state. As it was, it seemed easy enough; everything yielded before his touch. Then he became conscious that somehow – how, he never could remember – the chest was open. He unlocked his door, and, taking the chest on his shoulder, carried it up to the turret-room, the door of which also he unlocked. Even at the time he was amazed at his own strength, and wondered whence it had come. His mind, lost in conjecture, was too far off to realize more immediate things.

He knew that the chest was enormously heavy. He seemed, in a sort of vision which lit up the absolute blackness around, to see the two sturdy servant men staggering under its great weight. He locked himself again in the turret-room, and laid the opened chest on a table, and in the darkness began to unpack it, laying out the contents, which were mainly of metal and glass – great pieces in strange forms – on another table. He was conscious of being still asleep, and of acting rather in obedience to some unseen and unknown command than in accordance with any reasonable plan, to be followed by results which he understood. This phase completed, he proceeded to arrange in order the component parts of some large instruments, formed mostly of glass. His fingers seemed to have acquired a new and exquisite subtlety and even a volition of their own. Then weariness of brain came upon him; his head sank down on his breast, and little by little everything became wrapped in gloom.

He awoke in the early morning in his bedroom, and looked around him, now clear-headed, in amazement. In its usual place on the strong table stood the great steel-hooped chest without lock or key. But it was now locked. He arose quietly and stole to the turret-room. There everything was as it had been on the previous evening. He looked out of the window where high in the air flew, as usual, the giant kite. He unlocked the wicket gate of the turret stair and went out on the roof. Close to him was the great coil of cord on its reel. It was humming in the morning breeze, and when he touched the string it sent a quick thrill through hand and arm. There was no sign anywhere that there had been any disturbance or displacement of anything during the night.

Utterly bewildered, he sat down in his room to think. Now for the first time he *felt* that he was asleep and dreaming. Presently he fell asleep again, and slept for a long time. He awoke hungry and made a hearty meal. Then towards evening, having locked himself in, he fell asleep again. When he woke he was in darkness, and was quite at sea as to his whereabouts. He began feeling about the dark room and was recalled to the consequences of his position by the breaking of a large piece of glass. Having obtained a light, he discovered this to be a glass wheel, part of an elaborate piece of mechanism which he must in his sleep have taken from the chest, which was now opened. He had once again opened it whilst asleep, but he had no recollection of the circumstances.

Caswall came to the conclusion that there had been some sort of dual action of his mind, which might lead to some catastrophe or some discovery of his secret plans; so he resolved to forego for a while the pleasure of making discoveries regarding the chest. To this end, he applied himself to quite another matter – an investigation of the other treasures and rare objects in his collections. He went amongst them in simple, idle curiosity, his main object being to discover some strange item which he might use for experiments with the kite. He had already resolved to try some runners other than those made of paper. He had a vague idea that with such a force as the great kite straining at its leash, this might be used to lift to the altitude of the kite itself heavier articles. His first experiment with articles of little but increasing weight was eminently successful. So he added by degrees more and more weight, until he found out that the lifting power of the kite was considerable. He then determined to take a step further, and send to the kite some of the articles which lay in the steel-hooped chest. The last time he had opened it in sleep, it had not been shut again, and he had inserted a wedge so that he could open it at will. He made examination of the contents, but came to the conclusion that the glass objects were unsuitable. They were too light for testing weight, and they were so frail as to be dangerous to send to such a height.

So he looked around for something more solid with which to experiment. His eye caught sight of an object which at once attracted him. This was a small copy of one of the ancient Egyptian gods – that of Bes, who represented the destructive power of nature. It was so bizarre and mysterious as to commend itself to his mad humour. In lifting it from the cabinet, he was struck by its great weight in proportion to its size. He made accurate examination of it by the aid of some instruments, and came to the conclusion that it was carved from a lump of lodestone. He remembered that he had read somewhere of an ancient Egyptian god cut from a similar substance, and, thinking it over, he came to the conclusion that he must have read it in Sir Thomas Brown's *Popular Errors*, a book of the seventeenth century. He got the book from the library, and looked out the passage:

'A great example we have from the observation of our learned friend, Mr *Graves*, in an Egyptian idol cut out of Loadstone and found among the *Mummies*; which still retains its attraction, though probably taken out of the mine about two thousand years ago.'

The strangeness of the figure, and its being so close akin to his own nature, attracted him. He made from thin wood a large circular runner, and in front of it placed the weighty god, sending it up to the flying kite along the throbbing cord.

13

OOLANGA'S HALLUCINATIONS

During the last few days Lady Arabella had been getting exceedingly impatient. Her debts, always pressing, were growing to an embarrassing amount. The only hope she had of comfort in life was a good marriage; but the good marriage on which she had fixed her eye did not seem to move quickly enough – indeed, it did not seem to move at all – in the right direction. Edgar Caswall was not an ardent wooer. From the very first he seemed *difficile*, but he had been keeping to his own room ever since his struggle with Mimi Watford. On that occasion Lady Arabella had shown him in an unmistakable way what her feelings were; indeed, she had made it known to him, in a more overt way than pride should allow, that she wished to help and support him. The moment when she had gone across the room to stand beside him in his mesmeric struggle, had been the very limit of her voluntary action. It was quite bitter enough, she felt, that he did not come to her, but now that she had made that advance, she felt that any withdrawal on his part would, to a woman of her class, be nothing less than a flaming insult. Had she not classed herself with his negro servant, an unreformed savage? Had she not shown her preference for him at the festival of his home-coming? Had she not. . . . Lady Arabella was cold-blooded and she was prepared to go through all that might be necessary of indifference, and even insult, to become chatelaine of Castra Regis. In the meantime, she would show no hurry – she must wait. She might, in an unostentatious way, come to him again. She knew him now, and could make a keen guess at his desires with regard to Lilla Watford. With that secret in her possession, she could bring pressure to bear on Caswall which would make it no easy matter for him to evade her. The great difficulty was how to get near him. He was shut up within his Castle, and guarded by a defence of convention which she could not pass without danger of ill repute to herself. Over this question she thought and thought for days and nights. At last she decided that the only way would be to go to him openly at Castra Regis. Her rank and position would make such a thing possible, if carefully done. She could explain matters afterwards if necessary. Then when they were alone, she would use her arts and her experience to make him commit himself. After all, he was only a man, with a man's dislike of difficult or awkward situations. She felt quite sufficient confidence in her own womanhood to carry her through any difficulty which might arise.

360

From Diana's Grove she heard each day the luncheon-gong from Castra Regis sound, and knew the hour when the servants would be in the back of the house. She would enter the house at that hour, and, pretending that she could not make anyone hear her, would seek him in his own rooms. The tower was, she knew, away from all the usual sounds of the house, and moreover she knew that the servants had strict orders not to interrupt him when he was in the turret chamber. She had found out, partly by the aid of an opera-glass and partly by judicious questioning, that several times lately a heavy chest had been carried to and from his room, and that it rested in the room each night. She was, therefore, confident that he had some important work on hand which would keep him busy for long spells.

Meanwhile, another member of the household at Castra Regis had schemes which he thought were working to fruition. A man in the position of a servant has plenty of opportunity of watching his betters and forming opinions regarding them. Oolanga was in his way a clever, unscrupulous rogue, and he felt that with things moving round him in this great household there should be opportunities of self-advancement. Being unscrupulous and stealthy – and a savage – he looked to dishonest means. He saw plainly enough that Lady Arabella was making a dead set at his master, and he was watchful of the slightest sign of anything which might enhance this knowledge. Like the other men in the house, he knew of the carrying to and fro of the great chest, and had got it into his head that the care exercised in its porterage indicated that it was full of treasure. He was for ever lurking around the turret-rooms on the chance of making some useful discovery. But he was as cautious as he was stealthy, and took care that no one else watched him.

It was thus that the negro became aware of Lady Arabella's venture into the house, as she thought, unseen. He took more care than ever, since he was watching another, that the positions were not reversed. More than ever he kept his eyes and ears open and his mouth shut. Seeing Lady Arabella gliding up the stairs towards his master's room, he took it for granted that she was there for no good, and doubled his watching intentness and caution.

Oolanga was disappointed, but he dared not exhibit any feeling lest it should betray that he was hiding. Therefore he slunk downstairs again noiselessly, and waited for a more favourable opportunity of furthering his plans. It must be borne in mind that he thought that the heavy trunk was full of valuables, and that he believed that Lady Arabella had come to try to steal it. His purpose of using for his own advantage the combination of these two ideas was seen later in the day. Oolanga secretly followed her home. He was an expert at this game, and succeeded admirably on this occasion. He watched her enter the private gate of Diana's Grove, and then, taking a roundabout course and keeping out of her sight, he at last overtook her in a thick part of the Grove where no one could see the meeting.

Lady Arabella was much surprised. She had not seen the negro for several days, and had almost forgotten his existence. Oolanga would have been startled had he known and been capable of understanding the real value placed on him, his beauty, his worthiness, by other persons, and compared it with the value in these matters in which he held himself. Doubtless Oolanga had his dreams like other men. In such cases he saw himself as a young sun-god, as beautiful as the eye of dusky or even white womanhood had ever dwelt upon. He would have been filled with all noble and captivating qualities – or those regarded as such in his Africa home. Women would have loved him, and would have told him so in the overt and fervid manner usual in affairs of the heart in the shadowy depths of the forest of the Gold Coast.

Oolanga came close behind Lady Arabella, and in a hushed voice, suitable to the importance of his task, and in deference to the respect he had for her and the place, began to unfold the story of his love. Lady Arabella was not usually a humorous person, but no man or woman of the white race could have checked the laughter which rose spontaneously to her lips. The circumstances were too grotesque, the contrast too violent, for subdued mirth. The man a debased and primitive specimen and of an ugliness which was simply devilish; the woman of high degree, beautiful, accomplished. She thought that her first moment's consideration of the outrage – it was nothing less in her eyes – had given her the full material for thought. But every instant after threw new and varied lights on the affront. Her indignation was too great for passion; only irony or satire would meet the situation. Her cold, cruel nature helped, and she did not shrink to subject this ignorant savage to the merciless fire-lash of her scorn.

Oolanga was dimly conscious that he was being flouted; but his anger was no less keen because of the measure of his ignorance. So he gave way to it, as does a tortured beast. He ground his great teeth together, raved, stamped, and swore in barbarous tongues and with barbarous imagery. Even Lady Arabella felt it was well she was within reach of help, or he might have offered her brutal violence – even have killed her.

'Am I to understand,' she said with cold distain, so much more effective to wound than hot passion, 'that you are offering me your love? *Your –* love?'

For reply he nodded his head. The scorn of her voice, in a sort of baleful hiss, sounded – and felt – like the lash of a whip.

'And you dared! you – a savage – a slave – the basest thing in the world of vermin! Take care! I don't value your worthless life more than I do that of a rat or a spider. Don't let me ever see your hideous face here again, or I shall rid the earth of you.'

As she was speaking, she had taken out her revolver and was pointing it at him. In the immediate presence of death his impudence forsook him, and he made a weak effort to justify himself. His speech was short, consisting of single words. To Lady Arabella it sounded mere gibberish but it was in his own dialect, and meant love, marriage, wife. From the intonation of the words, she guessed, with her woman's quick intuition, at their meaning; but she quite failed to follow, when, becoming more pressing, he continued to urge his suit in a mixture of the grossest animal passion and ridiculous threats. He warned her that he knew she had tried to steal his master's treasure, and that he had caught her in the act. But if she would be his, he would share the treasure with her, and they would live in luxury in the African forests. But, if she refused, he would tell his master, who would flog and torture her and then give her to the police, who would kill her.

14

BATTLE RENEWED

The consequences of that meeting in the dusk of Diana's Grove were acute and far-reaching, and not only to the two engaged in it. From Oolanga, this might have been expected by anyone who knew the character of his type. To such, there are two passions that are inexhaustible and insatiable – vanity and that which they are pleased to call love. Oolanga left the Grove with an absorbing hatred in his heart. His lust and greed were afire, while his vanity had been wounded to the core. Lady Arabella's icy nature was not so deeply stirred, though she was in a seething passion. More than ever she was set upon bringing Edgar Caswall to her feet. The obstacles she had encountered, the insults she had endured, were only a fuel to the purpose of revenge which consumed her.

As she sought her own rooms in Diana's Grove, she went over the whole subject again and again, always finding in the face of Lilla Watford a key to a problem which puzzled her – the problem of a way to turn Caswall's powers – his very existence – to aid her purpose.

When in her boudoir, she wrote a note, taking so much trouble over it

363

that she destroyed, and re-wrote, till her dainty waste-basket was half-full of torn sheets of note-paper. When quite satisfied, she copied out the last sheet afresh, and then carefully burned all the spoiled fragments. She put the copied note in an emblazoned envelope, and directed it to Edgar Caswall at Castra Regis. This she sent off by one of her grooms. The letter ran:

'Dear Mr Caswall, –

'I want to have a chat with you on a subject in which I believe you are interested. Will you kindly call for me one day after lunch – say at three or four o'clock, and we can walk a little way together. Only as far as Mercy Farm, where I want to see Lilla and Mimi Watford. We can take a cup of tea at the Farm. Do not bring your African servant with you, as I am afraid his face frightens the girls. After all, he is not pretty, is he? I have an idea you will be pleased with your visit this time.

'Yours sincerely,
'ARABELLA MARCH.'

At half-past three next day, Edgar Caswall called at Diana's Grove. Lady Arabella met him on the roadway outside the gate. She wished to take the servants into her confidence as little as possible. She turned when she saw him coming, and walked beside him towards Mercy Farm, keeping step with him as they walked. When they got near Mercy, she turned and looked around her, expecting to see Oolanga or some sign of him. He was, however, not visible. He had received from his master peremptory orders to keep out of sight – an order for which the African scored a new offence up against her. They found Lilla and Mimi at home and seemingly glad to see them, though both the girls were surprised at the visit coming so soon after the other.

The proceedings were a repetition of the battle of souls of the former visit. On this occasion, however, Edgar Caswall had only the presence of Lady Arabella to support him – Oolanga being absent; but Mimi lacked the support of Adam Salton, which had been of such effective service before. This time the struggle for supremacy of will was longer and more determined. Caswall felt that if he could not achieve supremacy, he had better give up the idea, so all his pride was enlisted against Mimi. When they had been waiting for the door to be opened, Lady Arabella, believing in a sudden attack, had said to him in a low voice, which somehow carried conviction:

'This time you should win. Mimi is, after all, only a woman. Show her no mercy. That is weakness. Fight her, beat her, trample on her – kill her if need be. She stands in your way, and I hate her. Never take your eyes off her. Never mind Lilla – she is afraid of you. You are already her master. Mimi will try to make you look at her cousin. There lies defeat. Let nothing take your attention from Mimi, and you will win. If she is overcoming you, take my hand and hold it hard whilst you are looking into her eyes. If she is too strong for you, I shall interfere. I'll make a diversion, and under cover of it you must retire unbeaten, even if not victorious. Hush! they are coming.'

The two girls came to the door together. Strange sounds were coming up over the Brow from the west. It was the rustling and crackling of the dry reeds and rushes from the low lands. The season had been an unusually dry one. Also the strong east wind was helping forward enormous flocks of birds, most of them pigeons with white cowls. Not only were their wings whirring, but their cooing was plainly audible. From such a multitude of birds the mass of sound, individually small, assumed the volume of a storm. Surprised at the influx of birds, to which they had been strangers so long, they all looked towards Castra Regis, from whose high tower the great kite had been flying as usual. But even as they looked, the cord broke, and the great kite fell headlong in a series of sweeping dives. Its own weight and the aerial force opposed to it, which caused it to rise, combined with the strong easterly breeze, had been too much for the great length of cord holding it.

Somehow, the mishap to the kite gave new hope to Mimi. It was as though the side issues had been shorn away, so that the main struggle was thenceforth on simpler lines. She had a feeling in her heart, as though some religious chord had been newly touched. It may, of course, have been that with the renewal of the bird voices a fresh courage, a fresh belief in the good issue of the struggle came too. In the misery of silence, from which they had all suffered for so long, any new train of thought was almost bound to be a boon. As the inrush of birds continued, their wings beating against the crackling rushes, Lady Arabella grew pale, and almost fainted.

'What is that?' she asked suddenly.

To Mimi, born and bred in Siam, the sound was strangely like an exaggeration of the sound produced by a snake-charmer.

Edgar Caswall was the first to recover from the interruption of the falling kite. After a few minutes he seemed to have quite recovered his *sang-froid*, and was able to use his brains to the end which he had in view. Mimi too quickly recovered herself, but from a different cause. With her it was a deep religious conviction that the struggle round her was of the powers of Good and Evil, and that Good was triumphant. The very appearance of the snowy birds, with the cowls of Saint Columba, heightened the impression. With this conviction strong upon her, she continued the strange battle with fresh vigour. She seemed to tower over Caswall, and he to give back before her oncoming. Once again her vigorous passes drove him to the door. He was just going out backward when Lady Arabella, who had been gazing at him with fixed eyes, caught his hand and tried to stop his movement. She was, however, unable to do any good, and so, holding hands, they passed out together. As they did so, the strange music which had so alarmed Lady Arabella suddenly stopped. Instinctively they all looked towards the tower of Castra Regis, and saw that the workmen had refixed the kite, which had risen again and was beginning to float out to its former station.

As they were looking, the door opened and Michael Watford came into the room. By that time all had recovered their self-possession, and there was nothing out of the common to attract his attention. As he came in, seeing inquiring looks all around him, he said:

'The new influx of birds is only the annual migration of pigeons from Africa. I am told that it will soon be over.'

The second victory of Mimi Watford made Edgar Caswall more moody than ever. He felt thrown back on himself, and this, added to his absorbing interest in the hope of a victory of his mesmeric powers, became a deep and settled purpose of revenge. The chief object of his animosity was, of course, Mimi, whose will had overcome his, but it was obscured in greater or lesser degree by all who had opposed him. Lilla was next to Mimi in his hate – Lilla, the harmless, tender-hearted, sweet-natured girl, whose heart was so full of love for all things that in it was no room for the passions of ordinary life – whose nature resembled those doves of St Columba, whose colour she wore, whose appearance she reflected. Adam Salton came next – after a gap; for against him Caswall had no direct animosity. He regarded him as an interference, a difficulty to be got rid of or destroyed. The young Australian had been so discreet that the most he had against him was his knowledge of what had been. Caswall did not understand him, and to such a nature as his, ignorance was a cause of alarm, of dread.

Caswall resumed his habit of watching the great kite straining at its cord, varying his vigils in this way by a further examination of the mysterious treasures of his house especially Mesmer's chest. He sat much on the roof of the tower, brooding over his thwarted passion. The vast extent of his possessions, visible to him at that altitude, might, one would have thought, have restored some of his complacency. But the very extent of his ownership, thus perpetually brought before him, created a fresh sense of grievance. How was it, he thought, that with so much at command that others wished for, he could not achieve the dearest wishes of his heart?

In this state of intellectual and moral depravity, he found a solace in the renewal of his experiments with the mechanical powers of the kite. For a couple of weeks he did not see Lady Arabella, who was always on the watch for a chance of meeting him; neither did he see the Watford girls, who studiously kept out of his way. Adam Salton simply marked time, keeping ready to deal with anything that might affect his friends. He called at the farm and heard from Mimi of the last battle of wills, but it had only one consequence. He got from Ross several more mongooses, including a second king-cobra killer, which he generally carried with him in its box whenever he walked out.

Mr Caswall's experiments with the kite went on successfully. Each day he tried the lifting of greater weight, and it seemed almost as if the machine had a sentience of its own, which was increasing with the obstacles placed before it. All this time the kite hung in the sky at an enormous height. The wind was steadily from the north, so the trend of the kite was to the south. All day long, runners of increasing magnitude were sent up. These were only of paper or thin cardboard, or leather, or other flexible materials. The great height at which the kite hung made a great concave curve in the string, so that as the runners went up they made a flapping sound. If one laid a finger on the string, the sound answered to the flapping of the runner in a sort of hollow intermittent murmur. Edgar Caswall, who was now wholly obsessed by the kite and all belonging to it, found a distinct resemblance between that intermittent rumble and the snake charming music produced by the pigeons flying through the dry reeds.

One day he made a discovery in Mesmer's chest which he thought he would utilize with regard to the runners. This was a great length of wire, 'fine as human hair', coiled round a finely made wheel, which ran to a wondrous distance freely, and as lightly. He tried this on runners, and found it worked admirably. Whether the runner was alone, or carried something much more weighty than itself, it worked equally well. Also it was strong enough and light enough to draw back the runner without undue strain. He tried this a good many times successfully, but it was now growing dusk and he found some difficulty in keeping the runner in sight. So he looked for something heavy enough to keep it still. He placed the Egyptian image of Bes on the fine wire, which crossed the wooden ledge which protected it. Then, the darkness growing, he went indoors and forgot all about it.

He had a strange feeling of uneasiness that night – not sleeplessness, for he seemed conscious of being asleep. At daylight he rose, and as usual looked out for the kite. He did not see it in its usual position in the sky, so looked round the points of the compass. He was more than astonished when presently he saw the missing kite struggling as usual against the controlling cord. But it had gone to the further side of the tower, and now hung and strained *against the wind* to the north. He thought it so strange that he determined to investigate the phenomenon, and to say nothing about it in the meantime.

In his many travels, Edgar Caswall had been accustomed to use the sextant, and was now an expert in the matter. By the aid of this and other instruments, he was able to fix the position of the kite and the point over which it hung. He was startled to find that exactly under it – so far as he could ascertain – was Diana's Grove. He had an inclination to take Lady Arabella into his confidence in the matter, but he thought better of it and wisely refrained. For some reason which he did not try to explain to himself, he was glad of his silence, when, on the following morning, he found, on looking out, that the point over which the kite then hovered was Mercy Farm. When he had verified this with his instruments, he sat before the window of the tower, looking out and thinking. The new locality was more to his liking than the other; but the why of it puzzled him all the same. He spent the rest of the day in the turret-room, which he did not leave all day. It seemed to him that he was now drawn by forces which he could not control – of which, indeed, he had no knowledge – in directions which he did not understand, and which were without his own volition. In sheer helpless inability to think the problem out satisfactorily, he called up a servant and told him to tell Oolanga that he wanted to see him at once in the turret-room. The answer came back that the African had not been seen since the previous evening.

Caswall was now so irritable that even this small thing upset him. As he was distrait and wanted to talk to somebody, he sent for Simon Chester, who came at once, breathless with hurrying and upset by the unexpected summons. Caswall bade him sit down, and when the old man was in a less uneasy frame of mind, he again asked him if he had ever seen what was in Mesmer's chest or heard it spoken about. Chester admitted that he had once, in the time of 'the then Mr Edgar', seen the chest open, which, knowing something of its history and guessing more, so upset him that he had fainted. When he recovered, the chest was closed. From that time the then Mr Edgar had never spoken about it again.

When Caswall asked him to describe what he had seen when the chest was open, he got very agitated, and, despite all his efforts to remain calm, he suddenly went off into a faint. Caswall summoned servants, who applied the usual remedies. Still the old man did not recover. After the lapse of a considerable time, the doctor who had been summoned made his appearance. A glance was sufficient for him to make up his mind. Still, he knelt down by the old man, and made a careful examination. Then he rose to his feet, and in a hushed voice said:

'I grieve to say, sir, that he has passed away.'

15

ON THE TRACK

Those who had seen Edgar Caswall familiarly since his arrival, and had already estimated his cold-blooded nature of something of its true value, were surprised that he took so to heart the death of Old Chester. The fact was that not one of them had guessed correctly at his character. They thought, naturally enough, that the concern which he felt was that of a master for a faithful old servant of his family. They little thought that it was merely the selfish expression of his disappointment, that he had thus lost the only remaining clue to an interesting piece of family history – one which was now and would be for ever wrapped in mystery. Caswall knew enough about the life of his ancestor in Paris to wish to know more fully and more thoroughly all that had been. The period covered by that ancestor's life in Paris was one inviting every form of curiosity.

Lady Arabella, who had her own game to play, saw in the *métier* of sympathetic friend, a series of meetings with the man she wanted to secure. She made the first use of the opportunity the day after old Chester's death; indeed, as soon as the news had filtered in through the back door of Diana's Grove. At that meeting, she played her part so well that even Caswall's cold nature was impressed.

Oolanga was the only one who did not credit her with at least some sense of fine feeling in the matter. In emotional, as in other matters, Oolanga was distinctly a utilitarian, and as he could not understand anyone feeling grief except for his own suffering, pain, or for the loss of money, he could not understand anyone simulating such an emotion except for show intended to deceive. He thought that she had come to Castra Regis again for the opportunity of stealing something, and was determined that on this occasion the chance of pressing his advantage over her should not pass. He felt, therefore, that the occasion was one for extra carefulness in the watching of all that went on. Ever since he had come to the conclusion that Lady Arabella was trying to steal the treasure-chest, he suspected nearly everyone of the same design, and made it a point to watch all suspicious persons and places. As Adam was engaged on his own researches regarding Lady Arabella, it was only natural that there should be some crossing of each other's tracks. This is what did actually happen.

Adam had gone for an early morning survey of the place in which he was interested, taking with him the mongoose in its box. He arrived at the gate of Diana's Grove just as Lady Arabella was preparing to set out for Castra Regis on what she considered her mission of comfort. Seeing Adam from her window going through the shadows of the trees round the gate, she thought that he must be engaged on some purpose similar to her own. So, quickly making her toilet, she quietly left the house, and, taking advantage of every shadow and substance which could hide her, followed him on his walk.

Oolanga, the experienced tracker, followed her, but succeeded in hiding his movements better than she did. He saw that Adam had on his shoulder a mysterious box, which he took to contain something valuable. Seeing that Lady Arabella was secretly following Adam, he was confirmed in this idea. His mind – such as it was – was fixed on her trying to steal, and he credited her at once with making use of this new opportunity.

In this walk, Adam went into the grounds of Castra Regis, and Oolanga saw her follow him with great secrecy. He feared to go closer, as now on both sides of him were enemies who might make discovery. When he realized that Lady Arabella was bound for the Castle, he devoted himself to following her with singleness of purpose. He therefore missed seeing that Adam branched off the track and returned to the high road.

That night Edgar Caswall had slept badly. The tragic occurrence of the day was on his mind, and he kept waking and thinking of it. After an early breakfast, he sat at the open window watching the kite and thinking of many things. From his room he could see all round the neighbourhood, but the two places that interested him most were Mercy Farm and Diana's Grove. At first the movements about those spots were of a humble kind – those that belong to domestic service or agricultural needs – the opening of doors and windows, the sweeping and brushing, and generally the restoration of habitual order.

From his high window – whose height made it a screen from the observation of others – he saw the chain of watchers move into his own grounds, and then presently break up – Adam Salton going one way and Lady Arabella, followed by the nigger, another. Then Oolanga disappeared amongst the trees; but Caswall could see that he was still watching. Lady Arabella, after looking around her, slipped in by the open door, and he could, of course, see her no longer.

Presently, however, he heard a light tap at his door, then the door opened slowly, and he could see the flash of Lady Arabella's white dress through the opening.

16

A VISIT OF SYMPATHY

Caswall was genuinely surprised when he saw Lady Arabella, though he need not have been, after what had already occurred in the same way. The look of surprise on his face was so much greater than Lady Arabella had expected – though she thought she was prepared to meet anything that might occur – that she stood still, in sheer amazement. Cold-blooded as she was and ready for all social emergencies, she was nonplussed how to go on. She was plucky, however, and began to speak at once, although she had not the slightest idea what she was going to say.

'I came to offer you my very warm sympathy with the grief you have so lately experienced.'

'My grief? I'm afraid I must be very dull; but I really do not understand.'

Already she felt at a disadvantage, and hesitated.

'I mean about the old man who died so suddenly – your old . . . retainer.'

Caswall's face relaxed something of its puzzled concentration.

'Oh, he was only a servant; and he had overstayed his three-score-and-ten years by something like twenty years. He must have been ninety!'

'Still, as an old servant. . . .'

Caswall's words were not so cold as their inflection.

'I never interfere with servants. He was kept on here merely because he had been so long on the premises. I suppose the steward thought it might make him unpopular if the old fellow had been dismissed.'

How on earth was she to proceed on such a task as hers if this was the utmost geniality she could expect? So she at once tried another tack – this time a personal one.

'I am sorry I disturbed you. I am really not unconventional – though certainly no slave to convention. Still there are limits . . . it is bad enough to intrude in this way, and I do not know what you can say or think of the time selected for the intrusion.'

After all, Edgar Caswall was a gentleman by custom and habit, so he rose to the occasion.

'I can only say, Lady Arabella, that you are always welcome at any time you may deign to honour my house with your presence.'

She smiled at him sweetly.

'Thank you *so* much. You *do* put one at ease. My breach of convention

371

makes me glad rather than sorry. I feel that I can open my heart to you about anything.'

Forthwith she proceeded to tell him about Oolanga and his strange suspicions of her honesty. Caswall laughed and made her explain all the details. His final comment was enlightening.

'Let me give you a word of advice: If you have the slightest fault to find with that infernal negro, shoot him at sight. A swelled-headed negro, with a bee in his bonnet, is one of the worst difficulties in the world to deal with. So better make a clean job of it, and wipe him out at once!'

'But what about the law, Mr Caswall?'

'Oh, the law doesn't concern itself much about dead negroes. A few more or less do not matter. To my mind it's rather a relief!'

'I'm afraid of you,' was her only comment, made with a sweet smile and in a soft voice.

'All right,' he said, 'let us leave it at that. Anyhow, we shall be rid of one of them!'

'I don't love negroes any more than you do,' she replied, 'and I suppose one mustn't be too particular where that sort of cleaning up is concerned.' Then she changed in voice and manner, and asked genially: 'And now tell me, am I forgiven?'

'You are, dear lady – if there is anything to forgive.'

As he spoke, seeing that she had moved to go, he came to the door with her, and in the most natural way accompanied her downstairs. He passed through the hall with her and down the avenue. As he went back to the house, she smiled to herself.

'Well, that is all right. I don't think the morning has been altogether thrown away.'

And she walked slowly back to Diana's Grove.

Adam Salton followed the line of the Brow, and refreshed his memory as to the various localities. He got home to Lesser Hill just as Sir Nathaniel was beginning lunch. Mr Salton had gone to Walsall to keep an early appointment; so he was all alone. When the meal was over – seeing in Adam's face that he had something to speak about – he followed into the study and shut the door.

When the two men had lighted their pipes, Sir Nathaniel began.

'I have remembered an interesting fact about Diana's Grove – there is, I have long understood, some strange mystery about that house. It may be of some interest, or it may be trivial, in such a tangled skein as we are trying to unravel.'

'Please tell me all you know or suspect. To begin, then, of what sort is the mystery – physical, mental, moral, historical, scientific, occult? Any kind of hint will help me.'

'Quite right. I shall try to tell you what I think; but I have not put my thoughts on the subject in sequence, so you must forgive me if due order is not observed in my narration. I suppose you have seen the house at Diana's Grove?'

'The outside of it; but I have that in my mind's eye, and I can fit into my memory whatever you may mention.'

'The house is very old – probably the first house of some sort that stood there was in the time of the Romans. This was probably renewed – perhaps several times at later periods. The house stands, or, rather, used to stand here when Mercia was a kingdom – I do not suppose that the basement can be later than the Norman Conquest. Some years ago, when I was President of the Mercian Archæological Society, I went all over it very carefully. This was when it was purchased by Captain March. The house had then been done up, so as to be suitable for the bride. The basement is very strong – almost as strong and as heavy as if it had been intended as a fortress. There are a whole series of rooms deep underground. One of them in particular struck me. The room itself is of considerable size, but the masonry is more than massive. In the middle of the room is a sunk well, built up to floor level and evidently going deep underground. There is no windlass nor any trace of there ever having been any – no rope – nothing. Now, we know that the Romans had wells of immense depth, from which the water was lifted by the "old rag rope"; that at Woodhull used to be nearly a thousand feet. Here, then, we have simply an enormously deep well-hole. The door of the room was massive, and was fastened with a lock nearly a foot square. It was evidently intended for some kind of protection to someone or something; but no one in those days had ever heard of anyone having been allowed even to see the room. All this is *à propos* of a suggestion on my part that the well-hole was a way by which the White Worm (whatever it was) went and came. At that time I would have had a search made – even excavation if necessary – at my own expense, but all suggestions were met with a prompt and explicit negative. So, of course, I took no further step in the matter. Then it died out of recollection – even of mine.'

'Do you remember, sir,' asked Adam, 'what was the appearance of the room where the well-hole was? Was there furniture – in fact, any sort of thing in the room?'

'The only thing I remember was a sort of green light – very clouded, very dim – which came up from the well. Not a fixed light, but intermittent and irregular – quite unlike anything I had ever seen.'

'Do you remember how you got into the well-room? Was there a separate door from outside, or was there any interior room or passage which opened into it?'

'I think there must have been some room with a way into it. I remember going up some steep steps; they must have been worn smooth by long use or something of the kind, for I could hardly keep my feet as I went up. Once I stumbled and nearly fell into the well-hole.'

'Was there anything strange about the place – any queer smell, for instance?'

'Queer smell – yes! Like bilge or a rank swamp. It was distinctly nauseating; when I came out I felt as if I had just been going to be sick. I shall try back on my visit and see if I can recall any more of what I saw or felt.'

'Then perhaps, sir, later in the day you will tell me anything you may chance to recollect.'

'I shall be delighted, Adam. If your uncle has not returned by then, I'll join you in the study after dinner, and we can resume this interesting chat.'

17

THE MYSTERY OF 'THE GROVE'

That afternoon Adam decided to do a little exploring. As he passed through the wood outside the gate of Diana's Grove, he thought he saw the African's face for an instant. So he went deeper into the undergrowth, and followed along parallel to the avenue to the house. He was glad that there was no workman or servant about, for he did not care that any of Lady Arabella's people should find him wandering about her grounds. Taking advantage of the denseness of the trees, he came close to the house and skirted round it. He was repaid for his trouble, for on the far side of the house, close to where the rocky frontage of the cliff fell away, he saw Oolanga crouched behind the irregular trunk of a great oak. The man was so intent on watching someone, or something, that he did not guard against being himself watched. This suited Adam, for he could thus make scrutiny at will.

The thick wood, though the trees were mostly of small girth, threw a heavy shadow, so that the steep declension, in front of which grew the tree behind which the African lurked, was almost in darkness. Adam drew as close as he could, and was amazed to see a patch of light on the ground before him; when he realized what it was, he was determined more than ever to follow on the quest. The negro had a dark lantern in his hand, and was throwing the light down the steep incline. The glare showed a series of stone steps, which ended in a low-lying heavy iron door fixed against the side of the house. All the strange things he had heard from Sir Nathaniel, and all those, little and big, which he had himself noticed, crowded into his mind in a chaotic way. Instinctively he took refuge behind a thick oak stem, and set himself down to watch what might occur.

After a short time it became apparent that the African was trying to find out what was behind the heavy door. There no way of looking in, for the door fitted tight into the massive stone slabs. The only opportunity for the entrance of light was through a small hole between the great stones above the door. This hole was too high up to look through from the ground level. Oolanga, having tried standing tip-toe on the highest point near, and holding the lantern as high as he could, threw the light round the edges of the door to see if he could find anywhere a hole or a flaw in the metal through which he could obtain a glimpse. Foiled in this, he brought from the shrubbery a plank, which he leant against the top of the door, and then climbed up with great dexterity. This did not bring him near enough to the window-hole to look in, or even to throw the light of the lantern through it, so he climbed down and carried the plank back to the place from which he had got it. Then he concealed himself near the iron door and waited, manifestly with the intent of remaining there till someone came near. Presently Lady Arabella, moving noiselessly through the shade, approached the door. When he saw her close enough to touch it, Oolanga stepped forward from his concealment, and spoke in a whisper, which through the gloom sounded like a hiss.

'I want to see you, missey — soon and secret.'

'What do you want?'

'You know well, missey; I told you already.'

She turned on him with blazing eyes, the green tint in them glowing like emeralds.

'Come, none of that. If there is anything sensible which you wish to say to me, you can see me here, just where we are, at seven o'clock.'

He made no reply in words, but, putting the backs of his hands together, bent lower and lower till his forehead touched the earth. Then he rose and went slowly away.

Adam Salton, from his hiding-place, saw and wondered. In a few minutes he moved from his place and went home to Lesser Hill, fully determined that seven o'clock would find him in some hidden place behind Diana's Grove.

At a little before seven Adam stole softly out of the house and took the back-way to the rear of Diana's Grove. The place seemed silent and deserted, so he took the opportunity of concealing himself near the spot whence he had seen Oolanga trying to investigate whatever was concealed behind the iron door. He waited, perfectly still, and at last saw a gleam of white passing soundlessly through the undergrowth. He was not surprised when he recognized the colour of Lady Arabella's dress. She came close and waited, with her face to the iron door. From some place of concealment near at hand Oolanga appeared, and came close to her. Adam noticed, with surprised amusement, that over his shoulder was the box with the mongoose. Of course the African did not know that he was seen by anyone, least of all by the man whose property he had with him.

Silent-footed as he was, Lady Arabella heard him coming, and turned to meet him. It was somewhat hard to see in the gloom, for, as usual, he was all in black, only his collar and cuffs showing white. Lady Arabella opened the conversation which ensued between the two.

'What do you want? To rob me, or murder me?'

'No, to lub you!'

This frightened her a little, and she tried to change the tone.

'Is that a coffin you have with you? If so, you are wasting your time. It would not hold me.'

When a nigger suspects he is being laughed at, all the ferocity of his nature comes to the front; and this man was of the lowest kind.

'Dis ain't no coffin for nobody. Dis box is for you. Somefin you lub. Me give him to you!'

Still anxious to keep off the subject of affection, on which she believed him to have become crazed, she made another effort to keep his mind elsewhere.

'Is this why you want to see me?' He nodded. 'Then come round to the other door. But be quiet. I have no desire to be seen so close to my own house in conversation with a – a – a – a nigger like you!'

She had chosen the word deliberately. She wished to meet his passion with another kind. Such would, at all events, help to keep him quiet. In the deep gloom she could not see the anger which suffused his face. Rolling eyeballs and grinding teeth are, however, sufficient signs of anger to be decipherable in the dark. She moved round the corner of the house to her right. Oolanga was following her, when she stopped him by raising her hand.

'No, not that door,' she said; 'that is not for niggers. The other door will do well enough for you!'

Lady Arabella took in her hand a small key which hung at the end of her watch-chain, and moved to a small door, low down, round the corner, and a little downhill from the edge of the Brow. Oolanga, in obedience to her gesture, went back to the iron door. Adam looked carefully at the mongoose box as the African went by, and was glad to see that it was intact. Unconsciously, as he looked, he fingered the key that was in his waistcoat pocket. When Oolanga was out of sight, Adam hurried after Lady Arabella.

18

EXIT OOLANGA

The woman turned sharply as Adam touched her shoulder.

'One moment whilst we are alone. You had better not trust that negro!' he whispered.

Her answer was crisp and concise:

'I don't.'

'Forewarned is forearmed. Tell me if you will – it is for your own protection. Why do you mistrust him?'

'My friend, you have no idea of that man's impudence. Would you believe that he wants me to marry him?'

'No!' said Adam incredulously, amused in spite of himself.

'Yes, and wanted to bribe me to do it by sharing a chest of treasure – at least, he thought it was – stolen from Mr Caswall. Why do you mistrust him, Mr Salton?'

'Did you notice that box he had slung on his shoulder? That belongs to me. I left it in the gun-room when I went to lunch. He must have crept in and stolen it. Doubtless he thinks that it, too, is full of treasure.'

'He does!'

'How on earth do you know?' asked Adam.

'A little while ago he offered to give it to me – another bribe to accept him. Faugh! I am ashamed to tell you such a thing. The beast!'

Whilst they had been speaking, she had opened the door, a narrow iron one, well hung, for it opened easily and closed tightly without any creaking or sound of any kind. Within all was dark; but she entered as freely and with as little misgiving or restraint as if it had been broad daylight. For Adam, there was just sufficient green light from somewhere for him to see that there was a broad flight of heavy stone steps leading upward; but Lady Arabella, after shutting the door behind her, when it closed tightly without a clang, tripped up the steps lightly and swiftly. For an instant all was dark, but there came again the faint green light which enabled him to see the outlines of things. Another iron door, narrow like the first and fairly high, led into another large room, the walls of which were of massive stones, so closely joined together as to exhibit only one smooth surface. This presented the appearance of having at one time been polished. On the far side, also smooth like the walls, was the reverse of a wide, but not high, iron door. Here there was a little more light, for the high-up aperture over the door opened to the air.

Lady Arabella took from her girdle another small key, which she inserted in a keyhole in the centre of a massive lock. The great bolt seemed wonderfully hung, for the moment the small key was turned, the bolts of the great lock moved noiselessly and the iron doors swung open. On the stone steps outside stood Oolanga, with the mongoose box slung over his shoulder. Lady Arabella stood a little on one side, and the African, accepting the movement as an invitation, entered in an obsequious way. The moment, however, that he was inside, he gave a quick look around him.

'Much death here – big death. Many deaths. Good, good!'

He sniffed around as if he was enjoying the scent. The matter and manner of his speech were so revolting that instinctively Adam's hand wandered to his revolver, and, with his finger on the trigger, he rested satisfied that he was ready for any emergency.

There was certainly opportunity for the nigger's enjoyment, for the open well-hole was almost under his nose, sending up such a stench as almost made Adam sick, though Lady Arabella seemed not to mind it at all. It was like nothing that Adam had ever met with. He compared it with all the noxious experiences he had ever had – the drainage of war hospitals, of slaughterhouses, the refuse of dissecting rooms. None of these was like it, though it had something of them all, with, added, the sourness of chemical waste and the poisonous effluvium of the bilge of a water-logged ship whereon a multitude of rats had been drowned.

Then, quite unexpectedly, the negro noticed the presence of a third person – Adam Salton! He pulled out a pistol and shot at him, happily missing. Adam was himself usually a quick shot, but this time his mind had been on something else and he was not ready. However, he was quick to carry out an intention, and he was not a coward. In another moment both men were in grips. Beside them was the dark well-hole, with that horrid effluvium stealing up from its mysterious depths.

Adam and Oolanga both had pistols; Lady Arabella, who had not one, was probably the most ready of them all in the theory of shooting but that being impossible, she made her effort in another way. Gliding forward, she tried to seize the African; but he eluded her grasp, just missing, in doing so, falling into the mysterious hole. As he swayed back to firm

378

foothold, he turned his own gun on her and shot. Instinctively Adam leaped at his assailant; clutching at each other, they tottered on the very brink.

Lady Arabella's anger, now fully awake; was all for Oolanga. She moved towards him with her hands extended, and had just seized him when the catch of the locked box – due to some movement from within – flew open, and the king-cobra-killer flew at her with a venomous fury impossible to describe. As it seized her throat, she caught hold of it, and, with a fury superior to its own, tore it in two just as if it had been a sheet of paper. The strength used for such an act must have been terrific. In an instant, it was hurled into the well-hole. In another instant she had seized Oolanga, and with a swift rush had drawn him, her white arms encircling him, down with her into the gaping aperture.

Adam saw a medley of green and red lights blaze in a whirling circle, and as it sank down into the well, a pair of blazing green eyes became fixed, sank lower and lower with frightful rapidity, and disappeared, throwing upward the green light which grew more and more vivid every moment. As the light sank into the noisome depths, there came a shriek which chilled Adam's blood – a prolonged agony of pain and terror which seemed to have no end.

Adam Salton felt that he would never be able to free his mind from the memory of those dreadful moments. The gloom which surrounded that horrible charnel pit, which seemed to go down to the very bowels of the earth, conveyed from far down the sights and sounds of the nethermost hell. The ghastly fate of the African as he sank down to his terrible doom, his black face growing grey with terror, his white eyeballs, now like veined bloodstone, rolling in the helpless extremity of fear. The mysterious green light was in itself a *milieu* of horror. And through it all the awful cry came up from that fathomless pit, whose entrance was flooded with spots of fresh blood. Even the death of the fearless little snake-killer – so fierce, so frightful, as if stained with a ferocity which told of no living force above earth, but only of the devils of the pit – was only an incident. Adam was in a state of intellectual tumult, which had no parallel in his experience. He tried to rush away from the horrible place; even the baleful green light, thrown up through the gloomy well-shaft, was dying away as its source sank deeper into the primeval ooze. The darkness was closing in on him in overwhelming density – darkness in such a place and with such a memory of it!

He made a wild rush forward – slipped on the steps in some sticky, acrid-smelling mass and, falling forward, felt his way into the inner room, where the well-shaft was not.

Then he rubbed his eyes in sheer amazeent. Up the stone steps from the narrow door by which he had entered, glided the white-clad figure of Lady Arabella, the only colour to be seen on her being bloodmarks on her face and hands and throat. Otherwise, she was calm and unruffled, as when earlier she stood aside for him to pass in through the narrow iron door.

19

AN ENEMY IN THE DARK

Adam Salton went for a walk before returning to Lesser Hill; he felt that it might be well, not only to steady his nerves, shaken by the horrible scene, but to get his thoughts into some sort of order, so as to be ready to enter on the matter with Sir Nathaniel. He was a little embarrassed as to telling his uncle, for affairs had so vastly progressed beyond his original view that he felt a little doubtful as to what would be the old gentleman's attitude when he should hear of the strange events for the first time. Mr Salton would certainly not be satisfied at being treated as an outsider with regard to such things, most of which had points of contact with the inmates of his own house. It was with an immense sense of relief that Adam heard that his uncle had telegraphed to the housekeeper that he was detained by business at Walsall, where he would remain for the night; and that he would be back in the morning in time for lunch.

When Adam got home after his walk, he found Sir Nathaniel just going to bed. He did not say anything to him then of what had happened, but contented himself with arranging that they would talk together in the early morning, as he had much to say that would require serious attention.

Strangely enough he slept well, and awoke at dawn with his mind clear and his nerves in their usual unshaken condition. The maid brought up, with his early morning cup of tea, a note which had been found in the letter-box. It was from Lady Arabella, and was evidently intended to put him on his guard as to what he should say about the previous evening. He read it over carefully several times, before he was satisfied that he had taken in its full import.

'Dear Mr Salton, –
    'I cannot go to bed until I have written to you, so you must forgive me if I disturb you, and at an unseemly time. Indeed, you must also forgive me

if, in trying to do what is right, I err in saying too much or too little. The fact is that I am quite upset and unnerved by all that has happened in this terrible night. I find it difficult even to write; my hands shake so that they are not under control, and I am trembling all over with memory of the horrors we saw enacted before our eyes. I am grieved beyond measure that I should be, however remotely, a cause of this horror coming to you. Forgive me if you can, and do not think too hardly of me. This I ask with confidence, for since we shared together the danger – the very pangs – of death, I feel that we should be to one another something more than mere friends, that I may lean on you and trust you, assured that your sympathy and pity are for me. You really must let me thank you for the friendliness, the help, the confidence, the real aid at a time of deadly danger, and deadly fear which you showed me. That awful man – I shall see him for ever in my dreams. His black malignant face will shut out all memory of sunshine and happiness. I shall eternally see his evil eyes as he threw himself into that well-hole in a vain effort to escape from the consequences of his own misdoing. The more I think of it, the more apparent it seems to me that he had premeditated the whole thing – of course, except his own horrible death.

'Perhaps you have noticed a fur collar I occasionally wear. It is one of my most valued treasures – an ermine collar studded with emeralds. I had often seen the negro's eyes gleam covetously when he looked at it. Unhappily, I wore it yesterday. That may have been the cause that lured the poor man to his doom. On the very brink of the abyss he tore the collar from my neck – that was the last I saw of him. When he sank into the hole, I was rushing to the iron door, which I pulled behind me. When I heard that soul-sickening yell, which marked his disappearance in the chasm, I was more glad than I can say that my eyes were spared the pain and horror which my ears had to endure.

'When I tore myself out of the negro's grasp as he sank into the well-hole, I realized what freedom meant. Freedom! Freedom! Not only from that noisome prison-house, which has now such a memory, but from the more noisome embrace of that hideous monster. Whilst I live, I shall always thank you for my freedom. A woman must sometimes express her gratitude; otherwise it becomes too great to bear. I am not a sentimental girl, who merely likes to thank a man; I am a woman who knows all, of bad as well as good, that life can give. I have known what it is to love and to lose. But you must not let me bring any unhappiness into your life. I must live on – as I have lived – alone, and, in addition, bear with other woes the memory of this latest insult and horror. In the meantime, I must get away as quickly as possible from Diana's Grove. In the morning I shall go up to town, where I shall remain for a week – I cannot stay longer, as business affairs demand my presence here. I think, however, that a week in the rush of busy London, surrounded with multitudes of commonplace people, will help to soften – I cannot expect total obliteration – the terrible images of the bygone night. When I can sleep easily – which will be, I hope, after a day or two – I shall be fit to return home and take up again the burden which will, I suppose, always be with me.

'I shall be most happy to see you on my return – or earlier, if my good fortune sends you on any errand to London. I shall stay at the Mayfair Hotel. In that busy spot we may forget some of the dangers and horrors we have shared together. Adieu, and thank you, again and again, for all your kindness and consideration to me.

'ARABELLA MARCH.'

Adam was surprised by this effusive epistle, but he determined to say nothing of it to Sir Nathaniel until he should have thought it well over. When Adam met Sir Nathaniel at breakfast, he was glad that he had taken time to turn things over in his mind. The result had been that not only was he familiar with the facts in all their bearings, but he had already so far differentiated them that he was able to arrange them in his own mind according to their values. Breakfast had been a silent function, so it did not interfere in any way with the process of thought.

So soon as the door was closed, Sir Nathaniel began:

'I see, Adam, that something has occurred, and that you have much to tell me.'

'That is so, sir. I suppose I had better begin by telling you all I know – all that has happened since I left you yesterday?'

Accordingly Adam gave him details of all that had happened during the previous evening. He confined himself rigidly to the narration of circumstances, taking care not to colour events by any comment of his own, or any opinion of the meaning of things which he did not fully understand. At first, Sir Nathaniel seemed disposed to ask questions, but shortly gave this up when he recognized that the narration was concise and self-explanatory. Thenceforth, he contented himself with quick looks and glances, easily interpreted, or by some acquiescent motions of his hands, when such could be convenient, to emphasize his idea of the correctness of any inference. Until Adam ceased speaking, having evidently come to an end of what he had to say with regard to this section of his story, the elder man made no comment whatever. Even when Adam took from his pocket Lady Arabella's letter, with the manifest intention of reading it, he did not make any comment. Finally, when Adam folded up the letter and put it, in its envelope, back in his pocket, as an intimation that he had now quite finished, the old diplomatist carefully made a few notes in his pocket-book.

382

'Your narrative, my dear Adam, is altogether admirable. I think I may now take it that we are both well versed in the actual facts, and that our conference had better take the shape of a mutual exchange of ideas. Let us both ask questions as they may arise; and I do not doubt that we shall arrive at some enlightening conclusions.'

'Will you kindly begin, sir? I do not doubt that, with your longer experience, you will be able to dissipate some of the fog which envelops certain of the things which we have to consider.'

'I hope so, my dear boy. For a beginning, then, let me say that Lady Arabella's letter makes clear some things which she intended – and also some things which she did not intend. But, before I begin to draw deductions, let me ask you a few questions. Adam, are you heart-whole, quite heart-whole, in the matter of Lady Arabella?'

His companion answered at once, each looking the other straight in the eyes during question and answer.

'Lady Arabella, sir, is a charming woman, and I should have deemed it a privilege to meet her – to talk to her – even – since I am in the confessional – to flirt a little with her. But if you mean to ask if my affections are in any way engaged, I can emphatically answer "No!" – as indeed you will understand when presently I give you the reason. Apart from that, there are the unpleasant details we discussed the other day.'

'Could you – would you mind giving me a reason now? It will help us to understand what is before us, in the way of difficulty.'

'Certainly, sir. My reason, on which I can fully depend, is that I love another woman!'

'That clinches it. May I offer my good wishes, and, I hope, my congratulations?'

'I am proud of your good wishes, sir, and I thank you for them. But it is too soon for congratulations – the lady does not even know my hopes yet. Indeed, I hardly knew them myself, as definite, till this moment.'

'I take it then, Adam, that at the right time I may be allowed to know who the lady is?'

Adam laughed a low, sweet laugh, such as ripples from a happy heart.

'There need not be an hour's, a minute's delay. I shall be glad to share my secret with you, sir. The lady, sir, whom I am so happy as to love, and in whom my dreams of life-long happiness are centred, is Mimi Watford!'

'Then, my dear Adam, I need not wait to offer congratulations. She is indeed a very charming young lady. I do not think I ever saw a girl who united in such perfection the qualities of strength of character and sweetness of disposition. With all my heart, I congratulate you. Then I may take it that my question as to your heart-wholeness is answered in the affirmative?'

'Yes; and now, sir, may I ask in turn why the question?'

'Certainly! I asked because it seems to me that we are coming to a point where my questions might be painful to you.'

'It is not merely that I love Mimi, but I have reason to look on Lady Arabella as her enemy,' Adam continued.

'Her enemy?'

'Yes. A rank and unscrupulous enemy who is bent on her destruction.'

Sir Nathaniel went to the door, looked outside it and returned, locking it carefully behind him.

20

METABOLISM

'Am I looking grave?' asked Sir Nathaniel inconsequently when he re-entered the room.

'You certainly are, sir.'

'We little thought when first we met that we should be drawn into such a vortex. Already we are mixed up in robbery, and probably murder, but – a thousand times worse than all the crimes in the calendar – in an affair of ghastly mystery which has no bottom and no end – with forces of the most unnerving kind, which had their origin in an age when the world was different from the world which we know. We are going back to the origin of superstition – to an age when dragons tore each other in their slime. We must fear nothing – no conclusion, however improbable, almost impossible it may be. Life and death is hanging on our judgment, not only for ourselves, but for others whom we love. Remember, I count on you as I hope you count on me.'

'I do, with all confidence.'

'Then,' said Sir Nathaniel, 'let us think justly and boldly and fear nothing, however terrifying it may seem. I suppose I am to take as exact in every detail your account of all the strange things which happened whilst you were in Diana's Grove?'

'So far as I know, yes. Of course I may be mistaken in recollection of some detail or another, but I am certain that in the main what I have said is correct.'

'You feel sure that you saw Lady Arabella seize the negro round the neck, and drag him down with her into the hole?'

'Absolutely certain, sir, otherwise I should have gone to her assistance.'

'We have then an account of what happened from an eye-witness whom we trust – that is yourself. We have also another account, written by Lady Arabella under her own hand. These two accounts do not agree. Therefore we must take it that one of the two is lying.'

'Apparently, sir.'

'And that Lady Arabella is the liar!'

'Apparently – as I am not.'

'We must, therefore, try to find a reason for her lying. She has nothing to fear from Oolanga, who is dead. Therefore the only reason which could actuate her would be to convince someone else that she was blameless. This "someone" could not be you, for you had the evidence of your own eyes. There was no one else present; therefore it must have been an absent person.'

'That seems beyond dispute, sir.'

'There is only one other person whose good opinion she could wish to keep – Edgar Caswall. He is the only one who fills the bill. Her lies point to other things besides the death of the African. She evidently wanted it to be accepted that his falling into the well was his own act. I cannot suppose that she expected to convince you, the eye-witness; but if she wished later on to spread the story, it was wise of her to try to get your acceptance of it.'

'That is so!'

'Then there were other matters of untruth. That, for instance, of the ermine collar embroidered with emeralds. If an understandable reason be required for this, it would be to draw attention away from the green lights which were seen in the room, and especially in the well-hole. Any unprejudiced person would accept the green lights to be the eyes of a great snake, such as tradition pointed to living in the well-hole. In fine, therefore, Lady Arabella wanted the general belief to be that there was no snake of the kind in Diana's Grove. For my own part, I don't believe in a partial liar – this art does not deal in veneer; a liar is a liar right through. Self-interest may prompt falsity of the tongue; but if one prove to be a liar, nothing that he says can ever be believed. This leads us to the conclusion that because she said or inferred that there was no snake, we should look for one – and expect to find it, too.

'Now, let me digress. I live, and have for many years lived, in Derbyshire, a county more celebrated for its caves than any other county in England. I have been through them all, and am familiar with every turn of them; as also with other great caves in Kentucky, in France, in Germany, and a host of other places – in many of these are tremendously deep caves of narrow aperture, which are valued by intrepid explorers, who descend narrow gullets of abysmal depth – and sometimes never return. In many of the caverns in the Peak I am convinced that some of the smaller passages were used in primeval times as the lairs of some of the great serpents of legend and tradition. It may have been that such caverns were formed in the usual geologic way – bubbles or flaws in the earth's crust – which were later used by the monsters of the period of the young world. It may have been, of course, that some of them were worn originally by water; but in time they all found a use when suitable for living monsters.

'This brings us to another point, more difficult to accept and understand than any other requiring belief in a base not usually accepted, or indeed entered on – whether such abnormal growths could have ever changed in their nature. Some day the study of metabolism may progress so far as to enable us to accept structural changes proceeding from an intellectual or moral base. We may lean towards a belief that great animal strength may be a sound base for changes of all sorts. If this be so, what could be a more fitting subject than primeval monsters whose strength was such as to allow a survival of thousands of years? We do not know yet if brain can increase and develop independently of other parts of the living structure.

'After all, the mediæval belief in the Philosopher's Stone which could transmute metals, has its counterpart in the accepted theory of metabolism which changes living tissue. In an age of investigation like our own, when we are returning to science as the base of wonders – almost of miracles – we should be slow to refuse to accept facts, however impossible they may seem to be.

'Let us suppose a monster of the early days of the world – a dragon of the prime – of vast age running into thousands of years, to whom had been conveyed in some way – it matters not – a brain just sufficient for the beginning of growth. Suppose the monster to be of incalculable size and of a strength quite abnormal – a veritable incarnation of animal strength. Suppose this animal is allowed to remain in one place, thus being removed from accidents of interrupted development; might not, would not this creature, in process of time – ages, if necessary – have that rudimentary intelligence developed? There is no impossibility in this; it is only the natural process of evolution. In the beginning, the instincts of animals are confined to alimentation, self-protection, and the multiplication of their species. As time goes on and the needs of life become more complex, power follows need. We have been long accustomed to consider growth as applied almost exclusively to size in its various aspects. But Nature, who has no doctrinaire ideas, may equally apply it to concentration. A developing thing may expand in any given way or form. Now, it is a scientific law that increase implies gain and loss of various kinds; what a thing gains in one direction it may lose in another. May it not be that

Mother Nature may deliberately encourage decrease as well as increase – that it may be an axiom that what is gained in concentration is lost in size? Take, for instance, monsters that tradition has accepted and localized, such as the Worm of Lambton or that of Spindleston Heugh. If such a creature were, by its own process of metabolism, to change much of its bulk for intellectual growth, we should at once arrive at a new class of creature – more dangerous, perhaps, than the world has ever had any experience of – a force which can think, which has no soul and no morals, and therefore no acceptance of responsibility. A snake would be a good illustration of this, for it is cold-blooded, and therefore removed from the temptations which often weaken or restrict warm-blooded creatures. If, for instance, the Worm of Lambton – if such ever existed – were guided to its own ends by an organized intelligence capable of expansion, what form of creature could we imagine which would equal it in potentialities of evil? Why, such a being would devastate a whole country. Now, all these things require much thought, and we want to apply the knowledge usefully, and we should therefore be exact. Would it not be well to resume the subject later in the day?'

'I quite agree, sir. I am in a whirl already; and I want to attend carefully to what you say; so that I may try to digest it.'

Both men seemed fresher and better for the 'easy', and when they met in the afternoon each of them had something to contribute to the general stock of information. Adam, who was by nature of a more militant disposition than his elderly friend, was glad to see that the conference at once assumed a practical trend. Sir Nathaniel recognized this, and, like an old diplomatist, turned it to present use.

'Tell me now, Adam, what is the outcome, in your own mind, of our conversation?'

'That the whole difficulty already assumes practical shape; but with added dangers, that at first I did not imagine.'

'What is the practical shape, and what are the added dangers? I am not disputing, but only trying to clear my own ideas by the consideration of yours – '

So Adam went on:

'In the past, in the early days of the world, there were monsters who were so vast that they could exist for thousands of years. Some of them must have overlapped the Christian era. They may have progressed intellectually in process of time. If they had in any way so progressed, or even got the most rudimentary form of brain, they would be the most dangerous things that ever were in the world. Tradition says that one of these monsters lived in the Marsh of the East, and came up to a cave in Diana's Grove, which was also called the Lair of the White Worm. Such creatures may have grown down as well as up. They *may* have grown into, or something like, human beings. Lady Arabella March is of snake nature. She has committed crimes to our knowledge. She retains something of the vast strength of her primal being – can see in the dark – has the eyes of a snake. She used the nigger, and then dragged him through the snake's hole down to the swamp; she is intent on evil, and hates some one we love. Result . . .'

'Yes, the result?'

'First, that Mimi Watford should be taken away at once – then – '

'Yes?'

'The monster must be destroyed.'

'Bravo! That is a true and fearless conclusion. At whatever cost, it must be carried out.'

'At once?'

'Soon, at all events. That creature's very existence is a danger. Her presence in this neighbourhood makes the danger immediate.'

As he spoke, Sir Nathaniel's mouth hardened and his eyebrows came down till they met. There was no doubting his concurrence in the resolution, or his readiness to help in carrying it out. But he was an elderly man with much experience and knowledge of law and diplomacy. It seemed to him to be a stern duty to prevent anything irrevocable taking place till it had been thought out and all was ready. There were all sorts of legal cruxes to be thought out, not only regarding the taking of life, even of a monstrosity in human form, but also of property. Lady Arabella, be she woman or snake or devil, owned the ground she moved in, according to British law, and the law is jealous and swift to avenge wrongs done within its ken. All such difficulties should be – must be – avoided for Mr Salton's sake, for Adam's own sake, and, most of all, for Mimi Watford's sake.

Before he spoke again, Sir Nathaniel had made up his mind that he must try to postpone decisive action until the circumstances on which they depended – which, after all, were only problematical – should have been tested satisfactorily, one way or another. When he did speak, Adam at first thought that his friend was wavering in his intention, or 'funking' the responsibility. However, his respect for Sir Nathaniel was so great that he would not act, or even come to a conclusion on a vital point, without his sanction.

He came close and whispered in his ear:

'We will prepare our plans to combat and destroy this horrible menace, after we have cleared up some of the more baffling points. Meanwhile, we must wait for the night – I hear my uncle's footsteps echoing down the hall.'

Sir Nathaniel nodded his approval.

21

GREEN LIGHT

When old Mr Salton had retired for the night, Adam and Sir Nathaniel returned to the study. Things went with great regularity at Lesser Hill, so they knew that there would be no interruptions to their talk.

When their cigars were lighted Sir Nathaniel began.

'I hope, Adam, that you do not think me either slack or changeable of purpose. I mean to go through this business to the bitter end – whatever it may be. Be satisfied that my first care is, and shall be, the protection of Mimi Watford. To that I am pledged; my dear boy, we who are interested are all in the same danger. That semi-human monster out of the pit hates and means to destroy us all – you and me certainly, and probably your uncle. I wanted especially to talk with you to-night, for I cannot help thinking that the time is fast coming – if it has not come already – when we must take your uncle into our confidence. It was one thing when fancied evils threatened, but now he is probably marked for death, and it is only right that he should know all.'

'I am with you, sir. Things have changed since we agreed to keep him out of the trouble. Now we dare not; consideration for his feelings might cost his life. It is a duty – and no light or pleasant one, either. I have not a shadow of doubt that he will want to be one with us in this. But remember, we are his guests; his name, his honour, have to be thought of as well as his safety.'

'All shall be as you wish, Adam. And now as to what we are to do? We cannot murder Lady Arabella off-hand. Therefore we shall have to put things in order for the killing, and in such a way that we cannot be taxed with a crime.'

'It seems to me, sir, that we are in an exceedingly tight place. Our first difficulty is to know where to begin. I never thought this fighting an antediluvian monster would be such a complicated job. This one is a woman, with all a woman's wit, combined with the heartlessness of a *cocotte*. She has the strength and impregnability of a diplodocus. We may be sure that in the fight that is before us there will be no semblance of fair-play. Also that our unscrupulous opponent will not betray herself!'

'That is so – but being feminine, she will probably over-reach herself. Now, Adam, it strikes me that, as we have to protect ourselves and others against feminine nature, our strong game will be to play our masculine against her feminine. Perhaps we had better sleep on it. She is a thing of the night; and the night may give us some ideas.'

So they both turned in.

Adam knocked at Sir Nathaniel's door in the grey of the morning, and, on being bidden, came into the room. He had several letters in his hand. Sir Nathaniel sat up in bed.

'Well!'

'I should like to read you a few letters, but, of course, I shall not send them unless you approve. In fact' – with a smile and a blush – 'there are several things which I want to do; but I hold my hand and my tongue till I have your approval.'

'Go on!' said the other kindly. 'Tell me all, and count at any rate on my sympathy, and on my approval and help if I can see my way.'

Accordingly Adam proceeded:

'When I told you the conclusions at which I had arrived, I put in the foreground that Mimi Watford should, for the sake of her own safety, be removed – and that the monster which had wrought all the harm should be destroyed.

'Yes, that is so.'

'To carry this into practice, sir, one preliminary is required – unless harm of another kind is to be faced. Mimi should have some protector whom all the world would recognize. The only form recognized by convention is marriage!'

Sir Nathaniel smiled in a fatherly way.

'To marry, a husband is required. And that husband should be you.'

'Yes, yes.'

'And the marriage should be immediate and secret – or, at least, not spoken of outside ourselves. Would the young lady be agreeable to that proceeding?'

'I do not know, sir!'

'Then how are we to proceed?'

'I suppose that we – or one of us – must ask her.'

'Is this a sudden idea, Adam, a sudden resolution?'

'A sudden resolution, sir, but not a sudden idea. If she agrees, all is well and good. The sequence is obvious.'

'And it is to be kept a secret amongst ourselves?'

'I want no secret, sir, except for Mimi's good. For myself, I should like to shout it from the housetops! But we must be discreet; untimely knowledge to our enemy might work incalculable harm.'

'And how would you suggest, Adam, that we could combine the momentous question with secrecy?'

Adam grew red and moved uneasily.

'Someone must ask her – as soon as possible!'

'And that someone?'

'I thought that you, sir, would be so good!'

'God bless my soul! This is a new kind of duty to take on – at my life of life. Adam, I hope you know that you can count on me to help in any way I can!'

'I have already counted on you, sir, when I ventured to make such a suggestion. I can only ask,' he added, 'that you will be more than ever kind to me – to us – and look on the painful duty as a voluntary act of grace, prompted by kindness and affection.'

'Painful duty!'

'Yes,' said Adam boldly. 'Painful to you, though to me it would be all joyful.'

'It is a strange job for an early morning! Well, we all live and learn. I suppose the sooner I go the better. You had better write a line for me to take with me. For, you see, this is to be a somewhat unusual transaction, and it may be embarrassing to the lady, even to myself. So we ought to have some sort of warrant, something to show that we have been mindful of her feelings. It will not do to take acquiescence for granted – although we act for her good.'

'Sir Nathaniel, you are a true friend; I am sure that both Mimi and I shall be grateful to you for all our lives – however long they may be!'

So the two talked it over and agreed as to points to be borne in mind by the ambassador. It was striking ten when Sir Nathaniel left the house, Adam seeing him quietly off.

As the young man followed him with wistful eyes – almost jealous of the privilege which his kind deed was about to bring him – he felt that his own heart was in his friend's breast.

The memory of that morning was like a dream to all those concerned in it. Sir Nathaniel had a confused recollection of detail and sequence, though the main facts stood out in his memory boldly and clearly. Adam Salton's recollection was of an illimitable wait, filled with anxiety, hope, and chagrin, all dominated by a sense of the slow passage of time and accompanied by vague fears. Mimi could not for a long time think at all, or recollect anything, except that Adam loved her and was saving her from a terrible danger. When she had time to think, later on, she wondered when she had any ignorance of the fact that Adam loved her, and that she loved him with all her heart. Everything, every recollection however small, every feeling, seemed to fit into those elemental facts as though they had all been moulded together. The main and crowning recollection was her saying good-bye to Sir Nathaniel, and entrusting to him loving messages, straight from her heart, to Adam Salton, and of his bearing when – with an impulse which she could not check – she put her lips to his and kissed him. Later, when she was alone and had time to think, it was a passing grief to her that she would have to be silent, for a time, to Lilla on the happy events of that strange mission.

She had, of course, agreed to keep all secret until Adam should give her leave to speak.

The advice and assistance of Sir Nathaniel was a great help to Adam in carrying out his idea of marrying Mimi Watford without publicity. He went with him to London, and, with his influence, the young man obtained the licence of the Archbishop of Canterbury for a private marriage. Sir Nathaniel then persuaded old Mr Salton to allow his nephew to spend a few weeks with him at Doom Tower, and it was here that Mimi became Adam's wife. But that was only the first step in their plans; before going further, however, Adam took his bride off to the Isle of Man. He wished to place a stretch of sea between Mimi and the White Worm, while things matured. On their return, Sir Nathaniel met them and drove them at once to Doom, taking care to avoid any one that he knew on the journey.

Sir Nathaniel had taken care to have the doors and windows shut and locked – all but the door used for their entry. The shutters were up and the blinds down. Moreover, heavy curtains were drawn across the windows. When Adam commented on this, Sir Nathaniel said in a whisper:

'Wait till we are alone, and I'll tell you why this is done; in the meantime not a word or a sign. You will approve when we have had a talk together.'

They said no more on the subject till after dinner, when they were ensconced in Sir Nathaniel's study, which was on the top storey. Doom Tower was a lofty structure, situated on an eminence high up in the Peak. The top commanded a wide prospect, ranging from the hills above the Ribble to the near side of the Brow, which marked the northern bound of ancient Mercia. It was of the early Norman period, less than a century younger than Castra Regis. The windows of the study were barred and locked, and heavy dark curtains closed them in. When this was done not a gleam of light from the tower could be seen from outside.

When they were alone, Sir Nathaniel explained that he had taken his old friend, Mr Salton, into full confidence, and that in future all would work together.

'It is important for you to be extremely careful. In spite of the fact that your marriage was kept secret, as also your temporary absence, both are known.'

'How? To whom?'

'How, I know not; but I am beginning to have an idea.'

'To her?' asked Adam, in momentary consternation.

Sir Nathaniel shivered preceptibly.

'The White Worm – yes!'

Adam noticed that from now on, his friend never spoke of Lady Arabella otherwise, except when he wished to divert the suspicion of others.

Sir Nathaniel switched off the electric light, and when the room was pitch dark, he came to Adam, took him by the hand, and led him to a seat set in the southern window. Then he softly drew back a piece of the curtain and motioned his companion to look out.

Adam did so, and immediately shrank back as though his eyes had opened on pressing danger. His companion set his mind at rest by saying in a low voice:

'It is all right; you may speak, but speak low. There is no danger here – at present!'

Adam leaned forward, taking care, however, not to press his face against the glass. What he saw would not under ordinary circumstances have caused concern to anybody. With his special knowledge, it was appalling – though the night was now so dark that in reality there was little to be seen.

On the western side of the tower stood a grove of old trees, of forest dimensions. They were not grouped closely, but stood a little apart from each other, producing the effect of a row widely planted. Over the tops of them was seen a green light, something like the danger signal at a railway-crossing. It seemed at first quite still; but presently, when Adam's eye became accustomed to it, he could see that it moved as if trembling. This at once recalled to Adam's mind the light quivering above the well-hole in the darkness of that inner room at Diana's Grove, Oolanga's awful shriek, and the hideous black face, now grown grey with terror, disappearing into the impenetrable gloom of the mysterious orifice. Instinctively he laid his hand on his revolver, and stood up ready to protect his wife. Then, seeing that nothing happened, and that the light and all outside the tower remained the same, he softly pulled the curtain over the window.

Sir Nathaniel switched on the light again, and in its comforting glow, they began to talk freely.

22

AT CLOSE QUARTERS

'She has diabolical cunning,' said Sir Nathaniel. 'Ever since you left, she had ranged along the Brow and wherever you were accustomed to frequent. I have not heard whence the knowledge of your movements came to her, nor have I been able to learn any data whereon to found an opinion. She seems to have heard both of your marriage and your absence; but I gather, by inference, that she does not actually know where you and Mimi are, or of your return. So soon as the dusk falls, she goes out on her rounds, and before dawn covers the whole ground round the Brow, and away up into the heart of the Peak. The White Worm, in her own proper shape, certainly has great facilities for the business on which she is now engaged. She can look into windows of any ordinary kind. Happily, this house is beyond her reach, if she wishes – as she manifestly does – to remain unrecognized. But, even at this height, it is wise to show no lights, lest she might learn something of our presence or absence.'

'Would it not be well, sir, if one of us could see this monster in her real shape at close quarters? I am willing to run the risk – for I take it there would be no slight risk in the doing. I don't suppose anyone of our time has seen her close and lived to tell the tale.'

Sir Nathaniel held up an expostulatory hand.

'Good God, lad, what are you suggesting? Think of your wife, and all that is at stake.'

'It is of Mimi that I think – for her sake that I am willing to risk whatever is to be risked.'

Adam's young bride was proud of her man, but she blanched at the thought of the ghastly White Worm. Adam saw this and at once reassured her.

'So long as her ladyship does not know whereabout I am, I shall have as much safety as remains to us; bear in mind, my darling, that we cannot be too careful.'

Sir Nathaniel realized that Adam was right; the White Worm had no supernatural powers and could not harm them until she discovered their hiding-place. It was agreed, therefore, that the two men should go together.

When the two men slipped out by the back door of the house, they walked cautiously along the avenue which trended towards the west. Everything was pitch dark – so dark that at times they had to feel their way by the palings and tree-trunks. They could still see, seemingly far in front of them and high up, the baleful light which at the height and distance seemed like a faint line. As they were now on the level of the ground, the light seemed infinitely higher than it had from the top of the tower. At the sight Adam's heart fell; the danger of the desperate enterprise which he had undertaken burst upon him. But this feeling was shortly followed by another which restored him to himself – a fierce loathing, and a desire to kill, such as he had never experienced before.

They went on for some distance on a level road, fairly wide, from which the green light was visible. Here Sir Nathaniel spoke softly, placing his lips to Adam's ear for safety.

'We know nothing whatever of this creature's power of hearing or smelling, though I presume that both are of no great strength. As to seeing, we may presume the opposite, but in any case we must try to keep in the shade behind the tree-trunks. The slightest error would be fatal to us.'

Adam only nodded, in case there should be any chance of the monster seeing the movement.

After a time that seemed interminable, they emerged from the circling wood. It was like coming out into sunlight by comparison with the misty blackness which had been around them. There was light enough to see by, though not sufficient to distinguish things at a distance. Adam's eyes sought the green light in the sky. It was still in about the same place, but its surroundings were more visible. It was now at the summit of what seemed to be a long white pole, near the top of which were two pendent white masses, like rudimentary arms or fins. The green light, strangely enough, did not seem lessened by the surrounding starlight, but had a clearer effect and a deeper green. Whilst they were carefully regarding this – Adam with the aid of an opera-glass – their nostrils were assailed by a horrid stench, something like that which rose from the well-hole in Diana's Grove.

By degrees, as their eyes got their right focus, they saw an immense towering mass that seemed snowy white. It was tall and thin. The lower part was hidden by the trees which lay between, but they could follow the tall white shaft and the duplicate green lights which topped it. As they looked there was a movement – the shaft seemed to bend, and the line of green light descended amongst the trees. They could see the green light twinkle as it passed between the obstructing branches.

Seeing where the head of the monster was, the two men ventured a little further forward, and saw that the hidden mass at the base of the shaft was composed of vast coils of the great serpent's body, forming a base from which the upright mass rose. As they looked, this lower mass moved, the glistening folds catching the moonlight, and they could see that the monster's progress was along the ground. It was coming towards them at a swift pace, so they turned and ran, taking care to make as little noise as possible, either by their footfalls, or by disturbing the undergrowth close to them. They did not stop or pause till they saw before them the high tower of Doom.

23

IN THE ENEMY'S HOUSE

Sir Nathaniel was in the library next morning, after breakfast, when Adam came to him carrying a letter.

'Her ladyship doesn't lose any time. She has begun work already!'

Sir Nathaniel, who was writing at a table near the window, looked up.

'What is it?' said he.

Adam held out the letter he was carrying. It was in a blazoned envelope.

'Ha!' said Sir Nathaniel, 'from the White Worm! I expected something of the kind.'

'But,' said Adam, 'how could she have known we were here? She didn't know last night.'

'I don't think we need trouble about that, Adam. There is so much we do not understand. This is only another mystery. Suffice it that she does know – perhaps it is all the better and safer for us.'

'How is that?' asked Adam, with a puzzled look.

'General process of reasoning, my boy; and the experience of some years in the diplomatic world. This creature is a monster without heart or consideration for anything or anyone. She is not nearly so dangerous in the open as when she has the dark to protect her. Besides, we know, by our own experience of her movements, that for some reason she shuns publicity. In spite of her vast bulk and abnormal strength, she is afraid to attack openly. After all, she is only a snake and with a snake's nature, which is to keep low and squirm, and proceed by stealth and cunning. She will never attack when she can run away, although she knows well that running away would probably be fatal to her. What is the letter about?'

Sir Nathaniel's voice was calm and self-possessed. When he was engaged in any struggle of wits he was all diplomatist.

'She asks Mimi and me to tea this afternoon at Diana's Grove, and hopes that you also will favour her.'

Sir Nathaniel smiled.

'Please ask Mrs Salton to accept for us all.'

'She means some deadly mischief. Surely – surely it would be wiser not.'

'It is an old trick that we learn early in diplomacy, Adam – to fight on ground of your own choice. It is true that she suggested the place on this occasion; but by accepting it we make it ours. Moreover, she will not be able to understand our reason for doing so, and her own bad conscience –if she has any, bad or good – and her own fears and doubts will play our game for us. No, my dear boy, let us accept, by all means.'

Adam said nothing, but silently held out his hand, which his companion shook; no words were necessary.

When it was getting near tea-time, Mimi asked Sir Nathaniel how they were going.

'We must make a point of going in state. We want all possible publicity.' Mimi looked at him inquiringly. 'Certainly, my dear, in the present circumstances publicity is part of safety. Do not be surprised if, whilst we are at Diana's Grove, occasional messages come for you – for all or any of us.'

'I see!' said Mrs Salton. 'You're taking no chances.'

'None, my dear. All I have learned at foreign courts, and amongst civilized and uncivilized people, is going to be utilized within the next couple of hours.'

Sir Nathaniel's voice was full of seriousness, and it brought to Mimi in a convincing way the awful gravity of the occasion.

In due course, they set out in a carriage drawn by a fine pair of horses, who soon devoured the few miles of their journey. Before they came to the gate, Sir Nathaniel turned to Mimi.

'I have arranged with Adam certain signals which may be necessary if certain eventualities occur. These need be nothing to do with you directly. But bear in mind that if I ask you or Adam to do anything, do not lose a second in the doing of it. We must try to pass off such moments with an appearance of unconcern. In all probability, nothing requiring such care will occur. The White Worm will not try force, though she has so much of it to spare. Whatever she may attempt to-day, of harm to any of us, will be in the way of secret plot. Some other time she may try force, but – if I am able to judge such a thing – not to-day. The messengers who may ask for any of us will not be witnesses only, they may help to stave off danger.' Seeing query in her face, he went on: 'Of what kind the danger may be, I know not, and cannot guess. It will doubtless be some ordinary circumstance; but none the less dangerous on that account. Here we are at the gate. Now, be careful in all matters, however small. To keep your head is half the battle.'

There were a number of men in livery in the hall when they arrived. The doors of the drawing-room were thrown open, and Lady Arabella came forth and offered them cordial welcome. This having been got over, Lady Arabella led them into another room where tea was served.

Adam was acutely watchful and suspicious of everything, and saw on the far side of this room a panelled iron door of the same colour and configuration as the outer door of the room where was the well-hole wherein Oolanga had disappeared. Something in the sight alarmed him, and he quietly stood near the door. He made no movement, even of his eyes, but he could see that Sir Nathaniel was watching him intently, and, he fancied, with approval.

They all sat near the table spread for tea, Adam still near the door. Lady Arabella fanned herself, complaining of heat, and told one of the footmen to throw all the outer doors open.

Tea was in progress when Mimi suddenly started up with a look of fright on her face; at the same moment, the men became cognizant of a thick smoke which began to spread through the room – a smoke which made those who experienced it gasp and choke. The footmen began to edge uneasily towards the inner door. Denser and denser grew the smoke, and more acrid the smell. Mimi, towards whom the draught from the open door wafted the smoke, rose up choking, and ran to the inner door, which she threw open to its fullest extent, disclosing on the outside a curtain of thin silk, fixed to the doorposts. The draught from the open door swayed the thin silk towards her, and in her fright she tore down the curtain, which enveloped her from head to foot. Then she ran through the still open door, heedless of the fact that she could not see where she was going. Adam, followed by Sir Nathaniel, rushed forward and joined her – Adam catching his wife by the arm and holding her tight. It was well that he did so, for just before her lay the black orifice of the well-hole, which, of course, she could not see with the silk curtain round her head. The floor was extemely slippery; something like thick black oil had been spilled where she had to pass; and closer to the edge of the hole her feet shot from under her, and she stumbled forward towards the well-hole.

When Adam saw Mimi slip, he flung himself backward, still holding her. His weight told, and he dragged her up from the hole and they fell together on the floor outside the zone of slipperiness. In a moment he had raised her up, and together they rushed out through the open door into the sunlight, Sir Nathaniel close behind them. They were all pale except the old diplomatist, who looked both calm and cool. It sustained and cheered Adam and his wife to see him thus master of himself. Both managed to follow his example to the wonderment of the footmen, who saw the three who had just escaped a terrible danger walking together gaily, as, under the guiding pressure of Sir Nathaniel's hand, they turned to re-enter the house.

Lady Arabella, whose face had blanched to a deadly white, now resumed her ministrations at the tea-board as though nothing unusual had happened. The slop-basin was full of half-burned brown paper, over which tea had been poured.

Sir Nathaniel had been narrowly observing his hostess, and took the first opportunity afforded him of whispering to Adam:

'The real attack is to come – she is too quiet. When I give my hand to your wife to lead her out, come with us – and caution her to hurry. Don't lose a second, even if you have to make a scene. Hs-s-s-h!'

Then they resumed their places close to the table, and the servants, in obedience to Lady Arabella's order, brought in fresh tea.

Thence on, that tea-party seemed to Adam, whose faculties were at their utmost intensity, like a terrible dream. As for poor Mimi, she was so overwrought both with present and future fear, and with horror at the danger she had escaped, that her faculties were numb. However, she was braced up for a trial, and she felt assured that whatever might come she would be able to go through with it. Sir Nathaniel seemed just as usual – suave, dignified, and thoughtful – perfect master of himself.

To her husband, it was evident that Mimi was ill at ease. The way she kept turning her head to look around her, the quick coming and going of the colour of her face, her hurried breathing, alternating with periods of suspicious calm, were evidences of mental perturbation. To her, the attitude of Lady Arabella seemed compounded of social sweetness and personal consideration. It would be hard to imagine more thoughtful and tender kindness towards an honoured guest.

When tea was over and the servants had come to clear away the cups, Lady Arabella, putting her arm round Mimi's waist, strolled with her into an adjoining room, where she collected a number of photographs which were scattered about, and, sitting down beside her guest, began to show them to her. While she was doing this, the servants closed all the doors of the suite of rooms, as well as that which opened from the room outside – that of the well-hole into the avenue. Suddenly, without any seeming cause, the light in the room began to grow dim. Sir Nathaniel, who was sitting close to Mimi, rose to his feet, and, crying, 'Quick!' caught hold of her hand and began to drag her from the room. Adam caught her other hand, and between them they drew her through the outer door which the servants were beginning to close. It was difficult at first to find the way, the darkness was so great; but to their relief when Adam whistled shrilly, the carriage and horses, which had been waiting in the angle of the avenue, dashed up. Her husband and Sir Nathaniel lifted – almost threw – Mimi into the carriage. The postilion plied whip and spur, and the vehicle, rocking with its speed, swept through the gate and tore up the road. Behind them was a hubbub – servants rushing about, orders being shouted out, doors shutting, and somewhere, seemingly far back in the house, a strange noise. Every nerve of the horses was strained as they dashed recklessly along the road. The two men held Mimi between them, the arms of both of them round her as though protectingly. As they went, there was a sudden rise in the ground; but the horses, breathing heavily, dashed up it at racing speed, not slackening their pace when the hill fell away again, leaving them to hurry along the downgrade.

It would be foolish to say that neither Adam nor Mimi had any fear in returning to Doom Tower. Mimi felt it more keenly than her husband, whose nerves were harder, and who was more inured to danger. Still she bore up bravely, and as usual the effort was helpful to her. When once she was in the study in the top of the turret, she almost forgot the terrors which lay outside in the dark. She did not attempt to peep out of the window; but Adam did – and saw nothing. The moonlight showed all the surrounding country, but nowhere was to be observed that tremulous line of green light.

The peaceful night had a good effect on them all; danger, being unseen, seemed far off. At times it was hard to realize that it had ever been. With courage restored, Adam rose early and walked along the Brow, seeing no change in the signs of life in Castra Regis. What he did see, to his wonder and concern, on his returning homeward, was Lady Arabella, in her tight-fitting white dress and ermine collar, but without her emeralds; she was emerging from the gate of Diana's Grove and walking towards the Castle. Pondering on this and trying to find some meaning in it, occupied his thoughts till he joined Mimi and Sir Nathaniel at breakfast. They began the meal in silence. What had been had been, and was known to them all. Moreover, it was not a pleasant topic.

A fillip was given to the conversation when Adam told of his seeing Lady Arabella on her way to Castra Regis. They each had something to say of her, and of what her wishes or intentions were towards Edgar Caswall. Mimi spoke bitterly of her in every aspect. She had not forgotten – and never would – never could – the occasion when, to harm Lilla, the woman had consorted with the negro. As a social matter, she was disgusted with her for following up the rich landowner – 'throwing herself at his head so shamelessly,' was how she expressed it. She was interested to know that the great kite still flew from Caswall's tower. But beyond such matters she did not try to go. The only comment she made was of strongly expressed surprise at her ladyship's 'cheek' in ignoring her own criminal acts, and her impudence in taking it for granted that others had overlooked them also.

24

A STARTLING PROPOSITION

The more Mimi thought over the late events, the more puzzled she was. What did it all mean – what could it mean, except that there was an error of fact somewhere. Could it be possible that some of them – all of them had been mistaken, that there had been no White Worm at all? On either side of her was a belief impossible of reception. Not to believe in what seemed apparent was to destroy the very foundations of belief . . . yet in old days there had been monsters on the earth, and certainly some people had believed in just such mysterious changes of identity. It was all very strange. Just fancy how any stranger – say a doctor – would regard her, if she were to tell him that she had been to a tea-party with an antediluvian monster, and that they had been waited on by up-to-date men-servants.

Adam had returned, exhilarated by his walk, and more settled in his mind than he had been for some time. Like Mimi, he had gone through the phase of doubt and inability to believe in the reality of things, though it had not affected him to the same extent. The idea, however, that his wife was suffering ill-effects from her terrible ordeal, braced him up. He remained with her for a time, then he sought Sir Nathaniel in order to talk over the matter with him. He knew that the calm common sense and self-reliance of the old man, as well as his experience, would be helpful to them all.

Sir Nathaniel had come to the conclusion that, for some reason which he did not understand, Lady Arabella had changed her plans, and, for the present at all events, was pacific. He was inclined to attribute her changed demeanour to the fact that her influence over Edgar Caswall was so far increased, as to justify a more fixed belief in his submission to her charms.

As a matter of fact, she had seen Caswall that morning when she visited Castra Regis, and they had had a long talk together, during which the possibility of their union had been discussed. Caswall, without being enthusiastic on the subject, had been courteous and attentive; as she had walked back to Diana's Grove, she almost congratulated herself on her new settlement in life. That the idea was becoming fixed in her mind, was shown by a letter which she wrote later in the day to Adam Salton, and sent to him by hand. It ran as follows:

'Dear Mr Salton, –
'I wonder if you would kindly advise, and, if possible, help me in a

matter of business. I have been for some time trying to make up my mind to sell Diana's Grove, I have put off and put off the doing of it till now. The place is my own property, and no one has to be consulted with regard to what I may wish to do about it. It was bought by my late husband, Captain Adolphus Ranger March, who had another residence, The Crest, Appleby. He acquired all rights of all kinds, including mining and sporting. When he died, he left his whole property to me. I shall feel leaving this place, which has become endeared to me by many sacred memories and affections – the recollection of many happy days of my young married life, and the more than happy memories of the man I loved and who loved me so much. I should be willing to sell the place for any fair price – so long, or course, as the purchaser was one I liked and of whom I approved. May I say that you yourself would be the ideal person. But I dare not hope for so much. It strikes me, however, that among your Australian friends may be someone who wishes to make a settlement in the Old Country, and would care to fix the spot in one of the most historic regions in England, full of romance and legend, and with a never-ending vista of historical interest – an estate which, though small, is in perfect condition and with illimitable possibilities of development, and many doubtful – or unsettled – rights which have existed before the time of the Romans or even Celts, who were the original possessors. In addition, the house has been kept up to the *dernier cri*. Immediate possession can be arranged. My lawyers can provide you, or whoever you may suggest, with all business and historical details. A word from you of acceptance or refusal is all that is necessary, and we can leave details to be thrashed out by our agents. Forgive me, won't you, for troubling you in the matter, and believe me, yours very sincerely,

'ARABELLA MARCH.'

Adam read this over several times, and then, his mind being made up, he went to Mimi and asked if she had any objection. She answered – after a shudder – that she was, in this, as in all things, willing to do whatever he might wish.

'Dearest, I am willing that you should judge what is best for us. Be quite free to act as you see your duty, and as your inclination calls. We are in the hands of God, and He has hitherto guided us, and will do so to His own end.'

From his wife's room Adam Salton went straight to the study in the tower, where he knew Sir Nathaniel would be at that hour. The old man was alone, so, when he had entered in obedience to the 'Come in', which answered his query, he closed the door and sat down beside him.

'Do you think, sir, that it would be well for me to buy Diana's Grove?'

'God bless my soul!' said the old man, startled, 'why on earth would you want to do that?'

'Well, I have vowed to destroy that White Worm, and my being able to do whatever I may choose with the Lair would facilitate matters and avoid complications.'

Sir Nathaniel hesitated longer than usual before speaking. He was thinking deeply.

'Yes, Adam, there is much common sense in your suggestion, though it startled me at first. I think that, for all reasons, you would do well to buy the property and to have the conveyance settled at once. If you want more money than is immediately convenient, let me know, so that I may be your banker.'

'Thank you, sir, most heartily; but I have more money at immediate call than I shall want. I am glad you approve.'

'The property is historic, and as time goes on it will increase in value. Moreover, I may tell you something, which indeed is only a surmise, but which, if I am right, will add great value to the place.' Adam listened. 'Has it ever struck you why the old name, "The Lair of the White Worm", was given? We know that there was a snake which in early days was called a worm; but why white?'

'I really don't know, sir; I never thought of it. I simply took it for granted.'

'So I did at first – long ago. But later I puzzled my brain for a reason.'

'And what was the reason, sir?'

'Simply and solely because the snake or worm *was* white. We are near the county of Stafford, where the great industry of china-burning was originated and grew. Stafford owes much of its wealth to the large deposits of the rare china clay found in it from time to time. These deposits become in time pretty well exhausted; but for centuries Stafford adventurers looked for the special clay, as Ohio and Pennsylvania farmers and explorers looked for oil. Anyone owning real estate on which china clay can be discovered strikes a sort of gold mine.'

'Yes, and then – ' The young man looked puzzled.

'The original "Worm" so-called, from which the name of the place came, had to find a direct way down to the marshes and the mud-holes. Now, the clay is easily penetrable, and the original hole probably pierced a bed of china clay. When once the way was made it would become a sort of highway for the Worm. But as much movement was necessary to ascend such a great height, some of the clay would become attached to its rough skin by attrition. The downway must have been easy work, but the ascent was different, and when the monster came to view in the upper world, it would be fresh from contact with the white clay. Hence the

403

name, which has no cryptic significance, but only fact. Now, if that surmise be true – and I do not see why not – there must be a deposit of valuable clay – possibly of immense depth.'

Adam's comment pleased the old gentleman.

'I have it in my bones, sir, that you have struck – or rather reasoned out – a great truth.'

Sir Nathaniel went on cheerfully. 'When the world of commerce wakes up to the value of your find, it will be as well that your title to ownership has been perfectly secured. If anyone ever deserved such a gain, it is you.'

With his friend's aid, Adam secured the property without loss of time. Then he went to see his uncle, and told him about it. Mr Salton was delighted to find his young relative already constructively the owner of so fine an estate – one which gave him an important status in the county. He made many anxious enquiries about Mimi, and the doings of the White Worm, but Adam reassured him.

The next morning, when Adam went to his host in the smoking-room, Sir Nathaniel asked him how he proposed to proceed with regard to keeping his vow.

'It is a difficult matter which you have undertaken. To destroy such a monster is something like one of the labours of Hercules, in that not only its size and weight and power of using them in little-known ways are against you, but the occult side is alone an unsurpassable difficulty. The Worm is already master of all the elements except fire – and I do not see how fire can be used for the attack. It has only to sink into the earth in its usual way, and you could not overtake it if you had the resources of the biggest coal-mine in existence. But I daresay you have mapped out some plan in your mind,' he added courteously.

'I have, sir. But, of course, it may not stand the test of practice.'

'May I know the idea?'

'Well, sir, this was my argument: At the time of the Chartist trouble, an idea spread amongst financial circles that an attack was going to be made on the Bank of England. Accordingly, the directors of that institution consulted many persons who were supposed to know what steps should be taken, and it was finally decided that the best protection against fire – which is what was feared – was not water but sand. To carry the scheme into practice a great store of fine sea-sand – the kind that blows about and is used to fill hour-glasses – was provided throughout the building, especially at the points liable to attack, from which it could be brought into use.

'I propose to provide at Diana's Grove, as soon as it comes into my possession, an enormous amount of such sand, and shall take an early occasion of pouring it into the well-hole, which it will in time choke. Thus

Lady Arabella, in her guise of the White Worm, will find herself cut off from her refuge. The hole is a narrow one, and is some hundreds of feet deep. The weight of the sand this can contain would not in itself be sufficient to obstruct; but the friction of such a body working against it would be tremendous.'

'One moment. What use would the sand be for destruction?'

'None, directly; but it would hold the struggling body in place till the rest of my scheme came into practice.'

'And what is the rest?'

'As the sand is being poured into the well-hole, quantities of dynamite can also be thrown in!'

'Good. But how would the dynamite explode – for, of course, that is what you intend. Would not some sort of wire or fuse be required for each parcel of dynamite?'

Adam smiled.

'Not in these days, sir. That was proved in New York. A thousand pounds of dynamite, in sealed canisters, was placed about some workings. At the last a charge of gunpowder was fired, and the concussion exploded the dynamite. It was most successful. Those who were non-experts in high explosives expected that every pane of glass in New York would be shattered. But, in reality, the explosive did no harm outside the area intended although sixteen acres of rock had been mined and only the supporting walls and pillars had been left intact. The whole of the rocks were shattered.'

Sir Nathaniel nodded approval.

'That seems a good plan – a very excellent one. But if it has to tear down so many feet of precipice, it may wreck the whole neighbourhood.'

'And free it for ever from a monster,' added Adam, as he left the room to find his wife.

25

THE LAST BATTLE

Lady Arabella had instructed her solicitors to hurry on with with conveyance of Diana's Grove, so no time was lost in letting Adam Salton have formal possession of the estate. After his interview with Sir Nathaniel, he had taken steps to begin putting his plan into action. In order to accumulate the necessary amount of fine sea-sand, he ordered the

405

steward to prepare for an elaborate system of top-dressing all the grounds. A great heap of the sand, brought from bays on the Welsh coast, began to grow at the back of the Grove. No one seemed to suspect that it was there for the purpose other than what had been given out.

Lady Arabella, who alone could have guessed, was now so absorbed in her matrimonial pursuit of Edgar Caswall, that she had neither time nor inclination for thought extraneous to this. She had not yet moved from the house, though she had formally handed over the estate.

Adam put up a rough corrugated-iron shed behind the Grove, in which he stored his explosives. All being ready for his great attempt whenever the time should come, he was now content to wait, and, in order to pass the time, interested himself in other things – even in Caswall's great kite, which still flew from the high tower of Castra Regis.

The mound of fine sand grew to proportions so vast as to puzzle the bailiffs and farmers round the Brow. The hour of the intended cataclysm was approaching apace. Adam wished – but in vain – for an opportunity, which would appear to be natural, of visiting Caswall in the turret of Castra Regis. At last, one morning, he met Lady Arabella moving towards the Castle, so he took his courage *à deux mains* and asked to be allowed to accompany her. She was glad, for her own purposes, to comply with his wishes. So together they entered, and found their way to the turret-room. Caswall was much surprised to see Adam come to his house, but lent himself to the task of seeming to be pleased. He played the host so well as to deceive even Adam. They all went out on the turret roof, where he explained to his guests the mechanism for raising and lowering the kite, taking also the opportunity of testing the movements of the multitudes of birds, how they answered almost instantaneously to the lowering or raising of the kite.

As Lady Arabella walked home with Adam from Castra Regis, she asked him if she might make a request. Permission having been accorded, she explained that before she finally left Diana's Grove, where she had lived so long, she had a desire to know the depth of the well-hole. Adam was really happy to meet her wishes, not from any sentiment, but because he wished to give some valid and ostensible reason for examining the passage of the Worm, which would obviate any suspicion resulting from his being on the premises. He brought from London a Kelvin sounding apparatus, with a sufficient length of piano-wire for testing any probable depth. The wire passed easily over the running wheel, and when this was once fixed over the hole, he was satisfied to wait till the most advantageous time for his final experiment.

In the meantime, affairs had been going quietly at Mercy Farm. Lilla, of course, felt lonely in the absence of her cousin, but the even tenor of life went on for her as for others. After the first shock of parting was over, things went back to their accustomed routine. In one respect, however, there was a marked difference. So long as home conditions had remained unchanged, Lilla was content to put ambition far from her, and to settle down to the life which had been hers as long as she could remember. But Mimi's marriage set her thinking; naturally, she came to the conclusion that she too might have a mate. There was not for her much choice – there was little movement in the matrimonial direction at the farmhouse. She did not approve of the personality of Edgar Caswall, and his struggle with Mimi had frightened her; but he was unmistakably an excellent *parti*, much better than she could have any right to expect. This weighs much with a woman, and more particularly one of her class. So, on the whole, she was content to let things take their course, and to abide by the issue.

As time went on, she had reason to believe that things did not point to happiness. She could not shut her eyes to certain disturbing facts, amongst which were the existence of Lady Arabella and her growing intimacy with Edgar Caswall; as well as his own cold and haughty nature, so little in accord with the ardour which is the foundation of a young maid's dreams of happiness. How things would, of necessity, alter if she were to marry, she was afraid to think. All told, the prospect was not happy for her, and she had a secret longing that *something* might occur to upset the order of things as at present arranged.

When Lilla received a note from Edgar Caswall asking if he might come to tea on the following afternoon, her heart sank within her. If it was only for her father's sake, she must not refuse him or show any disinclination which he might construe into incivility. She missed Mimi more than she could say or even dared to think. Hitherto, she had always looked to her cousin for sympathy, for understanding, for loyal support. Now she and all these things, and a thousand others – gentle, assuring, supporting – were gone. And instead there was a horrible aching void.

For the whole afternoon and evening, and for the following forenoon, poor Lilla's loneliness grew to be a positive agony. For the first time she began to realize the sense of her loss, as though all the previous suffering had been merely a preparation. Everything she looked at, everything she remembered or thought of, became laden with poignant memory. Then on the top of all was a new sense of dread. The reaction from the sense of security, which had surrounded her all her life, to a never-quited apprehension, was at times almost more than she could bear. It so filled her with fear that she had a haunting feeling that she would as soon die as live. However, whatever might be her own feelings, duty had to be done, and as she had been brought up to consider duty first, she braced herself to go through, to the very best of her ability, what was before her.

Still, the severe and prolonged struggle for self-control told upon Lilla. She looked, as she felt, ill and weak. She was really in a nerveless and prostrate condition, with black circles round her eyes, pale even to her lips, and with an instinctive trembling which she was quite unable to repress. It was for her a sad mischance that Mimi was away, for her love would have seen through all obscuring causes, and have brought to light the girl's unhappy condition of health. Lilla was utterly unable to do anything to escape from the ordeal before her; but her cousin, with the experience of her former struggles with Mr Caswall and of the condition in which these left her, would have taken steps – even peremptory ones, if necessary – to prevent a repetition.

Edgar arrived punctually to the time appointed by herself. When Lilla, through the great window, saw him approaching the house, her condition of nervous upset was pitiable. She braced herself up, however, and managed to get through the interview in its preliminary stages without any perceptible change in her normal appearance and bearing. It had been to her an added terror that the black shadow of Oolanga, whom she dreaded, would follow hard on his master. A load was lifted from her mind when he did not make his usual stealthy approach. She had also feared, though in lesser degree, lest Lady Arabella should be present to make trouble for her as before.

With a woman's natural forethought in a difficult position, she had provided the furnishing of the tea-table as a subtle indication of the social difference between her and her guest. She had chosen the implements of service, as well as all the provender set forth, of the humblest kind. Instead of arranging the silver teapot and china cups, she had set out an earthen teapot, such as was in common use in the farm kitchen. The same idea was carried out in the cups and saucers of thick homely delft, and in the cream-jug of similar kind. The bread was of simple whole-meal, home-baked. The butter was good, since she had made it herself, while the preserves and honey came from her own garden. Her face beamed with satisfaction when the guest eyed the appointments with a supercilious glance. It was a shock to the poor girl herself, for she enjoyed offering to a guest the little hospitalities possible to her; but that had to be sacrificed with other pleasures.

Caswall's face was more set and iron-clad than ever – his piercing eyes seemed from the very beginning to look her through and through. Her heart quailed when she thought of what would follow – of what would be the end, when this was only the beginning. As some protection, though it could be only of a sentimental kind, she brought from her own room the photographs of Mimi, of her grandfather, and of Adam Salton, whom by now she had grown to look on with reliance, as a brother whom she could trust. She kept the pictures near her heart, to which her hand naturally strayed when her feelings of constraint, distrust or fear became so poignant as to interfere with the calm which she felt was necessary to help her through her ordeal.

At first Edgar Caswall was courteous and polite, even thoughtful; but after a little while, when he found her resistance to his domination grow, he abandoned all forms of self-control and appeared in the same dominance as he had previously shown. She was prepared, however, for this, both by her former experience, and the natural fighting instinct within her. By this means, as the minutes went on, both developed the power and preserved the equality in which they had begun.

Without warning the psychic battle between the two individualities began afresh. This time both the positive and negative causes were all in favour of the man. The woman was alone and in bad spirits, unsupported; nothing at all was in her favour except the memory of the two victorious contests; whereas the man, though unaided, as before, by either Lady Arabella or Oolanga, was in full strength, well rested, and in flourishing circumstance. It is not, therefore, to be wondered at that his native dominance of character had full opportunity of asserting itself. He began his preliminary stare with a conscious sense of power, and, as it appeared to have immediate effect on the girl, he felt an ever-growing conviction of ultimate victory.

After a little Lilla's resolution began to flag. She felt that the contest was unequal – that she was unable to put forth her best efforts. As she was an unselfish person, she could not fight so well in her own battle as in that of someone whom she loved and to whom she was devoted. Edgar saw the relaxing of the muscles of face and brow, and the almost collapse of the heavy eyelids which seemed tumblng downward in sleep. Lilla made gallant efforts to brace her dwindling powers, but for a time unsuccessfully. At length there came an interruption, which seemed like a powerful stimulant. Through the wide window she saw Lady Arabella enter the plain gateway of the farm, and advance towards the hall door. She was clad as usual in tight-fitting white, which accentuated her thin, sinuous figure.

The sight did for Lilla what no voluntary effort could have done. Her eyes flashed, and in an instant she felt as though a new life had suddenly developed within her. Lady Arabella's entry, in her usual unconcerned, haughty, supercilious way, heightened the effect, so that when the two stood close to each other battle was joined. Mr Caswall, too, took new courage from her coming, and all his masterfulness and power came back to him. His looks, intensified, had more obvious effect than had been noticeable that day. Lilla seemed at last overcome by his dominance. Her face became red and pale – violently red and ghastly pale – by rapid turns. Her strength seemed gone. Her knees collapsed, and she was actually sinking on the floor, when to her surprise and joy Mimi came into the room, running hurriedly and breathing heavily.

Lilla rushed to her, and the two clasped hands. With that, a new sense of power, greater than Lilla had ever seen in her, seemed to quicken her cousin. Her hand swept in the air in front of Edgar Caswall, seeming to drive him backward more and more by each movement, till at last he seemed to be actually hurled through the door which Mimi's entrance had left open, and fell at full length on the gravel path without.

Then came the final and complete collapse of Lilla, who, without a sound, sank down on the floor.

26

FACE TO FACE

Mimi was greatly distressed when she saw her cousin lying prone. She had a few times in her life seen Lilla on the verge of fainting, but never senseless; and now she was frightened. She threw herself on her knees beside Lilla, and tried, by rubbing her hands and other measures commonly known, to restore her. But all her efforts were unavailing. Lilla still lay white and senseless. In fact, each moment she looked worse; her breast, that had been heaving with the stress, became still, and the pallor of her face grew like marble.

At these succeeding changes Mimi's fright grew, till it altogether mastered her. She succeeded in controlling herself only to the extent that she did not scream.

Lady Arabella had followed Caswall, when he had recovered sufficiently to get up and walk – though stumblingly – in the direction of Castra Regis. When Mimi was quite alone with Lilla and the need for effort had ceased, she felt weak and trembled. In her own mind, she attributed it to a sudden change in the weather – it was momentarily becoming apparent that a storm was coming on.

She raised Lilla's head and laid it on her warm young breast, but all in vain. The cold of the white features thrilled through her, and she utterly collapsed when it was borne in on her that Lilla had passed away.

The dusk gradually deepened and the shades of evening closed in, but Mimi did not seem to notice or to care. She sat on the floor with her arms round the body of the girl whom she loved. Darker and blacker grew the sky as the coming storm and the closing night joined forces. Still she sat on – alone – tearless – unable to think. Mimi did not know how long she sat there. Though it seemed to her that ages had passed, it could not have been more than half an hour. She suddenly came to herself, and was surprised to find that her grandfather had not returned. For a while she lay quiet, thinking of the immediate past. Lilla's hand was still in hers, and to her surprise it was still warm. Somehow this helped her consciousness, and without any special act of will she stood up. She lit a lamp and looked at her cousin. There was no doubt that Lilla was dead; but when the lamplight fell on her eyes, they seemed to look at Mimi with intent – with meaning. In this state of dark isolation a new resolution came to her, and grew and grew until it became a fixed definite purpose. She would face Caswall and call him to account for his murder of Lilla – that was what she called it to herself. She would also take steps – she knew not what or how – to avenge the part taken by Lady Arabella.

In this frame of mind she lit all the lamps in the room, got water and linen from her room, and set about the decent ordering of Lilla's body. This took some time; but when it was finished, she put on her hat and cloak, put out the lights, and set out quietly for Castra Regis.

As Mimi drew near the Castle, she saw no lights except those in and around the tower room. The lights showed her that Mr Caswall was there, so she entered by the hall door, which as usual was open, and felt her way in the darkness up the staircase to the lobby of the room. The door was ajar, and the light from within showed brilliantly through the opening. She saw Edgar Caswall walking restlessly to and fro in the room, with his hands clasped behind his back. She opened the door without knocking and walked right into the room. As she entered, he ceased walking, and stared at her in surprise. She made no remark, no comment, but continued the fixed look which he had seen on her entrance.

For a time silence reigned, and the two stood looking fixedly at each other. Mimi was the first to speak.

'You murderer! Lilla is dead!'

'Dead! Good God! When did she die?'

'She died this afternoon, just after you left her.'

'Are you sure?'

'Yes – and so are you – or you ought to be. You killed her!'

'I killed her! Be careful what you say!'

'As God sees us, it is true; and you know it. You came to Mercy Farm on purpose to break her – if you could. And the accomplice of your guilt, Lady Arabella March, came for the same purpose.'

411

'Be careful, woman,' he said hotly. 'Do not use such names in that way, or you shall suffer for it.'

'I am suffering for it – have suffered for it – shall suffer for it. Not for speaking the truth, as I have done, but because you two, with devilish malignity, did my darling to death. It is you and your accomplice who have to dread punishment, not I.'

'Take care!' he said again.

'Oh, I am not afraid of you or your accomplice,' she answered spiritedly. 'I am content to stand by every word I have said, every act I have done. Moreover, I believe in God's justice. I fear not the grinding of His mills; if necessary I shall set the wheels in motion myself. But you don't care for God, or believe in Him. Your God is your great kite, which cows the birds of a whole district. But be sure that His hand, when it rises, always falls at the appointed time. It may be that your name is being called even at this very moment at the Great Assize. Repent while there is still time. Happy you, if you may be allowed to enter those mighty halls in the company of the pure-souled angel whose voice has only to whisper one word of justice, and you disappear for ever into everlasting torment.'

The sudden death of Lilla caused consternation among Mimi's friends and well-wishers. Such a tragedy was totally unexpected, as Adam and Sir Nathaniel had been expecting the White Worm's vengeance to fall upon themselves.

Adam, leaving his wife free to follow her own desires with regard to Lilla and her grandfather, busied himself with filling the well-hole with the fine sand prepared for the purpose, taking care to have lowered at stated intervals quantities of the store of dynamite, so as to be ready for the final explosion. He had under his immediate supervision a corps of workmen, and was assisted by Sir Nathaniel, who had come over for the purpose, and all were now staying at Lesser Hill.

Mr Salton, too, showed much interest in the job, and was constantly coming in and out, nothing escaping his observation.

Since her marriage to Adam and their coming to stay at Doom Tower, Mimi had been fettered by fear of the horrible monster at Diana's Grove. But now she dreaded it no longer. She accepted the fact of its assuming at will the form of Lady Arabella. She had still to tax and upbraid her for her part in the unhappiness which had been wrought on Lilla, and for her share in causing her death.

One evening when Mimi entered her own room, she went to the window and threw an eager look round the whole circle of sight. A single glance satisfied her that the White Worm *in propriâ personâ* was not visible. So she sat down in the window-seat and enjoyed the pleasure of a full view, from which she had been so long cut off. The maid who waited on her had told her that Mr Salton had not yet returned home, so she felt free to enjoy the luxury of peace and quiet.

As she looked out of the window, she saw something thin and white move along the avenue. She thought she recognized the figure of Lady Arabella, and instinctively drew back behind the curtain. When she had ascertained, by peeping out several times, that the lady had not seen her, she watched more carefully, all her instinctive hatred flooding back at the sight of her. Lady Arabella was moving swiftly and stealthily, looking back and around her at intervals, as if she feared to be followed. This gave Mimi an idea that she was up to no good, so she determined to seize the occasion for watching her in more detail.

Hastily putting on a dark cloak and hat, she ran downstairs and out into the avenue. Lady Arabella had moved, but the sheen of her white dress was still to be seen among the young oaks around the gateway. Keeping in shadow, Mimi followed, taking care not to come so close as to awake the other's suspicion, and watched her quarry pass along the road in the direction of Castra Regis.

She followed on steadily through the gloom of the trees, depending on the glint of the white dress to keep her right. The wood began to thicken, and presently, when the road widened and the trees grew farther back, she lost sight of any indication of her whereabouts. Under the present conditions it was impossible for her to do any more, so, after waiting for a while still hidden in the shadow, to see if she could catch another glimpse of the white frock, she determined to go on slowly towards Castra Regis, and trust to the chapter of accidents to pick up the trail again. She went on slowly, taking advantage of every obstacle and shadow to keep herself concealed. At last she entered on the grounds of the Castle, at a spot from which the windows of the turret were dimly visible, without having seen again any sign of Lady Arabella.

Meanwhile, during most of the time that Mimi Salton had been moving warily along in the gloom, she was in reality being followed by Lady Arabella, who had caught sight of her leaving the house and had never again lost touch with her. It was a case of the hunter being hunted. For a time Mimi's many turnings, with the natural obstacles that were perpetually intervening, caused Lady Arabella some trouble; but when she was close to Castra Regis, there was no more possibility of concealment, and the strange double following went swiftly on.

When she saw Mimi close to the hall door of Castra Regis and ascending the steps, she followed. When Mimi entered the dark hall and felt her way up the staircase, still, as she believed, following Lady Arabella, the latter kept on her way. When they reached the lobby of the turret-room, Mimi believed that the object of her search was ahead of her.

413

Edgar Caswall sat in the gloom of the great room, occasionally stirred to curiosity when the drifting clouds allowed a little light to fall from the storm-swept sky. But nothing really interested him now. Since he had heard of Lilla's death, the gloom of his remorse, emphasized by Mimi's upbraiding, had made more hopeless his cruel, selfish, saturnine nature. He heard no sound, for his normal faculties seemed benumbed.

Mimi, when she came to the door, which stood ajar, gave a light tap. So light was it that it did not reach Caswall's ears. Then, taking her courage in both hands, she boldly pushed the door and entered. As she did so, her heart sank, for now she was face to face with a difficulty which had not, in her state of mental perturbation, occurred to her.

27

ON THE TURRET ROOF

The storm which was coming was already making itself manifest, not only in the wide scope of nature, but in the hearts and natures of human beings. Electrical disturbance in the sky and the air is reproduced in animals of all kinds, and particularly in the highest type of them all – the most receptive – the most electrical. So it was with Edgar Caswall, despite his selfish nature and coldness of blood. So it was was Mimi Salton, despite her unselfish, unchanging devotion for those she loved. So it was even with Lady Arabella, who, under the instincts of a primeval serpent, carried the ever-varying wishes and customs of womanhood, which is always old – and always new.

Edgar, after he had turned his eyes on Mimi, resumed his apathetic position and sullen silence. Mimi quietly took a seat a little way apart, whence she could look on the progress of the coming storm and study its appearance throughout the whole visible circle of the neighbourhood. She was in brighter and better spirits than she had been for many days past. Lady Arabella tried to efface herelf behind the now open door.

Without, the clouds grew thicker and blacker as the storm-centre came closer. As yet the forces, from whose linking the lightning springs, were held apart, and the silence of nature proclaimed the calm before the storm. Caswall felt the effect of the gathering electric force. A sort of wild exultation grew upon him, such as he had sometimes felt just before the breaking of a tropical storm. As he became conscious of this, he raised his head and caught sight of Mimi. He was in the grip of an emotion greater than himself; in the mood in which he was he felt the need upon him of doing some desperate deed. He was now absolutely reckless, and as Mimi was associated with him in the memory which drove him on, he wished that she too should be engaged in this enterprise. He had no knowledge of the proximity of Lady Arabella, and thought that he was far removed from all he knew and whose interests he shared – alone with the wild elements, which were being lashed to fury, and with the woman who had struggled with him and vanquished him, and on whom he would shower the full measure of his hate.

The fact was that Edgar Caswall was, if not mad, close to the border-line. Madness in its first stage – monomania – is a lack of proportion. So long as this is general, it is not always noticeable, for the uninspired onlooker is without the necessary means of comparison. But in mono-mania the errant faculty protrudes itself in a way that may not be denied. It puts aside, obscures, or takes the place of something else – just as the head of a pin placed before the centre of the iris will block out the whole scope of vision. The most usual form of monomania has commonly the same beginning as that from which Edgar Caswall suffered – an over-large idea of self-importance. Alienists, who study the matter exactly, probably know more of human vanity and its effects than do ordinary men. Caswall's mental disturbance was not hard to identify. Every asylum is full of such cases – men and women, who, naturally selfish and egotistical, so appraise to themselves their own importance that every other circumstance in life becomes subservient to it. The disease supplies in itself the material self-magnification. When the decadence attacks a nature naturally proud and selfish and vain, and lacking both the aptitude and habit of self-restraint, the development of the disease is more swift, and ranges to farther limits. It is such persons who become imbued with the idea that they have the attributes of the Almighty – even that they themselves are the Almighty.

Mimi had a suspicion – or rather, perhaps, an intuition – of the true state of things when she heard him speak, and at the same time noticed the abnormal flush on his face, and his rolling eyes. There was a certain want of fixedness of purpose which she had certainly not noticed before – a quick, spasmodic utterance which belongs rather to the insane than to those of intellectual equilibrium. She was a little frightened, not only by his thoughts, but by his staccato way of expressing them.

Caswall moved to the door leading to the turret-stair by which the roof was reached, and spoke in a peremptory way, whose tone alone made her feel defiant.

'Come! I want you.'

She instinctively drew back – she was not accustomed to such words, more especially to such a tone. Her answer was indicative of a new contest.

'Why should I go? What for?'

He did not at once reply – another indication of his overwhelming egotism. She repeated her questions; habit reasserted itself, and he spoke without thinking the words which were in his heart.

'I want you, if you will be so good, to come with me to the turret-roof. I am much interested in certain experiments with the kite, which would be, if not a pleasure, at least a novel experience to you. You would see something not easily seen otherwise.'

'I will come,' she answered simply; Edgar moved in the direction of the stair, she following close behind him.

She did not like to be left alone at such a height, in such a place, in the darkness, with a storm about to break. Of himself she had no fear; all that had been seemed to have passed away with her two victories over him in the struggle of wills. Moreover, the more recent apprehension – that of his madness – had also ceased. In the conversation of the last few minutes he seemed so rational, so clear, so unaggressive, that she no longer saw reason for doubt. So satisfied was she that even when he put out a hand to guide her to the steep, narrow stairway, she took it without thought in the most conventional way.

Lady Arabella, crouching in the lobby, behind the door, heard every word that had been said, and formed her own opinion of it. It seemed evident to her that there had been some *rapprochement* between the two who had so lately been hostile to each other, and that made her furiously angry. Mimi was interfering with her plans! She had made certain of her capture of Edgar Caswall, and she could not tolerate even the lightest and most contemptuous fancy on his part which might divert him from the main issue. When she became aware that he wished Mimi to come with him to the roof and that she had acquiesced, her rage got beyond bounds. She became oblivious to any danger there might be in a visit to such an exposed place at such a time, and to all lesser considerations, and made up her mind to forestall them. She stealthily and noiselessly crept through the wicket, and, ascending the stair, stepped out on the roof. It was bitterly cold, for the fierce gusts of the storm which swept round the turret drove in through every unimpeded way, whistling at the sharp corners and singing round the trembling flag-staff. The kite-string and the wire which controlled the runners made a concourse of weird sounds which somehow, perhaps from the violence which surrounded them, acting on their length, resolved themselves into some kind of harmony – a fitting accompaniment to the tragedy which seemed about to begin.

Mimi's heart beat heavily. Just before leaving the turret-chamber she

416

had a shock which she could not shake off. The lights of the room had momentarily revealed to her, as they passed out, Edgar's face, concentrated as it was whenever he intended to use his mesmeric power. Now the black eyebrows made a thick line across his face, under which his eyes shone and glittered ominously. Mimi recognized the danger, and assumed the defiant attitude that had twice already served her so well. She had a fear that the circumstances and the place were against her, and she wanted to be forearmed.

The sky was now somewhat lighter than it had been. Either there was lightning afar off, whose reflections were carried by the rolling clouds, or else the gathered force, though not yet breaking into lightning, had an incipient power of light. It seemed to affect both the man and the woman. Edgar seemed altogether under its influence. His spirits were boisterous, his mind exalted. He was now at his worst; madder than he had been earlier in the night.

Mimi, trying to keep as far from him as possible, moved across the stone floor of the turret-room, and found a niche which concealed her. It was not far from Lady Arabella's place of hiding.

Edgar, left alone on the centre of the turret-roof, found himself altogether his own master in a way which tended to increase his madness. He knew that Mimi was close at hand, though he had lost sight of her. He spoke loudly, and the sound of his own voice, though it was carried from him on the sweeping wind as fast as the words were spoken, seemed to exalt him still more. Even the raging of the elements round him appeared to add to his exaltation. To him it seemed that these manifestations were obedient to his own will. He had reached the sublime of his madness; he was now in his own mind actually the Almighty, and whatever might happen would be the direct carrying out of his own commands. As he could not see Mimi, nor fix whereabout she was, he shouted loudly:

'Come to me! You shall see now what you are despising, what you are warring against. All that you see is mine – the darkness as well as the light. I tell you that I am greater than any other who is, or was, or shall be. When the Master of Evil took Christ up on a high place and showed Him all the kingdoms of the earth, he was doing what he thought no other could do. He was wrong – he forgot *Me*. I shall send you light, up to the very ramparts of heaven. A light so great that it shall dissipate those black clouds that are rushing up and piling around us. Look! Look! At the very touch of my hand that light springs into being and mounts up – and up – and up!'

He made his way whilst he was speaking to the corner of the turret whence flew the giant kite, and from which the runners ascended. Mimi looked on, appalled and afraid to speak lest she should precipitate some calamity. Within the niche Lady Arabella cowered in a paroxysm of fear.

Edgar took up a small wooden box, through a hole in which the wire of the runner ran. This evidently set some machinery in motion, for a sound as of whirring came. From one side of the box floated what looked like a piece of stiff ribbon, which snapped and crackled as the wind took it. For a few seconds Mimi saw it as it rushed along the sagging line to the kite. When close to it, there was a loud crack, and a sudden light appeared to issue from every chink in the box. Then a quick flame flashed along the snapping ribbon, which glowed with an intense light – a light so great that the whole of the countryside around stood out against the background of black driving clouds. For a few seconds the light remained, then suddenly disappeared in the blackness around. It was simply a magnesium light, which had been fired by the mechanism within the box and carried up to the kite. Edgar was in a state of tumultuous excitement, shouting and yelling at the top of his voice and dancing about like a lunatic.

This was more than Lady Arabella's curious dual nature could stand – the ghoulish element in her rose triumphant, and she abandoned all idea of marriage with Edgar Caswall, gloating fiendishly over the thought of revenge.

She must lure him to the White Worm's hole – but how? She glanced around and quickly made up her mind. The man's whole thoughts were absorbed by his wonderful kite, which he was showing off, in order to fascinate her imaginary rival, Mimi.

On the instant she glided through the darkness to the wheel whereon the string of the kite was wound. With deft fingers she unshipped this, took it with her, reeling out the wire as she went, thus keeping, in a way, in touch with the kite. Then she glided swiftly to the wicket, through which she passed, locking the gate behind her as she went.

Down the turret-stair she ran quickly, letting the wire run from the wheel which she carried carefully, and, passing out of the hall door, hurried down the avenue with all her speed. She soon reached her own gate, ran down the avenue, and with her key opened the iron door leading to the well-hole.

She felt satisfied with herself. All her plans were maturing, or had already matured. The Master of Castra Regis was within her grasp. The woman whose interference she had feared, Lilla Watford, was dead. Truly, all was well, and she felt that she might pause a while and rest. She tore off her clothes, with feverish fingers, and in full enjoyment of her natural freedom, stretched her slim figure in animal delight. Then she lay down on the sofa – to await her victim! Edgar Caswall's life blood would more than satisfy her for some time to come.

28

THE BREAKING OF THE STORM

When Lady Arabella had crept away in her usual noiseless fashion, the two others remained for a while in their places on the turret-roof: Caswall because he had nothing to say, Mimi because she had much to say and wished to put her thoughts in order. For quite a while – which seemed interminable – silence reigned between them. At last Mimi made a beginning – she had made up her mind how to act.

'Mr Caswall,' she said loudly, so as to make sure of being heard through the blustering of the wind and the perpetual cracking of the electricity.

Caswall said something in reply, but his words were carried away on the storm. However, one of her objects was effected: she knew now exactly whereabout on the roof he was. So she moved close to the spot before she spoke again, raising her voice almost to a shout.

'The wicket is shut. Please to open it. I can't get out.'

As she spoke, she was quietly fingering a revolver which Adam had given to her in case of emergency and which now lay in her breast. She felt that she was caged like a rat in a trap, but did not mean to be taken at a disadvantage, whatever happened. Caswall also felt trapped, and all the brute in him rose to the emergency. In a voice which was raucous and brutal – much like that which is heard when a wife is being beaten by her husband in a slum – he hissed out, his syllables cutting through the roaring of the storm:

'You came of your own accord – without permission, or even asking it. Now you can stay or go as you choose. But you must manage it for yourself; I'll have nothing to do with it.'

Her answer was spoken with dangerous suavity:

'I am going. Blame yourself if you do not like the time and manner of it. I daresay Adam – my husband – will have a word to say to you about it!'

'Let him say, and be damned to him, and to you too! I'll show you a light. You shan't be able to say that you could not see what you were doing.'

As he spoke, he was lighting another piece of the magnesium ribbon, which made a blinding glare in which everything was plainly discernible, down to the smallest detail. This exactly suited Mimi. She took accurate note of the wicket and its fastening before the glare had died away. She took her revolver out and fired into the lock, which was shivered on the instant, the pieces flying round in all directions, but happily without causing hurt to anyone. Then she pushed the wicket open and ran down the narrow stair, and so to the hall door. Opening this also, she ran down the avenue, never lessening her speed till she stood outside the door of Lesser Hill. The door was opened at once on her ringing.

'Is Mr Adam Salton in?' she asked.

'He has just come in, a few minutes ago. He has gone up to the study,' replied a servant.

She ran upstairs at once and joined him. He seemed relieved when he saw her, but scrutinized her face keenly. He saw that she had been in some concern, so led her over to the sofa in the window and sat down beside her.

'Now, dear, tell me all about it!' he said.

She rushed breathlessly through all the details of her adventure on the turret-roof. Adam listened attentively, helping her all he could, and not embarrassing her by any questioning. His thoughtful silence was a great help to her, for it allowed her to collect and organize her thoughts.

'I must go and see Caswall to-morrow, to hear what he has to say on the subject.'

'But, dear, for my sake, don't have any quarrel with Mr Caswall. I have had too much trial and pain lately to wish it increased by any anxiety regarding you.'

'You shall not, dear – if I can help it – please God,' he said solemnly, and he kissed her.

Then, in order to keep her interested so that she might forget the fears and anxieties that had disturbed her, he began to talk over the details of her adventure, making shrewd comments which attracted and held her attention. Presently, *inter alia*, he said:

'That's a dangerous game Caswall is up to. It seems to me that that young man – though he doesn't appear to know it – is riding for a fall!'

'How, dear? I don't understand.'

'Kite flying on a night like this from a place like the tower of Castra Regis is, to say the least of it, dangerous. It is not merely courting death or other accident from lightning, but it is bringing the lightning into where he lives. Every cloud that is blowing up here – and they all make for the highest point – is bound to develop into a flash of lightning. That kite is up in the air and is bound to attract the lightning. Its cord makes a road for it on which to travel to earth. When it does come, it will strike the top of the tower with a weight a hundred times greater than a whole park of artillery, and will knock Castra Regis into pieces. Where it will go after that, no one can tell. If there should be any metal by which it can travel, such will not only point the road, but be the road itself.'

'Would it be dangerous to be out in the open air when such a thing is taking place?' she asked.

'No, little woman. It would be the safest possible place – so long as one was not in the line of the electric current.'

'Then, do let us go outside. I don't want to run into any foolish danger – or, far more, to ask you to do so. But surely if the open is safest, that is the place for us.'

Without another word, she put on again the cloak she had thrown off, and a small, tight-fitting cap. Adam too, put on his cap, and, after seeing that his revolver was all right, gave her his hand, and they left the house together.

'I think the best thing we can do will be to go round all the places which are mixed up in this affair.'

'All right, dear, I am ready. But, if you don't mind, we might go first to Mercy. I am anxious about grandfather, and we might see that – as yet, at all events – nothing has happened there.'

So they went on the high-hung road along the top of the Brow. The wind here was of great force, and made a strange booming noise as it swept high overhead; though not the sound of cracking and tearing as it passed through the woods of high slender trees which grew on either side of the road. Mimi could hardly keep her feet. She was not afraid; but the force to which she was opposed gave her a good excuse to hold on to her husband extra tight.

At Mercy there was no one up – at least, all the lights were out. But to Mimi, accustomed to the nightly routine of the house, there were manifest signs that all was well, except in the little room on the first floor, where the blinds were down. Mimi could not bear to look at that, to think of it. Adam understood her pain, for he had been keenly interested in poor Lilla. He bent over and kissed her, and then took her hand and held it hard. Thus they passed on together, returning to the high road towards Castra Regis.

At the gate of Castra Regis they were extra careful. When drawing near, Adam stumbled upon the wire that Lady Arabella had left trailing on the ground.

Adam drew his breath at this, and spoke in a low, earnest whisper:

'I don't want to frighten you, Mimi dear, but wherever that wire is there is danger.'

'Danger! How?'

'That is the track where the lightning will go; at any moment, even now whilst we are speaking and searching, a fearful force may be loosed upon us. Run on, dear; you know the way to where the avenue joins the high road. If you see any sign of the wire, keep away from it, for God's sake. I shall join you at the gateway.'

'Are you going to follow that wire alone?'

'Yes, dear. One is sufficient for that work. I shall not lose a moment till I am with you.'

'Adam, when I came with you into the open, my main wish was that we should be together if anything serious happened. You wouldn't deny me that right, would you dear?'

'No, dear, not that or any right. Thank God that my wife has such a wish. Come; we will go together. We are in the hands of God. If He wishes, we shall be together at the end, whenever or wherever that may be.'

They picked up the trail of the wire on the steps and followed it down the avenue, taking care not to touch it with their feet. It was easy enough to follow, for the wire, if not bright, was self-coloured, and showed clearly. They followed it out of the gateway and into the avenue of Diana's Grove.

Here a new gravity clouded Adam's face, though Mimi saw no cause for fresh concern. This was easily enough explained. Adam knew of the explosive works in progress regarding the well-hole, but the matter had been kept from his wife. As they stood near the house, Adam asked Mimi to return to the road, ostensibly to watch the course of the wire, telling her that there might be a branch wire leading somewhere else. She was to search the undergrowth, and if she found it, was to warn him by the Australian native 'Coo-ee!'

Whilst they were standing together, there came a blinding flash of lightning, which lit up for several seconds the whole area of earth and sky. It was only the first note of the celestial prelude, for it was followed in quick succession by numerous flashes, whilst the crash and roll of thunder seemed continuous.

Adam, appalled, drew his wife to him and held her close. As far as he could estimate by the interval between lightning and thunder-clap, the heart of the storm was still some distance off, so he felt no present concern for their safety. Still, it was apparent that the course of the storm was moving swiftly in their direction. The lightning flashes came faster and faster and closer together; the thunder-roll was almost continuous, not stopping for a moment – a new crash beginning before the old one had ceased. Adam kept looking up in the direction where the kite strained and struggled at its detaining cord, but, of course, the dull evening light prevented any distinct scrutiny.

At length there came a flash so appallingly bright that in its glare Nature seemed to be standing still. So long did it last, that there was time to distinguish its configuration. It seemed like a mighty tree inverted, pendent from the sky. The whole country around within the angle of vision

422

was lit up till it seemed to glow. Then a broad ribbon of fire seemed to drop on the tower of Castra Regis just as the thunder crashed. By the glare, Adam could see the tower shake and tremble, and finally fall to pieces like a house of cards. The passing of the lightning left the sky again dark, but a blue flame fell downwards from the tower, and, with inconceivable rapidity, running along the ground in the direction of Diana's Grove, reached the dark silent house, which in the instant burst into flame at a hundred different points.

At the same moment there rose from the house a rending, crashing sound of woodwork, broken or thrown about, mixed with a quick scream so appalling that Adam, stout of heart as he undoubtedly was, felt his blood turn into ice. Instinctively, despite the danger and their consciousness of it, husband and wife took hands and listened, trembling. *Something* was going on close to them, mysterious, terrible, deadly! The shrieks continued, though less sharp in sound, as though muffled. In the midst of them was a terrific explosion, seemingly from deep in the earth.

The flames from Castra Regis and from Diana's Grove made all around almost as light as day, and now that the lightning had ceased to flash, their eyes, unblinded, were able to judge both perspective and detail. The heat of the burning house caused the iron doors to warp and collapse. Seemingly of their own accord, they fell open, and exposed the interior. The Saltons could now look through to the room beyond, where the well-hole yawned, a deep narrow circular chasm. From this the agonized shrieks were rising, growing ever more terrible with each second that passed.

But it was not only the heart-rending sound that almost paralysed poor Mimi with terror. What she saw was sufficient to fill her with evil dreams for the remainder of her life. . . .

Some of these fragments were covered with scaled skin as of a gigantic lizard or serpent. Once, in a sort of lull or pause, the seething contents of the hole rose, after the manner of a bubbling spring, and Adam saw part of the thin form of Lady Arabella, forced up to the top amid a mass of slime, and what looked as if it had been a monster torn into shreds. Several times some masses of enormous bulk were forced up through the well-hole with inconceivable violence, and, suddenly expanding as they came into large space, disclosed sections of the White Worm which Adam and Sir Nathaniel had seen looking over the trees with its enormous eyes of emerald-green flickering like great lamps in a gale.

At last the explosive power, which was not yet exhausted, evidently reached the main store of dynamite which had been lowered into the Worm's hole. The result was appalling. The ground for far around quivered and opened in long, deep chasms, whose edges shook and fell in, throwing up clouds of sand which fell back and hissed amongst the rising water. The heavily built house shook to its foundations. Great stones were thrown up as from a volcano, some of them, great masses of hard stone, squared and grooved with implements wrought by human hands, breaking up and splitting in mid-air as though riven by some infernal power. Trees near the house – and therefore presumably in some way above the hole, which sent up clouds of dust and steam and fine sand mingled, and which carried an appalling stench which sickened the spectators – were torn up by the roots and hurled into the air. By now, flames were bursting violently from all over the ruins, so dangerously that Adam caught up his wife in his arms, and ran with her from the promimity of the flames.

Then almost as quickly as it had begun, the whole cataclysm ceased, though a deep-down rumbling continued intermittently for some time. Then silence brooded over all – silence so complete that it seemed in itself a sentient thing – silence which seemed like incarnate darkness, and conveyed the same idea to all who came within its radius. To the young people who had suffered the long horror of that awful night, it brought relief – relief from the presence or the fear of all that was horrible – relief which seemed perfected when the red rays of sunrise shot up over the far eastern sea, bringing a promise of a new order of things with the coming day.

*　*　*

His bed saw little of Adam Salton for the remainder of that night. He and Mimi walked hand in hand in the brightening dawn round by the brow to Castra Regis and on to Lesser Hill. They did so deliberately, in an attempt to think as little as possible of the terrible experiences of the night. The morning was bright and cheerful, as a morning sometimes is after a devastating storm. The clouds, of which there were plenty in evidence, brought no lingering idea of gloom. All nature was bright and joyous, being in striking contrast to the scenes of wreck and devastation, the effects of obliterating fire and lasting ruin.

The only evidence of the once stately pile of Castra Regis and its inhabitants was a shapeless huddle of shattered architecture, dimly seen as the keen breeze swept aside the cloud of acrid smoke which marked the site of the once lordly castle. As for Diana's Grove, they looked in vain for a sign which had a suggestion of permanence. The oak trees of the Grove were still to be seen – some of them – emerging from a haze of smoke, the great trunks solid and erect as ever, but the larger branches broken and twisted and rent, with bark stripped and chipped, and the smaller branches broken and dishevelled looking from the constant stress and threshing of the storm.

Of the house as such, there was, even at the short distance from which they looked, no trace. Adam resolutely turned his back on the devastation and hurried on. Mimi was not only upset and shocked in many ways, but she was physically 'dog tired', and falling asleep on her feet. Adam took her to her room and made her undress and get into bed, taking care that the room was well lighted both by sunshine and lamps. The only obstruction was from a silk curtain, drawn across the window to keep out the glare. He sat beside her, holding her hand, well knowing that the comfort of his presence was the best restorative for her. He stayed with her till sleep had overmastered her wearied body. Then he went softly away. He found his uncle and Sir Nathaniel in the study, having an early cup of tea, amplified to the dimensions of a possible breakfast. Adam explained that he had not told his wife that he was going over the horrible places again, lest it should frighten her, for the rest and sleep in ignorance would help her and make a gap of peacefulness between the horrors.

Sir Nathaniel agreed.

'We know, my boy,' he said, 'that the unfortunate Lady Arabella is dead, and that the foul carcase of the Worm has been torn to pieces – pray God that its evil soul will never more escape from the nethermost hell.'

They visited Diana's Grove first, not only because it was nearer, but also because it was the place where most description was required, and Adam felt that he could tell his story best on the spot. The absolute destruction of the place and everything in it seen in the broad daylight was almost inconceivable. To Sir Nathaniel, it was as a story of horror full and complete. But to Adam it was, as it were, only on the fringes. He knew what was still to be seen when his friends had got over the knowledge of externals. As yet, they had only seen the outside of the house – or rather, where the outside of the house once had been. The great horror lay within. However, age – and the experience of age – counts.

A strange, almost elemental, change in the aspect had taken place in the time which had elapsed since the dawn. It would almost seem as if Nature herself had tried to obliterate the evil signs of what had occurred. True, the utter ruin of the house was made even more manifest in the searching daylight; but the more appalling destruction which lay beneath was not visible. The rent, torn, and dislocated stonework looked worse than before; the upheaved foundations, the piled-up fragments of masonry, the fissures in the torn earth – all were at the worst. The Worm's hole was still evident, a round fissure seemingly leading down into the very bowels of the earth. But all the horrid mass of slime and the sickening remnants of violent death were gone. Either some of the latter explosions had thrown up from the deep quantities of water which, though foul and corrupt itself, had still some cleansing power left, or else the writhing mass which

425

stirred from far below had helped to drag down and obliterate the items of horror. A grey dust, partly of fine sand, partly of the waste of the falling ruin, covered everything, and, though ghastly itself, helped to mask something still worse.

After a few minutes of watching, it became apparent to the three men that the turmoil far below had not yet ceased. At short irregular intervals the hell-broth in the hole seemed as if boiling up. It rose and fell again and turned over, showing in fresh form much of the nauseous detail which had been visible earlier. The worst parts were the great masses of the flesh of the monstrous Worm, in all it red and sickening aspect. Such fragments had been bad enough before, but now they were infinitely worse. Corruption comes with startling rapidity to beings whose destruction has been due wholly or in part to lightning – the whole mass seemed to have become all at once corrupt! The whole surface of the fragments, once alive, was covered with insects, worms, and vermin of all kinds. The sight was horrible enough, but, with the awful smell added, was simply unbearable. The Worm's hole appeared to breathe forth death in its most repulsive forms. The friends, with one impulse, moved to the top of the Brow, where a fresh breeze from the sea was blowing up.

At the top of the Brow, beneath them as they looked down, they saw a shining mass of white, which looked strangely out of place amongst such wreckage as they had been viewing. It appeared so strange that Adam suggested trying to find a way down, so that they might see it more closely.

'We need not go down; I know what it is,' Sir Nathaniel said. 'The explosions of last night have blown off the outside of the cliffs – that which we see is the vast bed of china clay through which the Worm originally found its way down to its lair. I can catch the glint of the water of the deep quags far down below. Well, her ladyship didn't deserve such a funeral – or such a momument.'

*   *   *

The horrors of the last few hours had played such havoc with Mimi's nerves, that a change of scene was imperative – if a permanent breakdown was to be avoided.

'I think,' said old Mr Salton, 'it is quite time you young people departed for that honeymoon of yours!' There was a twinkle in his eye as he spoke.

Mimi's soft shy glance at her stalwart husband, was sufficient answer.

Dracula's Guest

To
MY SON

Publisher's Note

This collection of stories by Bram Stoker was first published in 1914. Later a special edition of 1000 numbered copies was issued for souvenir presentation to the audience at the Prince of Wales Theatre, London, on the occasion of the 250th London performance of the play *Dracula* – on 14 September 1927. When each member of the audience opened his or her mystery packet, he found not only a copy of *Dracula's Guest* but also, inside the book's cover, a black bat, powered by elastic, which flew out as the book was opened. . . .

Preface

A few months before the lamented death of my husband
– I might say even as the shadow of death was over him –
he planned three series of short stories for publication,
and the present volume is one of them. To his original list
of stories in this book, I have added an hitherto
unpublished episode from *Dracula*. It was originally
excised owing to the length of the book, and may prove
of interest to the many readers of what is considered my
husband's most remarkable work. The other stories have
already been published in English and American
periodicals. Had my husband lived longer, he might have
seen fit to revise this work, which is mainly from the
earlier years of his strenuous life. But, as fate has
entrusted to me the issuing of it, I consider it fitting and
proper to let it go forth practically as it was left by him.

FLORENCE BRAM STOKER

DRACULA'S GUEST

When we started for our drive the sun was shining brightly on Munich, and the air was full of the joyousness of early summer. Just as we were about to depart, Herr Delbrück (the maître d'hôtel of the Quatre Saisons, where I was staying) came down, bareheaded, to the carriage and, after wishing me a pleasant drive, said to the coachman, still holding his hand on the handle of the carriage door:

'Remember you are back by nightfall. The sky looks bright but there is a shiver in the north wind that says there may be a sudden storm. But I am sure you will not be late.' Here he smiled, and added, 'for you know what night it is.'

Johann answered with an emphatic, 'Ja, mein Herr,' and, touching his hat, drove off quickly. When we had cleared the town, I said, after signalling him to stop:

'Tell me, Johann, what is tonight?'

He crossed himself, as he answered laconically: 'Walpurgisnacht.' Then he took out his watch, a great, old-fashioned German silver thing as big as a turnip, and looked at it, with his eyebrows gathered together and a little impatient shrug of his shoulders. I realized that this was his way of respectfully protesting against the unnecessary delay, and sank back in the carriage, merely motioning him to proceed. He started off rapidly, as if to make up for lost time. Every now and then the horses seemed to throw up their heads and sniffed the air suspiciously. On such occasions I often looked round in alarm. The road was pretty bleak, for we were traversing a sort of high, wind-swept plateau. As we drove, I saw a road that looked but little used, and which seemed to dip through a little, winding valley. It looked so inviting that, even at the risk of offending him, I called Johann to a stop – and when he had pulled up, I told him I would like to drive down that road. He made all sorts of excuses, and frequently crossed himself as he spoke. This somewhat piqued my curiosity, so I asked him various questions. He answered

431

fencingly, and repeatedly looked at his watch in protest. Finally I said:

'Well, Johann, I want to go down this road. I shall not ask you to come unless you like; but tell me why you do not like to go, that is all I ask.' For answer he seemed to throw himself off the box, so quickly did he reach the ground. Then he stretched out his hands appealingly to me, and implored me not to go. There was just enough of English mixed with the German for me to understand the drift of his talk. He seemed always just about to tell me something – the very idea of which evidently frightened him; but each time he pulled himself up, saying, as he crossed himself: 'Walpurgis-nacht!'

I tried to argue with him, but it was difficult to argue with a man when I did not know his language. The advantage certainly rested with him, for although he began to speak in English, in a very crude and broken kind, he always got excited and broke into his native tongue – and every time he did so, he looked at his watch. Then the horses became restless and sniffed the air. At this he grew very pale, and, looking around in a frightened way, he suddenly jumped forward, took them by the bridles and led them on some twenty feet. I followed, and asked why he had done this. For answer he crossed himself, pointed to the spot we had left and drew his carriage in the direction of the other road, indicating a cross, and said, first in German, then in English: 'Buried him – him what killed themselves.'

I remembered the old custom of burying suicides at cross-roads: 'Ah! I see, a suicide. How interesting!' But for the life of me I could not make out why the horses were so frightened.

Whilst we were talking, we heard a sort of sound between a yelp and a bark. It was far away; but the horses got very restless, and it took Johann all his time to quiet them. He was pale, and said, 'It sounds like a wolf – but yet there are no wolves here now.'

'No?' I said, questioning him; 'isn't it long since the wolves were so near the city?'

'Long, long,' he answered, 'in the spring and summer; but with the snow the wolves have been here not so long.'

Whilst he was petting the horses and trying to quiet them, dark clouds drifted rapidly across the sky. The sunshine passed away, and a breath of cold wind seemed to drift past us. It was only a breath, however, and more in the nature of a warning than a fact, for the sun came out brightly again. Johann looked under his lifted hand at the horizon and said:

'The storm of snow, he comes before long time.' Then he looked at his watch again, and, straightway holding his reins firmly – for the horses were still pawing the ground restlessly and shaking their heads – he climbed to his box as though the time had come for proceeding on our journey.

432

I felt a little obstinate and did not at once get into the carriage.

'Tell me,' I said, 'about this place where the road leads,' and I pointed down.

Again he crossed himself and mumbled a prayer, before he answered, 'It is unholy.'

'What is unholy?' I inquired.

'The village.'

'Then there is a village?'

'No, no. No one lives there hundreds of years.' My curiosity was piqued, 'But you said there was a village.'

'There was.'

'Where is it now?'

Whereupon he burst into a long story in German and English, so mixed up that I could not quite understand exactly what he said, but roughly I gathered that long ago, hundreds of years, men had died there and been buried in their graves; and sounds were heard under the clay, and when the graves were opened, men and women were found rosy with life, and their mouths red with blood. And so, in haste to save their lives (ay, and their souls! – and here he crossed himself) those who were left fled away to other places, where the living lived, and the dead were dead and not – not something. He was evidently afraid to speak the last words. As he proceeded with his narration, he grew more and more excited. It seemed as if his imagination had got hold of him, and he ended in a perfect paroxysm of fear – white-faced, perspiring, trembling and looking round him, as if expecting that some dreadful presence would manifest itself there in the bright sunshine on the open plain. Finally, in an agony of desperation, he cried:

'Walpurgisnacht!' and pointed to the carriage for me to get in. All my English blood rose at this, and, standing back, I said:

'You are afraid, Johann – you are afraid. Go home; I shall return alone; the walk will do me good.' The carriage door was open. I took from the seat my oak walking-stick – which I always carry on my holiday excursions – and closed the door, pointing back to Munich, and said, 'Go home, Johann – Walpurgisnacht doesn't concern Englishmen.'

The horses were now more restive than ever, and Johann was trying to hold them in, while excitedly imploring me not to do anything so foolish. I pitied the poor fellow, he was deeply in earnest; but all the same I could not help laughing. His English was quite gone now. In his anxiety he had forgotten that his only means of making me understand was to talk my language, so he jabbered away in his native German. It began to be a little tedious. After giving the direction, 'Home!' I turned to go down the cross-road into the valley.

With a despairing gesture, Johann turned his horses towards Munich. I leaned on my stick and looked after him. He went slowly along the road for a while: then there came over the hill a man tall and thin. I could see so much in the distance. When he drew near the horses, they began to jump and kick about, then to scream with terror. Johann could not hold them in; they bolted down the road, running away madly. I watched them out of sight, then looked for the stranger, but I found that he, too, was gone.

With a light heart I turned down the side road through the deepening valley to which Johann had objected. There was not the slightest reason, that I could see, for his objection; and I daresay I tramped for a couple of hours without thinking of time or distance, and certainly without seeing a person or a house. So far as the place was concerned, it was desolation itself. But I did not notice this particularly till, on turning a bend in the road, I came upon a scattered fringe of wood; then I recognized that I had been impressed unconsciously by the desolation of the region through which I had passed.

I sat down to rest myself, and began to look around. It struck me that it was considerably colder than it had been at the commencement of my walk – a sort of sighing sound seemed to be around me, with, now and then, high overhead, a sort of muffled roar. Looking upwards I noticed that great thick clouds were drifting rapidly across the sky from North to South at a great height. There were signs of coming storm in some lofty stratum of the air. I was a little chilly, and, thinking that it was the sitting still after the exercise of walking, I resumed my journey.

The ground I passed over was now much more picturesque. There were no striking objects that the eye might single out; but in all there was a charm of beauty. I took little heed of time and it was only when the deepening twilight forced itself upon me that I began to think of how I should find my way home. The brightness of the day had gone. The air was cold, and the drifting of clouds high overhead was more marked. They were accompanied by a sort of far-away rushing sound, through which seemed to come at intervals that mysterious cry which the driver had said came from a wolf. For a while I hesitated. I had said I would see the deserted village, so on I went, and presently came on a wide stretch of open country, shut in by hills all around. Their sides were covered with trees which spread down to the plain, dotting, in clumps, the gentler slopes and hollows which showed here and there. I followed with my eye the winding of the road, and saw that it curved close to one of the densest of these clumps and was lost behind it.

As I looked there came a cold shiver in the air, and the snow began to fall. I thought of the miles and miles of bleak country I had passed, and then hurried on to seek the shelter of the wood in front. Darker and darker grew the sky, and faster and heavier fell the snow, till the earth before and around me was a glistening white carpet the further edge of which was lost in misty vagueness. The road was here but crude, and when on the level its boundaries were not so marked, as when it passed through the cuttings; and in a little while I found that I must have strayed from it, for I missed underfoot the hard surface, and my feet sank deeper in the grass and moss. Then the wind grew stronger and blew with ever increasing force, till I was fain to run before it. The air became icy-cold, and in spite of my exercise I began to suffer. The snow was falling so thickly and whirling around me in such rapid eddies that I could hardly keep my eyes open. Every now and then the heavens were torn asunder by vivid lightning, and in the flashes I could see ahead of me a great mass of trees, chiefly yew and cypress all heavily coated with snow.

I was soon amongst the shelter of the trees, and there, in comparative silence, I could hear the rush of the wind overhead. Presently the blackness of the storm had become merged in the darkness of the night. By-and-by the storm seemed to be passing away: it now only came in fierce puffs or blasts. At such moments the weird sound of the wolf appeared to be echoed by many similar sounds around me.

Now and again, through the black mass of drifting cloud, came a straggling ray of moonlight, which lit up the expanse, and showed me that I was at the edge of a dense mass of cypress and yew trees. As the snow had ceased to fall, I walked out from the shelter and began to investigate more closely. It appeared to me that, amongst so many old foundations as I had passed, there might be still standing a house in which, though in ruins, I could find some sort of shelter for a while. As I skirted the edge of the copse, I found that a low wall encircled it, and following this I presently found an opening. Here the cypresses formed an alley leading up to a square mass of some kind of building. Just as I caught sight of this, however, the drifting clouds obscured the moon, and I passed up the path in darkness. The wind must have grown colder, for I felt myself shiver as I walked; but there was hope of shelter, and I groped my way blindly on.

I stopped, for there was a sudden stillness. The storm had passed; and, perhaps in sympathy with nature's silence, my heart seemed to cease to beat. But this was only momentarily; for suddenly the moonlight broke through the clouds, showing me that I was in a graveyard, and that the square object before me was a great massive tomb of marble, as white as the snow that lay on and all around it. With the moonlight there came a fierce sigh of the storm, which appeared to resume its course with a long, low howl, as of many dogs or wolves. I was awed and shocked, and felt the cold perceptibly grow upon me till it seemed to grip me by the heart. Then while the flood of moonlight still fell on the marble tomb, the storm gave further evidence of renewing, as though it was returning on its track. Impelled by some sort of fascination, I approached the sepulchre to see what it was, and why such a thing stood alone in such a place. I walked around it, and read, over the Doric door, in German:

COUNTESS DOLINGEN OF GRATZ
IN STYRIA
SOUGHT AND FOUND DEATH
1801

On top of the tomb, seemingly driven through the solid marble – for the structure was composed of a few vast blocks of stone – was a great iron spike or stake. On going to the back I saw, graven in great Russian letters:

'The dead travel fast.'

There was something so weird and uncanny about the whole thing that it gave me a turn and made me feel quite faint. I began to wish, for the first time, that I had taken Johann's advice. Here a thought struck me, which came under almost mysterious circumstances and with a terrible shock. This was Walpurgis Night!

Walpurgis Night, when, according the belief of millions of people, the devil was abroad – when the graves were opened and the dead came forth and walked. When all evil things of earth and air and water held revel. This very place the driver had specially shunned. This was the depopulated village of centuries ago. This was where the suicide lay; and this was the place where I was alone – unmanned, shivering with cold in a shroud of snow with a wild storm gathering again upon me! It took all my philosophy, all the religion I had been taught, all my courage, not to collapse in a paroxysm of fright.

And now a perfect tornado burst upon me. The ground shook as though thousands of horses thundered across it; and this time the storm bore on its icy wings, not snow, but great hailstones which drove with such violence that they might have come from the thongs of Balearic slingers – hailstones that beat down leaf and branch and made the shelter of the cypresses of no more avail than though their stems were standing-corn. At the first I had rushed to the nearest tree; but I was soon fain to leave it and seek the only spot that seemed to afford refuge, the deep Doric doorway of the marble tomb. There, crouching against the massive bronze door, I gained a certain amount of protection from the beating of the hailstones, for now they only drove against me as they ricocheted from the ground and the side of the marble.

As I leaned against the door, it moved slightly and opened inwards. The shelter of even a tomb was welcome in that pitiless tempest, and I was about to enter it when there came a flash of forked-lightning that lit up the whole expanse of the heavens. In the instant, as I am a living man, I saw, as my eyes were turned into the darkness of the tomb, a beautiful woman, with rounded cheeks and red lips, seemingly sleeping on a bier. As the thunder broke overhead, I was grasped as by the hand of a giant and hurled out into the storm. The whole thing was so sudden that, before I could realize the shock, moral as well as physical, I found the hailstones beating me down. At the same time I had a strange, dominating feeling that I was not alone. I looked towards the tomb. Just then there came another blinding flash, which seemed to strike the iron stake that surmounted the tomb and to pour through to the earth, blasting and crumbling the marble, as in a burst of flame. The dead woman rose for a moment of agony, while she was lapped in the flame, and her bitter scream of pain was drowned in the thundercrash. The last thing I heard was this mingling of dreadful sound, as again I was seized by the giant-grasp and dragged away, while the hailstones beat on me, and the air around seemed reverberant with the howling of wolves. The last sight that I remembered was a vague, white, moving mass, as if all the graves around me had sent out the phantoms of their sheeted-dead, and that they were closing in on me through the white cloudiness of the driving hail.

*   *   *

Gradually there came a sort of vague beginning of consciousness; then a sense of weariness that was dreadful. For a time I remembered nothing; but slowly my senses returned. My feet seemed positively racked with pain, yet I could not move them. They seemed to be numbed. There was an icy feeling at the back of my neck and all down my spine, and my ears, like my feet, were dead, yet in torment; but there was in my breast a sense of warmth which was, by comparison, delicious. It was a nightmare – a physical nightmare, if one may use such an expression; for some heavy weight on my chest made it difficult for me to breathe.

This period of semi-lethargy seemed to remain a long time, and as it faded away I must have slept or swooned. Then came a sort of loathing, like the first stage of sea-sickness, and a wild desire to be free from something – I knew not what. A vast stillness enveloped me, as though all the world were asleep or dead – only broken by the low panting as of some animal close to me. I felt a warm rasping at my throat, then came a consciousness of the awful truth, which chilled me to the heart and sent the blood surging up through my brain. Some great animal was lying on me and now licking my throat. I feared to stir, for some instinct of prudence bade lie still; but the brute seemed to realize that there was now some change in me, for it raised its head. Through my eyelashes I saw above me the two great flaming eyes of a gigantic wolf. Its sharp white teeth gleamed in the gaping red mouth, and I could feel its hot breath fierce and acrid upon me.

For another spell of time I remembered no more. Then I became conscious of a low growl, followed by a yelp, renewed again and again. Then, seemingly very far away, I heard a 'Holloa! holloa!' as of many voices calling in unison. Cautiously I raised my head and looked in the direction whence the sound came; but the cemetery blocked my view. The wolf still continued to yelp in a strange way, and a red glare began to move round the grove of cypresses, as though following the sound. As the voices drew closer, the wolf yelped faster and louder. I feared to make either sound or motion. Nearer came the red glow, over the white pall which stretched into the darkness around me. Then all at once from beyond the trees there came at a trot a troop of horsemen bearing torches. The wolf rose from my breast and made for the cemetery. I saw one of the horsemen (soldiers by their caps and their long military cloaks) raise his carbine and take aim. A companion knocked up his arm, and I heard the ball whizz over my head. He had evidently taken my body for that of the wolf. Another sighted the animal as it slunk away, and a shot followed. Then, at a gallop, the troop rode forward – some towards me, others following the wolf as it disappeared amongst the snow-clad cypresses.

As they drew nearer I tried to move, but was powerless, although I could see and hear all that went on around me. Two or three of the soldiers jumped from their horses and knelt beside me. One of them raised my head, and placed his hand over my heart.

'Good news, comrades!' he cried. 'His heart still beats!'

Then some brandy was poured down my throat; it put vigour into me, and I was able to open my eyes fully and look around. Lights and shadows were moving among the trees, and I heard men call to one another. They drew together, uttering frightened exclamations; and the lights flashed as the others came pouring out of the cemetery pell-mell, like men possessed. When the further ones came close to us, those who were around me asked them eagerly:

'Well, have you found him?'

The reply rang out hurriedly:

'No! no! Come away quick – quick! This is no place to stay, and on this of all nights!'

'What was it?' was the question, asked in all manner of keys. The answer came variously and all indefinitely as though the men were moved by some common impulse to speak, yet were restrained by some common fear from giving their thoughts.

'It – it – indeed!' gibbered one, whose wits had plainly given out for the moment.

'A wolf – and yet not a wolf!' another put in shudderingly.

'No use trying for him without the sacred bullet,' a third remarked in a more ordinary manner.

'Serve us right for coming out on this night! Truly we have earned our thousand marks!' were the ejaculations of a fourth.

'There was blood on the broken marble,' another said after a pause – 'the lightning never brought that there. And for him – is he safe? Look at his throat! See, comrades, the wolf has been lying on him and keeping his blood warm.'

The officer looked at my throat and replied:

'He is all right; the skin is not pierced. What does it all mean? We should never have found him but for the yelping of the wolf.'

'What became of it?' asked the man who was holding up my head, and who seemed the least panic-stricken of the party, for his hands were steady and without tremor. On his sleeve was the chevron of a petty officer.

'It went to its home,' answered the man, whose long face was pallid, and who actually shook with terror as he glanced around him fearfully. 'There are graves enough there in which it may lie. Come, comrades – come quickly! Let us leave this cursed spot.'

The officer raised me to a sitting posture, as he uttered a word of command; then several men placed me upon a horse. He sprang to the saddle behind me, took me in his arms, gave the word to advance; and, turning our faces away from the cypresses, we rode away in swift, military order.

As yet my tongue refused its office, and I was perforce silent. I must have fallen asleep; for the next thing I remembered was finding myself standing up, supported by a soldier on each side of me. It was almost broad daylight, and to the north a red streak of sunlight was reflected, like a path of blood, over the waste of snow. The officer was telling the men to say nothing of what they had seen, except that they found an English stranger, guarded by a large dog.

'Dog! that was no dog,' cut in the man who had exhibited such fear. 'I think I know a wolf when I see one.'

The young officer answered calmly: 'I said a dog.'

'Dog!' reiterated the other ironically. It was evident that his courage was rising with the sun; and, pointing to me, he said, 'Look at his throat. Is that the work of a dog, master?'

Instinctively I raised my hand to my throat, and as I touched it I cried out in pain. The men crowded round to look, some stooping down from their saddles; and again there came the calm voice of the young officer:

'A dog, as I said. If aught else were said we should only be laughed at.'

I was then mounted behind a trooper, and we rode on into the suburbs of Munich. Here we came across a stray carriage, into which I was lifted, and it was driven off to the Quatre Saisons – the young officer accompanying me, whilst a trooper followed with his horse, and the others rode off to their barracks.

When we arrived, Herr Delbrück rushed so quickly down the steps to meet me, that it was apparent he had been watching within. Taking me by both hands he solicitously led me in. The officer saluted me and was turning to withdraw, when I recognized his purpose, and insisted that he should come to my rooms. Over a glass of wine I warmly thanked him and his brave comrades for saving me. He replied simply that he was more than glad, and that Herr Delbrück had at the first taken steps to make all the searching party pleased; at which ambiguous utterance the maître d'hôtel smiled, while the officer pleaded duty and withdrew.

'But Herr Delbrück,' I inquired, 'how and why was it that the soldiers searched for me?'

He shrugged his shoulders, as if in depreciation of his own deed, as he replied:

'I was so fortunate as to obtain leave from the commander of the regiment in which I served, to ask for volunteers.'

'But how did you know I was lost?' I asked.

'The driver came hither with the remains of his carriage, which had been upset when the horses ran away.'

'But surely you would not send a search-party of soldiers merely on this account?'

'Oh, no!' he answered; 'but even before the coachman arrived, I had this telegram from the Boyar whose guest you are,' and he took from his pocket a telegram which he handed to me, and I read:

'*Bistritz.*

'Be careful of my guest – his safety is most precious to me. Should aught happen to him, or if he be missed, spare nothing to find him and ensure his safety. He is English and therefore adventurous. There are often dangers from snow and wolves at night. Lose not a moment if you suspect harm to him. I answer your zeal with my fortune.

DRACULA.'

As I held the telegram in my hand, the room seemed to whirl around me; and, if the attentive maître d'hôtel had not caught me, I think I should have fallen. There was something so strange in all this, something so weird and impossible to imagine, that there grew on me a sense of my being in some way the sport of opposite forces – the mere vague idea of which seemed in a way to paralyse me. I was certainly under some form of mysterious protection. From a distant country had come, in the very nick of time, a message that took me out of the danger of the snow-sleep and the jaws of the wolf.

THE JUDGE'S HOUSE

When the time for his examination drew near Malcolm Malcolmson made up his mind to go somewhere to read by himself. He feared the attractions of the seaside, and also he feared completely rural isolation, for of old he knew its charms, and so he determined to find some unpretentious little town where there would be nothing to distract him. He refrained from asking suggestions from any of his friends, for he argued that each would recommend some place of which he had knowledge, and where he would already have acquaintances. As Malcolmson wished to avoid friends he had no wish to encumber himself with the attention of friends' friends, and so he determined to look out for a place for himself. He packed a portmanteau with some clothes and all the books he required, and then took ticket for the first name on the local time-table which he did not know.

When at the end of three hours' journey he alighted at Benchurch, he felt satisfied that he had so far obliterated his tracks as to be sure of having a peaceful opportunity of pursuing his studies. He went straight to the one inn which the sleepy little place contained, and put up for the night. Benchurch was a market town, and once in three weeks was crowded to excess, but for the remainder of the twenty-one days it was as attractive as a desert. Malcolmson looked around the day after his arrival to try to find quarters more isolated than even so quiet an inn as 'The Good Traveller' afforded. There was only one place which took his fancy, and it certainly satisfied his wildest ideas regarding quiet; in fact, quiet was not the proper word to apply to it – desolation was the only term conveying any suitable idea of its isolation. It was an old rambling, heavy-built house of the Jacobean style, with heavy gables and windows, unusually small, and set higher than was customary in such houses, and was surrounded with a high brick wall massively built. Indeed, on examination, it looked more like a fortified house than an ordinary dwelling. But all these things pleased Malcolmson. 'Here,' he thought, 'is the very spot I have been looking for, and if I can get opportunity of using it I shall be happy.' His joy was increased when he realized beyond doubt that it was not at present inhabited.

From the post-office he got the name of the agent, who was rarely surprised at the application to rent a part of the old house. Mr Carnford, the local lawyer and agent, was a genial old gentleman, and frankly confessed his delight at anyone being willing to live in the house.

'To tell you the truth,' said he, 'I should be only too happy, on behalf of the owners, to let anyone have the house rent free for a term of years if only to accustom the people here to see it inhabited. It has been so long empty that some kind of absurd prejudice has grown up about it, and this can be best put down by its occupation – if only,' he added with a sly glance at Malcolmson, 'by a scholar like yourself, who wants its quiet for a time.'

Malcolmson thought it needless to ask the agent about the 'absurd prejudice'; he knew he would get more information, if he should require it, on that subject from other quarters. He paid his three months' rent, got a receipt, and the name of an old woman who would probably undertake to 'do' for him, and came away with the keys in his pocket. He then went to the landlady of the inn, who was a cheerful and most kindly person, and asked her advice as to such stores and provisions as he would be likely to require. She threw up her hands in amazement when he told her where he was going to settle himself.

'Not in the Judge's House!' she said, and grew pale as she spoke. He explained the locality of the house, saying that he did not know its name. When he had finished the answered:

'Ay, sure enough – sure enough the very place! It is the Judge's House sure enough.' He asked her to tell him about the place, why so called, and what there was against it. She told him that it was so called locally because it had been many years before – how long she could not say, as she was herself from another part of the country, but she thought it must have been a hundred years or more – the abode of a judge who was held in great terror on account of his harsh sentences and his hostility to prisoners at Assizes. As to what there was against the house itself she could not tell.

She had often asked, but no one could inform her; but there was a general feeling that there was *something*, and for her own part she would not take all the money in Drinkwater's Bank and stay in the house an hour by herself. Then she apologized to Malcolmson for her disturbing talk.

'It is too bad of me, sir, and you – and a young gentleman, too – if you will pardon me saying it, going to live there all alone. If you were my boy – and you'll excuse me for saying it – you wouldn't sleep there a night, not if I had to go there myself and pull the big alarm bell that's on the roof!' The good creature was so manifestly in earnest, and was so kindly in her intentions, that Malcolmson, although amused, was touched. He told her kindly how much he appreciated her interest in him, and added:

'But, my dear Mrs Witham, indeed you need not be concerned about me! A man who is reading for the Mathematical Tripos has too much to think of to be disturbed by any of these mysterious "somethings", and his work is of too exact and prosaic a kind to allow of his having any corner in his mind for mysteries of any kind. Harmonical Progression, Permutations and Combinations, and Elliptic Functions have sufficient mysteries for me!' Mrs Witham kindly undertook to see after his commissions, and he went himself to look for the old woman who had been recommended to him. When he returned to the Judge's House with her, after an interval of a couple of hours, he found Mrs Witham herself waiting with several men and boys carrying parcels, and an upholsterer's man with a bed in a car, for she said, though tables and chairs might be all very well, a bed that hadn't been aired for mayhap fifty years was not proper for young bones to lie on. She was evidently curious to see the inside of the house; and though manifestly so afraid of the 'somethings' that at the slightest sound she clutched on to Malcolmson, whom she never left for a moment, went over the place.

After his examination of the house, Malcolmson decided to take up his abode in the great dining-room, which was big enough to serve for all his requirements; and Mrs Witham, with the aid of the charwoman, Mrs Dempster, proceeded to arrange matters. When the hampers were brought in and unpacked, Malcolmson saw that with much kind forethought she had sent from her own kitchen sufficient provisions to last for a few days. Before going she expressed all sorts of kind wishes; and at the door turned and said:

'And perhaps, sir, as the room is big and draughty it might be well to have one of those big screens put round your bed at night – though, truth to tell, I would die myself if I were to be so shut in with all kinds of – of "things", that put their heads round the sides, or over the top, and look on me!' The image which she had called up was too much for her nerves, and she fled incontinently.

Mrs Dempster sniffed in a superior manner as the landlady disappeared, and remarked that for her own part she wasn't afraid of all the bogies in the kingdom.

'I'll tell you what it is, sir,' she said; 'bogies is all kinds and sorts of things – except bogies! Rats and mice, and beetles; and creaky doors, and loose slates, and broken panes, and stiff drawer handles, that stay out when you pull them and then fall down in the middle of the night. Look at the wainscot of the room! It is old – hundreds of years old! Do you think there's no rats and beetles there! And do you imagine, sir, that you won't see none of them! Rats is bogies, I tell you, and bogies is rats; and don't you get to think anything else!'

'Mrs Dempster,' said Malcolmson gravely, making her a polite bow, 'you know more than a Senior Wrangler! And let me say, that, as a mark of esteem for your indubitable soundness of head and heart, I shall, when I go, give you possession of this house, and let you stay here by yourself for the last two months of my tenancy, for four weeks will serve my purpose.'

'Thank you kindly, sir!' she answered, 'but I couldn't sleep away from home a night. I am in Greenhow's Charity, and if I slept a night away from my rooms I should lose all I have got to live on. The rules is very strict; and there's too many watching for a vacancy for me to run any risks in the matter. Only for that, sir, I'd gladly come here and attend to you altogether during your stay.'

'My good woman,' said Malcolmson hastily, 'I have come here on purpose to obtain solitude; and believe me that I am grateful to the late Greenhow for having so organized his admirable charity – whatever it is – that I am perforce denied the opportunity of suffering a form of temptation! Saint Anthony himself could not be more rigid on the point!'

The old woman laughed harshly. 'Ah, you young gentlemen,' she said, 'you don't fear for naught; and belike you'll get all the solitude you want here.' She set to work with her cleaning; and by nightfall, when Malcolmson returned from his walk – he always had one of his books to study as he walked – he found the room swept and tidied, a fire burning in the old hearth, the lamp lit, and the table spread for supper with Mrs Witham's excellent fare. 'This is comfort, indeed,' he said, as he rubbed his hands.

When he had finished his supper, and lifted the tray to the other end of the great oak dining-table, he got out his books again, put fresh wood on the fire, trimmed his lamp, and set himself down to a spell of real hard work. He went on without pause till about eleven o'clock, when he knocked off for a bit to fix his fire and lamp, and to make himself a cup of tea. He had always been a tea-drinker, and during his college life had sat late at work and had taken tea late. The rest was a great luxury to him, and he enjoyed it with a sense of delicious, voluptuous ease. The renewed fire leaped and sparkled, and threw quaint shadows through the great old room; and as he sipped his hot tea he revelled in a sense of isolation from his kind. Then it was that he began to notice for the first time what a noise the rats were making.

'Surely,' he thought, 'they cannot have been at it all the time I was reading. Had they been, I must have noticed it!' Presently, when the noise increased, he satisfied himself that it was really new. It was evident that at first the rats had been frightened at the presence of a stranger, and the light of fire and lamp; but that as the time went on they had grown bolder and were now disporting themselves as was their wont.

How busy they were! and hark to the strange noises! Up and down behind the old wainscot, over the ceiling and under the floor they raced, and gnawed, and scratched! Malcolmson smiled to himself as he recalled to mind the saying of Mrs Dempster, 'Bogies is rats, and rats is bogies!' The tea began to have its effect of intellectual and nervous stimulus, he saw with joy another long spell of work to be done before the night was past, and in the sense of security which it gave him, he allowed himself the luxury of a good look round the room. He took his lamp in one hand, and went all around, wondering that so quaint and beautiful an old house had been so long neglected. The carving of the oak on the panels of the wainscot was fine, and on and round the doors and windows it was beautiful and of rare merit. There were some old pictures on the walls, but they were coated so thick with dust and dirt that he could not distinguish any detail of them, though he held his lamp as high as he could over his head. Here and there as he went round he saw some crack or hole blocked for a moment by the face of a rat with its bright eyes glittering in the light, but in an instant it was gone, and a squeak and a scamper followed. The thing that most struck him, however, was the rope of the great alarm bell on the roof, which hung down in a corner of the room on the right-hand side of the fireplace. He pulled up close to the hearth a great high-backed carved oak chair, and sat down to his last cup of tea. When this was done he made up the fire, and went back to his work, sitting at the corner of the table, having the fire to his left. For a little while the rats disturbed him somewhat with their perpetual scampering, but he got accustomed to the noise as one does to the ticking of a clock or to the roar of moving water; and he became so immersed in his work that everything in the world, except the problem which he was trying to solve, passed away from him.

He suddenly looked up, his problem was still unsolved, and there was in the air that sense of the hour before the dawn, which is so dread to doubtful life. The noise of the rats had ceased. Indeed it seemed to him

445

that it must have ceased but lately and that it was the sudden cessation which had disturbed him. The fire had fallen low, but still it threw out a deep red glow. As he looked he started in spite of his *sang froid*.

There on the great high-backed carved oak chair by the right side of the fireplace sat an enormous rat, steadily glaring at him with baleful eyes. He made a motion to it as though to hunt it away, but it did not stir. Then he made the motion of throwing something. Still it did not stir, but showed its great white teeth angrily, and its cruel eyes shone in the lamplight with an added vindictiveness.

Malcolmson felt amazed, and seizing the poker from the hearth ran at it to kill it. Before, however, he could strike it, the rat, with a squeak that sounded like the concentration of hate, jumped upon the floor, and, running up the rope of the alarm bell, disappeared in the darkness beyond the range of the green-shaded lamp. Instantly, strange to say, the noisy scampering of the rats in the wainscot began again.

By this time Malcolmson's mind was quite off the problem; and as a shrill cock-crow outside told him of the approach of morning, he went to bed and to sleep.

He slept so sound that he was not even waked by Mrs Dempster coming in to make up his room. It was only when she had tidied up the place and got his breakfast ready and tapped on the screen which closed in his bed that he woke. He was a little tired still after his night's hard work, but a strong cup of tea soon freshened him up and, taking his book, he went out for his morning walk, bringing with him a few sandwiches lest he should not care to return till dinner time. He found a quiet walk between high elms some way outside the town, and here he spent the greater part of the day studying his Laplace. On his return he looked in to see Mrs Witham and to thank her for her kindness. When she saw him coming through the diamond-paned bay window of her sanctum she came out to meet him and asked him in. She looked at him searchingly and shook her head as she said:

'You must not overdo it, sir. You are paler this morning than you should be. Too late hours and too hard work on the brain isn't good for any man! But tell me, sir, how did you pass the night? Well, I hope? But my heart! sir, I was glad when Mrs Dempster told me this morning that you were all right and sleeping sound when she went in.'

'Oh, I was all right,' he answered smiling, 'the "somethings" didn't worry me, as yet. Only the rats; and they had a circus, I tell you, all over the place. There was one wicked looking old devil that sat up on my own chair by the fire, and wouldn't go till I took the poker to him, and then he ran up the rope of the alarm bell and got to somewhere up the wall or the ceiling – I couldn't see where, it was so dark.'

446

'Mercy on us,' said Mrs Witham, 'an old devil, and sitting on a chair by the fireside! Take care, sir! take care! There's many a true word spoken in jest.'

'How do you mean? Pon my word I don't understand.'

'An old devil! The old devil, perhaps. There! sir, you needn't laugh,' for Malcolmson had broken into a hearty peal. 'You young folks thinks it easy to laugh at things that makes older ones shudder. Never mind, sir! never mind! Please God, you'll laugh all the time. It's what I wish you myself!' and the good lady beamed all over in sympathy with his enjoyment, her fears gone for a moment.

'Oh, forgive me!' said Malcolmson presently. 'Don't think me rude; but the idea was too much for me – that the old devil himself was on the chair last night!' And at the thought he laughed again. Then he went home to dinner.

This evening the scampering of the rats began earlier; indeed it had been going on before his arrival, and only ceased whilst his presence by its freshness disturbed them. After dinner he sat by the fire for a while and had a smoke; and then, having cleared his table, began to work as before. Tonight the rats disturbed him more than they had done on the previous night. How they scampered up and down and under and over! How they squeaked, and scratched, and gnawed! How they, getting bolder by degrees, came to the mouths of their holes and to the chinks and cracks and crannies in the wainscoting till their eyes shone like tiny lamps as the firelight rose and fell. But to him, now doubtless accustomed to them, their eyes were not wicked; only their playfulness touched him. Sometimes the boldest of them made sallies out on the floor or along the mouldings of the wainscot. Now and again as they disturbed him Malcolmson made a sound to frighten them, smiting the table with his hand or giving a fierce 'Hsh, hsh', so that they fled straightway to their holes.

And so the early part of the night wore on; and despite the noise Malcolmson got more and more immersed in his work.

All at once he stopped, as on the previous night, being overcome by a sudden sense of silence. There was not the faintest sound of gnaw, or scratch, or squeak. The silence was as of the grave. He remembered the odd occurrence of the previous night, and instinctively he looked at the chair standing close by the fireside. And then a very odd sensation thrilled through him.

There, on the great old high-backed carved oak chair beside the fireplace sat the same enormous rat, steadily glaring at him with baleful eyes.

Instinctively he took the nearest thing to his hand, a book of

447

logarithms, and flung it at it. The book was badly aimed and the rat did not stir, so again the poker performance of the previous night was repeated; and again the rat, being closely pursued, fled up the rope of the alarm bell. Strangely too, the departure of this rat was instantly followed by the renewal of the noise made by the general rat community. On this occasion, as on the previous one, Malcolmson could not see at what part of the room the rat disappeared, for the green shade of his lamp left the upper part of the room in darkness, and the fire had burned low.

On looking at his watch he found it was close on midnight; and, not sorry for the *divertissement*, he made up his fire and made himself his nightly pot of tea. He had got through a good spell of work, and thought himself entitled to a cigarette; and so he sat on the great oak chair before the fire and enjoyed it. Whilst smoking he began to think that he would like to know where the rat disappeared to, for he had certain ideas for the morrow not entirely disconnected with a rat-trap. Accordingly he lit another lamp and placed it so that it would shine well into the right-hand corner of the wall by the fireplace. The he got all the books he had with him, and placed them handy to throw at the vermin. Finally he lifted the rope of the alarm bell and placed the end of it on the table, fixing the extreme end under the lamp. As he handled it he could not help noticing how pliable it was, especially for so strong a rope, and one not in use. 'You could hang a man with it,' he thought to himself. When his preparations were made he looked around, and said complacently:

'There now, my friend, I think we shall learn something of you this time!' He began his work again, and though as before somewhat disturbed at first by the noise of the rats, soon lost himself in his propositions and problems.

Again he was called to his immediate surroundings suddenly. This time it might not have been the sudden silence only which took his attention; there was a slight movement of the rope, and the lamp moved. Without stirring, he looked to see if his pile of books was within range, and then cast his eye along the rope. As he looked he saw the great rat drop from the rope on the oak armchair and sit there glaring at him. He raised a book in his right hand, and taking careful aim, flung it at the rat. The latter, with a quick movement, sprang aside and dodged the missile. He then took another book, and a third, and flung them one after another at the rat, but each time unsuccessfully. At last, as he stood with a book poised in his hand to throw, the rat squeaked and seemed afraid. This made Malcolmson more than ever eager to strike, and the book flew and struck the rat a resounding blow. It gave a terrified squeak, and turning on his pursuer a look of terrible malevolence, ran up the chair-back and made a great jump to the rope of the alarm bell and ran up it like lightning.

The lamp rocked under the sudden strain, but it was a heavy one and did not topple over. Malcolmson kept his eyes on the rat, and saw it by the light of the second lamp leap to a moulding of the wainscot and disappear through a hole in one of the great pictures which hung on the wall, obscured and invisible through its coating of dirt and dust.

'I shall look up my friend's habitation in the morning,' said the student, as he went over to collect his books. 'The third picture from the fireplace; I shall not forget.' He picked up the books one by one, commenting on them as he lifted them. '*Conic Sections* he does not mind, nor *Cycloidal Oscillations*, nor the *Principia*, nor *Quaternions*, nor *Thermodynamics*. Now for the book that fetched him!' Malcolmson took it up and looked at it. As he did so he started, and a sudden pallor overspread his face. He looked round uneasily and shivered slightly, as he murmured to himself:

'The Bible my mother gave me! What an odd coincidence.' He sat down to work again, and the rats in the wainscot renewed their gambols. They did not disturb him, however; somehow their presence gave him a sense of companionship. But he could not attend to his work, and after striving to master the subject on which he was engaged gave it up in despair, and went to bed as the first streak of dawn stole in through the eastern window.

He slept heavily but uneasily, and dreamed much; and when Mrs Dempster woke him late in the morning he seemed ill at ease, and for a few minutes did not seem to realize exactly where he was. His first request rather surprised the servant.

'Mrs Dempster, when I am out today I wish you would get the steps and dust or wash those pictures – specially that one the third from the fireplace – I want to see what they are.'

Late in the afternoon Malcolmson worked at his books in the shaded walk, and the cheerfulness of the previous day came back to him as the day wore on, and he found that his reading was progressing well. He had worked out to a satisfactory conclusion all the problems which had as yet baffled him, and it was in a state of jubilation that he paid a visit to Mrs Witham at 'The Good Traveller'. He found a stranger in the cosy sitting-room with the landlady, who was introduced to him as Dr Thornhill. She was not quite at ease, and this, combined with the doctor's plunging at once into a series of questions, made Malcolmson come to the conclusion that his presence was not an accident, so without preliminary he said:

'Dr Thornhill, I shall with pleasure answer you any question you may choose to ask me if you will answer me one question first.'

The doctor seemed surprised, but he smiled and answered at once, 'Done! What is it?'

'Did Mrs Witham ask you to come here and see me and advise me?'

449

Dr Thornhill for a moment was taken aback, and Mrs Witham got fiery red and turned away; but the doctor was a frank and ready man, and he answered at once and openly.

'She did: but she didn't intend you to know it. I suppose it was my clumsy haste that made you suspect. She told me that she did not like the idea of your being in that house all by yourself, and that she thought you took too much strong tea. In fact, she wants me to advise you if possible to give up the tea and the very late hours. I was a keen student in my time, so I suppose I may take the liberty of a college man, and without offence, advise you not quite as a stranger.'

Malcolmson with a bright smile held out his hand. 'Shake! as they say in America,' he said. 'I must thank you for your kindness and Mrs Witham too, and your kindness deserves a return on my part. I promise to take no more strong tea – no tea at all till you let me – and I shall go to bed tonight at one o'clock at latest. Will that do?'

'Capital,' said the doctor. 'Now tell us all that you noticed in the old house,' and so Malcolmson then and there told in minute detail all that had happened in the last two nights. He was interrupted every now and then by some exclamation from Mrs Witham, till finally when he told of the episode of the Bible the landlady's pent-up emotions found vent in a shriek; and it was not till a stiff glass of brandy and water had been administered that she grew composed again. Dr Thornhill listened with a face of growing gravity, and when the narrative was complete and Mrs Witham had been restored he asked:

'The rat always went up the rope of the alarm bell?'

'Always.'

'I suppose you know,' said the doctor after a pause, 'what the rope is?'

'No!'

'It is,' said the doctor slowly, 'the very rope which the hangman used for all the victims of the Judge's judicial rancour!' Here he was interrupted by another scream from Mrs Witham, and steps had to be taken for her recovery. Malcolmson having looked at his watch, and found that it was close to his dinner hour, had gone home before her complete recovery.

When Mrs Witham was herself again she almost assailed the doctor with angry questions as to what he meant by putting such horrible ideas into the poor young man's mind. 'He has quite enough there already to upset him,' she added. Dr Thornhill replied:

'My dear madam, I had a distinct purpose in it! I wanted to draw his attention to the bell rope, and to fix it there. It may be that he is in a highly overwrought state, and has been studying too much, although I am bound to say that he seems as sound and healthy a young man, mentally and bodily, as ever I saw – but then the rats – and that suggestion of the devil!' The doctor shook his head and went on. 'I would have offered to go and stay the first night with him but that I felt sure it would have been a cause of offence. He may get in the night some strange fright or hallucination; and if he does I want him to pull that rope. All alone as he is it will give us warning, and we may reach him in time to be of service. I shall be sitting up pretty late tonight and shall keep my ears open. Do not be alarmed if Benchurch gets a surprise before morning.'

'Oh, doctor, what do you mean? What do you mean?'

'I mean this; that possibly – nay, more probably – we shall hear the great alarm bell from the Judge's House tonight,' and the doctor made about as effective an exit as could be thought of.

When Malcolmson arrived home he found that it was a little after his usual time, and Mrs Dempster had gone away – the rules of Greenhow's Charity were not to be neglected. He was glad to see that the place was bright and tidy with a cheerful fire and a well-trimmed lamp. The evening was colder than might have been expected in April, and a heavy wind was blowing with such rapidly-increasing strength that there was every promise of a storm during the night. For a few minutes after his entrance the noise of the rats ceased; but so soon as they became accustomed to his presence they began again. He was glad to hear them, for he felt once more the feeling of companionship in their noise, and his mind ran back to the strange fact that they only ceased to manifest themselves when that other – the great rat with the baleful eyes – came upon the scene. The reading-lamp only was lit and its green shade kept the ceiling and the upper part of the room in darkness, so that the cheerful light from the hearth spreading over the floor and shining on the white cloth laid over the end of the table was warm and cheery. Malcolmson sat down to his dinner with a good appetite and a buoyant spirit. After his dinner and a cigarette he sat steadily down to work, determined not to let anything disturb him, for he remembered his promise to the doctor, and made up his mind to make the best of the time at his disposal.

For an hour or so he worked all right, and then his thoughts began to wander from his books. The actual circumstances around him, the calls on his physical attention, and his nervous susceptibility were not to be denied. By this time the wind had become a gale, and the gale a storm. The old house, solid though it was, seemed to shake to its foundations, and the storm roared and raged through its many chimneys and its queer old gables, producing strange, unearthly sounds in the empty rooms and corridors. Even the great alarm bell on the roof must have felt the force of the wind, for the rope rose and fell slightly, as though the bell were moved

451

a little from time to time, and the limber rope fell on the oak floor with a hard and hollow sound.

As Malcolmson listened to it he bethought himself of the doctor's words, 'It is the rope which the hangman used for the victims of the Judge's judicial rancour', and he went over to the corner of the fireplace and took it in his hand to look at it. There seemed a sort of deadly interest in it, and as he stood there he lost himself for a moment in speculation as to who these victims were, and the grim wish of the Judge to have such a ghastly relic ever under his eyes. As he stood there the swaying of the bell on the roof still lifted the rope now and again; but presently there came a new sensation – a sort of tremor in the rope, as though something was moving along it.

Looking up instinctively Malcolmson saw the great rat coming slowly down towards him, glaring at him steadily. He dropped the rope and started back with a muttered curse, and the rat turning ran up the rope again and disappeared, and at the same instant Malcolmson became conscious that the noise of the rats, which had ceased for a while, began again.

All this set him thinking, and it occurred to him that he had not investigated the lair of the rat or looked at the pictures, as he had intended. He lit the other lamp without the shade, and, holding it up went and stood opposite the third picture from the fireplace on the right-hand side where he had seen the rat disappear on the previous night.

At the first glance he started back so suddenly that he almost dropped the lamp, and a deadly pallor overspread his face. His knees shook, and heavy drops of sweat came on his forehead, and he trembled like an aspen. But he was young and plucky, and pulled himself together, and after the pause of a few seconds stepped forward again, raised the lamp, and examined the picture which had been dusted and washed, and now stood out clearly.

It was of a judge dressed in his robes of scarlet and ermine. His face was strong and merciless, evil, crafty, and vindictive, with a sensual mouth, hooked nose of ruddy colour, and shaped like the beak of a bird of prey. The rest of the face was of a cadaverous colour. The eyes were of peculiar brilliance and with a terribly malignant expression. As he looked at them, Malcolmson grew cold, for he saw there the very counterpart of the eyes of the great rat. The lamp almost fell from his hand, he saw the rat with its baleful eyes peering out through the hole in the corner of the picture, and noted the sudden cessation of the noise of the other rats. However, he pulled himself together, and went on with his examination of the picture.

The Judge was seated in a great high-backed carved oak chair, on the right-hand side of a great stone fireplace where, in the corner, a rope hung down from the ceiling, its end lying coiled on the floor. With a feeling of something like horror, Malcolmson recognized the scene of the room as it stood, and gazed around him in an awestruck manner as though he expected to find some strange presence behind him. Then he looked over to the corner of the fireplace – and with a loud cry he let the lamp fall from his hand.

There, in the Judge's arm-chair, with the rope hanging behind, sat the rat with the Judge's baleful eyes, now intensified with a fiendish leer. Save for the howling of the storm without there was silence.

The fallen lamp recalled Malcolmson to himself. Fortunately it was of metal, and so the oil was not spilt. However, the practical need of attending to it settled at once his nervous apprehensions. When he had turned it out, he wiped his brow and thought for a moment.

'This will not do,' he said to himself. 'If I go on like this I shall become a crazy fool. This must stop! I promised the doctor I would not take tea. Faith, he was pretty right! My nerves must have been getting into a queer state. Funny I did not notice it. I never felt better in my life. However, it is all right now, and I shall not be such a fool again.'

Then he mixed himself a good stiff glass of brandy and water and resolutely sat down to his work.

It was nearly an hour when he looked up from his book, disturbed by a sudden stillness. Without, the wind howled and roared louder than ever, and the rain drove in sheets against the windows, beating like hail on the glass; but within there was no sound whatever save the echo of the wind as it roared in the great chimney, and now and then a hiss as a few raindrops found their way down the chimney in the lull of the storm. The fire had fallen low and had ceased to flame, though it threw out a red glow. Malcolmson listened attentively, and presently heard a thin, squeaking noise, very faint. It came from the corner of the room where the rope hung down, and he thought it was the creaking of the rope on the floor as the swaying of the bell raised and lowered it. Looking up, however, he saw in the dim light the great rat clinging to the rope and gnawing it. The rope was already nearly gnawed through – he could see the lighter colour where the strands were laid bare. As he looked the job was completed, and the severed end of the rope fell clattering on the oaken floor, whilst for an instant the great rat remained like a knob or tassel at the end of the rope, which now began to sway to and fro. Malcolmson felt for a moment another pang of terror as he thought that now the possibility of calling the outer world to his assistance was cut off, but an intense anger took its place, and seizing the book he was reading he hurled it at the rat. The blow was well aimed, but before the missile could reach him the rat dropped off and struck the floor with a soft thud.

Malcolmson instantly rushed over towards him, but it darted away and disappeared in the darkness of the shadows of the room. Malcolmson felt that his work was over for the night, and determined then and there to vary the monotony of the proceedings by a hunt for the rat, and took off the green shade of the lamp so as to insure a wider spreading light. As he did so the gloom of the upper part of the room was relieved, and in the new flood of light, great by comparison with the previous darkness, the pictures on the wall stood out boldly. From where he stood, Malcolmson saw right opposite to him the third picture on the wall from the right of the fireplace. He rubbed his eyes in surprise, and then a great fear began to come upon him.

In the centre of the picture was a great irregular patch of brown canvas, as fresh as when it was stretched on the frame. The background was as before, with chair and chimney-corner and rope, but the figure of the Judge had disappeared.

Malcolmson, almost in a chill of horror, turned slowly round, and then he began to shake and tremble like a man in a palsy. His strength seemed to have left him, and he was incapable of action or movement, hardly even of thought. He could only see and hear.

There, on the great high-backed carved oak chair sat the Judge in his robes of scarlet and ermine, with his baleful eyes glaring vindictively, and a smile of triumph on the resolute, cruel mouth, as he lifted with his hands a *black cap*. Malcolmson felt as if the blood was running from his heart, as one does in moments of prolonged suspense. There was a singing in his ears. Without, he could hear the roar and howl of the tempest, and through it, swept on the storm, came the striking of midnight by the great chimes in the market place. He stood for a space of time that seemed to him endless still as a statue, and with wide-open, horror-struck eyes, breathless. As the clock struck, so the smile of triumph on the Judge's face intensified, and at the last stroke of midnight he placed the black cap on his head.

Slowly and deliberately the Judge rose from his chair and picked up the piece of the rope of the alarm bell which lay on the floor, drew it through his hands as if he enjoyed its touch, and then deliberately began to knot one end of it, fashioning it into a noose. This he tightened and tested with his foot, pulling hard at it till he was satisfied and then making a running noose of it, which he held in his hand. Then he began to move along the table on the opposite side to Malcolmson keeping his eyes on him until he had passed him, when with a quick movement he stood in front of the door. Malcolmson then began to feel that he was trapped, and tried to think of what he should do. There was some fascination in the Judge's eyes, which he never took off him, and he had, perforce, to look. He saw the Judge approach – still keeping between him and the door – and raise the noose and throw it towards him as if to entangle him. With a great effort he made a quick movement to one side, and saw the rope fall beside him, and heard it strike the oaken floor. Again the Judge raised the noose and tried to ensnare him, ever keeping his baleful eyes fixed on him, and each time by a mighty effort the student just managed to evade it. So this went on for many times, the Judge seeming never discouraged nor discomposed at failure, but playing as a cat does with a mouse. At last in despair, which had reached its climax, Malcolmson cast a quick glance round him. The lamp seemed to have blazed up, and there was a fairly good light in the room. At the many rat-holes and in the chinks and crannies of the wainscot he saw the rats' eyes; and this aspect, that was purely physical, gave him a gleam of comfort. He looked around and saw that the rope of the great alarm bell was laden with rats. Every inch of it was covered with them, and more and more were pouring through the small circular hole in the ceiling whence it emerged, so that with their weight the bell was beginning to sway.

Hark! it had swayed till the clapper had touched the bell. The sound was but a tiny one, but the bell was only beginning to sway, and it would increase.

At the sound the Judge, who had been keeping his eyes fixed on Malcolmson, looked up, and a scowl of diabolical anger overspread his face. His eyes fairly glowed like hot coals, and he stamped his foot with a sound that seemed to make the house shake. A dreadful peal of thunder broke overhead as he raised the rope again, whilst the rats kept running up and down the rope as though working against time. This time, instead of throwing it, he drew close to his victim, and held open the noose as he approached. As he came close there seemed something paralysing in his very presence, and Malcolmson stood rigid as a corpse. He felt the Judge's icy fingers touch his throat as he adjusted the rope. The noose tightened – tightened. Then the Judge, taking the rigid form of the student in his arms, carried him over and placed him standing in the oak chair, and stepping up beside him, put his hand up and caught the end of the swaying rope of the alarm bell. As he raised his hand the rats fled squeaking, and disappeared through the hole in the ceiling. Taking the end of the noose which was round Malcolmson's neck he tied it to the hanging-bell rope, and then descending pulled away the chair.

* * *

When the alarm bell of the Judge's House began to sound a crowd soon assembled. Lights and torches of various kinds appeared, and soon a silent crowd was hurrying to the spot. They knocked loudly at the door, but there was no reply. Then they burst in the door, and poured into the great dining-room, the doctor at the head.

There at the end of the rope of the great alarm bell hung the body of the student, and on the face of the Judge in the picture was a malignant smile.

THE SQUAW

Nurnberg at the time was not so much exploited as it has been since then. Irving had not been playing *Faust*, and the very name of the old town was hardly known to the great bulk of the travelling public. My wife and I being in the second week of our honeymoon, naturally wanted someone else to join our party, so that when the cheery stranger, Elias P. Hutcheson, hailing from Isthmian City, Bleeding Gulch, Maple Tree County, Neb. turned up at the station at Frankfort, and casually remarked that he was going on to see the most all-fired old Methuselah of a town in Yurrup, and that he guessed that so much travelling alone was enough to send an intelligent, active citizen into the melancholy ward of a daft house, we took the pretty broad hint and suggested that we should join forces. We found, on comparing notes afterwards, that we had each intended to speak with some diffidence or hesitation so as not to appear too eager, such not being a good compliment to the success of our married life; but the effect was entirely marred by our both beginning to speak at the same instant – stopping simultaneously and then going on together again. Anyhow, no matter how, it was done; and Elias P. Hutcheson became one of our party. Straightway Amelia and I found the pleasant benefit; instead of quarrelling, as we had been doing, we found that the restraining influence of a third party was such that we now took every opportunity of spooning in odd corners. Amelia declares that ever since she has, as the result of that experience, advised all her friends to take a friend on the honeymoon. Well, we 'did' Nurnberg together, and much enjoyed the racy remarks of our Transatlantic friend, who, from his quaint speech and his wonderful stock of adventures, might have stepped out of a novel. We kept for the last object of interest in the city to be visited the Burg, and on the day appointed for the visit strolled round the outer wall of the city by the eastern side.

The Burg is seated on a rock dominating the town and an immensely deep fosse guards in on the northern side. Nurnberg has been happy in that it was never sacked; had it been it would certainly not be so spick and span perfect as it is at present. The ditch has not been used for centuries, and now its base is spread with tea-gardens and orchards, of which some of the trees are of quite respectable growth. As we wandered round the wall, dawdling in the hot July sunshine, we often paused to admire the views spread before us, and in especial the great plain covered with towns and villages and bounded with a blue line of hills, like a landscape of Claude Lorraine. From this we always turned with new delight to the city itself, with its myriad of quaint old gables and acre-wide red roofs dotted with dormer windows, tier upon tier. A little to our right rose the towers of the Burg, and nearer still, standing grim, the Torture Tower, which was, and is, perhaps, the most interesting place in the city. For centuries the tradition of the Iron Virgin of Nurnberg has been handed down as an instance of the horrors of cruelty of which man is capable; we had long looked forward to seeing it; and here at last was its home.

In one of our pauses we leaned over the wall of the moat and looked down. The garden seemed quite fifty or sixty feet below us, and the sun pouring into it with an intense, moveless heat like that of an oven. Beyond rose the grey, grim wall seemingly of endless height, and losing itself right and left in the angles of bastion and counterscarp. Trees and bushes crowned the wall, and above again towered the lofty houses on whose massive beauty Time has only set the hand of approval. The sun was hot and we were lazy; time was our own, and we lingered, leaning on the wall. Just below us was a pretty sight – a great black cat lying stretched in the sun, whilst round her gambolled prettily a tiny black kitten. The mother would wave her tail for the kitten to play with, or would raise her feet and push away the little one as an encouragement to further play. They were just at the foot of the wall, and Elias P. Hutcheson, in order to help the play, stooped and took from the walk a moderate sized pebble.

'See!' he said, 'I will drop it near the kitten, and they will both wonder where it came from.'

'Oh, be careful,' said my wife: 'you might hit the dear little thing!'

'Not me, ma'am,' said Elias P. 'Why, I'm as tender as a Maine cherry-tree. Lor, bless ye, I wouldn't hurt the poor pooty little critter more'n I'd scalp a baby. An' you may bet your variegated socks on that! See, I'll drop it fur away on the outside so's not to go near her!' Thus saying, he leaned over and held his arm out at full length and dropped the stone. It may be

457

that there is some attractive force which draws lesser matters to greater; or more probably that the wall was not plump but sloped to its base – we not noticing the inclination from above; but the stone fell with a sickening thud that came up to us through the hot air, right on the kitten's head, and shattered out its little brains then and there. The black cat cast a swift upward glance, and we saw her eyes like green fire fixed an instant on Elias P. Hutcheson; and then her attention was given to the kitten, which lay still with just a quiver of her tiny limbs, whilst a thin red stream trickled from a gaping wound. With a muffled cry, such as a human being might give, she bent over the kitten licking its wounds and moaning. Suddenly she seemed to realize that it was dead, and again threw her eyes up at us. I shall never forget the sight, for she looked the perfect incarnation of hate. Her green eyes blazed with lurid fire, and the white, sharp teeth seemed to almost shine through the blood which dabbled her mouth and whiskers. She gnashed her teeth, and her claws stood out stark and at full length on every paw. Then she made a wild rush up the wall as if to reach us, but when the momentum ended fell back, and further added to her horrible appearance for she fell on the kitten, and rose with her black fur smeared with its brains and blood. Amelia turned quite faint, and I had to lift her back from the wall. There was a seat close by in shade of a spreading plane-tree, and here I placed her whilst she composed herself. Then I went back to Hutcheson, who stood without moving, looking down on the angry cat below.

As I joined him, he said:

'Wall, I guess that air the savagest beast I ever see – 'cept once when an Apache squaw had an edge on a half-breed what they nicknamed "Splinters" 'cos of the way he fixed up her papoose which he stole on a raid just to show that he appreciated the way they had given his mother the fire torture. She got that kinder look so set on her face that it jest seemed to grow there. She followed Splinters mor'n three year till at last the braves got him and handed him over to her. They did say that no man, white or Injun, had ever been so long a-dying under the tortures of the Apaches. The only time I ever see her smile was when I wiped her out. I kem on the camp just in time to see Splinters pass in his checks, and he wasn't sorry to go either. He was a hard citizen, and though I never could shake with him after that papoose business – for it was bitter bad, and he should have been a white man, for he looked like one – I see he had got paid out in full. Durn me, but I took a piece of his hide from one of his skinnin' posts an' had it made into a pocket-book. It's here now!' and he slapped the breast pocket of his coat.

Whilst he was speaking the cat was continuing her frantic efforts to get up the wall. She would take a run back and then charge up, sometimes

458

reaching an incredible height. She did not seem to mind the heavy fall which she got each time but started with renewed vigour; and at every tumble her appearance became more horrible. Hutcheson was a kind-hearted man – my wife and I had both noticed little acts of kindness to animals as well as to persons – and he seemed concerned at the state of fury to which the cat had wrought herself.

'Wall, now!' he said, 'I du declare that that poor little critter seems quite desperate. There! there! poor thing, it was all an accident – though that won't bring back your little one to you. Say! I wouldn't have had such a thing happen for a thousand! Just shows what a clumsy fool of a man can do when he tries to play! Seems I'm too darned slipperhanded to even play with a cat. Say Colonel!' – it was a pleasant way he had to bestow titles freely – 'I hope your wife don't hold no grudge against me on account of this unpleasantness? Why, I wouldn't have had it occur on no account.'

He came over to Amelia and apologized profusely, and she with her usual kindness of heart hastened to assure him that she quite understood that it was an accident. Then we all went again to the wall and looked over.

The cat missing Hutcheson's face had drawn back across the moat, and was sitting on her haunches as though ready to spring. Indeed, the very instant she saw him she did spring, and with a blind unreasoning fury, which would have been grotesque, only that it was so frightfully real. She did not try to run up the wall, but simply launched herself at him as though hate and fury could lend her wings to pass straight through the great distance between them. Amelia, womanlike, got quite concerned, and said to Elias P. in a warning voice:

'Oh! you must be very careful. That animal would try to kill you if she were here; her eyes look like positive murder.'

He laughed out jovially. 'Excuse me, ma'am,' he said, 'but I can't help laughin'. Fancy a man that has fought grizzlies an' Injuns bein' careful of bein' murdered by a cat!'

When the cat heard him laugh, her whole demeanour seemed to change. She no longer tried to jump or run up the wall, but went quietly over, and sitting again beside the dead kitten began to lick and fondle it as though it were alive.

'See!' said I, 'the effect of a really strong man. Even that animal in the midst of her fury recognizes the voice of a master, and bows to him!'

'Like a squaw!' was the only comment of Elias P. Hutcheson, as we moved on our way round the city fosse. Every now and then we looked over the wall and each time saw the cat following us. At first she had kept going back to the dead kitten, and then as the distance grew greater took it in her mouth and so followed. After a while, however, she abandoned

459

this, for we saw her following all alone; she had evidently hidden the body somewhere. Amelia's alarm grew at the cat's persistence, and more than once she repeated her warning; but the American always laughed with amusement, till finally, seeing that she was beginning to be worried, he said:

'I say, ma'am, you needn't be skeered over that cat. I go heeled, I du!' Here he slapped his pistol pocket at the back of his lumbar region. 'Why sooner'n have you worried, I'll shoot the critter, right here, an' risk the police interferin' with a citizen of the United States for carrying arms contrairy to reg'lations!' As he spoke he looked over the wall, but the cat on seeing him, retreated, with a growl, into a bed of tall flowers, and was hidden. He went on: 'Blest if that ar critter ain't got more sense of what's good for her than most Christians. I guess we've seen the last of her! You bet, she'll go back now to that busted kitten and have a private funeral of it, all to herself!'

Amelia did not like to say more, lest he might, in mistaken kindness to her, fulfil his threat of shooting the cat: and so we went on and crossed the little wooden bridge leading to the gateway whence ran the steep paved roadway between the Burg and the pentagonal Torture Tower. As we crossed the bridge we saw the cat again down below us. When she saw us her fury seemed to return, and she made frantic efforts to get up the steep wall. Hutcheson laughed at he looked down at her, and said:

'Good-bye, old girl. Sorry I injured your feelin's, but you'll get over it in time! So long!' And then we passed through the long, dim archway and came to the gate of the Burg.

When we came out again after our survey of this most beautiful old place which not even the well-intentioned efforts of the Gothic restorers of forty years ago have been able to spoil – though their restoration was then glaring white – we seemed to have quite forgotten the unpleasant episode of the morning. The old lime tree with its great trunk gnarled with the passing of nearly nine centuries, the deep well cut through the heart of the rock by those captives of old, and the lovely view from the city wall whence we heard, spread over almost a full quarter of an hour, the multitudinous chimes of the city, had all helped to wipe out from our minds the incident of the slain kitten.

We were the only visitors who had entered the Tortured Tower that morning – so at least said the old custodian – and as we had the place all to ourselves were able to make a minute and more satisfactory survey than would have otherwise been possible. The custodian, looking to us as the sole source of his gains for the day, was willing to meet our wishes in any way. The Torture Tower is truly a grim place, even now when many thousands of visitors have sent a stream of life, and the joy that follows

460

life, into the place; but at the time I mention it wore its grimmest and most gruesome aspect. The dust of ages seemed to have settled on it, and the darkness and the horror of its memories seem to have become sentient in a way that would have satisfied the Pantheistic souls of Philo or Spinoza. The lower chamber where we entered was seemingly, in its normal state, filled with incarnate darkness; even the hot sunlight streaming in through the door seemed to be lost in the vast thickness of the walls, and only showed the masonry rough as when the builder's scaffolding had come down, but coated with dust and marked here and there with patches of dark stain which, if walls could speak, could have given their own dread memories of fear and pain. We were glad to pass up the dusty wooden staircase, the custodian leaving the outer door open to light us somewhat on our way; for to our eyes the one long-wick'd, evil-smelling candle stuck in a sconce on the wall gave an inadequate light. When we came up through the open trap in the corner of the chamber overhead, Amelia held on to me so tightly that I could actually feel her heart beat. I must say for my own part that I was not surprised at her fear, for this room was even more gruesome than that below. Here there was certainly more light, but only just sufficient to realize the horrible surroundings of the place. The builders of the tower had evidently intended that only they who should gain the top should have any of the joys of light and prospect. There, as we had noticed from below, were ranges of windows, albeit of mediæval smallness, but elsewhere in the tower were only a very few narrow slits such as were habitual in places of mediæval defence. A few of these only lit the chamber, and these so high up in the wall that from no part could the sky be seen through the thickness of the walls. In racks, and leaning in disorder against the walls, were a number of headsmen's swords, great double-handed weapons with broad blade and keen edge. Hard by were several blocks whereon the necks of the victims had lain, with here and there deep notches where the steel had bitten through the guard of flesh and shored into the wood. Round the chamber, placed in all sorts of irregular ways, were many implements of torture which made one's heart ache to see – chairs full of spikes which gave instant and excruciating pain; chairs and couches with dull knobs whose torture was seemingly less, but which, though slower, were equally efficacious; racks, belts, boots, gloves, collars, all made for compressing at will; steel baskets in which the head could be slowly crushed into a pulp if necessary; watchmen's hooks with long handle and knife that cut at resistance – this a speciality of the old Nurnberg police system; and many, many other devices for man's injury to man. Amelia grew quite pale with the horror of things, but fortunately did not faint, for being a little overcome she sat down on a torture chair, but jumped up again with a shriek, all tendency to faint gone. We both pretended that it was the injury done to her dress by the dust of the chair, and the rusty spikes which had upset her, and Mr Hutcheson acquiesced in accepting the explanation with a kind-hearted laugh.

But the central object in the whole of this chamber of horrors was the engine known as the Iron Virgin, which stood near the centre of the room. It was a rudely-shaped figure of a woman, something of the bell order, or, to make a closer comparison, of the figure of Mrs Noah in the children's Ark, but without that slimness of waist and perfect *rondeur* of hip which marks the aesthetic type of the Noah family. One would hardly have recognized it as intended for a human figure at all had not the founder shaped on the forehead a rude semblance of a woman's face. This machine was coated with rust without, and covered with dust; a rope was fastened to a ring in the front of the figure, about where the waist should have been, and was drawn through a pulley, fastened on the wooden pillar which sustained the flooring above. The custodian pulling this rope showed that a section of the front was hinged like a door at one side; we then saw that the engine was of considerable thickness, leaving just room enough inside for a man to be placed. The door was of equal thickness and of great weight, for it took the custodian all his strength, aided though he was by the contrivance of the pulley, to open it. This weight was partly due to the fact that the door was of manifest purpose hung so as to throw its weight downwards, so that it might shut of its own accord when the strain was released. The inside was honeycombed with rust – nay more, the rust alone that come through time would hardly have eaten so deep into the iron walls; the rust of the cruel stains was deep indeed! It was only, however, when we came to look at the inside of the door that the diabolical intention was manifest to the full. Here were several long spikes, square and massive, broad at the base and sharp at the points, placed in such a position that when the door should close the upper ones would pierce the eyes of the victim, and the lower ones his heart and vitals. The sight was too much for poor Amelia, and this time she fainted dead off, and I had to carry her down the stairs, and place her on a bench outside till she recovered. That she felt it to the quick was afterwards shown by the fact that my eldest son bears to this day a rude birthmark on his breast, which has, by family consent, been accepted as representing the Nurnberg Virgin.

When we got back to the chamber we found Hutcheson still opposite the Iron Virgin; he had been evidently philosophizing, and now gave us the benefit of his thought in the shape of a sort of exordium.

'Wall, I guess I've been learnin' somethin' here while madam has been gettin' over her faint. 'Pears to me that we're a long way behind the times on our side of the big drink. We uster think out on the plains that the Injun could give us points in tryin' to make a man uncomfortable; but I guess your old mediæval law-and-order party could raise him every time. Splinters was pretty good in his bluff on the squaw, but this here young miss held a straight flush all high on him. The points of them spikes air sharp enough still, though even the edges air eaten out by what uster be on them. It'd be a good thing for our Indian section to get some specimens of this here play-toy to send round to the Reservations jest to knock the stuffin' out of the bucks, and the squaws too, by showing them as how old civilization lays over them at their best. Guess but I'll get in that box a minute jest to see how it feels!'

'Oh no! no!' said Amelia. 'It is too terrible!'

'Guess, ma'am, nothin's too terrible to the explorin' mind. I've been in some queer places in my time. Spent a night inside a dead horse while a prairie fire swept over me in Montana Territory – an' another time slept inside a dead buffler when the Comanches was on the war path an' I didn't keer to leave my kyard on them. I've been two days in a caved-in tunnel in the Billy Broncho gold mine in New Mexico, an' was one of the four shut up for three parts of a day in the caisson what slid over on her side when we was settin' the foundations of the Buffalo Bridge. I've not funked an odd experience yet, an' I don't propose to begin now!'

We saw that he was set on the experiment, so I said: 'Well, hurry up, old man, and get through it quick!'

'All right, General,' said he, 'but I calculate we ain't quite ready yet. The gentlemen, my predecessors, what stood in that thar canister, didn't volunteer for the office – not much! And I guess there was some ornamental tyin' up before the big stroke was made. I want to go into this thing fair and square, so I must get fixed up proper first. I daresay this old galoot can rise some string and tie me up accordin' to sample?'

This was said interrogatively to the old custodian, but the latter, who understood the drift of his speech, though perhaps not appreciating to the full the niceties of dialect and imagery, shook his head. His protest was, however, only formal and made to be overcome. The American thrust a gold piece into his hand, saying: 'Take it, pard! it's your pot; and don't be skeer'd. This ain't no necktie party that you're asked to assist in!' He produced some thin frayed rope and proceeded to bind our companion with sufficient strictness for the purpose. When the upper part of his body was bound, Hutcheson said:

'Hold on a moment, Judge. Guess I'm too heavy for you to tote into the canister. You jest let me walk in, and then you can wash up regardin' my legs!'

Whilst he was speaking he had backed himself into the opening which

463

was just enough to hold him. It was a close fit and no mistake. Amelia looked on with fear in her eyes, but she evidently did not like to say anything. Then the custodian completed his task by tying the American's feet together so that he was now absolutely helpless and fixed in his voluntary prison. He seemed to really enjoy it, and the incipient smile which was habitual to his face blossomed into actuality as he said:

'Guess this here Eve was made out of the rib of a dwarf! There ain't much room for a full-grown citizen of the United States to hustle. We uster make our coffins more roomier in Idaho Territory. Now, Judge, you jest begin to let this door down, slow, on to me. I want to feel the same pleasure as the other jays had when those spikes began to move toward their eyes!'

'Oh no! no! no!' broke in Amelia hysterically. 'It is too terrible! I can't bear to see it! – I can't! I can't!' But the American was obdurate. 'Say, Colonel,' said he, 'why not take Madame for a little promenade? I wouldn't hurt her feelin's for the world; but now that I am here, havin' kem eight thousand miles, wouldn't it be too hard to give up the very experience I've been pinin' and pantin' fur? A man can't get to feel like canned goods every time! Me and the Judge here'll fix up this thing in no time, an' then you'll come back, an' we'll all laugh together!'

Once more the resolution that is born of curiosity triumphed, and Amelia stayed holding tight to my arm and shivering whilst the custodian began to slacken slowly inch by inch the rope that held back the iron door. Hutcheson's face was positively radiant as his eyes followed the first movement of the spikes.

'Wall!' he said, 'I guess I've not had enjoyment like this since I left Noo York. Bar a scrap with a French sailor at Wapping – an' that warn't much of a picnic neither – I've not had a show fur real pleasure in this dod-rotted Continent, where there ain't no b'ars nor no Injuns, an' wheer nary man goes heeled. Slow there, Judge! Don't you rush this business! I want a show for my money this game – I du!'

The custodian must have had in him some of the blood of his predecessors in that ghastly tower, for he worked the engine with deliberate and excruciating slowness which after five minutes, in which the outer edge of the door had not moved half as many inches, began to overcome Amelia. I saw her lips whiten, and felt her hold upon my arm relax. I looked around an instant for a place whereon to lay her, and when I looked at her again found that her eye had become fixed on the side of the Virgin. Following its direction I saw the black cat crouching out of sight. Her green eyes shone like danger lamps in the gloom of the place, and their colour was heightened by the blood which still smeared her coat and reddened her mouth. I cried out:

'The cat! look out for the cat!' for even then she sprang out before the engine. At this moment she looked like a triumphant demon. Her eyes blazed with ferocity, her hair bristled out till she seemed twice her normal size, and her tail lashed about as does a tiger's when the quarry is before it. Elias P. Hutcheson when he saw her was amused, and his eyes positively sparkled with fun as he said:

'Darned if the squaw hain't got on all her war paint! Jest give her a shove off if she comes any of her tricks on me, for I'm so fixed everlastingly by the boss, that durn my skin if I can keep my eyes from her if she wants them! Easy there, Judge! don't you slack that ar rope or I'm euchered!'

At this moment Amelia completed her faint, and I had to clutch hold of her round the waist or she would have fallen to the floor. Whilst attending to her I saw the black cat crouching for a spring, and jumped up to turn the creature out.

But at that instant, with a sort of hellish scream, she hurled herself, not as we expected at Hutcheson, but straight at the face of the custodian. Her claws seemed to be tearing wildly as one sees in the Chinese drawings of the dragon rampant, and as I looked I saw one of them light on the poor man's eye, and actually tear through it and down his cheek, leaving a wide band of red where the blood seemed to spurt from every vein.

With a yell of sheer horror which came quicker than even his sense of pain, the man leaped back, dropping as he did so the rope which held back the iron door. I jumped for it, but was too late, for the cord ran like lightning through the pulley-block, and the heavy mass fell forward from its own weight.

As the door closed I caught a glimpse of our poor companion's face. He seemed frozen with terror. His eyes stared with horrible anguish as if dazed, and no sound came from his lips.

And then the spikes did their work. Happily the end was quick, for when I wrenched open the door they had pierced so deep that they had locked in the bones of the skull through which they had crushed, and actually tore him – it – out of his iron prison till, bound as he was, he fell at full length with a sickly thud upon the floor, the face turning upward as he fell.

I rushed to my wife, lifted her up and carried her out, for I feared for her very reason if she should wake from her faint to such a scene. I laid her on the bench outside and ran back. Leaning against the wooden column was the custodian moaning in pain whilst he held his reddening handkerchief to his eyes. And sitting on the head of the poor American was the cat, purring loudly as she licked the blood which trickled through the gashed socket of his eyes.

I think no one will call me cruel because I seized one of the old executioner's swords and shore her in two as she sat.

THE SECRET OF THE GROWING GOLD

When Margaret Delandre went to live at Brent's Rock the whole neighbourhood awoke to the pleasure of an entirely new scandal. Scandals in connection with either the Delandre family or the Brents of Brent's Rock, were not few; and if the secret history of the county had been written in full both names would have been found well represented. It is true that the status of each was so different that they might have belonged to different continents – or to different worlds for the matter of that – for hitherto their orbits had never crossed. The Brents were accorded by the whole section of the country a unique social dominance, and had ever held themselves as high above the yeoman class to which Margaret Delandre belonged, as a blue-blooded Spanish hidalgo out-tops his peasant tenantry.

The Delandres had an ancient record and were proud of it in their way as the Brents were of theirs. But the family had never risen above yeomanry; and although they had been once well-to-do in the good old times of foreign wars and protection, their fortunes had withered under the scorching of the free trade sun and the 'piping times of peace'. They had, as the elder members used to assert, 'stuck to the land', with the result that they had taken root in it, body and soul. In fact, they, having chosen the life of vegetables, had flourished as vegetation does – blossomed and thrived in the good season and suffered in the bad. Their holding, Dander's Croft, seemed to have been worked out, and to be typical of the family which had inhabited it. The latter had declined generation after generation, sending out now and again some abortive shoot of unsatisfied energy in the shape of a soldier or sailor, who had worked his way to the minor grades of the services and had there stopped, cut short either from unheeding gallantry in action or from that destroying cause to men without breeding or youthful care – the recognition of a position above them which they feel unfitted to fill. So, little by little, the family dropped lower and lower, the men brooding and dissatisfied, and drinking themselves into the grave, the women drudging at home, or marrying beneath them – or worse. In process of time all disappeared, leaving only two in the Croft, Wykham Delandre and his sister Margaret. The man and woman seemed to have inherited in masculine and feminine form respectively the evil tendency of their race, sharing in common the principles, though manifesting them in different ways, of sullen passion, voluptuousness and recklessness.

The history of the Brents had been something similar, but showing the causes of decadence in their aristocratic and not their plebeian forms. They, too, had sent their shoots to the wars; but their positions had been different and they had often attained honour – for without flaw they were gallant, and brave deeds were done by them before the selfish dissipation which marked them had sapped their vigour.

The present head of the family – if family it could now be called when one remained of the direct line – was Geoffrey Brent. He was almost a type of worn out race, manifesting in some ways its most brilliant qualities, and in others its utter degradation. He might be fairly compared with some of those antique Italian nobles whom the painters have preserved to us with their courage, their unscrupulousness, their refinement of lust and cruelty – the voluptuary actual with the fiend potential. He was certainly handsome, with that dark, aquiline, commanding beauty which women so generally recognize as dominant. With men he was distant and cold; but such a bearing never deters woman-kind. The inscrutable laws of sex have so arranged that even a timid woman is not afraid of a fierce and haughty man. And so it was that there was hardly a woman of any kind or degree, who lived within view of Brent's Rock, who did not cherish some form of secret admiration for the handsome wastrel. The category was a wide one, for Brent's Rock rose up steeply from the midst of a level region and for a circuit of a hundred miles it lay on the horizon, with its high old towers and steep roofs cutting the level edge of wood and hamlet, and far-scattered mansions.

So long as Geoffrey Brent confined his dissipations to London and Paris and Vienna – anywhere out of sight and sound of his home – opinion was silent. It is easy to listen to far off echoes unmoved, and we can treat them with disbelief, or scorn, or disdain, or whatever attitude of coldness may suit our purpose. But when the scandal came close home it was another matter; and the feelings of independence and integrity which is in people of every community which is not utterly spoiled, asserted itself and demanded that condemnation should be expressed. Still there was a certain reticence in all, and no more notice was taken of the existing facts than was absolutely necessary. Margaret Delandre bore herself so fearlessly and so openly – she accepted her position as the justified companion of Geoffrey Brent so naturally that people came to believe that she was secretly married to him, and therefore thought it wiser to hold their tongues lest time should justify her and also make her an active enemy.

The one person who, by his interference, could have settled all doubts was debarred by circumstances from interfering in the matter. Wykham Delandre had quarrelled with his sister – or perhaps it was that she had quarrelled with him – and they were on terms not merely of armed neutrality but of bitter hatred. The quarrel had been antecedent to Margaret going to Brent's Rock. She and Wykham had almost come to blows. There had certainly been threats on one side and on the other, and in the end Wykham, overcome with passion, had ordered his sister to leave his house. She had risen straightway, and, without waiting to pack up even her own personal belongings, had walked out of the house. On the threshold she had paused for a moment to hurl a bitter threat at Wykham that he would rue in shame and despair to the last hour of his life his act of that day. Some weeks had since passed; and it was understood in the neighbourhood that Margaret had gone to London, when she suddenly appeared driving out with Geoffrey Brent, and the entire neighbourhood knew before nightfall that she had taken up her abode at the Rock. It was no subject of surprise that Brent had come back unexpectedly, for such was his usual custom. Even his own servants never knew when to expect him, for there was a private door, of which he alone had the key, by which he sometimes entered without anyone in the house being aware of his coming. This was his usual method of appearing after a long absence.

Wykham Delandre was furious at the news. He vowed vengeance – and to keep his mind level with his passion drank deeper than ever. He tried several times to see his sister, but she contemptuously refused to meet him. He tried to have an interview with Brent and was refused by him also. Then he tried to stop him in the road, but without avail, for Geoffrey was not a man to be stopped against his will. Several actual encounters took place between the two men, and many more were threatened and avoided. At last Wykham Delandre settled down to a morose, vengeful acceptance of the situation.

Neither Margaret nor Geoffrey was of a pacific temperament, and it was not long before there began to be quarrels between them. One thing would lead to another, and wine flowed freely at Brent's Rock. Now and again the quarrels would assume a bitter aspect, and threats would be exchanged in uncompromising language that fairly awed the listening servants. But such quarrels generally ended where domestic altercations do, in reconciliation, and in a mutual respect for the fighting qualities proportionate to their manifestation. Fighting for its own sake is found by a certain class of persons, all the world over, to be a matter of absorbing interest, and there is no reason to believe that domestic conditions minimize its potency. Geoffrey and Margaret made occasional absences from Brent's Rock, and on each of these occasions Wykham Delandre also absented himself; but as he generally heard of the absence too late to be of any service, he returned home each time in a more bitter and discontented frame of mind than before.

At last there came a time when the absence from Brent's Rock became longer than before. Only a few days earlier there had been a quarrel, exceeding in bitterness anything which had gone before; but this, too, had been made up, and a trip on the Continent had been mentioned before the servants. After a few days Wykham Delandre also went away, and it was some weeks before he returned. It was noticed that he was full of some new importance – satisfaction, exaltation – they hardly knew how to call it. He went straightway to Brent's Rock, and demanded to see Geoffrey Brent, and on being told that he had not yet returned, said, with a grim decision which the servants noted:

'I shall come again. My news is solid – it can wait!' and turned away. Week after week went by, and month after month; and then there came a rumour, certified later on, that an accident had occurred in the Zermatt valley. Whilst crossing a dangerous pass the carriage containing an English lady and the driver had fallen over a precipice, the gentleman of the party, Mr Geoffrey Brent, having been fortunately saved as he had been walking up the hill to ease the horses. He gave information, and search was made. The broken rail, the excoriated roadway, the marks where the horses had struggled on the decline before finally pitching over into the torrent – all told the sad tale. It was a wet season, and there had been much snow in the winter, so that the river was swollen beyond its usual volume, and the eddies of the stream were packed with ice. All search was made, and finally the wreck of the carriage and the body of one horse were found in an eddy of the river. Later on the body of the driver was found on the sandy, torrent-swept waste near Täsch; but the body of the lady, like that of the other horse, had quite disappeared, and was – what was left of it by that time – whirling amongst the eddies of the Rhone on its way down to the Lake of Geneva.

Wykham Delandre made all the inquiries possible, but could not find any trace of the missing woman. He found, however, in the books of the various hotels the name of 'Mr and Mrs Geoffrey Brent'. And he had a stone erected at Zermatt to his sister's memory, under her married name, and a tablet put up in the church at Bretten, the parish in which both Brent's Rock and Dander's Croft were situated.

There was a lapse of nearly a year, after the excitement of the matter had worn away, and the whole neighbourhood had gone on its accustomed way. Brent was still absent, and Delandre more drunken, more morose, and more revengeful than before.

Then there was a new excitement. Brent's Rock was being made ready for a new mistress. It was officially announced by Geoffrey himself in a letter to the Vicar, that he had been married some months before to an Italian lady, and that they were then on their way home. Then a small army of workmen invaded the house; and hammer and plane sounded, and a general air of size and paint pervaded the atmosphere. One wing of the old house, the south, was entirely re-done; and then the great body of the workmen departed, leaving only materials for the doing of the old hall when Geoffrey Brent should have returned, for he had directed that the decoration was only to be done under his own eyes. He had brought with him accurate drawings of a hall in the house of his bride's father, for he wished to reproduce for her the place to which she had been accustomed. As the moulding had all to be re-done, some scaffolding poles and boards were brought in and laid on one side of the great hall, and also a great wooden tank or box for mixing the lime, which was laid in bags beside it.

When the new mistress of Brent's Rock arrived the bells of the church rang out, and there was a general jubilation. She was a beautiful creature, full of the poetry and fire and passion of the South; and the few English words which she had learned were spoken in such a sweet and pretty broken way that she won the hearts of the people almost as much by the music of her voice as by the melting beauty of her dark eyes.

Geoffrey Brent seemed more happy than he had ever before appeared; but there was a dark, anxious look on his face that was new to those who knew him of old, and he started at times as though at some noise that was unheard by others.

And so months passed and the whisper grew that at last Brent's Rock was to have an heir. Geoffrey was very tender to his wife, and the new bond between them seemed to soften him. He took more interest in his tenants and their needs than he had ever done; and works of charity on his part as well as on his sweet young wife's were not lacking. He seemed to have set all his hopes on the child that was coming, and as he looked deeper into the future the dark shadow that had come over his face seemed to die gradually away.

All the time Wykham Delandre nursed his revenge. Deep in his heart had grown up a purpose of vengeance which only waited an opportunity to crystallize and take a definite shape. His vague idea was somehow centred in the wife of Brent, for he knew that he could strike him best through those he loved, and the coming time seemed to hold in its womb the opportunity for which he longed. One night he sat alone in the living-room of his house. It had once been a handsome room in its way, but time and neglect had done their work and it was now little better than a ruin, without dignity or picturesqueness of any kind. He had been drinking heavily for some time and was more than half stupefied. He thought he heard a noise as of someone at the door and looked up. Then he called half savagely to come in; but there was no response. With a muttered blasphemy he renewed his potations. Presently he forgot all around him, sank into a daze, but suddenly awoke to see standing before him someone or something like a battered, ghostly edition of his sister. For a few moments there came upon him a sort of fear. The woman before him, with distorted features and burning eyes seemed hardly human, and the only thing that seemed a reality of his sister, as she had been, was her wealth of golden hair, and this was now streaked with grey. She eyed her brother with a long, cold stare; and he, too, as he looked and began to realize the actuality of her presence, found the hatred of her which he had had, once again surging up in his heart. All the brooding passion of the past year seemed to find a voice at once as he asked her:

'Why are you here? You're dead and buried.'

'I am here, Wykham Delandre, for no love of you, but because I hate another even more than I do you!' A great passion blazed in her eyes.

'Him?' he asked, in so fierce a whisper that even the woman was for an instant startled till she regained her calm.

'Yes, him!' she answered. 'But make no mistake, my revenge is my own; and I merely use you to help me to it.' Wykham asked suddenly:

'Did he marry you?'

The woman's distorted face broadened out in a ghastly attempt at a smile. It was a hideous mockery, for the broken features and seamed scars took strange shapes and strange colours, and queer lines of white showed out as the straining muscles pressed on the old cicatrices.

'So you would like to know! It would please your pride to feel that your sister was truly married! Well, you shall not know. That was my revenge on you, and I do not mean to change it by a hair's breadth. I have come here to-night simply to let you know that I am alive, so that if any violence be done me where I am going there may be a witness.'

'Where are you going?' demanded her brother.

'That is my affair! and I have not the least intention of letting you know!' Wykham stood up, but the drink was on him and he reeled and fell. As he lay on the floor he announced his intention of following his sister; and with an outburst of splenetic humour told her that he would follow her through the darkness by the light of her hair, and of her beauty. At this she turned on him, and said that there were others beside him that would rue her hair and her beauty too. 'As he will,' she hissed; 'for the hair remains though the beauty be gone. When he withdrew the lynch-pin and sent us over the precipice into the torrent, he had little thought of my beauty. Perhaps his beauty would be scarred like mine were he whirled, as I was, among the rocks of the Visp, and frozen on the ice pack in the drift of the river. But let him beware! His time is coming!' and with a fierce gesture she flung open the door and passed out into the night.

* * *

Later on that night, Mrs Brent, who was but half-asleep, became suddenly awake and spoke to her husband:

'Geoffrey, was not that the click of a lock somewhere below our window?'

But Geoffrey – though she thought that he, too, had started at the noise – seemed sound asleep, and breathed heavily. Again Mrs Brent dozed; but this time awoke to the fact that her husband had arisen and was partially dressed. He was deadly pale, and when the light of the lamp which he had in his hand fell on his face, she was frightened at the look in his eyes.

'What is it, Geoffrey? What dost thou?' she asked.

'Hush! little one,' he answered, in a strange, hoarse voice. 'Go to sleep. I am restless, and wish to finish some work I left undone.'

'Bring it here, my husband,' she said; 'I am lonely and I fear when thou art away.'

For reply he merely kissed her and went out, closing the door behind him. She lay awake for a while, and then nature asserted itself, and she slept.

Suddenly she started broad awake with the memory in her ears of a smothered cry from somewhere not far off. She jumped up and ran to the door and listened, but there was no sound. She grew alarmed for her husband, and called out: 'Geoffrey! Geoffrey!'

After a few moments the door of the great hall opened, and Geoffrey appeared at it, but without his lamp.

'Hush!' he said, in a sort of whisper, and his voice was harsh and stern. 'Hush! Get to bed! I am working, and must not be disturbed. Go to sleep, and do not wake the house!'

With a chill in her heart – for the harshness of her husband's voice was new to her – she crept back to bed and lay there trembling, too frightened to cry, and listened to every sound. There was a long pause of silence, and then the sound of some iron implement striking muffled blows! Then

472

there came a clang of a heavy stone falling, followed by a muffled curse. Then a dragging sound, and then more noise of stone on stone. She lay all the while in an agony of fear, and her heart beat dreadfully. She heard a curious sort of scraping sound; and then there was silence. Presently the door opened gently, and Geoffrey appeared. His wife pretended to be asleep; but through her eyelashes she saw him wash from his hands something white that looked like lime.

In the morning he made no allusion to the previous night, and she was afraid to ask any question.

From that day there seemed some shadow over Geoffrey Brent. He neither ate nor slept as he had been accustomed, and his former habit of turning suddenly as though someone were speaking from behind him revived. The old hall seemed to have some kind of fascination for him. He used to go there many times in the day, but grew impatient if anyone, even his wife, entered it. When the builder's foreman came to inquire about continuing his work Geoffrey was out driving; the man went into the hall, and when Geoffrey returned the servant told him of his arrival and where he was. With a frightful oath he pushed the servant aside and hurried up to the old hall. The workman met him almost at the door; and as Geoffrey burst into the room he ran against him. The man apologized:

'Beg pardon, sir, but I was just going out to make some inquiries. I directed twelve sacks of lime to be sent here, but I see there are only ten.'

'Damn the ten sacks and the twelve too!' was the ungracious and incomprehensible rejoinder.

The workman looked surprised, and tried to turn the conversation.

'I see, sir, there is a little matter which our people must have done; but the governor will of course see it set right at his own cost.'

'What do you mean?'

'That 'ere 'arth-stone, sir: some idiot must have put a scaffold pole on it and cracked it right down the middle, and it's thick enough you'd think to stand hanythink.' Geoffrey was silent for quite a minute, and then said in a constrained voice and with much gentler manner:

'Tell your people that I am not going on with the work in the hall at present. I want to leave it as it is for a while longer.'

'All right sir. I'll send up a few of our chaps to take away these poles and lime bags and tidy the place up a bit.'

'No! No!' said Geoffrey, 'leave them where they are. I shall send and tell you when you are to get on with the work.' So the foreman went away, and his comment to his master was:

'I'd send in the bill, sir, for the work already done. 'Pears to me that money's a little shaky in that quarter.'

Once or twice Delandre tried to stop Brent on the road, and, at last, finding that he could not attain his object rode after the carriage, calling out:

'What has become of my sister, your wife?' Geoffrey lashed his horses into a gallop, and the other, seeing from his white face and from his wife's collapse almost into a faint that his object was attained, rode away with a scowl and a laugh.

That night when Geoffrey went into the hall he passed over to the great fireplace, and all at once started back with a smothered cry. Then with an effort he pulled himself together and went away, returning with a light. He bent down over the broken hearth-stone to see if the moonlight falling through the storied window had in any way deceived him. Then with a groan of anguish he sank to his knees.

There, sure enough, through the crack in the broken stone were protruding a multitude of threads of golden hair just tinged with grey!

He was disturbed by a noise at the door, and looking round, saw his wife standing in the doorway. In the desperation of the moment he took action to prevent discovery, and lighting a match at the lamp, stooped down and burned away the hair that rose through the broken stone. Then rising nonchalantly as he could, he pretended surprise at seeing his wife beside him.

For the next week he lived in an agony; for, whether by accident or design, he could not find himself alone in the hall for any length of time. At each visit the hair had grown afresh through the crack, and he had to watch it carefully lest his terrible secret should be discovered. He tried to find a receptacle for the body of the murdered woman outside the house, but someone always interrupted him; and once, when he was coming out of the private doorway, he was met by his wife, who began to question him about it, and manifested surprise that she should not have before noticed the key which he now reluctantly showed her. Geoffrey dearly and passionately loved his wife, so that any possibility of her discovering his dread secrets, or even of doubting him, filled him with anguish; and after a couple of days had passed, he could not help coming to the conclusion that, at least, she suspected something.

That very evening she came into the hall after her drive and found him there sitting moodily by the deserted fireplace. She spoke to him directly.

'Geoffrey, I have been spoken to by that fellow Delandre, and he says horrible things. He tells to me that a week ago his sister returned to his house, the wreck and ruin of her former self, with only her golden hair as of old, and announced some fell intention. He asked me where she is – and oh, Geoffrey, she is dead, she is dead! So how can she have returned? Oh! I am in dread, and I know not where to turn!'

For answer, Geoffrey burst into a torrent of blasphemy which made her shudder. He cursed Delandre and his sister and all their kind, and in especial he hurled curse after curse on her golden hair.

'Oh, hush! hush!' she said, and was then silent, for she feared her husband when she saw the evil effect of his humour. Geoffrey in the torrent of his anger stood up and moved away from the hearth; but suddenly stopped as he saw a new look of terror in his wife's eyes. He followed their glance, and then he too, shuddered – for there on the broken hearth-stone lay a golden streak as the point of the hair rose through the crack.

'Look, look!' she shrieked. 'Is it some ghost of the dead! Come away – come away!' and seizing her husband by the wrist with the frenzy of madness, she pulled him from the room

That night she was in a raging fever. The doctor of the district attended her at once, and special aid was telegraphed for to London. Geoffrey was in despair, and in his anguish at the danger of his young wife almost forgot his own crime and its consequences. In the evening the doctor had to leave to attend to others; but he left Geoffrey in charge of his wife. His last words were:

'Remember, you must humour her till I come in the morning, or till some other doctor has her case in hand. What you have to dread is another attack of emotion. See that she is kept warm. Nothing more can be done.'

Late in the evening, when the rest of the household had retired. Geoffrey's wife got up from her bed and called to her husband.

'Come!' she said. 'Come to the old hall! I know where the gold comes from! I want to see it grow!'

Geoffrey would fain have stopped her, but he feared for her life or reason on the one hand, and lest in a paroxysm she should shriek out her terrible suspicion, and seeing that it was useless to try to prevent her, wrapped a warm rug around her and went with her to the old hall. When they entered, she turned and shut the door and locked it.

'We want no strangers amongst us three tonight!' she whispered with a wan smile.

'We three! nay we are but two,' said Geoffrey with a shudder; he feared to say more.

'Sit here,' said his wife as she put out the light. 'Sit here by the hearth and watch the gold growing. The silver moonlight is jealous! See, it steals along the floor towards the gold – our gold!' Geoffrey looked with growing horror, and saw that during the hours that had passed the golden hair had protruded further through the broken hearth-stone. He tried to hide it by placing his feet over the broken place; and his wife, drawing her chair beside him, leant over and laid her head on his shoulder.

'Now do not stir, dear,' she said; 'let us sit still and watch. We shall find the secret of the growing gold!' He passed his arm round her and sat silent; and as the moonlight stole along the floor she sank to sleep.

He feared to wake her; and so sat silent and miserable as the hours stole away.

Before his horror-struck eyes the golden-hair from the broken stone grew and grew; and as it increased, so his heart got colder and colder, till at last he had not power to stir, and sat with eyes full of terror watching his doom.

* * *

In the morning when the London doctor came, neither Geoffrey nor his wife could be found. Search was made in all the rooms, but without avail. As a last resource the great door of the old hall was broken open, and those who entered saw a grim and sorry sight.

There by the deserted hearth Geoffrey Brent and his young wife sat cold and white and dead. Her face was peaceful, and her eyes were closed in sleep; but his face was a sight that made all who saw it shudder, for there was on it a look of unutterable horror. The eyes were open and stared glassily at his feet, which were twined with tresses of golden hair, streaked with grey, which came through the broken hearth-stone.

THE GIPSY PROPHECY

'I really think,' said the doctor, 'that, at any rate, one of us should go and try whether or not the thing is an imposture.'

'Good!' said Considine. 'After dinner we will take our cigars and stroll over to the camp.'

Accordingly, when the dinner was over, and the *La Tour* finished, Joshua Considine and his friend, Dr Burleigh, went over to the east side of the moor, where the gipsy encampment lay. As they were leaving, Mary

Considine, who had walked as far as the end of the garden where it opened into the laneway, called after her husband:

'Mind, Joshua, you are to give them a fair chance, but don't give them any clue to a fortune – and don't you get flirting with any of the gipsy maidens – and take care to keep Gerald out of harm.'

For answer Considine held up his hand, as if taking a stage oath, and whistled the air of the old song, 'The Gipsy Countess'. Gerald joined in the strain, and then, breaking into merry laughter, the two men passed along the laneway to the common, turning now and then to wave their hands to Mary, who leaned over the gate, in the twilight, looking after them.

It was a lovely evening in the summer; the very air was full of rest and quiet happiness, as though an outward type of the peacefulness and joy which made a heaven of the home of the young married folk. Considine's life had not been an eventful one. The only disturbing element which he had ever known was in his wooing of Mary Winston, and the long-continued objection of her ambitious parents, who expected a brilliant match for their only daughter. When Mr and Mrs Winston had discovered the attachment of the young barrister, they had tried to keep the young people apart by sending their daughter away for a long round of visits, having made her promise not to correspond with her lover during her absence. Love, however, had stood the test. Neither absence nor neglect seemed to cool the passion of the young man, and jealousy seemed a thing unknown to his sanguine nature; so, after a long period of waiting, the parents had given in, and the young folk were married.

They had been living in the cottage a few months, and were just beginning to feel at home. Gerald Burleigh, Joshua's old college chum, and himself a sometime victim of Mary's beauty, had arrived a week before to stay with them for so long a time as he could tear himself away from his work in London.

When her husband had quite disappeared Mary went into the house, and, sitting down at the piano, gave an hour to Mendelssohn.

It was but a short walk across the common, and before the cigars required renewing the two men had reached the gipsy camp. The place was as picturesque as gipsy camps – when in villages and when business is good – usually are. There were some few persons round the fire, investing their money in prophecy, and a large number of others, poorer or more parsimonious, who stayed just outside the bounds but near enough to see all that went on.

As the two gentlemen approached, the villagers, who knew Joshua, made way a little, and a pretty, keen-eyed gipsy girl tripped up and asked to tell their fortunes. Joshua held out his hand, but the girl, without seeming to see it, stared at his face in a very odd manner. Gerald nudged him:

'You must cross her hand with silver,' he said. 'It is one of the most important parts of the mystery.' Joshua took from his pocket a half-crown and held it out to her, but, without looking at it, she answered:

'You have to cross the gipsy's hand with gold.'

Gerald laughed. 'You are at a premium as a subject,' he said. Joshua was of the kind of man – the universal kind – who can tolerate being stared at by a pretty girl, so, with some little deliberation, he answered:

'All right; here you are, my pretty girl; but you must give me a real good fortune for it,' and he handed her a half sovereign, which she took, saying:

'It is not for me to give good fortune or bad, but only to read what the Stars have said.' She took his right hand and turned it palm upward; but the instant her eyes met it she dropped it as though it had been red hot, and, with a startled look, glided swiftly away. Lifting the curtain of the large tent, which occupied the centre of the camp, she disappeared within.

'Sold again!' said the cynical Gerald. Joshua stood a little amazed, and not altogether satisfied. They both watched the large tent. In a few moments there emerged from the opening not the young girl, but a stately looking woman of middle age and commanding presence.

The instant she appeared the whole camp seemed to stand still. The clamour of tongues, the laughter and noise of the work were, for a second or two, arrested, and every man or woman who sat, or crouched, or lay, stood up and faced the imperial looking gipsy.

'The Queen, of course,' murmured Gerald. 'We are in luck tonight.' The gipsy Queen threw a searching glance around the camp, and then, without hesitating an instant, came straight over and stood before Joshua.

'Hold out your hand,' she said in a commanding tone.

Again Gerald spoke, *sotto voce*: 'I have not been spoken to in that way since I was at school.'

'Your hand must be crossed with gold.'

'A hundred per cent, at this game,' whispered Gerald, as Joshua laid another half sovereign on his upturned palm.

The gipsy looked at the hand with knitted brows; then suddenly looking up into his face, said:

'Have you a strong will – have you a true heart that can be brave for one you love?'

'I hope so; but I am afraid I have not vanity enough to say "yes".'

'Then I will answer for you; for I read resolution in your face – resolution desperate and determined if need be. You have a wife you love?'

'Yes,' emphatically.

'Then leave her at once – never see her face again. Go from her now, while love is fresh and your heart is free from wicked intent. Go quick – go far, and never see her face again!'

Joshua drew away his hand quickly, and said, 'Thank you!' stiffly but sarcastically, as he began to move away.

'I say!' said Gerald, 'you're not going like that, old man; no use in being indignant with the Stars or their prophet – and, moreover, your sovereign – what of it? At least, hear the matter out.'

'Silence, ribald!' commanded the Queen, 'you know not what you do. Let him go – and go ignorant, if he will not be warned.'

Joshua immediately turned back. 'At all events, we will see this thing out,' he said. 'Now, madam, you have given me advice, but I paid for a fortune.'

'Be warned!' said the gipsy. 'The Stars have been silent for long; let the mystery still wrap them round.'

'My dear madam, I do not get within touch of a mystery every day, and I prefer for my money knowledge rather than ignorance. I can get the latter commodity for nothing when I want any of it.'

Gerald echoed the sentiment. 'As for me I have a large and unsaleable stock on hand.'

The gipsy Queen eyed the two men sternly, and then said: 'As you wish. You have chosen for yourself, and have met warning with scorn, and appeal with levity. On your own head be the doom!'

'Amen!' said Gerald.

With an imperious gesture the Queen took Joshua's hand again, and began to tell his fortune.

'I see here the flowing of blood; it will flow before long; it is running in my sight. It flows through the broken circle of a severed ring.'

'Go on!' said Joshua, smiling. Gerald was silent.

'Must I speak plainer?'

'Certainly; we commonplace mortals want something definite. The Stars are a long way off, and their words get somewhat dulled in the message.'

The gipsy shuddered, and then spoke impressively. 'This is the hand of a murderer – the murderer of his wife!' She dropped the hand and turned away.

Joshua laughed. 'Do you know,' he said, 'I think if I were you I should prophesy some jurisprudence into my system. For instance, you say "this hand is the hand of a murderer." Well, whatever it may be in the future – or potentially – it is at present not one. You ought to give your prophecy in such terms as "the hand which will be a murderer's", or rather, "the

479

hand of one who will be the murderer of his wife". The Stars are really not good on technical questions.'

The gipsy made no reply of any kind, but, with drooping head and despondent mien, walked slowly to her tent, and, lifting the curtain, disappeared.

Without speaking the two men turned homewards, and walked across the moor. Presently, after some little hesitation, Gerald spoke.

'Of course, old man, this is all a joke; a ghastly one, but still a joke. But would it not be well to keep it to ourselves?'

'How do you mean?'

'Well, not tell your wife. It might alarm her.'

'Alarm her! My dear Gerald, what are you thinking of? Why, she would not be alarmed or afraid of me if all the gipsies that ever didn't come from Bohemia agreed that I was to murder her, or even to have a hard thought of her, whilst so long as she was saying "Jack Robinson".'

Gerald remonstrated. 'Old fellow, women are superstitious – far more than we men are; and, also they are blessed – or cursed – with a nervous system to which we are strangers. I see too much of it in my work not to realize it. Take my advice and do not let her know, or you will frighten her.'

Joshua's lips unconsciously hardened as he answered: 'My dear fellow, I would not have a secret from my wife. Why, it would be the beginning of a new order of things between us. We have no secrets from each other. If we ever have, then you may begin to look out for something odd between us.'

'Still,' said Gerald, 'at the risk of unwelcome interference, I say again be warned in time.'

'The gipsy's very words,' said Joshua. 'You and she seem quite of one accord. Tell me, old man, is this a put-up thing? You told me of the gipsy camp – did you arrange it all with Her Majesty?' This was said with an air of bantering earnestness. Gerald assured him that he only heard of the camp that morning; but he made fun of every answer of his friend, and, in the process of this raillery, the time passed, and they entered the cottage.

Mary was sitting at the piano but not playing. The dim twilight had waked some very tender feelings in her breast, and her eyes were full of gentle tears. When the men came in she stole over to her husband's side and kissed him. Joshua struck a tragic attitude.

'Mary,' he said in a deep voice, 'before you approach me, listen to the words of Fate. The Stars have spoken and the doom is sealed.'

'What is it, dear? Tell me the fortune, but do not frighten me.'

'Not at all, my dear; but there is a truth which it is well that you should know. Nay, it is necessary so that all your arrangements can be made beforehand, and everything be decently done and in order.'

'Go on, dear; I am listening.'

'Mary Considine, your effigy may yet be seen at Madame Tussaud's. The juris-imprudent Stars have announced their fell tidings that this hand is red with blood – your blood. Mary! Mary! my God!' He sprang forward, but too late to catch her as she fell fainting on the floor.

'I told you,' said Gerald. 'You don't know them as well as I do.'

After a little while Mary recovered from her swoon, but only to fall into strong hysterics, in which she laughed and wept and raved and cried, 'Keep him from me – from me, Joshua, my husband,' and many other words of entreaty and of fear.

Joshua Considine was in a state of mind bordering on agony, and when at last Mary became calm he knelt by her and kissed her feet and hands and hair and called her all the sweet names and said all the tender things his lips could frame. All that night he sat by her bedside and held her hand. Far through the night and up to the early morning she kept waking from sleep and crying out as if in fear, till she was comforted by the consciousness that her husband was watching beside her.

Breakfast was late that morning, but during it Joshua received a telegram which required him to drive over to Withering, nearly twenty miles. He was loth to go; but Mary would not hear of his remaining, and so before noon he drove off in his dog-cart alone.

When he was gone Mary retired to her room. She did not appear at lunch, but when afternoon tea was served on the lawn under the great weeping willow, she came to join her guest. She was looking quite recovered from her illness of the evening before. After some casual remarks, she said to Gerald: 'Of course it was very silly about last night, but I could not help feeling frightened. Indeed I would feel so still if I let myself think of it. But, after all, these people may only imagine things, and I have got a test that can hardly fail to show that the prediction is false – if indeed it be false,' she added sadly.

'What is your plan?' asked Gerald.

'I shall go myself to the gipsy camp, and have my fortune told by the Queen.'

'Capital. May I go with you?'

'Oh, no! That would spoil it. She might know you and guess at me, and suit her utterance accordingly. I shall go alone this afternoon.'

When the afternoon was gone Mary Considine took her way to the gipsy encampment. Gerald went with her as far as the near edge of the common, and returned alone.

Half-an-hour had hardly elapsed when Mary entered the drawing-room, where he lay on a sofa reading. She was ghastly pale and was in a state of extreme excitement. Hardly had she passed over the threshold

481

when she collapsed and sank moaning on the carpet. Gerald rushed to aid her, but by a great effort she controlled herself and motioned him to be silent. He waited, and his ready attention to her wish seemed to be her best help, for, in a few minutes, she had somewhat recovered, and was able to tell him what had passed.

'When I got to the camp,' she said, 'there did not seem to be a soul about. I went into the centre and stood there. Suddenly a tall woman stood beside me. "Something told me I was wanted!" she said. I held out my hand and laid a piece of silver on it. She took from her neck a small golden trinket and laid it there also, and then, seizing the two, threw them into the stream that ran by. The she took my hand in hers and spoke: "Naught but blood in this guilty place," and turned away. I caught hold of her and asked her to tell me more. After some hesitation, she said: "Alas! alas! I see you lying at your husband's feet, and his hands are red with blood".'

Gerald did not feel at all at ease, and tried to laugh it off. 'Surely,' he said, 'this woman has a craze about murder.'

'Do not laugh,' said Mary, 'I cannot bear it,' and then, as if with a sudden impulse, she left the room.

Not long after Joshua returned, bright and cheery, and as hungry as a hunter after his long drive. His presence cheered his wife, who seemed much brighter, but she did not mention the episode of the visit to the gipsy camp, so Gerald did not mention it either. As if by tacit consent the subject was not alluded to during the evening. But there was a strange, settled look on Mary's face, which Gerald could not but observe.

In the morning Joshua came down to breakfast later than usual. Mary had been up and about the house from an early hour; but as the time drew on she seemed to get a little nervous and now and again threw around an anxious look.

Gerald could not help noticing that none of those at breakfast could get on satisfactorily with their food. It was not altogether that the chops were tough, but that the knives were all so blunt. Being a guest, he, of course, made no sign; but presently saw Joshua draw his thumb across the edge of his knife in an unconscious sort of way. At the action Mary turned pale and almost fainted.

After breakfast they all went out on the lawn. Mary was making up a bouquet, and said to her husband, 'Get me a few of the tea-roses, dear.'

Joshua pulled down a cluster from the front of the house. The stem bent, but was too tough to break. He put his hand in his pocket to get his knife; but in vain. 'Lend me your knife, Gerald,' he said. But Gerald had not got one, so he went into the breakfast room and took one from the table. He came out feeling its edge and grumbling. 'What on earth has happened to all the knives – the edges seem all ground off?' Mary turned away hurriedly and entered the house.

Joshua tried to sever the stalk with the blunt knife as country cooks sever the necks of fowl – as schoolboys cut twine. With a little effort he finished the task. The cluster of roses grew thick, so he determined to gather a great bunch.

He could not find a single sharp knife in the sideboard where the cutlery was kept, so he called Mary, and when she came, told her the state of things. She looked so agitated and so miserable that he could not help knowing the truth, and, as if astounded and hurt, asked her:

'Do you mean to say that *you* have done it?'

She broke in, 'Oh, Joshua, I was so afraid.'

He paused, and a set, white look came over his face. 'Mary!' said he, 'is this all the trust you have in me? I would not have believed it.'

'Oh, Joshua! Joshua!' she cried entreatingly, 'forgive me,' and wept bitterly.

Joshua thought a moment and then said: 'I see how it is. We shall better end this or we shall all go mad.'

He ran into the drawing-room.

'Where are you going?' almost screamed Mary.

Gerald saw what he meant – that he would not be tied to blunt instruments by the force of a superstition, and was not surprised when he saw him come out through the French window, bearing in his hand a large Ghourka knife, which usually lay on the centre table, and which his brother had sent him from Northern India. It was one of those great hunting-knives which worked such havoc, at close quarters with the enemies of the loyal Ghourkas during the mutiny, of great weight but so evenly balanced in the hand as to seem light, and with an edge like a razor. With one of these knives a Ghourka can cut a sheep in two.

When Mary saw him come out of the room with the weapon in his hand she screamed in an agony of fright, and the hysterics of last night were promptly renewed.

Joshua ran toward her, and, seeing her falling, threw down the knife and tried to catch her.

However, he was just a second too late, and the two men cried in horror simultaneously as they saw her fall upon the naked blade.

When Gerald rushed over he found that in falling her left hand had struck the blade, which lay partly upwards on the grass. Some of the small veins were cut through, and the blood gushed freely from the wound. As he was tying it up he pointed out to Joshua that the wedding ring was severed by the steel.

They carried her fainting to the house. When, after a while, she came out, with her arm in a sling, she was peaceful in her mind and happy. She said to her husband:

'The gipsy was wonderfully near the truth; too near for the real thing ever to occur now, dear.'

Joshua bent over and kissed the wounded hand.

THE COMING OF ABEL BEHENNA

The little Cornish port of Pencastle was bright in the early April, when the sun had seemingly come to stay after a long and bitter winter. Boldly and blackly the rock stood out against a background of shaded blue, where the sky fading into mist met the far horizon. The sea was of true Cornish hue – sapphire, save where it became deep emerald green in the fathomless depths under the cliffs, where the seal caves opened their grim jaws. On the slopes the grass was parched and brown. The spikes of furze bushes were ashy grey, but the golden yellow of their flowers streamed along the hillside, dipping out in lines as the rock cropped up, and lessening into patches and dots till finally it died away all together where the sea winds swept round the jutting cliffs and cut short the vegetation as though with an ever-working aerial shears. The whole hillside, with its body of brown and flashes of yellow, was just like a colossal yellow-hammer.

The little harbour opened from the sea between towering cliffs, and behind a lonely rock, pierced with many caves and blow-holes through which the sea in storm time sent its thunderous voice, together with a fountain of drifting spume. Hence, it wound westwards in a serpentine course, guarded at its entrance by two little curving piers to left and right. These were roughly built of dark slates placed endways and held together with great beams bound with iron hands. Thence, it flowed up the rocky bed of the stream whose winter torrents had of old cut out its way amongst the hills. This stream was deep at first, with here and there, where it widened, patches of broken rock exposed at low water, full of holes where crabs and lobsters were to be found at the ebb of the tide. From amongst the rocks rose sturdy posts, used for warping in the little coasting vessels which frequented the port. Higher up, the stream still flowed deeply, for the tide ran far inland, but always calmly for all the force of the wildest storm was broken below. Some quarter mile inland the stream was deep at high water, but at low tide there were at each side patches of the same broken rock as lower down, through the chinks of which the sweet water of the natural stream trickled and murmured after the tide had ebbed away. Here, too, rose mooring posts for the fishermen's boats. At either side of the river was a row of cottages down almost on the level of high tide. They were pretty cottages, strongly and snugly built, with trim narrow gardens in front, full of old-fashioned plants, flowering currants, coloured primroses, wall-flower, and stone-crop. Over the fronts of many of them climbed clematis and wisteria. The window sides and door posts of all where as white as snow, and the little pathway to each was paved with light coloured stones. At some of the doors were tiny porches, whilst at others were rustic seats cut from tree trunks or from old barrels; in nearly every case the window ledges were filled with boxes or pots of flowers or foliage plants.

Two men lived in cottages exactly opposite each other across the stream. Two men, both young, both good-looking, both prosperous, and who had been companions and rivals from their boyhood. Abel Behenna was dark with the gipsy darkness which the Phœnician mining wanderers left in their tracks; Eric Sanson – which the local antiquarian said was a corruption of Sagamanson – was fair, with the ruddy hue which marked the path of the wild Norseman. These two seemed to have singled out each other from the very beginning to work and strive together, to fight for each other and to stand back to back in all endeavours. They had now put the coping-stone on their Temple of Unity by falling in love with the same girl. Sarah Trefusis was certainly the prettiest girl in Pencastle, and there was many a young man who would gladly have tried his fortune with her, but that there were two to contend against, and each of these the strongest and most resolute man in the port – except the other. The average young man thought that this was very hard, and on account of it bore no good will to either of the three principals: whilst the average young woman who had, lest worse should befall, to put up with the grumbling of her sweetheart, and the sense of being only second best which it implied, did not either, be sure, regard Sarah with friendly eye. Thus it came, in the course of a year or so, for rustic courtship is a slow process, that the two men and woman found themselves thrown much together. They were all satisfied, so it did not matter, and Sarah, who was vain and something frivolous, took care to have her revenge on both men and women in a quiet way. When a young woman in her 'walking out' can only boast one not-quite-satisfied young man, it is no particular pleasure to her to see her escort cast sheep's eyes at a better-looking girl supported by two devoted swains.

At length there came a time which Sarah dreaded, and which she had tried to keep distant – the time when she had to make her choice between the two men. She liked them both, and, indeed, either of them might have satisfied the ideas of even a more exacting girl. But her mind was so constituted that she thought more of what she might lose, than of what she might gain; and whenever she thought she had made up her mind she became instantly assailed with doubts as to the wisdom of her choice. Always the man whom she had presumably lost became endowed afresh with a newer and more bountiful crop of advantages than had ever arisen from the possibility of his acceptance. She promised each man that on her birthday she would give him his answer, and that day, the 11th of April, had now arrived. The promises had been given singly and confidentially, but each was given to a man who was not likely to forget. Early in the morning she found both men hovering round her door. Neither had taken the other into his confidence, and each was simply seeking an early opportunity of getting his answer, and advancing his suit if necessary. Damon, as a rule, does not take Pythias with him when making a proposal; and in the heart of each man his own affairs had a claim far above any requirements of friendship. So, throughout the day, they kept seeing each other out. The position was doubtless somewhat embarrassing to Sarah, and though the satisfaction of her vanity that she should be thus adored was very pleasing, yet there were moments when she was annoyed with both men for being so persistent. Her only consolation at such moments was that she saw, through the elaborate smiles of the other girls when in passing they noticed her door thus doubly guarded, the jealousy which filled their hearts. Sarah's mother was a person of commonplace and sordid ideas, and, seeing all along the state of affairs, her one intention, persistently expressed to her daughter in the plainest words, was to so arrange matters that Sarah should get all that was possible out of both men. With this purpose she had cunningly kept herself as far as possible in the background in the matter of her daughter's wooings, and watched in silence. At first Sarah had been indignant with her for her sordid views; but, as usual, her weak nature gave way before persistence, and she had now got to the stage of acceptance. She was not surprised when her mother whispered to her in the little yard behind the house:–

'Go up the hillside for a while; I want to talk to these two. They're both red-hot for ye, and now's the time to get things fixed!' Sarah began a feeble remonstrance, but her mother cut her short.

'I tell ye, girl, that my mind is made up! Both these men want ye, and only one can have ye, but before ye choose it'll be so arranged that ye'll have all that both have got! Don't argy, child! Go up the hillside, and when ye come back I'll have it fixed – I see a way quite easy!' So Sarah went up the hillside through the narrow paths between the golden furze, and Mrs Trefusis joined the two men in the living-room of the little house.

She opened the attack with the desperate courage which is in all mothers when they think for their children, however mean the thoughts may be.

'Ye two men, ye're both in love with my Sarah!'

Their bashful silence gave consent to the barefaced proposition. She went on:

'Neither of ye has much!' Again they tacitly acquiesced in the soft impeachment.

'I don't know that either of ye could keep a wife!' Though neither said a word their looks and bearing expressed distinct dissent. Mrs Trefusis went on:

'But if ye'd put what ye both have together ye'd make a comfortable home for one of ye – and Sarah!' She eyed the men keenly, with her cunning eyes half shut, as she spoke; then satisfied from her scrutiny that the idea was accepted she went on quickly, as if to prevent argument:

'The girl likes ye both, and mayhap it's hard for her to choose. Why don't ye toss up for her? First put your money together – ye've each got a bit put by, I know. Let the lucky man take the lot and trade with it a bit, and then come home and marry her. Neither of ye's afraid, I suppose! And neither of ye'll say that he won't do that much for the girl that ye both say ye love!'

Abel broke the silence:

'It don't seem the square thing to toss for the girl! She wouldn't like it herself, and it doesn't seem – seem respectful like to her – ' Eric interrupted. He was conscious that his chance was not so good as Abel's in case Sarah should wish to choose between them:

'Are ye afraid of the hazard?'

'Not me!' said Abel, boldly. Mrs Trefusis, seeing that her idea was beginning to work, followed up the advantage.

'It is settled that ye put yer money together to make a home for her, whether ye toss for her or leave it for her to choose?'

'Yes,' said Eric quickly, and Abel agreed with equal sturdiness. Mrs Trefusis' little cunning eyes twinkled. She heard Sarah's step in the yard, and said:

487

'Well! here she comes, and I leave it to her.' And she went out.

During her brief walk on the hillside Sarah had been trying to make up her mind. She was feeling almost angry with both men for being the cause of her difficulty, and as she came into the room said shortly:

'I want to have a word with you both – come to the Flagstaff Rock, where we can be alone.' She took her hat and went out of the house up the winding path to the steep rock crowned with a high flagstaff, where once the wreckers' fire basket used to burn. This was the rock which formed the northern jaw of the little harbour. There was only room on the path for two abreast, and it marked the state of things pretty well when, by a sort of implied arrangement, Sarah went first, and the two men followed, walking abreast and keeping step. By this time, each man's heart was boiling with jealousy. When they came to the top of the rock, Sarah stood against the flagstaff, and the two young men stood opposite her. She had chosen her position with knowledge and intention, for there was no room for anyone to stand beside her. They were all silent for a while; then Sarah began to laugh and said:–

'I promised the both of you to give you an answer to-day. I've been thinking and thinking and thinking, till I began to get angry with you both for plaguing me so; and even now I don't seem any nearer than ever I was to making up my mind.' Eric said suddenly:

'Let us toss for it, lass!' Sarah showed no indignation whatever at the proposition; her mother's eternal suggestion had schooled her to the acceptance of something of the kind, and her weak nature made it easy to her to grasp at any way out of the difficulty. She stood with downcast eyes idly picking at the sleeve of her dress, seeming to have tacitly acquiesced in the proposal. Both men instinctively realizing this pulled each a coin from his pocket, spun it in the air, and dropped his other hand over the palm on which it lay. For a few seconds they remained thus, all silent; then Abel, who was the more thoughtful of the men, spoke:

'Sarah! is this good?' As he spoke he removed the upper hand from the coin and placed the latter back in his pocket. Sarah was nettled.

'Good or bad, it's good enough for me! Take it or leave it as you like,' she said, to which he replied quickly:

'Nay lass! Aught that concerns you is good enow for me. I did but think of you lest you might have pain or disappointment hereafter. If you love Eric better nor me, in God's name say so, and I think I'm man enow to stand aside. Likewise, if I'm the one, don't make us both miserable for life!' Face to face with a difficulty, Sarah's weak nature proclaimed itself; she put her hands before her face and began to cry, saying–

'It was my mother. She keeps telling me!' The silence which followed was broken by Eric, who said hotly to Abel:

'Let the lass alone, can't you? If she wants to choose this way, let her. It's good enough for me – and for you, too! She's said it now, and must abide by it!' Hereupon Sarah turned upon him in sudden fury, and cried:

'Hold your tongue! what is it to you, at anyrate?' and she resumed her crying. Eric was so flabbergasted that he had not a word to say, but stood looking particularly foolish, with his mouth open and his hands held out with the coin still between them. All were silent till Sarah, taking her hands from her face laughed hysterically and said:

'As you two can't make up your minds, I'm going home!' and she turned to go.

'Stop,' said Abel, in an authoritative voice. 'Eric, you hold the coin, and I'll cry. Now, before we settle it, let us clearly understand: the man who wins takes all the money that we both have got, brings it to Bristol and ships on a voyage and trades with it. Then he comes back and marries Sarah, and they two keep all, whatever there may be, as the result of the trading. Is this what we understand?'

'Yes,' said Eric.

'I'll marry him on my next birthday,' said Sarah. Having said it the intolerably mercenary spirit of her action seemed to strike her, and impulsively she turned away with a bright blush. Fire seemed to sparkle in the eyes of both men. Said Eric: 'A year so be! The man that wins is to have one year.'

'Toss!' cried Abel, and the coin spun in the air. Eric caught it, and again held it between his outstretched hands.

'Heads!' cried Abel, a pallor sweeping over his face as he spoke. As he leaned forward to look Sarah leaned forward too, and their heads almost touched. He could feel her hair blowing on his cheek, and it thrilled through him like fire. Eric lifted his upper hand; the coin lay with its head up. Abel stepped forward and took Sarah in his arms. With a curse Eric hurled the coin far into the sea. Then he leaned against the flagstaff and scowled at the others with his hands thrust deep into his pockets. Abel whispered wild words of passion and delight into Sarah's ears, and as she listened she began to believe that fortune had rightly interpreted the wishes of her secret heart, and that she loved Abel best.

Presently Abel looked up and caught sight of Eric's face as the last ray of sunset struck it. The red light intensified the natural ruddiness of his complexion, and he looked as though he were steeped in blood. Abel did not mind his scowl, for now that his own heart was at rest he could feel unalloyed pity for his friend. He stepped over meaning to comfort him, and held out his hand, saying:

'It was my chance, old lad. Don't grudge it me. I'll try to make Sarah a happy woman, and you shall be a brother to us both!'

'Brother be damned!' was all the answer Eric made, as he turned away. When he had gone a few steps down the rocky path he turned and came back. Standing before Abel and Sarah, who had their arms round each other, he said:

'You have a year. Make the most of it! And be sure you're in time to claim your wife! Be back to have your banns up in time to be married on the 11th April. If you're not, I tell you I shall have my banns up, and you may get back too late.'

'What do you mean, Eric? You are mad!'

'No more mad than you are, Abel Behenna. You go, that's your chance! I stay, that's mine! I don't mean to let the grass grow under my feet. Sarah cared no more for you than for me five minutes ago, and she may come back to that five minutes after you're gone! You won by a point only – the game may change.'

'The game won't change!' said Abel shortly. 'Sarah, you'll be true to me? You won't marry till I return?'

'For a year!' added Eric, quickly, 'that's the bargain.'

'I promise for the year,' said Sarah. A dark look came over Abel's face, and he was about to speak but he mastered himself and smiled.

'I mustn't be too hard or get angry to-night! Come, Eric! we played and fought together. I won fairly. I played fairly all the game of our wooing! You know that as well I do; and now when I am going away, I shall look to my old and true comrade to help me when I am gone!'

'I'll help you none,' said Eric, 'so help me God!'

'It was God helped me,' said Abel simply.

'Then let Him go on helping you,' said Eric angrily. 'The Devil is good enough for me!' and without another word he rushed down the steep path and disappeared behind the rocks.

When he had gone Abel hoped for some tender passage with Sarah, but the first remark she made chilled him.

'How lonely it all seems without Eric!' and this note sounded till he had left her at home – and after.

Early on the next morning Abel heard a noise at his door, and on going out saw Eric walking rapidly away: a small canvas bag full of gold and silver lay on the threshold; on a small slip of paper pinned to it was written:

'Take the money and go. I stay. God for you! The Devil for me! Remember the 11th of April. – ERIC SANSON.' That afternoon Abel went off to Bristol, and a week later sailed on the *Star of the Sea* bound for Pahang. His money – including that which had been Eric's – was on board in the shape of a venture of cheap toys. He had been advised by a shrewd old mariner of Bristol whom he knew, and who knew the ways of the

Chersonese, who predicted that every penny invested would be returned with a shilling to boot.

As the year wore on Sarah became more and more disturbed in her mind. Eric was always at hand to make love to her in his own persistent, masterful manner, and to this she did not object. Only one letter came from Abel, to say that his venture had proved successful, and that he had sent some two hundred pounds to the bank at Bristol, and was trading with fifty pounds still remaining in goods for China, whither the *Star of the Sea* was bound and whence she would return to Bristol. He suggested that Eric's share of the venture should be returned to him with his share of the profits. This proposition was treated with anger by Eric, and as simply childish by Sarah's mother.

More than six months had since then elapsed, but no other letter had come, and Eric's hopes which had been dashed down by the letter from Pahang, began to rise again. He perpetually assailed Sarah with an 'if!' If Abel did not return, would she then marry him? If the 11th April went by without Abel being in the port, would she give him over? If Abel had taken his fortune, and married another girl on the head of it, would she marry him, Eric, as soon as the truth were known? And so on in an endless variety of possibilities. The power of the strong will and the determined purpose over the woman's weaker nature became in time manifest. Sarah began to lose her faith in Abel and to regard Eric as a possible husband; and a possible husband is in a woman's eye different to all other men. A new affection for him began to arise in her breast, and the daily familiarities of permitted courtship furthered the growing affection. Sarah began to regard Abel as rather a rock in the road of her life, and had it not been for her mother's constantly reminding her of the good fortune already laid by in the Bristol Bank she would have tried to have shut her eyes altogether to the fact of Abel's existence.

The 11th April was Saturday, so that in order to have the marriage on that day it would be necessar that the banns should be called on Sunday, 22nd March. From the beginning of that month Eric kept perpetually on the subject of Abel's absence, and his outspoken opinion that the latter was either dead or married began to become a reality to the woman's mind. As the first half of the month wore on Eric became more jubilant, and after church on the 15th he took Sarah for a walk to the Flagstaff Rock. There he asserted himself strongly:

'I told Abel, and you too, that if he was not here to put up his banns in time for the eleventh, I would put up mine for the twelfth. Now the time has come when I mean to do it. He hasn't kept his word' – here Sarah struck in out of her weakness and indecision:

'He hasn't broken it yet!' Eric ground his teeth with anger.

'If you mean to stick up for him,' he said, as he smote his hands savagely on the flagstaff, which sent forth a shivering murmur, 'well and good. I'll keep my part of the bargain. On Sunday I shall give notice of the banns, and you can deny them in the church if you will. If Abel is in Pencastle on the eleventh, he can have them cancelled, and his own put up; but till then, I take my course, and woe to anyone who stands in my way!' With that he flung himself down the rocky pathway, and Sarah could not but admire his Viking strength and spirit, as, crossing the hill, he strode away along the cliffs towards Bude.

During the week no news was heard of Abel, and on Saturday Eric gave notice of the banns of marriage between himself and Sarah Trefusis. The clergyman would have remonstrated with him, for although nothing formal had been told to the neighbours, it had been understood since Abel's departure that on his return he was to marry Sarah; but Eric would not discuss the question.

'It is a painful subject, sir,' he said with a firmness which the parson, who was a very young man, could not but be swayed by. 'Surely there is nothing against Sarah or me. Why should there be any bones made about the matter?' The parson said no more, and on the next day he read out the banns for the first time amidst an audible buzz from the congregation. Sarah was present, contrary to custom, and though she blushed furiously enjoyed her triumph over the other girls whose banns had not yet come. Before the week was over she began to make her wedding dress. Eric used to come and look at her at work and the sight thrilled through him. He used to say all sorts of pretty things to her at such times, and there were to both delicious moments of love-making.

The banns were read a second time on the 29th, and Eric's hope grew more and more fixed though there were to him moments of acute despair when he realized that the cup of happiness might be dashed from his lips at any moment, right up to the last. At such times he was full of passion – desperate and remorseless – and he ground his teeth and clenched his hands in a wild way as though some taint of the old Berserker fury of his ancestors still lingered in his blood. On the Thursday of that week he looked in on Sarah and found her, amid a flood of sunshine, putting finishing touches to her white wedding gown. His own heart was full of gaiety, and the sight of the woman who was so soon to be his own so occupied, filled him with a joy unspeakable, and he felt faint with languorous ecstasy. Bending over he kissed Sarah on the mouth, and then whispered in her rosy ear –

'Your wedding dress, Sarah! And for me!' As he drew back to admire her she looked up saucily, and said to him –

'Perhaps not for you. There is more than a week yet for Abel!' and then cried out in dismay, for with a wild gesture and a fierce oath Eric dashed out of the house, banging the door behind him. The incident disturbed Sarah more than she could have thought possible, for it awoke all her fears and doubts and indecision afresh. She cried a little, and put by her dress, and to soothe herself went to sit for a while on the summit of the Flagstaff Rock. When she arrived she found there a little group anxiously discussing the weather. The sea was calm and the sun bright, but across the sea were strange lines of darkness and light, and close in to shore the rocks were fringed with foam, which spread out in great white curves and circles as the currents drifted. The wind had backed, and came in sharp, cold puffs. The blow-hole, which ran under the Flagstaff Rock, from the rocky bay without to the harbour within, was booming at intervals, and the seagulls were screaming ceaselessly as they wheeled about the entrance of the port.

'It looks bad,' she heard an old fisherman say to the coastguard. 'I seen it just like this once before, when the East Indiaman *Coromandel* went to pieces in Dizzard Bay!' Sarah did not wait to hear more. She was of a timid nature where danger was concerned, and could not bear to hear of wrecks and disasters. She went home and resumed the completion of her dress, secretly determined to appease Eric when she should meet him with a sweet apology – and to take the earliest opportunity of being even with him after her marriage.

The old fisherman's weather prophecy was justified. That night at dusk a wild storm came on. The sea rose and lashed the western coasts from Skye to Scilly and left a tale of disaster everywhere. The sailors and fishermen of Pencastle all turned out on the rocks and cliffs and watched eagerly. Presently, by a flash of lightning, a 'ketch' was seen drifting under only a jib about half-a-mile outside the port. All eyes and all glasses were concentrated on her, waiting for the next flash, and when it came a chorus went up that it was the *Lovely Alice*, trading between Bristol and Penzance, and touching at all the little ports between. 'God help them!' said the harbour-master, 'for nothing in this world can save them when they are between Bude and Tintagel and the wind on shore!' The coastguards exerted themselves, and, aided by brave hearts and willing hands, they brought the rocket apparatus up on the summit of the Flagstaff Rock. Then they burned blue lights so that those on board might see the harbour opening in case they could make any effort to reach it. They worked gallantly enough on board; but no skill or strength of man could avail. Before many minutes were over the *Lovely Alice* rushed to her doom on the great island rock that guarded the mouth of the port. The screams of those on board were faintly borne on the tempest as they flung themselves into the sea in a last chance for life. The blue lights were kept burning, and eager eyes peered into the depths of the waters in case any face could be seen; and ropes were held ready to fling out in aid. But never a face was seen, and the willing arms rested idle. Eric was there amongst his fellows. His old Icelandic origin was never more apparent than in that wild hour. He took a rope, and shouted in the ear of the harbour-master:

'I shall go down on the rock over the seal cave. The tide is running up, and someone may drift in there!'

'Keep back, man!' came the answer. 'Are you mad? One slip on that rock and you are lost: and no man could keep his feet in the dark on such a place in such a tempest!'

'Not a bit,' came the reply. 'You remember how Abel Behenna saved me there on a night like this when my boat went on the Gull Rock. He dragged me up from the deep water in the seal cave, and now someone may drift in there again as I did,' and he was gone into the darkness. The projecting rock hid the light on the Flagstaff Rock, but he knew his way too well to miss it. His boldness and sureness of foot standing to him, he shortly stood on the great round-topped rock cut away beneath by the action of the waves over the entrance of the seal cave, where the water was fathomless. There he stood in comparative safety, for the concave shape of the rock beat back the waves with their own force, and though the water below him seemed to boil like a seething cauldron, just beyond the spot there was a space of almost calm. The rock, too, seemed here to shut off the sound of the gale, and he listened as well as watched. As he stood there ready, with his coil of rope poised to throw, he thought he heard below him, just beyond the whirl of the water, a faint, despairing cry. He echoed it with a shout that rang into the night. Then he waited for the flash of lightning, and as it passed flung his rope out into the darkness where he had seen a face rising through the swirl of the foam. The rope was caught, for he felt a pull on it, and he shouted again in his mighty voice:

'Tie it round your waist, and I shall pull you up.' Then when he felt that it was fast he moved along the rock to the far side of the sea cave, where the deep water was something stiller, and where he could get foothold secure enough to drag the rescued man on the overhanging rock. He began to pull, and shortly he knew from the rope taken in that the man he was now rescuing must soon be close to the top of the rock. He steadied himself for a moment, and drew a long breath, that he might at the next effort complete the rescue. He had just bent his back to the work when a flash of lightning revealed to each other the two men – the rescuer and the rescued.

Eric Sanson and Abel Behenna were face to face – and none knew of the meeting save themselves; and God.

On the instant a wave of passion swept through Eric's heart. All his hopes were shattered, and with the hatred of Cain his eyes looked out. He saw in the instant of recognition the joy in Abel's face that his was the hand to succour him, and this intensified his hate. Whilst the passion was on him he started back, and the rope ran out between his hands. His moment of hate was followed by an impulse of his better manhood, but it was too late.

Before he could recover himself, Abel encumbered with the rope that should have aided him, was plunged with a despairing cry back into the darkness of the devouring sea.

Then, feeling all the madness and the doom of Cain upon him, Eric rushed back over the rocks, heedless of the danger and eager only for one thing – to be amongst other people whose living noises would shut out that last cry which seemed to ring still in his ears. When he regained the Flagstaff Rock the men surrounded him, and through the fury of the storm he heard the harbour-master say:–

'We feared you were lost when we heard a cry! How white you are! Where is your rope? Was there anyone drifted in?'

'No one,' he shouted in answer, for he felt that he could never explain that he had let his old comrade slip back into the sea, and at the very place and under the very circumstances in which that comrade had saved his own life. He hoped by one bold lie to set the matter at rest for ever. There was no one to bear witness – and if he should have to carry that still white face in his eyes and that despairing cry in his ears for evermore – at least none should know of it. 'No one,' he cried, more loudly still. 'I slipped on the rock, and the rope fell into the sea!' So saying he left them, and, rushing down the steep path, gained his own cottage and locked himself within.

The remainder of that night he passed lying on his bed – dressed and motionless – staring upwards, and seeming to see through the darkness a pale face gleaming wet in the lightning, with its glad recognition turning to ghastly despair, and to hear a cry which never ceased to echo in his soul.

In the morning the storm was over and all was smiling again, except that the sea was still boisterous with its unspent fury. Great pieces of wreck drifted into the port, and the sea around the island rock was strewn with others. Two bodies also drifted into the harbour – one the master of the wrecked ketch, the other a strange seaman whom no one knew.

Sarah saw nothing of Eric till the evening, and then he only looked in for a minute. He did not come into the house, but simply put his head in through the open window.

'Well, Sarah,' he called out in a loud voice, though to her it did not ring truly, 'is the wedding dress done? Sunday week, mind! Sunday week!'

495

Sarah was glad to have the reconciliation so easy; but, womanlike, when she saw the storm was over and her own fears groundless, she at once repeated the cause of offence.

'Sunday so be it,' she said without looking up, 'if Abel isn't there on Saturday!' Then she looked up saucily, though her heart was full of fear of another outburst on the part of her impetuous lover. But the window was empty; Eric had taken himself off, and with a pout she resumed her work. She saw Eric no more till Sunday afternoon, after the banns had been called the third time, when he came up to her before all the people with an air of proprietorship which half-pleased and half-annoyed her.

'Not yet, mister!' she said, pushing him away, as the other girls giggled. 'Wait till Sunday next, if you please – the day after Saturday!' she added, looking at him saucily. The girls giggled again, and the young men guffawed. They thought it was the snub that touched him so that he became as white as a sheet as he turned away. But Sarah, who knew more than they did, laughed, for she saw triumph through the spasm of pain that overspread his face.

The week passed uneventfully; however, as Saturday drew nigh Sarah had occasional moments of anxiety, and as to Eric he went about at night-time like a man possessed. He restrained himself when others were by, but now and again he went down amongst the rocks and caves and shouted aloud. This seemed to relieve him somewhat, and he was better able to restrain himself for some time after. All Saturday he stayed in his own house and never left it. As he was to be married on the morrow, the neighbours thought it was shyness on his part, and did not trouble or notice him. Only once was he disturbed, and that was when the chief boatman came to him and sat down, and after a pause said:

'Eric, I was over in Bristol yesterday. I was in the ropemaker's getting a coil to replace the one you lost the night of the storm, and there I saw Michael Heavens of this place, who is a salesman there. He told me that Abel Behenna had come home the week ere last on the *Star of the Sea* from Canton, and that he had lodged a sight of money in the Bristol Bank in the name of Sarah Behenna. He told Michael so himself – and that he had taken passage on the *Lovely Alice* to Pencastle. Bear up, man,' for Eric had with a groan dropped his head on his knees, with his face between his hands. 'He was your old comrade, I know, but you couldn't help him. He must have gone down with the rest that awful night. I thought I'd better tell you, lest it might come some other way, and you might keep Sarah Trefusis from being frightened. They were good friends once, and women take these things to heart. It would not do to let her be pained with such a thing on her wedding day!' Then he rose and went away, leaving Eric still sitting disconsolately with his head on his knees.

'Poor fellow!' murmured the chief boatman to himself; 'he takes it to heart. Well, well! right enough! They were true comrades once, and Abel saved him!'

The afternoon of that day, when the children had left school, they strayed as usual on half-holidays along the quay and the paths by the cliffs. Presently some of them came running in a state of excitement to the harbour, where a few men were unloading a coal ketch, and a great many were superintending the operation. One of the children called out:

'There is a porpoise in the harbour mouth! We saw it come through the blow-hole! It had a long tail, and was deep under the water!'

'It was no porpoise,' said another; 'it was a seal; but it had a long tail! It came out of the seal cave!' The other children bore various testimony, but on two points they were unanimous – it, whatever 'it' was, had come through the blow-hole deep under the water, and had a long, thin tail – a tail so long that they could not see the end of it. There was much unmerciful chaffing of the children by the men on this point, but as it was evident that they had seen something, quite a number of persons, young and old, male and female, went along the high paths on either side of the harbour mouth to catch a glimpse of this new addition to the fauna of the sea, a long-tailed porpoise or seal. The tide was now coming in. There was a slight breeze, and the surface of the water was rippled so that it was only at moments that anyone could see clearly into the deep water. After a spell of watching a woman called out that she saw something moving up the channel, just below where she was standing. There was a stampede to the spot, but by the time the crowd had gathered the breeze had freshened, and it was impossible to see with any distinctness below the surface of the water. On being questioned the woman described what she had seen, but in such an incoherent way that the whole thing was put down as an effect of imagination; had it not been for the children's report she would not have been credited at all. Her semi-hysterical statement that what she saw was 'like a pig with the entrails out' was only thought anything of by an old coastguard, who shook his head but did not make any remark. For the remainder of the daylight this man was seen always on the bank, looking into the water, but always with disappointment manifest on his face.

Eric arose early on the next morning – he had not slept all night, and it was a relief to him to move about in the light. He shaved himself with a hand that did not tremble, and dressed himself in his wedding clothes. There was a haggared look on his face, and he seemed as though he had grown years older in the last few days. Still there was a wild, uneasy light of triumph in his eyes, and he kept murmuring to himself over and over again:

'This is my wedding-day! Abel cannot claim her now – living or dead! –

497

living or dead! Living or dead!' He sat in his arm-chair, waiting with an uncanny quietness for the church hour to arrive. When the bell began to ring he arose and passed out of his house, closing the door behind him. He looked at the river and saw the tide had just turned. In the church he sat with Sarah and her mother, holding Sarah's hand tightly in his all the time, as though he feared to lose her. When the service was over they stood up together, and were married in the presence of the entire congregation; for no one left the church. Both made the responses clearly – Eric's being even on the defiant side. When the wedding was over Sarah took her husband's arm, and they walked away together, the boys and younger girls being cuffed by their elders into a decorous behaviour, for they would fain have followed close behind their heels.

The way from the church led down to the back of Eric's cottage, a narrow passage being between it and that of his next neighbour. When the bridal couple had passed through this the remainder of the congregation, who had followed them at a little distance, were startled by a long, shrill scream from the bride. They rushed through the passage and found her on the bank with wild eyes, pointing to the river bed opposite Eric Sanson's door.

The falling tide had deposited there the body of Abel Behenna stark upon the broken rocks. The rope trailing from its waist had been twisted by the current round the mooring post, and had held it back whilst the tide had ebbed away from it. The right elbow had fallen in a chink in the rock, leaving the hand outstretched toward Sarah, with the open palm upward as though it were extended to receive hers, the pale drooping fingers open to the clasp.

All that happened afterwards was never quite known to Sarah Sanson. Whenever she would try to recollect there would become a buzzing in her ears and a dimness in her eyes, and all would pass away. The only thing that she could remember of it all – and this she never forgot – was Eric's breathing heavily, with his face whiter than that of the dead man, as he muttered under his breath:

'Devil's help! Devil's faith! Devil's price!'

THE BURIAL OF THE RATS

Leaving Paris by the Orleans road, cross the Enceinte, and, turning to the right, you find yourself in a somewhat wild and not at all savoury district. Right and left, before and behind, on every side rise great heaps of dust and waste accumulated by the process of time.

Paris has its night as well as its day life, and the sojourner who enters his hotel in the Rue de Rivoli or the Rue St Honoré late at night or leaves it early in the morning, can guess, in coming near Montrouge – if he has not done so already – the purpose of those great waggons that look like boilers on wheels which he finds halting everywhere as he passes.

Every city has its peculiar institutions created out of its own needs; and one of the most notable institutions of Paris is its rag-picking population. In the early morning – and Parisian life commences at an early hour – may be seen in most streets standing on the pathway opposite every court and alley and between every few houses, as still in some American cities, even in parts of New York, large wooden boxes into which the domestics or tenement-holders empty the accumulated dust of the past day. Round these boxes gather and pass on, when the work is done, to fresh fields of labour and pastures new, squalid hungry-looking men and women, the implements of whose craft consist of a coarse bag or basket slung over the shoulder and a little rake with which they must turn over and probe and examine in the minutest manner the dustbins. They pick up and deposit in their baskets, by aid of their rakes, whatever they may find, with the same facility as a Chinaman uses his chopsticks.

Paris is a city of centralization – and centralization and classification are closely allied. In the early times, when centralization is becoming a fact, its forerunner is classification. All things which are similar or analogous become grouped together, and from the grouping of groups rises one whole or central point. We see radiating many long arms with innumerable tentaculae, and in the centre rises a gigantic head with a comprehensive brain and keen eyes to look on every side and ears sensitive to hear – and a voracious mouth to swallow.

Other cities resemble all the birds and beasts and fishes whose appetites and digestions are normal. Paris alone is the analogical apotheosis of the octopus. Product of centralization carried to an *ad absurdum*, it fairly represents the devil fish; and in no respects is the resemblance more curious than in the similarity of the digestive apparatus.

Those intelligent tourists who, having surrendered their individuality into the hands of Messrs Cook or Gaze, 'do' Paris in three days, are often puzzled to know how it is that the dinner which in London would cost about six shillings, can be had for three francs in a café in the Palais Royal. They need have no more wonder if they will but consider the classification which is a theoretic speciality of Parisian life, and adopt all round the fact from which the chiffonier has his genesis.

The Paris of 1850 was not like the Paris of to-day, and those who see the Paris of Napoleon and Baron Haussmann can hardly realize the existence of the state of things forty-five years ago.

Amongst other things, however, which have not changed are those districts where the waste is gathered. Dust is dust all the world over, in every age, and the family likeness of dust-heaps is perfect. The traveller, therefore, who visits the environs of Montrouge can go back in fancy without difficulty to the year 1850.

In this year I was making a prolonged stay in Paris. I was very much in love with a young lady who, though she returned my passion, so far yielded to the wishes of her parents that she had promised not to see me or to correspond with me for a year. I, too, had been compelled to accede to these conditions under a vague hope of parental approval. During the term of probation I had promised to remain out of the country and not to write to my dear one until the expiration of the year.

Naturally the time went heavily with me. There was not one of my own family or circle who could tell me of Alice, and none of her own folk had, I am sorry to say, sufficient generosity to send me even an occasional word of comfort regarding her health and well-being. I spent six months wandering about Europe, but as I could find no satisfactory distraction in travel, I determined to come to Paris, where, at least, I would be within easy hail of London in case any good fortune should call me thither before the appointed time. That 'hope deferred maketh the heart sick' was never better exemplified than in my case, for in addition to the perpetual longing to see the face I loved there was always with me a harrowing anxiety lest some accident should prevent me showing Alice in due time that I had, throughout the long period of probation, been faithful to her trust and my own love. Thus, every adventure which I undertook had a fierce pleasure of its own, for it was fraught with possible consequences greater than it would have ordinarily borne.

Like all travellers I exhausted the places of most interest in the first month of my stay, and was driven in the second month to look for amusement whithersoever I might. Having made sundry journeys to the better-known suburbs, I began to see that there was a *terra incognita*, in so far as the guide book was concerned, in the social wilderness lying between these attractive points. Accordingly I began to systematize my researches, and each day took up the thread of my exploration at the place where I had on the previous day dropped it.

In the process of time my wanderings led me near Montrouge, and I saw that hereabouts lay the Ultima Thule of social exploration – a country as little known as that round the source of the White Nile. And so I determined to investigate philosophically the chiffonier – his habitat, his life, and his means of life.

The job was an unsavoury one, difficult of accomplishment, and with little hope of adequate reward. However, despite reason, obstinacy prevailed, and I entered into my new investigation with a keener energy than I could have summoned to aid me in any investigation leading to any end, valuable or worthy.

One day, late in a fine afternoon, toward the end of September, I entered the holy of holies of the city of dust. The place was evidently the recognized abode of a number of chiffoniers, for some sort of arrangement was manifested in the formation of the dust heaps near the road. I passed amongst these heaps, which stood like orderly sentries, determined to penetrate further and trace dust to its ultimate location.

As I passed along I saw behind the dust heaps a few forms that flitted to and fro, evidently watching with interest the advent of any stranger to such a place. The district was like a small Switzerland, and as I went forward my tortuous course shut out the path behind me.

Presently I got into what seemed a small city or community of chiffoniers. There were a number of shanties or huts, such as may be met with in the remote parts of the Bog of Allan – rude places with wattled walls, plastered with mud and roofs of rude thatch made from stable refuse – such places as one would not like to enter for any consideration, and which even in water-colour could only look picturesque if judiciously treated. In the midst of these huts was one of the strangest adaptations – I cannot say habitations – I had ever seen. An immense old wardrobe, the colossal remnant of some boudoir of Charles VII, or Henry II, had been converted into a dwelling-house. The double doors lay open, so that the entire ménage was open to public view. In the open half of the wardrobe was a common sitting-room of some four feet by six, in which sat, smoking their pipes round a charcoal brazier, no fewer than six old soldiers of the First Republic, with their uniforms torn and worn threadbare. Evidently they were of the *mauvais sujet* class; their bleary eyes and limp jaws told plainly of a common love of absinthe; and their eyes had that haggard, worn look of slumbering ferocity which follows hard in the wake of drink. The other side stood as of old, with its shelves intact, save that they were cut to half their depths, and in each shelf, of which there were six, was a bed made with rags and straw. The half-dozen of worthies who inhabited this structure looked at me curiously as I passed; and when I looked back after going a little way I saw their heads together in a whispered conference. I did not like the look of this at all, for the place was very lonely, and the men looked very, very villainous. However, I did not see any cause for fear, and went on my way, penetrating further and further into the Sahara. The way was tortuous to a degree, and from going round in a series of semi-circles, as one goes in skating with the Dutch roll, I got rather confused with regard to the points of the compass.

When I had penetrated a little way I saw, as I turned the corner of a half-made heap, sitting on a heap of straw an old soldier with threadbare coat.

'Hallo!' said I to my self; 'the First Republic is well represented here in its soldiery.'

As I passed him the old man never even looked up at me, but gazed on the ground with stolid persistency. Again I remarked to myself: 'See what a life of rude warfare can do! This old man's curiosity is a thing of the past.'

When I had gone a few steps, however, I looked back suddenly, and saw that curiosity was not dead, for the veteran had raised his head and was regarding me with a very queer expression. He seemed to me to look very like one of the six worthies in the press. When he saw me looking he dropped his head; and without thinking further of him I went on my way, satisfied that there was a strange likeness between these old warriors.

Presently I met another old soldier in a similar manner. He, too, did not notice me whilst I was passing.

By this time it was getting late in the afternoon, and I began to think of retracing my steps. Accordingly I turned to go back, but could see a number of tracks leading between different mounds and could not ascertain which of them I should take. In my perplexity I wanted to see someone of whom to ask the way, but could see no one. I determined to go on a few mounds further and so try to see someone – not a veteran.

I gained my object, for after going a couple of hundred yards I saw before me a single shanty such as I had seen before – with, however, the difference that this was not one for living in, but merely a roof with three walls open in front. From the evidences which the neighbourhood exhibited I took it to be a place for sorting. Within it was an old woman wrinkled and bent with age; I approached her to ask the way.

She rose as I came close and I asked her my way. She immediately commenced a conversation; and it occurred to me that here in the very centre of the Kingdom of Dust was the place to gather details of the history of Parisian rag-picking – particularly as I could do so from the lips of one who looked like the oldest inhabitant.

I began my inquiries, and the old woman gave me most interesting answers – she had been one of the ceteuces who sat daily before the guillotine and had taken an active part among the women who signalized themselves by their violence in the revolution. While we were talking she said suddenly: 'But m'sieur must be tired standing,' and dusted a rickety old stool for me to sit down. I hardly liked to do so for many reasons; but the poor old woman was so civil that I did not like to run the risk of hurting her by refusing, and moreover the conversation of one who had been at the taking of the Bastille was so interesting that I sat down and so our conversation went on.

While we were talking an old man – older and more bent and wrinkled even than the woman – appeared from behind the shanty. 'Here is Pierre,' said she. 'M'sieur can hear stories now if he wishes, for Pierre was in everything, from the Bastille to Waterloo.' The old man took another stool at my request and we plunged into a sea of revolutionary reminiscences. This old man, albeit clothed like a scarecrow, was like any one of the six veterans.

I was now sitting in the centre of the low hut with the woman on my left hand and the man on my right, each of them being somewhat in front of me. The place was full of all sorts of curious objects of lumber, and of many things that I wished far away. In one corner was a heap of rags which seemed to move from the number of vermin it contained, and in the other a heap of bones whose odour was something shocking. Every now and then, glancing at the heaps, I could see the gleaming eyes of some of the rats which infested the place. These loathsome objects were bad enough, but what looked even more dreadful was an old butcher's axe with an iron handle stained with clots of blood leaning up against the wall on the right-hand side. Still, these things did not give me much concern. The talk of the two old people was so fascinating that I stayed on and on, till the evening came and the dust heaps threw dark shadows over the vales between them.

After a time I began to grow uneasy. I could not tell how or why, but somehow I did not feel satisfied. Uneasiness is an instinct and means warning. The psychic faculties are often the sentries of the intellect, and when they sound alarm the reason begins to act, although perhaps not consciously.

This was so with me. I began to bethink me where I was and by what surrounded, and to wonder how I should fare in case I should be attacked; and then the thought suddenly burst upon me, although without any overt cause, that I was in danger. Prudence whispered: 'Be still and make no sign,' and so I was still and made no sign, for I knew that four cunning eyes were on me. 'Four eyes – if not more.' My God, what a horrible thought! The whole shanty might be surrounded on three sides with villains! I might be in the midst of a band of such desperadoes as only half a century of periodic revolution can produce.

With a sense of danger my intellect and observation quickened, and I grew more watchful than was my wont. I noticed that the old woman's eyes were constantly wandering towards my hands. I looked at them too, and saw the cause – my rings. On my left little finger I had a large signet and on the right a good diamond.

I thought that if there was any danger my first care was to avert suspicion. Accordingly I began to work the conversation round to rag-picking – to the drains – of the things found there; and so by easy stages to jewels. Then, seizing a favourable opportunity, I asked the old woman if she knew anything of such things. She answered that she did, a little. I held out my right hand, and, showing her the diamond, asked her what she thought of that. She answered that her eyes were bad, and stooped over my hand. I said as nonchalantly as I could: 'Pardon me! You will see better thus!' and taking it off handed it to her. An unholy light came into her withered old face, as she touched it. She stole one glance at me swift and keen as a flash of lightning.

She bent over the ring for a moment, her face quite concealed as though examining it. The old man looked straight out of the front of the shanty before him, at the same time fumbling in his pockets and producing a screw of tobacco in a paper and a pipe, which he proceeded to fill. I took advantage of the pause and the momentary rest from the searching eyes on my face to look carefully round the place, now dim and shadowy in the gloaming. There still lay all the heaps of varied reeking foulness; there the terrible blood-stained axe leaning against the wall in the right hand corner, and everywhere, despite the gloom, the baleful glitter of the eyes of the rats. I could see them even through some of the chinks of the boards at the back low down close to the ground. But stay! these latter eyes seemed more than usually large and bright and baleful!

For an instant my heart stood still, and I felt in that whirling condition of mind in which one feels a sort of spiritual drunkenness, and as though the body is only maintained erect in that there is no time for it to fall before recovery. Then, in another second, I was calm – coldly calm, with all my energies in full vigour, with a self-control which I felt to be perfect and with all my feeling and instincts alert.

Now I knew the full extent of my danger: I was watched and surrounded by desperate people! I could not even guess at how many of them were lying there on the ground behind the shanty, waiting for the moment to strike. I knew that I was big and strong, and they knew it, too. They knew also, as I did, that I was an Englishman and would make a fight for it; and so we waited. I had, I felt, gained an advantage in the last few seconds, for I knew my danger and understood the situation. Now, I thought is the test of my courage – the enduring test: the fighting test may come later!

The old woman raised her head and said to me in a satisfied kind of way:

'A very fine ring, indeed – a beautiful ring! Oh, me! I once had such rings, plenty of them, and bracelets and earrings! Oh! for in those fine days I led the town a dance! But they've forgotten me now! They've forgotten me! They? Why they never heard of me! Perhaps their grandfathers remember me, some of them!' and she laughed a harsh, croaking laugh. And then I am bound to say that she astonished me, for she handed me back the ring with a certain suggestion of old-fashioned grace which was not without its pathos.

The old man eyed her with a sort of sudden ferocity, half rising from his stool, and said to me suddenly and hoarsely:

'Let me see!'

I was about to hand the ring when the old woman said:

'No! no, do not give it to Pierre! Pierre is eccentric. He loses things; and such a pretty ring!'

'Cat!' said the old man, savagely. Suddenly the old woman said, rather more loudly than was necessary:

'Wait! I shall tell you something about a ring.' There was something in the sound of her voice that jarred upon me. Perhaps it was my hyper-sensitiveness, wrought up as I was to such a pitch of nervous excitement, but I seemed to think that she was not addressing me. As I stole a glance round the place I saw the eyes of the rats in the bone heaps, but missed the eyes along the back. But even as I looked I saw them again appear. The old woman's 'Wait!' had given me a respite from attack, and the men had sunk back to their reclining posture.

'I once lost a ring – a beautiful diamond hoop that had belonged to a queen, and which was given to me by a farmer of the taxes, who afterwards cut his throat because I sent him away. I thought it must have been stolen, and taxed my people; but I could get no trace. The police came and suggested that it had found its way to the drain. We descended – I in my fine clothes, for I would not trust them with my beautiful ring! I know more of the drains since then, and of rats, too! but I shall never forget the horror of that place – alive with blazing eyes, a wall of them just outside the light of our torches. Well, we got beneath my house. We searched the outlet of the drain, and there in the filth found my ring, and we came out.

'But we found something else before we came! As we were coming toward the opening a lot of sewer rats – human ones this time – came towards us. They told the police that one of their number had gone into the drain, but had not returned. He had gone in only shortly before we had, and, if lost, could hardly be far off. They asked help to seek him, so we turned back. They tried to prevent me going, but I insisted. It was a new excitement, and had I not recovered my ring? Not far did we go till we came on something. There was but little water, and the bottom of the drain was raised with brick, rubbish, and much matter of the kind. He had made a fight for it, even when his torch had gone out. But they were too many for him! They had not been long about it! The bones were still warm; but they were picked clean. They had even eaten their own dead ones and there were bones of rats as well as of the man. They took it cool enough those other – the human ones – and joked of their comrade when they found him dead, though they would have helped him living. Bah! what matters it – life or death?'

'And you had no fear?' I asked her.

'Fear!' she said with a laugh. 'Me have fear? Ask Pierre! But I was younger then, and, as I came through that horrible drain with its wall of greedy eyes, always moving with the circle of the light from the torches, I did not feel easy. I kept on before the men, though! It is a way I have! I never let the men get it before me. All I want is a chance and a means! And they ate him up – took every trace away except the bones; and no one knew it, nor no sound of him was ever heard!' Here she broke into a chuckling fit of the ghastliest merriment which it was ever my lot to hear and see. A great poetess describes her heroine singing: 'Oh! to see or hear her singing! Scarce I know which is the divinest.'

And I can apply the same idea to the old crone – in all save the divinity, for I scarce could tell which was the most hellish – the harsh, malicious, satisfied, cruel laugh, or the leering grin, and the horrible square opening of the mouth like a tragic mask, and the yellow gleam of the few discoloured teeth in the shapeless gums. In that laugh and with that grin and the chuckling satisfaction I knew as well as if it had been spoken to me in words of thunder that my murder was settled, and the murderers only bided the proper time for its accomplishment. I could read between the lines of her gruesome story the commands to her accomplices. 'Wait,' she seemed to say, 'bide your time. I shall strike the first blow. Find the weapon for me, and I shall make the opportunity! He shall not escape! Keep him quiet, and then no one will be wiser. There will be no outcry, and the rats will do their work!'

It was growing darker and darker; the night was coming. I stole a glance round the shanty, still all the same! The bloody axe in the corner, the heaps of filth, and the eyes on the bone heaps and in the crannies of the floor.

Pierre had been still ostensibly filling his pipe; he now struck a light and began to puff away at it. The old woman said:

'Dear heart, how dark it is! Pierre, like a good lad, light the lamp!'

Pierre got up and with the lighted match in his hand touched the wick of a lamp which hung at one side of the entrance to the shanty, and which had a reflector that threw the light all over the place. It was evidently that which was used for the sorting at night.

'Not that, stupid! Not that! The lantern!' she called out to him.

He immediately blew it out, saying: 'All right, mother, I'll find it,' and he hustled about the left corner of the room – the old woman saying through the darkness:

'The lantern! the lantern! Oh! That is the light that is most useful to us poor folks. The lantern was the friend of the revolution! It is the friend of the chiffonier! It helps us when all else fails.'

Hardly had she said the word when there was a kind of creaking of the whole place, and something was steadily dragged over the roof.

Again I seemed to read between the lines of her words. I knew the lesson of the lantern.

'One of you get on the roof with a noose and strangle him as he passes out if we fail within.'

As I looked out of the opening I saw the loop of a rope outlined black against the lurid sky. I was now, indeed, beset!

Pierre was not long in finding the lantern. I kept my eyes fixed through the darkness on the old woman. Pierre struck his light, and by its flash I saw the old woman raise from the ground beside her where it had mysteriously appeared, and then hide in the folds of her gown, a long sharp knife or dagger. It seemed to be like a butcher's sharpening iron fined to a keen point.

The lantern was lit.

'Bring it here, Pierre,' she said. 'Place it in the doorway where we can see it. See how nice it is! It shuts out the darkness from us; it is just right!'

Just right for her and her purposes! It threw all its light on my face, leaving in gloom the faces of both Pierre and the woman, who sat outside of me on each side.

I felt that the time of action was approaching; but I knew now that the first signal and movement would come from the woman, and so watched her.

I was all unarmed, but I had made up my mind what to do. At the first movement I would seize the butcher's axe in the right-hand corner and fight my way out. At least, I would die hard. I stole a glance round to fix its exact locality so that I could not fail to seize it at the first effort, for then, if ever, time and accuracy would be precious.

Good God! It was gone! All the horror of the situation burst upon me; but the bitterest thought of all was that if the issue of the terrible position should be against me Alice would infallibly suffer. Either she would believe me false – and any lover, or any one who has ever been one, can

507

imagine the bitterness of the thought – or else she would go on loving long after I had been lost to her and to the world, so that her life would be broken and embittered, shattered with disappointment and despair. The very magnitude of the pain braced me up and nerved me to bear the dread scrutiny of the plotters.

I think I did not betray myself. The old woman was watching me as a cat does a mouse; she had her right hand hidden in the folds of her gown, clutching, I knew, that long, cruel-looking dagger. Had she seen any disappointment in my face she would, I felt, have known that the moment had come, and would have sprung on me like a tigress, certain of taking me unprepared.

I looked out into the night, and there I saw new cause for danger. Before and around the hut were at a little distance some shadowy forms; they were quite still, but I knew that they were all alert and on guard. Small chance for me now in that direction.

Again I stole a glance round the place. In moments of great excitement and of great danger, which is excitement, the mind works very quickly, and the keenness of the faculties which depend on the mind grows in proportion. I now felt this. In an instant I took in the whole situation. I saw that the axe had been taken through a small hole made in one of the rotten boards. How rotten they must be to allow of such a thing being done without a particle of noise.

The hut was a regular murder-trap, and was guarded all around. A garroter lay on the roof ready to entangle me with his noose if I should escape the dagger of the old hag. In front the way was guarded by I know not how many watchers. And at the back was a row of desperate men – I had seen their eyes still through the crack in the boards of the floor, when last I looked – as they lay prone waiting for the signal to start erect. If it was to be ever, now for it!

As nonchalantly as I could I turned slightly on my stool so as to get my right leg well under me. Then with a sudden jump, turning my head, and guarding it with my hands, and with the fighting instinct of the knights of old, I breathed my lady's name, and hurled myself against the back wall of the hut.

Watchful as they were, the suddenness of my movement surprised both Pierre and the old woman. As I crashed through the rotten timbers I saw the old woman rise with a leap like a tiger and heard her low gasp of baffled rage. My feet lit on something that moved, and as I jumped away I knew that I had stepped on the back of one of the row of men lying on their faces outside the hut. I was torn with nails and splinters, but otherwise unhurt. Breathless I rushed up the mound in front of me, hearing as I went the dull crash of the shanty as it collapsed into a mass.

It was a nightmare climb. The mound, though but low, was awfully steep, and with each step I took the mass of dust and cinders tore down with me and gave way under my feet. The dust rose and choked me; it was sickening, fœtid, awful; but my climb was, I felt, for life or death, and I struggled on. The seconds seemed hours; but the few moments I had in starting, combined with my youth and strength, gave me a great advantage, and though several forms struggled after me in deadly silence which was more dreadful than any sound, I easily reached the top. Since then I have climbed the cone of Vesuvius, and as I struggled up that dreary steep amid the sulphurous fumes the memory of that awful night at Montrouge came back to me so vividly that I almost grew faint.

The mound was one of the tallest in the region of dust, and as I struggled to the top, panting for breath and with my heart beating like a sledge-hammer, I saw away to my left the dull red gleam of the sky, and nearer still the flashing of lights. Thank God! I knew where I was now and where lay the road to Paris!

For two or three seconds I paused and looked back. My pursuers were still well behind me, but struggling up resolutely, and in deadly silence. Beyond, the shanty was a wreck – a mass of timber and moving forms. I could see it well, for flames were already bursting out; the rags and straw had evidently caught fire from the lantern. Still silence there! Not a sound! These old wretches could die game, anyhow.

I had no time for more than a passing glance, for as I cast an eye round the mound preparatory to making my descent I saw several dark forms rushing round on either side to cut me off on my way. It was now a race for life. They were trying to head me on my way to Paris, and with the instinct of the moment I dashed down to the right-hand side. I was just in time, for, though I came as it seemed to me down the steep in a few steps, the wary old men who were watching me turned back, and one, as I rushed by into the opening between the two mounds in front, almost struck me a blow with that terrible butcher's axe. There could surely not be two such weapons about!

Then began a really horrible chase. I easily ran ahead of the old men, and even when some younger ones and a few women joined in the hunt I easily distanced them. But I did not know the way, and I could not even guide myself by the light in the sky, for I was running away from it. I had heard that, unless of conscious purpose, hunted men turn always to the left, and so I found it now; and so, I suppose, knew also my pursuers, who were more animals than men, and with cunning or instinct had found out such secrets for themselves: for on finishing a quick spurt, after which I intended to take a moment's breathing space, I suddenly saw ahead of me two or three forms swiftly passing behind a mound to the right.

I was in the spider's web now indeed! But with the thought of this new danger came the resource of the hunted, and so I darted down the next turning to the right. I continued in this direction for some hundred yards, and then, making a turn to the left again, felt certain that I had, at any rate, avoided the danger of being surrounded.

But not of pursuit, for on came the rabble after me, steady, dogged, relentless, and still in grim silence.

In the greater darkness the mounds seemed now to be somewhat smaller than before, although – for the night was closing – they looked bigger in proportion. I was now well ahead of my pursuers, so I made a dart up the mound in front.

Oh joy of joys! I was close to the edge of this inferno of dust heaps. Away behind me the red light of Paris was in the sky, and towering up behind rose the heights of Montmartre – a dim light, with here and there brilliant points like stars.

Restored to vigour in a moment, I ran over the few remaining mounds of decreasing size, and found myself on the level land beyond. Even then, however, the prospect was not inviting. All before me was dark and dismal, and I had evidently come on one of those dank, low-lying waste places which are found here and there in the neighbourhood of great cities. Places of waste and desolation, where the space is required for the ultimate agglomeration of all that is noxious, and the ground is so poor as to create no desire of occupancy even in the lowest squatter. With eyes accustomed to the gloom of the evening, and away now from the shadows of those dreadful dust heaps, I could see much more easily than I could a little while ago. It might have been, of course, that the glare in the sky of the lights of Paris, though the city was some miles away, was reflected here. Howsoever it was, I saw well enough to take bearings for certainly some little distance around me.

In front was a bleak, flat waste that seemed almost dead level, with here and there the dark shimmering of stagnant pools. Seemingly far off on the right, amid a small cluster of scattered lights, rose a dark mass of Fort Montrouge, and away to the left in the dim distance, pointed with stray gleams from cottage windows, the lights in the sky showed the locality of Bicêtre. A moment's thought decided me to take to the right and try to reach Montrouge. There at least would be some sort of safety, and I might possibly long before come on some of the cross roads which I knew. Somewhere, not far off, must lie the strategic road made to connect the outlying chain of forts circling the city.

Then I looked back. Coming over the mounds, and outlined black against the glare of the Parisian horizon, I saw several moving figures, and still a way to the right several more deploying out between me and my destination. They evidently meant to cut me off in this direction, and so my choice became constricted; it lay now between going straight ahead or turning to the left. Stooping to the ground, so as to get the advantage of the horizon as a line of sight, I looked carefully in this direction, but could detect no sign of my enemies. I argued that as they had not guarded or were not trying to guard that point, there was evidently danger to me there already. So I made up my mind to go straight on before me.

It was not an inviting prospect, and as I went on the reality grew worse. The ground became soft and oozy, and now and again gave way beneath me in a sickening kind of way. I seemed somehow to be going down, for I saw round me places seemingly more elevated than where I was, and this in a place which from a little way back seemed dead level. I looked around, but could see none of my pursuers. This was strange, for all along these birds of the night had followed me through the darkness as well as though it was broad daylight. How I blamed myself for coming out in my light-coloured tourist suit of tweed. The silence, and my not being able to see my enemies, whilst I felt that they were watching me, grew appalling, and in the hope of some one not of this ghastly crew hearing me I raised my voice and shouted several times. There was not the slightest response; not even an echo rewarded my efforts. For a while I stood stock still and kept my eyes in one direction. On one of the rising places around me I saw something dark move along, then another, and another. This was to my left, and seemingly moving to head me off.

I thought that again I might with my skill as a runner elude my enemies at this game, and so with all my speed darted forward.

Splash!

My feet had given way in a mass of slimy rubbish, and I had fallen headlong into a reeking, stagnant pool. The water and the mud in which my arms sank up to the elbows was filthy and nauseous beyond description, and in the suddenness of my fall I had actually swallowed some of the filthy stuff, which nearly choked me, and made me gasp for breath. Never shall I forget the moments during which I stood trying to recover myself almost fainting from the fœtid odour of the filthy pool, whose white mist rose ghostlike around. Worst of all, with the acute despair of the hunted animal when he sees the pursuing pack closing on him, I saw before my eyes whilst I stood helpless the dark forms of my pursuers moving swiftly to surround me.

It is curious how our minds work on odd matters even when the energies of thought are seemingly concentrated on some terrible and pressing need. I was in momentary peril of my life: my safety depended on my action, and my choice of alternatives coming now with almost every step I took, and yet I could not but think of the strange dogged

511

persistency of these old men. Their silent resolution, their steadfast, grim, persistency even in such a cause commanded, as well as fear, even a measure of respect. What must they have been in the vigour of their youth. I could understand now that whirlwind rush on the bridge of Arcola, that scornful exclamation of the Old Guard at Waterloo! Unconscious cerebration has its own pleasures, even at such moments; but fortunately it does not in any way clash with the thought from which action springs.

I realized at a glance that so far I was defeated in my object, my enemies as yet had won. They had succeeded in surrounding me on three sides, and were bent on driving me off to the left hand, where there was already some danger for me, for they had left no guard. I accepted the alternative – it was a case of Hobson's choice and run. I had to keep the lower ground, for my pursuers were on the higher places. However, though the ooze and broken ground impeded me my youth and training made me able to hold my ground, and by keeping a diagonal line I not only kept them from gaining on me but even began to distance them. This gave me new heart and strength, and by this time habitual training was beginning to tell and my second wind had come. Before me the ground rose slightly. I rushed up the slope and found before me a waste of watery slime, with a low dyke or bank looking black and grim beyond. I felt that if I could but reach that dyke in safety I could there, with solid ground under my feet and some kind of path to guide me, find with comparative ease a way out of my troubles. After a glance right and left and seeing no one near, I kept my eyes for a few minutes to their rightful work of aiding my feet whilst I crossed the swamp. It was rough, hard work, but there was little danger, merely toil; and a short time took me to the dyke. I rushed up the slope exulting; but here again I met a new shock. On either side of me rose a number of crouching figures. From right and left they rushed at me. Each body held a rope.

The cordon was nearly complete. I could pass on neither side, and the end was near.

There was only one chance, and I took it. I hurled myself across the dyke, and escaping out of the very clutches of my foes threw myself into the stream.

At any other time I should have thought that water foul and filthy, but now it was as welcome as the most crystal stream to the parched traveller. It was a highway of safety!

My pursuers rushed after me. Had only one of them held the rope it would have been all up with me, for he could have entangled me before I had time to swim a stroke; but the many hands holding it embarrassed and delayed them, and when the rope struck the water I heard the splash well behind me. A few minutes' hard swimming took me across the stream. Refreshed with the immersion and encouraged by the escape, I climbed the dyke in comparative gaiety of spirits.

From the top I looked back. Through the darkness I saw my assailants scattering up and down along the dyke. The pursuit was evidently not ended, and again I had to choose my course. Beyond the dyke where I stood was a wild, swampy space very similar to that which I had crossed. I determined to shun such a place, and thought for a moment whether I would take up or down the dyke. I thought I heard a sound – the muffled sound of oars, so I listened, and then shouted.

No response; but the sound ceased. My enemies had evidently got a boat of some kind. As they were on the up side of me I took the down path and began to run. As I passed to the left of where I had entered the water I heard several splashes, soft and stealthy, like the sound a rat makes as he plunges into the stream, but vastly greater; and as I looked I saw the dark sheen of the water broken by the ripples of several advancing heads. Some of my enemies were swimming the stream also.

And now behind me, up the stream, the silence was broken by the quick rattle and creak of oars; my enemies were in hot pursuit. I put my best leg foremost and ran on. After a break of a couple of minutes I looked back, and by a gleam of light through the ragged clouds I saw several dark forms climbing the bank behind me. The wind had now begun to rise, and the water beside me was ruffled and beginning to break in tiny waves on the bank. I had to keep my eyes pretty well on the ground before me, lest I should stumble, for I knew that to stumble was death. After a few minutes I looked back behind me. On the dyke were only a few dark figures, but crossing the waste, swampy ground were many more. What new danger this portended I did not know – could only guess. Then as I ran it seemed to me that my track kept ever sloping away to the right. I looked up ahead and saw that the river was much wider than before, and that the dyke on which I stood fell quite away, and beyond it was another stream on whose near bank I saw some of the dark forms now across the marsh. I was on an island of some kind.

My situation was now indeed terrible, for my enemies had hemmed me in on every side. Behind came the quickening roll of the oars, as though my pursuers knew that the end was close. Around me on every side was desolation; there was not a roof or light, as far as I could see. Far off to the right rose some dark mass, but what it was I knew not. For a moment I paused to think what I should do, not for more, for my pursuers were drawing closer. Then my mind was made up. I slipped down the bank and took to the water. I struck out straight ahead so as to gain the current by clearing the backwater of the island, for such I presume it was, when I had passed into the stream. I waited till a cloud came driving across the moon and leaving all in darkness. Then I took off my hat and laid it softly on the water floating with the stream, and a second after dived to the right and struck out under water with all my might. I was, I suppose, half a minute under water, and when I rose came up as softly as I could, and turning, looked back. There went my light brown hat floating merrily away. Close behind it came a rickety old boat, driven furiously by a pair of oars. The moon was still partly obscured by the drifting clouds, but in the partial light I could see a man in the bows holding aloft ready to strike what appeared to me to be that same dreadful pole-axe which I had before escaped. As I looked the boat drew closer, closer, and the man struck savagely. The hat disappeared. The man fell forward, almost out of the boat. His comrades dragged him in but without the axe, and then as I turned with all my energies bent on reaching the further bank, I heard the fierce whirr of the muttered 'Sacré!' which marked the anger of my baffled pursuers.

That was the first sound I had heard from human lips during all this dreadful chase, and full as it was of menace and danger to me it was a welcome sound for it broke that awful silence which shrouded and appalled me. It was as though an overt sign that my opponents were men and not ghosts, and that with them I had, at least, the chance of a man, though but one against many.

But now that the spell of silence was broken the sounds came thick and fast. From boat to shore and back from shore to boat came quick question and answer, all in the fiercest whispers. I looked back – a fatal thing to do – for in the instant someone caught sight of my face, which showed white on the dark water, and shouted. Hands pointed to me, and in a moment or two the boat was under way, and following hard after me. I had but a little way to go, but quicker and quicker came the boat after me. A few more strokes and I would be on the shore, but I felt the oncoming of the boat, and expected each second to feel the crash of an oar or other weapon on my head. Had I not seen that dreadful axe disappear in the water I do not think that I could have won the shore. I heard the muttered curses of those not rowing and the laboured breath of the rowers. With one supreme effort for life or liberty I touched the bank and sprang up it. There was not a single second to spare, for hard behind me the boat grounded and several dark forms sprang after me. I gained the top of the dyke, and keeping to the left ran on again. The boat put off and followed down the stream. Seeing this I feared danger in this direction, and quickly turning, ran down the dyke on the other side, and after passing a short stretch of marshy ground gained a wild, open flat country and sped on.

Still behind me came on my relentless pursuers. Far away, below me, I saw the same dark mass as before, but now grown closer and greater. My heart gave a great thrill of delight, for I knew that it must be the fortress of Bicêtre, and with new courage I ran on. I had heard that between each and all of the protecting forts of Paris there are strategic ways, deep sunk roads, where soldiers marching should be sheltered from an enemy. I knew that if I could gain this road I would be safe, but in the darkness I could not see any sign of it, so, in blind hope of striking it, I ran on.

Presently I came to the edge of a deep cut, and found that down below me ran a road guarded on each side by a ditch of water fenced on either side by a straight, high wall.

Getting fainter and dizzier, I ran on; the ground got more broken — more and more still, till I staggered and fell, and rose again, and ran on in the blind anguish of the hunted. Again the thought of Alice nerved me. I would not be lost and wreck her life: I would fight and struggle for life to the bitter end. With a great effort I caught the top of the wall. As, scrambling like a catamount, I drew myself up, I actually felt a hand touch the sole of my foot. I was now on a sort of causeway, and before me I saw a dim light. Blind and dizzy, I ran on, staggered, and fell, rising, covered with dust and blood.

'Halt là!'

The words sounded like a voice from heaven. A blaze of light seemed to enwrap me, and I shouted with joy.

'Qui va là?' The rattle of musketry, the flash of steel before my eyes. Instinctively I stopped, though close behind me came a rush of my pursuers.

Another word or two, and out from a gateway poured, as it seemed to me, a tide of red and blue, as the guard turned out. All around seemed blazing with light, and the flash of steel, the clink and rattle of arms, and the loud, harsh voices of command. As I fell forward, utterly exhausted, a soldier caught me. I looked back in dreadful expectation, and saw the mass of dark forms disappearing into the night. Then I must have fainted. When I recovered my senses I was in the guard room. They gave me brandy, and after a while I was able to tell them something of what had passed. Then a commissary of police appeared, apparently out of the empty air, as is the way of the Parisian police officer. He listened attentively, and then had a moment's consultation with the officer in command. Apparently they were agreed, for they asked me if I were ready now to come with them.

'Where to?' I asked, rising to go.

'Back to the dust heaps. We shall, perhaps, catch them yet!'

'I shall try!' said I.

He eyed me for a moment keenly, and said suddenly:—

515

'Would you like to wait a while or till tomorrow, young Englishman?' This touched me to the quick, as, perhaps, he intended, and I jumped to my feet.

'Come now!' I said; 'now! now! An Englishman is always ready for his duty!'

The commissary was a good fellow, as well as a shrewd one; he slapped my shoulder kindly. 'Brave garçon!' he said. 'Forgive me, but I knew what would do you most good. The guard is ready. Come!'

And so, passing right through the guard room, and through a long vaulted passage, we were out into the night. A few of the men in front had powerful lanterns. Through courtyards and down a sloping way we passed out through a low archway to a sunken road, the same that I had seen in my flight. The order was given to get at the double, and with a quick, springing stride, half run, half walk, the soldiers went swiftly along. I felt my strength renewed again – such is the difference between hunter and hunted. A very short distance took us to a low-lying pontoon bridge across the stream, and evidently very little higher up than I had struck it. Some effort had evidently been made to damage it, for the ropes had all been cut, and one of the chains had been broken. I heard the officer say to the commissary:

'We are just in time! A few more minutes, and they would have destroyed the bridge. Forward, quicker still!' and on we went. Again we reached a pontoon on the winding stream; as we came up we heard the hollow boom of the metal drums as the effort to destroy the bridge was again renewed. A word of command was given, and several men raised their rifles.

'Fire!' A volley rang out. There was a muffled cry, and the dark forms dispersed. But the evil was done, and we saw the far end of the pontoon swing into the stream. This was a serious delay, and it was nearly an hour before we had renewed ropes and restored the bridge sufficiently to allow us to cross.

We renewed the chase. Quicker, quicker we went towards the dust heaps.

After a time we came to a place that I knew. There were the remains of a fire – a few smouldering wood ashes still cast a red glow, but the bulk of the ashes were cold. I knew the site of the hut and the hill behind it up which I had rushed, and in the flickering glow the eyes of the rats still shone with a sort of phosphorescence. The commissary spoke a word to the officer, and he cried:

'Halt!'

The soldiers were ordered to spread around and watch, and then we commenced to examine the ruins. The commissary himself began to lift away the charred boards and rubbish. These the soldiers took and piled together. Presently he started back, then bent down and rising beckoned me.

'See!' he said.

It was a gruesome sight. There lay a skeleton face downwards, a woman by the lines – an old woman by the coarse fibre of the bone. Between the ribs rose a long spike-like dagger made from a butcher's sharpening knife, its keen point buried in the spine.

'You will observe,' said the commissary to the officer and to me as he took out his note book, 'that the woman must have fallen on her dagger. The rats are many here – see their eyes glistening among that heap of bones – and you will also notice' – I shuddered as he placed his hand on the skeleton – 'that but little time was lost by them, for the bones are scarcely cold!'

There was no other sign of any one near, living or dead; and so deploying again into line the soldiers passed on. Presently we came to the hut made of the old wardrobe. We approached. In five of the six compartments was an old man sleeping – sleeping so soundly that even the glare of the lanterns did not wake them. Old and grim and grizzled they looked, with their gaunt, wrinkled, bronze faces and their white moustaches.

The officer called out harshly and loudly a word of command, and in an instant each one of them was on his feet before us and standing at 'attention!'

'What do you here?'

'We sleep,' was the answer.

'Where are the other chiffoniers?' asked the commissary.

'Gone to work.'

'And you?'

'We are on guard!'

'Peste!' laughed the officer grimly, as he looked at the old men one after the other in the face and added with cool deliberate cruelty: 'Asleep on duty! Is this the manner of the Old Guard? No wonder, then, a Waterloo!'

By the gleam of the lantern I saw the grim old faces grown deadly pale, and almost shuddered at the look in the eyes of the old men as the laugh of the soldiers echoed the grim pleasantry of the officer.

I felt in that moment that I was in some measure avenged.

For a moment they looked as if they would throw themselves on the taunter, but years of their life had schooled them and they remained still.

'You are but five,' said the commissary: 'where is the sixth?' The answer came with a grim chuckle.

'He is there!' and the speaker pointed to the bottom of the wardrobe.

'He died last night. You won't find much of him. The burial of the rats is quick!'

The commissary stooped and looked in. Then he turned to the officer and said calmly:

'We may as well go back. No trace here now; nothing to prove that man was the one wounded by your soldiers' bullets! Probably they murdered him to cover up the trace. See!' again he stooped and placed his hands on the skeleton. 'The rats work quickly and there are many. These bones are warm!'

I shuddered, and so did many more of those around me.

'Form!' said the officer, and so in marching order, with the lanterns swinging in front and the manacled veterans in the midst, with steady tramp we took ourselves out of the dust heaps and turned backward to the fortress of Bicêtre.

* * *

My year of probation has long since ended, and Alice is my wife. But when I look back upon that trying twelvemonth one of the most vivid incidents that memory recalls is that associated with my visit to the City of Dust.

A DREAM OF RED HANDS

The first opinion given to me regarding Jacob Settle was a simple descriptive statement, 'He's a down-in-the-mouth chap': but I found that it embodied the thoughts and ideas of all his fellow-workmen. There was in the phrase a certain easy tolerance, an absence of positive feeling of any kind, rather than any complete opinion, which marked pretty accurately the man's place in public esteem. Still, there was some dissimilarity between this and his appearance which unconsciously set me thinking, and by degrees, as I saw more of the place and the workmen, I came to have a special interest in him. He was, I found, for ever doing kindnesses, not involving money expenses beyond his humble means, but in the manifold ways of forethought and forbearance and self-repression which are of the truer charities of life. Women and children trusted him implicitly, though, strangely enough, he rather shunned them, except when anyone was sick, and then he made his appearance to help if he could, timidly and awkwardly. He led a very solitary life, keeping house by himself in a tiny cottage, or rather hut, of one room, far on the edge of the moorland. His existence seemed so sad and solitary that I wished to cheer it up, and for the purpose took the occasion when we had both been sitting up with a child, injured by me through accident, to offer to lend him books. He gladly accepted, and as we parted in the grey of the dawn I felt that something of mutual confidence had been established between us.

The books were always most carefully and punctually returned, and in time Jacob Settle and I became quite friends. Once or twice as I crossed the moorland on Sundays I looked in on him; but on such occasions he was shy and ill at ease so that I felt diffident about calling to see him. He would never under any circumstances come into my own lodgings.

One Sunday afternoon, I was coming back from a long walk beyond the moor, and as I passed Settle's cottage stopped at the door to say 'How do you do?' to him. As the door was shut, I thought that he was out, and merely knocked for form's sake, or through habit, not expecting to get any answer. To my surprise, I heard a feeble voice from within, though what was said I could not hear. I entered at once, and found Jacob lying half-dressed upon his bed. He was as pale as death, and the sweat was simply rolling off his face. His hands were unconsciously gripping the bedclothes as a drowning man holds on to whatever he may grasp. As I came in he half arose, with a wild, hunted look in his eyes, which were wide open and staring, as though something of horror had come before him; but when he recognized me he sank back on the couch with a smothered sob of relief and closed hs eyes. I stood by him for a while, quite a minute or two, while he gasped. Then he opened his eyes and looked at me, but with such a despairing, woeful expression that, as I am a living man, I would have rather seen that frozen look of horror. I sat down beside him and asked after his health. For a while he would not answer me except to say that he was not ill; but then, after scrutinizing me closely, he half arose on his elbow and said:

'I thank you kindly, sir, but I'm simply telling you the truth. I am not ill, as men call it, though God knows whether there be not worse sicknesses than doctors know of. I'll tell you, as you are so kind, but I trust that you won't even mention such a thing to a living soul, for it might work me more and greater woe. I am suffering from a bad dream.'

'A bad dream!' I said, hoping to cheer him; 'but dreams pass away with the light – even with waking.' There I stopped, for before he spoke I saw the answer in his desolate look round the little place.

'No! no! that's all well for people that live in comfort and with those they love around them. It is a thousand times worse for those who live alone and have to do so. What cheer is there for me, waking here in the silence of the night, with the wide moor around me full of voices and full of faces that make my waking a worse dream than my sleep? Ah, young sir, you have no past that can send its legions to people the darkness and the empty space, and I pray the good God that you may never have!' As he spoke, there was such an almost irresistible gravity of conviction in his manner that I abandoned my remonstrance about his solitary life. I felt that I was in the presence of some secret influence which I could not fathom. To my relief, for I knew not what to say, he went on:

'Two nights past have I dreamed it. It was hard enough the first night, but I came through it. Last night the expectation was in itself almost worse than the dream – until the dream came, and then it swept away every remembrance of lesser pain. I stayed awake till just before the dawn, and then it came again, and ever since I have been in such an agony as I am sure the dying feel, and with it all the dread of to-night.' Before he had got to the end of the sentence my mind was made up, and I felt that I could speak to him more cheerfully.

'Try and get to sleep early tonight – in fact, before the evening has passed away. The sleep will refresh you, and I promise you there will not be any bad dreams after to-night.' He shook his head hopelessly, so I sat a little longer and then left him.

When I got home I mady my arrangements for the night, for I had made up my mind to share Jacob Settle's lonely vigil in his cottage on the moor. I judged that if he got to sleep before sunset he would wake well before midnight, and so, just as the bells of the city were striking eleven, I stood opposite his door armed with a bag, in which were my supper, an extra large flask, a couple of candles, and a book. The moonlight was bright, and flooded the whole moor, till it was almost as light as day; but ever and anon black clouds drove across the sky, and made a darkness which by comparison seemed almost tangible. I opened the door softly, and entered without waking Jacob, who lay asleep with his white face upward. He was still, and again bathed in sweat. I tried to imagine what visions were passing before those closed eyes which could bring with them the misery and woe which were stamped on the face, but fancy failed me, and I waited for the awakening. It came suddenly, and in a fashion which touched me to the quick, for the hollow groan that broke from the man's white lips as he half arose and sank back was manifestly the realization or completion of some train of thought which had gone before.

'If this be dreaming,' said I to myself, 'then it must be based on some very terrible reality. What can have been that unhappy fact that he spoke of?'

While I thus spoke, he realized that I was with him. It struck me as strange that he had no period of that doubt as to whether dream or reality surrounded him which commonly marks an unexpected environment of waking men. With a positive cry of joy, he seized my hand and held it in his two wet, trembling hands, as a frightened child clings on to someone whom it loves. I tried to soothe him:

'There, there! it is all right. I have come to stay with you to-night, and together we will try to fight this evil dream.' He let go my hand suddenly, and sank back on his bed and covered his eyes with his hands.

'Fight it? – the evil dream! Ah! no, sir, no! No mortal power can fight that dream, for it comes from God – and is burned in here;' and he beat upon his forehead. Then he went on:

'It is the same dream, ever the same, and yet it grows in its power to torture me every time it comes.'

'What is the dream?' I asked, thinking that the speaking of it might give him some relief, but he shrank away from me, and after a long pause said:

'No, I had better not tell it. It may not come again.'

There was manifestly something to conceal from me – something that lay behind the dream, so I answered:

'All right. I hope you have seen the last of it. But if it should come again, you will tell me, will you not? I ask, not out of curiosity, but because I think it may relieve you to speak.' He answered with what I thought was almost an undue amount of solemnity:

'If it comes again, I shall tell you all.'

Then I tried to get his mind away from the subject to more mundane things, so I produced supper, and made him share it with me, including the contents of the flask. After a little he braced up, and when I lit my cigar, having given him another, we smoked a full hour, and talked of many things. Little by little the comfort of his body stole over his mind, and I could see sleep laying her gentle hands on his eyelids. He felt it, too, and told me that now he felt all right, and I might safely leave him; but I told him that, right or wrong, I was going to see in the daylight. So I lit my other candle, and began to read as he fell asleep.

By degrees I got interested in my book, so interested that presently I was startled by its dropping out of my hands. I looked and saw that Jacob was still asleep, and I was rejoiced to see that there was on his face a look of unwonted happiness, while his lips seemed to move with unspoken words. Then I turned to my work again, and again woke, but this time to feel chilled to my very marrow by hearing the voice from the bed beside me:

521

'Not with those red hands! Never! never!' On looking at him, I found that he was still asleep. He woke, however, in an instant, and did not seem surprised to see me; there was again that strange apathy as to his surroundings. Then I said:

'Settle, tell me your dream. You may speak freely, for I shall hold your confidence sacred. While we both live I shall never mention what you may choose to tell me.'

He replied:

'I said I would; but I had better tell you first what goes before the dream, that you may understand. I was a schoolmaster when I was a very young man; it was only a parish school in a little village in the West Country. No need to mention any names. Better not. I was engaged to be married to a young girl whom I loved and almost reverenced. It was the old story. While we were waiting for the time when we could afford to set up house together, another man came along. He was nearly as young as I was, and handsome, and a gentleman, with all a gentleman's attractive ways for a woman of our class. He would go fishing, and she would meet him while I was at my work in school. I reasoned with her and implored her to give him up. I offered to get married at once and go away and begin the world in a strange country; but she would not listen to anything I could say, and I could see that she was infatuated with him. Then I took it on myself to meet the man and ask him to deal well with the girl, for I thought he might mean honestly by her, so that there might be no talk or chance of talk on the part of others. I went where I should meet him with none by, and we met!' Here Jacob Settle had to pause, for something seemed to rise in his throat, and he almost gasped for breath. Then he went on:

'Sir, as God is above us, there was no selfish thought in my heart that day. I loved my pretty Mabel too well to be content with a part of her love, and I had thought of my own unhappiness too often not to have come to realize that, whatever might come to her, my hope was gone. He was insolent to me – you, sir, who are a gentleman, cannot know, perhaps, how galling can be the insolence of one who is above you in station – but I bore with that. I implored him to deal well with the girl, for what might be only a pastime of an idle hour with him might be the breaking of her heart. For I had never had a thought of her truth, or that the worst of harm could come to her – it was only the unhappiness to her heart I feared. But when I asked him when he intended to marry her his laughter galled me so that I lost my temper and told him that I would not stand by and see her life made unhappy. Then he grew angry too, and in his anger said such cruel things of her that then and there I swore he should not live to do her harm. God knows how it came about, for in such moments of passion it is hard to remember the steps from a word to a blow, but I found myself standing over his dead body, with my hands crimson with the blood that welled from his torn throat. We were alone and he was a stranger, with none of his kin to seek for him and murder does not always out – not all at once. His bones may be whitening still, for all I know, in the pool of the river where I left him. No one suspected his absence, or why it was, except my poor Mabel, and she dared not speak. But it was all in vain, for when I came back again after an absence of months – for I could not live in the place – I learned that her shame had come and that she had died in it. Hitherto I had been borne up by the thought that my ill deed had saved her future, but now, when I learned that I had been too late, and that my poor love was smirched with that man's sin, I fled away with the sense of my useless guilt upon me more heavily than I could bear. Ah! sir, you that have not done such a sin don't know what it is to carry it with you. You may think that custom makes it easy to you, but it is not so. It grows and grows with every hour, till it becomes intolerable, and with it growing, too, the feeling that you must for ever stand outside Heaven. You don't know what that means, and I pray God that you never may. Ordinary men, to whom all things are possible, don't often, if ever, think of Heaven. It is a name, and nothing more, and they are content to wait and let things be, but to those who are doomed to be shut out for ever you cannot think what it means, you cannot guess or measure the terrible endless longing to see the gates opened, and to be able to join the white figures within.

'And this brings me to my dream. It seemed that the portal was before me, with great gates of massive steel with bars of the thickness of a mast, rising to the very clouds, and so close that between them was just a glimpse of a crystal grotto, on whose shining walls were figured many white-clad forms with faces radiant with joy. When I stood before the gate my heart and my soul were so full of rapture and longing that I forgot. And there stood at the gate two mighty angels with sweeping wings, and, oh! so stern of countenance. They held each in one hand a flaming sword, and in the other the latchet, which moved to and fro at their lightest touch. Nearer were figures all draped in black, with heads covered so that only the eyes were seen, and they handed to each who came white garments such as the angels wear. A low murmur came that told that all should put on their own robes, and without soil, or the angels would not pass them in, but would smite them down with the flaming swords. I was eager to don my own garment, and hurriedly threw it over me and stepped swiftly to the gate; but it moved not, and the angels, loosing the latchet, pointed to my dress. I looked down, and was aghast, for the whole robe was smeared with blood. My hands were red; they glittered with the blood that dripped from them as on that day by the river

523

bank. And then the angels raised their flaming swords to smite me down, and the horror was complete – I awoke. Again, and again, and again, that awful dream comes to me. I never learn from the experience, I never remember, but at the beginning the hope is ever there to make the end more appalling; and I know that the dream does not come out of the common darkness where the dreams abide, but that it is sent from God as a punishment! Never, never shall I be able to pass the gate, for the soil on the angel garments must ever come from these bloody hands!'

I listened as in a spell as Jacob Settle spoke. There was something so far away in the tone of his voice – something so dreamy and mystic in the eyes that looked as if through me at some spirit beyond – something so lofty in his very diction and in such marked contrast to his workworn clothes and his poor surroundings that I wondered if the whole thing were not a dream.

We were both silent for a long time. I kept looking at the man before me in growing wonderment. Now that his confession had been made, his soul, which had been crushed to the very earth, seemed to leap back again to uprightness with some resilient force. I suppose I ought to have been horrified with his story, but, strange to say, I was not. It certainly is not pleasant to be made the recipient of the confidence of a murderer, but this poor fellow seemed to have had, not only so much provocation, but so much self-denying purpose in his deed of blood that I did not feel called upon to pass judgment upon him. My purpose was to comfort, so I spoke out with what calmness I could, for my heart was beating fast and heavily:

'You need not despair, Jacob Settle. God is very good, and His mercy is great. Live on and work on in the hope that some day you may feel that you have atoned for the past.' Here I paused, for I could see that sleep, natural sleep this time, was creeping upon him. 'Go to sleep,' I said; 'I shall watch with you here, and we shall have no more evil dreams tonight.'

He made an effort to pull himself together, and answered:

'I don't know how to thank you for your goodness to me this night, but I think you had best leave me now. I'll try to sleep this out; I feel a weight off my mind since I have told you all. If there's anything of the man left in me, I must try and fight out life alone.'

'I'll go to-night, as you wish it,' I said; 'but take my advice, and do not live in such a solitary way. Go among men and women; live among them. Share their joys and sorrows, and it will help you to forget. This solitude will make you melancholy mad.'

'I will!' he answered, half unconsciously, for sleep was overmastering him.

I turned to go, and he looked after me. When I had touched the latch I dropped it, and coming back to the bed, held out my hand. He grasped it with both his as he rose to a sitting posture, and I said my good-night, trying to cheer him:

'Heart, man, heart! There is work in the world for you to do, Jacob Settle. You can wear those white robes yet and pass through that gate of steel!'

Then I left him.

A week later I found his cottage deserted, and on asking at the works was told that he had 'gone north', no one exactly knew whither.

Two years afterwards, I was staying for a few days with my friend Dr Munro in Glasgow. He was a busy man, and could not spare much time for going about with me, so I spent my days in excursions to the Trossachs and Loch Katrine and down the Clyde. On the second last evening of my stay I came back somewhat later than I had arranged, but found that my host was late too. The maid told me that he had been sent for to the hospital – a case of accident at the gas-works, and the dinner was postponed for an hour; so telling her I would stroll down to find her master and walk back with him, I went out. At the hospital I found him washing his hands preparatory to starting for home. Casually, I asked him what his case was.

'Oh, the usual thing! A rotten rope and men's lives of no account. Two men were working in a gasometer, when the rope that held their scaffolding broke. It must have occurred just before the dinner hour, for no one noticed their absence till the men had returned. There was about seven feet of water in the gasometer, so they had a hard fight for it, poor fellows. However, one of them was alive, just alive, but we have had a hard job to pull him through. It seems that he owes his life to his mate, for I have never heard of greater heroism. They swam together while their strength lasted, but at the end they were so done up that even the lights above, and the men slung with ropes, coming down to help them, could not keep them up. But one of them stood on the bottom and held up his comrade over his head, and those few breaths made all the difference between life and death. They were a shocking sight when they were taken out, for that water is like a purple dye with the gas and the tar. The man upstairs looked as if he had been washed in blood. Ugh!'

'And the other?'

'Oh, he's worse still. But he must have been a very noble fellow. That struggle under the water must have been fearful; one can see that by the way the blood has been drawn from the extremities. It makes the idea of the *Stigmata* possible to look at him. Resolution like this could, you would think, do anything in the world. Ay! it might almost unbar the gates of Heaven. Look here, old man, it is not a very pleasant sight, especially just before dinner, but you are a writer, and this is an odd case. Here is something you would not like to miss, for in all human probability you will never see anything like it again.' While he was speaking he had brought me into the mortuary of the hospital.

On the bier lay a body covered with a white sheet, which was wrapped close round it.

'Looks like a chrysalis, don't it? I say, Jack, if there be anything in the old myth that a soul is typified by a butterfly, well, then the one that this chrysalis sent forth was a very noble specimen and took all the sunlight on its wings. See here!' He uncovered the face. Horrible, indeed, it looked, as though stained with blood. But I knew him at once, Jacob Settle! My friend pulled the winding sheet further.

The hands were crossed on the purple breast as they had been reverently placed by some tender-hearted person. As I saw them my heart throbbed with a great exultation, for the memory of his harrowing dream rushed across my mind. There was no stain now on those poor, brave hands, for they were blanched white as snow.

And somehow as I looked I felt that the evil dream was all over. That noble soul had won a way through the gate at last. The white robe had now no stain from the hands that had put it on.

CROOKEN SANDS

Mr Arthur Fernlee Markam, who took what was known as the Red House above the Mains of Crooken, was a London merchant, and being essentially a cockney, thought it necessary when he went for the summer holidays to Scotland to provide an entire rig-out as a Highland chieftain, as manifested in chromolithographs and on the music-hall stage. He had once seen in the Empire the Great Prince – 'The Bounder King' – bring down the house by appearing as 'The MacSlogan of that Ilk', and singing the celebrated Scotch song, 'There's naething like haggis to mak a mon dry!' and he had ever since preserved in his mind a faithful image of the picturesque and warlike appearance which he presented. Indeed, if the true inwardness of Mr Markam's mind on the subject of his selection of Aberdeenshire as a summer resort were known, it would be found that in the foreground of the holiday locality which his fancy painted stalked the many hued figure of the MacSlogan of that Ilk. However, be this as it may, a very kind fortune – certainly so far as external beauty was concerned – led him to the choice of Crooken Bay. It is a lovely spot, between Aberdeen and Peterhead, just under the rock-bound headland whence the long, dangerous reefs known as the Spurs run out into the North Sea. Between this and the 'Mains of Crooken' – a village sheltered by the northern cliffs – lies the deep bay, backed with a multitude of bent-grown dunes where the rabbits are to be found in thousands. Thus at either end of the bay is a rocky promontory, and when the dawn or the sunset falls on the rocks of red syenite the effect is very lovely. The bay itself is floored with level sand and the tide runs far out, leaving a smooth waste of hard sand on which are dotted here and there the stake nets and bag nets of the salmon fishers. At one end of the bay there is a little group or cluster of rocks whose heads are raised something above high water, except when in rough weather the waves come over them green. At low tide they are exposed down to sand level; and here is perhaps the only little bit of dangerous sand on this part of the eastern coast. Between the rocks, which are apart about some fifty feet, is a small quicksand, which, like the Goodwins, is dangerous only with the incoming tide. It extends outwards till it is lost in the sea, and inwards till it fades away in the hard sand of the upper beach. On the slope of the hill which rises beyond the dunes, midway between the Spurs and the Port of Crooken, is the Red House. It rises from the midst of a clump of fir-trees which protect it on three sides, leaving the whole sea front open. A trim old-fashioned garden stretches down to the roadway, on crossing which a grassy path, which can be used for light vehicles, threads a way to the shore, winding amongst the sand hills.

When the Markam family arrived at the Red House after their thirty-six hours of pitching on the Aberdeen steamer *Ban Righ* from Blackwall, with the subsequent train to Yellon and drive of a dozen miles, they all agreed that they had never seen a more delightful spot. The general satisfaction was more marked as at that very time none of the family were, for several reasons, inclined to find favourable anything or any place over the Scottish border. Though the family was a large one, the prosperity of the business allowed them all sorts of personal luxuries, amongst which was a wide latitude in the way of dress. The frequency of the Markam girls' new frocks was a source of envy to their bosom friends and of joy to themselves.

527

Arthur Fernlee Markam had not taken his family into his confidence regarding his new costume. He was not quite certain that he should be free from ridicule, or at least from sarcasm, and as he was sensitive on the subject, he thought it better to be actually in the suitable environment before he allowed the full splendour to burst upon them. He had taken some pains to insure the completeness of the Highland costume. For the purpose he had paid many visits to 'The Scotch All-Wool Tartan Clothing Mart' which had been lately established in Copthall-court by the Messrs MacCallum More and Roderick MacDhu. He had anxious consultations with the head of the firm – MacCallum as he called himself, resenting any such additions as 'Mr' or 'Esquire'. The known stock of buckles, buttons, straps, brooches and ornaments of all kinds were examined in critical detail; and at last an eagle's feather of sufficiently magnificent proportions was discovered, and the equipment was complete. It was only when he saw the finished costume, with the vivid hues of the tartan seemingly modified into comparative sobriety by the multitude of silver fittings, the cairngorm brooches, the philibeg, dirk and sporran that he was fully and absolutely satisfied with his choice. At first he had thought of the Royal Stuart dress tartan, but abandoned it on the MacCallum pointing out that if he should happen to be in the neighbourhood of Balmoral it might lead to complications. The MacCallum, who, by the way, spoke with a remarkable cockney accent, suggested other plaids in turn; but now that the other question of accuracy had been raised, Mr Markam foresaw difficulties if he should by chance find himself in the locality of the clan whose colours he had usurped. The MacCallum at last undertook to have, at Markam's expense, a special pattern woven which would not be exactly the same as any existing tartan, though partaking of the characteristics of many. It was based on the Royal Stuart, but contained suggestions as to simplicity of pattern from the Macalister and Ogilvie clans, and as to neutrality of colour from the clans of Buchanan, Macbeth, Chief of Macintosh and Macleod. When the specimen had been shown to Markam he had feared somewhat lest it should strike the eye of his domestic circle as gaudy; but as Roderick MacDhu fell into perfect ecstasies over its beauty he did not make any objection to the completion of the piece. He thought, and wisely, that if a genuine Scotchman like MacDhu liked it, it must be right – especially as the junior partner was a man very much of his own build and appearance. When the MacCallum was receiving his cheque – which, by the way, was a pretty stiff one – he remarked:

'I've taken the liberty of having some more of the stuff woven in case you or any of your friends should want it.' Markam was gratified, and told him that he should be only too happy if the beautiful stuff which they had originated between them should become a favourite, as he had no doubt it would in time. He might make and sell as much as he would.

Markam tried the dress on in his office one evening after the clerks had all gone home. He was pleased, though a little frightened, at the result. The MacCallum had done his work thoroughly, and there was nothing omitted that could add to the martial dignity of the wearer.

'I shall not, of course, take the claymore and the pistols with me on ordinary occasions,' said Markam to himself as he began to undress. He determined that he would wear the dress for the first time on landing in Scotland, and accordingly on the morning when the *Ban Righ* was hanging off the Girdle Ness lighthouse, waiting for the tide to enter the port of Aberdeen, he emerged from his cabin in all the gaudy splendour of his new costume. The first comment he heard was from one of his own sons, who did not recognize him at first.

'Here's a guy! Great Scott! It's the governor!' And the boy fled forthwith and tried to bury his laughter under a cushion in the saloon. Markam was a good sailor and had not suffered from the pitching of the boat, so that his naturally rubicund face was even more rosy by the conscious blush which suffused his cheeks when he had found himself at once the cynosure of all eyes. He could have wished that he had not been so bold for he knew from the cold that there was a big bare spot under one side of his jauntily worn Glengarry cap. However, he faced the group of strangers boldly. He was not, outwardly, upset even when some of the comments reached his ears.

'He's off his bloomin' chump,' said a cockney in a suit of exaggerated plaid.

'There's flies on him,' said a tall thin Yankee, pale with sea-sickness, who was on his way to take up his residence for a time as close as he could get to the gates of Balmoral.

'Happy thought! Let us fill our mulls; now's the chance!' said a young Oxford man on his way home to Inverness. But presently Mr Markam heard the voice of his eldest daughter.

'Where is he? Where is he?' and she came tearing along the deck with her hat blowing behind her. Her face showed signs of agitation, for her mother had just been telling her of her father's condition; but when she saw him she instantly burst into laughter so violent that it ended in a fit of hysterics. Something of the same kind happened to each of the other children. When they had all had their turn Mr Markam went to his cabin and sent his wife's maid to tell each member of the family that he wanted to see them at once. They all made their appearance, suppressing their feelings as well as they could. He said to them very quietly:

'My dears, don't I provide you all with ample allowances?'

'Yes, father!' they all answered gravely, 'no one could be more generous!'

'Don't I let you dress as you please?'

'Yes, father!' – this a little sheepishly.

'Then, my dears, don't you think it would be nicer and kinder of you not to try and make me feel uncomfortable, even if I do assume a dress which is ridiculous in your eyes, though quite common enough in the country where we are about to sojourn?' There was no answer except that which appeared in their hanging heads. He was a good father and they all knew it. He was quite satisfied and went on:

'There, now, run away and enjoy yourselves! We shan't have another word about it.' Then he went on deck again and stood bravely the fire of ridicule which he recognized around him, though nothing more was said within his hearing.

The astonishment and the amusement which his get-up occasioned on the *Ban Righ* was, however, nothing to that which it created in Aberdeen.

The boys and loafers, and women with babies, who waited at the landing shed, followed *en masse* as the Markam party took their way to the railway station; even the porters with their old-fashioned knots and their new-fashioned barrows, who await the traveller at the foot of the gang-plank, followed in wondering delight. Fortunately the Peterhead train was just about to start, so that the martyrdom was not unnecessarily prolonged. In the carriage the glorious Highland costume was unseen, and as there were but few persons at the station at Yellon, all went well there. When, however, the carriage drew near the Mains of Crooken and the fisher folk had run to their doors to see who it was that was passing, the excitement exceeded all bounds. The children with one impulse waved their bonnets and ran shouting behind the carriage; the men forsook their nets and their baiting and followed; the women clutched their babies and followed also. The horses were tired after their long journey to Yellon and back, and the hill was steep, so that there was ample time for the crowd to gather and even to pass on ahead.

Mrs Markam and the elder girls would have liked to make some protest or to do something to relieve their feelings of chagrin at the ridicule which they saw on all faces, but there was a look of fixed determination on the face of the seeming Highlander which awed them a little, and they were silent. It might have been that the eagle's feather, even when arising above the bald head, the cairngorm brooch even on the fat shoulder, and the claymore, dirk and pistols, even when belted round the extensive pauch and protruding from the stocking on the sturdy calf, fulfilled their existence as symbols of martial and terrifying import! When the party arrived at the gate of the Red House there awaited them a crowd of

530

Crooken inhabitants, hatless and respectfully silent; the remainder of the population was painfully toiling up the hill. The silence was broken by only one sound, that of a man with a deep voice.

'Man! but he's forgotten the pipes!'

The servants had arrived some days before, and all things were in readiness. In the glow consequent on a good lunch after a hard journey all the disagreeables of travel and all the chagrin consequent on the adoption of the obnoxious costume were forgotten.

That afternoon Markam, still clad in full array, walked through the Mains of Crooken. He was all alone, for, strange to say, his wife and both daughters had sick headaches, and were, as he was told, lying down to rest after the fatigue of the journey. His eldest son, who claimed to be a young man, had gone out by himself to explore the surroundings of the place, and one of the boys could not be found. The other boy, on being told that his father had sent for him to come for a walk, had managed – by accident, of course – to fall into the water butt, and had to be dried and rigged out afresh. His clothes not having been as yet unpacked this was of course impossible without delay.

Mr Markam was not quite satisfied with his walk. He could not meet any of his neighbours. It was not that there were not enough people about, for every house and cottage seemed to be full; but the people when in the open were either in their doorways some distance behind him, or on the roadway a long distance in front. As he passed he could see the tops of heads and the whites of eyes in the windows or round the corners of doors. The only interview which he had was anything but a pleasant one. This was with an odd sort of old man who was hardly ever heard to speak except to join in the 'Amens' in the meeting-house. His sole occupation seemed to be to wait at the window of the post-office from eight o'clock in the morning till the arrival of the mail at one, when he carried the letterbag to a neighbouring baronial castle. The remainder of his day was spent on a seat in a draughty part of the port, where the offal of the fish, the refuse of the bait, and the house rubbish was thrown, and where the ducks were accustomed to hold high revel.

When Saft Tammie beheld him coming he raised his eyes, which were generally fixed on the nothing which lay on the roadway opposite his seat, and, seeming dazzled as if by a burst of sunshine, rubbed them and shaded them with his hand. Then he started up and raised his hand aloft in a denunciatory manner as he spoke:–

' "Vanity of vanities, saith the preacher. All is vanity." Mon, be warned in time! "Behold the lilies of the field, they toil not, neither do they spin, yet Solomon in all his glory was not arrayed like one of these." Mon! Mon! Thy vanity is as the quicksand which swallows up all which comes within its spell. Beware vanity! Beware the quicksand, which yawneth for thee, and which will swallow thee up! See thyself! Learn thine own vanity! Meet thyself face to face, and then in that moment thou shalt learn the fatal force of thy vanity. Learn it, know it, and repent ere the quicksand swallow thee!' Then without another word he went back to his seat and sat there immovable and expressionless as before.

Markam could not but feel a little upset by this tirade. Only that it was spoken by a seeming madman, he would have put it down to some eccentric exhibition of Scottish humour or impudence; but the gravity of the message – for it seemed nothing else – made such a reading impossible. He was, however, determined not to give in to ridicule, and although he had not yet seen anything in Scotland to remind him even of a kilt, he determined to wear his Highland dress. When he returned home, in less than half-an-hour, he found that every member of the family was, despite the headaches, out taking a walk. He took the opportunity afforded by their absence of locking himself in his dressing-room, took off the Highland dress, and putting on a suit of flannels, lit a cigar and had a snooze. He was awakened by the noise of the family coming in, and at once donning his dress made his appearance in the drawing-room for tea.

He did not go out again that afternoon; but after dinner he put on his dress again – he had, of course dressed for dinner as usual – and went by himself for a walk on the sea-shore. He had by this time come to the conclusion that he would get by degrees accustomed to the Highland dress before making it his ordinary wear. The moon was up and he easily followed the path through the sand-hills, and shortly struck the shore. The tide was out and the beach firm as a rock, so he strolled southwards to nearly the end of the bay. Here he was attracted by two isolated rocks some little way out from the edge of the dunes, so he strolled towards them. When he reached the nearest one he climbed it, and sitting there elevated some fifteen or twenty feet over the waste of sand, enjoyed the lovely, peaceful prospect. The moon was rising behind the headland of Pennyfold, and its light was just touching the top of the furthermost rock of the Spurs some three-quarters of a mile out; the rest of the rocks were the dark shadow. As the moon rose over the headland, the rocks of the Spurs and then the beach by degrees became flooded with light.

For a good while Mr Markam sat and looked at the rising moon and the growing area of light which followed its rise. Then he turned and faced eastwards and sat with his chin in his hand looking seawards, and revelling in the peace and beauty and freedom of the scene. The roar of London – the darkness and the strife and weariness of London life – seemed to have passed quite away, and he lived at the moment a freer and higher life. He looked at the glistening water as it stole its way over the flat waste of sand, coming closer and closer insensibly – the tide had turned. Presently he heard a distant shouting along the beach very far off.

'The fisherman calling to each other,' he said to himself and looked around. As he did so he got a horrible shock, for though just then a cloud sailed across the moon he saw, in spite of the sudden darkness around him, his own image. For an instant, on the top of the opposite rock he could see the bald back of the head and the Glengarry cap with the immense eagle's feather. As he staggered back his foot slipped, and he began to slide down towards the sand between the two rocks. He took no concern as to falling, for the sand was really only a few feet below him, and his mind was occupied with the figure or simulacrum of himself, which had already disappeared. As the easiest way of reaching *terra firma* he prepared to jump the remainder of the distance. All this had taken but a second, but the brain works quickly, and even as he gathered himself for the spring he saw the sand below him lying so marbly level shake and shiver in an odd way. A sudden fear overcame him; his knees failed, and instead of jumping he slid miserably down the rock, scratching his bare legs as he went. His feet touched the sand – went through it like water – and he was down below his knees before he realized that he was in a quicksand. Wildly he grasped at the rock to keep himself from sinking further, and fortunately there was a jutting spur or edge which he was able to grasp instinctively. To this he clung in grim desperation. He tried to shout, but his breath would not come, till after a great effort his voice rang out. Again he shouted, and it seemed as if the sound of his own voice gave him new courage, for he was able to hold on to the rock for a longer time than he thought possible – though he held on only in blind desperation. He was, however, beginning to find his grasp weakening, when, joy of joys! his shout was answered by a rough voice from just above him.

'God be thankit, I'm nae too late!' and a fisherman with great thigh-boots came hurriedly climbing over the rock. In an instant he recognized the gravity of the danger, and with a cheering 'Haud fast, mon! I'm comin'!' scrambled down till he found a firm foothold. Then with one strong hand holding the rock above, he leaned down, and catching Markam's wrist called out to him, 'Haud to me, mon! Haud to me wi' ither hond!'

Then he lent his great strength, and with a steady, sturdy pull, dragged him out of the hungry quicksand and placed him safe upon the rock. Hardly giving him time to draw breath, he pulled and pushed him – never letting him go for an instant – over the rock into the firm sand beyond it, and finally deposited him, still shaking from the magnitude of his danger, high upon the beach. Then he began to speak:

'Mon! but I was just in time. If I had no laucht at yon foolish lads and

533

begun to rin at the first you'd a bin sinkin' doon to the bowels o' the airth be the noo! Wully Beagrie thocht you was a ghaist, and Tom MacPhail swore ye was only like a goblin on a puddick-steel! "Na!" said I. "Yon's but the daft Englishman – the loony that had escapit frae the waxwarks." I was thinkin' that bein' strange and silly – if not a wholemade feel – ye'd no ken the ways o' the quicksan'! I shouted till warn ye, and then ran to drag ye aff, if need be. But God be thankit, be ye fule or only half-daft wi' yer vanity, that I was no that late!' and he reverently lifted his cap as he spoke.

Mr Markam was deeply touched and thankful for his escape from a horrible death; but the sting of the charge of vanity thus made once more against him came through his humility. He was about to reply angrily, when suddenly a great awe fell upon him as he remembered the warning words of the half-crazy letter-carrier: 'Meet thyself face to face, and repent ere the quicksand shall swallow thee!'

Here, too, he remembered the image of himself that he had seen and the sudden danger from the deadly quicksand that had followed. He was silent a full minute, and then said:

'My good fellow, I owe you my life!'

The answer came with reverence from the hardy fisherman, 'Na! Na! Ye owe that to God; but, as for me, I'm only too glad till be the humble instrument o' His mercy.'

'But you will let me thank you,' said Mr Markam, taking both the great hands of his deliverer in his and holding them tight. 'My heart is too full as yet, and my nerves are too much shaken to let me say much; but, believe me, I am very, very grateful!' It was quite evident that the poor old fellow was deeply touched, for the tears were running down his cheeks.

The fisherman said, with a rough but true courtesy:

'Ay, sir! thank me and ye will – if it'll do yer poor heart good. An' I'm thinking that if it were me I'd be thankful too. But, sir, as for me I need no thanks. I am glad, so I am!'

That Arthur Fernlee Markam was really thankful and grateful was shown practically later on. Within a week's time there sailed into Port Crooken the finest fishing smack that had ever been seen in the harbour of Peterhead. She was fully found with sails and gear of all kinds, and with nets of the best. Her master and men went away by the coach, after having left with the salmon-fisher's wife the papers which made her over to him.

As Mr Markam and the salmon-fisher walked together along the shore the former asked his companion not to mention the fact that he had been in such imminent danger, for that it would only distress his dear wife and children. He said that he would warn them all of the quicksand, and for that purpose he, then and there, asked questions about it till he felt that his information on the subject was complete. Before they parted he asked his companion if he had happened to see a second figure, dressed like himself on the other rock as he had approached to succour him.

'Na! Na!' came the answer, 'there is nae sic another fule in these parts. Nor has there been since the time o' Jamie Fleeman – him that was fule to the Laird o' Udny. Why, mon! sic a heathenish dress as ye have on till ye has nae been seen in these pairts within the memory o' mon. An' I'm thinkin' that sic a dress never was for sittin' on the cauld rock, as ye done beyont. Mon! but do ye no fear the rheumatism or the lumbagy wi' floppin' doon on to the cauld stanes wi' yer bare flesh? I was thinking that it was daft ye waur when I see ye the mornin' doon be the port, but it's fule or eediot ye maun be for the like o' thot!' Mr Markam did not care to argue the point, and as they were now close to his own home he asked the salmon-fisher to have a glass of whisky – which he did – and they parted for the night. He took good care to warn all his family of the quicksand, telling them that he had himself been in some danger from it.

All that night he never slept. He heard the hours strike one after the other; but try how he would he could not get to sleep. Over and over again he went through the horrible episode of the quicksand, from the time that Saft Tammie had broken his habitual silence to preach to him of the sin of vanity and to warn him. The question kept ever arising in his mind: 'Am I then so vain as to be in the ranks of the foolish?' and the answer ever came in the words of the crazy prophet: ' "Vanity of vanities! All is vanity." Meet thyself face to face, and repent ere the quicksand shall swallow thee!' Somehow a feeling of doom began to shape itself in his mind that he would yet perish in that same quicksand, for there he had already met himself face to face.

In the grey of the morning he dozed off, but it was evident that he continued the subject in his dreams, for he was fully awakened by his wife, who said:

'Do sleep quietly! That blessed Highland suit has got on your brain. Don't talk in your sleep, if you can help it!' He was somehow conscious of a glad feeling, as if some terrible weight had been lifted from him, but he did not know any cause of it. He asked his wife what he had said in his sleep, and she answered:

'You said it often enough, goodness knows, for one to remember it – "Not face to face! I saw the eagle plume over the bald head! There is hope yet! Not face to face!" Go to sleep! Do!' And then he did go to sleep, for he seemed to realize that the prophecy of the crazy man had not yet been fulfilled. He had not met himself face to face – as yet at all events.

He was awakened early by a maid who came to tell him that there was a fisherman at the door who wanted to see him. He dressed himself as quickly as he could – for he was not yet expert with the Highland dress – and hurried down, not wishing to keep the salmon-fisher waiting. He was surprised and not altogether pleased to find that his visitor was none other than Saft Tammie, who at once opened fire on him:

'I maun gang awa' t' the post; but I thocht that I would waste an hour on ye, and ca' roond just to see if ye waur still that fou wi' vanity as on the nicht gane by. An' I see that ye've no learned the lesson. Well! the time is comin', sure eneucht! However I have all the time i' the marnins to my ain sel', so I'll aye look roond jist till see how ye gang yer ain gait to the quicksan', and then to the de'il! I'm aff till ma wark the noo!' And he went straightway, leaving Mr Markam considerably vexed, for the maids within earshot were vainly trying to conceal their giggles. He had fairly made up his mind to wear on that day ordinary clothes, but the visit of Saft Tammie reversed his decision. He would show them all that he was not a coward, and he would go on as he had begun – come what might. When he came to breakfast in full martial panoply the children, one and all, held down their heads and the backs of their necks became very red indeed. As, however, none of them laughed – except Titus, the youngest boy, who was seized with a fit of hysterical choking and was promptly banished from the room – he could not reprove them, but began to break his egg with a sternly determined air. It was unfortunate that as his wife was handing him a cup of tea one of the buttons of his sleeve caught in the lace of her morning wrapper, with the result that the hot tea was spilt over his bare knees. Not unnaturally, he made use of a swear word, whereupon his wife, somewhat nettled, spoke out:

'Well, Arthur, if you will make such an idiot of yourself with that ridiculous costume what else can you expect? You are not accustomed to it – and you never will be!' In answer he began an indignant speech with: 'Madam!' but he got no further, for now that the subject was broached, Mrs Markam intended to have her say out. It was not a pleasant say, and, truth to tell, it was not said in a pleasant manner. A wife's manner seldom is pleasant when she undertakes to tell what she considers 'truths' to her husband. The result was that Arthur Fernlee Markam undertook, then and there, that during his stay in Scotland he would wear no other costume than the one she abused. Woman-like his wife had the last word – given in this case with tears:

'Very well, Arthur! Of course you will do as you choose. Make me as ridiculous as you can, and spoil the poor girls' chances in life. Young men don't seem to care, as a general rule, for an idiot father-in-law! But I must warn you that your vanity will some day get a rude shock – if indeed you are not before then in an asylum or dead!'

It was manifest after a few days that Mr Markam would have to take the major part of his outdoor exercise by himself. The girls now and again took a walk with him, chiefly in the early morning or late at night, or on a wet day when there would be no one about; they professed to be willing to go out at all times, but somehow something always seemed to occur to prevent it. The boys could never be found at all on such occasions, and as to Mrs Markam she sternly refused to go out with him on any consideration so long as he should continue to make a fool of himself. On the Sunday he dressed himself in his habitual broadcloth, for he rightly felt that church was not a place for angry feelings; but on Monday morning he resumed his Highland garb. By this time he would have given a good deal if he had never thought of the dress, but his British obstinacy was strong, and he would not give in. Saft Tammie called at his house every morning, and not being able to see him nor to have any message taken to him, used to call back in the afternoon when the letter-bag had been delivered and watched for his going out. On such occasions he never failed to warn him against his vanity in the same words which he had used at the first. Before many days were over Mr Markam had come to look upon him as little short of a scourge.

But the time the week was out the enforced partial solitude, the constant chagrin, and the never-ending brooding, which was thus engendered, began to make Mr Markam quite ill. He was too proud to take any of his family into his confidence, since they had in his view treated him very badly. Then he did not sleep well at night, and when he did sleep he had constantly bad dreams. Merely to assure himself that his pluck was not failing him he made it a practice to visit the quicksand at least once every day, he hardly ever failed to go there the last thing at night. It was perhaps this habit that wrought the quicksand with its terrible experience so perpetually into his dreams. More and more vivid these became, till on waking at times he could hardly realize that he had not been actually in the flesh to visit the fatal spot. He sometimes thought that he might have been walking in his sleep.

One night his dream was so vivid that when he awoke he could not believe that it had only been a dream. He shut his eyes again and again, but each time the vision, if it was a vision, or the reality, if it was a reality, would rise before him. The moon was shining full and yellow over the quicksand as he approached it; he could see the expanse of light shaken and disturbed and full of black shadows as the liquid sand quivered and trembled and wrinkled and eddied as was its wont between its pauses of marble calm. As he drew close to it another figure came towards it from the opposite side with equal footsteps. He saw that it was his own figure, his very self, and in silent terror, compelled by what force he knew not, he advanced – charmed as the bird is by the snake, mesmerized or hypnotized

– to meet this other self. As he felt the yielding sand closing over him he awoke in the agony of death, trembling with fear, and, strange to say, with the silly man's prophecy seeming to sound in his ears: ' "Vanity of vanities! All is vanity!" See thyself and repent ere the quicksand swallow thee!'

So convinced was he that this was no dream that he arose, early as it was, and dressing himself without disturbing his wife took his way to the shore. His heart fell when he came across a series of footsteps on the sands, which he at once recognized as his own. There was the same wide heel, the same square toe; he had no doubt now that he had actually been there, and half horrified, and half in a state of dreamy stupor, he followed the footsteps, and found them lost in the edge of the yielding quicksand. This gave him a terrible shock, for there were no return steps marked on the sand, and he felt that there was some dread mystery which he could not penetrate, and the penetration of which would, he feared, undo him.

In this state of affairs he took two wrong courses. Firstly he kept his trouble to himself, and as none of his family had any clue to it, every innocent word or expression which they used supplied fuel to the consuming fire of his imagination. Secondly he began to read books professing to bear upon the mysteries of dreaming and of mental phenomena generally, with the result that every wild imagination of every crank or half-crazy philosopher became a living germ of unrest in the fertilizing soil of his disordered brain. Thus negatively and positively all things began to work to a common end. Not the least of his disturbing causes was Saft Tammie, who had now become at certain times of the day a fixture at his gate. After a while, being interested in the previous state of this individual, he made inquiries regarding his past with the following result.

Saft Tammie was popularly believed to be the son of a laird in one of the counties round the Fifth of Forth. He had been partially educated for the ministry, but for some cause which no one ever knew threw up his prospects suddenly, and, going to Peterhead in its days of whaling prosperity, had there taken service on a whaler. Here off and on he had remained for some years, getting gradually more and more silent in his habits, till finally his shipmates protested against so taciturn a mate, and he had found service amongst the fishing smacks of the northern fleet. He had worked for many years at the fishing with always the reputation of being 'a wee bit daft', till at length he had gradually settled down at Crooken, where the laird, doubtless knowing something of his family history, had given him a job which practically made him a pensioner. The minister who gave the information finished thus:–

'It is a very strange thing, but the man seems to have some odd kind of gift. Whether it be that "second sight" which we Scotch people are so prone to believe in, or some other occult form of knowledge, I know not, but nothing of a disastrous tendency ever occurs in this place but the men with whom he lives are able to quote after the event some saying of his which certainly appears to have foretold it. He gets uneasy or excited – wakes up, in fact – when death is in the air!'

This did not in any way tend to lessen Mr Markam's concern, but on the contrary seemed to impress the prophecy more deeply on his mind. Of all the books which he had read on his new subject of study none interested him so much as a German one *Die Doppelgänger*, by Dr Heinrich von Aschenberg, formerly of Bonn. Here he learned for the first time of cases where men had led a double existence – each nature being quite apart from each other – the body being always a reality with one spirit, and a simulacrum with the other. Needless to say that Mr Markam realized this theory as exactly suiting his own case. The glimpse which he had of his own back the night of his escape from the quicksand – his own footmarks disappearing into the quicksand with no return steps visible – the prophecy of Saft Tammie about his meeting himself and perishing in the quicksand – all lent aid to the conviction that he was in his own person an instance of the doppelgänger. Being then conscious of a double life he took steps to prove its existence to his own satisfaction. To this end on one night before going to bed he wrote his name in chalk on the soles of his shoes. That night he dreamed of the quicksand, and of his visiting it – dreamed so vividly that on walking in the grey of the dawn he could not believe that he had not been there. Arising, without disturbing his wife, he sought his shoes.

The chalk signatures were undisturbed! He dressed himself and stole out softly. This time the tide was in, so he crossed the dunes and struck the shore on the further side of the quicksand. There, oh, horror of horrors! he saw his own footprints dying into the abyss!

He went home a desperately sad man. It seemed incredible that he, an elderly commercial man, who had passed a long and uneventful life in the pursuit of business in the midst of roaring, practical London, should thus find himself enmeshed in mystery and horror, and that he should discover that he had two existences. He could not speak of his trouble even to his own wife, for well he knew that she would at once require the fullest particulars of that other life – the one which she did not know; and that she would at the start not only imagine but charge him with all manner of infidelities on the head of it. And so his brooding grew deeper and deeper still. One evening – the tide then going out and the moon being at the full – he was sitting waiting for dinner when the maid announced that Saft Tammie was making a disturbance outside because he would not be let in to see him. He was very indignant, but did not like the maid to think that he had any fear on the subject, and so told her to bring him in. Tammie entered, walking more briskly than ever with his head up and a look of vigorous decision in the eyes that were so generally cast down. As soon as he entered he said:

'I have come to see ya once again – once again; and there ye sit, still just like a cockatoo on a pairch. Weel, mon, I forgie ye! Mind ye that, I forgie ye!' And without a word more he turned and walked out of the house, leaving the master in speechless indignation.

After dinner he determined to pay another visit to the quicksand – he would not allow even to himself that he was afraid to go. And so, about nine o'clock, in full array, he marched to the beach, and passing over the sands sat on the skirt of the nearer rock. The full moon was behind him and its light lit up the bay so that its fringe of foam, the dark outline of the headland, and the stakes of the salmon-nets were all emphasized. In the brilliant yellow glow the lights in the windows of Port Crooken and in those of the distant castle of the laird trembled like stars through the sky. For a long time he sat and drank in the beauty of the scene, and his soul seemed to feel a peace that it had not known for many days. All the pettiness and annoyance and silly fears of the past weeks seemed blotted out, and a new holy calm took the vacant place. In this sweet and solemn mood he reviewed his late action calmly, and felt ashamed of himself for his vanity and for the obstinacy which had followed it. And then and there he made up his mind that the present would be the last time he would wear the costume which had estranged him from those whom he loved, and which had caused him so many hours and days of chagrin, vexation, and pain.

But almost as soon as he arrived at this conclusion another voice seemed to speak within him and mockingly ask if he should ever get the chance to wear the suit again – that it was too late – he had chosen his course and must now abide the issue.

'It is not too late,' came the quick answer of his better self; and full of the thought, he rose up to go home and divest himself of the now hateful costume right away. He paused for one look at the beautiful scene. The light lay pale and mellow, softening every outline of rock and tree and house-top, and deepening the shadows into velvety-black, and lighting, as with a pale flame, the incoming tide, that now crept fringe-like across the flat waste of sand. Then he left the rock and stepped out for the shore.

But as he did so a frightful spasm of horror shook him, and for an instant the blood rushing to his head shut out all the light of the full moon. Once more he saw that fatal image of himself moving beyond the quicksand from the opposite rock to the shore. The shock was all the

540

greater for the contrast with the spell of peace which he had just enjoyed; and almost paralysed in every sense, he stood and watched the fatal vision and the wrinkly, crawling quicksand that seemed to writhe and yearn for something that lay between. There could be no mistake this time, for though the moon behind threw the face into shadow he could see there the same shaven cheeks as his own, and the small stubby moustache of a few weeks' growth. The light shone on the brilliant tartan, and on the eagle's plume. Even the bald space at one side of the Glengarry cap glistened, as did the cairngorm brooch on the shoulder and the tops of the silver buttons. As he looked he felt his feet slightly sinking, for he was still near the edge of the belt of quicksand, and he stepped back. As he did so the other figure stepped forward, so that the space between them was preserved.

So the two stood facing each other, as though in some weird fascination; and in the rushing of the blood through his brain Markam seemed to hear the words of the prophecy: 'See thyself face to face, and repent ere the quicksand swallow thee.' He did stand face to face with himself, and he had repented – and now he was sinking in the quicksand! The warning and prophecy were coming true.

Above him the seagulls screamed, circling round the fringe of the incoming tide, and the sound being entirely mortal recalled him to himself. On the instant he stepped back a few quick steps, for as yet only his feet were merged in the soft sand. As he did so the other figure stepped forward, and coming within the deadly grip of the quicksand began to sink. It seemed to Markam that he was looking at himself going down to his doom, and on the instant the anguish of his soul found vent in a terrible cry. There was at the same instant a terrible cry from the other figure, and as Markam threw up his hands the figure did the same. With horror-struck eyes he saw him sink deeper into the quicksand; and then, impelled by what power he knew not, he advanced again towards the sand to meet his fate. But as his more forward foot began to sink he heard again the cries of the seagulls which seemed to restore his benumbed faculties. With a mighty effort he drew his foot out of the sand which seemed to clutch it, leaving his shoe behind, and then in sheer terror he turned and ran from the place, never stopping till his breath and strength failed him, and he sank half swooning on the grassy path through the sandhills.

* * *

Arthur Markam made up his mind not to tell his family of his terrible adventure – until at least such time as he should be complete master of himself. Now that the fatal double – his other self – had been engulfed in the quicksand he felt something like his old peace of mind.

That night he slept soundly and did not dream at all; and in the morning was quite his old self. It really seemed as though his newer and worser self had disappeared for ever; and strangely enough Saft Tammie was absent from his post that morning and never appeared there again, but sat in his old place watching nothing, as of old, with lack-lustre eye. In accordance with his resolution he did not wear his Highland suit again, but one evening tied it up in a bundle, claymore, dirk and philibeg and all, and bringing it secretly with him threw it into the quicksand. With a feeling of intense pleasure he saw it sucked below the sand, which closed above it into marble smoothness. Then he went home and announced cheerily to his family assembled for evening prayers:

'Well! my dears, you will be glad to hear that I have abandoned my idea of wearing the Highland dress. I see now what a vain old fool I was and how ridiculous I made myself! You shall never see it again!'

'Where is it, father?' asked one of the girls wishing to say something so that such a self-sacrificing announcement as her father's should not be passed in absolute silence. His answer was so sweetly given that the girl rose from her seat and came and kissed him. It was:

'In the quicksand, my dear! and I hope that my worser self is buried there along with it – for ever.'

* * *

The remainder of the summer was passed at Crooken with delight by all the family, and on his return to town Mr Markam had almost forgotten the whole of the incident of the quicksand, and all touching on it, when one day he got a letter from the MacCallum More which caused him so much thought, though he said nothing of it to his family, and left it, for certain reasons, unanswered. It ran as follows:

'The MacCallum More and Roderick MacDhu.
    'The Scotch All-Wool Tartan Clothing Mart.
        'Copthall Court, E.C.,
            '30th September, 1892.
    'Dear Sir,
'I trust you will pardon the liberty which I take in writing to you, but I am desirous of making an inquiry, and I am informed that you have been sojourning during the summer in Aberdeenshire (Scotland, N.B.). My partner, Mr Roderick MacDhu – as he appears for business reasons on our bill-heads and in our advertisments, his real name being Emmanuel Moses Marks of London – went early last month to Scotland (N.B.) for a tour, but as I have only once heard from him, shortly after his departure, I am anxious lest any misfortune may have befallen him. As I have been

unable to obtain any news of him on making all inquiries in my power, I venture to appeal to you. His letter was written in deep dejection of spirit, and mentioned that he feared a judgment had come upon him for wishing to appear as a Scotchman on Scottish soil, as he had one moonlight night shortly after his arrival seen his 'wraith'. He evidently alluded to the fact that before his departure he had procured for himself a Highland costume similar to that which we had the honour to supply to you, with which, as perhaps you will remember, he was much struck. He may, however, never have worn it, as he was, to my knowledge, diffident about putting it on, and even went so far as to tell me that he would at first only venture to wear it late at night or very early in the morning, and then only in remote places, until such time as he should get accustomed to it. Unfortunately he did not advise me of his route so that I am in complete ignorance of his whereabouts; and I venture to ask if you may have seen or heard of a Highland costume similar to your own having been seen anywhere in the neighbourhood in which I am told you have recently purchased the estate which you temporarily occupied. I shall not expect an answer to this letter unless you can give me some information regarding my friend and partner, so pray do not trouble to reply unless there be cause. I am encouraged to think that he may have been in your neighbourhood as, though his letter is not dated, the envelope is marked with the postmark of "Yellon" which I find is in Aberdeenshire, and not far from the Mains of Crooken.

'I have the honour to be, dear sir.
        'Yours very respectfully,
            'JOSHUA SHEENY COHEN BENJAMIN
                '(The MacCallum More.)'